THE OCCURRENCES OF THAT NIGHT SIXTEEN YEARS AGO HAD ALL COME RUSHING BACK IN A FLOOD OF VIVID MEMORIES, AND THE BEAT OF TRASK'S HEART HAD PICKED UP SPEEDTOMATCHTHESUDDENFLOWOF ADRENALINE.

'David?' he said, making it a question.

Chung answered with a grim nod, simply that, and whisked him into the elevator. But as the doors slid shut on them and they were alone, he uttered those words which Trask most dreaded to hear: 'He's back.'

Trask didn't want to believe it. 'He?' he husked, knowing full well who *he* must be, the only one *he* could be. 'Harry?'

Chung nodded, shrugged helplessly, seemed lost for words. '*Something* of him,' he answered at last, 'who or whatever he is now. But yes, Ben, I'm talking about Harry. *Something* of Harry Keogh has come back to us . . .'

Brian Lumley was born in the coal-mining village of Hordern, County Durham. At the age of twenty-one, he was called up for National Service and was assigned to the Royal Military Police. He subsequently joined up and in his twenty-two years of service travelled widely.

A devotee of horror and fantasy fiction all his life, he began writing while still in the army in the 1960s, and his first stories were published in America. His early influence was that of H. P. Lovecraft's *Cthulhu Mythos* cycle of fiction. After returning to civilian life in 1981, Brian Lumley became a full-time writer and began working on his longer, more ambitious novels: first the *Psychomech* trilogy, then individual novels such as *Demogorgon* and *House of Doors*, culminating in the highly original series of bestselling Vampire novels, the five *Necroscope* books. *Blood Brothers*, *The Last Aerie* and *Bloodwars* are all published in ROC, and together they form his new trilogy, *Vampire World*, a spin-off from the *Necroscope* series. Also published in ROC are *Fruiting Bodies and Other Fungi* and *Return of the Deep Ones and Other Mythos Tales*.

With more than thirty books and over a hundred short stories published in English, Brian Lumley has also had his work translated into French, German, Italian, Spanish, Dutch, Japanese and, most recently, Polish. His story 'Fruiting Bodies' won the British Fantasy Award for the Best Short Story and he has also been the recipient of *Fear* Magazine's Award for *Necroscope III: The Source*.

VAMPIRE WORLD II
THE LAST AERIE

BRIAN LUMLEY

A ROC BOOK

ROC

Published by the Penguin Group
Penguin Books Ltd, 27 Wrights Lane, London W8 5TZ, England
Penguin Books USA Inc., 375 Hudson Street, New York, New York 10014, USA
Penguin Books Australia Ltd, Ringwood, Victoria, Australia
Penguin Books Canada Ltd, 10 Alcorn Avenue, Toronto, Ontario, Canada M4V 3B2
Penguin Books (NZ) Ltd, 182–190 Wairau Road, Auckland 10, New Zealand

Penguin Books Ltd, Registered Offices: Harmondsworth, Middlesex, England

First published 1993
5 7 9 10 8 6

 Roc is a trademark of Penguin Books Ltd

Typeset by Datix International Limited, Bungay, Suffolk
Printed in England by Clays Ltd, St Ives plc

Of all the bars at all the conventions
in all the world, you had to walk into mine.
Here's looking at you, kid!

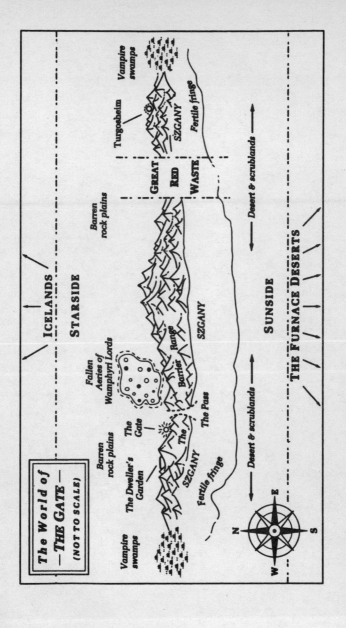

PART ONE

E-Branch

I

Harry's Passing

To the members of E-Branch, bad dreams were an occupational hazard; it was generally accepted that nightmares went with the work. Ben Trask, current head of the Branch, had always had his share of bad dreams. Indeed, since the Yulian Bodescu affair twelve years ago, he'd had more than his share. And only half of them when he was asleep. The sleeping ones were of the harmless variety: they frightened but couldn't kill you. They were engendered of the waking sort, which were very different: sometimes they *could* kill and worse. Because they were real.

As for this one, it wasn't so much a bad as a weird dream. And weirder because Trask was wide awake, having driven his car through the wee small hours of a rainy night into the heart of London, and parked it opposite E-Branch HQ ... without knowing why. And Trask was fussy about things like that; he generally liked to be responsible for his actions.

It was a Sunday in mid-February of 1990, one of those rare days when Trask could get away from his work and switch off, or rather switch on, to the normal world which existed outside the Branch. It should have been one of those days, anyway. But here he was, at E-Branch HQ in the middle of the sleeping city; and in the eye of his mind this weird dream which wouldn't go away, this daydream repeating over and over, like flickering frames from an old monochrome movie projected onto a window, so that he could see right through it. A ghost film; if he blinked his eyes rapidly it would vanish, however momentarily, and return just as soon as he relaxed:

A corpse, smouldering, with its fire-blackened arms flung wide; steaming head thrown back as in the final agony of death; tumbling end over end into a black void shot through with thin neon bars or ribbons of blue, green, and red light.

It was a tortured thing, yes, but dead now from all of its torments and no longer suffering; unknown and unknowable as the weird waking dream which it was. And yet there was something morbidly *familiar* about it; so that watching it, Trask's face was grey and his lips drawn back in a silent snarl from his strong, slightly yellow teeth. If only the corpse would stop tumbling for a moment and come into focus, give him a clearer shot of the blistered, silently screaming face . . .

Trask got out of his car into a sudden squall of leaden raindrops, as if some Invisible One had dipped his hands in water and scooped it into Trask's face. And muttering a curse as he turned up the collar of his overcoat, he glanced at the building across the street, craning his neck to peer up at the high windows of E-Branch. Up there he expected to see a light – just one, burning in a window set centrally in the length of the entire upper storey which was the Branch – lighting the room which housed the Duty Officer through his lonely night vigil. Well, he saw the Duty Officer's light, right enough, and keeping it company, three or four more which he hadn't expected. But he saw more than the lights, for even the rain couldn't wash away the tortured, monotonously tumbling figure from the screen of his mind.

4

Trask knew that if he were someone or thing other than who and what he was – head of a top-secret, in more than one way esoteric security organization – that the experience must surely scare the hell out of him. Except, well, he'd been scared by experts. Or, he might believe he was going mad. But there again, E-Branch was ... E-Branch. This thing he was experiencing, it must be in his mind, he supposed. It *had* to be, for there was no physical mechanism to account for it. Or was there?

Hallucination? Well, possibly. Someone could have got to him, fed him drugs, brainwashed him ... but to what end? Why bring him here in the dead of night? And why bring these other people here? (The extra lights up there, the shiny black MG Metro pulling into the kerb, and the bloke across the road – an E-Branch agent, surely? – even now running through the rain towards the Branch's back door entrance.) Why were they here?

'Sir?' A girl struggled stiffly, awkwardly out of the Metro. She was Anna Marie English, a Branch esper. English by name but never an English rose – nor any sort of rose by any other name – she was enervated, pallid, dowdy, a stray cat drowning in the rain. It was her talent, Trask knew, and he felt sorry for her. She was 'ecologically aware'; or as she herself was wont to put it, she was 'as one with the Earth'. When water tables declined and deserts expanded, so her skin dried out, became desiccated. When acid rains ate into Scandinavian forests, her dandruff fell like snow. In her dreams she heard whale species singing sadly of their decline and inevitable extinction, and she knew from her aching bones when the Japanese were slaughtering the dolphins. A human lodestone, she tracked illicit nuclear waste, monitored pollution, shrank from

5

yawning holes in the ozone as a coral polyp from a diver's probing spearpoint. Yes, she was an 'ecopath': she felt for the Earth and suffered all of its sicknesses, and unlike the rest of us *knew* that she, too, was dying from them.

Trask looked at her: she was twenty-four and looked fifty. Despite his pity, perhaps paradoxically, he thought of her in harsh, disassociated, almost disapproving terms – thick-lensed spectacles, liver spots, hearing aid, straggly-haired, crumpled blouse, splay-legged – and knew he disliked her because she mirrored the decline of the world. And that was *his* talent at work. Ben Trask was a human lie-detector: he recognized a lie when he saw, felt, heard, or otherwise perceived one as other men recognize a slap in the face; so that conversely, in the absence of falsehood he must acknowledge truth. Except Anna Marie English's truth was unbearable. If Greenpeace had her and could make the world believe in her, they would win their case in one ... though of course it would be lost at one and the same time. For they'd suspect that they were too late. But Trask also knew that it wasn't quite like that. The world was a huge creature and had been sorely wounded, and Anna Marie English was just too small to sustain so much damage. But while she was suffering almost beyond endurance, the Earth could go on taking it for a long time yet. This was Trask's view of it, anyway. He supposed it made him an optimist, which was something of a paradox in itself.

'Can you see it?' he said. 'Do you have any idea what it's all about?'

She looked at him and saw a mousey-haired, green-eyed man in his late thirties. Trask was about five feet ten, a little overweight and slope-shouldered, and wore what could only be described as a lugubrious expression. Perhaps it had to do with his talent: in a world where the plain truth was increasingly hard to find, it was no easy thing being a lie-detector. White lies, half-truths, and downright fables came at Trask from all directions, until sometimes he felt he didn't want to look any more.

But Anna Marie English had her own problems. Finally she nodded her bedraggled mop of a head. 'I see it, yes, but don't ask me what it's all about. I woke up, saw it, and knew I had to come here. That's all. But I've a hunch the world's a loser yet again.' Her voice was a coughing rasp.

'A hunch?'

'This thing isn't specific to me,' she frowned. 'This time I'm just ... an onlooker? It isn't hurting me. I feel for him, yes, but his fate doesn't seem to have made much impression on the world in general. Yet at the same time, somehow I think it makes the world less.'

'Do you know him?'

'I feel that I *should* know him, certainly,' she answered, simultaneously shaking her head. And ruefully, 'I know that I was watching him when I should have been watching the road. I went through two red lights at least!'

Trask nodded, took her by the elbow and guided her across the street. 'Let's join them and see if anyone else has a clue.' In fact he already had more than a clue but was unwilling to give it voice. If he was right, then just like the ecopath he could scarcely view this phenomenon as Earth-damaging. In fact it might even be a relief.

With Whitehall no more than a ten minute walk away, the torn front page from a discarded *Pravda* seemed strangely out of place where it spun slowly in the current of the flooded gutter, inching soggily and perhaps prophetically towards the iron-barred throat of a gurgling sump. But as if in defiance of the stinging rain, the night, and all other distractions, the phantom hologram continued to display itself wherever the glances of Trask and Anna Marie English happened to fall. It was there in the tiny unmanned foyer, playing on the neutral grey doors of the elevator as if projected there from their eyeballs; and when the doors hissed open to admit them, they took it with them into the cage to be carried up to the top floor offices of E-Branch HQ.

The rest of the building was a well-known hotel; bright lights at the front, and a uniformed doorman from the Corps of Commissionaires sheltering from the rain under his striped plastic canopy, or more likely inside taking a coffee with the night clerk now that all the guests were abed. But up here on the top floor . . .

This was a different world. And a weird one.

E-Branch: Ben Trask felt much the same about it now as he had fourteen years ago when he was first recruited, and as every Branch esper before and since. Alec Kyle, an old friend and ex-Head of Branch was dead and gone now, (*was he? And his body, too? Was that what this was all about?*) but he had come closest to it when he'd used to say, 'E-Branch? A bloody funny outfit, Ben! Science and sorcery − telemetry and telepathy − computerized probability patterns and precognition − gadgets and ghosts. We have access to all of these things . . . now.'

That 'now' had qualified it. For at the time, Kyle had been talking about Harry Keogh. And later he had *become* Harry Keogh; Keogh's mind in Kyle's body, anyway . . .

The cage jerked to a halt; its doors hissed open; Trask and the unnaturally aged 'girl', and the hologram, got out.

Hologram or phantom? Trask wondered. *Gadget . . . or ghost?* When he was a kid he'd believed in ghosts. Then for a time he hadn't. Now he worked for E-Branch and . . . sometimes he wished he were a kid again. For then it was all in the imagination.

Ian Goodly, the Night Duty Officer, was waiting for them in the corridor. Very tall, skeletally thin and gangly, he was a prognosticator or 'hunchman'. Grey and mainly gaunt-featured, Goodly's expression was usually grave; he rarely smiled; only his eyes – large, brown, warm and totally disarming – belied what must otherwise constitute a rather unfortunate first impression, that of a cadaverous mortician. 'Anna,' he offered the girl a polite nod. 'Ben?'

Trask returned the unspecified query. 'Do you see it, too?'

'We all do,' Goodly answered, his voice high-pitched and a little shrill, but not unusually so. And before Trask could say anything else: 'I guessed you'd be in. I've told them to wait for you in the Ops room.'

'How many of them?'

Goodly shrugged. 'Everyone within a thirty mile radius.'

Trask nodded. 'Thanks, Ian. I'll go and speak to them. And you'd better go back to keeping watch.'

Again Goodly's shrug. 'Very well, but apart from this it's going to be a quiet night. This thing is happening, and soon it will be finished. And then we'll see what we'll see.' He began to turn away.

Trask caught his arm and stopped him. 'Any ideas?'

Goodly sighed. 'I could give you . . . an "educated guess". But I suspect you'd prefer to let it play itself out, right?' Like all hunchmen, he was cautious about being too specific. The future didn't like being pinned down.

9

Someone had called the elevator; its doors closed and the indicator signalled its descent. As Goodly made to return to his watch, Trask uttered a belated, 'Right,' then turned left along the corridor and headed for the Ops room. And Anna Marie English limped along behind him.

In the Ops room they found their colleagues waiting for them. In front of the briefing podium an area had been cleared of chairs where eleven espers formed an inward-facing circle. Trask and the girl made thirteen. *A witch's dozen*, he thought, wryly. *We complete the coven.*

As the circle opened up and its members adjusted their positions the better to accommodate the latecomers, so Trask saw the point of the formation. The combined awareness of the espers added to the hologram's authentication: to experience the thing as a group was to focus it, lend it definition. And the hitherto nebulous mental projection expanded in a moment from a 3-D picture in Trask's mind's eye to a seemingly physical, apparently solid figure right there in front of him! But only *apparently* solid, for obviously it wasn't real.

The ring formed by the espers was maybe fifteen to eighteen feet in diameter; the location of the smouldering corpse where it tumbled backwards, head over heels, free of the floor, as on some invisible spit, was no more than ten feet away from any individual viewer. If it were solid – if it were 'here' at all – then the figure would have to be that of a child or a dwarf. But its proportions were those of a normal, adult human being. And so the apparition *was* some kind of hologram, viewed as from a considerably greater distance than was apparent. It was like a scene in a crystal ball: they were seeing something which had happened, or which was even now *in enactment*, somewhere else. And more than ever Trask believed he knew this ... victim? And more than ever he suspected that this was a scene from another world, even another universe.

On entering the room, the Head of Branch had noted the identities of the eleven. There was Millicent Cleary, a pretty little telepath whose talent was still developing. There seemed little doubt but that one day she would be a power in her own right, but right now she was vulnerable – telepathy could do that to a person – and Trask thought of her as the kid sister he'd never had. Then there was David Chung, a hugely talented locator and scryer. He was slight, wiry, slant-eyed and yellow as they come. But he was British from birth, a Londoner, and fiercely loyal to the Branch. All of them were loyal, or else the Branch would fail. Chung tracked Soviet stealth subs, IRA units in the field, drug-runners – especially the latter. Addiction had killed his parents, which was where his talent had its genesis. And it was still growing.

The precog Guy Teale stood to the left of Trask. Like Ian Goodly, he was 'gifted' in reading the future, a suspect talent at best. The future didn't like being read and had kicked back more than once. Teale was small, thin, jumpy. Easily startled, he lived on his nerves. His sometime partner Frank Robinson, a spotter who infallibly recognized other espers, stood next to him. Robinson was as blond as Teale was dark; boyish and freckled, he looked only nineteen or thereabouts, which was seven years short of the mark. The pair had worked with Trask on the Keogh job some six or seven months ago; they'd helped him corner the Necroscope in his house near Edinburgh, and burn the place to the ground. That had caused Harry to escape right out of this world to a place on the other side of the Perchorsk

Gate. Since then, everyone who knew the score had prayed that he wouldn't be back. And he hadn't been . . .

. . . *Until now?* Trask wondered. *Is this – image – is it Harry?* And he suspected that they were all wondering the same thing. And just like him, they'd all be glad that it was *only* an image.

Paul Garvey, a full-blown telepath, stood directly opposite Trask on the other side of the circle. He caught Trask's eye through the rotation of the projection and nodded almost imperceptibly. It was his acknowledgement of Trask's thought, which Garvey had 'heard'. Yes, they were all thinking pretty much the same thing.

Garvey was tall, well-built, and had been a good-looking thirty-five year old. But then, that time six months ago, he'd tackled a murderous swine called Johnny Found and lost most of the left side of his face. Since then some of the best plastic surgeons in England had worked on Garvey till he looked pretty good, but a real face is made of more than flesh. Garvey's was mostly tissue now, and the nerves didn't connect up too well. He could smile with the right side but not the left, and so avoided the travesty by not smiling at all.

It had happened when they were tracking Harry Keogh, who in turn had been tracking Found, a necromancer whose speciality was to molest women before and *after* they were dead. Garvey had made the mistake of finding Harry's quarry first, that was all. But the Necroscope had squared it; later, in a graveyard, the police had discovered Found's body so badly chewed up that he was barely recognizable. And despite everything else that was happening at the time – the fact that Harry had been a prime target – Garvey still reckoned he owed him for that.

As for Ben Trask, he reckoned they *all* owed Harry

Keogh something, the whole world. It would have been so easy for the Necroscope to release the plague of vampirism which he carried within himself upon all humanity and be emperor here, with an entire planet for his empire. But instead he'd let them hound him into exile in an alien world of vampires, where he would be just one more monster. Harry had let it happen, yes, before the *Thing* inside him could take full control.

But whenever Trask thought back on that, on the alien passions which had governed Harry – how he'd *looked* the last time Trask saw him, in the garden of his burning house not far from Edinburgh – then his own mixed emotions would sort themselves out in short order, and he would know it was for the best:

The lower half of Harry's figure had been mist-shrouded, visible only as a vague outline in the opaque, milky swirl of his vampire mist ... but the rest of him had been all too visible. He'd worn an entirely ordinary suit of dark, ill-fitting clothes which seemed two sizes too small for him, so that his upper torso sprouted from the trousers to form a blunt wedge. Framed by a jacket held together by one straining button, the bulk of Harry's rib-cage had been massively muscular.

His white, open-necked shirt had burst open down the front, revealing the ripple of his muscle-sheathed ribs and the deep, powerful throb of his chest; the shirt's collar had looked like a crumpled frill, insubstantial around the corded bulk of his leaden neck. His flesh was a sullen grey, dappled lurid orange and sick yellow by leaping fire and gleaming moonlight. And he towered all of a foot taller than Trask, quite literally dwarfing him. But his face –

– That had been the absolute embodiment of a waking nightmare! His halogen Hallowe'en eyes which had

seemed to drip sulphur. And his ... grin? A grin, was that what it had been? Maybe, in an alien vampire world called Starside on the other side of the Möbius Continuum. But here on Earth it had been the rabid slavering grimace of a great wolf; here it was teeth visibly elongating, curving up and out of gleaming gristle jaw-ridges to shear through gums which spurted splashes of hot ruby blood; here it was a writhing of scarlet lips, a flattening of convoluted snout, a yawning of mantrap jaws.

That face .... that mouth ... that crimson cavern of stalactite, stalagmite teeth, as jagged as shards of white, broken glass. What? Like the gates of hell? That and worse, for Harry had been Wamphyri!

Trask started massively as Anna Marie English, standing on his right, grasped his elbow and needlessly, breathlessly stated, 'Sir, he's moving away from us.'

She was right, as everyone there could see. The hologram of the corpse was getting smaller, falling or receding faster and faster towards a multi-hued, nebulous origin or destiny out of which the blue, green, and red ribbons of neon light reached like writhing tentacle arms to welcome it. The smoking, rotating figure dwindled; it became a mote, a speck; it disappeared!

And where it had been —

— An explosion! A sunburst of golden light, expanding silently, hugely, awesomely! So that the thirteen observers gasped and ducked down; and despite that it was in their group mind, they turned away from the blinding intensity of the glare and what flew out of it. All except Ben Trask, who shielded his eyes and shrank down a little but continued to watch — because he must know the truth. Trask, and also David Chung, who cried his astonishment, staggered and almost fell. But they had seen, both of them:

Those myriad golden splinters speeding outwards from the sunburst, angling this way and that, sentient, seeking, disappearing into as many unknown places. Those – pieces – of the Necroscope, Harry Keogh? All that remained of him? And as the last of them had zipped by Trask and vanished silently out of view – out into the corridor, apparently – so the streamers of blue, green and red metaphysical light had blinked out of being, returning the briefing room's illumination to normal.

Except ... that last golden dart had seemed so real. Why, Trask could have sworn that it had actually materialized right here in the Ops room, sentient and solid, before speeding out into the corridor and disappearing from view!

And now, within the room, thirteen startled, gaping, extraordinary human beings. But *perfectly* ordinary in comparison to what they had witnessed ...

Trask forced himself into action, stepped across the room to where David Chung was still mazed, staggering. He took hold of him, steadied him, snapped, 'David, are you all right?'

'No – yes,' the other answered. 'But he isn't.' He licked dry lips and closed his slack mouth, half-pointed and flapped a hand towards the centre of the room where the espers were moving about once more.

'Was it Harry?' Trask breathed.

Chung sighed heavily and collapsed a little into himself. 'Oh, yes. It was Harry, Ben. It *was* him.'

'The end of him?'

Chung nodded, opened his trembling hand and showed the other what he was holding: a pig-bristle hairbrush whose oval wooden plaque fitted snug in his palm. For a moment Trask was mystified ... then he understood. It was Chung's talent: he was a sympathetic tracker, a locator. Following the Bodescu affair Harry Keogh had stayed here at E-Branch HQ for a month, filling in the blank spaces. For a time he'd even considered taking on the position of Head of Branch. But with the loss of his wife and son, the Necroscope's world had collapsed and he'd moved on, become a recluse up in Scotland. The hairbrush had been his, one of several items he'd left behind.

'I've kept it all this time, since I was first recruited into the Branch,' Chung now explained to the other espers as they gathered round. 'This and one or two other pieces which were his. Six months ago, when the Russians reported Harry's escape through the Perchorsk Gate, I took out his things and tried to locate him. I mean, I obviously couldn't *locate* him, but it was just the same as when Jazz Simmons went through: I knew that Harry wasn't here, not in this world, but he wasn't dead either. He was in Starside.'

'And now?' It was Anna Marie English, worrying for her world, for herself.

Chung shook his head. 'Now he isn't.'

'Not in Starside?' one of the younger espers gasped. 'You mean he's come back? He's here?'

Again Chung shook his head, showed them the brush in his hand. 'This piece of wood, these few bristles, meant something, told me something. They told me that the Necroscope was alive; if not here, alive somewhere. Only let me pick up this brush or Harry's other things, and I knew it. Now ... it's just a hairbrush, no longer alive. And neither is Harry Keogh. He died a few moments ago, somewhere. And we all saw it.'

'Harry's dead.' Ben Trask made no bones of it. 'What we've just witnessed was him. Somehow, he found a way to let us know, give us peace of mind. That's how I see it, anyway.'

16

Ian Goodly came in with a pair of late arrivals: another esper and the Branch's Minister Responsible. The Minister was in his mid-forties, young for his job, but had a mind sharp as a knife. He was small and dapper, with keen blue eyes, and dark hair brushed back and plastered down. His blue suit was fashionable in the Corridors of Power; somehow his dress as a whole marked him as a person of class. In no way psychically talented, still the Minister was Branch; he too had felt the call – something had lured him here – until a moment ago, when it had stopped.

While Trask told the Minister what had happened, Goodly fetched coffee. Then for an hour, two, the entire group sat around and remembered Harry. They said very little but were satisfied just to be there. And despite that they should be jubilant, they weren't. And for all that a great plague had passed them by, most of them felt they'd lost a friend.

David Chung had put Harry's brush in his pocket; every now and then he would reach in and touch it with his fingertips. But it was just a brush now, wood and glue and bristle, inanimate, without being.

And that's how it would stay for sixteen long years . . .

A fortnight later Zek Föener called from her Greek island home in Zante. She'd put it off until it was unbearable, but in the end had to speak to Trask. 'Are we friends again, Ben?'

For all that she couldn't see him, he nodded and smiled. He knew that Zek would sense it, for she was a powerful telepath. 'After that job we did on Janos Ferenczy's creatures in the Med? We'll always be friends, Zek.'

'Despite that I helped him in the end?' Her voice was

17

a little distorted by the line but her anxiety was real enough. Trask's talent was working for him, so that her sincerity was as tangible as the steady beat of his own heart.

He shrugged, which she would also sense, and said, 'You're not the only one who helped Harry, Zek.'

'You, too? I somehow thought you would.'

'I took a chance,' he told her. 'If it had gone the other way ... I could have ended up the biggest traitor mankind has ever known! By now there might have been a new world order.'

'I know. I thought much the same thing. But it *was* Harry, after all.'

'Half of it was, anyway,' Trask answered.

'Actually, he died six, seven months ago,' she said.

'What?' She'd taken Trask by surprise.

'He was dead to us the moment he went through the Perchorsk Gate,' she explained. 'Or as good as. There was no way we were ever going to see him again. He'd used *both* of the Gates, the one in the Urals and the one in Romania. He couldn't come back; the grey holes would reject him.'

Trask had been happy to hear her voice, talk to Zek, but suddenly his mood was grim. She'd brought something up that he didn't like to think about. 'That's true as far as it goes,' he said, 'but his son used a different route. Harry had considered himself the master of the Möbius Continuum, but in fact he was a novice. Those are his words, not mine. Harry Junior was the real master. But if anyone knows that, you do: it's how he brought you and Jazz out of that place back here.'

There was a pause before she answered. 'The Dweller still worries you, right?'

'The Dweller?' Trask frowned. But in the next moment: 'Oh, yes, you mean Harry Junior. He worries me, right enough. The Perchorsk Gate worries me, and the resurgence of one of the Danube's tributaries near Radujevac in Romania. They all worry me, for they're all routes into this world from the world of the vampires.'

'But they're covered now, surely?'

'Harry Junior isn't.'

And now it was Trask's turn to sense the shake of a head. 'He won't be coming back,' Zek told him. 'He was Wamphyri, yes, but he was different. As different as the Lady Karen. As different as his father. He fought for his territory on Starside, and he'll stay there and keep it. He battled with the vampires, Ben, destroyed them, and to my knowledge he didn't create one out of himself. He kept no thralls, no lieutenants, no vampire lovers. Just friends. But they *did* love him, even as much as the Great Majority loved his father.'

She had reassured him. 'Zek, I know you've turned me down before,' he said, 'but I really think you and Jazz should come over here some time. Be our guests and stay in London a while at our expense, and tell us your story in full. No, you don't owe us anything, neither one of you. But you said it yourself: we're friends. And the pair of you have such a lot of information locked in your heads: about Starside, the Wamphyri, even things about Harry Keogh and his son, that only you know. The world's improving, Zek — not by leaps and bounds, not yet — but who knows ... maybe you can help it along the way? Or if not help it, protect it at least.'

And before she could answer him, 'I mean, it's not like it used to be, Zek, not any more. You were used, you and Jazz both — oh, and too many others — by Russia's E-Branch, and by ours, too. But lessons were learned and it isn't like that any more. We are learning all the time. I've thought about it a lot, and it's as if everything the Necroscope touched upon has been improved and changed forever. Before he'd even discovered the Möbius Continuum, he had to use Checkpoint Charlie in Berlin to get into East Germany and talk to Möbius in his Leipzig grave. And where's the checkpoint now, eh? As for Romania ... Do you see what I mean, Zek? It's as if mankind has turned over a new leaf, and all since Harry came along, or since he left us. But should we be surprised, really? I remember Harry once said, "There are a great many talents among the dead, and they have their ways of using them." But it was him who showed them how to talk to each other, connecting them up in their graves. Since then – just look around the world.

'Are they responsible, the teeming dead? Who knows what they've achieved, or how they did it? Communism is on its last legs, a dismal failure, and the world's a safer place. After we send the rest of our false ideological gods packing, then maybe we can start over: a grand restructuring, the ecology of Mother Earth herself. Right now the world *is* safer, but it's still not safe enough. Could you and Jazz help make it just a little bit safer, Zek? That's what I want you to think about. If not for me, for Harry. I mean, don't you reckon it's worth finishing the job that he started?'

'That's cheating, Ben,' she told him.

'Well, think about it anyway.'

Later, she did think about it. Zek and Jazz both. But they didn't go to London. It would take a long time for their wounds to heal, a long time before they would forgive the world's ESP-Branches ...

While sixteen years isn't a long time in the great scheme of things, still changes do occur. People, faces, places change; governments and organizations come and go;

causes and ideologies collapse and others spring into being. But establishments are wont to continue, if only because they are established.

Cold wars had come and gone; hot ones, too, however brief, localized; the world's Secret Services were always in demand. Even during periods of intense *perestroika* and *glasnost* (perhaps especially through such periods), that most esoteric of all services, E-Branch, had gone on, with Ben Trask continuing as Head of Branch. While some of his agents were no more and others had been recruited to take their places, the organization itself was an extremely successful establishment. There would always be work for the Branch, and if ever that should change ... the truth of it was that the government of the day probably wouldn't know what to do with the Branch's esoteric talents if they were disbanded. At least this way the espers could be seen to be working for the common good.

As for the current state of the world:

Communist China was slipping fast on the worndown heels of Russia into a bog of stagnation and economic decay, and the USSR itself was much less unified. Internally, Russia was still recovering from seventy years of self-inflicted wounds, but its occasional haemorrhages were all on the inside now, and issued from vastly reduced lesions. There was no longer even a remote threat of global conflict; the last remaining Superpower, the USA, was ultimately potent and alert, as were her allies. But more importantly, theirs was a generally benign alliance. And just as Ben Trask had once forecast, the world was a much safer place now; so much so that it had become a fad among political and historical commentators to attempt to identify the turning point and name the prime factors and movers:

The microchip; Lech Walesa; giant technological

spin-offs from the space race and the Star Wars programme; spies in the sky; Chernobyl; the total collapse of European Communism; President Reagan, Prime Minister Thatcher, and to some extent Premier Gorbachev; the war in the Gulf, where the entire world had watched with fascination, astonishment, and more than a little horror as uninspired warriors with outmoded, outgunned weapons were mown down under the previously unimaginable onslaught of outraged passions and superior technology.

And through all of this, no one except perhaps a handful of E-Branch members remembered Harry Keogh, Necroscope, or attributed anything of the current world order to his works. And other than that same small handful, no one credited the Great Majority, the teeming dead, with even the smallest part in it.

Which was the way things stood on that Monday morning in January 2006 when Trask arrived at E-Branch HQ in the heart of London, and found David Chung prowling to and fro in the foyer with a cellphone, waiting for him. Except it wasn't the cellphone which brought Trask up short as he entered the building but the look on Chung's face, and what he was holding in his other hand: an old hairbrush.

Harry Keogh's old hairbrush . . .

Before Trask saw that, however, he recognized Chung's urgency and commenced to say, 'Sorry, David, my carphone is on the blink. And anyway there's so much interference these days a man can't even think, let alone speak! Is there a problem? Were you trying to . . . contact . . . me?'

By then he'd seen the hairbrush and jerked to a halt. The occurrences of that night sixteen years ago had all come rushing back in a flood of vivid memories, and the beat of Trask's heart had picked up speed to match the sudden flow of adrenaline. 'David?' he said, making it a question.

Chung answered with a grim nod, simply that, and whisked him into the elevator. But as the doors slid shut on them and they were alone, he uttered those words which Trask had most dreaded to hear: 'He's back.'

Trask didn't want to believe it. 'He?' he husked, knowing full well who *he* must be, the only one *he* could be. 'Harry?'

Chung nodded, shrugged helplessly, seemed lost for words. '*Something* of him,' he answered at last, 'who or whatever he is now. But yes, Ben, I'm talking about Harry. *Something* of Harry Keogh has come back to us . . .'

II

Harry's Room

From the hotel manager's point of view, E-Branch didn't even exist. He occasionally forgot that the hotel had a top storey; which wasn't strange, for he'd never seen it. The occupants of that unknown uppermost level had their own elevator situated at the rear of the building, private stairs also at the rear, even their own fire escape. Indeed, 'they' owned the top floor, and so fell entirely outside the hotel's sphere of management and operation.

As to who 'they' were: international entrepreneurs, or so the hotel manager had been given to understand; nor was he alone in his ignorance. For from the outside looking in, very few would suspect that the building in toto was anything other than it purported to be: an hotel. Which was exactly the guise or aspect, or lack of such, which 'they' wished to convey. And so, except to its members, and to a select core of Very Important Persons in the Corridors of Power, who could be numbered on the fingers of one hand – only one of which, the Minister Responsible, knew the actual location of E-Branch HQ – the Branch simply did not exist.

Yet paradoxically E-Branch's existence and indeed its location were known of elsewhere in the world, to one organization at least and probably more than one. The Soviet equivalent knew of it certainly, and possibly China's mindspy organization too. They knew about E-

Branch HQ but made no great show of it – not yet. Let it suffice that the hotel had been earmarked and was a target; in the unlikely event of global conflict it would be an early casualty, simply because it gave the West too much of an edge.

This was of small concern: since the end of World War Two inner London itself had been a target, as were all centres of government, finance, and commerce worldwide, not to mention a thousand military establishments. And for that matter, so were the Russian and Chinese ESP-agencies targets, including Soviet HQ on Protze Prospekt in Moscow, next door to the State Biological Research Laboratories. Also the Soviet 'listening' cell in Mogocha near the Chinese border, where a team of telepaths kept an eye (or an ear) on the Yellow Peril; and likewise the Chinese outfit itself on Kwijiang Avenue, Chungking. The commencement of World War Three would be a hot time for espers, which was as good a reason as any why such agencies should work for its prevention. And so to all intents and purposes, *perestroika* and *glasnost* were still very much the order of the day.

Which was why it came as no surprise to Trask when Chung told him, 'Our "friends" on Protze Prospekt have confirmed it: something has come through the Perchorsk Gate. They've got it trapped there and want our help with it – urgently.' He used the term 'friends' loosely; the British and Soviet E-Branches had never been more than wary adversaries. In fact the Necroscope in his time had twice pared 'the Opposition' down to the bone. But ever since the Chernobyl disaster, the Russians had been far less reluctant to ask for outside help. They'd asked for it not only with that horror but also with the decommissioning and mothballing of a dozen more outdated, outmoded and positively lethal

25

nuclear reactors, and for ten years now the West had been helping them dispose of the rest of their seemingly endless toxic-waste junkyards. For Earth's sake, if for no other good reason.

As the elevator doors hissed open, letting them out into the main corridor, Trask said, 'I think you'd better start at the beginning. Let me see the whole picture. Also, let's have every available hand in on it. The Duty Officer, espers doing paperwork, administration: the whole shoot.'

But Chung had anticipated him. 'They're waiting for us in the Ops room. But only Millie Cleary knows what it's about. She was Duty Officer last night and took the call from Moscow just an hour ago. As for myself: I couldn't sleep and came in early. Then, passing Harry's room, I ... I sort of felt it. By which time the head of Soviet E-Branch had been on the blower asking to speak to you.'

'Harry's room?' Trask frowned.

They were heading down the corridor towards the Ops room. Chung took Trask's elbow and brought him to a halt, looked over the other's shoulder at a door behind him and nodded. 'Harry's room, yes,' he said. The expression on his face was curious, questioning.

Then Trask remembered. When Harry Keogh stayed here after the Bodescu affair, they'd given him a room of his own. Indeed the Necroscope had literally lived here, however briefly, until his wife's problem had become apparent. That had been ... what? A quarter century ago? And eight years after that he had been debriefed here, after his return from Starside. God, the passage of time: it made Trask feel old! Who was he kidding? Well past fifty he was getting old, and too fast!

He turned and looked at the door, which had its own faded plastic name plate:

Harry's Room

Trask frowned again, and said: 'You know, I don't think I've ever been in there? Well, not since Harry's time, anyway.' He looked at Chung and saw that he was suddenly pale; his mouth was tight and his slanted eyes were blinking rapidly. 'David?'

The other shook his head. 'It's nothing. Just this room, I think. You've never been in there? Well, you're not alone. The Necroscope used it for a while, since when . . .' He shrugged. 'The room housed a computer terminal for eight years, until we refitted. In fact the old machine is still in there, gathering dust. Then the room fell into disuse, and no one seems to have had *any* use for it at all! But now . . . I find myself wondering if it doesn't go deeper than that? I mean, it's always *cold* in that room, Ben. All of the espers feel it: it has an aura. The room itself doesn't seem to want anyone; it doesn't want to be messed with.' Chung stared hard at Trask. 'Haven't you felt it too?'

Trask looked blank. 'I don't think I've even noticed the room,' he said. 'I mean, I *have* noticed it − the name plate and all − but it hasn't made any impression. It's just a place I've lived with every day of my life all these years, without really seeing it.'

'That's exactly what I mean,' Chung answered. 'And all of the others say the same thing. Someone stuck that plate on the door God knows how long ago and since then it's been Harry's room and that's all. But ever since he returned to Starside . . . *we* might have forgotten Harry, or tried to, but it's like this room hasn't.'

A phrase the Necroscope had used came back to Trask, 'His last vestige on Earth?'

Chung shrugged. 'Something like that.'

Trask nodded and said, 'We'll look into it later. First I have to know what's been happening in Perchorsk.'

Waiting for Trask and Chung in the large Operations room, one half of which was an auditorium, a small group of espers occupied seats in the lower tier facing the stage and podium. As the Head of Branch entered, the low murmur of their voices reached out to him for a moment. Then the noise fell away, and showing their respect, they stood up. Trask waved them back into their seats, climbed steps up onto the stage with Chung following on behind. To one side of the podium, a table and chairs faced the audience. The two men seated themselves and Trask went straight into it:

'Being who and what you are, you probably know as much as I do about what's going on. Briefly: something has come through into Perchorsk from Starside. Now, we're each and every one *au fait* with the problem at Perchorsk, so it's no wonder our "colleagues" over there seem to have a flap on. *Anything* that comes through the Gate has to be highly suspect. Except this is more so, because David here tells me it's Harry Keogh . . .'

'. . . *Something* of the Necroscope,' Chung cut into their gasps and whispers. 'Something with powerful connections. We know Harry was – well, changing – but he would have to be changed completely to come back through the Gate. Grey holes don't do return tickets. Once through, that's it: there's no way back. Except maybe through the other Gate, into an underground river which rises again into the Danube. But this thing has come through into Perchorsk. Also, Harry Keogh is dead; we all *saw* him die that time sixteen years ago! Or was he simply undead? No, for he was already that before he went through the Gate. So . . . while my talent tells me it's Harry, my reasoning tells me it just can't be. Which means it has to be something like him, something *of* him.'

Trask took it up again. 'In a minute or two I'll be talking to Turkur Tzonov, the Opposition's top man. We know what his talent is: face to face, he reads minds – but *very* accurately! He'll want to speak to me on-screen, so I can only tell him the truth. That squares things up, because Turkur knows *my* talent and that he can't lie to me either! It's why the handful of conversations we've had in the past have always seemed tentative, lumbering, awkward things. And in all probability, this one, too. Right now: it looks like the Opposition will be asking for our help. Before that I want your ideas, want to know what we'll be dealing with if we offer our assistance. Lately, we haven't had too much on our plate. Nothing special, anyway. Well, with the exception of the Nightmare Zone. So maybe we're all just a wee bit rusty where the really important stuff is concerned. This could be just the opportunity we need to get our various talents out of neutral.'

He looked at their faces looking back at him: Millicent Cleary, who had taken the call from Moscow. Of all E-Branch's agents, Trask probably related most to Millie; he sympathized with her. Telepathy was her talent, and it was also her curse. She'd stayed single, as had most of the espers; but in any case they were already married – to the Branch. The job was one reason she was still single, anyway, and the other was her mind-reading.

For as Millie's telepathy had matured along with her body, so all thoughts of young love, marriage, and children had flown out of the window. What, be a telepath and know your lover's every thought? Even the bad thoughts, which we all have from time to time? And if kids should come along, perhaps pass the 'talent' on to them? No way, for just exactly like Trask himself, Millie had learned that for every basically pure mind out there, there were also the tainted ones, and for far too many of those there were totally corrupt minds, and that at the very limits of the human spectrum there were others so filled with acid that they ate inwards into themselves and outwards into the world in general. She *knew* what was out there, for it was her job to look into such minds. Sometimes even the worst of them.

Although she was a woman of thirty-eight now, Trask still thought of her as his kid sister. There'd been a sort of girl-next-door freshness about her, which galvanized his protective urges: a shyness and all-too-rare innocence; which at the same time permitted her to flash her green eyes, wrinkle her pretty nose, toss her head of copper hair and get really mad if necessary. Occasionally it was, and she'd never failed to stand up for her principles. Millie had retained all of these qualities. And somehow, despite the job, she'd managed to hold on to something of her innocence, too.

'Millie,' Trask said, 'did you pick up anything from your conversation with Tzonov?'

She shook her head. 'He sounded cool, superior, almost disdainful. He wasn't on-screen, just a voice on the line. If I had been able to see him, maybe — and maybe not. There was a lot of static. I mean, mental static.'

Trask said, 'There would be.' He rubbed his chin and scanned the other faces:

Anna Marie English. At twenty-four she had looked fifty. And amazingly, now that she was forty she still looked fifty! It said a lot for Mother Earth. Ecologically aware, English's 'disease' had been held in abeyance by the planet's partial recovery. She would be as good a place as any to start. Trask nodded his intention; a nod which she returned, however imperceptibly, before answering, 'Can we step through into Ops? Maybe use the screens and charts?'

Trask and Chung came back down off the dais, followed the other espers into the Ops section where they switched on table screens and illuminated walls. As shutters whirred into position covering the windows, so the room lit up; suddenly it took on a sort of cold, technological life of its own. On one large wall screen the Earth was shown in flat, stereographic projection, with colours which were lifelike as seen from space.

Anna Marie English went to the screen, paused and looked at the other espers, especially Trask. Her unlovely face was tinged blue in the glare of the projection, and her eyes were invisible behind the reflective sheen of her spectacles. The ecopath's voice was a rasp as she asked of no one in particular, 'Is our world under threat?' She shrugged and turned to the screen. 'I can only offer my opinion.'

The next step was one which everyone present understood well enough: sympathetic perception. She reached up and placed a trembling right hand over a mountainous region of Russia, the Urals some four hundred miles north of Sverdlovsk. And closing her eyes, she held her breath and leaned her physical and metaphysical weight on that one sensitive extension of herself. Several long seconds ticked by, and as many quiet heartbeats, before she straightened up, withdrew her hand and faced her colleagues again.

'Well?' Trask gave voice to all of their anxieties.

She took a deep breath and said, 'Perchorsk reads to me just exactly the way it did the last time I scanned it – menacing! The place itself is ... well, a dire threat, obviously. But I detected nothing of any additional hazard. I did sense something new, however. Something ... warm? In my opinion: if something, someone, has come through to our side, he, she, or it is harmless to our world, maybe even benevolent.'

Trask sighed. Like everyone else, he'd been holding his breath. He looked around. Who else could he use? David Chung was standing close to him, but he shook his head. 'I can only tell you what I've already told you: it feels like the Necroscope to me. *Like* him, but that's all.'

The precog Guy Teale had taken over Duty Officer from Millicent Cleary. As the group of espers had entered the Ops area, Teale had been summoned to duty by his pager, which was locked into Branch communications. Now he returned and said, 'It's the Opposition, Turkur Tzonov again. Still wanting to speak to you, sir.' He looked at Trask. 'I patched him through to the screen in here. When you're ready?'

'He can wait a minute more,' Trask growled. But he knew that if Tzonov was that impatient, this was at least as important as he suspected it to be. He looked at the others gathered round him. Ian Goodly seemed on the point of saying something. Knowing how reluctant 'hunchmen' usually are to air their talents, Trask prompted him, 'Ian?'

'I was waiting until Guy got back,' the gangling, cadaverous esper answered. 'Being likeminded, so to speak — both of us being precogs, prognosticators — I'm interested to get a second opinion.'

'Your own opinion will do for starters,' Trask told him.

Goodly shuffled uncomfortably, then shrugged. 'We're going to be involved,' he finally said. Trask turned towards Teale.

'Likewise,' said the other. 'Who or whatever it is that's come through —' He frowned and paused. '— No, *who*ever it is, he needs our help.'

'He?'

'That's my guess,' Teale answered. 'Educated, as always.'

'And that's it?'

'Heavily involved,' Goodly nodded. 'I see ... interesting times ahead.' He held up a hand. 'But don't ask me to look any deeper than that, Ben. Not yet. It's never safe, and right now it isn't necessary.'

Again Trask's sigh, this time of frustration. 'Right,' he said. 'No more guesswork, however informed. It's time we knew for sure. I'm going to speak to Tzonov. I would prefer all of you off-screen, however, so if you don't mind . . .?'

As they moved out of range, Trask made himself comfortable in a black, padded swivel chair before a large flat screen on a central console. But as Teale made to switch on the televiewer:

'Wait!' Trask stopped him. 'I want you to cover me, all of you. Let's play the Opposition at their own game and have some mental static around here. Tzonov's a damn fine, an extraordinary, mentalist. If I'm not covered he'll be able to read things in my head that even I don't know are there!'

And as they shielded him with the combined energy of their minds, Teale switched on.

The signal from Moscow unscrambled itself onto the opaque screen; a fuzzy hi-tech background blinked into being, while in the foreground sharp features under a high-domed, totally bald head faced Trask and held him with penetrating eyes. He stared back as the picture gained stability and clear, almost better-than-life contrast. On-screen the Russian's face was certainly larger than life: in order to make himself that much more impressive, he'd given his screen extra amplification. Which was scarcely necessary. The looks of the man were ... startling. But Ben Trask was a hard man to intimidate. It's not easy to impress a human lie-detector, a man who will instantly recognize even the most

33

remote distortion or elaboration. It was the reason Trask had always liked and been impressed by Harry Keogh; not so much by the Necroscope's awesome powers but by his humility, and his truth.

'Truth, Mr Trask?' Tzonov raised his right eyebrow. 'But there you have the advantage. As long as your agents keep you covered, you can lie to your heart's content and remain hidden in their static. As for myself, I have no such safeguard. Nor do I need one, not on this occasion. If I wanted to play games ... well, I'm sure you know I have enough clever chessmen, without my own personal involvement. So there we have it: I am here to ask a favour of you, not to lie to you or spy on you.' Tzonov's voice – well-modulated and without accent, and to all intents and purposes lacking in emotion – nevertheless contained the merest suggestion of a sneer.

Trask smiled back, however tightly. 'For someone who protests my advantage over his own "innocence", you picked that out of my mind easily enough, Tzonov. Naturally I'm concerned about the truth; I always have been and always will be. It happens to be my talent.' While he answered, he studied the other's face.

Turkur Tzonov was part-Turk, part-Mongol, all man. Without question he was an 'Alpha' male, a leader, an outstanding mind housed in an athlete's body. His grey eyes were the sort that could look at and into a man, or through him if the mind behind them considered him of little or no importance. It was a measure of Trask's stature that Tzonov's eyes looked *at* him, and not without respect.

The Russian's eyebrows were slim as lines pencilled on paper; upwards-slanting, they were silver-blond against the tanned, sharp-etched ridges of his brows. From the eyebrows up he was completely hairless, which was so in keeping with his other features as to make it appear that hair was never intended. Certainly his baldness wasn't a sign of ill-health or premature aging; the broad bronze dome of his head glowed with vitality to match the flesh of his face, where the only anomaly lay in the orbits of Tzonov's eyes. Deep-sunken and dark, their hollows seemed bruised from long hours of study or implacable concentration. Trask knew it was a symptom of the man's telepathy. Tzonov's nose was sharply hooked, which despite his light grey eyes might mark him as an Arab; except Trask suspected it had been broken in an accident or a fight. Probably the latter, for the head of Russia's E-Branch was a devotee of the martial arts. His mouth was well-fleshed if a little wide, above a chin which was strong and square. His cheeks were very slightly hollow, and his small, pointed ears lay flat to his head. The picture overall was of a too-perfect symmetry, where the left and right halves of the Russian's face seemed mirror images. In the majority of people this would be a disadvantage, Trask thought: the physical attractions of a face, its 'good looks', are normally defined by imperfections of balance. Turkur Tzonov to the contrary: paradoxically, he was a very attractive man.

The secret lay in the eyes, which were a fascination unto themselves. Trask could well understand the Branch's profile of this man, which detailed a long string of beautiful and intelligent female companions. None of them had voiced any complaint when he moved on; they had all remained 'loyal' to him in their various ways. Trask wondered if it were true loyalty, or simply that Tzonov knew too much about them. How could any woman speak out against a man who knows every detail of her pastlife? Only a stupid or insensitive or entirely innocent woman would dare, none of which were Tzonov's sort.

And now those near-hypnotic eyes – those telepathic eyes of Turkur Tzonov – were intent upon Trask as the two heads of British and Soviet ESP-Intelligence measured each other across a distance of more than fifteen hundred miles.

Trask's appraisal of the other had taken moments; possibly the Russian had read something of it in his mind; in any case there had been nothing there he could possibly object to. And if there had been, well he was the one who was asking for help. Trask nodded. 'So you have a problem, Turkur ... er, do you mind if I use your first name? I know you're still fond of the term "Comrade" over there, but we're hardly that.'

'Turkur, by all means,' the other shrugged and permitted himself the ghost of a smile. 'As for "Comrade": it's true our organizations have had their differences in the past, Mr Trask – or should that be Ben? But that is history and this is now, and the future is ... oh, a very big place! In a world scrutinized by alien intelligences, perhaps even under the threat of attack, we wouldn't find it so difficult to be Comrades. Am I right?'

His argument and the way he presented it were disarming, especially since Trask knew what he was talking about. Perhaps Trask knew even more than Tzonov thought. For instance, he knew or suspected that the – intruder? – from the other side was a man. And now there might be a way to confirm his suspicions.

'Is that what you think?' he said. 'That your visitor is a spy for the Wamphyri? Their advance guard, as it were? Someone working for Harry Keogh, perhaps?'

If his words caught the other off guard there was little outward sign of it: a single blink, and the almost imperceptible narrowing of cool grey eyes. Then Tzonov's answer. 'The reputation of your Branch is well-deserved, Ben. That is precisely what I think. It's at least a possibility. Between us we control talents with which to combat any such incursion; but until we know what the threat is, or that it definitely exists . . .' He let his words taper off.

'You haven't been able to fathom him, then?' Trask took it that Guy Teale had been correct: what had come through the Perchorsk Gate was a man.

'As yet we're not wholly in a position to fathom him, no,' Tzonov said. 'Rather, he is not in a position to be fathomed.'

'Can you explain that?'

'We're holding him *within* the Gate,' Tzonov obliged. 'At our end, just beyond the Perchorsk threshold. What? But do you think we've learned nothing from the lessons of the past? That we would simply let such a creature in without first considering our actions? A thing – *possibly* a man, which at least has the looks and present shape of a man – from the parallel dimension of the Wamphyri?'

'Holding him?' Trask couldn't help but frown. Since that time all those years ago when Harry Keogh had gone through the Gate, E-Branch had lost much of its interest in Perchorsk. It had been taken for granted that the Russians were adequately equipped to close the place down. Or if not that, certainly to deal with whatever might come through.

'Ah!' said Tzonov, nodding. And for the first time during their conversation he seemed surprised, and pleased. 'You don't know of the – precautions – which we've taken at Perchorsk.'

'We've always assumed you sealed the place up,' Trask told him. 'Permanently. Any responsible authority would have seen to it at once.'

'That had been tried before,' Tzonov answered with a

grim smile, 'before my time. But do you know, I'm told that it was far better to be in Perchorsk and living in fear, than out of that place and *not knowing* what was going on! And I believe it, for since then we've had the experience of an entirely separate but analogous comparison. I refer to Chernobyl, of course. You may recall that the Sarcophagus was a sealed unit, too – until they opened it up again ... *and* again! But the place is *still* alive and dangerous, and will continue to be for a long time to come. Which is why they must now open it yet again, a third time, in order to be certain they know what's happening. Well, Perchorsk was the same: we had to know what was happening.' He paused, and in a moment continued, 'We've taken precautions, of course. Such as these safeguards are, they have allowed us to contain this most recent visitor at our end of the Gate. So that we now have a choice: we can study him, if it's at all possible, or simply destroy him out of hand. I would prefer to study him.'

'And you want to let us in on it?' Trask kept his face expressionless. 'That would seem very big of you, if I didn't already know that you can't handle it on your own.' It was so, he knew; also that everything Tzonov had told him was the absolute truth. The needle on Trask's mental lie-detector hadn't so much as wavered. 'But what you haven't yet told me is the sort of help you expect from us. How about it, Turkur? What is it we've got that you need?'

'Several things,' the other accepted his reading, made no pointless attempt to deny the accuracy of Trask's deductions. 'Your Branch has a wealth of experience in such matters, for one thing. Not to mention a diversity of ESP talents. You yourself would be invaluable, Ben. Your ability to look at what we've got here and know the truth of it: whether our visitor is merely a man and harmless, or much more than a man and a monstrous threat. As I am sure you're aware, your talent is unique and we have nothing like you. Then there are your prognosticators – your "hunchmen" – Teale and Goodly. We too have a man who reads the future, our own precog, of course. Alas his talent is ...' Tzonov shrugged, '... middling at best. And I'm sure you're aware of that, too. But your men *are* the best! At the first sign of danger, they'd recognize it immediately. Indeed, it is their nature to know well in advance.'

It was Trask's thought to ask: *What is it about this man or thing that interests you? Why don't you just destroy it out of hand? What do you hope to gain from studying it?* But if he asked those questions and Tzonov chose to lie or obfuscate ... their new found rapport could be broken, and Trask knew now that he needed the cooperation of the Russian telepath as much as he himself was needed. Of course he did, for if David Chung was correct and the visitor was in some way revenant of Harry Keogh ...

'If you won't help us and we're obliged to work on this alone,' (it was as if Tzonov had got inside Trask's head, but Trask prayed that he hadn't), 'and if there's any profit in it ... then we alone reap the benefits. Can you really afford to refuse us? I should think you'd jump at the chance to help!'

He was right. If the visitor was like or 'of' Harry, he must never be allowed to fall so easily into the Opposition's hands. What a weapon they'd make of him! Before Trask let that happen, and if it should be necessary, why he'd kill the visitor himself!

'Very well,' he nodded, 'you shall have our cooperation. But this is a busy time, Turkur, and if we're to work together in Perchorsk there are things I have to see to here first. I'll get my Duty Officer to phone you back, within the hour, to make the necessary arrangements.'

'To phone me?' Tzonov raised his customary eyebrow. 'Is it not better to talk face to face?'

Trask smiled. 'The walls of trust are built by degrees, my friend. First pebbles, later boulders.'

The Russian nodded. 'And they are just as easily tumbled. Remove a pebble, and the whole wall breaks. That is one of our sayings.'

'Exactly,' Trask answered.

'Very well,' Tzonov agreed. 'My Duty Officer will stand by for your Duty Officer's call, for I too have things to put in order. Meanwhile, I shall look forward to working with you and yours.' His face disappeared from the screen and was replaced by white dazzle . . .

'Just the two of us,' Trask spoke to his precogs. 'Myself and one of you two. The flip of a coin.' He held a penny, his good-luck piece of pre-decimal coinage, between thumb and finger.

Ian Goodly shook his head; his high-pitched voice belied his mournful expression as he answered, 'No need for that, Ben. We already know.'

Guy Teale pulled a wry face. 'I'm staying here. That's how we see it, anyway.'

Trask shrugged and said to Goodly, 'Then you'd better get your things together. It won't be long.' His advice wasn't necessary, but between them the espers kept their conversations as near normal as possible. As the precogs left his office, Trask saw David Chung waiting in the corridor and called him in.

'David?'

'I'd like to come with you.'

'You think you'd be of use?'

'I'm fascinated to know the connection between this

thing and Harry Keogh.'

'And that's it?'

'More or less.'

Trask shook his head. 'You're one of our best, David, and I know you have enough to do right here. Also, I have to think of the Branch. If anything were to happen to us out there ... well, the organization would be weakened enough without losing you, too. Still, it's not my decision entirely; I've just been speaking to the Minister Responsible. He's okayed it, however reluctantly, but just for the two of us. So I'm afraid that's that. Incidentally, you'll be in the chair while I'm away. And if anything *was* to happen to us in Perchorsk, you'd most likely stay in the chair. So you see: there's no way we can also jeopardize the life of the heir apparent!'

Chung remained silent, standing there before Trask's desk, until the Head of Branch felt obliged to ask, 'Was there something else?'

Chung looked embarrassed. 'Don't you think it's possible you made a mistake when you were talking to Tzonov on-screen?'

'In what way?'

'When you asked him if he thought his visitor at Perchorsk might be a spy for the Wamphyri, possibly working for Harry? Up until then Harry Keogh hadn't been mentioned. It seemed to me an error, to bring up the question of the Necroscope.'

Trask shook his head. 'I only mentioned him by name, not by talent. I deliberately avoided even *thinking* of Harry's talents. But you see, you'd already put thoughts of Harry into my head. They were *in* there, fresh after sixteen years. Tzonov is possibly the world's finest telepath: his eyes look right into your mind. So even covered by all that static, I still wasn't sure he

41

wouldn't read something. The easy way out was to mention Harry, but slightly out of context. That way, Tzonov would "know" what I thought *he* thought and look no further. You see, David, through you we're reasonably certain that something of Harry Keogh has come back into our world. But the Opposition knows nothing of that, not yet.' He smiled. 'It's just one more reason why I won't take you east with us. You're much too valuable right where you are.'

He stood up and saw Chung to the door. Out there, the long central corridor was empty now, silent. Chung said, 'What about Harry's room?'

Trask nodded. 'It can't hurt to look inside. What was that you said about it? Always cold in there?'

As they walked down the corridor and paused at the door in question, Chung answered, 'Cold, yes. Always. The heating is on but the room stays cold.' He reached for the doorknob . . .

. . . And the door opened!

Both men gasped and started, then breathed mutual sighs of relief, glancing at each other sheepishly as the cleaning lady, Mrs Wills, came into the corridor. Armed with her appointments – galvanized bucket, short-bladed squeegee, mop and dusters – she perspired freely.

Sure that his shock was still registering, Trask made an effort to cover his embarrassment. 'Well . . . Mrs Wills doesn't look very cold,' he said. And speaking directly to the cleaning lady, 'Mr Chung was telling me how this room always feels too cold. How do you find it?'

Mrs Wills was a short, rather stout, fiftyish Londoner. Not especially bright, she was a hard worker and had a heart of gold. She was the only permanent member of staff who was in no way 'talented', and in all her fifteen years' service to the Branch she had never had the slightest idea what it was all about, except that its simple rules were for obeying and its people not for talking about. Indeed, Mrs Wills had been chosen for her singular lack of curiosity. Now her face lit up ruddily as she beamed first at Trask, then Chung: two of the gentlemen 'what she did for'.

Finally Trask's question got through to her. 'What, Mr 'Arry's room, sir? Cold, did yer say? Can't say I've noticed it meself. But the 'eating's working, all right!'

Concerned, she followed them in. At the back there was a recess with a sliding door, containing a wash basin, shower, and toilet. In front ... just a small overnight bedroom, maybe four paces by five, from the days when the top floor, too, had belonged to the hotel. The floor space along one wall was occupied by an obsolete computer console, with a chair and space below for the operator's feet, plus a second swivel chair and ample work surface. In a corner, a small wardrobe stood open; it was equipped with coat hangers, and shelving to one side.

Chung nodded to indicate the wardrobe's interior. 'Some of Harry's things,' he told Trask. 'A shirt of his, trousers and a jacket. A bit mothy by now, I should think. Plus a few other bits and pieces on the top shelf there. The other items were left behind −' (he glanced out of the corner of his eye at Mrs Wills, who had found a speck of dust to wipe from the computer console), '− by people we lost from time to time. I kept them . . . because I didn't like to destroy them. As a locator, I'd used them all in my time. Stuff belonging to Darcy Clarke, Ken Layard, Trev Jordan. These things formed my link with them in the field . . .'

As Chung talked Trask was looking into the wardrobe, but he wasn't seeing. Rather, he was feeling. And Chung was right: the room was cold. Or if not cold, empty. Despite the computer console, the wardrobe and its contents, it felt like an empty space, as if nothing was here. Not even Trask, Chung, and Mrs Wills. Trask felt like an echo of himself in this room, like a shadow. He felt if he stood here just a little while longer he might fade into the walls and disappear forever. The place was psychically charged, definitely. And the cold wasn't physical but metaphysical, psychological ... supernatural? Whichever, Trask shivered anyway.

Mrs Wills had finished with her dusting. 'There we are,' she said, drawing Trask back into himself. 'All spick-'n-span again. As my Jim's always saying, "Meg me love, whatever yer do, just be sure yer keeps 'Arry's room spick-'n-span." That's what my Jim always says.'

As she turned away Trask's jaw fell open and he glanced at Chung. Then she'd gone back out into the corridor, and the two espers were after her in a moment. 'Er, Mrs Wills.' Trask caught her by the elbow. 'Did you and, er, Jim – I mean, did you *know* Harry, then?'

Her hand flew to her mouth and her eyes went wide. 'Oh, my! Was I talking about Jim again? Oh, dear, I *am* sorry, sir! I mean, after all these years, yer'd think I'd let it be, now wouldn't yer?'

Trask raised his eyebrows, looked mystified, waited.

'See,' she said, 'my Jim was a talker. Lord, Jim could talk! Of a night before we'd go ter sleep, he'd just talk and talk and *talk*! About all and everything, and nothing very much. I used ter tell him, "Jim Wills, yer'll likely talk yerself ter death one day!" And bless him, he did. A heart attack, anyway. But ... well ... yer see, I was so used ter Jim's voice, that sometimes I 'ears it even now! And even if I never did know Mr 'Arry, whoever he is, it seems my Jim must 'ave known him, or 'eard of him, anyway. Truth is, my Jim says an 'ell of a lot of 'em knows – or knew – 'Arry Keogh.'

44

That did it. There may be plenty of Harrys in the world, but by Trask's reckoning there could only be one Harry Keogh. The Necroscope's second name had never been mentioned − or it shouldn't have been − in front of Mrs Wills. Her knowledge of his Christian name was easy to explain: she'd been reading it five days a week, plainly visible on the plaque on the door. But his surname? Trask glanced at Chung.

David Chung was thinking much the same thing as his boss. Through Harry, the espers of E-Branch had learned that death is not the end but a transition to incorporeality, immobility. The flesh may be weak and corruptible, but mind and will go beyond that. People, when they die, do not accompany their bodies into dissolution but become one with the Great Majority; and merging into a sort of limbo − a darkness where *thought* is the all − the minds of the teeming dead occupy themselves naturally with whatever was their passion in life. Great artists continue to visualize magnificent canvases, pictures they can never paint; architects plan faultless, world-spanning cities they can never build; scientists follow through the research they weren't able to complete in life, whose benefits can never be passed on to the living.

And Jim Wills, the cleaning lady's husband? In life he'd just overflowed with words; and the one he'd loved to talk to most of all . . . had been his wife. Was it so strange? And how many other lonely people 'hear' their absent loved ones talking to them, Trask wondered? But out loud he only said, 'What else has Jim told you, Mrs Wills?'

Perhaps there was a tear in the corner of her eye as she looked at him, but she hid it and smiled anyway. 'Only how I should be a good girl,' she said. 'And treat others the way I'd expect to be treated. And remember that Jim loved me, and only me, all his days.'

Trask nodded. 'That's all good advice,' he said, softly. 'But I meant about Harry. What did Jim tell you about Harry?'

She shrugged and sighed. 'Not much. Just ter look after his room and keep it spick-'n-span, that's all. "Meg, me love, whatever else goes ter the wall, you look after 'Arry's room," he says. And when I asks him why, he shrugs and says, "Well, yer never knows when he'll be needin' ter use it again, now does yer?"'

She looked at the two espers and smiled, and the tears were gone now. 'Anyway, that's what my Jim always says . . .'

PART TWO

Nestor's Story

———

I

Sunside

Three days earlier (by Earth's chronological system), at the dawn of a long Sunside 'day', the vampire Lord Nestor had gone to earth in the forest a mile or two north of the leper colony on the fringe of Sunside's prairie belt. In fear, loathing, and great trepidation — trembling, aye, even the necromancer Lord Nestor of the Wamphyri! — he had plunged headlong through the deep dark woods, away from the gold-stained horizon where the sun rose inexorably, menacingly in the south.

There in the gloom of the forest, stumbling into a stream, he had stripped naked and washed himself scrupulously clean in every part, until even his metamorphic vampire flesh was raw, red, and broken from his furious scrubbing. And in his shrinking mind (known also to his parasite vampire, of course) one terrifying thought eclipsing all others: that he'd spent last night among Szgany lepers, watched over by lepers, tended and fed by lepers, and . . . infected, perhaps? By lepers?

Leprosy: Great Bane of the Wamphyri! And Nestor had been with these stumbling, crumbling people from sundown to sunup, in their place, unconscious in one of their beds and covered by their blankets . . .

They'd discovered him where his crippled flyer had come down in the forest close by; they had touched him, lifted him up, taken him to their colony. Their wooden spoons had carried soup to Nestor's dribbling mouth, while his lungs had breathed air which theirs had breathed out! Their bandages and healing salves had covered his wounded face and eyes ... but what were ointments against the curse of leprosy? And so he had scrubbed his body raw, then dressed himself in his soiled leather clothing, and with something of his composure regained followed the stream east and a little north.

Mainly Nestor had walked in the shallow water, shaded by dense foliage along the banks. His eyes had been half-blinded by silver shot, and though the lepers had pricked most of the tiny poison pellets out of his flesh, it would be a while yet before his parasite leech could heal him completely. By sticking to the water he avoided obstacles: he couldn't crash into things and further damage himself. But always he'd been aware of the furnace sun's rising, however gradual, and had known he must find shelter before its lethal rays could strike through the trees and discover him there.

And shortly, where the stream slowed, broadened out and flowed deep over its bed, in a cave under a rocky vine-draped outcrop that jutted over the water, there Nestor had collapsed on a shingly ledge and stretched himself out to sleep, hopefully to regain his strength. But sleep was difficult; he was not long awake following a night's rest in the place of the lepers; his mind wove this way and that as he considered and reconsidered his position, his chances.

Actually, they were good: so long as he stayed here in this cave through the hours of daylight, he would survive. At sundown, avoiding the makeshift camps of Travellers, he would venture north, climb the barrier mountains by the light of the stars, and send out a mindcall through the passes in the peaks to his Lieutenant Zahar Lichloathe, once Sucksthrall.

Upon a time, Zahar had been Vasagi the Suck's man; now Nestor's, he had taken his necromancer master's cognomen for his own. Lichloathe was the name that the Wamphyri of Wrathstack had given Nestor out of respect for his talent, which lay in tormenting corpses for their secrets. But it was not that Nestor loathed the dead, rather that they loathed him. As for the Wamphyri: they had grown to respect him, perhaps even to fear him in however small a degree. For with Nestor, something had come among them which seemed worse than dying: the dark and harrowing art of necromancy, by use of which an adept might carry vengeance even beyond death itself. It was an awesome talent. But torturing the dead in Wrathstack was a far cry from this bed of pebbles in a cool dark cave.

So Nestor had lain there making his plans: to climb the barrier mountains and call for Zahar, who would come for him with a flyer to bear him back to the last aerie. Before then, however, a seemingly endless day and the best part of a night had lain ahead, and Nestor would be wise to rest his mind and body both. Yet still sleep eluded him.

In part, it was the agony of rapid metamorphic healing; worse far, it was the terror of dreams he knew he must dream: of sloughing flesh and a crumbling ruin of a man shunned and forgotten, perhaps walled-up and abandoned, fretting to dust little by little in some cold, lonely Starside niche or crevice. A man called Nestor.

So he'd tossed and turned in a fever upon his pebble bed, and as the day wore on the air had grown heavier and more oppressive. Beyond the low mouth of his cave, dragonflies had danced over the slow-flowing water, where sunbeams glanced and sparkled like gold and silver fire on the ripples. It had all seemed so very peaceful out there, harmless; there had been a time in some misty mythical past when it *was* quite harmless, he felt sure. But now –

– Nestor could almost hear the sunlight seething like a refuse pit! Only let him venture beyond the mouth of this cave into those soft yellow rays ... they would eat him alive like the metal-molding acids of the Szgany east of the Great Pass, whose skills in the forging of war-gauntlets alone kept them safe from the raids of the Wamphyri! The sunlight would kill him, reduce him to so much smoke and stench, to tar and sticky black bones. For Nestor was a vampire, and the sun his mortal enemy. And yet it had not always been like this. Except ... he couldn't remember when or how it had been different!

In Nestor's early days in the last aerie, towering tall over Starside's barren boulder plains, he had frequently suffered from sleeplessness. Then the place had been alien to him, and full of fearsome sounds: weird sighings, strange laughter, and screams – a great many of those. Eventually he'd discovered a trick, by means of which he might lull his jittery mind and thumping heart to sleep. It was a simple device: he would try to recall to memory details of that earlier time, before he became Wamphyri. All a waste of effort and useless as counting goats on a crag, for he rarely remembered anything of his life before those days he'd spent in the lonely home of Brad Berea, deep in the Sunside forest.

But in his cave by the gurgling stream, safe for the moment from his terror of the lepers and the sun alike, this time Nestor had tried a variation on the theme. He had attempted to recall all that had occurred *since* that night when he left the shelter of Brad Berea's cabin, to follow the coldly glittering Northstar and seek out the Wamphyri in Starside. And this time it had worked! Almost before Nestor could begin gathering his few vague memories of pre-Wamphyri times together, at last he had fallen asleep.

Except his device worked better than he'd supposed, so that even whilst sleeping the chain of thought which he had set in motion continued. Thus, as Nestor's body rested and his metamorphic flesh worked unseen to repair itself, his dreaming mind recounted in vivid detail all of his morbid story.

But few men would have called it dreaming . . .

At first it came in flashes:

Nestor's near-drowning . . . the burly Brad Berea fishing on the riverbank somewhere east of Twin Fords, and saving Nestor's life when his body came drifting, head-down in the water. Then Brad's cabin . . . his daughter, Glina, who had wanted Nestor for his body. Well, she'd wanted something more than that: a man to call her own, and fill her lonely days and nights. He had been all of a man, certainly . . . enough for any woman. As well, though, that she hadn't wanted a mind.

For Nestor had been an amnesiac. Damaged, his head broken, he had no memories, no past. Except a lone voice in the back of his mind, which was wont to repeat insistently, 'I am the Lord Nestor!' But only a notion, for obviously he was not Wamphyri. The sun didn't harm him; he ate common fare, like common men; his senses were less than a vampire's, indeed less than those of a whole man. No, it had been a fantasy, some lone fragment from lost times . . . Or a forecast?

Glina made him a man – in part, anyway – but never a whole man. Pondering a vanished past, Nestor's mind was wont to wander; lacking the cohesion of memory, his brain and body seemed detached, as if he lived by the will of another. Knowing Glina's flesh and having her (or rather, being made love to by her) became instinctive, an automatic thing; so that in fact there was nothing of love in it. But with blood racing in his veins and his shaft rocking to and fro within her, passion of a kind would light in his eyes, and emotion of a sort blaze up in his heart. But it was never love. Glina had known that.

And sometimes at the climax of Nestor's strange cold passion, as he jerked to a crescendo in her body, she had sensed that he would like to kill her. For then at the height of their sex, his hands would leave her breasts and seek her throat, so that she must protect herself. Sometimes, too, she would hear him speak a name: Misha.

Misha! It had been like a curse, bitter as a wormy apple on his tongue. So that Glina had hated this Misha without even knowing her, because Nestor had known and loved her. Yes, and she'd hurt him more than Glina ever could. Or so Brad Berea's homely daughter suspected . . .

Then came the night of the Wamphyri! . . . their flyers wafting high overhead . . . the propulsors of their warriors making thunder and stenches in the clear night air! But the house of Brad Berea was hidden in a forest thicket, camouflaged, secret, secure. The Wamphyri passed by like swift-fleeting clouds, heading north for the Northstar, to Starside across the barrier range.

But Nestor had seen them; he felt their weird allure; and in the back of his mind, as always, a small but insistent voice repeating, 'I am the Lord Nestor, of the Wamphyri!' A vampire Lord? Perhaps he had been, upon a time, and now by some freak of misfortune was changed back to a man. One way or the other, he had to know.

That night as the house slept, Nestor crept out into

the dark and took his leave of the Bereas. But trekking through the gloomy heart of the forest, he was never alone. Like a clot of blue ice frozen and glittering over the barrier mountains, the Northstar was both beacon and companion. For he knew that the star of ill-omen shone down not only on Sunside, but also on Starside and the last great aerie of the Wamphyri . . .

Towards dawn Nestor had found himself in the foothills – *and in the presence of monsters!*

A pair of Wamphyri Lords had come to fight a duel on Sunside, which Nestor witnessed. Wran Killglance was one (called Wran the Rage after his furies), and Vasagi the Suck the other. Vasagi's face was a nightmare in itself: with no mouth or chin as such, but a tapering trunk and flickering needle proboscis, like the siphon of some monstrous insect . . . but *worse* than a nightmare when Wran was done. For then Vasagi's face had looked like the hole which is left behind when a limb is wrenched from its socket, all bloody and dripping from its rim.

But Nestor had been more than just a witness; indeed, he had been part of the fight, and had probably saved Wran's life. For in his horror of the conflict – the animal *ferocity* which the enormously powerful combatants displayed – Nestor had temporarily forgotten his perverse desire to be a 'Lord' himself; and of the two who fought, Wran had at first seemed the least alien . . .

. . . At first, aye.

Later, with the flush of a false dawn flowing like molten gold along the far southern horizon, Wran had dragged Vasagi to the hillside and pegged him down to await the sun's rising. And while he worked, so he questioned Nestor about his part in all this, and discovered his motive: that he would be Wamphyri. At that, a grimly ironic scheme had entered Wran's mind. Here was one vampire about to die – Vasagi, and his leech still in him – and here a Szgany youth just itching to take his place! And why not? Wran owed him that much at least. It would be such a simple thing to arrange.

It had been arranged! Wran had sent Nestor on some small errand, and in his absence opened Vasagi's spine through skin, flesh, muscle, and ribs to find and drain his leech. For to a vampire the blood is the life, and the best vessel from which to drink it is another vampire's parasite – preferably an enemy's!

Drained and dying, finally the Suck's leech had deserted him and issued its egg. As Nestor returned, Wran caught up the small, skittering, pearly spheroid into his hand, to stare at it in grim satisfaction. He knew that if he, Wran, were a suitable vessel, then that Vasagi's egg would soak like quicksilver through his skin and inhabit him; but he already had a mature parasite leech of his own, which would devour any intruder in a trice.

Then, opening his fist to show Nestor the naked egg, Wran had called him closer. And as if blowing a kiss, he'd sent the thing flying into the other's gawping face!

It had taken nothing more than that: it was the quickest, easiest way to become a vampire. Not the virulent bite, which brings about lethargy, death, and undeath; and not sex, which likewise transmits *stuff* of the vampire between bodies. For in cases such as these the transition is only gradual. The victim *will* become a vampire – always, invariably – but not always Wamphyri. Ah, but when the egg *itself* is passed on . . .

The melding had caused Nestor such pain as he could never have believed possible without experiencing it. By the time he had recovered strength enough to crawl, the sun was very nearly up. But there on a bluff, Vasagi's flyer had waited, its spatulate head nodding this way and that in a soughing breeze off Sunside's forests, and Nestor had known what he must do.

Making his way to the flyer, he passed close to Vasagi, who still clung to life despite his hideous wounds. Then the Suck had begged him to loosen the pegs which held him fast to the hillside. For after all, Nestor already possessed Vasagi's egg and would soon become heir to his flyer. So what more could he want? Surely he could afford to spare his life, what little of it remained, and not leave him to melt in the sun?

Nestor had been naïve in the ways of the Wamphyri. If his egg were a mature leech, doubtless it would have caused him to laugh. But with his own agonies so fresh in his mind, he could scarcely bear the thought of another's. And such agonies: to slump into gurgling glue, vaporize to roiling smoke and stench, and steam away to nothing, like a slug tossed into a campfire! And so he'd paused a moment to loosen and yank free the Suck's pegs, before carrying on towards the patiently waiting flyer.

Before, there'd been a crossbow bolt transfixing the V of muscle between Vasagi's neck and shoulder. Nestor knew, for he was the one who had put it there (Wran had pulled it out when he pegged Vasagi down, just for the pleasure it gave him). Now the ironwood bolt lay in the bloodied dust, and Nestor's empty crossbow swung at his hip. Automatically, he had taken up the bolt and clipped it into its housing under the crossbow's tiller. For if he was really on his way to Starside, it would be as well to take a weapon along – especially now that he knew what to expect there! The crossbow should provide some security at least. For in all Sunside there was no finer shot than Nestor. So they had used to say back in ... back in ... back where? But Nestor no longer remembered.

Then he'd found Vasagi's bloodied battle gauntlet hanging by a thong from the flyer's saddle, where Wran had left it for him. But even then – with the deadly furnace sun so close to breaching the far horizon, and just as close to sending out its sighing, searing golden rays – still the flyer had known its would-be rider for a stranger and would not launch ...

... Until the crippled Vasagi sent a mind-call winging, to stir the beast to action: *Aye, you were ever a faithful creature. When I told you to stay, you stayed. But now you belong to another – it pleases me to give you to him – for a while, at least. And now it's time to fly or die. So fly ... fly!*

Only then, on Vasagi's command, had the flyer extended its wings; and as alveolate bones, membrane and muscle stretched in metamorphic flux, so the creature had launched itself aloft! A moment more, and then –

– Wind whipping in Nestor's face as his mount glided out and turned in a rising thermal over Sunside! And as its arched manta wings formed vast scoops or air-traps, so the beast rose up towards the peaks, where soon the sun would strike with hammers of gold. But Nestor was no longer afraid, not of anything. For welling up from deep within his changeling's mind and body, he'd heard the first discordant notes of a strange, savage and wonderful song – Wamphyri!

And *how* that silent song of metamorphosis had thrilled in his contaminated blood, for at last he had known he was on his way.

To Starside!

To the last aerie!

Wamphyri! *Wamphyyyyri ...!*

*

In Nestor's dream the past came alive with such imme-
diacy and in such vivid detail, it was as if he lived it
again. Indeed, as if it were happening even now:

With the reins trapped in his right hand, and gripping
the left-hand horn of twin pommels in the other, he
used his knees to cling tightly to the hump of the well-
rubbed leather saddle; and flattening himself down out
of the slipstream, he leaned a little forward into the
force of the blast. But even lacking fear and feeling a
wild exhilaration, still he hung on for dear life. The
wind in his face snatched at his breath and struck cold
against his clenched teeth; he found his position precari-
ous, to say the least, and jammed his heels firmly up
under the flyer's wings where they met its body, to give
himself more purchase.

But at least he was airborne and Starside bound at
last. And his weird mount, so heavy and unwieldy on
the ground? Now it glided like some prehistoric bird,
balancing itself on turbulent currents of air and steadily
gaining altitude. *Bravo!* Ah, but while *it* knew how to
fly, Nestor did not!

Perhaps he had known it, upon a time, but all long
forgotten now. Vague memories, revenant of some
elusive, shadowy past – of a flyer just like this one, all
crashed and broken on Sunside, screaming in lethal
sunlight as its skin cracked open to issue jets of steam,
and its fluids dripping free like the juices of a pig on a
spit – were all that remained. Maybe that was how he'd
got himself marooned and lost his memory in the first
place, by crashing his flyer on Sunside and banging his
head. It was an explanation, at least. Well, and now
he'd be a Lord again, and have new things to remember.
Ah, but new things to *learn* first, like flying!

As the mountainside fell away, and the furious bluster slackened, he leaned forward between the jutting

pommels and wiped at his streaming tears. And slitting his eyes, finally he could see again. Meanwhile in its search for thermals, the flyer had spiralled south; and there, far out across the furnace desert, Nestor spied a spear of yellow light lancing from the molten horizon, striking west upon the flanks of the gaunt grey mountains. Sunup, and Nestor's time on Sunside was at an end. 'North!' he shouted at his mount. 'North – Starside – the last aerie!'

From the west, all along the spine of the barrier range, the fan of fire crept closer and the mountains came alive with light. The yellow egg of the sun was set to hatch on the southern horizon, to let its golden bird of prey fly free!

But now, as if answering Nestor's cry however grudgingly, his flyer wheeled lumberingly north and seemed to hang there a moment in mid-air, suspended between the uppermost peaks. And as in a frenzy he cried, 'Faster, fly faster!', the beast commenced a leisurely drift inwards over peaks, ravines and plateau jumbles. Till finally, lowering its tapering neck and head, it slid gradually into a glide.

Nestor couldn't know it, but his mount found no great novelty in all this drama; it had flown this way before with Vasagi the Suck, and knew the route well enough; there was nothing new here except its rider, a feeble-seeming fellow at best. His thoughts were blunt as wedges, not needle-sharp, like the Suck's. He'd not once used his spurs, but sat there wan and wind-lashed in the saddle. Why he was here at all remained a mystery.

Perhaps Nestor sensed the flyer's slow, dull thoughts, and its low regard for himself. But with the sun at his heels he was done with gentling the beast! He snatched the dart from under his crossbow's tiller, leaned forward between the pommel horns and tickled the creature's spine, then concentrated his thoughts in a stream of abuse along its leathery neck and into its head. And he finished with a threat:

Make haste, now, or I'll crawl along your neck and stick this in your ear! The beast heard him; more than that, it felt the first hot breath of the sun upon its hindquarters, put its nose down and glided into the shadows of a pass. And safe from the sun at last, it sped for Starside.

Nestor breathed a sigh of relief, and in the next moment heard guttural laughter and a ringing cry: 'Bravo!'

It was Wran. He launched his flyer from the shadows of a ridge and came up alongside. 'You made it by a breath! What? On a count of ten, your beast's wings would have blackened and crisped to dust! Aye, and it's a long way down, Lord Nestor of the Wamphyri . . .'

His words carried on the air, but they were also in Nestor's mind. It was an art of the Wamphyri; at close range like this they were thought-thieves to a man, but some much better than others. Vasagi had been a veritable master of telepathy, while Wran's talent was merely middling. Now it was Nestor's turn:

Why did you wait?

Ahhh! Wran was taken by surprise, but recovered in a moment. *What? A mentalist, too? But is it you, Nestor, or simply the effect of Vasagi's egg? If the latter, then obviously you got a good one . . . considering its source, that is!* And again he laughed. *As to why I waited: simple curiosity. Frankly, I didn't think you'd make it. Since you have, and since I'm responsible for your — predicament? — it seems only right that I should escort you into Starside, introduce you and make explanation. For you're a cool one, Nestor, and in no way the fool I* first considered you. *The Suck was my enemy, but you'll make a useful ally. And what will you get out of it? Well believe me, you'll need all the friends you can get, in Wrathstack!*

Wrathstack? It was news to Nestor. But the suffix 'stack' had brought a flash of memory. Synonymous with 'aerie', it had painted a picture in his mind of the last great redoubt of the Wamphyri, called ... Karenstack? It had been, upon a time, of that he was sure. Also that he had been there before. But when, how?

His thoughts were so intense that Wran picked them from his mind without difficulty, and answered: *Many a Lord or Lady has dwelled there from time to time, I should think, since the early days of Turgo Zolte. I can't say, for I don't know Starside's history. But now the aerie has new tenants, and on the whole we call it Wrathstack after the Lady Wratha, who brought us here from Turgosheim in the east.* His thoughts had turned sour now.

She's your leader? Nestor was mainly innocent, careless in his choice of words.

She was, for a while, Wran growled in his head. *And with a strong man to ride and guide her ... who can say? She could be again. Well, a partner in leadership, at least. But that's for the future ...* Plainly, he'd grown tired of the conversation. *Now let's make haste. For I've been too long away. Aye, and things are wont to change in a hurry, in Wrathstack ...*

He drew ahead, put on a spurt and sent his flyer diving into the Great Pass, which split the barrier range in a dogleg north to south. Nestor followed (by his will, or purely of his beast's own inclination, he could not say) to hurtle above the bed of the pass at breakneck speed. The bend in the dogleg lay to the rear, a haze of yellow where the sun's lethal rays were trapped for now. Any danger of burning was past, and the hackles on Nestor's neck lay flat. The earlier exhilaration of his ride returned; feeling more in control, he began to enjoy it.

He urged his flyer on. *Faster, faster! Get in front. Show that sluggish creature how to fly!* His beast responded, pulled ahead, left Wran in its wake.

Hah! Wran called after him. *And so you see, he bred good creatures, old Vasagi. But on the other hand, why, there's not so much meat on you!* And then, less grudgingly: *Still, you do sit the beast well, so that what with your mentalism and all, I fancy you'll do all right.*

Nestor looked back and laughed, and cried out loud: 'I'll do better than all right!'

Oh, really? Wran pulled alongside again. *Well, I hope you do, but the odds are all against it. What you have to remember is this: in Wrathstack we're all vampires born. And me? Why, I might well have been born in the saddle!*

But this time his laughter was grating as iron in cold ashes as he swerved his flyer in towards Nestor's, caught it a glancing blow, and almost sent it crashing into the wall of the canyon! Turning side-on to fan the precipitous rock, the creature flattened like a leaf to scrape the weathered stone, and for a moment Nestor felt he'd be tilted into space. Then ... the danger was past and he could breathe again, and from up ahead:

So you'll do better than all right, will you? Maybe you will at that. But first you must live long enough, eh? It had been a lesson, and Nestor wouldn't forget it. Just one of several things which he wouldn't forget ... about Wran the Rage.

The end of the pass was now in sight, where the mountains sloped down to Starside's boulder plains. And on the left, just coming into view, the bulging, blinding dome of the half-buried sphere portal to the hell-lands. Nestor knew it without knowing how he knew; likewise the plume or finger of glowing, poisoned earth that pointed from the Gate out across the barren plains towards the Icelands. To him, these things were more than adequate confirmation that indeed he'd been here before. If only he could remember.

But he was given no time to ponder the enigma; for up ahead Wran swerved right, eastwards, away from the Gate and out towards Karenstack (no, Wrathstack, now), the last great aerie of the Wamphyri. Miles sped by beneath the manta flyers, where their moon- and star-cast shadows flowed like stains in the immemorial dust, or like clots of darkness over bald, domed boulders and riven earth alike. And looming in the north-east, vast monument to the evil of ages past, Wrathstack was a lone fang among the stumps of fallen stacks, where the shattered aeries of the olden Lords lay in tumbled disarray, littering the plain like corpses or rotted mushrooms petrified to stone.

And as if Wran read Nestor's mind again, though in fact he merely conversed, his question came ringing: 'Oh, and have you been here before, too, Lord Nestor?'

Aye, he had, the once at least. These jumbles of toppled stone, their configurations, seemed so familiar they were like memories in themselves; yet they failed to spark others in the aching void of Nestor's head. But he made no comment, neither speech nor thought, except to drive his beast that much faster and draw level again with his vampire companion.

Ahead loomed a stack (or the stump of one), three-quarters of a kilometre broad at its scree-littered base, rising to three hundred metres high by two hundred wide where its hollow neck was like the shattered bole of an ancient tree felled by lightning and turned to stone. The rest of it, the aerie that had been, lay in blocks like the knuckles of a skeletal spine stretched out across the plain. But it was only the first of many.

Side by side, Wran and Nestor rose up and flew across the mighty stump from side to side, and looked down into its yawning, hollowed maw. There were rooms down there, vast pits, and stairwells of bone and stone, and polished vats like the molds for making monsters. 'Exactly so!' cried Wran, picking up Nestor's thoughts again. 'For *this* was an aerie, upon a time! Why, it must have rivalled Wrathstack itself! In Turgosheim in the east, men and warriors have clashed, and blood been spilled, over many a lesser manse than this!'

Nestor looked across at him. 'And yet now ... why do you live lumped together in Wrathstack?'

'Ah-*hah!*' Wran cried. 'It must be the recluse in you, as it was in Vasagi. He, too, would have stayed on his own, if he could. It was because the Suck felt crowded in Turgosheim, that he came here with the rest of us to olden Starside. Or perhaps it's simply your longing for an aerie and territories of your own, which is an urge common among the Wamphyri. But you know what, Nestor? Why, I find myself half-willing to believe that the spirit of some olden creature – some vampire out of time – has indeed returned to inhabit you! In other words, you're a natural, lad, a natural!'

They sped on, gaining height over a wilderness of twisted bone and fretted rock ruins, over tortured cartilage relics and fire-blackened mounds, where other grand aeries had exploded in their bases and slumped down into themselves, forming pyramids of scree and rubble. And Wrathstack drawing ever closer, rearing on high, its uppermost towers, battlements, launching-bays and windows most of a kilometre high and more than an acre in cross-section.

And: 'Up now, up!' Wran shouted. 'Let the winds take you, where they spiral round this last great spire.'

Climb, Nestor commanded his flyer. *Follow on behind. Gain height. Form scoops with your wings, trap the air, and rise on the rising thermals.* It was all sound advice, but wasted; good practice but nothing more. His creature was experienced in all such matters.

And Wrathstack loomed closer still . . .

II

The Last Aerie

Less than a hundred metres from the wall of the colossal stack, both flyers discovered sighing currents of air and commenced a mighty rising spiral. And as they climbed, so Nestor benefited from Wran's knowledge of the place.

Down below, the Rage sent, in the nethermost levels, the very bowels of the place, that's Gorvi's domain. The dark and devious Gorvi the Guile. He keeps the wells, and has flightless warriors on the ground, to repel any would-be incursions. Hah! A pointless exercise! If ever we're attacked, it won't be from the ground. It's just a measure of the way he watches his back. We don't call him the Guile for nothing. Ah, see? Here he comes now, eager to know who won the duel and now returns victorious out of Sunside. But myself or Vasagi, what odds? It will make no difference to Gorvi. He'll be sour – he always is!

A flyer launched from a cavern mouth beneath an overhang of rock and came spiralling up behind. Fresh from resting, the creature fanned its manta wings and rapidly gained on Wran and Nestor's weary beasts. Nestor twisted in his saddle and looked back and down; his wide, curious eyes met Gorvi's only a wing-span to the left and a metre or two below, and he saw immediately how well the other's nickname suited him.

The Guile sat hunched, by no means cadaverous yet

remarkably corpse-like, scowling in his saddle. The dome of his head was shaven save for a single central lock, with a knot hanging to the rear. Dressed in black, with his cloak belling out like tattered wings, the contrast of his sallow features turned him to a leprous vulture settling to its prey. With eyes so deeply sunken they were little more than a crimson glimmer, yet shifty for all that, and hands clutching the reins like skinny claws, this was Gorvi. He seemed a sinister creature: but of course, for he was Wamphyri! And he didn't like the way Nestor stared back at him.

'What's this?' Gorvi finally called out to Wran. 'Some captive you've brought back out of Sunside? A new lieutenant, perhaps? Was he your second in the duel, Wran? And if so, did Vasagi have one also? If not . . . be sure there'll be some who say you cheated.'

Wran dropped back a little and settled lower, levelling with Gorvi. 'Do you think so?' he called across, scowling to match the other's scowl. 'They'll say I cheated, eh? Well as long as you're not one of them, you'll be safe. Or is it that you, too, would care to fly to Sunside with me, and try your luck in the gloomy forests?'

'I meant nothing by it.' Gorvi shrugged and reined back a little. 'I was making conversation, that's all. And so you've taken a prisoner. But a proud one, if I'm not mistaken.'

Again Nestor turned to look back at Gorvi, and this time his lip curled a little as he shouted, 'You want to know who I am, Gorvi the Guile? Then speak to me, not about me! My name's Nestor – Lord Nestor, of the Wamphyri – and the last thing I am is a captive!'

'Eh?' Gorvi was astonished, if not outraged. 'But –'

'– No buts!' Wran cut him short. 'Learn all about it at my reception. But until then, keep your nose out! I'm instructing the young Lord Nestor in the ways of the stack: its personalities and their responsibilities in the various levels which they inhabit. Our time is short. So begone!'

Gorvi reined in more yet, and fell to the rear. And Wran continued, proudly:

'These next levels up – a good many, as you see – are mine; mine and my brother Spiro's, wherein we control the main refuse pits and methane chambers. These are a great responsibility, a huge weight upon our shoulders ... which are broad to take it! If not for the diligence of the brothers Killglance, the stack would go without heat and light, eventually without inhabitants. Seven great levels – high-ceilinged, indeed cavernous, and likewise huge across – that is the extent of Madmanse. For we've named our place in memory of our old manse in Turgosheim, do you see? But new Madmanse is far and away superior to our haunted old promontory home in the east. And oh so well equipped!

'We have launching bays, vats for the brewing of creatures, and all manner of rooms, halls, and stables. In Turgosheim in the time of the tithe, fresh meat was hard to come by. We kept beasts to supplement our diet. But here? Sunside is a well-stocked larder, a hive full of honey, a bottomless well of sweet ... whatever.' And chuckling obscenely, he glanced across at Nestor.

As they spiralled higher still, Nestor began to shiver, for the cold was finding its way into his bones. Soon ... he'd no longer notice it too much. But for now he sat like an icicle in his saddle. In any case he was soon distracted, as out from a yawning launching bay sprang Spiro Killglance aboard a flyer of his own. 'Ho, brother!' he shouted gleefully across at Wran. 'So you've had it out and the Suck is no more. I for one never doubted the outcome. But how did you deal with him ... and who is your friend?' His eyebrows came together in a frown as first he stared, then glared, at Nestor.

Nestor in turn stared back, and committed Spiro's details to memory. Patently the brothers were twins, and possibly even identical, though certainly not in their mannerisms or mode of dress. For where Wran actually looked the Lord (as Nestor had always imagined Lords to be), Spiro seemed far more a vagabond or ruffian, removed from his brother as chalk from cheese. He was loutish, with a loose-hanging lower lip and mainly malign expression, and his 'clothes' were disreputable to say the least: a rag of leather for a shirt, a dirty breechclout, and a strip of cloth on his forehead to keep his unkempt hair out of his fiery scarlet eyes. Other than this, and the fact that Wran wore a small black wen upon his chin, the brothers were physically alike: tall, broad-shouldered, and a little overweight. They might even be said to be handsome – or perhaps 'handsome specimens'. Certainly they were not ugly, not in appearance, anyway.

'By now Vasagi's blood is boiling to slime!' Wran answered his brother's query. 'I drained his leech, then pegged him out on a hillside to await the sun's rising. As for this one,' he glanced again at Nestor, 'he was of use to me. At any rate, I count him an ally. He is the Lord Nestor.'

Spiro's eyebrows peaked. 'A Lord, did you say?'

'Indeed!' Wran answered. 'For he has the Suck's egg!'

'Ahhh!' sighed the other, in amaze. 'But ... you must tell me all.'

'All in good time,' Wran replied. 'But for now let's get on.' And to Nestor:

Where was I? Ah, yes, Madmanse, which now falls behind and below. And up ahead: Mangemanse, where Canker Canison crows to the moon; and higher still ...

*Suckscar! Hah! But now it shall have a new name, to go
with its new master. What do you say to that, Nestor?*

In Nestor's youth, he'd learned a trick to keep his
brother's thoughts out of his mind. Though his youth
and even his brother were forgotten to him now (except
he knew the latter as a vague and largely mythical
'enemy' dwelling on Sunside), the trick itself remained
accessible. It involved thinking obliquely, 'to one side'
of his main stream of thoughts, and so keeping his
secrets to himself. The art was an instinctive thing, and
useful now as never before. For Wran believed that
Vasagi had melted in the sun.

Perhaps he had, and perhaps not. But Nestor saw
how hazardous it could be to admit what he'd done:
namely, that he'd set Vasagi free after Wran had left
him for dead. Perhaps for a similar if not quite the same
reason, he should also leave well enough alone in the
re-naming of Vasagi's manse.

For which reason, finally: *Let the name stand,* he
answered Wran in his own mode. *Suckscar will suffice,
for now at least.*

But then, a moment more and he gasped aloud. For
suddenly Wran's meaning had sunk in! That Suckscar
should be named anew, with a name to suit ... himself!
Its new master! Lord Nestor of the Wamphyri! And
finally, no longer guarding his thoughts but letting
them fly free: *For now ... I really am Wamphyri!*

But: *Huh!* came Spiro's mental grunt. And to Wran:
*Brother, you're changeable as the winds chasing them-
selves around Wrathstack! I thought we'd arranged
that I should be master of Suckscar? That way, between
us, we'd control almost half the stack. And now?*

Now? Wran answered (and this time he was the one
to guard his thoughts, ensuring they went only to
Spiro). *Why, with this simpleton Nestor in place – if we*

can fix it – it will amount to much the same thing! That way, before too long and after we settle one or two other scores, why, you'll still be available to inhabit some other level, eh?

Then for a while, gradually receding, their chuckles hung black as sin and just as secretive, dwindling to nothing in the mental ether. And now there were four flyers, all strung out in a row, climbing towards the higher levels and bays . . .

'Nestor,' Wran eventually called aloud, as rocky caverns and ledges, fretted bone causeways, and external staircases of fused cartilage and stone slipped down and away into the abyss of air. 'There goes Mangemanse below. Only four levels, as you see. More than sufficient for the great hound who dwells there, and not much I can tell you about them. Their master's responsibilities are few; indeed, he seems to exist only to keep us apart! Wratha and the rest of us, I mean. But when we take to our beds, Canker is often on the prowl. He keeps more bitches than the rest of us – he has his needs, you know? – but his real mistress is the silver moon. Oh, you'll hear his howling soon enough, as he sings his devotions to his goddess on high! Still, it surprises me he's not here for my reception.'

'Ah, but other things are on his mind,' Spiro cut in across the blustery gulf. 'For Canker builds a thing of bones!'

'He builds . . . a what?' Wran shook his head and laughed his amaze.

'A device of pipes large and small, made from the hollow bones of warriors where he finds them littered on the boulder plains. He's spent the entire night with his lieutenants, flying to and fro, lifting up bones to his kennel.'

'But why? For what good reason? A device, you say? What sort of device?'

Spiro shrugged. 'An instrument – musical, he says.'

'Musical?' Wran was nonplussed. 'Like the Szgany troupe which Devetaki Skullguise kept in Masquemanse? Aye, they were musicians, but Canker? An instrument of hollow bones?'

'To help him in his devotions,' Spiro tried to explain. 'He swears the moon's deaf and can't hear him, or else she'd come down to be his lover. And so he's determined to sing all the louder, with the help of the thing which he fashions from these bones. How? Don't ask me – ask him! *Hah!* And to think, they call *us* the mad ones! But we only rage, we don't rave!'

'Suckscar!' Wran cried, forgetting in a moment Canker's doings. 'And these were Vasagi's levels: yours, now, Nestor. Or soon to be, we hope. Not much to tell; not much to *do*, in Suckscar, for the heavy duties are all below. But Vasagi was the expert in metamorphism: he could make *monsters!* His vats will be yours now, including the beasts which are brewing in them. But you'll doubtless fashion creatures of your own . . . given time, and with a little help. A favour for a favour, eh, Spiro?' He winked at his brother, gliding now to one side. 'We can all use a little help, from time to time. But in any case, enough of that; for you'll soon be exploring Suckscar to your heart's content.'

He lifted his head, looked on and up, and smiled a gaping smile. 'And now – to my reception!'

Three-quarters of a kilometre below, the collapsed mounds and shattered stacks of toppled aeries were stony jumbles on a pebble plain. South-west, majestic now, the barrier mountains were golden in their peaks; while central and to the east, the grey gradually faded to yellow. Hours yet, some thirty or more, before the sun would strike through the central peaks and play her rays on Wrathstack, and then only in these highest levels. Still and all, in other times the Wamphyri would be preparing for their long sleep, for even the thought of the sun was unbearable. Except now ... a victor had returned out of Sunside and desired his reception. It was only just, after all.

'Wrathspire!' cried Wran. 'And why not? For it is indeed the very spire of the stack, and Wratha's the Lady who dwells here. Her apartments are the loftiest and — dare I say it? — the lordliest. So where better to accept the grudging applause of my peers? And see, the Mistress herself awaits us ...'

Riding a gusting wind, Wran's flyer rounded a jagged natural buttress and settled towards a cavernous landing bay. The others were close behind: Spiro, then Gorvi jumping the queue, and finally Nestor. He was busy now, anxiously commanding his flyer: *Follow the others; stay in line; easy now ... easy!* But not so busy he could fail to notice the Lady Wratha, where she leaned against the carved bone balcony of an observation port above and to one side of the bay.

Even a glimpse was riveting, magnetic, so that Nestor's eyes felt compelled to linger upon her. That couldn't be, however, for Gorvi's flyer was already down and shuffling to one side, making room for Nestor's beast. Nestor's creature knew what it was about; balancing on the wind, it waited its turn. Its wings were arched into huge traps, thrusters extended forward to take the shock of landing. Briefly, Nestor experienced a moment of vertigo: the sheer height was appalling! He didn't look down but clung to reins and saddle, and wisely refrained from issuing any further commands.

Finally Gorvi's beast cleared the landing area, and Nestor's flyer inched forward and settled to the grainy rock. As thralls came forward to take the reins and lead the creature aside, Nestor slid gratefully to the ground. Except it wasn't the ground but the mouth of a cavern two thousand eight hundred feet high above the boulder plains! And even safe on the floor of the vast landing bay, still Nestor staggered.

Wran came from somewhere, took his arm, and whispered: 'Now is not the time to show weakness. Let me do the talking and all will go well.' Nestor was only too pleased to submit to this scheme; he was dizzy, awed, and had no words.

At the back of the landing bay, stone staircases with balustrades of bone climbed the rock wall to tunnels and balconies which in turn led to higher levels of honeycombed rock. Descending to the lower levels, other gangways passed through steep shafts or cartilage stairwells. But on high, looking down from one of the balconies, there stood Wratha. And lured by her presence, finally Nestor's eyes focused upon her. And she was a sight for sore eyes.

For her part, Wratha merely glanced at him, however speculatively, before speaking to Wran. 'The Lord Killglance, back from Sunside, I see, and all in one piece!' She raised an inquiring eyebrow. 'The Suck?'

'Need you ask?' Wran returned, smiling like a skull. 'Oh, I know your preferences, Wratha, but alas it isn't so. By now Vasagi's all rendered down, a stain on the hill where I pegged him out to await the rising sun. And indeed the sun was hot on our heels as we left.'

'We?' Again her eyes flickered over Nestor, and returned to Wran.

Wran glanced at Nestor. 'His is a story I can tell at my reception.'

Wratha nodded. 'Well, I prepared a feast for one of you, whoever was the victor. So now will you join me, in my apartments on high?'

The others, Gorvi and Spiro, were already on their way up a bone-embellished causeway. Wran and Nestor would follow them at once, but there came an interruption. From below, out of one of the sunken stairwells, the huge-shouldered figure of a man appeared, clad in the polished leather garb of a lieutenant. 'My Lady!' he called up to Wratha. 'I beg pardon for the intrusion, but . . . I believe it is my right?' His eyes under shaggy black brows were feral, scarlet in their cores. A true disciple of vampirism.

Wratha scowled down on him. 'Vasagi's man?'

'Indeed,' he replied. 'I am Gore Sucksthrall: first out of Sunside . . . first-made of Vasagi in Suckscar . . . now Keeper of the Vats. It seems my master's manse goes wanting a leader. If I am worthy of that honour, I would ascend.'

While Wratha and Gore exchanged words, the Lords on the stairs and in the landing bay paused to listen. As Gore finished, Gorvi the Guile (devious as his name implied), clapped his hands briefly and cried, 'Well said!' For he could smell trouble a mile away, and invariably encouraged it.

But Wran grasped Nestor's arm tightly and muttered, 'Damn it to hell! A complication . . .'

And Wratha nodded and called down: 'Well then, Gore Sucksthrall, maybe you'd better come up.' And sweeping her eyes over the others: 'But gentlemen, no gauntlets if you please. It is a rule I'm obliged to enforce. Certain of my creatures are easily disturbed . . . and volatile to say the least.' It was meant as a warning, not a threat; Wratha kept her small, personal warriors chained when she had visitors. But as she slipped away, her deceptively sweet laughter came floating down to them. And to a man they knew who was mistress here in the aerie's heights.

Through all of this, Nestor didn't take his eyes off her until the moment she drifted out of sight through an archway behind the balcony. Then he blinked, looked at Wran, and said, 'Wratha?' But it seemed as if her afterimage still burned on his retinas, and he could still see her there:

She was tall, even as tall (or as small, in company such as this) as Nestor himself, with hair black as night in plaits that fell to her shoulders. Around her neck, she wore a golden torque or harness, with ropes of black bat fur depending vertically to form a smoky curtain. Milky limbs gleamed as if oiled through the black stripes of fur, but her naked arms projected; likewise the points of her tilted breasts, a long pale oval of thigh, and a delicate knee.

The image was fading now, but Nestor continued to examine what remained of it. *Wratha's eyes had been least in evidence. Protected by a scarp of figured bone upon her brow, their fire had been subdued by the ornamentation of blue-glittering crystals fixed to her temples, and matching earrings in the furred lobes of her fleshy ears. But apart from the shell-like whorls of those Wamphyri ears, and the somewhat flattened aspect of a nose whose convolutions had not seemed too exaggerated – and the scarlet flicker of her split, vampire's tongue, of course – apart from those things, she might well have been Szgany.*

In short, she had looked more woman than a Lady of the Wamphyri as Nestor might have expected one to be . . . looked it, at least.

'Wratha the Risen, aye,' Wran answered sourly, starting up the stone stairs. But after two paces he paused, looked back at Nestor and said, 'What, does she interest you then? Stricken, are you? What, you?' He slapped his thigh and laughed, '*Hah!*' – and was sober again in

77

a moment. 'Better watch your step, Nestor. She fancies young men out of Sunside.'

Nestor, following behind, inquired: 'Something to fear?'

'Not really,' the other grunted, sweeping up the stairs. 'Not unless you make her angry. It's not a good idea, to make the Lady Wratha angry.'

And behind them both, Gore Sucksthrall followed in surly mood, saying nothing at all . . .

They climbed through three expansive levels to Wrathspire's Great Hall, where the Lady's thralls had prepared a table for five. The table was enormous: five feet wide and extending all of forty-five feet down the hall from Wratha's bone-throne, it could easily have accommodated three dozen people. At its head, upon a shallow platform and so slightly elevated, there stood Wratha's great chair, in which sat the Lady herself. The bone-throne was a monstrous, marvellous thing – the skeletal lower jaw of some vast, long-dead creature – which she had acquired along with the furniture and all other appurtenances of Wrathspire the day she'd arrived in this abandoned, derelict place out of Turgosheim. The stack had been derelict then, at least. But now, due chiefly to Wratha's industry, it had returned to loathsome life.

Already seated when her thralls ushered her guests into the Great Hall, Wratha came briefly to her feet and made apology of a sort:

'I had prepared for five; since it appears we're now six, my girls are setting an extra place – or perhaps two, for Canker may yet honour his obligations. Wran Killglance: as victor, you will take the chair directly opposite mine, at the guest's "head" of table. You others . . . may sit where you will.'

Female thralls scurried, finished setting places, then fled out of sight. Wran seated himself opposite Wratha at the end of the table as she had suggested, and indicated a seat to Nestor some three chairs away on his left. Nestor took the indicated chair and sat there wondering what to do with himself. The chair was built for a man, or more properly a Lord of the Wamphyri. Seated in it, he felt like a mere boy. In time his vampire leech, developed from Vasagi's egg, would attend to that: his metamorphic flesh would stretch and fill out. But for now . . . well at least he could try thinking like a Lord.

Spiro Killglance sat on Nestor's left, with some five or six chairs separating them. Opposite Spiro, Gore Sucksthrall took his place, and Gorvi the Guile edged into a chair across from Nestor. On the table in front of Wratha's guests, wooden platters, hollowed into shallow bowls, contained barbed stabbing spikes of soft gold. There were leather drinking jacks, and several large jugs of fired pottery patterned in the fashion of Sunside's Szgany, containing sweet water or weak wine for the jacks. Wratha knew better than to serve strong drink. Her own plate and cup were of gold; she likewise knew how to make her guests feel small and even unworthy.

The fare was scarcely extravagant: lightly braised hearts, kidneys, and livers of shads, and four suckling wolves roasted on spits and basted in a sauce of their mother's milk, urine, and blood. Individual or special requirements were not catered for; the food was simply an expression of Wratha's hospitality; the Wamphyri normally 'refuelled' themselves in the first hours after sundown, according to personal needs, habits, and tastes. That which at this hour would be breakfast to a Traveller, was therefore a mere novelty to them.

Nestor, on the other hand, was hungry. He had last eaten well before sundown, in the cabin of Brad Berea in the forest. In the time-scale of a parallel world beyond the Starside Gate (which Szgany and Wamphyri alike called the hell-lands, because since time immemorial no one had ever returned from them), that was the equivalent of four days. There was no way Nestor could know that, but he did know that since sundown he'd survived on a few nuts, and a piece of wild fruit in the woods; scarcely sufficient to keep body and soul together. Well, too late now to worry about his soul, but his body must go on at least.

Also, while his memory was still largely impaired prior to his time spent with the Bereas, his mind itself was completely healed and receptive – made receptive by his parasite egg, which demanded that he be strong and cunning – so that he was constantly learning. The ability, indeed the need to learn anew had been sparked within him. And with no background as such, an empty past, every smallest item of new information was soaking into his brain like rain into desiccated earth. While deep in his subconscious, thirsty seeds of ambition, knowledge, even memory – however misshapen or mutated from their source material – were waiting to spring to life. But he could not become wise, strong, Wamphyri, in a depleted body. And so he ate.

He ate with gusto, stabbing a slice of shad liver, which was in any case a Szgany delicacy, and doing it justice as he held it in his hand and tore at it with strong teeth. And such was his hunger that the meat never even touched his platter! Another slice followed, and a steaming kidney, whole, which he manoeuvred onto his plate without losing but a splash of gravy. Then a jack of wine, and tender flesh from a thigh of suckling wolf. The Szgany didn't eat wolf, but Nestor didn't know what the meat was. Whatever, he would have eaten it! It was strong and imparted strength. And while he ate, he studied his surroundings.

The Great Hall was all of a hundred and fifty feet long by sixty feet wide. It ran parallel with the south-facing wall of the stack, where windows had been cut through the solid rock to the chasm of open air that spanned the boulder plains all the way to the barrier mountains. In places, these deep embrasures in the wall of the spire were almost tunnels; in others, where the rock was thinner, they formed archways out onto high balconies of grafted bone, whose baffles of hide and cartilage were so constructed as to turn aside and deaden the buffeting of the wind. Framed in one such opening, Nestor observed the fluttering of a banner, which periodically displayed Wratha's sigil: a kneeling man in silhouette, with slumped shoulders and bowed head . . .

Each window was fitted with black bat-fur drapes which presently stood open, giving access to the pale dawn light. Many hours still to go before the sun shone on Wrathspire, by which time the curtains would be drawn. But from where Nestor sat, if he turned his head a little, he could see the morning mists of Sunside gathering in the gaunt grey peaks and passes, forming clouds and drifting free. The sight was nothing new to him, except . . . in previous times, he'd seen it from the other side. Perhaps at that – at these distant echoes and thoughts out of the past, of Sunside and what he had been there – Nestor felt something of poignancy for a life gone and forgotten forever, but all such emotions were rapidly fading now.

In two of the 'corners' of the mainly irregular hall, curtained areas hid Wratha's smaller, personal warriors from view. But in a third she had deliberately left the drapes open. At the sight of the creature shackled there, her guests were reminded yet again of Wratha's sovereignty in these dizzy aerial levels. Twice the size of a man and nine times heavier, with overlapping, inch-thick scales of blue-grey, chitin armour, the creature was mainly claws, jaws, and teeth. Going on all fours like a bear (despite that it once was a man, or men), it would occasionally rear upright, grunt and mutter questioningly, and shake its chains curiously – but purely out of habit.

During the daylight hours proper, when the sun was high and Wratha had taken to her bed, two of these beasts would be stationed in the stairwells near the launching bays, while the third would roam through Wrathspire top to bottom, guarding mainly against aerial incursions, but also patrolling Wratha's chambers. The Lady's lieutenants and thralls, some of whom had duties in these unsociable hours, had her scent upon them, of course, and so were safe. But as for any stranger . . .

Nestor's gaze was attracted to the dome of the ceiling, where on several occasions he'd sensed some strange, furtive activity. Now he saw what it was: a colony of giant Desmodus bats! For in the darkest corners and the gloom of deep ledges (from which locations their spillage could neither intrude nor disgust), Wrathspire's lesser *inhabitants* clung like dense black cobwebs or fragments of a shroud to walls and ceiling, causing the darkness to crawl there. Even as Nestor watched, a party of latecomers entered through a window, chittering shrilly as they dispersed to various parts of the living blanket. Vampires all, though not of the human strain, these were Wratha's familiars. And Nestor wondered – but in no way morbidly – if he would be heir to just such a colony, five levels down in Suckscar.

While making these observations, Nestor had continued to eat, until now he was replete. Sighing, he stripped
a last morsel of tender flesh from the thigh bone of a
wolf-cub, glanced round the table ... and paused in his
chewing. Every eye seemed rapt upon him: the way he
had disposed of his food. Finally he put down the
gleaming bone, ran his fingers through his hair to clean
them, and glanced at Wran questioningly. The Rage
seemed to find something amusing; he stifled a laugh
and merely grinned, and took another sip from his jack.
But Wratha, no less fascinated than the others, raised
an eyebrow and said:

'Well, at least one of us has an appetite!' Which
galvanized the rest of her guests to something of activity, at least. For now they, too, took up their skewers ...

In a little while, as all of them about the table joined
Nestor in swilling wine and picking at various tidbits,
Wratha stood up and rapped for attention. 'My Lords,'
she began, dryly, 'we are gathered here to honour a
special person upon a rare and special occasion.
Namely: the reception of Wran Killglance on his return
out of Sunside, where in the night he had business with
Vasagi the Suck. Alas, Vasagi is no more. I now call
upon Wran – called the Rage, and rightly – to tell us
all, and spare no detail of trial and triumph in the
telling.' She sat down. It had been a standard opening;
the Lords among them had all heard much the same
before in Turgosheim, usually from Vormulac Unsleep,
master of melancholy Vormspire.

Wran sat up straighter, and made as if to begin. At
which ... an interruption! It was a sound or series of
sounds: a burble of notes, piping trills, as of Sunside
birds – issuing from a stairwell. At first an odd fluting,
soon it turned to laughter, and then the two interspersed.
Curious whistles, and gales of raucous laughter! And:

'Canker Canison!' Wran scowled, before that one had even presented himself. But in another moment he appeared, with one of Wratha's thralls bowing him in. Nestor looked, saw him, and his jaw dropped. So this was the missing Lord. But a Lord? The others around the table were mainly human – or born of woman, at least – but this one? Oh, there was *something* of humanity in him, but there was a great deal more of something else!

Later, Nestor would learn a little of Canker's history, his unutterable *lineage*: that somewhere in his ancestry there had been a fox, dog or wolf. Whichever, the creature had probably strayed from its normal hunting grounds on Sunside or in the mountains and wandered into the swamps east of Turgosheim to drink. There it had become infected by a spore and emerged a vampire changeling. After that, the possibilities were several:

It had bitten or savaged someone, and so passed on a canine strain of vampirism. Or ... inside the beast, a leech had developed from the vampire spore, whose egg later transferred to a man or woman, who became Wamphyri and ascended in Turgosheim. Or ... some vampire had sired a litter on a dog bitch, she-wolf, or vixen; not necessarily by miscegenation, probably by biting the creature when she was pregnant. Or – in the case of someone like Canker – perhaps even sexually ...

Whichever, evidence of this – mongrel – ancestry had been apparent in the line ever since, and never more so than in Canker Canison. Standing upright and leaning forward (his normal posture), he was tall as a tall man but his limbs were all out of proportion. Shoulders, thighs and chest were massive, while forelegs were slender, sinewy, wolf-like.

Canker's hands ... were hands; but his knob-like,

thickly padded feet were plainly paws. Instead of nails, his hands and feet alike were equipped with claws. Face and head, while basically human, were also disturbingly doglike, with long jaws and canine teeth, triangular eyes, and pointed ears which were mobile, expressive, and thickly furred. Named after the disease of the inner ear which had driven his father baying mad and caused his suicide, Canker, by use of his metamorphism (also by physically sculpting them), had caused the lobes of his own ears to be fretted into curious and intricate designs, which included his sigil, a sickle moon.

Canker's hair was a wiry, foxy red; his eyes, too, though in dusk or darkness they could as easily turn yellow and feral. His gait was more a long-striding lope than a walk proper, and from time to time he would fall to all fours, then push himself upright with sinuous ease. When he laughed there was more than a hint of howling in it, and the gape of his jaws was enormous. Then, too, he would throw back his head and shake from tip to toe . . .

He was laughing now, mainly at the long-suffering expressions on the faces of his peers. But as the dogthing's laughter died away, so his spiky eyebrows came together in a frown over his long, much-convoluted snout, and his voice became a growling rumble. 'Eh, what? And have you started without me?'

'The first gold is on the peaks, Canker,' Wratha observed, without turning a hair. 'It is you who are late. For someone who observes the future in dreams, you scarcely seem to observe the present at all; you have no sense of occasion! But now that you are here, won't you be seated?'

'Late?' He sniffed the air, glancing here and there about the table. 'Am I? In which case you must excuse me. I serve the moon, as well you know, and my industry on Her behalf is great. In honour of my silver mistress in the sky, I am constructing . . . an instrument!' He lifted a bone flute to his moist mouth, blew several ear-piercing notes, then loped to a chair midway between Nestor and Spiro. And seating himself, Canker tossed down the flute upon the table. 'This was my inspiration.'

The flute rolled to a rocking standstill in the middle of the table between Nestor and Gorvi the Guile; the latter picked it up, examined it, and said: 'You found inspiration in this? A Szgany toy?'

'No.' Canker shook his head and scowled. 'Only the pattern is Szgany. But I made this flute – of bone! Szgany flutes are of reed, and they break too easily. This one's notes are purer, because the bore is perfect. Then, having made it, I remembered all the times I had flown over the boulder plains and seen the remains of olden battles. Why, in places the plains are a veritable boneyard! The wars of our ancestors were bloody indeed! Men and monsters alike have died out there, and for a thousand years their bones have bleached under the cold stars, made silver by the moon in Her passing.

'And I thought: those bones have worshipped Her, too, but all in silence. They have *worshipped* my silver mistress, whose light has shone on them through all the centuries! And remembering this flute – or Szgany toy, if you *insist*,' (he scowled at Gorvi), '– I knew what I must do. And I have started!

'In my house are many windows facing north, the Icelands, and the cold winds that blow. I shall build baffles there, in the central level, to gather the winds *within* my manse! There, too, I shall build my instrument.' He looked at the bone flute where Gorvi had put it down. 'For if a mere "toy" such as this, in combination with lungs such as mine, can make music fit for the ears of men . . . how then a mighty orchestra of bones, and the lungs of the very wind itself? So shall I worship Her on high, while Wrathstack thunders to the songs of the long dead and forgotten!' He fell quiet and glared all about the table.

Gorvi nodded and put the flute down, and murmured wrily, 'Fit for the ears of men, aye . . .'

'What?' Canker had heard him. *His* ears were sensitive to a fault.

But Gorvi only shrugged. 'I was merely . . . savouring the phrase? Your appreciation of music goes deeper than we had suspected, Canker.'

The other sat back again, loosely in his chair, and likewise shrugged. 'It's a means to an end, that's all: to lure my silver mistress from the sky, and make Her my mistress proper.' He held up a cautionary, protesting hand. 'No, no! Not the moon itself, but the one who dwells there, who . . . who *calls* to me.' He saw the looks that passed between them, gave himself a shake and sat up straighter.

Then too, as if for the first time, he noticed Nestor and Gore Sucksthrall. 'But what's this? Do common thralls and lieutenants attend your reception, Wran?' And turning his head the other way: 'Do you sup with servants, Wratha? Or is it perhaps that they're the main course?' And he leered at Nestor.

Wran said, 'Canker, you are plainly exhausted. Gore Sucksthrall here is a lieutenant, sure enough, but Nestor? This one has ascended: he has an egg. Indeed, he has Vasagi's egg, for the Suck has no more use for it! But I'm surprised you didn't sniff it out for yourself.'

'*Ahhh!* The vampire egg of Vasagi? This boy?' Canker leaned closer to Nestor and sniffed cautiously, as if at suspect meat. But in a moment: 'Yes, I see you're right!'

'And now if you'll hear me out, I'll tell all,' said Wran.

The others were all ears, except Nestor himself. He knew the tale well enough and could afford to let his attention wander a little. It didn't wander too far, however, for diagonally across the table, Gore Sucksthrall was glaring pure poison at him from furious, blazing eyes!

III

Lord Nestor of the Wamphyri

Wran kept it short:

'Vasagi and I, we flew off in different directions from Madmanse and Suckscar. Our arguments had been one too many, and our enmity seemed insurmountable. This was the only honourable way to settle it: man to man on Sunside. For weapons we had our gauntlets, nothing else. I saw Vasagi flying at a distance. We acknowledged each other, a nod of the head. And even at that range he sent a thought: *I hope you've said your last farewells, Wran. If not, too late now. For only one of us can return. Alas, it won't be you!*

'I thought to make some derisory answer but the distance was increasing. Despite Vasagi's superior mentalism, he probably wouldn't hear me; my range was not so extensive. In that respect, who among us is – or was – equal to Vasagi? Having no speech as such, his telepathy supplemented his ridiculous miming! Still, his words had served as a warning. Not that I feared him, you understand, but he had reminded me of his skill as a thought-thief. From then on, I would keep my own thoughts very well guarded.

'I landed on Sunside east of the great pass, and manoeuvred my flyer back into a thicket of tall trees growing on the hillside. In front was a bluff. When all was done I could call my creature forward and launch without hindrance. And then I waited.' He paused.

'You ... waited?' said Gorvi. 'You didn't hunt for him?'

Wran shook his head. 'My thought was that he would hunt for me. If I moved about, changing my location, it would only make his task more difficult. And the sooner we came together the better. And so I waited ... well, for a little while. But this was Sunside and I could smell the smoke of a Szgany campfire not long extinguished; so that suddenly, the urge was on me! Oh, it's true I was here for different game this night of nights, but I saw no harm in mixing business with pleasure.

'I went to my flyer and cautioned him to be still, quiet, and wait for me. I forbade any sort of commotion, for whatever reason. Then I headed east on foot, through the foothills. The smoke stench came from that direction; it was faint due to distance and the dispersal of small winds; its source might be as much as seven or eight miles away. That was nothing, for I had an entire night at my disposal. Also, I made no effort to hide my tracks but left a strong spoor. That way, if the Suck should discover my flyer, he would be able to follow my trail without difficulty. But I kept my thoughts constantly guarded, for if he sensed my confidence, it might caution him to keep back.

'Well, eventually I found a small family group of Travellers where they sheltered in a cavelet. My first knowledge of them came when I stumbled across the male having a piss in the dead of night a little way from the cave. When I found him he was half asleep ... *fully* asleep when I had done! The sleep of the undead. By now, enthralled, doubtless he's following me through the pass. Later I'll find him making his way to Wrathstack, wailing like a banshee and gnashing his teeth where he stumbles across the boulder plains. I hereby lay claim to him. But last night ...

'. . . Having had his blood, a good deal of it, now I would enjoy his woman. But first I must deal with his children, lest there be crying and a deal of confusion. There were two Szgany whelps, a girl and boy. The girl was six or seven; I smothered her in her sleep. Her brother was a bairn; I crushed his head. And their mother was . . . *succulent!*' Wran paused to glance at Wratha. 'But I won't be indelicate. You men can ask me later. For now I'll tell you only this: she lasted well . . .

'Later, I trekked back towards the place where I'd left my flyer. The boy child dangled from my belt, trailing blood, which made my spoor easier still to follow. And always I kept my mind shielded. But do you know, such had been my . . . *extravagance* with the woman, that I actually felt weary! It was as if I had raged, though in truth I had not. My *flesh* had raged a little, perhaps, but . . . such is the nature of lust. So that what with these excesses of mine, and all the trekking afoot – plus the fact that during the previous day I'd been excited by the prospect of the night ahead, and so had not slept as best I might – I felt depleted. Or perhaps I had supped too well on the blood of the man and what little I'd had from his wife – and the rest of what I had had from her – until I was replete in every sense and now must sleep it off.

'Except, somewhere out there in the night, Vasagi the Suck was likewise afoot. It gave me pause, but eventually I puzzled my way out of the dilemma.

'I hastened to my flyer and curled myself in a belly ridge where the thrusters are lodged. And before sleeping I commanded the beast that if someone approached, namely Vasagi the Suck, I was to be awakened at once. Or if not – if he came gliding and in great stealth or disguised in a mist, remaining hidden until the last moment – then that my creature must thrust me aside to safety, and roll or fall upon Vasagi and so crush him.

'But, no such incursion; I slept the best and possibly the longest sleep of my life! Then, awakening, I sensed sunup some hours away and knew that time was narrowing down. And still my business with the Suck remained unsettled. So . . . I would try to lure him one last time, and if that failed then I must resort to hunting him.

'I left my flyer, proceeded some small distance on foot, and there built a fire in the lee of a rocky outcrop. I commenced roasting the boy child upon a spit, and before too long felt a presence. The feeling was momentary, but strong. In the night and the dark I fancied I felt eyes upon me, perhaps from on high. And of course I wondered: had Vasagi passed fleetingly overhead? It would seem the most likely explanation; certainly the sweet smell of roasting bairn would be a vast attraction. If so, then he had surely seen me.

'I continued to roast my breakfast, and waited. And in a little while someone came! Ah, but he was clumsy, perhaps too eager? Above me in a nest of rounded boulders, I heard a pebble slither. Did he intend to jump down on me? Possibly. But I was ready, fully rested and wide awake . . . even eager! He came to his doom, be sure!

'Except – it wasn't Vasagi! It was this one!' And here Wran pointed dramatically at Nestor.

'However unwittingly, this strange night-prowling Szgany youth had distracted me when, concentrating upon *his* approach, I had failed to detect the Suck's! Or rather, Vasagi had utilized this one's clumsiness to mask his own far more sinister slither. And while I was confused, finally he attacked!

'Then . . .

'. . . Nestor shouted a warning! Also, he put a bolt in the Suck's shoulder. But can you credit it? The intervention of a Traveller, a Szgany youth, in a grand duel of vampire Lords? It was astonishing, and it was ironic! For to my way of thinking, it evened up the balance admirably. Vasagi had used this lad to get close to me, and paid for his deviousness when Nestor turned on him. But injured, the Suck was yet more dangerous. And in the fight which ensued I sustained grave injuries of my own, mainly to my back. I intend to keep the scars, to illustrate the extent of Vasagi's ferocity. Perhaps on some future occasion, you may even prevail upon me to display them for you . . .'

This time, when Wran's pause threatened to extend itself indefinitely, Gorvi the Guile put in: 'All very interesting, I readily submit, though none of it explains this Nestor's custody of Vasagi's egg. Was it won, or illegally . . . bequeathed? Which is to say, not by the Suck, but by his destroyer, Wran. You'll concede I have a point. For here sits Gore Sucksthrall, first-chosen lieutenant of Vasagi himself, and rightful aspirant to Suckscar. Must he now stand aside for this Nestor? An unusual procedure, to say the least.'

'*Bah!*' This from Wratha. 'What's so unusual, Gorvi? Think back on your own ascension, as I often think on mine. It's the getting there that's important, not the means. Aye, the *getting* there, and the *wanting* to be there! And yet . . . it would seem you've asked a valid question: was it done out of spite, maliciously conceived and contrived by Wran the Rage, or was Nestor receptive? And I ask another: if the latter, how so? For in all my days I've never yet heard of a Traveller who *desired* to be Wamphyri – not before the fact, at least.'

Canker Canison sat up straighter, slapped a hand flat on the table and barked: 'Only one person to ask!' And turning to Nestor, where so far he'd sat silent: 'You, Nestor. You have a vampire egg in you. But did you desire to be Wamphyri, or was it forced upon you?'

93

'What the hell odds does it make?' Wran roared, coming to his feet. 'Wratha has it right: it's *getting* there that counts. As for eggs: don't we bequeath them where we will? We do, when we have the choice. Well, when last I saw Vasagi the Suck, he had no choice. I pegged his broken body out to burn. And now I wish I'd let his leech and egg burn with him!'

'May I speak?' Gore Sucksthrall growled, but quietly. And when they looked at him:

'It seems to me that the Lord Wran engineered this thing,' Gore said. 'Not to thwart me – of course not, for I am nothing as yet – but to punish his old enemy the Lord Vasagi, who was my master. It would seem a grand jest, to transfer the Suck's egg to this ... this innocent. And of course, cowed by Wran and afraid of us all, this unworthy receptacle sits here, numb and dumb, and praying it's all a dream. Myself, I *would* aspire to Suckscar, and no question about it. Except a usurper has Vasagi's egg. Doubtless it was torn from my master's body, or fled him upon his death. Which seems to me the easiest way to regain it – and *now*, before the egg becomes a leech, or while the vampire is still a tadpole. Wherefore I challenge this Nestor to a trial of combat. The time, place and manner of his death, I leave to him.'

Gore was right. Deep in Nestor's core, Vasagi's seed was as yet a tadpole. Be that as it may, already it could sense the strength of its host – and his weaknesses. But the latter only served the parasite's purposes; rather, they worked to its benefit. Nestor had no history, nothing to cling to, and therefore no resistance to the seething metamorphosis taking place within him. On the other hand, his vampire had no real 'intelligence' as such; as yet embryonic, its sole purpose was to enhance the darker facets of its host, while simultaneously blunting his human compassion and deadening his sensibilities. In so doing, it honed to a razor's edge those skills necessary to Nestor's — and of course its own — survival. For above all else, the vampire is tenacious.

And Gore was quite wrong: instead of sitting there 'numb and dumb', Nestor had taken his small but deadly crossbow from his belt and into his lap, fitted its bolt, and now only required to load it. While the first of these actions had been easy, going all unseen behind and below the bulk of the great table, the last would take some small effort and could never be accomplished in secret, especially now that all eyes were on Nestor. He hesitated ... there was still time enough ... he would wait and see what he would see.

Canker, on Nestor's immediate left, had doubtless seen his furtive movements; he said nothing but simply said there, feral eyes blazing, holding his dog's breath and glancing from Nestor to Gore and back again. Gore had meanwhile put both of his huge hands flat on the table and looked about ready to stand up. *His* eyes were likewise feral — and full of murder. He had made his challenge; if it went unaccepted, or even unanswered by Nestor, plainly Gore would have the right to act.

Nestor sat stiff as a ramrod and looked at Gore. The man was a vampire; he had put on flesh and bulked out until he was almost as massive as a Lord; clad in heavy leather, he made two of Nestor. On the other hand, he was unarmed; even more important, he had no egg. Perhaps Nestor could talk him down. For as well as tenacious, the vampire is devious.

When it seemed the tableau could hold no longer — that Gore must now get up, come round the table, dispose of Nestor and claim his rights — that was when Nestor spoke. But even now alien stuff was at work in him, and as well as being tenacious and full of guile, in circumstances like these the vampire is often abrupt and aggressive:

'It happened much as Wran told it,' he began, in a voice deep, dark and arresting, 'yet also as you have it, Gore Sucksthrall. I was coming to Starside, the last aerie, to be a Lord. Except I believed I already *was* Wamphyri – or had been – and I had forgotten or been robbed of my inheritance. Why, I still believe it, even now! It was as if I cried out to be Wamphyri! All of which I made known to Wran the Rage. And I'm in Wran's debt, it's true, for in his own sweet way he ... *reminded* me, of certain procedures. So that however you would have it, the fact remains that I *am* now Wamphyri! And I caution you, Gore: be my thrall and live, or –'

'Or?' Gore was on his feet. 'What? I should become *your* thrall ... or?' He was grey as lead, puffed up, bloated with rage and lust. Lust for Nestor's blood, egg, life, all three. He licked his lips greedily, knotted his fists into clubs at his sides, thrust his head forward menacingly. For a moment his eyes stood out like yellow plums in his face. Then ...

... He moved! But as for coming *round* the table, nothing so refined. Gore Sucksthrall took the shortest route and came over it!

Platters large and small went flying, jugs of wine were hurled aside, as the lieutenant swung up onto the table, took one pace forward, and crouched down to launch himself full in Nestor's face. Nestor came to his feet, knocking his chair on its side as he threw himself backwards. And in his few remaining seconds, he loaded his crossbow. Roaring with rage, Gore was already in mid-flight; too late he saw the weapon in Nestor's hand; Nestor didn't have time or need to aim but merely pointed ... and pulled the trigger!

The bolt took Gore dead centre between the eyes, caved in the bridge of his nose, smashed through his brain and only came to a halt when its head bit through the back of his skull in a splintering of bone and splash of blood. Dead in mid-air, or as dead as a vampire can be while still he has a head, his mouth chomped and drooled vacuously as he flew. But his eyes no longer saw, and his outstretched hands were limp as rags.

Nestor stepped lithely aside as Gore crashed down upon the polished stone floor and skidded to a crumpled halt. Possibly he could survive even now, as a crippled mute if nothing else. Certainly his metamorphic flesh and bones would heal, and part of the brain repair itself at least. But Nestor's vampire nature was stirring to life, and he wasn't about to allow that. These Lords and Lady harboured doubts about his fitness to be one of them. Well, he *was* Wamphyri, and now as good a time as any to show them!

There was one large knife on the table for carving. Nestor could take Gore's head if he wanted it. But he saw another, far easier way.

Astonishingly, the fallen lieutenant had pushed himself up onto all fours. He was kneeling there, head-down, slopping blood and brains, and shaking like a palsied dog. And a stream of slurred, stuttering, meaningless words or noises was issuing from his morbidly grimacing mouth. Nestor dropped his crossbow to the floor, went to him, grasped his topknot with both hands and dragged him to a window. On hands and knees, Gore skidded in blood, drool, and brain fluid forward onto a fretted cartilage balcony. Nestor got behind him, put a foot firmly on his backside, and shoved. Part of the balcony shattered, and Gore took the pieces with him into space.

Out there, close to three thousand feet of unresisting

air, and at its bottom the scree jumbles, dirt and solid rock. When he hit, Gore Sucksthrall would shatter into so much mush and a fistful of jellied pieces. Gorvi the Guile's flightless guardian warriors would snarl and threaten over what few morsels they could salvage . . .

Nestor turned from the window, and on his way back to the table picked up his crossbow. Gorvi, malicious as ever, was the first to find his voice. Pointing at Nestor's weapon, he said, 'That is forbidden! Not only in Wrath-spire, but even throughout the entire aerie.'

Canker slapped the table and barked, 'But we all knew he had it. He's Szgany, isn't he? This is how they arm themselves. Szgany, aye, and a mere youth. It's just that we knew – or we supposed – that he'd never have the guts to use it!'

Nestor stood by his toppled chair, lifted his crossbow by its tiller overhead and said, 'If this weapon offends you, then it likewise offends me. So be it.' And he brought it down shatteringly on the table's rim, so as to break it into pieces. 'In any case, I've no more use for it. Not now that I have Vasagi's gauntlet.' And turning to Canker Canison: 'You are wrong, Canker. Perhaps I *was* Szgany, but no more.'

All of these had been good moves; coming in quick succession, and startling, they had fixed the attention of the others about the table. Frowning, they stared at Nestor in silence for long seconds. Then Wran grinned, however lopsidedly, and looked along the table at Wratha. 'Lady,' he said, 'I recall you were saying something about your own ascension? If the stories I've heard are true, that, too, was a bloody affair.'

On another occasion Wratha might well have taken offence, and even now it was her instinct to say: 'Oh, and what of your own and Spiro's and Gorvi's?' But for the moment her thoughts were elsewhere, so that she musingly answered, 'Those stories you've heard are true, aye.' Except she wasn't looking at Wran but at Nestor.

The newcomer was made of the right stuff. She could feel it in him. Why, given time, she might even feel him in her! And that was a pleasant thought (if one she kept guarded); for her male thralls, handsome creatures though some of them might be, were like mice in her bed, timid and creeping. When Nestor was fully ascendant, it was possible he'd make a worthy lover . . . not to mention an ally . . .

Wratha gave herself a mental shake, and turned her gaze to Wran. 'I was Szgany, and ascended in Turgosheim by my wits alone. When others would destroy me, *I* destroyed my so-called "master" and took his egg. All true . . . as is what I said but a moment ago: it's the *getting* there that counts.'

'Well?' Wran cried. 'And hasn't Nestor got there?'

'No.' She shook her head. 'Not yet a while. For being here and surviving here are different things. But . . . certainly he's on his way.' Then, nodding her approval and looking at them all in turn, Spiro, Canker, Gorvi, Wran, and lastly Nestor, finally she said:

'My Lords, I give you Lord Nestor of the Wamphyri — perhaps. But what say you?'

Canker accepted him readily enough. 'You must visit me in Mangemanse,' he barked. 'By all means come and inspect my instrument of bones!'

Wran and Spiro were well satisfied but didn't wish to display it, and so answered in unison, cautiously, 'Let's wait and see how all works out.'

Gorvi scowled, and said: 'It seems I'm a minority of one. But . . . very well, Nestor is a Lord — with one proviso! We'll give him five sunups and if he doesn't fit, then he goes back to Sunside. And to certain death.'

Wratha looked at Nestor and said, 'Well?'

He shrugged. 'I've no complaints.'

'Good!' she said. And to the others, lifting her goblet, 'A toast, then. To Lord Nestor of Suckscar: a successful ascension!'

'Success!' they chorused, lifting their jacks, Gorvi with some ill-grace. But before drinking, he couldn't resist adding: 'Success, aye. Or whatever . . .'

However alien in aspect Vasagi had been, Wratha the Risen had regarded him as something of an ally; hence his habitation of the levels closest to her own. Now, as Wran's reception broke up, the Killglance brothers offered to accompany the newcomer down into Suckscar before returning to their flyers.

Canker, whose Mangemanse levels lay directly below Nestor's, went with them. Coming up, he'd used exterior causeways, covered ledges, and dizzy bridges suspended from the underside of various flying buttresses. He could have flown, of course, but that would have meant saddling a flyer, a launching, landing, etcetera. And Canker, having only just remembered his appointment, had been late enough already. On the spur of the moment, out of grudging respect for the property of another – not to mention the very real threat of hostility from who or whatever the Suck had left in charge in his absence – Canker had chosen his vertiginous but otherwise unobtrusive route around Suckscar. Now that he knew Nestor, however, and with his permission on this occasion, a return descent through Suckscar seemed the easiest, most obvious route.

Oddly, as the four descended and Wran and Spiro led the way, proceeding a little ahead of Nestor, Canker stayed very much 'to heel' behind him. Glancing back on occasion, Nestor would find the other padding along in his wake, tongue lolling, for all the world like some grotesque, upright dog. But in no way a 'pet'. And yet in some ways that, too. For whenever Nestor paused, Canker would likewise come to a halt and cock his head on one side, as if he waited on some command or other! On the other hand, his half-human expression was difficult to gauge; Nestor had seen similar looks on the faces of wolves tracking their prey.

Through Wratha's launching bays they went, down massive stairs chiselled from the bed of a sloping shaft, towards the uppermost of Suckscar's levels. Here the brothers Killglance proceeded cautiously indeed, prompting Nestor to inquire: 'A problem?'

Glancing back at him in the gloom of the unlit stairwell, Spiro scowled and impatiently replied, 'What? And didn't you see Wratha's warriors? Do you think she's the only one who keeps guardians like that? Well let me tell you we *all* have them, and so did Vasagi!'

Canker at once put a hand on Nestor's shoulder, and thrusting his muzzle forwards snarled at Spiro, 'Then you should let Nestor go first! He has Vasagi's egg, after all. And just as I sniffed it out, so shall they. Why, anyone would suspect that Suckscar was yours now – yours and Wran's together – and not Nestor's at all!'

'Meaning?' Wran turned swiftly in the cramped confines of the sloping tunnel. His eyes had narrowed to slits of scarlet light.

But Nestor intervened, squeezing forwards and replying on Canker's behalf, 'Meaning simply that as Suckscar's new master, I *should* go first. Canker is right.'

'Indeed I am,' Canker growled, following close behind. And now the brothers brought up the rear.

Nestor went a little faster; he was eager to discover the extent of Vasagi's holdings, and just exactly what his inheritance would be. And as he went he noticed that even in the dim light of the tunnel, while he was fully aware of the darkness, still he could see almost as well as in broad daylight. Which could only be further evidence of his vampire change.

Eventually, reaching a landing and turning through thirty degrees — as light showed at the bottom of the shaft, where the echoes of their footsteps had preceded them — so other sounds came back. But these were the echoes of furtive movement. And now it was Nestor's turn to pause.

'No,' Canker growled in his ear. 'Go on. They will recognize you. Take my word for it. You *are* Wamphyri!'

On Sunside, Nestor had always had a way with dogs; he and his forgotten brother alike. As children, wild dogs had come to them out of the forest, not to harm them but to play; domesticated wolves, 'guard dogs', had permitted the very roughest of rough-and-tumbling without turning on them; wild wolves in the hills had sat still at their approach, and not slunk but moved cautiously, almost reluctantly out of their path. Nestor had never made anything of it; it was simply that canine creatures trusted him, and he in turn trusted them and was unafraid. And it was the same now with Canker Canison. Nestor believed what Canker said. And he understood why this — what, this monster? — stuck so close to him. Out of nothing, a relationship had been formed. Nestor wasn't sure if he appreciated it or not, but he trusted it, certainly.

He went unafraid down the stairwell to the bottom, only pausing when something stirred and flowed forward in a narrow archway at the very foot of the stairs. And 'something' was as good a way as any of describing it! It was different again from one of Wratha's personal guardians: black as night, shaped like a bat hanging from a ceiling, but upright, with its head at the top;

wider than a man, and a good deal taller; eyes which were crimson wedges in a furred, elongated head. A bat, probably – or what was once a bat – yet manlike, too. A composite creature, bred of Vasagi's vats, retaining sufficient intelligence to obey his commands. Or one command, at least. To guard this stairwell.

The thing was hard to discern; it seemed wrapped in darkness, shrouded in gloom, cloaked in its own smoky fur. But when it thrust its half-rodent, half-human face forward to hiss and spit saliva, its purpose and determination were obvious. And if Nestor and the others would go forward, the only way was past this guardian.

'Huh!' Canker coughed in Nestor's ear, gripped his shoulder. 'Not so grotesque. All of Vasagi's creatures are different ... he was always experimenting! I've not seen this one before. But go forward, present yourself.'

The monster was three paces away, still mainly hidden in its own gloom and that of the archway. Nestor took one tentative step along the now horizontal corridor – and the guardian flowed out of its niche, blocking the way! Also, it became more nearly visible. It *was* cloaked in darkness: in black, leathery membranous wings which folded across its body, overlapping. But where the folds hugged closest to flesh, there the darkness was alive with pink, wriggling worms!

Now the creature's jaws cracked open and yawned wide, and its teeth were visible like row upon row of long white needles, receding into its scarlet throat. Teeth like that could strip a man's flesh to the bone, leaving his face or limbs flensed in a moment. But even now the thing was not as awesome as Wratha's guardian beasts.

You are mine! Nestor told it. *I have Vasagi's egg. Stand aside, for I would pass. Likewise these men with*

103

me, who are my friends ... for now at least. He took another breathless pace forwards –

– And the creature flowed to meet him!

Its wings opened, but they were not wings. From its forearms and underarms, down the sides of its body to its knees or where knees would be in a man, a thick webbing of flesh formed furry blankets which were *like* wings on both sides of the creature's body. *Superficially,* they were wings. But in reality, they were traps!

On Sunside there were flowers which functioned similarly; they had spined, fleshy petals that closed on insect victims to devour them. But this thing wasn't designed to devour insects – and the Sunside flowers weren't intelligent and mobile!

Under the 'wings' before they closed on Nestor, he saw that the pink worms were merely the tips of a nest of lashing tentacles based around the dark orifice of a grinding, suctorial mouth. The thing had *two* mouths, only one of which was in its face. Then the tentacles locked him in, trapping his arms and crushing him to that more immediate mouth where its huge, quivering lips *tasted* him!

For a moment – a single moment – Nestor was deaf, dumb, and blind. He was nauseated by the smell of rotting meat, the stench of an open stomach, the slick feel on his skin of some bio-acidic solution. A single moment ... before the guardian released him, folded its flaps and flowed back from him in a confused fashion, blinked furnace eyes hesitantly, then shuffled backwards into its niche and cowered down.

Nestor might have staggered a little, but Canker had come forward and was holding his elbow. 'Excellent!' the dog-thing growled. 'Vasagi's beast acknowledges its new master.'

Nestor's skin was crawling from head to toe, but he

104

and Canker went on. And behind them, the thing in the dark archway opened its flaps again, lashed its tentacles and hissed menacingly as Wran and Spiro followed — until Nestor turned and cautioned it: *Be quiet! Did I not say that these men were with me?*

And as the thing fell silent and shrank back, so the four proceeded down into Suckscar . . .

At the end of the short corridor, two more of Vasagi's creatures were tethered in niches set back a little from the main passage. They were not too unlike Wratha's personal guardians: brutal, ferocious things that howled and gibbered, tearing at their chains as Nestor and the others came into view. Their new master spoke to them at once, saying:

'I am the Lord Nestor of the Wamphyri. Vasagi's egg — and *all* of Vasagi's things — are mine. Now what *is* this commotion? Desist . . . or suffer!' It was enough; the warriors sniffed him out and at once fell silent, shuffling uncomfortably in their places.

Wran and Spiro were frankly astonished. Being Wamphyri, of course they too could have calmed the beasts . . . given sufficient time to threaten, cajole, and work on them. But Nestor had no experience of such things; even with Vasagi's egg, still he was a newcomer here; and yet he instinctively, almost automatically fitted into place. 'Yes,' Wran told him, 'I think you'll do very well indeed, in Suckscar.' But his scarlet eyes were shrouded. For it seemed to Wran that perhaps Nestor would do just a little *too* well here . . .

Thralls and lieutenants alike had heard the rowing warriors. Two of the latter came at the run just as Nestor and the others entered Suckscar's main hall. They were massive men, as are all the chosen lieutenants of the Wamphyri, so that Nestor felt dwarfed between his three companions and these newcomers. But the lieutenants, seeing Canker, Wran and Spiro, skidded to a halt, looked at each other, and approached more cautiously.

While they were still out of earshot, Canker whined, 'Now comes the real test. For these are not dumb beasts but men, and they have brains that think. Better let me handle it, for now at least.'

'Who goes there?' said one, the biggest of the two. 'You Lords are trespassers! Unless Gore Sucksthrall accompanies you – and possibly even then – you have no business here. Vasagi would never have deigned to invite you.' He pointed at Nestor and scowled. 'And what, pray, is that?'

Despite Canker's warning, Nestor narrowed his eyes and made to step forward; but the dog-thing got in his way. 'You lads had better listen,' he coughed. 'The Suck's no more, for Wran the Rage killed him. Which I don't need to tell you, for I'm sure someone at least must have been at a window, waiting for Vasagi to return out of Sunside. Ah, but while the Suck is gone, his egg goes on, for it fled into Nestor here – or the *Lord* Nestor, to you.'

Their mouths fell open. But after a moment the bigger one spoke up again. 'Oh, really? And this one's come to claim Suckscar, right? Well, Lords Canker, Wran, Spiro, no disrespect to you, but I am Zahar, Third-in-Command in Suckscar after Gore. And I say to you that I *myself* could eat this one!' He prodded Nestor in the chest with a hard finger. 'And as for when Gore Sucksthrall sees him . . .'

He threw back his head and laughed, and went to prod Nestor again. But Nestor was lightning fast; he caught the offending finger in a clenched fist and bent it back all in one movement, so that it broke with a loud crack! Then, as Zahar howled and fell to his knees, Nestor kicked him as hard as he could in the throat, which served to silence him and send him sprawling. In another moment, Nestor was down beside him on one knee, pinning his topknot to the stone floor; and in the next the sharp point of Nestor's six-inch knife was pricking the bulge of the lieutenant's throbbing Adam's apple.

Before, the knife in Nestor's belt had seemed barely significant; a piffling toothpick, the Wamphyri Lords and Lady had ignored it. Like his crossbow, he wouldn't dare consider using it against such as them. Ah, but their thralls were a different matter!

'Gore Sucksthrall is dead!' Nestor snarled. 'I killed him! Now swear allegiance to me — and at once — or follow him into eternity!'

'Gak ... gak ... urk!' said Zahar, holding up a trembling hand and arm. It might have been threatening or pleading, that hand, for it was the one with a dangling digit; whichever, Nestor couldn't take any chances. He slashed at the tendons in the joint of the elbow, which showed through where leather sleeves came together, and the arm flopped uselessly to the floor. And fast as thought, Nestor caught the crippled hand and took the finger, so that its stump had barely started to spurt as he came lithely to his feet.

Zahar writhed like a crippled snake on the floor, hissing and coughing but making no sensible noises whatsoever. His inability to answer made no difference, for as Nestor now told him: 'Good! Then you are now my man. Now watch!' And he deliberately gashed his own thumb, and let the blood drip into the joint of Zahar's arm and onto his bloody hand. 'See now: blood of my own Wamphyri flesh. The power of renewal, so that your arm may heal itself and your hand be whole again. Why, I have even honoured you, Zahar; you could as well be a bloodson ... well, of sorts! But my bloodson and not Vasagi's, for Vasagi is no more. And so a fatherly word of warning: from this time forward *cower* as you approach me! And when you stand in my presence, be sure to make no threatening movements. For if you do, the first will be the last. Remember: even now you would be dead, except I need you to run my manse.'

Nestor turned his back on the writhing, crippled Zahar and faced the second of the two. And he saw how Canker had held him back, when he might have come to Zahar's aid. Then, raising an eyebrow, as if in faint surprise, Nestor said: 'What's this? Do you molest a man of mine, Canker?' Canker released the lieutenant at once, and Nestor offered his hand and forearm in the old Szgany greeting.

The other was young, not long out of Sunside; but already he was inches taller than Nestor, broad, well-muscled, grey of flesh and feral-eyed: a vampire in his own right. Not Wamphyri, no, but given a hundred years he might be. If he lived. He spoke up, but falteringly: 'I'm Grig Sucksthrall ... or I was.'

He sensed the authority in Nestor – and possibly the presence of Vasagi's egg, too – and was awed and disadvantaged by the hot eyes of so many Lords looking on. Then, remembering the ways of Sunside, he fumblingly went to grasp Nestor's proferred forearm. But no, Nestor grasped Grig's hand instead and pressed Zahar's severed digit into his palm. And as Grig's jaw dropped, Nestor told him:

'Eat it! Accept my food and live, and take shelter with me in Suckscar – or deny me now and suffer the consequences. But what's this? Do you tremble? Ah, don't worry! I shall not kill you but set you free on the boulder plains, to take your chances with the lowest of the low and live like a trog in a crevice. How shall it be?'

Grig looked at the bloody finger in his grey hand, then at Zahar who had struggled to a seated position, where now he was bent forward, rocking himself to and fro and moaning. And finally: 'Lord,' he told Nestor, 'Zahar is my friend . . . !'

'Friend? Friend?' Nestor looked astonished. 'And am I to be known as the Lord Nestor, who gives shelter to friends? No, I desire no friends in my house but only thralls and obedient lieutenants — who eat or go hungry at my command!' He stared hard, severely at the other. 'For the last time, then: what's it to be?'

There and then Grig ate Zahar's finger. And because Nestor held his gaze the while, he scarcely grimaced at all . . .

IV

Suckscar

Nestor sent Grig and Zahar off to tend to the latter's damaged hand and arm. And then the four Lords explored Suckscar.

Wran, Spiro, and Canker had all been here before — but just the once — the day they arrived here along with Wratha, Vasagi and their lieutenants, a handful of flyers and another of warriors, out of the east. Then, mainly at Wratha's direction or insistence (the great stack had been sorely in need of repairs and maintenance, which she'd wanted set to rights at once), they'd moved in and laid claim to the various levels. And Suckscar had become Vasagi's.

He had named the five levels which made up his section of the stack out of admiration for their dramatic external appearance: they were deeply scarred from front to back (or south to north) with massive downward slanting gouges, almost as if the sun rising over the barrier mountains had steamed their outer layers away like vampire flesh. But in fact the sun had never risen so high as to light on Suckscar's levels; it was simply the result of the natural tilt of the rock layers, which were somewhat softer here, and the weathering of centuries and even millennia. Now these five levels, set immediately over Canker Canison's Mangemanse, belonged to Nestor, and he explored them eagerly.

In the first level he saw the great communal hall,

where common thralls dwelled in caverns in the outer immensity of the perimeter wall, and a sweeping rock-hewn staircase the width of the hall itself led up to Vasagi the Suck's once-private chambers. At the top and to the sides of the staircase were warriors or guardians of a unique design, which in function were similar to the creature in the stairwell encountered during the descent from Wratha's landing-bays. They *looked* like thick brown rugs sewn up from the skins of bears, but rugs don't creep.

As Nestor had climbed the stairs, so these creatures had flowed inwards along the upper steps, closing on him. But their stealth was such that when, half-way up, he paused to stare at them ... the things were only rugs again! At which Canker Canison, who accompanied Nestor, had sniffed the air and gone more cautiously, pointing out: 'More of the Suck's things, aye. He was a master of metamorphism, that one ...'

Then Nestor had climbed diagonally, almost threateningly, towards the closest of the two guardians, commanding it: *Come on then, and we'll see what manner of creature you are!* And creepingly, silently, the creature had flowed down from above; likewise its twin on the other side, converging on him ...

... Until the last moment, when suddenly they reared up! And then Nestor saw just how thick they were: like doughy blankets of flesh – like great bears, yes, but with their skeletal frames extruded and their flesh spread out, thick in the centre and thin as membrane at the edges – with great bands of grey muscle rippling on the underside. And bearlike in their general structuring, too, except their legs and arms were boneless, supported only by springy cartilage; but sufficiently agile to lift and thrust themselves upon hapless victims.

More: Nestor saw their mouths. Like the guardian in

111

the stairwell, they had more than sufficient of those; or precisely sufficient, considering Vasagi's purpose in creating them. For all these creatures consisted of was mouth, stomach and crushing muscle, and tiny red eyes, hidden in the topside fur. The mouths were many, small, red and suctorial, without teeth that Nestor could see; or if they were toothed then these were small and inconspicuous; but the drool which they issued smoked where it touched stone, so that Nestor knew it was acidic. And then he understood.

Wrapped in a creature such as this, a man would be completely immobilized — fixed like a fly in honey, smothered and softened by digestive juices — and finally slurped away until his flensed bones were discarded in a clattering heap! But Nestor was no such victim.

His egg, by now the merest tadpole of a leech, was strong and growing stronger by the moment. Its strength was Nestor's, who was strong in his own right. Suckscar's guardian creatures had been Vasagi's and now were his, all of them. And they must be made to understand that he'd suffer no more threats, not in his own house!

Standing his ground, he coughed up a great gob of phlegm to spit into the poisonous heart of the monster rearing before him! And turning on his heel, he pointed a commanding, threatening finger and issued a mind-blast that sent the other beast shrinking back from him: *BEGONE!*

Something of Vasagi was in him, and just like the Suck's other weird constructs, these things knew it. They collapsed like piles of fur to the steps, and bellied back from Nestor, grovellingly to their accustomed places. And now there was no one and nothing in Suckscar to say no him.

Canker was impressed, and followed even closer to

heel as they went up to Vasagi's old rooms over the great hall. Behind them, Wran and Spiro were nowhere in sight. They were exploring on their own, a fact which had not gone unnoticed by Nestor. As well to suffer their rudeness . . . for now at least.

At the top of the wide flight, cartilage balconies extended left and right, grafted to ledges in the rock which spanned half-way across the great hall just below the ceiling. Up here, Nestor would be able to move about, keeping watch over the industries of common thralls and lieutenants alike. Tunnels in the walls at the rear of the ledges led to lesser rooms, galleries, storehouses, dizzy observation platforms supported by cartilage buttresses, and landing bays and stables in the outer 'skin' of the aerie, whose rock had been worn into those deep and impressive scars for which the manse was named. From the outermost turret, looking hard right (due south), Nestor spied the barrier mountains golden in their peaks, while on high the clouds over teetering Wrathspire were lined with silver and hazy with deadly sunlight. Such observations helped with his orientation: temporal, spatial and mundane, all three. For just as he had begun to think of himself as invincible, he was reminded of his mortality and the sun's destructive power. And when he'd momentarily considered himself magnificent, the stack's awesome majesty had reduced him to a flea. From which time forward his excitement was somewhat reduced . . .

This was as well, for after the view from the platforms, landing-bays and bartizans, Nestor found Vasagi's rooms something of a disappointment; patently the Suck had not been one for luxuries but within Wamphyri parameters had been satisfied with a life of austerity. His bed was of stone slabs raised up, with a large depression hollowed in the middle and filled with the cured furs of Sunside animals. Beneath the bed was a fire hole containing a few scattered ashes. A blackened bone flue angled off from the head of the bed to join with another above a massive fireplace in the vastly thick outer wall. In a curtained corner niche, a dark-stained hole angled down into the floor, from which issued the occasional draught of fresh air. It was just as well that the other end of this hole vacated in some lofty, inaccessible exit over the abyss, for it had been Vasagi's toilet.

From another room, hewn deeper into the stack's porous outer sheath, a large, deep, circular window fitted with cartilage baffles gazed out in a north-easterly direction, showing on the one hand the barrier range dwindling into distance, and on the other the far, dark-blue sheen of the aurora-lit Icelands horizon. There were rooms with wooden tables and chairs, and others with benches cut in the walls. A large sloping hall was enclosed behind an east-facing wall with a row of window holes admitting a maximum of light – and of air! Before being walled-in, this draughty gallery had been one of the manse's great scars; during the period of Vasagi's occupation at least, it had become his studio. This was where the Suck had worked on the 'designs' of his metamorphic creatures, before he gave them life in his vats. And as Nestor examined the huge and intricate paintings, he felt glad Vasagi had not invested *all* of them in flesh.

The east wing of this one level had now been explored, and Nestor and Canker returned to the sweeping staircase down into the great hall. But as they descended a cry rang out, and Canker was galvanized into activity. 'Hah! I had expected it,' he growled. 'The brothers Killglance, scavenging!'

'What?' Nestor looked at him. 'You can only mean

pillaging, surely? But I am the master here, and all that is here is mine. Would they dare?'

Canker snorted. 'Wratha was right: being here and existing here are different things. Unless you are sure of a person or thing, never invite him or it into your house! If you must, make sure he, or it, enters of his own free will. Which is to say: he faces the consequences of any transgressions, whether of his making or of yours! Letting the brothers in here, why, that was like giving them a licence to work their will! Remember: Wran the Rage killed Vasagi. Already he may consider himself entitled to whatever's on offer, while you as yet merely aspire.' He shrugged. 'In my way, I tried to warn you.'

'From now on I shall value your warnings,' Nestor told him. 'But right now I may require your help! Here they come.'

Wran and Spiro had emerged from one of the tunnels into the great hall. Behind them, they dragged female thralls with their clothes stripped mainly from them and hanging in rags. The women were vociferous in their protests; here in Suckscar, they knew what was their lot . . . but in Madmanse?

Hurrying towards Wran, Spiro, and their struggling prizes, Zahar and Grig went to intercept. Back from seeing to the former's wounds, they seemed affronted by the twins' rapaciousness. But these were the Killglance brothers, Lords of the Wamphyri; if things turned nasty, Nestor's lieutenants wouldn't stand a chance. Still, it said a lot for Zahar that even with a dangling arm and damaged hand he now knew where his loyalties lay. For the moment at least . . .

Laughing, the Lords faced down the would-be defenders of Suckscar; but Spiro grew calm in a moment, his grin becoming a scowl as Zahar and Grig drew closer.

Until at last he queried: 'Oh? And is there a problem?' Giving his captive a back-hander in the face, he sent her skittering among a crowd of cowering thralls where they'd emerged from their various places. So far, Suckscar's 'people' had kept well out of it; they had guessed that the Lord Vasagi was no more, but had not known the nature of their new master. Curiosity is a powerful force, however, especially among vampires. A good many of them were here now, anxious to discover what was their lot.

'Make or break!' Canker coughed in Nestor's ear, where they too closed on the frozen tableau. 'It's come sooner than I thought. Gore Sucksthrall was the best of Vasagi's men, and he's dead. These others are useless to you, and the Killglance brothers are fiends in a fight. I . . . I *like* your cut, Nestor, but this is not my problem. It's up to you now: a "diplomatic solution" – cowardice, if you like – or a beating, and possibly death.'

'Or something else,' Nestor answered, in a voice empty of emotion, cold as the winds off the Icelands. 'Watch your back.'

'Eh?' Canker glanced to the rear, and saw Nestor's furry familiars flowing across the hall's flags behind them.

'Even without you,' Nestor told him in that same emotionless voice, 'I am not alone. And I'm not about to be beaten.'

Canker paused a moment, then threw back his head to howl like a mad thing and shake from head to toe. And catching up with Nestor, he said: 'Why, now I like your cut even more, my crafty Lord Nestor – not to mention the odds! Very well, we stand together.'

'Well?' Spiro took a threatening pace towards Grig, who had now come to a halt.

And Wran – still smiling, for the moment – told

Zahar: 'Man, if you persist in blocking my way, there's a very strong chance I'll eat your heart right here and now, off this immaculately clean floor.'

'Gentlemen,' Nestor growled, coming upon them. 'I see you found my women, and picked out two of the comeliest to show me what is my get. That was thoughtful of you. But now, alas, matters have come to a head and I must show you off my property. As you see, two of my creatures are here to make sure you have not forgotten the way out.' And in his mind: *Rear up! Menace them! Issue your smoking juices!*

He stepped aside, Canker likewise – and the guardians of the staircase at once flowed forward, reared upright, presented their muscular underbellies and dripped acid! Wran released his captive; both he and his brother crouched down, looked this way and that; their crimson eyes now blazed with fires so hot they almost smoked. Then:

'Do ... you ... *threaten?*' No longer a 'gentleman', Wran looked about to explode, indeed to rage.

'Threaten?' Nestor put on a surprised expression. 'In what way? I merely provide you with an escort from my place. For as I have said, matters are coming to a head.'

'What matters?' Spiro snarled, clasping his brother's arm as if to hold him in place.

'Why, only that the sun is up,' Nestor answered. 'You've a little time to spare, of course, but if you would collect your flyers from Wratha's landing-bay, and return to Madmanse without – inconvenience – then it's time you were on your way.'

Wran's captive had wriggled away from him; she hid behind Nestor, clutching his jacket. The brothers fumed; they glared at each other, at Canker, and at Nestor with his knife in his belt, but mainly at his familiars. Wran and Spiro were not equipped for war, and even Nestor's common thralls had now taken heart, hissing and creeping closer.

'*Hah!*' Spiro snarled. 'Not a threat?'

'In no way,' Nestor answered. 'I invited you in here, and you entered of your own free will. What sort of hospitality, to threaten you now? Also, Wran is responsible for my being here. I would be in his debt — except of course, I saved his life on Sunside, and so we're even. And while we talk the sun is risen, soon to burn on Wrathspire. I was thinking of your safety, and only that.'

Wran took a deep breath, held it a moment, then slapped his thigh and burst out laughing, however harshly. 'A prodigy!' he cried, through gritted teeth. 'A babe out of Sunside, grown to a man in a single morning, and master now of an aerie manse! Well, and didn't I say you'd do *well* in Suckscar?'

'Indeed you did.' Nestor gestured to indicate the way out, and in so doing cleared a path for them across the floor of the great hall, towards the tunnel stairs to Wratha's landing-bays. 'And so I shall. But each of us in his own place, and yours is in Madmanse.'

The brothers left; they took their time walking across the floor, but they left. Behind them, Nestor's staircase guardians flowed across the flags, leaving a whiff of acid stench in the air. And ahead of them:

Nestor sent a thought to the dark-furred bat-thing in its archway niche. *The men who approach: let them pass, then spit at them, hiss, and shepherd them up and out of Suckscar! From this time forward, they shall not pass again.*

Nestor's male and female thralls, his lieutenants, most of his people — and all of them vampires — were gathered to him now. Knowing that things were afoot, they'd converged on the great hall from their various work

118

places. He stepped up onto a table and turned in a circle, letting all of them see him clearly. Their babble ceased in a moment.

'Look well,' he told them, 'and remember: I am the Lord Nestor, Master of Suckscar. You are my people. Should there be those among you who do not wish to be mine, who may not desire my food, protection, or the comforts of my house, then by all means choose a window and make your exit. For in future, that is how I shall punish any rebellious creature of mine: a long last screaming flight, and a few stains on the scoriac scree. So much for mere dissension ... but as for treachery or insurgence —' He let his gaze wander, to settle on his carpet creatures where they flowed with scarcely a ripple up the stairs to their accustomed places. '— The guardians of my staircase have their needs ...

'And so I make it simple: my word is law. One law for all, and whosoever breaks it gets broken in his turn. So be it.'

Nestor looked down on the faces closest to the table, and said, 'Canker, Zahar, Grig.' He held out his arms to help them up. And of Canker: 'This one, Canker Canison, Master of Mangemanse, is my friend.' He held up his hand. 'Ah, no, it bestows no privileges upon him but merely grants that Canker is *not* my enemy! You will respect him but not obey him.' Canker shrugged, grinned, and nodded appreciatively.

'As for these two,' Nestor glanced at Zahar and Grig each in turn, 'they are my lieutenants, whose word next to mine is law. Zahar is the senior and my right-hand man; *his* arm shall grow stronger, and his hand yet more heavy.'

Nestor considered what he had said and nodded. He was satisfied. But one final command, and a warning, seemed in order. 'I shall see you about, and you shall see me ... but when you least expect it. And now it seems your various works go wanting, while you stand idle and gawping. Let him who has no work learn how to fly, and quickly!'

The crowd dispersed, hastened by Zahar and Grig, who got down among them from the table. Only the two mistreated vampire women held back, examining their bruises and glancing sideways at Nestor. He saw that they were young and very beautiful, and said to them, 'Vasagi's rooms were cold, but mine will be warm. His hearth has no fire, and his bed is hard. These things are mine now. Put them in order, and wait for me ...'

A moment later, when they were alone, Canker danced like a dog on its hind legs and chortled, 'Excellent, all *excellent!* And I no longer fear for you. The surly Suck's no more, and my new neighbour is much to my liking. Why I can see us now: scampering like pups on Sunside, chasing the chickens to and fro!' He became serious, and whined pleadingly, 'But now let me beg you, come down with me into Mangemanse and see my great work: that instrument fashioned of bones, with which I'll lure my silver mistress down from the moon.'

Nestor considered it for a moment, then shook his head. 'Later, perhaps — *if* you'll show me the way down and promise to speak on my behalf to whatever guards the way! But first I must explore all of Suckscar. For after all, this is just one level. I've now seen the east wing of just *one* level, and the north, south, and west wings still unseen! And four more levels to go!' It was hard to keep the elation out of his voice. The vampire is territorial; Nestor's territories, along with his expectations, were expanding fast.

Canker was downcast. 'Ah! Of course. But already it seems you've been here forever, and I feel that I have known you that long at least. Also, it's my instinct that you'll be fascinated by that which these so-called "colleagues" of ours despise. And it will be splendid to have a visitor in Mangemanse who I can trust.'

'As soon as I've at least stuck my head in each corridor, room, hall and workshop, then I shall visit you,' Nestor promised. 'No matter the hour.'

'Excellent!' Canker was delighted. 'I shall expect you before nightfall.'

'And should I enter of my own free will?' Nestor's voice was cold, his expression blank.

Canker looked at him, stared into his eyes. Perhaps there was a hint of red in them even now, as early as this. 'Tut-tut! We are friends!'

'As Wran was my friend?'

'No, as I am your friend!'

'So be it,' said Nestor.

'Very well,' Canker answered. 'Now we proceed directly to your nethermost level, where I shall show you the stairwell and pass down into Mangemanse. And on the way down, I'll advise my creatures as you suggest.'

Nestor looked all about the great hall. A few thralls were busy in a kitchen to one side; a female swept the floor; industrious sounds echoed from various side-tunnels and passageways. The Lord Nestor had issued a warning against sloth, and it was obvious that his people had taken it seriously.

'Zahar!' he called out, as Canker led the way towards a stone-hewn stairwell. 'Attend me.' And to Canker: 'I need him. When you have gone, he shall accompany me on my tour of Suckscar.'

'Good!' said the other. 'That way, you will seem to have purpose and not be seen wandering aimlessly.'

'I *do* have purpose!' Nestor retorted. 'I shall be seen to be interested in everything, and where things don't work, they shall be put to rights. Even if they *do* work, but I don't like the way they work, I shall change them.'

'A new broom sweeps clean,' said Canker. 'And a new Lord of the Wamphyri commands respect.' He shook his head and frowned, and great shaggy red eyebrows met over the bridge of his nose. 'But still I can't get over how quickly you're settling in. Maybe there's more to that story of yours than meets the eye: about your having been Wamphyri before, and forgotten it. Could it be you're someone's bloodson, I wonder? Is it possible that somewhere in your ancestry some Lord took a Sunside girl, and the issue had nothing of the vampire in him except the desire to be Wamphyri?'

Nestor nodded, shook his head, shrugged. 'I don't know. 'You could be right. But I do know this: if I haven't always been Wamphyri, certainly I have always wanted to be.'

Then Zahar joined them and they proceeded down into the lower levels . . .

After Canker had gone, Zahar took Nestor on his tour.

'How many rooms do I have?' Nestor inquired.

'You have stables, storerooms and a granary, a slaughterhouse and cold store,' Zahar answered. 'You have kitchens and rooms for dining, quarters for your thralls, workshops and a laundry, and launching-bays. You have a hall of metamorphosis, with great vats hollowed in the floor and cages in the walls for your warriors. And of course you have your own rooms over the great hall. But how many? I doubt if anyone ever counted them, Lord!'

'Oh? Then have it done,' Nestor answered at once. 'I want them counted, listed, and mapped.'

'Mapped?'

'Aye, on skins. Five skins in frames, one for each

level, all accurately marked with the location of every room, chamber, hall, whatever. With arrows showing north, south, etcetera, and all landmark curiosities clearly displayed. For it strikes me a man could get lost in Suckscar, which would never do. But with a map, I may check my route before I go abroad from my rooms. Is all understood?'

'Yes, Lord,' Zahar answered. 'I know a man, a thrall. On Sunside he drew maps of the Traveller trails. Likewise here in Suckscar, except he drew them for Vasagi. When the Suck raided, he knew where he was going.'

'Good!' said Nestor. 'A useful man, that. Later, you must send him to me.' And after a moment, 'Now tell me, Zahar, where should I look first?' He sounded tired now, and Zahar noted the fact ... also that they were quite alone in Suckscar's nether levels.

Hugging his wounded arm and hand, finally Zahar answered, 'Vasagi's vats ... may be of interest. Creatures of his – or yours, Lord – are waxing even now.' He looked at his arm and hand. And so did Nestor. The bleeding had stopped; Zahar's metamorphic vampire flesh was healing him; he would soon be good as new.

'To the vats, then,' said Nestor. Before retiring, he would see what Vasagi the Suck had fashioned. But the idea of bed was appealing now, and the long Starside 'day' still lay ahead. For some time to come Nestor would continue to sleep like a Traveller, until his change was complete. But after that the sun (its presence in the sky over Sunside) would act on him like a poisonous drug, compelling him to sleep in his dark, shadowy room, with the curtains drawn against the light.

They climbed up to the centre level, then made their way north-west through a maze of passageways and halls to a place where the rock was of a volcanic origin. The ancient lava was pitted like the alveolate bones of birds; and in a vast, low-ceilinged hall, long-escaped gasses had left cavernous pits in the grained, fibrous floor. Except for these sunken 'vats' the floor had been levelled; the vats had been lined with clay and sealed with tar from Sunside's tar pits. This was where Vasagi and doubtless many other Lords of the Old Wamphyri before him had bred their warriors and familiars. And as Zahar had said, some of the Suck's constructs were waxing even now.

From a swirl of gluey fluids, a great colourless eye gazed vacuously up at Nestor where he stood at the rim of a vat. The metamorphic liquid in the vat was almost opaque; the creature it covered was little more than a vague outline, like a series of submerged rocks covered with spines; only the quivering of the grey-green surface told of life. And the mindless gazing and swivelling of the eye, of course.

'A warrior,' Zahar informed quietly, tonelessly, almost as if he feared to breathe, where he stood directly behind Nestor at the vat's rim. 'A replacement. Vasagi lost several in Traveller traps on Sunside. Some of the tribes are very well organized under brave leaders. The Szgany Lidesci are clever indeed, and will pay heavily for their cleverness – eventually.'

Nestor's vampire was alert, alive, wriggling frantically in his body and mind. It sharpened his previously dull and damaged wits, expanded his five mundane senses and awareness to their present limits, issued warnings he couldn't ignore. He did not need to glance over his shoulder to know that Zahar was only an inch away, and that his good arm and hand hung down on a parallel with Nestor's spine. He could almost *feel* the pent pressure in that hand and arm, and certainly he could 'hear' the deadly design of Zahar's mind. A lunge forward, a shove, was all that was needed.

124

Nestor stepped aside, and his motion was so swift that it left Zahar stumbling a little. And merely glancing at him, Nestor said, 'What is this liquid?'

At the end of the vat was a ramp sloping down and disappearing into the murk and slop. It was flanked by narrow stone steps. Nestor moved towards that end, and behind him he heard Zahar take a deep breath. But inside Nestor, his vampire was still at work, and what was instinct to it became instinct to him. So that even before Zahar spoke, he knew what the fluids were: the metamorphic juices of life! This vat was a cold womb for the foetal fashionings of a vampire thing. And Vasagi the Suck had been both father and mother to the contents. The liquids were the white of the egg which sustains the yellow chick, a plasma soup of lymph and protoplasm, derived mainly from innocent blood but contaminated or 'fertilized' with Vasagi's own urine, blood, spittle and sperm.

'It is the sweet juice of forty Travellers, all squeezed by Vasagi!' said Zahar, his throat clogged with weird emotion, perhaps pleasurable anticipation? 'It feeds his creature, oils its joints, and defines its very allegiance. Emerging from its vat, it would know *him* at once. In another sunup and sundown, it *will* emerge . . .' He let his voice tail off.

And Nestor looked at him. 'But the question is, will it know me?'

Zahar shrugged, and struggled with himself not to smile. His thoughts were sinister and Nestor knew it. He also knew a little about Nature: the way the Travellers imprint wolves by midwifing the bitches and supplanting the dog fathers, so that the whelp grows up as guardian to child and man. It was one of those memories which occasionally sprang to mind, unbidden out of a mainly forgotten past.

But who could take chances with a creature such as this? What? Approach such a thing with outstretched hand as it woke to monstrous life and vacated its vat? Best to imprint it now, and stamp his own seal over whatever remained of Vasagi's. He couldn't know it, but the thought was not original to him. Or it was, but it had been spurred by the process of metamorphosis taking place within him.

He looked at Zahar again. 'A man must be careful in this place,' he said, apparently innocently. 'It would seem a dire thing, even perilous, to put a foot wrong and fall into a vat such as this!'

'Indeed, Lord,' Zahar agreed, with just the suspicion of a smirk.

'But —' said Nestor, his voice hardening, '— I am not a man. I am Wamphyri!' And he slowly, very deliberately stripped off his clothes, even discarding his belt and knife, to step down naked into the tepid swirl and sluggish gurgle. And fixing Zahar with his eyes, in which the spark of red was now grown to an ember, he moved alongside the bulk of the waxing warrior and touched it with his hands.

You are mine! he told it. *All which was Vasagi's is mine! That which he was is now in me ... I have eaten him! And you are my creature for ever and ever.*

The ripples in the fluids became small waves as the warrior flexed its great body. Palps with claws which were as yet of soft, flexible chitin closed on Nestor, and various appendages lifted out of the glue to clasp him — but gently! He was ... examined. And accepted. The thing lay still again, and its uppermost eye regarded Nestor with something of fixation, and perhaps something of fear.

You are a good creature, he told it then, *and I shall care for you and feed you well. When you are ready to be born, call me and I shall attend to it myself ...*

And leaving the thing to wax and wallow, he waded to the steps, climbed them, and stepped up onto the level floor; and stood there with the muck dripping from him in small puddles, gazing at Zahar with eyes as cold as the warrior's. But oh so much more knowing.

'Take off your leather jacket,' he told him.

'What?' Zahar stepped back a pace, his Adam's apple wobbling. His eyes went from Nestor to the thing in the vat and back again. 'My jacket, Lord?'

'Are you hard of hearing?' Nestor's voice was harsh. 'Your jacket – now!'

'Yes, Lord!' Zahar stripped it off, let it fall.

'Now your shirt of cloth,' said Nestor.

'Lord,' Zahar gibbered. 'You may be Wamphyri – no, you *are* Wamphyri, assuredly! – but I am just a common thrall. A lieutenant, aye, and a vampire of course, but just a man for all that. To me these special liquids are a poison. If I were to do as you have done and plunge myself into them, be sure I would not surface! And even if I did, your warrior would roll on me with its spines.'

Nestor held out a hand for the shirt. 'And yet these were the things you would have wished on me, just a few moments ago. Indeed, it was even your thought to push me in! Did you think I would not know? Now one last time: your shirt.'

Zahar needed help with it; Nestor dragged the shirt from the grey flesh of his back; for a moment they stood there, the little master calm and his great thrall trembling. And finally Nestor dried himself on the shirt.

'This is loathsome stuff,' he said. 'I would not ask any man to swim in it, and certainly not a brave and loyal lieutenant. But neither do I want it on my body.' And smiling now, however sardonically: 'Better put on your jacket, Zahar. Why, shivering like that, you'll catch a chill.'

'Yes, Lord.' Zahar sighed, lowered his head in relief and took up his jacket; and Nestor tossed the soiled shirt aside.

And dressing himself, Nestor said, 'Zahar, think on this: you had better mend your ways, and soon. There will be no more warnings. The next time I have reason to rebuke you, I will be speaking to meat on a hook in my cold store.'

'Yes, Lord,' Zahar said again. And he knew it was true . . .

'Will you sleep now, Lord?' Zahar inquired as they went up two levels to Suckscar's great hall.

'Yes,' Nestor answered. 'My limbs ache; my head hurts; I'm not quite myself.'

'It's your change,' Zahar told him. 'I've heard about such things. In some it is a long process, but you . . . your eyes are red even now! And the morning just begun. I think you will be a very powerful Lord.'

'I'm tired,' Nestor told him, 'and yet I am not tired. My body is astir. I want to laugh, but fear I might not stop! Ah, but then I could cry, too, except tears are unseemly in Wamphyri eyes. Also, I lust after . . . *things*, without quite knowing what they are. I am proud of Suckscar –' he turned suddenly on Zahar, '– be sure to guard it well for me, while I sleep!'

'As always, Lord.'

'I must have, oh, several hours of sleep. Six, seven . . . eight should be more than enough. Then come to me and wake me, you or Grig. And so we shall continue until I know Suckscar – and all of my thralls, and the work which they perform, and all there is to know – like the lines in the palm of my own hand.'

'It shall be done, Lord.'

'And be *aware!*' Nestor told him. 'The other Lords –

and perhaps a certain Lady, too — think I'm easy meat. Set a watch and see to it that the men are alert. Prowl among them when it is quiet, and if you catch one idling . . . punish him!'

'Yes, Lord.'

'About Canker Canison . . .'

'Yes, Lord?'

'I trust him, for now. For he's a great dog, and I have a way with dogs. But even the best trained dog may make mistakes. These are my orders: he is only to enter Suckscar when I myself am to house and awake. Is that understood?'

'Yes, Lord.'

'Good! As for the rest: I trust Gorvi not at all. And the brothers Killglance are deranged. Well, so is Canker for that matter. But crazy like a fox, aye!'

'And the Lady Wratha?'

'We shall see what we shall see. She is very beautiful.' Nestor was uncertain. 'She *is* a Lady.'

'*Huh!*' Zahar felt obliged to return; and, when Nestor looked at him: 'I have heard stories, Lord.'

'Then tell me all,' said Nestor. 'But some other time.'

They were at the foot of the staircase where it swept up to Nestor's apartments. 'Sleep well, Lord Nestor of the Wamphyri,' said Zahar.

'Be sure of it,' Nestor answered, and climbed the stairs.

A fire burned in his hearth; there was water in an earthen bowl; the two girls were in his bed, already asleep. After washing himself, Nestor climbed in with them. One of them murmured and reached for his member. He brushed her hand away. Time now for sleep. Time for the other later.

And between the vampire girls, soft and warm and musty, he slept like a dead man. Or one who is undead, anyway . . .

V

Mangemanse – Spiders – Canker's Moon Lure

When Nestor woke up the girls were still there, still
asleep. Neither Grig nor Zahar had come to awaken
him, for he had not slept out his full eight hours. The
thing inside him had awakened him, for it had needs of
its own; rather, its needs were now Nestor's. It required
to grow, wherefore he was required to be up and about,
active, a vampire. And now he must take sustenance
not only for himself, but also for his leech, his parasite.

Nestor had eaten well in Wrathspire and shouldn't
be hungry, yet deep inside him there was a different
hunger. In his stretching bones an ache; in his loins a
ripeness requiring an outlet; and in this core which
he'd never even known was a part of him, a great
emptiness, a gnawing red hunger. It was blind and it
was insistent, and he knew that it was red. It was salt
and it was life and it was death . . . and undeath. Now
that he was Wamphyri, it was his weird, unnatural
nature.

His vampire women slept on. The soft loose breasts
of one were in his face; the other was behind him, a leg
draped across his thigh, the pubic covering of her
quiescent core rough where it pressed against skin
which grew ever more sensitive, even to the texture of
shadows and the breath of bats. In the silence, Nestor
could hear the hearts of the women pumping, the coursing of the blood in their veins.

From below, through the honeycombed rock of Suckscar, he felt the motion of thralls where they patrolled, the murmur of far-off voices, the hum or chitter . . . of great bats, yes! His own Desmodus colony, where they clustered in the crevices of a dark lodge of their own. While from outside, from above –

– He could feel the *sear* of the sun on Wrathspire! Which was one of the several things that had awakened him. His skin, previously itchy from the touch of the musty hair of the woman sleeping behind him, now crawled. He knew that the sun was up, burning on Wrathspire, and that his own days of sunlight were gone forever.

For a moment there was panic as all the memories of the last few hours of his life crowded where none had been before – as they ordered themselves and firmed from what *might* have been spumy dreamstuff into the rock of reality – and he knew where and what he was. Panic, as his own heart pounded a little faster, his limbs stiffened to immobility, and all of his vampire awareness reached out like a mist from him, like a presence in its own right, to gauge the day for danger. But there was no danger for this was his place, Suckscar, and all that it contained was his.

Everything . . .

'Umph!' The girl in front of him murmured, as she turned a little and one of her soft nipples brushed his lips. And for a moment he remembered Sunside. He saw it in the eye of his mind, a reflection from the screen of his impaired memory: a misty riverbank in the still of evening, not far from Brad Berea's lonely cabin in the forest. The place where Brad's homely daughter Glina – an innocent in her own right, mainly – had taught him what little he knew and used his body for her pleasure, while in turn giving him pleasure.

It had not been love (not on his part) but lust. Perhaps not even that, but need. For he was a young man, and his body an engine geared to life. But that was then and this was now, when his needs were the amplified needs of the Wamphyri! What had been a pulse, a throb, a fire in his blood ... was now an agony, a driving force, the cap of a volcano straining against the pent pressures of the magma core. And these girls were not homely but very lovely. They were vampires with vampire stuff in them, which had changed and enhanced them, even as it now enhanced Nestor's emotions – specifically, his lust.

He sucked the girl's nipple into his mouth, felt it grow hard, and grew hard himself between her thighs. Still sleeping, she snatched air in a sharp gasp, parted her legs, reached down and guided him in. Her wet core was like an automatic thing, a creature in its own right; its slippery sheath sucked at Nestor like a pouting mouth, so that he need hardly move at all! Reaching down, he pushed at the second girl's hip until her leg slid off his thigh, then parted her bush and sought her bud with his fingers. Her reaction was instinctive, immediate. Gasping, she opened herself, reared against him, and sucked at his hand. It was drawn in to the wrist, where the neck of her vulva tightened on him like a soft leather sleeve.

Nestor wanted to feel the girl he was in, to explore and know all of her. He freed his hand from the furry trap behind him and heard the girl moan. She was waking up. He rolled onto the one he faced and took the initiative, driving deeply into her flesh as if to split her. She, too, was coming awake. The free girl was kissing his ear, the tips of her divided tongue licking and wriggling inside it, while her hand moved between his legs, rolling his balls in her palm.

132

His tongue was drawn down a convulsing throat. Resilient breasts flattened under his chest and he squeezed their bulge with his upper arms. The second girl was now kneeling between his legs, rubbing Nestor's back with her breasts; her hands were under him and his partner, toying and teasing around the area of their sexual organs, manipulating both of them. Nestor moaned, wanting it to last, but it couldn't. And when he came it was as if fire jetted from him, which also activated an orgasm in his frantically writhing partner.

'Mine now!' sighed the second girl, catching his hips and rolling him over. And still jerking, trickling semen, drowning in the sweet, singing agony of his flesh, Nestor felt her sucking mouth come down on him, eager for the last drop. Then:

'Fuck me! *Me* now!' she gurgled, sliding her small, pointed breasts up his chest in a trail of semen from her mouth, lowering her moistly shuddering flesh onto his shaft, and shuffling her tight round backside in an ecstasy of erotic motion until he had slithered in . . .

So it continued, and at least one of Nestor's needs was satisfied, but neither the first nor the last of them. A need, then, and the needs of his vampire women, too. A rare day when they'd enjoyed Vasagi's so-called 'lovemaking' – feeling his organ expanding into their bodies to fill them, while his hollow siphon proboscis of needle-tipped chitin slid into breast, neck, cheek or root of tongue, to draw off blood and heighten his unthinkable pleasure – but they had enjoyed Nestor's. So had Nestor, despite that only one need had been served . . . so far.

And when finally exhausted all three lay still, *still* his hunger was there, like a raw red wound inside him. Some of the metamorphic ache of flesh and bones had subsided, yes, or been dulled by excess; but as Nestor drifted into a second, deeper sleep, his nameless hunger remained . . .

. . . And was absent when he woke up.

Replete, he started awake! Grig's hand was on his shoulder. And Grig's mouth was a dark hole in his grey face, open as if a hinge had snapped in his jaw!

'What?' said Nestor. And then he saw what.

His women had not woken up. The one with the small, firm breasts lay there, breathing but feebly, ashen and cold, completely exposed where Grig had laid back the bedcovers. But the other was motionless, corpse-like, without a breath of life in her body.

And: 'What?' Nestor said again, trying to understand.

'That one, Marla, will live, Lord,' Grig told him, pointing at the ashen one. 'But the other, Carmen . . . she must sleep for some time.'

'Sleep?'

'Undeath,' said Grig. 'In your sleep, you drained her. You took from her and you gave to her. She was a vampire thrall but mainly human. When she wakes up she will still be a vampire but mainly inhuman. Essence of your leech is in her. Eventually, if she is allowed to continue she will be Wamphyri!'

Nestor tried hard to grasp the principle. But the intricacies of vampirism were such that even with his own vampire's instinct, still he was confused. He stood up, took the undead girl's hand in his, let it flop loosely, lifelessly back among the furs. 'On Sunside,' he said, speaking slowly and mainly to himself, 'when the Wamphyri make their thralls, they are *only* thralls! So what's so different here?' He looked at Grig accusingly. 'And why do you understand when I do not?'

'I have been here some time, Lord,' Grig answered,

'and I have learned. There were things which Vasagi did, and things which he did not do. He bred vampires — *not* Wamphyri! On Sunside, in the hunt, the Lords take women for their pleasure and the comforts they give; also for their blood, of course. *Some* of their blood. They also take men, for thralls, lieutenants, and for the provisioning of the manse. The difference is this: they don't kill them. They take a little, give something back. The fever gets into their Szgany victims, who are then brought back here or make their own way. Or they are discovered by the Travellers and put to death on Sunside. Except . . .' He searched for words, and Nestor grew impatient.

'Yes, except?'

'Except, if a man or woman is drained — if so much blood is taken that he or she "dies" — then the vampire, *your* vampire, compensates, gives more of itself. The more you take, the more you give. And after the sleep of undeath, the transition is that much faster.'

Nestor looked at the 'dead' girl again, but with a different expression on his face. 'She could be . . . *Wamphyri?*' He glanced at Grig and held up a hand to still his tongue. 'Yes, I know: *if* she is allowed to continue . . .'

He looked at the other woman. 'But this one, Marla . . . is only a thrall.'

'But a *weak* thrall, Lord,' Grig nodded. 'For your hunger was very great. The furs are soaked red where your thirst ran over! She needs food, soup, meat. In order to serve you again, she must first recover.'

Suddenly Nestor felt bloated. Suddenly he was aware of his red hands, face, even his eyes. He was still a novice and had taken too much. While his system was changing, it had not yet had time to adjust or prepare itself for such a gorging. His ascendant leech had been

135

too eager! He reeled beside the bed, clutching the high stone headboard for support. And indicating Carmen, he choked out: 'Deal with that. The provisioning.' But as Grig lifted her up light as a leaf: 'No, wait! Lie her in state somewhere, until I can think. Then return and care for this one, this Marla. But for the moment –' Nestor's gorge was beginning to heave, '– *leave me alone!*'

And as Grig carried Carmen from the room, Lord Nestor of the Wamphyri groped his way blindly to the curtained niche in the corner, and almost but not quite made it . . .

Nestor and Grig went down into Mangemanse. At least, Grig *would* have accompanied his master, if he had been allowed. But where a deep dark stairwell descended in a steep, narrow spiral into black bowels of rock, and a recess in the wall facing the shaft housed a second bat-thing guardian, there Nestor took his lieutenant's arm to bring him to a halt. And he pointed out a sigil carved in a flagstone at the head of the steps. It was Canker's mark: a sickle moon.

Then, as if at some signal, though none had been given, a growl echoed up from below and was followed by a single, ululating howl, which slowly died away. The guardian showed alarm, flowed forward in its niche and hissed, but Nestor cautioned it: *Be quiet, all is well.*

And: 'Lord?' Grig looked at him uncertainly, and waited.

'Canker and I have an agreement,' Nestor told him. 'When in future we visit, we go alone, of our own free will. It was not my intention that you would accompany me further than this point, but that you'd wait here until I return. Then you shall show me Suckscar, taking over where Zahar left off. For there remains a great deal to be seen, and I want to know all. Meanwhile, move about and make yourself useful by all means, but stay within earshot of this stairwell. When I return, I shall call for you.'

'Yes, Lord. But –'

'But?'

Grig looked at the steps leading down, and at the nitre-streaked walls. 'That is an odorous place, Lord: a kennel, by all accounts. Are you sure you would see it?'

And again, as if at some command, the unseen creature howled far below, and a wave – an almost visible reek – of animal musk came wafting up out of darkness. There was ordure in the smell, strong urine, the stench of some feral beast's lair. Grig turned to Nestor again, and said, 'Lord?'

'That howling . . . was not a man,' said Nestor.

Grig shook his head. 'No, Lord. Canker Canison makes creatures in his own image . . .'

Nestor shrugged. 'Still, I made a promise, and I must be known by my word. Also, Canker will make a powerful ally. Well, an ally of sorts.' He started down the deeply hollowed steps. 'Wait for me, and when I return, answer my call.'

'Yes, Lord.'

And Nestor proceeded down into Mangemanse . . .

The spiral staircase was deep. Nestor went cautiously; his Wamphyri eyes were now so changed that he saw almost as well as in daylight. There was no more howling, but an aura of expectancy. Without even knowing he did it, Nestor sent his vampire awareness ahead of him, probing the root of the shaft. Something was down there, but keeping well back, and keeping quiet now.

And Nestor sent: *I am the Lord Nestor. Your master, Canker Canison, has asked me to attend him. Who harms me dies! If not by my hand, by Canker's certainly.*

Snuffles echoed up to him, but that was all.

At the foot of the steps ... Nestor was appalled! To the left, a natural cave led back into darkness absolute, in which feral eyes — huge, yellow, malevolent — glared for a moment, then blinked out. But this was not the source of his concern. That was the veritable *midden* which lay in a second, smaller cave, to the right.

The reeking dung of some large beast, possibly the thing with the yellow eyes, was piled in slumping heaps out of which grew squat, corpse-white mushrooms; while around and in between the piles swirled sickening green puddles of piss! Nestor stood on a narrow, raised, unpolluted path midway between the two, the unknown guardian on the one hand and its despicable *depository* on the other. But if this was how Canker kept Mangemanse generally ... then it well deserved its name!

And holding his breath, he proceeded along a corridor towards an area where a row of tiny round windows let in a little grey light from the west, and also the wind which hummed a different tune through each orifice, and sucked away the stench of the stairwell midden. Perhaps this was where Canker had derived the inspiration for his instrument. But now, as Nestor left the windows behind and their song dwindled in his ears, so the way ahead turned inwards from the outer sheath and into the rock of the stack proper, and the corridor grew dark again.

Striding out, Nestor found himself listening to the *slap, slap, slap* of his own footsteps on the worn stone; but when he came to a sudden, breathless halt, he knew that he heard much more than that. For from somewhere not too far behind sounded a soft and regular — yet strangely irregular — padding, and the panting of a loping fox or wolf ... both of which paused only a split second after Nestor paused.

One of two things: he was either being tracked, as prey, or he'd acquired a wary escort. Looking back, he saw the corridor disappearing into the gloom of its own curve, its walls glowing with a dim phosphorescence of their own; and in the core of darkness between the walls, at a height about central to a man's thigh, those yellow eyes. The guardian of Canker's stairwell, but escorting him ... or stalking him? And his concentrated vampire senses detected a thought which sped by him in a moment into Mangemanse:

Something is here: a trespasser, a sneaking thing ... and human! It - he - pretends to know you and have business here, but I don't trust him! No, he cannot be the one you mentioned, your friend. Only command me, and he shall be no more! It was never a human thought but a beast's: the ill-formed message of a beast-mind, a dog or great wolf, but having far more of intelligence than any warrior or guardian so far encountered. Something of panic set in then, or if not true panic, an instinctive reaction to danger: a deadly cold, emotionless desperation, causing Nestor to shut down his own probes and emanations and withdraw into himself at once, like a shadow merging into deeper shadows. It was his vampire, of course — its sense of self-preservation — which now directed his actions. But if there was any sort of telepathic answer to the tracker's murderous suggestion, that too was shut out, leaving Nestor naked and alone with his own fancies and imaginings. Perhaps it were best to try contacting the dog-Lord, except ... could he trust Canker now? Could he *really* trust him?

A few more swift, silent paces brought him to a junction like the hub of a great wheel, with spoke passageways or rooms leading off. Choosing the first room on the right and slipping quietly in through its arched entrance, Nestor put his back to the wall and waited. It had been his parasite's instinct to cast the merest pulse of a probe ahead of him into the room — sufficient to discern no human or inimical animal inhabitant, at least, but no more than that — and then he was inside.

Whatever followed him must pass close by. Depending on the nature of the beast, and if it failed to detect him, Nestor had two choices: to let it carry on, and then escape back along the way he'd come, or to leap upon the creature and try to kill it. To that end, his knife was in his hand. And standing there with his back to the cold stone wall, scarcely daring to breathe, Nestor looked all about his bolthole to discover its contents, function, and any other exits or escape routes which might exist. Of the latter, there were none: the place was quite simply a dry cave with a high ceiling, crumbling ledges, gloomy niches, and no obvious evidence that it had ever been inhabited or furnished ... by men. But it did have its own function, and it did provide habitation of sorts. For spiders!

Their black webs, half as thick as a man's little finger, didn't become visible until Nestor craned his neck to stare up through a great many irregularly concentric tiers of crumbling sandstone ledges — like the interior of some crooked, burned-out chimney — receding to the ceiling high overhead. Then the webs looked like intricately patterned cracks in the darkness, no two patterns alike, all of them faintly luminescent; layer upon layer of them, bridging the gaps between the ledges as they receded with them into the heights of the place.

And he was still staring at them, pondering their meaning, when they began to shiver and tremble, all in unison, like the dewy webs of much smaller, commoner forest and plains species when their makers shake them to trap mites. Following which, the truth of it became obvious.

Ever since childhood, Nestor had known something of the Wamphyri; Szgany legends had been full of them, despite that in those days the Old Wamphyri were no more. When Nestor had played with other Traveller children, he had always taken the part of a vampire Lord — indeed, as a child he *had* truly desired to be Wamphyri — so that it was not so very strange that these were the only genuinely material things which he remembered from those forgotten days of yore.

He had been familiar with all the Wamphyri myths, and had known about their powers. Their mentalism, and their ability to conjure mists out of their bodies; their familiars, the bats of Starside, great and small, which they commanded. But there was another part of the legend which was less well-known: the way they used lesser creatures (such as the bat, and the great red bat-eating spiders of Starside caverns) to spy for them and perform ... other functions. One such myth had been that the Wamphyri used spider silk to spin their clothing, while another hinted that they kept the corpses of victims wrapped in spider-shrouds, which preserved their meat for eating.

Such memories sprang to mind now, perhaps enhanced and given substance by his new vampire instinct. So that even without knowing the mechanics of the thing, Nestor knew that something of these ancient beliefs was true. He also knew why the as-yet-unseen spiders in the ledges of the cave were shaking their webs: to trap whatever intruder had entered into their place, namely himself. It was an automatic thing and natural; in any case he was no cavern bat to go flitting to his death in the shimmering heights!

He scarcely felt threatened – not by spiders, however large – but nevertheless turned more fully towards the doorway . . . and in that same moment became aware of the furtive slap of padded feet, and a low panting which issued from the mouth of the long corridor back to the stairwell. Whatever it was that stalked him, it was here even now. And Nestor gripped his knife that much tighter, and stayed hidden in the shadows of the doorway until the thing began to emerge into the hub of the cavern system. Then, seeing it come slowly, cautiously into view . . .

. . . He took a last deep breath and held it, and *continued* to hide in the shadows. And the knife in his hand felt like a brittle twig, and his flesh soft as the pulp of fungi, as the Thing more fully emerged, lowered its face to the floor where he had stepped – and sniffed with a drooling snout more than a foot long!

Nestor had seen his share of Grey Ones, the wolves of the barrier mountains, but never a one like this. Something of the wolf was in it, certainly, but very little of Nature. No, for this was a creature spawned of Canker's vats. And it had been bred in something of Canker's 'image', at that. Lupine, yes, but fox-red, too, its lope was nightmarish; *made* nightmarish by the fact of its six legs! The first four of these moved like the legs of any ordinary tame dog or wolf, in diagonal agreement, but the pair that brought up the rear moved *in tandem* with the centre pair, like the small deer of Sunside's forests when startled to flight; yet all with a sinuous grace. The thing was something less than eight feet long from snout to tip of tail, stood maybe thirty-six inches off the ground, and must have weighed in excess of four hundred pounds. The pads of its paws were larger than Nestor's hands, with claws that clicked against stone where the flags of the floor were uneven.

And its head and face were ... quite monstrous. Again, they reminded Nestor of a wolf – their *dimensions* were those of a huge wolf, certainly – but the furtive, unblinking intelligence behind the burning sulphur of the eyes, and the colour of its fur, that was all fox. In combination, the feral talents of the two animals would be formidable.

They *were* formidable!

The guardian took another weird, loping pace forward; its long snout again touched the floor where Nestor had paused, and sniffed; and the long, sensitive ears swivelled to point at him in his hiding place. He would draw further back but didn't dare move. This creature wasn't something he could shout at and subdue. It wasn't one of his own but Canker Canison's, over which he had no claim or control at all. It had allowed him to enter this place 'of his own free will'. But that didn't mean it had to let him out again.

Nestor had instinctively, automatically shuttered his eyes. Still the yellow orbs of the wolf-thing found the red flush of his own, and grew large in its sloping face as its entire body aimed itself like an arrow at his doorway. Then, growling low in its throat, stiff-legged, and salivating from jaws like an ivory mantrap, the thing advanced.

And it was no more than five of Nestor's paces away when he felt a tap on his shoulder!

Any ordinary man might have fainted at that touch; even the bravest Szgany Traveller would have cried out; but Nestor was no longer Szgany, no longer a Traveller. He was Wamphyri! He moved but a fraction, turning his body only an inch or two at most, but his knife-hand moved like greased lightning. And he slashed unerringly at whatever had touched him.

The keen edge of his blade bit into but didn't quite cut the rope-like thing touching his upper left shoulder. Instead, the weapon seemed *attracted* to that slender, hairy strand, and in order to retrieve it he must wrench sharply downwards; which only served to bring him into further contact with the thread of gluey spider silk. Slapping against the sleeve of his jacket from shoulder to elbow, it adhered at once – and began to vibrate!

Nestor glanced out of the door; the wolf-thing had come to a halt and was crouched down snarling only two paces – or a single bound – away! Its sleek muscles were bunching even now. While descending from above, a foot or two overhead . . .

. . . A great red spider crept effortlessly, head-first down the strand; and in the walls, the ruby-glinting eyes of others were visible where they swung from ledge to ledge, coming to investigate the nature of their victim. But there are spiders and there are spiders. Relatives of these creatures dwelled on Sunside, too, in deep caverns from which they emerged at dusk to fashion their webs and trap moths. That species was three to four inches long, with a bite that was poisonous but rarely fatal. It produced a numbness and even partial paralysis, accompanied by dizziness and vomiting, but lasting only three or four hours at most. That was Sunside, however, while this was Starside; these aerie spiders were at least four times longer, with forty or fifty times the bulk!

Nestor gave his arm a desperate yank and his sleeve was torn away down the stitches, to dangle there on the adhesive thread. The violence of the movement shook the spider loose; it flopped to the floor and at once rolled itself into a ball; without pause, Nestor kicked it straight into the face of the wolf-thing. And as Canker's creature reared back and yelped, he stepped into the open with his knife-arm upraised.

'What's all this?' Canker whiningly queried, loping forward across the open span of the hub. 'Is it the Lord Nestor? What, and do you threaten my creatures?' He grinned.

'Do I . . . *what*?' Nestor was astonished, and angry.

'*Hah!*' Canker barked. 'Or do they threaten you, eh?'

The great spider scurried by them into the darkness of the cave, and Canker's 'guard-dog' shrank down and grovelled, then backed off with its tail between its legs. Canker scowled at it and said, 'Well done!' Then pointed and added, 'And now begone!' The creature turned and slunk away, returning the way it had come.

'Your dog would have attacked me!' Nestor accused. 'And your spiders *did* attack me!'

'On the first count, wrong,' said Canker. 'My "dog", as you have it, was instructed to follow you and see you came to no harm. He was only suspicious because you were so furtive, whereas I had said you would be bold! And on the second count, also wrong, because the great red spiders are only "mine" insofar as they dwell here. I don't – can't – command them; they are what they are and do what they do. But . . . you have spiders of your own, surely? Or should I say, there *are* spiders, in Suckscar. Ah, but I note your confusion! As yet you've not explored your manse to the full, and so you fail to understand the special functions of creatures such as this. Well, that's easily put to rights; let me show you.'

He led the way back into the spider cavern, but Nestor stayed where he was. 'What?' Canker glanced back at him. 'Do you hold back? No need for caution now, Nestor. Indeed quite the opposite! The more noise the better!' And with that he barked and capered, and laughed in his mad-dog fashion within the cave. The echoes of his actions went up, and dust rilled down, and high overhead the luminous webs stopped shivering and grew still.

'Blind!' Canker laughed. 'Or very nearly. Ah, but they *hear* well enough! Why, you must have crept in here, Nestor, that they should mistake you for something small. But quite obviously we noisy creatures are not bats, and so the spiders are fled to their high niches. But come, see, and understand.'

He loped through the cavern, across a floor inches deep in defunct, cast-off webs which had lost both their glow and adhesion, to a corner which was festooned in dusty drapes of spider silk. And behind these shrouding curtains . . .

'. . . There!' said Canker, pointing.

And now Nestor saw that the old Szgany legends were true. For there against the wall stood a geometrical structure, like a small section cut through a beehive honeycomb. Six hexagonal tubes formed the base, with five more on top, then four, three, two and one. A pyramid of tubes. Storage tubes of wax, produced and fashioned by the spiders, in which to preserve . . . what?

The tubes were almost seven feet long by two feet across the bore. Nestor approached the pyramid and brushed dust away from wax which was not quite opaque. The tube he had chosen was in the row of three, about shoulder high, the fourth in height from the floor. And lodged within, all wrapped in silk threads except for his face – was that a human figure?

Well, sub-human anyway. For it was a brown and leathery trog from Starside's caverns under the barrier

146

mountains, apparently mummified and more than a little shrivelled. But dead? Nestor fancied he saw the faint flutter of an eyelid and the merest twitch of a protuberant lip. Also, the wall of the waxy tube directly above his face was misty, as from shallow breathing.

'Bravo!' said Canker. 'Your developing vampire instinct: you chose to examine the one cell currently in use.'

'Cell?' Nestor looked at him, and Canker shrugged.

'Hatchery, then.'

Nestor frowned, shook his head, and Canker sighed. Then, leading the way back out: 'Now listen,' he said, 'and I shall explain. The spiders fashion these combs in size according to their prey. Here in Mangemanse — and throughout the aerie in general — we, the Wamphyri, provide the prey, wherefore the tubes are man-sized.

'The process is simple: We hunt on Sunside, or in this case on Starside, down in the bottoms beyond the sucking sphere of white light.'

'The hell-lands Gate?' (Again Nestor's resurgent memory.)

'Indeed, in the trog caverns where the earth shines. Hell-lands Gate, did you say? Aye, I've heard my thralls call it by that name, when I've brought them out of Sunside. Let me begin again:

'We hunt on Sunside, and take thralls, lieutenants, women! But not everyone can be a thrall or lieutenant, and sometimes a woman can get used up too quickly. Of course, there is always the provisioning: a manse has its needs no less than its inhabitants. I have warriors to feed, and familiars. And then there are my common vampire thralls and my men. But what use to keep a surfeit of flesh around, especially if it be useless, surly, or ugly?

'Well, I have cold storage rooms, as do we all. But . . .

147

I prefer my meat red and afoot when I can have it. Right now, I don't have much use for the spiders, none of us do. But in time of siege, if that should ever come to pass – and well it might, for we have powerful enemies in the east – or if ever fresh blood should prove hard to come by ... then the aerie's spiders come into their own.

'For they have a bite which will put a man to sleep as easily as my own – *ha, ha!* Except men will rise from my bite, if I wish it, while the spider bite will freeze them for long and long. It is not undeath, no, but similar in its way. It does not make vampires but simply preserves ... meat. And so you see the value of the spiders. Bitten by them and wrapped in their cocoons, a man is slowed down, down, down and lasts a year or more. So that if the time comes when I may not journey abroad, well, so what? My larder is full at home. Oh, *ha, ha!* I have thirty men preserved in this way; aye, and even a handful of women ...

'The antidote is produced by the female when her eggs are due to hatch. It lets blood flow freely in the incubator: that is, the body of the victim, in which she has laid her eggs. In men, these are deposited in the gut; and even as the antidote stirs the victim to agonized life, so the hatchlings are busy eating their way out!

'Ah, but of course that is not allowed to happen! As soon as a man is stilled and cocooned – before eggs can be laid in him – I have him removed from this place to my larder. Later, when I require him up and about, it's the work of a moment to have a female administer the antidote. What could be simpler?'

Walking with Canker through the hollow, echoing maze of Mangemanse's upper level, Nestor offered a shrug. Deep inside, perhaps something of the old Nestor rebelled; if so, his parasite quickly subdued it. 'It seems simple enough,' he finally answered. 'Except ... do you keep trogs in your larder, too?'

'Eh?' Canker frowned. 'Ah! — that one back there? No, no — he is not for eating. Not by me, at least! But you see, the spiders look after me, and I must look after the spiders. That trog you saw, he is a receptacle, a hatchery. What, and should I let the beasts die out? No, of course not, for they serve me too well. The trog's dull life is burgeoning even now, and so is a new generation of grubs, burrowing in his innards.

'But enough of that. Let's down into Mangemanse proper, and see what's to be seen.' They had reached the north-eastern corner of the stack, where windows looked out on mile upon mile of barren boulder plains and a distant, dark-blue horizon, cold and sombre under the occasional writhing wisp of auroral sheen. Here a wide staircase led down, and as Nestor followed on close behind the dog-Lord, his first view of Canker's great hall surprised him more than just a little. Here at least, Mangemanse was not what he'd supposed it would be ...

If Nestor had been puzzled by Canker's remark about descending into Mangemanse 'proper', he was puzzled no more. Up above, in the level immediately below his own Suckscar, the aura had been one of emptiness, desolation, abandonment. Ah, but all deliberately contrived! Nestor saw that now: that the upper level had been kept that way — gloomy, echoing, guarded, and forbidding — *because* of its proximity to the one-time manse of Vasagi the Suck. There was nothing up there which a neighbour would covet, just empty rooms, mazy corridors, a cave of spiders (of which Vasagi, and now Nestor, had sufficient of his own) and a ferocious guardian equipped not only with a physical 'voice', but also with a cunning intelligence and a strong telepathic connection with its master. That level was a gantlet, a place to be approached with great caution and suspicion, if not actual fear and trepidation; though who in his right mind would want to run such a gantlet in the first place, Nestor couldn't say. Perhaps those 'powerful enemies in the east' which Canker had mentioned. But down here:

As opposed to a midden, stink-hole or kennel, Mangemanse 'proper' was immaculate, which in the richness and variety of its appointments by far outdid the austerity and dingy furnishings of Suckscar! The walls were hung with tapestries, hunting scenes mainly, at which well-clothed vampire women worked even now, stitching and embellishing. A kitchen in an alcove to one side issued mouth-watering aromas and billowing wafts of smoke and steam into a chimney hole in the ceiling. More windows, cut high in the walls, let in all that was required of light; since these faced well away from the sun and towards the north-east, their ornate baffles, screens and bat-fur curtains were kept mainly open, aerating the place.

Canker pointed out a great high archway in an inner wall; surmounted by a recently cemented keystone bearing his sickle-moon sigil, this was the entrance to his private apartments. He made no attempt to show Nestor inside, but explained: 'I keep a watcher just within who has no eyes and so works by smell alone. This makes him extra vigilant, and he accepts only me and mine. Instant death to anyone else – friend, foe, whatever – who so much as puts a toe across that threshold. Be advised: that is one place where you must never go, neither of your own free will nor by invitation, not even mine! No, for you are a Lord of the Wamphyri in your own right; be sure he would sniff out your leech and fall on you in a moment!'

They left Canker's great hall and struck out north through a maze of well-kept corridors and lesser halls. And in a while, as they proceeded:

'It was a mistake to come here,' said Nestor, musingly.

'How so?' Canker coughed.

'Because it makes me realize how much of my own place goes unseen, as yet unexplored! But since we seem to have struck up something of a friendship, it would have been impolite of me to refuse you.'

'Impolite?' Canker grinned, but ruefully. 'Precious little of politics here, Nestor! What rules the Wamphyri make are for breaking; their "chivalry" is a sham; if a Lord can lie and go undetected, be sure he'll never tell the truth. If you find one you think you can trust, odds are he's made a fool of you. When a Lord laughs with you, make sure he doesn't continue when your back is turned. And any bargain you may strike, strike it twice and make doubly sure you nail it down!'

Nestor looked at him earnestly. 'Oh, and is your chivalry — the friendship which you've shown me — a sham, Canker? Do you also lie? In trusting you, am I a fool? Do you laugh with me, or behind my back?'

'I'm as big a liar as the rest,' the dog-Lord answered, carelessly. 'As for chivalry: let a man cross me, I'll ambush and gut him at my first opportunity! Comradeship and laughter? There are laughs and there are laughs. But you ...' He paused in his loping, caught Nestor's arms and looked him straight in the eye, very seriously, with his great shaggy head cocked a little on one side. 'You ... are *different*. To answer your question: no, I'll not betray you. But you're not yet full-fledged; and when your leech rides ascendant, well, it could yet be a question of who betrays who.'

By now they had crossed the span of Mangemanse to

151

reach a cold and blustery cavern in the north-facing wall. Out there, seen through a series of small round window holes, the distant horizon was of a variegated blue and purple, shimmering through amethyst to indigo and back again, under the weave of the Icelands aurora.

But here inside the cavern – once a long, low-ceilinged landing bay by its looks – this was where Canker had been at work on his 'musical instrument'. Nestor gazed in open astonishment at the gleaming white jumble where Canker stepped proudly, carefully among the various half-finished assemblies, and marvelled at the dog-Lord's industry, that he had conceived of and commenced to build such a thing.

It was of alveolate bones, of course, many of them thin as a man's arm, while others were vast beyond reason: the leg and thigh-bones of warrior creatures of the Old Wamphyri who, in ages past, had warred with each other and ridden their vampire beasts to battle and death out across the boulder plains more than two thousand feet below. For in those days there had been many aeries, whose Lords and Ladies were forever feuding. And so the littered gullies and dried-out river beds of Starside's bottoms formed a monstrous ossuary.

Now: Canker had started to carve these hollowed relics of bygone ages, to pierce them and fit the holes with oiled, sliding plugs, and to join the resulting – flutes? – together in series from large bones to small. He had strapped them side by side with leather fastenings, their open ends facing the blustery gulf beyond the landing-bay. While in the mouth of the bay itself, there a series of massive baffles – the oarlike scapulae of monsters – were held in position by ropes and turned on pivots at Canker's command. And indeed there seemed something of order in his work, which was why Nestor marvelled.

'There,' said Canker, gratified. 'I see it in your face: you acknowledge my skill in the construction of this work! Ah, and one day you'll applaud my artistry, too, as I orchestrate the very winds and cause these bones to sound! But ... would you like a demonstration? Stand back then, and you shall see. Oh, it's not perfected, not yet by a long shot. But one day, one day.'

And as Nestor looked on, Canker loosened the baffle-ropes where they were coiled on capstans ...

VI

The Bonesong – Wratha – Carmen

In all the levels of the last great aerie of the Wamphyri – in echoing halls which now were mainly empty except for drowsy vampire guards and watchkeeping monsters, in winding, mazy corridors and stairwells, storerooms, communal and private places – the *sound* gradually became apparent. It might be the sighing of the wind flowing down from the Icelands, drawn by the sun rising over Sunside, where even now mists had been lured up from foothills and crags to obscure the yellow peaks of the barrier range. It might be a mewling of monsters waxing in their vats, things which had been men and now were less (or more?) than men, giving hideous voice and readying themselves for their new roles. It might be the scorching of the sun on the south-facing flanks of Wrathspire itself, as if its rays ate like acid into the harrowed rock of morbid centuries.

It might have been any or all of these things, a combination of sounds amplified by the comparative quiet and the aching acoustic hollowness of the kilometre-high stack, but it was none of them. It was, instead, a sounding of bones. It was Canker Canison at his first fumbling trial run, adjusting the baffles which directed the gusting dawn winds through the maze of grotesque bone pipes which was his moon lure. And it sounded, however faintly at first, in every inch of the stack from Gorvi's basement apartments to the tip of the topmost turret of Wrathspire itself.

Down in Guilesump, the water in Gorvi's wells seemed to tremble on the surface as from some internal stirring. Dust, falling in rills, formed curtains like drifting smoke or the weird weave of Iceland's auroras without their phosphorescent sheen. The Guile's watchmen turned wondering eyes upwards to cavern ceilings, only to blink and feel the sting as the fine grey dust settled into them.

In Madmanse, the brothers Wran and Spiro Killglance slept and dreamed their red dreams, but all disturbed and distorted by the sound. Half-waking, Wran aimed a sluggish thought at unseen but suspect guardian creatures which he supposed were quarrelling: *Be still! Stop fighting! Keep watch! Or should I simply dissolve you in the vats and start again?* Having issued the threat, he returned to his hideous dreaming. But still the sound was there.

And Spiro cried out — once, twice, sharply and fearfully from his bed — and whined: 'Eygor, our father which we murdered! But ... are you here, too? Does your uneasy spirit prowl the last aerie, the new Madmanse, just as it stalked the corridors of that haunted old place in Turgosheim? So be it! I am not afraid. For there's no power in your eyes now. You may not destroy me with a glance!' All very defiant and brave-sounding. Bravo! But Spiro's voice had faded to a dry, mumbling croak at the end. And there was no answer except the bonesong.

In Suckscar, Zahar and Grig shared the duties of Lieutenant of the Guard the better to keep an eye on the common thrall pickets and watchmen; for Nestor's orders (his dire threats and warnings) had not gone astray. Currently, Grig was half-asleep on a bench not far from where Nestor had left him on his descent into Mangemanse, and Zahar nursed his crippled but rapidly healing arm and hand as he crept up on watchmen to catch them out.

To them the wail and throb and thunder of Canker's music seemed a song of grave foreboding; issuing from Mangemanse, it might easily spell trouble and even death for their new master, who seemed bent on suicide in those unknown levels of kennel-stench and canine perversion. Aye, for even among the Wamphyri, Canker was perverse. Not that Zahar and Grig would worry much over Nestor's demise, but more about their own futures if such were the case.

And overhead, in Wrathspire, Wratha tossed in her bed and called out wearily for her love-thrall to attend her. He came, shuddering, from his fur-draped bench in a niche, massaged her back with trembling hands, and told her, 'Hush, now! Rest easy, Lady. No harm befalls.' Her vampire lover was young and strong, but not as strong as he had been and no longer so young. He ate like a shad but his weight went down ounce by ounce; his cheeks were sinking in upon themselves; his nerves were breaking. And the smile he must smile for Wratha was often as not a grimace ... but not when she could see it, only when he practised. For in his heart of hearts he knew it would not be long before the Lady sought a replacement; knew also what had befallen the one who had gone before him. Wrathspire had its requirements and little went to waste. There was always the provisioning ...

To Wratha's love-thrall the bonesong was the merest hum vibrating upwards through the rock under his feet and into him: a loose window baffle perhaps, thrumming in a crosswind. But to Wratha it was something else. Her acute Wamphyri senses, which numbered more than five, loaned it new accent and meaning, especially in her vampire sleep. It was an accusing voice which howled out of the past, and was borne to her on beams of sunlight from far across the barrier mountains.

'The sun is risen and smiles her sick, yellow smile at me,' she whispered, her voice all trembly, drowsy and dreaming, as her thrall's clever hands soothed her a little. 'Aye, smiling ... even as she smiled at Karl the Crag that time, and turned his hair to smoke, and burned his eyes out! I can hear him crying out to me, demanding revenge! His voice is in the sun, which burns on Wrathspire even now.' And perspiring, yet with something of a shiver in her voice, she queried: 'Are the drapes drawn? *Are* they?'

'Yes, Lady. Throughout all of Wrathspire. Except ... this room has no drapes, for there are no windows. You rarely sleep where the sun can find you, Lady.'

'True,' she sighed in answer, drifting deeper into fevered dreams. 'But I nightmare wherever I sleep ...'

In Mangemanse, Nestor leaned back against a curved inner buttress with his hands clapped to his ringing ears. There stood Canker like a huge upright dog, outlined against the deep blue sheen of the northern horizon. With four baffle-ropes wrapped around each arm, he tried desperately hard, and uselessly, to control all of the wind inlets at once. The result for the last six or seven minutes had been an absolute cacophony, until Nestor could stand it no longer. Now, pale and shaken, he watched the laughing dog-Lord releasing rope after rope, until the numerous cartilage baffles were set loose to pivot and turn at will, knocked to and fro by the mindless wind.

Then for a while it was even worse. Several of the bellows between the baffles and the organ assemblies ruptured as great blasts of uncontrolled air tore into them; an eight foot tall baffle was wrenched loose from its seating in a splintering of cartilage and went clattering away along the outer wall of the stack and down into the abyss; one of the assemblies, virtually a pyramid of bones, began vibrating so violently that its bindings snapped, setting free a dozen or more mighty white tubes to go rolling and bouncing this way and that across the floor of the one-time landing bay. Canker, hastily winding ropes on capstans, had to dance to avoid being knocked off his feet.

At last the chaos was over and there came a blissful surcease. And despite the moaning of the wind round the last aerie, the 'silence' was such that it was deafening. Furious about the damage, Canker stamped and roared, and finally turned to where Nestor staggered wan and very nearly deafened against the buttress.

'Did you hear? Did you see?' The dog-thing barked. On the one hand his fury was still plain to see, but on the other he seemed partially satisfied at least. 'And what did you think?'

'Think?' Nestor answered. 'Have you left me a brain with which to think?'

'Was it that bad?' Canker was at once crestfallen.

'Bad is not the word for what it was!'

'Aye, you are right.' The other nodded. 'Too much for one man to handle, I think. But it was the first time I'd tried it, after all. Perhaps when I've repaired it, next time you'd care to give me a hand?'

Nestor shook his aching head, but carefully. 'I think not. Compose your orchestra of lieutenants and thralls, Canker. For even the strongest friendship has its breaking point.'

'But you'll admit the thing has possibilities?'

'Will it make music? Will it lure your mythical Lady down from the moon? Is that what you're asking?'

For a moment Canker's face turned yet more bestial

and his jaws gaped wide, snarling . . . but in the next his expression was sad. 'Mythical, Nestor?' he half-panted, half-whined. '*Huh!* I might have expected that from the others, but not from you. I tell you I have dreamed of her, and she *must* be from the moon! Where else, all dressed in silver, with her yellow hair and blue eyes? Have you not seen how the moon tumbles blue and yellow through the skies: blue in those parts which are turned to the Icelands, and yellow in the half that is lit by the furnace sun? And sometimes silver head to toe when the sun is down and the aurora flutters pale in the north? Do you not know that I am an oneiro-mancer and can read the future in dreams? Until you can readily understand such things, don't speak to me of myths and fancies.'

'I didn't mean to offend you,' Nestor told him. 'And in any case, who am I to say you're wrong? I can't even remember my own past – well, except in brief, meaning-less flashes – let alone read the future!'

Canker came to him and clapped his shoulder. 'I am not offended. We are friends, you and I, and must always speak the truth to one another. That's how it shall be. But tell me, how may I learn the music? I mean, I understand the principle, but have no idea of the tune. It is for dancing, am I right? And for singing? Well I can sing, you may believe it! And I dance in a fashion, though not like you Szgany sing and dance.'

'The tune?' Nestor was puzzled. 'But I'm sure there's more than one tune. I think I know a few notes of several. Bring me a flute out of Sunside and I'll teach you.'

'A song of love, of devotion, of worship!' Canker yelped his excitement. 'That is what I require. I shall imitate your most beautiful tune, and fit my song to it. Then, eventually, I'll lure my silver mistress down from the moon!'

Moon madness! Nestor thought, but kept the thought well hidden . . .

On their way back to the midden stairwell to Suckscar, Nestor was quiet a while before saying: 'Something is amiss here.'

'Eh?' Canker looked at him where they paused in the passageway to the foot of the stairs, where lurked the six-legged wolf creature. 'Something amiss? In what way?'

'It was my impression . . . that is, I was given to understand –' Nestor paused for a moment, and finished in a rush: '– that you lived like a beast!' And backing away a little from the other: 'If we are to be true friends, then surely I can say these things?'

Canker threw back his head and laughed, and was serious in a moment. 'That is an image which I have deliberately fostered. And after all, I *am* a beast! But so are they all. And you too, Nestor, or you will be. But yes, I understand your meaning. My reason for this lifelong subterfuge is simple: survival! If my so-called colleagues think there is nothing to covet in Mange-manse, then they will covet nothing. If they believe I dwell in a pigsty, they will surely stay out of it. Just as long as they consider me a strange, mad creature, I have little to fear from them; for quite obviously I am harmless – that is, as long as I'm left to my own devices and not threatened. When abroad, hunting on Sunside, I ravage and rage and pose a dire threat, to females especially. There seems no purpose to the things I do. Ah, but there *is* a purpose! Certainly I achieve some gratification, some small satisfaction, from certain acts which others might consider gross. But more than that I perpetuate my image, the light in which those others see me.' He paused.

'Here in Mangemanse, however, as you have seen and as I trust you will keep to yourself, things are very different. My place is clean, neither a kennel nor a midden except in its approaches, which is a deliberate contrivance. What is more, I would hazard a guess that in its appointments – its staff, equipment, furnishings and facilities – Mangemanse is superior to almost any other house in all this great stack! Well, with the exception, perhaps, of Wrathspire. For indeed Wratha the Risen likes her little luxuries. But only let some vile intruder enter by this route – or by any route, up, down or sideways – and he's bound to think as you thought when first you ventured here into stench and ordure, and so proceed no farther. Thus are my credentials, and my manse's security, established.'

'And shall remain so,' Nestor nodded. 'Also, I know your state of mind ... I think.'

'My state of mind?' Canker raised a shaggy red eyebrow.

'Your attitude in this respect,' Nestor answered. 'I seem to remember that sometimes on Sunside, if a guard-dog or -wolf is tethered or kennelled for too long in one place, then he may become "kennel-proud"; which is to say he'll suffer no other creature within the boundary of his territory. Whenever this occurs, only the dog's master may command him within that perimeter or bring him safely out of it. Add to this the fact that the Wamphyri are notoriously territorial ...'

'Your reasoning is sound,' Canker nodded. 'You are saying that perhaps I am suffering from this kennel-proudness, and it could be that you are right. Except there's a flaw in it, for it doesn't explain why I invited *you* to come down here. Unless for "master" we substitute the word "friend". But understand this: one thing I am proud of is my ancestry, however mongrel. The dog, even the fox – and especially the wolf – they are all of them noble beasts. Don't you agree?'

'Certainly,' said Nestor, though he was not convinced. But best to keep the dog-Lord happy.

'For the wolf is a hunter who lives in the wild and relies solely upon his own skill,' Canker went on. 'The fox is colourful, crafty beyond measure, a sneak thief and merciless killer. And as for the dog when he is trained? What more faithful creature exists in all the world?'

Nestor was surprised. 'Do the Wamphyri keep dogs?'

'It's not unknown. In Turgosheim, several Lords keep dogs, aye. They keep them as pets, and occasionally for the hunting. Ah, but it's common knowledge that the Szgany of Sunside keep a great many dogs, for the security which they give! Not only to guard their encampments against hostile strangers, but also for early warning of Wamphyri raiders. As for myself ... why, Mangemanse is full of dogs! They are my children!'

'Your chil –?'

'Oh, ha-ha!' Canker capered. 'I have wives, Nestor, a good many. And they've borne me a good many pups. Ah, you've likely heard it said that girls stolen out of Sunside don't last too long in Mangemanse, eh? Not so? Well, that's the way they tell it, anyway. But it's untrue. Just because I kill on Sunside – and remember, Canker has killed *with his member*, lad! – that's not to say I do it in Mangemanse. What, I should worry my girl thralls to death like a wild dog among goats? Not at all. They are my wives who pleasure me. But none outside Mangemanse knows it. Except you, for you have seen. They work in my kitchens, at my tapestries, in my laundry and butcher shop, even in the pens and launching bays. As for my yelping bloodsons: what better way to build an army, and staff it with faithful lieutenants, than to ensure they're of your own blood? And so another legend brought to its knees. I *am* a beast, aye ... when it suits me to be one!'

Nestor nodded slowly and said, 'Any who think you are mad, Canker Canison, quite obviously they are mad.'

But as he made his way up into Suckscar alone, he thought to himself: *As for your silver mistress in the moon ... well, there's madness and there's madness ...*

At the start of the next sunup, Nestor's vampire came into its true ascendancy. In the interim, for a period equivalent to five days in the world beyond the glaring hell-lands Gate, he had expended furious and frightening Wamphyri energies exploring, charting and reorganizing Suckscar. And in that same period he had grown, changed, taken on a shape which was like yet unlike his own, the shape of a true Lord of the Wamphyri. His excessive activity was like a fever in his blood, which would not let him rest; it was the Change That Shapes; it was his rapid metamorphosis into something other than the Nestor he had been. And as the furnace sun rose up again beyond the barrier range to banish the shadows from the mountains, then it was that his vampire leech became fully ascendant.

The speed with which the change had occurred was astonishing, the activity of his parasite amazing. He would launch out from his manse upon his flyer, and when the others saw him circling Wrathstack, or soaring over Wrathspire itself, laughing into the wind, then they would wonder at it. But the fact of it was that Vasagi the Suck had been a master of metamorphism, and the answer lay in the genetic make-up of his egg. In that and in Nestor's urgency to *be* Wamphyri!

Then, too, the other side of his morbid ancestry came

into play. But morbid only in the sense of its infinitely dark possibilities, not in the nature of the one who had explored, possessed and used them; a man called Harry Keogh, Necroscope. In his own world a parallel universe away (and later in this one, too) Nestor's father had been beloved of the teeming dead, the Great Majority. How could it have been otherwise? For Harry had been a lone candle glimmering in their eternal darkness, a warm spot in the chill of their unbeing, the only man of all living men who could talk to them and give them comfort. And more, he had been the only one who could die for them. In the end he had done just that: died for the dead and the living alike, for all the generations that were and those yet to come in two worlds. Except ... his end had signalled a monstrous beginning, and Nestor was just another link in the endless chain.

Thus Harry's darkest talent, or an even darker one, had been inherited by this Gypsy son of his, just as it had been passed on to Nestor's brother, Nathan. But in Nestor the dark side was ascendant, and the dead would never love him. Indeed those who had passed beyond, and should *be* beyond all fear and feeling, would very soon fear him above all other living, dead, and undead creatures. Fear him, yes, together with all of his works. Because some of them would even *feel* the works of the vampire Lord Nestor!

Nothing of which was known to Nestor himself, for the Necroscope Harry Keogh had died when he was still a child, and Nestor had long since forgotten Nathan as a brother and now thought of him only as some hated rival or grim enemy out of the past. But Harry Keogh's talent was in him for all that, or a hideously warped version of it at least.

Lord Nestor of the Wamphyri – Necroscope? No, never.

But necromancer? Ah, indeed . . .

It started like this:

Nestor was out flying. It seemed the only way to ease his spirit, still the weird tides surging in his blood and calm his burgeoning Wamphyri passions. Out there in the crisp, cold air, under fading ice-chip stars, feeling the rush of the slipstream over his flyer's head and neck, he could forget . . . things. And that in itself was strange, for in truth he had very little to forget. Except perhaps the rushing whirlpool of numbers spiralling in his head, that madly whirling vortex which on occasion he dreamed of even now. The vortex and its treacherous origin: the mind of his olden enemy on Sunside.

For upon a time Nestor had loved; the ache was still there in his heart, and the hatred. He had loved, and had been rejected. Or rather, his olden enemy had stolen her away. That was as much as he remembered of it; that and the fact that afterwards . . . well, he had not been the same. Nor would he ever be the same again. For his change then had been physical, wrought of a damaged mind and body, while his change now was psychical, of the spirit. Indeed there was very little of the human spirit left in him. But an inhuman spirit?

And so Nestor rode out upon his flyer and bared his teeth and laughed into the wind, even though he felt that the laughter wasn't entirely his. But the gold was back on the peaks of the barrier mountains and he dared not fly too high. Soon the tallest towers of Wrathspire would be bathed in yellow glare, and all of Wratha's curtains closed against the light of day. That was still several hours away, however, and for the moment Nestor displayed his newly acquired mastery of flight, urging his beast into intricate aerial configurations in and out of Wrathspire's hollow turrets and fretted rock needles.

Then . . . he saw the Lady Wratha herself.

She was in a turret, watching him at his play and keeping her thoughts hidden. Nestor had sensed her there before, on several occasions, but had never seen her. Seeing her now, distracted by her presence, he momentarily lost control of his flyer and came close to striking a bartizan. But his mount, concerned for its own skin as well as its master's, instinctively avoided the collision.

Hearing Wratha's laughter, Nestor wheeled his flyer in a tight circle, alighted on a quarter-acre of roof like a small, sloping plateau, dismounted and went striding towards her turret observation post. 'Funny, was it?' he queried angrily. 'To distract me, so that I might easily have crashed, wrecked my flyer and gone tumbling over the edge to a certain death?'

From somewhere behind and below her there sounded a warning, echoing rumble and the clatter of scrabbling claws. The turret must conceal a stairwell down into Wrathspire. It was one of the Lady's exits onto the roof. And Wratha had brought up an escort with her, one of her small personal warriors.

Now her laughter, gay as a girl's, died away. 'Oh, and do you find me a distraction, then, Nestor?' Wratha's expression was almost but not quite innocent as she stepped from the turret to display herself in her revealing robe of black bat-fur ropes. 'But a pleasant one, I trust. Anyway, there was nothing malicious in it. This is my place, after all, and I often look out from here. Oh, I've watched you once or twice, and monitored your change. Aye, and I like what I've seen of you.'

Nestor came to a halt ten paces away as something dark rose up behind her, adding its darkness to the shadows inside the turret. And then he asked himself: *Has she deliberately lured me here?* Nestor had left his gauntlet behind, hanging from his flyer's saddle. Well, and what odds? Even with his gauntlet he'd stand no slightest chance against even a small warrior. These were some of the thoughts that passed rapidly through his head as he stood glaring at the Lady and the shadowy shape in the turret behind her. But in the next moment:

Ridiculous! he thought. *What am I thinking of? I land on another's territory unbidden and of my own free will, approach her in anger, and at once consider murderous combat – with a warrior? Madness! Quite obviously this white heat inside my body and head is burning up my brain!*

His thoughts were confused, a jumble, entirely unguarded. And: 'Aha!' said Wratha. 'And so he rises!'

Nestor was taken aback. He glanced this way and that and saw nothing. 'Who rises?'

She smiled at him wickedly, teasingly perhaps. 'Why, your leech, my young Lord! Your parasite. He – or it – rises to ascendancy.'

It explained a lot and was the only clue Nestor needed. 'I . . . I had wondered,' he said, lamely.

'Don't we all,' she answered, 'when first we feel the fever heat, the boundless energy, the furious passion? But looking at you now . . . oh, it's perfectly obvious! Your leech is risen and is as one with you. Yes, you are Wamphyri. You need not concern yourself with getting there any longer, Nestor. You *are* there! And soon your fever will cool and leave you fully forged and in command. Or so you'll believe, anyway.'

Her words shocked him in one way, pleased him in another. But shocked, pleased or both, still some spiteful or prideful urge caused him to reply: 'And was there ever any doubt?'

'Possibly not.' She tossed her head.

'Possibly?' He shook his head. 'No, *definitely* not! And if the change had been slower, d'you think I would have submitted to Gorvi the Guile's time limit and let them throw me out? *Hah!* Gorvi setting limits, indeed! What? They would have to invade me in my manse and drag me out of it first. And believe me, the Suck had monsters no less than your own! Well, and they're mine now.'

She clapped her hands. 'You have such energy, Nestor! And all from your leech. But if you weren't so strong, the change would not have been so fast. And so you see, you and your parasite fit each other like a hand in a glove. You are ... strong, aye.' Her eyes beneath their scarp lingered on him. 'But just look at you. You were a boy, and now you're a man. You were – oh, a good six-footer. But now you're six and a half! You were handsome ... well, half-handsome, I suppose, but lacking style. And now you're dark, sinister, seductively powerful. Every inch a true Lord of the Wamphyri. Come, step closer.'

He did so, saying: 'Canker is not dark, sinister, seductive. He is a monster. Gorvi is gaunt as death and devious to a fault. Only Wran fits my picture of a true Lord, and he is overweight and has a wen! What's more, I suspect that he and Spiro are mad. So all in all, it strikes me there's nothing glorious about the Wamphyri. Not this bunch, anyway.'

'But their passions are glorious,' she answered quietly, her voice husky where she laid a trembling hand upon his arm and felt the blood coursing and the muscles bunching. 'And am I not glorious?'

'You are very beautiful,' he answered, 'or would appear to be. And yet ... I have heard tales.'

'Would appear to be? Tales?' Her voice was suddenly cold as she drew back from him. 'What tales?' Sensing her changing emotions, Wratha's guardian creature rumbled and glared green-eyed at Nestor from the darkness of the turret. Knowing that the thing would react instantly to her slightest command, he took a precautionary pace to the rear and towards his flyer where it nodded vacantly some small distance away.

'Just tales,' he answered. 'The way you keep your eyes hidden beneath that scarp of bone; the blue crystals in your temples, to cool the furnace of your glance; the lie of your flesh, which is not a girl's but a hag's. Aye, all of these things and more. For as I understand it the Wamphyri, especially their Ladies, are often deceptive in appearance . . .'

For a moment she was silent, then:

'Listen to me,' she told him, but with nothing of anger. 'Listen and learn. In an hundred years – or even two hundred, if you are fortunate – you will be an old man. But will you look like one? Of course not, because you are Wamphyri! Vain, as most of us are, you will look much as you look now. It is how you will keep yourself. And it is how I have kept myself. What? Would you have me wrinkle to a prune when I can look the way I do? For remember: the blood is the life, and it is also the youth! It is my gift to look this way forever, and so I shall. It is my nature . . . and yours. But I may tell you this, my handsome Lord Nestor: Wratha was never a hag. I was beautiful, and I still am. Except . . .

'. . . You have made it very plain to me that you don't appreciate beauty, so begone.' Her voice had turned sour. 'This is my roof and I did not give you permission to land here. It would serve you right if I loosed my guardian creature upon you.'

She began to turn away, until Nestor stepped forward and on impulse caught her hand. Then, immediately, she turned to him . . . and deliberately fell into his arms!

Her eyes beneath the scarp on her forehead were ablaze, firing the figured bone with red. She half-shuttered them, but not so much as to subdue their scarlet allure. The ropes of her robe parted to display first the tips, then the quivering globes of her proud breasts, and her breath was sweet as Nestor lowered his mouth to drink from hers – but sweet as blood, not honey. It made no difference; there *was* no difference, not to Nestor, not now. Indeed it seemed entirely possible that honey would be bitter by comparison.

And as he kissed her and fondled her breasts, the furious heat inside him threatened to overflow and boil him from within. So hot indeed that Wratha felt it, too, and knew her danger. She would not be raped up here on her own roof, not with all the fading stars peeping down ... and not with a huge and empty bed in her rooms below! But all of that must wait. She had no desire to appear easy meat.

So that finally, when his kisses and fondling threatened to engulf her despite her feigned reticence: *Come!* She pulled herself breathlessly away and issued her mental command. *Protect me!*

Being so close to her, Nestor heard her mind-call – and witnessed its result. Her creature came.

It was one of the warriors which Nestor had seen in Wrathspire's great hall: nine feet tall when upright, yet squat for its height. A thing of inch-thick, blue-grey chitin armour. A thing of claws, jaws, and dagger teeth. Its face was huge and slate-grey, rat-like, flattened and sloping from chin to forehead; yet almost human, too. What, almost? Nestor knew better than that: that indeed the thing had *been* human, upon a time. But its eyes were set too far apart, at the sides, giving it a wide angle of vision. It had short hind legs, long reaching arms, and a shambling but energetic gait – as Nestor now saw.

For roaring like a rutting shad, but five times louder, the creature bore down on him where he backed off from Wratha and turned to run for his flyer. He might even have made it, but in his haste tripped and went to one knee. And Wratha's warrior was on him! Then . . .

. . . *HOLD!* She sent a mind-blast. *Do him no harm but simply detain him!*

The thing stopped snorting and bellowing at once; it grabbed Nestor around the waist and by his shoulder, and picked him up – literally, as if he were some Szgany child's toy! It drew him close and gazed at him, turning its loathsome head this way and that the better to observe him. And holding him in mid-air while Wratha approached, it breathed upon him.

The stench was awful! Nestor held his breath; he also held still and made no move or protest, but simply waited for death. For if that was Wratha's purpose, certainly no one could deny her now. But it was not her purpose.

She approached and looked up at him almost curiously. He gradually eased his head to one side, away from the face of the monster and its gaping jaws, and stared down at her whey-faced. He was totally defenceless; he knew that he was at her mercy, and death only a bite away. But he was also Wamphyri.

'So it looks like . . . like I'm not going to live for two hundred years after all,' he said. And if it had been possible, he might even have shrugged.

For a moment Wratha said nothing but merely smiled. And he saw how cold that smile of hers was. But in another moment she brightened, gave herself a shake, and said: 'Men have always been my problem. As a Szgany girl, as Karl the Crag's thrall in Cragspire, even as Wratha the Risen in the dark and rocky gorge of Turgosheim. Why, it was because of weak and malicious men that I fled west to this last great aerie, where even now they're the bane of my life; these dullards with their manses in my stack. But you . . . are not a dullard, and I think I prefer you alive. It could be I'm making a mistake, but –' *Take him to his flyer.*

Her warrior obeyed, stood Nestor on his feet close to his mount, and pushed him in that direction. Stumbling, he caught up the reins and hauled himself up into the saddle. And as he urged his beast to flight:

Visit me again, some time, Wratha sent. Amazingly, there was never a hint of enmity or malice in her voice.

What, of my own free will? he replied, sarcasm dripping from his mind. A moment later, his flyer's thrusters uncoiled, sending mount and rider skimming down the gentle slope of the plateau.

She laughed in his mind. *Well, then, invite me down into Suckscar. For I've only ever been there the once. And we are neighbours, after all.*

But I'm the one with warriors, in Suckscar, he answered.

And now he sensed her shrug, but also her frustration. *So be it, my handsome Lord Nestor. But I'm sure we'll meet again some time.*

He shot out over the precipitous rim of the last aerie, and ordered his mount home. He had women of his own there, a gaggle of them. What need had he of Wratha the Risen? But on the other hand . . . the needs of the Wamphyri are great, and Wratha shone in his mind like some strange dark jewel. How could his thralls compare with her? The promise he'd felt when he held her in his arms had been . . . limitless. He knew that her fire could match his any time.

All of which were thoughts that Nestor kept hidden as well as he could, but perhaps not well enough. For as his flyer dipped below the rim, so Wratha's tinkling mind-laughter came to him again. And in the cup of his burning hand the feel of her silky breasts, and on his lips the taste of her tainted kiss . . .

In Suckscar, Zahar was waiting on the return of his Lord. When Nestor landed his flyer in the yawning weathered socket of his personal landing-bay, his first lieutenant was there to take the reins and guide the floundering beast to its pen. Nestor could see that the man wanted words with him, and so waited until his flyer was penned. Then:

'Lord,' said Zahar, joining him and entering into Suckscar proper, and following him to his rooms. 'There is a matter . . .'

'Oh? And what is it?' Nestor turned on the sweeping stone stairs and stared at him. And read trouble in his feral eyes. 'Out with it, Zahar.'

'It is . . . the Lady Carmen, Lord.'

Nestor gave a start. 'The Lady Car . . . ?' And he paused with the name unspoken. But he knew well enough what – and who – Zahar was talking about. And: 'Carmen,' he finally said. 'Yes. And what of her?' And again he knew the answer before it came.

'It is sunup, Lord. It's unlikely she'll rise up from her bench through sunup. But when the sun goes down, as the last light fades on the crags of the barrier mountains, and their shadows creep across the boulder plains towards the Icelands, then . . .'

'We shall have a Lady in our manse,' Nestor finished it for him, and slowly nodded. 'And for now – how goes it with her?'

'How goes it?' Zahar raised an eyebrow. 'She is dead, Lord. Or undead, as we say. She sleeps her sleep. Afterwards – perhaps even a long time afterwards, when she is risen up – she will suffer the Change That

173

Shapes, just as you are suffering it. Then she will be a true Lady, and Mistress of Suckscar.'

'On whose authority?' Nestor snapped.

'Why, on yours, Lord! For there's no denying it, you have brought her into being. And she will be Wamphyri.'

Nestor pulled at his right earlobe. 'I had forgotten her. No, I had put her from my mind. It seemed a cruel way to use her: to use her, even unto undeath, and then destroy her.'

'But that was then, Lord, and this is now. Perhaps you see things differently ... now?'

Nestor stood tall, gritted his teeth. 'I cannot have a Lady in my house. My women, yes, but not a Lady. The provisioning is the answer. See to it.' He made to turn away, but Zahar said:

'Lord? The provisioning?'

'Yes. Is something amiss?'

'Very much so! She is Wamphyri, Lord. If your thralls eat of her ... it could be problematic.'

'Grind her down, fool!' Nestor snarled, as the growing but inexperienced thing within sent him conflicting messages. 'For be sure she won't be up to infecting anything in the smallest of small pieces!'

'But indeed she *will*, Lord,' said Zahar, very quietly and grimly. 'On Sunside, the Szgany stake vampires through their hearts; they cut off their heads and burn them to ashes. And they are only vampires, not Wamphyri!'

Nestor knew all of this. He remembered it the moment his lieutenant was through speaking the words. He had known how the Szgany would have dealt with him, if they'd caught him after he left Brad Berea's house in the forest; or how, at that time, he had *thought* they would deal with him. And now he felt a fool in front of

174

Zahar. But if his lieutenant was so full of knowledge, perhaps he might have ideas, too. So Nestor asked him: 'What, then, do you suggest?'

'Take her to the barrier mountains now.' Zahar was eager; he didn't fancy serving two masters, or one master and one mistress, in Suckscar. 'Lie her down in a place where the sun will strike in just a few hours' time. After that . . . your work will be done.'

'No,' said Nestor, 'your work will be done. Should I keep dogs and do my own barking?'

Zahar bowed. 'As you will, Lord.'

'Then be about it.'

'Yes, Lord.' He turned to go, but Nestor caught his arm.

'Wait! Take me to her. I would look upon this Carmen one last time. If I'm to destroy a thing, it's as well I know what I'm destroying.'

And Zahar took him to where Carmen lay in state.

Looking at her on the cold, raised stone slab where she lay, Nestor felt no pity. He had thought he would – had remembered that once long ago he'd known how to – but no longer knew how to. Carmen was . . . she was flesh.

But for all that she had lain here for more than one hundred hours – where a massive window ten feet deep had been cut through solid rock to face east, and the winds blew in without hindrance – she was not 'cold' flesh. Or she was, but not the clay-cold of death. She was the grey, unwrinkled, undecayed and unending flesh of undeath.

'If you had . . .' Zahar started and paused. 'If this situation had been initiated twenty-four hours earlier, Lord, by now she would be up and about. This close to sunup, her rising is delayed . . .' He fell silent.

'I have made love to this woman,' Nestor mused, sombrely.

'You loved her to death, Lord,' Zahar reminded him.

And Nestor made up his mind. 'She is dead,' he said. 'Do with her as you have described.'

And to Carmen, placing his hand upon her brow: *Farewell.*

Whaaaat? Her answer rang in his mind like a cracked bell, sending him staggering. *Fareweeeellllll? But I'm not going anywhere, Nestoooor – I'm coming baaaack!*

'Ahhh!' he cried out loud, lurching like a drunkard. 'She speaks to me!'

'But that can't be.' Zahar's jaw fell open as he took his master's arm. 'See, she still sleeps, and will continue to do so until the change wakes her. Or until the sun finds her wanting. Carmen *is* dead, until she wakes or dies the true death.'

'Fool!' Nestor ranted, pointing a trembling finger at the shrouded figure on the raised slab. 'I tell you she spoke. And she . . . *knows* me!'

And: *Oh, yesss. I know you now,* Carmen told him inside his head. *You are Nestor of the Wamphyri – my would-be muuurderer!*

No would-be about it! 'Take her!' Nestor gasped, as he was sent staggering yet again. 'Take her now, to the barrier mountains. You do it – you, Zahar. Do it now, and make sure it's done well!'

And Zahar did it.

That was how it had started . . .

And in his fevered dreams where he lay in a dark, damp cave under the bank of a Sunside river, Nestor shuddered as he often shuddered in his sleep. Proof, perhaps, that something of the old Nestor lingered on deep inside.

Or perhaps not. Perhaps he shuddered simply in recognition of his own monstrousness.

176

Whichever, for a while after that he dreamed no more. And slowly, so laboriously slowly, his metamorphic vampire flesh worked to heal his wounds. While beyond the low mouth of the cave, the river water sparkled, and Sunside's dawn grew to a full day . . .

PART THREE

The Opposition

I

Perchorsk

___

It had been snowing heavily in Moscow when the disklike British Airways VTOL Hawk stooped down through its landing window and Ben Trask, Ian Goodly, and one hundred and ten other 'businessmen' disembarked. Turkur Tzonov himself had met them off the plane; by-passing customs, he'd seen his guests out of the airport and into a brand new, Moscow-built, Ford-Volga *Premier*, their transport to a small military airport ten kilometres out of the city. From there they'd travelled by jet-copter all the way, with a fuelling stop in Kirov before the streamlined wasp of an aircraft turned onto a more nearly northerly heading over Berezniki, and set out to parallel the snow-capped Urals for a further two hundred miles. In all, the journey from London to Perchorsk had taken two hours fifty-five minutes, and it was 6:00 p.m. local time as the aircraft switched back to hover-mode, sidestepped between gloomy peaks under lowering clouds, and gentled down into the dull grey Perchorsk ravine.

Back in Moscow, at the airports and between them, Tzonov had been a courteous, efficient escort. Full of mainly solicitous inquiries – about the weather in London (the winter was proving to be a hard one all over Europe), the physical wellbeing of his guests following their flight from England, the quality of service in-flight, and so on – the head of Soviet ESPionage had

181

made an energetic but paradoxically empty or at best ephemeral host. Ephemeral because his comments and questions were mainly meaningless, and empty because he studiously avoided mentioning the real reason why Trask and Goodly were here.

Trask believed he knew why: when Tzonov required to know anything really important, he would probably pick it right out of their minds; at least, he would *expect* to be able to do so. But, in any case, he wouldn't attempt it until after they'd seen Perchorsk's prisoner; it would be pointless to try to discover their opinions before they'd had sufficient time to form them. Which meant that for the time being the Russian would continue in his guise of companionably disarming escort and guide.

Nevertheless (and despite that the British mindspies had taken certain precautions against Tzonov's probing), they deliberately avoided thinking about Harry Keogh. This required an effort of mental vigilance which would not be easy to maintain over a protracted period of time, but short term it wasn't too difficult: there was in any case more than sufficient to focus their minds upon without concerning themselves with any conjectural connection between Perchorsk's alien intruder and a man who had been dead for all of sixteen years.

From Moscow to Perchorsk, Tzonov had been mainly silent. Having explained how his work had kept him busy the previous night right through until the early hours, immediately after take-off he'd stretched out his legs, reclined in his seat and fallen asleep – apparently. Thus his guests, the only other passengers aboard the small, short-range, military reconnaissance aircraft, had been left to their own devices. For Trask this was no problem: following Tzonov's example, he slept for an hour, leaving the precog Goodly awake to read what he dared of their immediate future. While up front in the bubble cockpit, the pilot and co-pilot in their dowdy, ill-fitting Army Aviator jump suits would glance back every now and then, nodding at Goodly and smiling blank, ostensibly affable smiles.

But now, as the jet-copter descended into the Perchorsk ravine and Goodly shook Trask awake, so Turkur Tzonov stirred and a few seconds later sat up without so much as a yawn. And all three stared out through clear wraparound flexon panels in the cabin's walls and floor, down into the depths of the gorge, and watched its slate-grey scarps and crags floating up around them towards the fading light of the bitter cold Urals night. While down below:

There were lights in the pass; a helicopter landing zone was marked by a circle of yellow strobes rotating clockwise on the concrete plateau of a dam's wide wall; searchlights illuminated the chopper's vertical descent, their glare mirrored in a weaving silver lattice on the surface of an otherwise leaden lake. All of which was reflected from ice-sheathed rock scarps, and made scintillant in the refraction of freezing spray from the shining arcs of four huge spouts of water erupting from conduits in the lower dam wall.

Shading their eyes, Trask and Goodly glanced at each other and thought much the same thought: that there were far too many lights, a veritable dazzle of them! Perhaps someone had decided that they shouldn't see too much: a futile exercise in camouflage at best; American spysats had had the Perchorsk ravine mapped out in fine detail for close on twenty years now. Impossible to hide something as big as this from electronic eyes-in-the-sky capable of reading headline newsprint from orbits a hundred miles up! And in any case, what was there to hide? Nothing, not any longer. Or if anything, a potential pesthole of truly gigantic proportions, but one which the Russians had well under control ... didn't they? It had always been assumed that they did. Until now ...

A 'defensive system' which had backfired from day one, the Perchorsk Projekt had been intended as the USSR's answer to America's SDI or Star Wars scenario. The object was to create an impenetrable dome of destructive energy twenty miles high in the sky, which would 'kill off' any and all incoming enemy missiles. An umbrella, so that no one in the whole wide world could ever again threaten to rain on Mother Russia's parade. As soon as it had proved itself in an exhaustive series of tests, a device such as this would on its own elevate the USSR to an unassailable position as the planet's Number One Superpower.

That was what Perchorsk had been all about ... until its epic failure had jeopardized not only the USSR but the entire human race. As Trask came more fully awake he started to think back more clearly on what he knew of the whole can of worms:

The Russians had built and tested the Projekt — tested it just the once, and disastrously — back in the early eighties. But despite their best efforts at technological camouflaging, the results of that test were seen and recorded not only by American spy satellites but also by friendly forces on the ground. And when all of the reports had been processed ...

... At the time, and while no one had known *exactly* what was going on down there in the guts of the Perchorsk ravine, still it had been sufficient to kick-start the USA's Space Defense Initiative into real being. And in small, powerful, very secretive circles throughout the Western World there had taken place a good many worried discussions about such things as APB (accelerated particle beam) 'shields', nuclear- or plasma-powered lasers, even about a theoretical 'Magma Motor' which might tap the gravitational energies at Earth's core.

Finally the first-hand report of a western sympathizer had come leaking out of one of the logging camps east of Perchorsk. Trask had been privy to the contents of the document and remembered them to this day. Not the work of an educated man, indeed that of a peasant in forced exile – a 'relocated' ex-Ukrainian dissident – still the wording had been vivid and evocative.

It had been a bright clear night, with the shimmer of *aurora borealis* like a pale shifting curtain in the northern sky. The observer, a lumberjack out hunting near the mountain pass, had been aware as always of the distant hum of giant turbines, transmitted through the earth from the Projekt some four kilometres away. But as the whine of the engines had wound itself up, the man had stopped and looked back through the evergreens – to see the rim of the Perchorsk ravine bathed in a wash of flickering light like pale foxfire!

Suddenly, it had seemed that the night held its breath ... only to expel it in a great gasp or sigh. And as the whining of the turbines had climbed higher yet, a beam of pure white light had shot up from the ravine, turning night to day as it bounded into the sky! A *pulse* of light, which lasted just long enough to leave its after-image burning on the eyeballs and then was gone. And in its wake –

– A bright clear night ... until then. But as the weird white searchlight had blinked into and out of being and Perchorsk's turbines fell abruptly silent, so a hot wind had blown down from the crags, and within the hour clouds had boiled up out of nowhere to rain a strange warm rain. Then, as if intensified by the rain, a smell of burning – an acrid, electrical burning, like ozone maybe? – had seemed to permeate the damp night air. But before that, indeed within minutes of the flash of light itself, there had been the sirens. Perchorsk's sirens, like the voice of the ravine wailing its agonies. But in fact they were the agonies of men.

There had been an accident, a big one. And for the next fortnight . . . helicopters shuttling in and out, ambulances in the mountain passes, and men in radiation suits decontaminating the walls of the ravine. And the one whisper that got out as local Soviet authorities moved to shut down certain 'fifth column elements' in the logging camps was this: blowback! The Perchorsk experiment had discharged itself into the sky, all right, but at the same time it had backfired into the underground complex that housed it. And like some fantastic, free-wheeling incinerator – melting men and machinery alike – it had almost blown the lid off the place before burning itself out!

After that . . . Trask remembered several things which the Soviets had not been able to cover up: like the apparent mass migration of many of their top-flight doctors, mainly radiation specialists, from Moscow, Omsk, and Sverdlovsk, into the understaffed and ill-equipped frontier hospitals in Beresovo, Ukhta and Izhma. No one had experienced much difficulty figuring out what that was all about: as well as all of the dead, they must have taken a good many badly injured men out of the ravine. Since when the experiment if not Perchorsk itself had been abandoned.

And so there had been only the one test firing, but one too many. The damage it caused had been permanent, and Turkur Tzonov was correct to liken Perchorsk to the Chernobyl Sarcophagus. Trask would go even further; in his mind both places had much in common with Pandora's box: they each harboured plagues which, in their diverse ways, might oh so easily have endangered and even doomed the entire world. And one of them – Perchorsk itself – might do so even now . . .

The jet-copter's passengers sensed rather than felt its landing as the aircraft gentled to a touchdown on the dam wall. Just as surely, Trask's thoughts also came back to earth. Looking out through windows already blurred by a thin sheath of ice formed from the mist of the dam's cascade, he made out a figure in a white parka waiting in the safety margin beyond the lethal glimmer of the fan. Then the high-pitched whining of the rotors wound down to a reassuring *whup, whup, whup*, and the co-pilot came hunch-shouldered from the cockpit to let down a curving side panel into preformed steps.

Signalling that they should watch their heads, Tzonov ushered Trask and Goodly down onto a rubber-clad surface and guided them through the rotor's bluster towards the figure in the parka: a statuesque platinum blonde whose looks were classically Scandinavian. Smiling a welcome, she handed parkas to the British espers and helped them shrug into them. Then, turning to the head of Soviet E-Branch, she hugged him, covered his shoulders with a wing of her own hugely oversized parka, and hurried him towards an open jeep where a driver sat waiting. Smiling blandly, pampered and proud of it, Tzonov offered no slightest resistance to any of this. Trask and Goodly exchanged covert glances, and the latter raised a querying, even wistful eyebrow which Trask answered with a shrug. There was nothing for it but to follow on behind Tzonov and his lady.

Trask took the seat alongside the driver, which left his precog colleague to cram himself into the back of the vehicle with Tzonov and the girl, where they huddled like lovers. Quite obviously, they *were* lovers. Introductions would be out of the question over the throb of the jet-copter's engine, the stuttering cough of its idling rotors, and the clatter of the jeep's exhaust; Tzonov didn't even attempt it but confined himself to hugging the girl and whispering something in her ear. Her answering laughter was whipped away by turbulence from the rotors as the jeep turned right off the dam wall onto a road dynamited from the face of the ravine.

A hundred and fifty yards up the precipitous road, the driver brought his vehicle to a halt on a level hardstanding and leaned on his horn until massive, motorized, steel-jawed doors under a frowning overhang rumbled open. It was the way into Perchorsk, the 'throat' of the subterranean complex. And as a swath of light blazed out and the jeep drove through it into a brightly illuminated interior, so the jaws closed again, shutting out the gaunt ravine from view. Finally the jeep's motor was switched off and its row faded to an almost painful silence.

At last Trask and Goodly could hear themselves think, and now they must guard against *others* hearing them think. As they climbed out of the jeep, Tzonov said, 'Welcome to the Perchorsk Projekt ... or rather, to the system of passageways and caverns which once housed it. For now, of course, the Projekt exists in name only, and the complex houses something else entirely.'

From the jet-copter to this place – these outer environs of the Perchorsk complex – had taken no more than a minute and a half maximum, but Trask was glad of his parka. Likewise Ian Goodly; in such a short time, the bitter cold of the ravine had seemed to eat right into his bones. Both men rubbed their hands briskly and Trask turned to the girl. 'We really ought to thank you for these excellent garments, Miss, er ... ?'

'Dam!' She held out her hand and grinned mischievously. 'No, not a swear-word, just my name! Sigrid Dam – or Siggi, to my friends.' Like Tzonov's, her accent was scarcely noticeable. What there was of it wasn't Russian, but Trask believed he'd detected ... what, a Swedish lilt? Or Danish? Possibly. The surname was Danish, certainly.

'Ben Trask,' he smiled. 'And this is my colleague, Ian Goodly. I'm sure we'll enjoy being your friends.'

As she shook hands with the gaunt, gloomy-seeming precog, Turkur Tzonov snapped his fingers, exchanged concerned glances with all three and exclaimed: 'Ah! Unforgivable! What must you think of me, to forget the introductions? But ... there was no opportunity ... you must forgive me, my dear.' And turning more fully to his guests: 'Siggi is ... my constant companion.'

'A mutually stimulating friendship, I'm sure,' Trask said, and tried desperately to keep his thoughts to himself. But with a girl like this (no, a *woman* like this, as he now saw), it was difficult not to envy his Russian counterpart.

Sigrid Dam was thirtyish, taller than average, and (Trask guessed) slim and athletic under that parka. The garment seemed cut for a giant and covered her like a poncho half-way down her thighs, yet still looked stylish on Siggi. But then, she would probably have the same effect on a potato sack. From the bottom of the parka down, her long tapering legs were clad in shimmering black ski-pants, while beneath it she wore a matching black top. The wide bottoms of the pants formed bells over fur-lined calf-boots.

Under expressive blonde eyebrows, Siggi's eyes were the deep blue of summer fjords; her mouth was perfectly shaped if a little cold; her nose was just a fraction tip-tilted, hinting at a strong, even aggressive personality.

189

All in all, and while her skin was marginally paler than Tzonov's, the general impression which Trask received was much the same: one of radiant good health. And yet ... the picture was marred; something didn't add up. Something about her eyes, maybe? Trask thought he knew what it was but would wait and see what developed.

And meanwhile he wondered about Siggi's relationship with Tzonov — their real relationship. That is, he wondered if it *was* real. In which case ...

Just seeing this woman in the company of Turkur Tzonov (and despite that they were *not* opposites), Trask could easily understand their mutual attraction. In a world full of mainly mundane, unexceptional people, a pair such as this would naturally gravitate together. Why, they might easily be the leading roleplayers in a Hollywood epic from Trask's youth: people too rare or beautiful to even exist — except among their contemporaries in a surreal, celluloid world apart.

Trask caught her looking at him ... what, appreciatively? At which moment she blinked and said: 'Anyway, it's Turkur you must thank for the parkas. They were his idea. Your overcoats may be just the thing in London, but we're fifteen to twenty degrees colder here!'

Goodly turned to Tzonov, and in his somewhat fluting voice said, 'It's all very considerate of you. You seem to have taken our welfare so much into account — and all so far in advance.' There was something in his wording which caused Trask to glance at him.

But Tzonov merely grinned. 'Ah, yes, of course. Your *penchant* for the future, Mr Goodly — er, Ian?' And then to his woman, by way of explanation: 'Ian is a precog, Siggi.'

She clapped her hands. 'But in that case ... perhaps you had foreseen the provision of the parkas?'

Goodly shook his head, shrugged apologetically. 'Far too specific,' he said.

'Anyway,' Turkur was enjoying this, 'I didn't arrange for the parkas until twenty minutes before we landed!'

And Trask thought (but to himself), *Oh? When you were supposed to be sleeping?* He'd known, of course, that Tzonov wasn't asleep ... but if not asleep, what then? Merely resting? Or had he been talking to Siggi Dam? Now Trask saw how everything fitted. Like the pale purple in the orbits of Siggi's eyes, which betrayed her telepathy – but only to someone who knew his business. To most other men that slightly bruised look would only serve to complement her sensuality, might even be mistaken for a symptom of her dissipation lingering over after the excesses of a long night. Once again he was aware of her sharp glance, but this time she was frowning.

Goodly offered a rare if somewhat tortured smile. 'And so Siggi's a powerful telepath. I thought so. But such beauty and talent combined! It hardly seems fair! I suppose I should have foreseen it –' he looked at Tzonov: '– that you two would be a perfect match.'

'Birds of a feather?' Tzonov answered his smile. 'Aren't we all?' And to Siggi, before anyone could say anything else: 'My dear, will you see our guests to their rooms? It won't be the Ritz, I'm afraid, but as Siggi pointed out this isn't London. An hour or so on your own – time enough to clean up and rest a while after your journey? – and then I'll collect you for a tour of the place.'

Trask nodded. 'During which ... will we get to see your visitor?'

'Certainly,' Tzonov answered. 'And a lot more than that into the bargain. This is a fascinating place, Ben, with a fascinating history. But with all the good will

191

and the *glasnost* in the world, it's not the sort of place you get to see every day . . .'

A few minutes later in the privacy of their 'rooms' – a pair of steel-walled, interconnected cells, more like – Trask and Goodly conversed in lowered tones. Despite that in accommodation this austere it was difficult to see where bugs could be hidden, Goodly had already checked his own room. Using a tiny detector which doubled as a pocket calculator, he'd satisfied himself that the place was clean. Then he'd gone through into Trask's – what, compartment? – to sit on his lumpy army bed and watch the other wet-shaving over a dented aluminium washhand basin. As they talked, their glances met in the mirror over the basin.

Seeing the detector, Trask had just this moment pulled a wry face and given his head a shake, sending bubbles of shaving foam flying. 'That's not necessary,' he said. 'I'd know it if something was other than it appears to be. It's all as you see it: cheap and nasty but clean as can be. The same goes for our hosts, too: they're squeaky clean – so far.'

Goodly raised an eyebrow. 'You find no fault with their behaviour?'

Trask tidied up his short grey sideburns. 'Not really. Do you? Ask yourself this: what welcome would we have given Tzonov if we'd known in advance that he was coming to London?'

Goodly shrugged. 'Our best men would have been on the job from square one. With their science and sorcery, they'd be all over him!'

'Even if he was there to do us a favour?'

Goodly raised an eyebrow. 'In which case we'd let him get it done, and *then* –'

'– We'd be all over him with our science and sorcery

192

'... yes, I agree. So maybe he'll be more interested in us later.'

Goodly nodded and said, 'I'm sure he will ...' And after a moment, 'You know he wasn't sleeping in the chopper.'

'Tzonov?' Trask dried his face. 'No, he'd simply chosen to withdraw. Turkur Tzonov has a talent, Ian, one which he's used to using. But with us he can't, and still expect our cooperation. So in the close confines of the jet-copter he opted out, backed off and chose to "sleep" right through the flight. That way he wouldn't be tempted to look at us – or look *into* us – face to face. It seems he genuinely needs our help and doesn't want to scare us off. Well, and it isn't without precedence. There was a time when the Opposition's top man worked alongside ours on the Bodescu affair, too.'

'That was before Tzonov's time,' Goodly pointed out. '*And* it was a disaster! Our Branches don't work well together.'

Trask put on his shirt. 'Is that what you foresee: a disaster?'

Goodly looked more gaunt and morose than ever. 'Ben, you know as well as anyone that I'm frightened of my talent. Most precogs are. The future has an uncanny knack of doing what we expect but not how we expect it. I read it sparingly, and not too far ahead, because ... well, like Turkur Tzonov's motives, it's not to be trusted. No, I don't foresee a disaster – not yet anyway – but it won't be a joyride either ...'

Trask studied his grave face. 'So, can we simply say that you're ... uneasy?'

Goodly nodded. 'Uneasy, yes. Look at it this way: my knowledge of the future springs from the past and the present. With me it's a sort of unconscious extrapolation, where I "remember" what's still to come like you remember your dreams: with fuzzy edges and lacking in fine detail. But despite that a dream will rapidly fade; if it's a good one it can set you up for the rest of the day, where by the same token a nightmare will only upset you and make you irritable. Well, that's how I feel right now: itchy and irritable. Now keep that in mind and concentrate on what we know of Tzonov, his psychological profile.'

Trask said, musingly, 'I know something about his *physical* profile: we should have known about this Siggi Dam! She wasn't in his file and so has to be a recent conquest.'

Goodly shook his head and said, 'Yes, but I'm not talking about her. I'm talking about Tzonov's mind, the way he thinks. He's proud, dedicated, and a bad loser. That's the thread that connects his past, present, and future. It's what steered him to where he is now: head of Russia's E-Branch. And it's what makes me itchy.'

Trask couldn't see where this was leading. 'Explain?'

'Proud,' Goodly pressed. 'Of himself, of his abilities, and definitely of his country, despite its Humpty Dumpty act: that it fell so badly apart the rest of us have scarcely been able to put it together again. Proud and dedicated: to his talent, his job, and to the security of Mother Russia. Proud, dedicated, and a very poor loser, who knows the entire history of his organization from Gregor Borowitz, Dragosani and the Chateau Bronnitsy, right up to the present moment in every minute detail. Knows all of its triumphs and especially its tragedies ... *and* knows who to blame for most of them!'

'Harry Keogh?'

Goodly shook his head, then changed his mind and nodded. 'If not Harry, the ones he was working for,' he said. 'Namely, us. E-Branch.'

'Revenge? He intends to use us, then punish us?'

Goodly shrugged. 'He's a true son of Mother Russia, this Turkur Tzonov. He can't bear it that she's the world's sick old lady. He bears a grudge against everyone who had a hand in her decline, despite that the actual breakdown was no one's fault but her own. And so in his own field, he'll do whatever he can to even up the score.'

'But not until afterwards,' Trask said.

'Eh?'

'After he's used us – and only then if he can get clean away with it. You're right, of course. I notice it whenever he uses the word "glasnost", meaning openness: the fact that it's the one word that doesn't ring true. But we know he's looking for a position in the party's Demokratik Politburo and so follows Premier Gustav Turchin's line – but only because he *has* to, not because he's a true believer in world unity. Oh, Turkur Tzonov's no one-man resurgence of old-style hardline communism, no, but he is ambitious. And you're probably right that his ambitions extend to the entire USSR. Or what used to be the USSR. He would like to see Russia out there in the race again, with himself in the driving seat, and he'd relish the opportunity to run over a few toes and settle some old scores on his way up the main drag. Which to put it another way is like saying he's … what, a patriot?'

Goodly nodded. 'From his point of view, anyway.'

'And from ours?'

'He's dangerous –' Goodly answered, '– but not just yet. And that's the other thing about his psychological profile: the fact that only a very thin wire separates his genius from downright instability. And just like a tightrope, that's a wire we daren't jerk about too much. So for the moment, while I admit I'm itchy, I'm not yet sweating.'

'And when you start to sweat?'

The precog nodded, promising: 'You'll be the first to know it.'

Looking at Goodly, Trask made no reply. He knew that the precog would be right, but he couldn't help wishing he didn't look so much like a mortician . . .

Later, Tzonov guided his guests through Perchorsk's labyrinth of corridors and levels down towards its core, which the handful of men who knew of its existence had christened 'the Gate'.

'You probably know the background to all of this as well as I do,' he said. 'I was a mere youth at the time, an avid student of ESPionage at the Moscow academy. I knew nothing of all this; my forte was metaphysics, not physics. Anyway, when they tested their device it backfired, and the energy it released was unbelievable! In the immediate vicinity of the pile matter flowed like water, and radiating outwards from it . . . I'm told there were three kinds of "heat". Nuclear radiation, though not as much as one might expect; then the physical heat of combustion; and finally an alien heat which warped, melted and fused things together, but without burning.'

Tzonov paused to open a door-sized hatch in a steel bulkhead, ushered Trask and Goodly through and followed on behind. 'As for the radioactivity,' he continued on the other side, 'it has been cleared up now. A very few hotspots remain. But don't worry, we shall of course avoid them. There are several places we cannot avoid, however, which define various zones of contamination: the areas in which those common — and alien — heat energies which I mentioned expended themselves. This corridor is an example of "common" heat, the sort that burns.'

Beyond the bulkhead door, the corridor reached out ahead, wound to the left and receded from sight. Strip lighting in the ceiling loaned everything a blue-tinged sheen and flicker, humming electrically where sections of old neon tube were starting to short out. Despite the absence of tracks, platform, benches, still Trask found the place strangely reminiscent of a certain neglected London tube station in the wee small hours, one which he must have used frequently fifteen years ago before they were all refitted, but couldn't name or bring to mind now except as an echo of this place.

But there was one other big difference between some nameless underground station of the early Nineties and this place: evidence of that terrific physical heat which Tzonov had mentioned, sufficient to blacken and even partially *melt* the rough rock of the ceiling, until it had run down like lava to solidify on the cooler metal of wall panels and bulky steel stanchions. Underfoot, rubber floor tiles had burned through to naked steel plates which themselves were buckled right out of alignment; while in the walls, veins and drips and splashes of red, fused copper were all that remained of ancient wiring.

Leading the way, Tzonov nodded curtly to a group of lab-smocked scientists where they leaned against a pock-marked wall and compared notes. 'They still study this place as avidly – should I perhaps say as morbidly? – as ever,' he wryly commented, when the scientists had been left behind. 'They measure, examine, photograph and sample, without ever reaching any positive conclusion other than the one Viktor Luchov reached all those years ago: that when the blowback occurred the pile ate itself and mundane matter bent inwards and outwards, and even backwards, in space-time – until it warped through the "wall" of this universe and created the Gate.'

Tzonov glanced at his guests and quickly added: 'Oh, don't worry, I'm not going to give too much away! What? Why, our best physicists have been working at it for twenty years and getting nowhere, so don't take it as an insult if I doubt that you two will discover the secrets of the universe in a few short hours, days, or even weeks! Anyway, your agent Michael J. Simmons was here that time; and the Necroscope Harry Keogh too, before you chased him out of this world. Surely one or both of them have already filled in most of the blank spots for you.'

Trask shook his head. 'Harry was never able to stay here too long,' he said, looking the Russian straight in the eye. 'And even he had to admit that the math was too much for him. The Gate was an accident, when the universe suffered a power surge and its computer crashed. That was how he explained it, anyway. As for Jazz Simmons: he never returned to England and lives in the Greek islands still. In those days our Department of Dirty Tricks pulled a fast one on him. He's never forgiven us, and I for one don't blame him. The same must be said for Zek Föener, but in her case it was your people who gave her the runaround.'

Tzonov shrugged. Trask had given him the opportunity to read his mind, and he hadn't wasted it. Every word the British esper had spoken had been the truth, as he saw it. 'Well, times change,' the Russian said. And by way of changing the subject: 'So actually, this is all quite new to you?'

'Most of it,' Trask told him. 'The sight and feel of it, certainly. A picture is better than a hundred words. The physical reality is better than a blueprint.'

'Oh?' Tzonov raised a thin eyebrow as he came to a halt at the head of a flight of aluminium stairs, which from their bright sheen were a recent fitment. 'It's better to see something than to have an accurate description? Well, I take your meaning, of course, and normally would agree with you. Except there are things here which were better sight unseen. They lie in an area that suffered the other sort of heat, which may only be experienced in the melting pot of space-time. If it were my choice I would not show such things to you, but since they lie between us and the Gate . . .' He shrugged again and led the way down the stairs. 'I'm told that Viktor Luchov called these the magmass levels.'

'Magmass?' Ian Goodly was trembling slightly where he followed on after the others on uncertain legs, descending into a dimly lit region between levels proper. Trask sensed the tremor in his colleague's voice and guessed it was his talent working. Well, Tzonov had tried to warn them. And:

'Yes,' the Russian answered, but very quietly now, as he came to a halt. And quite unnecessarily, he pointed. 'Magmass. Now you can have the "sight" and "feel" of it, and perhaps you will even feel something of what it must have been like, when Perchorsk was gutted like a soft-bellied fish.'

Trask and Goodly looked, and knew that they had entered a region of sheerest fantasy. They stared into the dim recesses of a weird chaos, a vastly disordered cavern or vault, where the lighting was deliberately subdued so as to hide the most monstrous effects. For certainly what little could be seen was frightening, or disconcerting to say the least. It was as if the stairs had carried them out of this universe into a place where human laws no longer applied, where geometry and substance and science itself had failed . . . and the magmass had taken over.

Tzonov was on the move again, and drawn in his footsteps the British espers followed, silent where they gazed on these creations of drugged hallucination and madness. Down through a tangle of warped plastic, fused stone and blistered metal they passed, where on both sides amazingly consistent (in so much inconsistency) smooth-bored tunnels some two or three feet in diameter wound and twisted like the wormholes of ocean parasites in rotting coral, except they drove through solid rock, crumpled girders, and other, far less recognizable debris or residua.

And Trask thought: *It's like an alien alchemy! Some titan force tried to make everything one here, or change it all to a new unreality.*

Looking at him, Tzonov nodded. 'Yes,' he said. 'To change it, or deform it beyond all recognition. It's not so much that the various materials have been fused by heat and fire, rather that they've been *folded in* like a mass of dough, or Plasticine in the hands of a vast mad child. But this is only a small part of it, and I certainly won't show you the worst. No, for metal and plastic and rock were not the only materials which suffered this awful magmass change, but at least they are not . . . what? Biodegradable? I am sure you take my meaning.'

Goodly shuddered. 'What a horror!' he said.

Tzonov agreed. 'The more accessible areas were cleansed with hard acids, while other places were simply sealed off. A good many of the magmass moulds simply don't bear scrutiny.'

The stairs had descended to a bed of magmass, levelling into a catwalk along a vertical wall of unbroken rock like the face of a cliff. Seen over the aluminium handrails and through the metal lattice of the walkway, the floor was chaotically humped and anomalous, where different materials were so mixed as to have no individual identity whatsoever. And looping the loop —

twisting and twining through all the warped, congealed mass of this earthly yet hideously immundane material – there ran those weird wormhole energy channels which had carried the flux of a nightmarish nuclear cancer through the heart of Perchorsk, reducing it to this.

Looking at it (and Trask found that he must look at it, that his eyes were drawn to it as in some morbid fascination), he began to feel nauseous and was sure that Goodly must feel the same. Until suddenly, looming on the left of the walkway and bringing a sense of renewed reality, a perfectly circular opening appeared in the face of the wall of warped rock. Here the catwalk turned left into the mouth of the shaft, widened out to become a rubber-coated stairway, then continued its descent towards a region of eerie illumination down below.

'The core,' Tzonov informed his guests tonelessly as a group of armed, uniformed soldiers came clattering up through the shaft, heading in the opposite direction. 'The hole or cavern which was eaten out of the solid rock when the atomic pile imploded and formed the Gate: a most unnatural cavern, as you will see. The guard has just now been changed and these soldiers released from duty. Ah, but see how eager they are! The core is not a pleasant place. And even though the Gate is now secure, made safe to the very best of our ability, still we guard it. One can never tell . . .'

At the lower end of the shaft there was a railed landing, this time of steel and supported on steel stanchions. Flanked by Trask and Goodly, Tzonov went to the rail and leaned on it, staring grimly at the scene below. He had called this place a 'cavern' of sorts, but a most unnatural one. Now the British espers could see why.

It was *like* being in a cavern, but there was no way one might mistake it for any ordinary sort of cave. The solid rock had been hollowed out in the shape of a perfect sphere, a giant bubble in the very roots of the Ural Mountains – but a bubble well over a hundred and twenty feet in diameter! The curving, shiny-black wall all around was glass-smooth except for the worm-holes which riddled it everywhere, even in the domed ceiling. Where the three men were standing, the mouth of the shaft pointed downwards at forty-five degrees directly at the centre of the space – the core itself – which was occupied by what looked like a huge steel ball supported on a tripod of massive hydraulic rams. The ball would have to be a little more than thirty feet in diameter.

'Inside it, the Gate,' Tzonov explained. 'We cased it in carbon steel a foot thick, welded together in three sections. The rams support the sections and can apply massive pressure to keep them welded together, if it were ever necessary. But within the shell ... the Gate supports itself, floating there dead centre, right where it was born on the night of the accident, when the test was aborted.'

Trask looked at him in the painful blue-white glare of faulty strip lighting. 'And that's where you've trapped your visitor? In there? Inside the Gate?'

'Obviously. No way we can let him through, until we know what we're dealing with.'

'I think it's time we saw him,' Trask said. 'How long has he been here?'

'Four days,' Tzonov told him. 'After Premier Turchin himself was informed, I was the first to know of his arrival. Ordered here from Moscow, I saw, assessed, contacted you. You know the rest. You'll understand, of course, that the complex isn't my ordinary place of work. Until now my interest in Perchorsk has been purely academic.' (He had made a simple mistake! Trask saw the lie immediately, but knew that it wouldn't be to his advantage to point it out. He said nothing, letting Tzonov continue:) 'When one considers the esoteric aspect of this latest incident ... obviously I was the right man for the job.'

Goodly seemed puzzled. 'But four days, in there? He must be starving!'

Tzonov looked at him reprovingly. 'Do you think we're all barbarians, then? He has been fed, of course. Indeed, it was an opportunity we really couldn't afford to miss: to find out what he eats. Oh yes, for other creatures have come through the Gate before this one, Ian, whose appetites were ... well, suspect to say the least!' Without another word he led the way down steel steps to a perimeter walkway, and out over a wide gantry catwalk to the enigmatic, shining ball of carbon steel ...

II

The Visitor, and a Visit

———————

Around the steel sphere, encircling it like an inner ring
of Saturn, but so close as to almost touch the ball itself,
the railed catwalk was maybe ten feet wide; it was
equipped with consoles, computers, viewscreens. A
handful of scientists and technicians were seated at a
master console; others moved around the core's catwalk
carefully measuring and examining, concentrating on
their various instruments and tasks.

Crossing the gantry, Trask had absorbed all he could
of the so-called 'cavern'. There were no soldiers in
attendance at the core itself, but a trio of emplacements
on the perimeter under the inward curving walls were
manned and equipped with high velocity cannons, and
the battery directly opposite the master console was
further equipped with a small tracked vehicle bearing a
dull metal container and the obscene, squat-nozzled
hoses of what could only be a flamethrower unit. Well
read in what few documents were available concerning
the Perchorsk Gate, Trask knew enough to appreciate
the significance of all of these 'precautions'.

Likewise he understood the meaning of a trio of
scaffolding towers which reached up from the curving
floor higher than the gantry, consoles and central sphere
itself, to where a triangular framework suspended from
the ceiling joined them up and strengthened the structure. Central in this metal web, a nest of carboys was

connected to a sprinkler system whose outlets were aimed down onto the inner walkway and gantry. Should the system be activated, a hard acid rain would drench this entire area. So much for scientists, consoles, and catwalk! Draconian but effective, the system left no room for speculation about the inimical nature of what these people might be called upon to deal with down here.

And everywhere Trask looked, the claustrophobic wall of the bubble cavern formed a shiny-black backdrop, glass-smooth except for the wormholes riddling it through all its quarters, in the upward curving floor, encircling walls, and domed ceiling alike; that dull black glitter of all-enclosing, seemingly endless surface, alive with its myriad firefly reflections of the inadequate lighting system: like standing in the heart of some strange dark crystal. As for what Turkur Tzonov had said – that the core was not a 'pleasant' place – well, that had to be the understatement of the century! Trask knew that if he were a Russian soldier, he'd consider Perchorsk a punishment posting!

As the three men approached the master console, so one of the seated scientists turned, saw them, and gave a small, involuntary start. He reached out and flipped a switch. View-screens dissolved at once into white static and dazzling oscillations, quiet conversations tailed into silence, all heads turned and cold stares greeted the newcomers. Tzonov, smiling thinly, told Trask and Goodly: 'As you see, they don't even trust me yet, let alone you two! They consider me "muscle" – like the KGB – and here in the United Soviet States we don't yet have your own degree of cooperation between mind and muscle. Also, they are scientists, while we are mere metaphysicians, *fakirs* in whom they have no great faith. Fortunately *we* know that we are more truly mind than they could ever give us credit for. And in any case, no one here may gainsay me.'

His smile went out like a light turned off as he snapped some order in Russian at the console controller. The man sat there staring at him for a moment, but Tzonov's authority – and his eyes – had already won the battle of wills. The scientist's lips twitched a little in the left-hand corner as he switched the screens on again. And:

'Our visitor,' said Tzonov.

It was sudden, but the British espers had been expecting something like it and were able to cover their astonishment. At first the white dazzle – a backdrop of pure white, a veritable snowfield – got in the way, but as their eyes adjusted to the blaze and focused on the man on the screens, they saw that he was Harry Keogh – or Alec Kyle – or both of them. He *was* the Necroscope, or a twenty-year-old version of him, anyway!

Harry Junior! Trask and Goodly could scarcely be blamed for thinking the selfsame thought, which they kept to themselves as best they could. As it happened they were right in one sense, and totally wrong in another; but out of the corner of his eye Trask saw Turkur Tzonov's satisfied nod, and wondered if the telepath had zoomed in on them. Tzonov didn't keep him in suspense.

'I think so, too,' he said, an indicator that Trask could stop trying to conceal his suspicions and give his full attention to the scene in the scanners. He did so.

Goodly, on the other hand, chose to hide his thoughts and feelings behind a screen of questions. 'Closed circuit TV? You have cameras on the inside?'

'How observant!' Tzonov let his sarcasm drip; he'd seen through the precog's ploy at once. 'Yes, of course. Miniature cameras, trained on the area immediately

206

behind the steel section. The metal is ten inches thick, armoured on the inside; what you see on the screen there is no more than four or five feet from where you're standing; if you hammered on the panel you could give him a headache.'

Despite that Goodly knew he'd been rumbled, he clung to his pretext. 'How do you feed him?'

Tzonov pointed. 'You see that groove in the metal? Not merely a groove but a hatch, a door, hermetically sealed and magnetically locked. Down at the bottom there, that circular mark is an even smaller door, through which we pass food. Of course, we don't do it while he's awake but when he's sleeping. And now that he's satisfied to eat what we give him, we could just as easily poison him. Or we might pump lethal gas in there, or squirt acid at him. We *might* do so even now, if we can't satisfy ourselves that he's just a man . . .'

During which conversation, Trask had taken the opportunity to satisfy *himself* (albeit erroneously) that first impressions must be correct: this was Harry Keogh Junior, the son of the Necroscope, who as an infant had spirited his ailing mother away into an alien dimension. He looked maybe ten years younger than he should, but there again he'd come to manhood in a different world. Still, the discrepancy was such as to cause Trask to frown. He felt that he wasn't seeing the whole picture. As for what he *was* seeing:

The man in the viewscreen was seated cross-legged on what was barely discernible as a white floor. It seemed no different to the rest of his surroundings, except his thighs and backside flattened out when pressed against it. And the rest of his surroundings . . . were white. There was little more to say of that tunnel between worlds: it was a glaring white expanse joining up our universe to some other. It was the Gate.

Again Trask examined the visitor, and discovered another anomaly, however small. Alec Kyle's (or Harry Keogh's?) hair had been brown and plentiful, naturally wavy. This one's hair was blond and shining, like damp straw, with grey streaks to both sides which gave him a look of intelligence or erudition well in advance of his years. And his hair was long, falling to his shoulders, giving him something of the appearance of a Viking. Moreover his eyes were of a sapphire blue, where Kyle/Keogh's had been as brown as his hair. Trask was certain that genetically this was Alec Kyle's son, but at the same time he seemed to have inherited his – what, spiritual? – father's colours! As for the rest of his features: there could be no denying that this was the son of the Necroscope.

As if the visitor had suddenly heard or sensed something, he thrust himself upright until his sandalled feet flattened to the white 'floor', and looked directly into the eye of a scanner; all of which was performed in a dreary slow-motion which must be an effect of the Gate. A technician adjusted the picture until the whole man was revealed, his eyes narrowed and brow furrowed where he stood with his gaze slightly elevated into the camera.

Trask couldn't gauge his height but suspected he'd be a six-footer. He had an athlete's body: broad shoulders, narrow waist, powerful arms and legs. His eyes might be very slightly slanted, or it could simply be a result of his currently suspicious, frowning expression. His nose was straight and seemed small under a broad forehead flanked by high cheekbones. Over a square chin which jutted a little (though not aggressively, Trask thought), his mouth was full and tended to slant downwards a fraction to the left. In others this might suggest a certain cynicism, but not in him. Rather the opposite: there was an air of patience, inevitability, even of vulnerability about him beyond that of a creature trapped in an unknown, unknowable environment.

Now that he relaxed a little – his expression changing, eyes opening wider and frown melting away – Trask saw something else which could only be revenant of Harry: a natural innocence and compassion, the soulfulness of the mind behind the face. So that without being Keogh's spitting image, still the visitor *felt* like him. And as that fact dawned, Trask knew that it wasn't so much what he'd seen when first he looked at this one, rather what he'd experienced inside that made him sure of his identity. Gut feelings on the one hand, supported by Trask's weird talent on the other, which could not be confused or mistaken. This *was* the Necroscope's son. So ... why was it, he wondered, that something continued to bother him?

As for the visitor's clothes:

He was clad in a fringed jacket with a high collar and wide lapels, and in trousers which were tight at the knee and flared at the calves to fit snug over soft leather boots. The outfit was almost 'wild west' in cut, yet flowing and Gypsyish at the same time, and its material was a finely patterned skin or leather – like alligator hide. Soft, sand-coloured, flexible, it looked comfortable if a little worn and dusty.

Then Trask noticed the earring in his left ear: a queer twist of yellow metal, only an inch long and presumably gold. But if Trask had been frowning before, now the lines deepened on his brow. He knew the significance of that odd shape, knew what it was: the Möbius Strip, the metaphysical symbol which had been Harry Keogh's passport to another world. It was the final piece in the puzzle, which validated all the rest and caused them to click into place. Trask put it to the back of his mind at

209

once, something else to be hidden in the hypnotic abyss behind his eyes.

And that, in a nutshell, was the visitor. Overall, there was nothing in his clothing, manner, or appearance in general to suggest the haughty aggressive arrogance, physical superiority, and awesome metamorphic arts of the Wamphyri. So that despite Trask's other, perhaps ulterior political motives, he knew that his prime purpose in being here – the validation of the visitor as a man and *only* a man – had been justified.

'Off!' Tzonov's voice cut into his thoughts, causing Trask to start. As the screens blinked into a grey opacity, he turned to the Russian and answered his gaze ... and was at once aware of its bite! *Now* the telepath would read his or Goodly's mind, if he could. Like the colours of a chameleon, his eyes changed until their grey so diluted itself as to drain them of colour, while yet their pupils seemed to enlarge to magnifying lenses which on another occasion might look right into Trask's mind. But not this time. For as the Russian's gaze fastened on his eyes, so something deep in Trask's brain snapped into action and channelled the other's telepathy down an empty tunnel.

Tzonov knew it in a moment without knowing how it was done: that Trask was impervious. Or perhaps not impervious: his mind was accessible but blank! And Goodly's pale smile told him the same thing, that his mind too had been – secured? 'Hypnotism!' the Russian finally grunted, his bottom jaw falling open. And seeing Trask's expression, he knew that he'd guessed correctly. 'You've been hypnotized! If I so much as look at you ... your minds switch off!'

He clapped a hand to his forehead and ground his teeth, then grew calm in a moment and actually forced a smile, until he became aware of the core's scientists

210

worriedly staring at him. 'You . . . may get back to your work,' he told them, turning on his heel and starting unsteadily back along the gantry.

Trask and Goodly looked at each other, then followed on behind. Tzonov paused and waited for them at the bottom of the ramp through the entrance tunnel. As they came up the steps he said, 'All very clever, but it wasn't part of our deal. I have held to my part.' He was in control again, but cold as a mid-winter Siberian blizzard.

Trask said, 'And we'll hold to ours. But it wasn't part of the deal to have you in our minds. Did you ever consider simply asking?'

Tzonov pursed his lips. 'At times . . . at times I'm almost given to believe that my telepathy isn't just a tool. Sometimes I feel that *I* am the tool, and my talent the master. And I have to admit: it's hard to own or be owned by such a talent without using it. If I was presumptuous, then I'm sorry. It's just that it seemed the easiest way, that's all.' And Trask knew that he was telling the truth.

The Russian saw it in his face, relaxed, nodded and said: 'Very well, I'm asking. Is he what he seems to be, just a man, the son of Harry Keogh? Or is he an imitation – a spy, decoy, or invader from another world – and something we should destroy without delay?'

'He's a man,' Trask answered at once, but he was careful to leave Tzonov's 'just' out of his reply. 'And I believe he's Harry's son, yes.'

Tzonov sighed. 'I read as much in your minds almost without trying,' he said. 'Yet when I tried . . .'

Goodly spoke up, saying: 'That was your mistake, Turkur. We can't be forced. We can offer up the information voluntarily, or else be taken by surprise, tricked, eavesdropped. But face to face . . . the moment your

211

eyes lock on, post-hypnotic commands take over, we shut up shop, and our minds go blank.' Telling him didn't hurt; Tzonov would work it out for himself quickly enough.

'Ah!' he said, smiling his thin smile, which fell away at once. 'But ... it will be difficult to work together in circumstances such as these.' He began to turn away.

But Trask said, 'Under your rules it would be impossible! Our minds are our own, Turkur.'

The Russian looked at him. 'But you have the advantage,' he said, an edge of frustration in his voice. 'If I lie – if what I say is not the *precise* truth – you'll know it immediately!'

'Then try not to lie,' Trask answered, starting up the tunnel towards the magmass levels. 'It shouldn't be too hard. After all, you've been doing all right so far ...'

On their way back to quarters, Trask said: 'I think it's time you answered a few questions, Turkur. For example: since you are able to look at your visitor any time you want to – face to face, on screen – why haven't you read his mind? Why did you need me to tell you about him, the truth of him?'

Tzonov shrugged. 'Perhaps you've answered your own question. Perhaps he, too, has been hypnotized! Believe me I would *love* to read his mind, but can't! It could be interference from the sphere's "skin", its event horizon, which lies between the visitor and the wall of his steel cell. Maybe it's related to the slow-motion effect which you observed when he stood up, I don't know. But whichever, his mind is likewise a blank wall to me, just like your own. Perhaps when we bring him through to this side things will be different. We must wait and see.'

'That was my next question,' Trask said. 'When will you bring him through?'

Tzonov knew he couldn't lie, and so replied with an ambiguous: 'Soon.' Then, as Trask and Goodly reached their door, he looked at them and said, 'Siggi, of course, will find no great difficulty in reading your minds. Her talent does not rely on eye to eye contact.'

'But only if we should relax our guard,' Goodly told him. 'I mean, if she catches us with our pants down. Which wouldn't be cricket, now would it?'

Tzonov laughed. 'Our Great Cultural Difference! Cricket! The rules of the game! The fact that you have them, and we do not!'

'Also that we have "ladies",' Goodly answered, 'while you have only "comrades".' And as Tzonov's smile turned sour, the British espers passed through into their adjoining rooms and closed the door on him . . .

Later: the four ate together in Perchorsk's mess hall, where a so-called 'executive dining area' had been screened off for the use of officers and scientists, to separate them from the common soldiers. As the hour was late, they were in any case alone. The heating of the hall was only just adequate, but Siggi Dam seemed perfectly comfortable despite that her dress was almost Mediterranean, a fact which Trask and Goodly couldn't help but notice after Tzonov had helped her out of her coat. Following which they studiously avoided paying her too much attention.

She wore a short, tight, figure-hugging skirt, in combination with a fashionable wide-shouldered bolero waistcoat held together by a single button, over a chiffon blouse open to the waist. Her cleavage was all too evident and the dark stains of her nipples were like patterns on the pale blue chiffon. If it was her intention to distract, it certainly worked; the espers tried not to be too *gauche* but found themselves making a point of

213

talking face to face with Tzonov, which kept their hypnotic implants primed. And in a little while Trask sensed that Siggi was no longer trying to read them.

But to be absolutely sure, he smiled at her and said, 'In a place as unnaturally cold and unfriendly as this, I'm sure your presence must raise the temperature by several degrees at least!' While this was a genuine compliment, his very deliberate afterthought was anything but: *God, what I wouldn't give to fuck your face!*

Then, still smiling, he waited with numbed nerves for her slap – but instead she returned his smile, inclined her head, and said, 'Why, thank you, Ben!'

Other conversation was sparse during the meal, which like the accommodation wasn't exactly the Ritz. For all that, Trask suspected that some poor Soviet Citizen's Army cook had made a special effort here. You could cut the meat despite its cryptic origin, and instead of the dubiously de-bugged bottled 'spring water' to be found in most Russian cities these days, the Coca-Cola was fresh, cool, sparkling.

'The quality of our food,' Tzonov commented, almost disinterestedly (perhaps apologetically?) 'continues to improve with the ecology.'

All thanks due to the West, Trask thought, but to himself. Pointless to further damage the Russian's pride. The fact was, though, that without the help of Germany, France, Great Britain and the USA of course, the body of the USSR would be a vast and ugly mutant thing dying of its sores. As it was, the most dangerous of the reactors had been closed down and mothballed, the worst of the industrial pollution was now under control, Siberian forests and wild life were flourishing once more, and even the so-called 'Aral Desert' was regaining something of its old water table. Ask Anna Marie English and she'd gladly detail a thousand other small miracles.

Trask finished off only a little of his fairly tasteless pudding and Goodly hardly touched his, a spoonful at best. The Russians didn't even make that much effort. But finally Tzonov yawned and said: 'I'm for bed. Tomorrow will be a busy day. We should all sleep as best we can. Myself, I find it claustrophobic down here. I like to picture myself out in the open, in an orchard counting the plums, and sleep comes easier. You might like to try it.'

Goodly looked at him, ignored his advice and concentrated on the one word: 'Tomorrow?' Behind his grey, sunken features, the precog's mind was likewise hollow. Perhaps even more than it should be. And his voice felt hollow, too, as he asked, 'Is that when you're letting him come through?'

The head of Russian E-Branch yawned again, but just like the first one it was a lie. Trask shrugged inside and told himself it was simply Tzonov's excuse to be alone with Siggi. Who could blame him anyway? But then, as the cook came to take away their dishes, suddenly Trask was unaccustomedly sleepy. And he knew in a moment why he hadn't wanted his pudding.

After that ... it was an effort to get himself and Goodly back to their rooms and onto their beds before the dark flooded in. And Goodly never did get an answer to his question concerning the visitor: about when they'd be letting him through the Gate into Perchorsk. It made no difference for he'd known the answer anyway, except he'd known it just ten seconds too late. And so had Trask.

Now, falling headlong into the great black hole of sleep, they both knew it was going to be tonight, within the hour, as soon as they were out of the way.

And then they *were* out of the way ...

*

Ben Trask wasn't much of a dreamer. At least he didn't often remember his dreams, for which he was grateful. The ones that stuck were usually nightmares, which came to him as a result of his job. On occasion, he still nightmared about Yulian Bodescu, corrupted in his mother's womb and born into a life of necromancy and vampirism. Or he might dream that he was back in the Greek islands, up against Janos Ferenczy, last of an infamous bloodline. Or he might see the Necroscope again, as he'd seen him that time in the garden of Harry's Edinburgh home, before he'd fled into Starside through the Perchorsk Gate. And so it can be seen why Trask wasn't much of a one for dreaming.

Once, the Branch had employed its own oneiro-mancer: a man who not only translated other people's dreams but used his own to gauge his and others' destinies. He had worked for E-Branch for three years, and then stopped dreaming – and a week later died of a brain tumour. Time and again, it had been shown how the future resisted the tampering of mere men. And by exactly the same degree, Ben Trask resisted dreaming.

He would resist it just as stringently now, if he hadn't been weakened by the drugged food. But as it was he found himself drawn into the dream and trapped there – by a voice. But a voice with a difference, with an aura. An aura that reminded Trask of his dreams of Harry Keogh.

At first there was only the velvet darkness of deep sleep, criss-crossed by the flashes of instantly forgotten thoughts or half-formed visions, transient as meteor trails in a night sky. But there was nothing really visual about it. Then . . . the aura was there like cigarette smoke, curling in Trask's mind, acrid with the touch – or the taint? – of the one who'd first drawn and then exhaled it. Or maybe acrid wasn't the right word: *redolent* of him, perhaps . . .

216

A curl of smoke, but intent, sentient, probing. And as the aura of the other sensed Trask and settled like a fog all about him, so he felt himself brushed by the eddies of a powerful rushing force, tugged and whirled in the mental currents of some weird cyclone of the mind. It *was* a whirlwind, a vortex, and as it drew Trask in, so he saw or sensed its composition: numbers!

A numbers vortex! It was as if the continuous printout of some colossal computer had spiralled up into the air like a gigantic inverted flypaper, burning away until the numbers were left to spin on their own. Flying free, they too burned with an inner fire; they glowed like neon as esoteric equations sought to resolve themselves, evolving or mutating into metaphysical maths. A nodding, cone-shaped tornado of writhing numbers snatched Trask up and hurled him aloft, just one more cypher in a rapidly rotating wall of agonized algebraic symbols and coruscating calculi.

But just as a storm has its calm 'eye' at the centre of the tumult, so the numbers vortex obscured and protected its sentient core: another mind, which Trask felt warm against his own as soon as he touched it. Except it wasn't simply that he felt it, but also that he felt he *knew* it!

'Who ...?' he said, dismissing his post-hypnotic mind-guard and opening himself to the other's probe. 'What...?'

A friend, came back the answer. *Or one who would be your friend, if you will have me.*

And despite that the telepathic voice was warm, uncertain, and even a little afraid, still Trask shuddered in his sleep. It was as if someone had walked on his grave – *exactly* like that – and for the first time in his life he fully appreciated the meaning of that old cliché. For this was how it must feel to be dead and have someone talk to you! A single word, thought, idea, floated to the surface of Trask's mind:

'Necroscope!'

For a moment there was a hushed silence. Then: *And is that such a dreadful thing to be? I can feel it in your voice that you think so.*

Even drugged, asleep, Trask knew who he was talking to — the only one he could possibly be talking to — so that before considering or attempting to curb his reply, he found himself answering: 'But your father *was* a dreadful thing, in the end!'

Ahhh! You knew my father? My real father? There was hope in the voice, eagerness and excitement, but all fading away in a moment. *And I see that you feared him, too, just like everyone else in this place.*

'In the end we all feared him, yes,' Trask repeated. 'But in the beginning, he was my friend.'

And you ... can tell me about him? Something of hope had returned.

'Oh, yes, I know about him,' Trask answered. 'I know a lot about him. More than most men. Most *living* men, anyway.' Which seemed to say it all.

Ahhh! Again that strange, sad sigh. And in another moment: *We'll talk again. But not now. There are mentalists here. They watch and listen. I see you have a mindguard. Use it!*

The voice faded away, leaving Trask to cry out after it, 'Wait, wait!' But it was useless; the numbers vortex snatched him up again and dragged him into its whirling wall. Buffeted this way and that in a spiral of mad maths, Trask was rocked, shocked, shaken ...

... Shaken awake!

'Easy, Ben! Easy!' Ian Goodly's worried expression loomed into focus. The precog sat on the edge of Trask's bed, gripped his arms and continued to caution him.

'They think we're still out for the count. And as long as they continue to believe it, we can talk.'

'Ian!' Trask grasped the other's wrists, stared up into his pale face. 'I was dreaming.'

'Nightmaring, more like!' Goodly retorted. 'Who were you calling after?'

'You wouldn't believe me if I told you!' Trask struggled upright, gently fingered his brow. 'God ... headache!'

'That mousse, or whatever it was supposed to be.' Goodly nodded. 'Or rather, what was in it.' He stepped through into his room, ran water, returned with a fizzing glass. 'Good old American knowhow.'

'Eh?' Trask drank.

'Alka-Seltzer.'

'Ah!' Trask looked at him, focusing a little easier now. 'So what happened to your precognition?'

'Nothing, it worked fine.'

'You *knew* they'd mickey us?' Trask's jaw fell.

'But not until it was too late, after the first spoonful.'

Trask tut-tutted his disgust.

'And your own faultless talent?' Goodly raised an eyebrow.

Trask's expression changed, grew rueful. 'Much the same as yours, I suppose: it came too late.' He sighed. 'I guessed Tzonov's "tiredness" was a lie, but what the hell, *obviously* he wanted to be alone with Siggi! So I wasn't seeing or thinking straight. Something was — yes, I have to admit it — distracting me. But by the time I was a couple of mouthfuls into that pudding . . .'

'That's when you knew.' Goodly grimaced. 'Because by then she was able to relax. We'd taken the poisoned bait. Except ... well, we only took a little of it. I expect the dose was carefully measured; a full portion of that pudding would probably have put us both down for the entire night.'

Trask frowned. 'Run that by me again? About Siggi, I mean?'

And Goodly said, 'That's what she does, and it's why she's here. Siggi Dam's no ordinary telepath, Ben. It's my guess she carries as much mind-smog around with her as any of the undead you ever went up against. What makes me think so? Simply that I can't read a damn thing of her future. Nothing!'

Trask stroked his chin. 'Mind-smog? Static? She produces it?'

'To order. That's my bet, anyway. It throws the talents of other espers out of kilter. It's why my advance knowledge went into reverse and your instinctive lie-detector blew a fuse.' He nodded and managed to look more mournful yet. 'As if she wasn't a big enough distraction already. Physically, that is.'

Trask got up, crossed to his washbasin and ran cold water, splashed his face with it. 'Certainly it would explain why she isn't listed,' he grunted. 'A new player we know nothing about. Her telepathy warns her when another esper is near, and then she hides behind her mind-smog. Turkur Tzonov's secret weapon. We had too much of an edge, so he shipped Siggi in to blunt us down a bit. I knew there was something I should ask myself the first time I saw her, namely: what the hell's a nice girl like her doing in a dump like this? Keeping Tzonov company? Maybe, but she's no bimbo. Given that she has a mind, there have to be ten thousand better places to be!' Squinting in the room's poor light, he glanced at his wrist-watch.

'You were out for an hour and forty minutes,' Goodly told him. 'You still would be, if I hadn't woken you up. Myself . . . I was out for half an hour.'

'You're resistant?'

'I only tasted that stuff,' again Goodly's grimace. 'But

you know, the Bulgarians were expert "chemists" all of thirty, forty years ago. Designer drugs? Old hat to them and the Opposition. Anyway, I went down fighting it and kept fighting it. If I hadn't, my drugged sleep might well have merged into normal sleep. But I knew what had happened and wanted desperately to be awake! I used my mental alarm clock: that's a trick of mine to wake myself up at any hour of the day or night. Before going to sleep, I just tell myself when I want to be up. Which is what I did. But as I was coming out of it, someone entered the room. So I just closed my eyes and mind and lay there. Whoever it was must have been satisfied. After he or they left I tried to wake you but couldn't, so I took a look around on my own.'

'You did what?'

Goodly shrugged. 'Why shouldn't I? We're not prisoners. And if Tzonov can play dirty tricks, why shouldn't we? So I went walkabout.'

'In the Projekt?'

'Here and there.' The precog's face wasn't so much gaunt as grim now, and Trask saw things in his eyes that worried him.

'So what did you find?'

'I saw a lot of stuff you're not going to like, Ben,' the other told him. 'Stuff that you won't like one little bit . . .'

Nathan ... Kiklu?

'Tell me about it.' Trask sighed his relief as the pounding in his skull receded a little.

'It's night now up top,' Goodly told him. 'The very dead of night. And down here, except for essential duties, everyone is asleep. Also, we're "guests" as opposed to interlopers – or we're supposed to be – with no special orders attaching to us. And anyway they think, thought, we were out of the picture. So I wasn't interfered with as I did my rounds. Well, not until I descended through the magmass levels to the core. That's where I was picked up and escorted back here. But before then ...

'Ben, what do we know of this place? I mean, in connection with Harry Keogh, the last time he was here?'

Trask shrugged. 'We had pretty good liaison with the Reds at that time. They were "Reds" then, just waking up to the fact that they were in it up to their necks. Harry Keogh had become a vampire: he carried a plague in his blood that could run rampant across the face of the Earth. And using this thing called the Möbius Continuum, he could travel instantaneously from one place to another like you and I go from room to room. He could be, and was, in the Greek islands, Hong Kong, Nicosia, Detroit, Macau, and here in Perchorsk, all in the space of an hour. Our locators – Russian and

Chinese locators, too – were out of their heads trying to follow his movements . . .' Trask paused. 'But why am I telling you this? You were with the Branch and know it as well as I do.'

'Tell it anyway,' Goodly urged.

Trask struggled into his jacket. 'Very well, but on our way.'

'We're going to see Tzonov?'

'Damn right!' Trask growled. 'And to find out what he's up to with his visitor.' And to himself: *With my visitor? The one I spoke to in a dream? Or was it just a dream?*

'This place is a maze,' Goodly warned. 'How do we know where they are? How will we find them?'

'Wherever the action is – where they're *not* sleeping – that's where we'll find them,' Trask answered. He led the way out into the corridor, which was even dimmer now and yet more eerie, and headed for the core. 'But you asked me to refresh your memory on Perchorsk, at the time when Harry went through the Gate.' His voice fell to a whisper:

'Well, we were the ones who told Soviet E-Branch that the Necroscope would probably try it. He'd already used the Romanian route and so was stuck with this one. The Russians assured us he wouldn't make it; forewarned, they would be waiting for him with a lot more firepower than he or anyone – *anything* – could possibly handle. Since we couldn't be sure exactly what that signified, we were obliged to take their word for it. One thing for sure, though: they really believed they could stop him.'

'Except they didn't,' Goodly took it up. 'He tried to go through on a motorcycle – first through the Möbius Continuum, then through the Gate – with that poor vampirized girl, Penny, riding pillion. He made it but . . .

the girl was shaken loose on this side. She came down on electrified steel plates under an acid rain. A terrible way to go, even for a vampire.'

Trask nodded. 'Eventually the Russians told us what had happened. They had to, for they were scared to death he'd come back again! After what Harry had done to them in earlier times – the havoc he'd wreaked with their E-Branch – they wanted to ingratiate themselves. It could be they were going to need our help ... badly! And so they told us the whole thing. But they also told us about their new "failsafe" system. My God! Talk about Chernobyl!

'But on the other hand, who could blame them? They'd had more than enough of things coming through that Gate. The next time anything stuck its ugly face in here, they were going to blow its head off and close the Gate for good! But it was the way they were going to do it. Two nuclear warheads, one timed to explode inside the Gate, close to the opening into the parallel world of the vampires, and the other set to go off just beyond that portal, on Starside itself! It was just typical of Russian thinking at the time: destroy the invader if possible, wreck his lines of resupply, devastate his home ground. Also, with any luck the Gate itself might be destroyed at the same time.

'When we heard about it and after we asked our scientists what sort of side effects there might be, all hell broke loose! What, set off a nuclear device inside a black hole – or a grey one – right here on Earth, right in the earth? Unthinkable! We could be playing with the forces that hold the very universe in place! We started negotiations ... but too late. Harry had been gone for some time by then, and it seems he'd been keeping busy on Starside. What happened here in Perchorsk that fateful night ... no one knows for sure. Most of the

224

survivors were out of it before the missiles were actually fired. But the story they had to tell ... well, it was the work of the Necroscope, all right. It had to be him, for who else could return Perchorsk's dead to life?'

The two had penetrated the upper magmass levels into an area where neither of them had set foot before. Visible in the distorted matter-melt of walls and floor, weird moulds had been scooped from metal, plastic, and the very rock itself as if by fire or furious acid. Blow-torch scorching and the discoloration of chemical reaction were apparent everywhere.

Goodly paused, his gaze hardening in the poor light. With a nod of his head, he directed Trask's eyes to these inarticulate yet vaguely frightening shapes in the magmass. And despite that Trask's last words had been a statement of fact as opposed to a question proper, still the precog answered them in his fashion, by taking up the story again:

'The dead woke up, that's what happened. The dead of Perchorsk in their glass, rock or metal cysts – the *magmass* dead, fused with machinery, tools, whatever they'd been working with; rotting or mummified semi-mechanical *things*, who'd been melted and sealed up in the original explosion – broke out! Dead men, whose warped composite bodies might just fit the twisted shapes of these terrible magmass moulds. And *they* fired the missiles into the open Gate!'

Trask nodded, his voice hushed as he answered: 'According to the Russians, anyway. But it could only have been Harry who gave the orders. He was dying on Starside – he even gathered us all together to *watch* him die, that time at E-Branch HQ in London – but his deadspeak voice bridged the gap from another world to this place, and called up the dead just one more time in an attempt to close the Gate. *That* sort of dead, yes ...'

225

He looked again at the magmass moulds, then quickly looked away. 'Mercifully, our scientists were wrong. Whatever the Gate is – whatever it's made of – it was too tough for the Soviet nukes. It seemed to eat them up: no repercussions whatsoever. We can't even be sure that they went off. There was no blow-back, nothing. Perhaps they should have anticipated that; after all, the Gate is a one-way ticket.'

Goodly took his arm, turned this way and that, said, 'We must have missed a turning. Somewhere back there . . . is something you ought to see. And anyway, I don't think we'll find Tzonov and his visitor along here.'

As they began to retrace their steps, Trask asked: 'So why did you want to go over all of that again?'

'To get it straight in my head,' the other answered. 'I'm pretty good with the future, but the past sometimes eludes me. And anyway, you skipped the most interesting part. I'm talking about when Chingiz Khuv was in charge here, and sent Jazz Simmons through into Starside.'

The magmass was behind them now. The tunnel ahead looked more than ever like some old London underground, with several confusing, branching passageways. Finally they drew level with a recess on the left, containing a bulkhead door marked with a radiation hazard sign. 'Ah!' Goodly nodded. 'This is it.'

Trask glanced at the warning, looked again and shook his head. 'A barefaced lie to keep out the incurably curious, such as you and me,' he said. 'But radiation? It would suffice for most people, certainly!' And as Goodly spun the wheel to free the hatch, and pushed it back on squealing hinges: 'What about when Jazz went through?'

Goodly stepped into darkness, turned on the lights.

Trask followed him into . . . a storeroom? The place was like a warehouse, with other rooms leading off and stacked steel shelving on every hand. Then Trask saw what the shelves contained, and Goodly said:

'E-Branch didn't get much out of Jazz Simmons when Harry Junior brought him back. Can't say I blame him, not after what Intelligence and the Branch had done to him. We had to send a man out to Zante just to speak to him! But he did say that –'

Trask cut him off: '– That Chingiz Khuv had been planning an invasion of Starside?' He looked again at the shelves. 'Yes, he did say that. And now?'

Goodly shrugged and joined him in examining the armaments stacked on the shelves, a stockpile of small and not so small-arms: flamethrowers, grenades, automatic rifles, hand guns and ammunition. And: 'What do you think?' he said.

'If you can't destroy the Gate,' Trask answered, 'first secure and defend it, and then prepare to invade it! Who knows what you might find on the other side? Something to swing the balance in your favour? A means of achieving your ambition: to even the score and grow Big in the world again? But is this the Russian Premier's philosophy . . . or is it just Tzonov's? Is he trying to work this trick on his own, do you think? I know he was lying when he said that up until Nathan's arrival his interest in this place was purely academic.'

'Whichever,' Goodly said, 'I think this visitor from Starside has come through at just the right time. If he hadn't, we wouldn't have seen all of this . . .'

'Which might seem to beg a further question,' Trask added. 'Who was it who *really* wanted us in on this? Turkur Tzonov, or Premier Gustav Turchin? Were we invited merely on the whim of the one, or on the command of The Boss himself so that we'd be in on it and just as much to blame if it went wrong?'

. 'Probably the latter,' Goodly answered, 'and Tzonov has to make the best of it. It would explain the lack of security: we were *supposed* to see everything, and Tzonov daren't hide that fact. So from the technicians' and scientists' point of view, we appear as free agents. But in reality Tzonov's keeping us on a leash, only letting us see what he wants us to see.'

'Until now,' Trask growled. 'Let's get out of here. I don't want to be found in this place, and I don't want Turkur Tzonov to know we've seen it . . .'

They left the storeroom with no time to spare; a technician, yawning, bespectacled, barely awake, came into view around the curve of the corridor. He must be going on night shift down in the core. As they drew level Trask stepped in front of him and said, 'Er, Turkur Tzonov?'

'Uh?' The other looked at them, blinked sleep out of his eyes. 'You looking for Tzonov?' He nodded. 'But not here. Back there, er, fifty steps? Passage on right. Is there. But could be dangerous. The intruder.'

'Thanks,' Trask smiled. 'This is a big place. We got lost.'

The other shrugged and blinked again. 'Is no problem.'

They went their own ways, but as soon as they were out of earshot Goodly whispered: 'See what I mean? There don't appear to be any guards in the place, and very little of suspicion in respect of our being here. Earlier, down at the core, the scientists were more opposed to Tzonov's presence than to ours. I think they see *him* as the intruder! They don't want the military or people of Tzonov's dubious, cloak-and-dagger character down here at all! They'd like to study the visitor their way, as scientists. Not his way, whatever that will prove to be.' It was the way he said it that caused Trask to glance at him.

'You said you were picked up at the core,' Trask said. 'Did you see anything down there?'

'Enough,' Goodly answered, but darkly.

'Enough?'

'Enough to make me suspect that our man isn't going to have an easy time of it. I saw them bring him through. His food must have been drugged, too. When they opened the door his arm flopped out. He was unconscious. They dragged him through and put him in a cage.'

'What? A cage?'

'Like a big birdcage, yes.'

The two turned down the indicated passage on the right, followed it for fifteen or so paces, then turned right again and found themselves outside another steel door. But this time it was guarded. A young soldier leaned against the wall with a rifle over his shoulder. When the espers came into view he stood up and adopted a sloppy position of attention, but as Trask approached the door he stepped in his way. 'No go,' he said.

'We were invited,' Trask told him, face to face. 'We have to see Turkur Tzonov.'

The soldier frowned, scratched his chin, and said, 'No,' but without malice. Goodly had stepped to one side of the uniformed man and now made to pass around him. But as the soldier moved to intercept him, so the door opened. Tzonov stepped into view, and the orbits of his eyes were that much deeper, darker. No need to inquire what he had been doing, or trying to do. He saw them at once, but his face showed little or no evidence of surprise.

'Ah! Ben, Ian,' he said. 'I was going to send for you, but it seems you've beaten me to it.'

'I hope you have some answers, Turkur,' Trask told him, coldly, as the Russian stepped aside and ushered them past him into the laboratory beyond the steel door. 'And I hope they're good ones. Because if they're not . . .' His voice tailed off as he gazed all about, until his eyes found what he was looking for.

In one corner of the large, well-lit room, a tiled, sunken area like a small swimming pool had been cut from the living rock. Beyond it the walls of the man-made cave rose sheer out of the basin to a high, roughly hewn ceiling. The cage Goodly had mentioned stood central in the tiled depression itself, and there were steps leading down to it. Set in the walls of the sunken area, nozzles pointed inwards towards the cage. As soon as Trask had absorbed this last detail, he recognized its function. This was not and had never been intended as a swimming pool. This was an acid bath.

There were two scientists in the room, both of them young, inexperienced, definitely cowed — by Tzonov's presence, Trask correctly assumed. They sat on chairs at the rim of the sunken area with millboards, notepaper, and pens. As yet they didn't seem to be doing too much writing, which Trask understood readily enough. Tzonov himself had pinpointed the difficulty here: these people were scientists and he was a metaphysician. They didn't even believe what he had been trying to do. They were a token force of the small scientific community here, representatives of their fraternity against the parapsychological or 'supernatural' nature of Tzonov's.

Crossing the floor to the sunken area, Trask told Tzonov, 'What you did to us constitutes a serious assault. You've introduced harmful foreign agencies, drugs, into our bodies. Your lot have always been good at that sort of thing, ever since the Bulgarians showed you how. It was a mistake, however, for we'll bring charges.'

The Russian tut-tutted. 'Come, now! Harmful? On the contrary: they were totally harm*less!* Do you feel any ill effects? Of course not. Moreover, by now your bodies are already voiding the drug, and so you could never prove it. Here and now, face to face, *I* accept what you say, of course. For there's no way I can lie to you. But how would that stand up in an international court of law? Ordinary people don't believe in our talents, Ben! So your threat is meaningless. And in any case, it was done for your own safety.'

The three paused at the rim of the sunken area, where the two Englishmen looked their host scornfully in the face, especially Trask. The sharp edge of his talent was never keener. He looked, saw, knew that Tzonov had told a half-truth. Something of it had been for his and Goodly's safety, but mainly it had been to keep them out of the way. Tzonov wasn't lying, but he wasn't telling the whole truth either.

'We don't have to prove it to take action on it,' Goodly spoke up, his face and voice animated for once. 'If courts of law are out, there are always other ways. You aren't the only one with a powerful organization behind you. There are things which we, too, can do that could never be handled by a court of law. If you doubt me, better go and do a little homework on British E-Branch.'

There had been a half-smile on Tzonov's face. Now it fell away. 'I'll do what I have to do,' he said, 'to protect myself and my country from any threat. Whether it comes from an alien world or an alien ideology. And I won't let anyone stand in my way. But on this occasion, I had you two put out of the way in order to protect you. This thing,' he jerked his head to indicate the cage, 'is the unknown! In the past, other things which seemed harmless have come through into Perchorsk, and brought death and madness with them. Not only a threat to my country but to yours, too. Indeed, a threat to the entire world.'

'We're not complaining about your patriotism, Turkur,' Trask told him. 'Only about your zeal.' He started down the steps into the sunken area. 'And what would Premier Turchin say, I wonder, if he knew you were up to stuff like that? As for what you said about alien ideologies: tsk-tsk! Is democracy so alien to you, then? And would Turchin fall into line with your thoughts on that, too, I wonder?'

Goodly and Tzonov followed him down, the latter cautioning: 'Be careful! I know you believe he's just a man — Harry Keogh's son, but without his father's powers — and it seems I have to agree with you. But we still can't be sure. If he's Wamphyri . . . that could well be the very last thing you discover about him!' There was malice in his voice, almost a wish, perhaps a death wish: for Trask and Goodly. In mentioning Premier Turchin, advocate general of Russia's New Democracy, Trask had obviously touched a raw nerve.

A chair stood opposite the cage, with its backrest facing the steel bars. Tzonov's chair, but Trask sat down and crossed his arms on the backrest, and rested his chin on his arms. And sighing, he peered at the man from the other side of the Gate. Trask was no telepath; there was no way he could know for sure what the other was thinking, but he guessed anyway. Something of it, at least. It was written in the visitor's slumped posture: the way he sat cross-legged dead centre of the cage, arms by his sides, hands curled beside his feet, head down in utter dejection.

Tzonov came and stood on Trask's right, looking sideways and down on him. Trask avoided his glance, but in any case his hypnotic guard was up and Tzonov couldn't read him. As long as Trask was careful, he could think what he liked and know that his thoughts were inviolate. Until Siggi Dam came back on the scene, anyway. Then ... she and Tzonov might conceivably work something out between them. As for right now: Trask could hazard a guess at the reason for her absence. Tzonov didn't want her mind-smog interfering with what he'd been doing here.

'So,' Trask said, 'you've had him ... how long? An hour and a half? And after you woke him up, what then? Did you sit here looking at him, trying to get inside his head, talking to him? In how many languages, and with what result? What, nothing? And is that why you decided to send for us?'

Tzonov said, 'We've X-rayed him, and taken blood, urine, tissue, and other samples. A comprehensive range of tests. So far he's come through all of them. He looks normal, human. But I repeat, this is not conclusive proof. He came from the world beyond the Gate and could be anything but human. Now, the fact is you know far more about that other world than we do. Your beloved Harry told you all about it; well, a great deal about it. That is one of the reasons why you are here: because you might see and recognize something in him that we would miss.

'As for my telepathy: useless, on this one. Eye to eye, I meet a whirl, a swirl, a vortex which spins so rapidly that it shines! His mind is impenetrable. I had thought it might be an effect of his being on the other side of the event horizon, but I was wrong. Now that he's on our side, it's just the same. It seems he's one of those rare individuals who can't be read.'

'Not so rare among Sunside's Travellers,' Trask answered. 'Many of them are skilled in physical and mental camouflage. Hunted by vampires, it's been a matter of survival, evolution, for them. In our world the Eskimos have an extra layer of fat, to combat the cold. So the Travellers are resistant to telepathic probes, to combat the Wamphyri.' He didn't mention that Harry was the same in the end, after he'd become a vampire.

In any case, what he had said was news to Tzonov. 'Ah!' the Russian sighed — before his tone hardened. 'But couldn't you have mentioned this before? It's hardly a classic example of cooperation!'

'True,' Trask answered, 'but then, over the course of the last few hours the pebbles in our "wall of trust" have suffered no small amount of subsidence. Indeed, you could even say that the wall is teetering!'

Tzonov ignored the jibe, began to pace to and fro behind Trask where he continued to stare at the visitor in his cage. 'So,' the Russian mused, 'this ability of his — this talent? — to deflect my telepathy, is a natural thing. In which case, he will have to learn our language.'

And Goodly added, 'Or we can learn his. That shouldn't be too hard: Romanian with a smattering of Slavonic, Germanic, and true Romany. A good linguist, preferably an empath, could pick it up in a week. We have just such a man in London.'

'Oh?' Tzonov paused in his pacing and met Goodly face to face. 'And are we gullible as well as incompetent? Perhaps we should simply give our visitor to you, to take back to London with you! And perhaps with your help he could also develop his father's powers, eh? No, Mr Goodly, I think I can choose just such an empath from the members of my own branch.'

Goodly smiled wryly. 'So much for first name terms,' he said.

It was exactly the sort of diversion Trask had been looking for. He wasn't a telepath, but someone had spoken to him in his dreams. Now, concentrating his mind, he thought at the visitor: *Who are you? What's your name? Do you know that you're in danger, that the people in this place — especially this man — will either find a way to use you, or keep you imprisoned, or even kill you?*

He wasn't hoping for any kind of answer, but:

The man in the cage didn't move his body an inch, but his head lifted a fraction and his deep blue eyes looked straight into Trask's. And:

Don't! the answer came back, causing Trask to start in his chair. *I understand all of this, but say nothing, do nothing! Tzonov's talent is huge!*

'What?' The Russian esper spun on his heel, away from Goodly, grasped Trask's shoulder and stared at the visitor, whose head was back on his chest. And again he hissed: 'What was *that*?' In his effort of concentration, his forehead had creased into a hundred wrinkles.

'Eh?' Trask looked up at him, his hypnotic shield firmly back in place. 'What was what?'

Tzonov released his shoulder, took two paces to the bars and grasped them. 'You!' he spat the word at the visitor. 'Did you speak?' He shook the bars until the man in the cage looked up. 'On your feet!' Tzonov shouted. 'Speak to me!'

The visitor sat there, looked sad, puzzled.

Trask stood up and went to Tzonov. 'If he can't understand you, where's the sense in shouting at him?'

Tzonov looked at him, frustration etched in every line of his face. 'You didn't hear him speak?'

Trask shook his head. 'Not a word.'

'In your mind?'

Trask took a pace to the rear and frowned, he hoped convincingly. 'Are you mad? You're the telepath, Turkur, not me!'

The Russian breathed deeply, regained control of himself. 'Then why do I feel that you're getting more out of this than I am? Perhaps it was a mistake to bring you here. I think I'll have to talk to a higher authority.'

'As you wish.' Trask shrugged. 'But before that, why don't you let me try to get through to him? I mean here and now – in front of you – all above board and out in the open, as they say?' The last thing he wanted right now was to be ordered out of the laboratory, even out of Perchorsk, leaving the visitor to Tzonov's tender mercies and methods.

Tzonov considered it, calmed down more yet, finally said: 'It can do no harm. He is after all my prisoner, and whatever he tells you he tells me.'

Trask sighed, 'My, how the wall crumbles!' and turned back to the visitor. Except this time he didn't dare play with telepathy; he must simply hope that the man in the cage was tuned in to all of this. 'Can you hear me?' he inquired in the warmest, calmest voice he could muster. 'Listen, we're your friends. We only want to find out about you. But how can we if you won't respond?'

Nothing. The visitor sat there as before.

'Perhaps I was mistaken,' Tzonov quietly commented, after a moment's silence. 'But when you were sitting there looking . . . at . . . him . . . !'

Stiffening his back and neck, the visitor had straightened up a little. He was looking at Trask, and there was something of interest in his eyes and expression in general. 'People are like animals,' Trask said in that same reassuring tone, without taking his eyes from the other's face. 'They know when they're up against a friend, an enemy, someone kind or someone . . . not so kind. Sunside's Travellers are probably highly sensitive in this respect. It's in the expression, the voice and eyes. Your eyes can be especially frightening, Turkur. They look under a man's skin, into his mind, his soul.'

He smiled and signalled that the caged man should stand up, and the other slowly got to his feet. 'There now,' Trask said, 'and maybe we can take it a step further, play Jane and Tarzan with him.' Placing his right palm flat on his chest, he said; 'Trask. Ben Trask.' Then, pointing at the other, he let his expression frame a question mark. And:

'Nathan,' said the other, hand on chest. 'Nathan Kiklu.'

'More than I got out of him in an hour!' Tzonov rasped.

'Then be quiet,' Trask told him, but in the same reasoned tone of voice,' and give me a chance to do a little better.'

He stuck a hand through the bars, and heard the Russian's sharp *hiss* of apprehension and warning. The visitor also heard it, and his eyes narrowed as his expression became suspicious. Trask turned his hand palm up, thrust it hard between the bars, offered it more forcefully. And the other relaxed, reached out and grasped Trask's wrist as he in turn grasped the visitor's. It was the Szgany handshake, as Trask remembered it from Harry Keogh's description of Sunside's nomads.

The contact did a lot for both men. It told Nathan Kiklu that Trask was his friend, also that he might indeed have been his father's. Where else could he have learned this greeting, if not from a Traveller or someone who knew the customs of Sunside? And to Trask it confirmed what he would quite happily – what he might already – have bet his life on: that the visitor was human. Entirely human. It was in the warmth of his touch, the conviction of his friendship, the irrefutable evidence of Trask's talent: that this was the real thing.

Finally they released each other, stepped back a little. And Trask softly said, 'Nathan, can you understand me? Do you understand anything of what I'm saying?' It was nothing short of a subterfuge, a red herring, a ploy to gain a little time. Trask already knew that the other understood a great deal, not only of his situation but also of the political intrigue going on around him. Or if not that, at least he recognized the principal players and had determined which side to come down on.

The other played up to it: he shrugged, tapped himself on the chest again, and said: 'Nathan?' His face was a picture of innocence.

Trask pointed into the palm of his left hand, and said: 'Hand.'

Nathan nodded. 'Hanta!'

'German!' Goodly said. 'Or as good as.'

Trask crouched down a little and touched his own foot. 'Fusse?'

Nathan looked blank. 'Bindera?'

Goodly said, 'In German, legs are *die Beine*.'

Trask reached inside his pocket, brought out something like the kernel of a large nut. He held it out to the man in the cage, but Tzonov stepped forward to grab his arm. 'What's this?'

'The best proof of his humanity that you're ever likely to see,' Trask told him. 'It's a clove of garlic!'

Nathan was interested. He reached through the bars and took the clove, held it to his nose and sniffed as if it were some exotic flower. And indeed it might seem to hold some rare fragrance for him, such was his expression. Then ... it was as if memories of old times had misted up his eyes as the previous soulful look returned.

238

Goodly said, 'Garlic: Knoblauch.'

And Nathan said, 'Kneblasch.'

Trask turned to Tzonov. 'So much for your concern about his humanity, Turkur. This one's no vampire. I'm wearing a silver ring, but he clasped forearms with me. And he treats garlic as if it were his national flower or emblem. That's a measure of his respect, which I for one understand readily enough.'

'Maybe you understand more than you're saying,' the other answered darkly. 'But . . . I'm grateful to you. You have made a start, at least. One which I can, what — capitalize? – upon. And now I must ask you to leave.'

'Leave?' Trask stared at him. Perhaps he stared too long and hard, until his suspicious, anxious thoughts were visible. But in any case, the Russian shook his smooth dome of a head.

'No, not Perchorsk, not just yet, anyway. You have shown a measure of goodwill in this thing, despite that you consider my methods draconian and unfair. And so I'm willing to forget our differences, for the present at least. I meant only that you should leave this laboratory, go back to your rooms, and get a good night's sleep. Tomorrow you may continue what you were doing, these language lessons. Meanwhile, I'll arrange to have someone flown in who knows Romanian and the romance languages in general, probably an empath.'

Goodly spoke up. 'What about Nathan's rights, Turkur? Or being an "alien", doesn't he have any? Think how you're treating him. Why, he can't even lie down in this birdcage, not in any comfort! Are you going to keep him here all night? Do you think it will impress him to take you into his confidence?'

Tzonov merely glanced at him, then offered an exasperated, irritated shrug. 'Do you two know how aggressive you are? Whenever I try to be flexible, you reply with criticism! But as I've tried to explain, these measures – this cage and cleansing area – are only temporary precautions until we can be sure of him. Even now we can't relax, not with one hundred per cent confidence, until the results of our tests are known. But acting on your reassurances ... yes, I am willing to ease up a little. Which is why I require you to leave. You see, I intend to move him – right now, tonight – to more suitable but nevertheless secure accommodation.'

Trask grunted a barely perceptible, 'Huh!' Following it with: 'And you don't want us to see where you're putting him, right?'

'That is part of it,' the Russian answered truthfully. 'But as for the rest: nothing has changed. It's for your own safety! You are my guests here. Think how it would look, how I would feel, if some harm should befall you.'

They might have argued the point but Tzonov was through with talking. He called for the soldier on the door, and the British espers were escorted back to their rooms. Left alone, they talked for a little while, but both men were weary now.

As Trask readied himself for bed, Goodly stuck his head into the room. 'What about him?' he said.

'What about who?'

'About the visitor, Nathan Kiklu ... or Nathan Keogh? One thing's certain: this isn't the Harry Junior who we knew. He's much too young, and we know that the Dweller was a vampire when last Harry saw him. But according to David Chung, something of the Necroscope has come back. So what do you think?'

'You saw him, didn't you?' Trask got into bed. 'Chung's right: Kiklu may be his name, but Keogh was his father. He's not the Dweller, no, but he is a son of Harry Keogh. I mean, he has Harry written all over him! Then there's that earring of his. Didn't you notice it?'

'I noticed it,' Goodly nodded. 'Harry's Möbius sigil, yes! Interesting times ahead, Ben. Interesting times.'

Trask was tempted to mention something else: that Nathan had spoken to him in his waking and dreaming hours alike. But spoken to him *in his mind*, when Trask wasn't even a telepath. He was tempted, but kept it to himself. A case of what Goodly didn't know, Goodly wouldn't think about. And in a place like this, what he wouldn't think about couldn't hurt him . . .

IV

Nathan and Siggi

While Trask and Goodly prepared for sleep, Turkur Tzonov spoke to Siggi Dam in her room. Pacing the floor before her where she lay sprawled on her bed, his attitude was far from romantic; in any case, what had passed before was mainly for show; they had been lovers some years ago, an affair which terminated when he discovered his rivals – or rather, how many rivals. Currently when they were brought together by their work, they were still 'lovers', but it was no longer the state of being, just the act.

'Some progress has been made, but not enough,' he told her. 'Tomorrow the British will want to see him again, and it would not be prudent to stop them. When we have some more of our own people here, that will be time enough. Meanwhile, it can't hurt to go through these tediously slow processes. After that we'll only let Trask talk to our visitor for an hour or so at a time, and always under supervision. Proving Nathan's humanity – and so far the results of our tests do appear positive in his favour – was only the first step. Discovering why he's here, and especially at this time . . . that is now our top priority.'

'You don't think it's just a coincidence?' Siggi sat up and stretched, arms above her head, breasts jutting, the platinum flow of her hair highlighting her strong jaw. Looking at her, Tzonov could almost wish he was free tonight.

'I think it most probably is a coincidence,' he answered, 'but best to be sure. What, the son – or *a* son – of the Necroscope, Harry Keogh, here in Perchorsk again? An outcast from Starside? Oh really? Or is he something else entirely? Did he escape here, or was he sent? And if the latter, why? And so it goes. We need answers to all these questions . . .'

Siggi had been asleep for an hour or two. Her night-gown was of very flimsy stuff: white chiffon, shot through with metallic silver lamé. Looking at her, again Tzonov caught himself wishing that he was free tonight. But no, he intended to supervise his soldiers – *his* soldiers, a hand-picked platoon which he had managed to infiltrate into this place over a period of time – in the removal and relocation of their arms cache to a secure, more discreet armoury on a disused magmass level below the core. In another hour or so, when only a handful of scientists remained on duty, then he'd be able to make a start.

And between times he had calls to make; not least to the Kremlin, to report the occurrences of the day, but also to his own E-Branch HQ on Protze Prospekt, to enlist the skills of an empath-linguist. These and several other administrative tasks would keep him amply occupied through the small hours, and in any case he was tired and felt the need to conserve his energies. In a purely physical sense Siggi could be very demanding. And there again, he had other plans for her . . .

It was not usual for Sigrid Dam to read the minds of her colleagues, but on this occasion she was curious about Turkur Tzonov's mental state. Normally he would be implacably stable, indeed unshakable, but occurrences over the last week seemed to have unnerved him in however small a degree. Siggi was his confidante, it could even be said his 'right-hand man' in the scheme he'd been hatching for several years now: to usurp the Soviet Premier and elevate Russia to world domination via the untapped resources of an alien world. The timing of the coup was crucial and hinged upon an invasion of the parallel world of Sunside/Starside. When the time was ripe Tzonov would make his move: first Premier Turchin's removal by use of some discreetly ephemeral poison, by which time Tzonov's seat on the Demokratik Politburo would have been secured. Then, with the esoteric resources of E-Branch for back-up, he would propose himself for Premier and almost certainly be elected. In the interim his soldiers would have invaded the world beyond the Perchorsk Gate, returning via the Romanian Gate with first-hand knowledge – and even the first fruits? – of whatever was on offer in that unknown, primitive, and incredibly dangerous place.

But Tzonov was well aware that he was not the first esper to plot political ... revitalization? And he knew only too well the difficulties his predecessors had come up against. The name of one such obstacle had become a curse among the rank and file of Soviet E-Branch: Harry Keogh. But for sixteen years now the man or monster known as the Necroscope had been banished from the face of the Earth, until finally he'd become little more than a myth, a legend, a bad dream. Old fears that one day he might return – fears shared by British E-Branch no less than its Soviet equivalent – had not been realized. Possibly the Necroscope was dead; certainly the British thought so. Or was it that Keogh had not been able, or simply hadn't desired, to return?

And now this visitor, this Nathan Kiklu.

A refugee from a vampire world? Or a spy for monstrous Wamphyri masters on Starside? That remained to be discovered. That and whatever else Tzonov could learn from him. The trick would be to ensure that the British espers didn't learn more. It rankled a little that they were here by order of Gustav Turchin on Tzonov's own recommendation; but in fact he'd believed they would be needed. Now that they were no longer required he must continue to be their host of sorts, and at the same time learn whatever he could from them, especially with regard to their previous knowledge of Sunside/Starside.

It was all very delicate, complicated, fraught with pitfalls. But until the visitor had been thoroughly interrogated and dealt with, and British E-Branch were out of here, and the whole seething cauldron had settled down somewhat, Tzonov must tread warily and hold his greater plans in abeyance ...

Many of these things in Turkur Tzonov's mind were 'overheard' by Siggi. Since she was already aware of their theme in general, they made no significant impact. But certain thoughts of his *had* impacted upon her: in particular, his vague but less than gallant reference to what he would term her promiscuity. Knowing Tzonov's psychological problem – his egocentricity, the fact that it bordered on egomania – Siggi was also aware of the paradox: that he was jealous and possessive beyond all reasonable bounds. It was the reason he changed partners so frequently. Only let one of his women display the slightest awareness of or interest in another man ... he would fly into a rage and the affair would be over. But Siggi also knew that if the day should ever dawn when Tzonov came up against a man who was his mental, physical, and political superior all three, then he'd be finished. So far that day was a long way off, but still his nerves showed ragged edges in the presence of men like Trask and Goodly. They may not be his physical equivalent, but mentally they were probably a match for him; it took some of the shine off his ego.

Tzonov had stopped pacing and was looking at her. 'Oh? Is there something . . . ?' Perhaps it was the look on her face.

She shook her head, changed her mind and nodded. 'Perhaps there is. Turkur, we're agreed that you are the leader and I am a mere follower however high in the ranks, and that in some not too distant future my loyalty shall be suitably rewarded. Not a very novel scenario, but still I've gone along with it in every respect; so much so that I'm probably guilty of treason against the state, and certainly against its Premier.'

He frowned and nodded. 'Both of us, Siggi, and E-Branch, and all of our agents and recruits, including certain Generals in the so-called "Citizen's Army". So what are you getting at?'

'Only this,' she answered, sitting up straighter. 'If I'm really your Second-in-Command, which is the next best thing to being your partner, then I wish you'd stop thinking of me as a slut!'

'Do I?' He looked surprised.

'You think of me as . . . promiscuous,' she answered, 'to say the very least. You can't even look at me without remembering your "rivals". But they weren't rivals, merely lovers, and briefly at that. If I were to dwell upon all of your conquests in a similar light, what would that make you? A lech, a rake, a bloated and diseased roué? Being male, perhaps it would please you to be so considered. But I'm a woman and it doesn't please me!'

His pale eyebrows came together as his frown grew more intense, curiosity turning to anger. 'My dear,' he said, his words very precise so as to make their meaning clear and unmistakable, 'promiscuity is not the word. That would simply mean that you were indiscriminate in your sexual relations. And I would never think of you as a slut, which for me describes a common person of very low intelligence, whose body is worthless. No, you've read me wrong. You are neither indiscriminate nor common, but simply . . . unbalanced.'

'*What?*' She stood up, faced him, shrugged into her dressing-gown and belted it tightly.

'Oh yes,' he insisted. 'It's all in the mind. I've known it for a long time, and I'm sure that you have, too. You're a nymphomaniac, Siggi. That is how I think of you, because it's what you are. Men hold this morbid fascination for you. Almost *all* men!'

'*Get out!*' she said. All the colour had drained from her face. 'In this instance, rank has no privileges. You're in my room, and I want you out of it! And I don't ever want to see you in it again!'

'Of course you don't.' He smiled thinly. 'Until the next time, when your needs overcome your disgust – of yourself!'

'Out!' she said again, and made to stride to the door. He caught her wrist, brought her to a halt. And his anger was as great as her own.

'Siggi, listen. This is nothing new but how it always was between us. It's the reason our relationship failed. But there are relationships and relationships. And there must be discipline in our working relationship! What you said a moment ago is true: in the eyes of all the dupes of this great country of ours and its so-called "demokratik system", we would be traitors. If our ties are weakened by sexual conflict, that's as it may be, but it must not be allowed to interfere with our purpose, our goal overall.'

She was calmer now. 'What, and am I a fool as well

as a slut? Of course we must continue to work together –
or fall together. But right now I would prefer you out of
here. I have to dress. And as for your thoughts about my
personal life, in future you can keep them to yourself.'

'That's where you have the advantage,' he told her.
'Your thoughts are guarded – hidden in mind-smog –
whereas you can read mine like the pages of an open
book!'

It was true, she knew. Telepathy was a two-edged
sword. If one was curious to look into another mind,
one must accept its contents. Tzonov could no more
disassociate himself from his thoughts than from his
limbs. They were a part of him.

And now he was thinking about this Nathan, and the
instructions which he had previously given to her. He
was about to issue a caution, one which she could read
in his mind (even as he himself had acknowledged) 'like
the pages of an open book'.

'Don't worry,' she told him, however grudgingly, as
she opened the door to let him out. 'I'll go to Nathan
and talk to him, see if I can worm my way past this
freakish talent of his. We seem to be two of a type, this
primitive and I. Perhaps our shields can be made to
cancel each other out. If it's at all possible, I'll get into
his mind for you.'

'Good!' Tzonov looked at Siggi one last time, luring her
eyes with his own. A wasted effort; her static got in the
way; he could only read her when she desired to be read.
And at the same time he'd left himself wide open. There
was another instruction, a final order in his mind . . . but he
was wise enough to leave it unspoken. It concerned Siggi
and Nathan: what she must *not* do when she was with him.

Closing the door in his face, she thought: *Fuck you!*
But she made sure she kept the thought to herself . . .

*

In her anger, Siggi was no less human than any other woman or man, and it was only after Tzonov had gone that she knew what she should have said to him: that the level of sexual activity in any normally healthy body is only as high or low as opportunity will allow. How many affairs die stillborn because their would-be authors are afraid to voice their feelings? But with a telepath . . . ? When Siggi met a man who wanted her, she knew it at once, as surely as if he had whispered in her ear! Why, sometimes it was as if he had shouted! And if he should have that special something that attracted her – that indefinable something, that sex appeal, which is different for all women, thereby allowing for relationships between all types – what then? Knowing what was available, was she supposed to ignore it?

But by the same token, and once the first flush of sexual excitement had burned itself out, she would also know the rest of her lover's thoughts. She knew too well the luscious, juicy, shivering lust that could turn to a weird disgust just as soon as a man had fired himself into her; knew also that the moment she read such a thing in a lover's mind – the first time he thought of her in such terms, in her entirety, as a darkly quaking, coarse-haired, sucking hole – then that the affair was over. Even if the thought was fleeting, transient, still it signalled the end, always. But while it was painful, Siggi had learned to accept it; she knew that another lover would come along soon enough and the first flush be reborn.

Ordinary lovers were fortunate, in a way. Because their minds were their own and inviolable – because they could not see the truth, the various disaffections and dissatisfactions gradually growing up between them – they tended to pretend it was always good and

249

unchanging, that their sex together would always be like the first time. It was a ploy that even worked for some of them, and their love lasted a lifetime. But only for a few, for even the blind are not deaf and dumb, too.

And yet Siggi was not without hope. Somewhere, sometime, she might meet a man like herself, whose mind was unfathomable, a secret thing known only to himself. And there was an old saying that was never far from her thoughts: what the eye doesn't see, the mind won't grieve. Two choices then: find a lover who would be satisfied quite simply to *love* her, in every sense of the word, or one with the skill (and the compassion?) to keep his baser thoughts to himself. Ah! – *and* of course the will to keep from reading her own!

And so ... a sex maniac? No. But a realist, an opportunist, a desperate searcher? And was Tzonov himself any different, any better? Siggi knew that he was not, but that unlike herself he had not yet come to terms with it. Nor could he while his ego intruded. He had called her a nymphomaniac because his *ego* demanded it. 'Obviously' there was a flaw in her psychological make-up, for any 'normal' woman couldn't possibly find time for other men, not while Turkur Tzonov was around. What were other men anyway, compared to him? Yet in Siggi's case ... her taste in all other matters was impeccable. Wherefore this was not a matter of taste but addiction. Hence his use of that word which describes a woman addicted to men ...

Such were the warped convolutions of Tzonov's thinking when facing a problem that challenged his ego. And such was Siggi's assessment of him as she prepared to interrogate, in her way, this visitor, this Nathan Kiklu.

As for Tzonov's unspoken 'instruction', that she conduct her interrogation on a purely impersonal level: she had never intended anything else. Nathan was from the alien world of Sunside/Starside, and scientific tests to the contrary, who could say what alien things might or might not lurk in his blood? His mind was of far greater concern than his body. But on the other hand ... perhaps Turkur should be made to understand how Siggi despised this sort of interference. She was her own person – or anyone else's to whom she might care to give herself.

Siggi dressed slowly and thoughtfully, and was careful to avoid any sort of uniformed or military appearance. She didn't want to seem aloof, or in any sense official, ascetic, clinical. She was the scented glove – or as the British might have it, the 'soft sell' – as opposed to the clenched fist, and must appear more girl than woman, more nurse than inquisitor. He wasn't an innocent, this man from the Gate; she had known that much from the first time she saw him on the viewscreens. But he was far too young, wild – and primitive, yes, as the place he'd come from – to be too well-versed in the ways and wiles of women. Especially the sophisticated women of Earth.

So thought Sigrid Dam, who could make mistakes just like any other woman. And of any other world ...

When she had finished dressing, she examined the result in her room's less than adequate mirror. Her choice of earth colours, despite that she knew they didn't compliment her own, had been deliberate; she didn't want to seem too bright or – alien? – to the visitor. According to what little the Soviet E-Branch knew of Sunside/Starside, it was a dull world, dark, dreary; which the pale browns and yellows of Nathan's clothes might seem to corroborate. A Gypsy world, peopled by nomadic tribes on one side of barrier mountains, and Wamphyri on the other.

All such knowledge, what little there was of it, had been supplied by the British in that brief period of esper *glasnost* following Harry Keogh's vampiric metamorphism and his escape to Starside, and Siggi well understood Tzonov's eagerness to learn more about the world beyond the Gate and its inhabitants. Not only to go one up on what the British already knew, but more as an important equation in his preparations. Of course, for this was the world he intended to conquer, to make it a new satellite of Mother Russia – unless it conquered first. And in that respect, she understood something of Tzonov's fears, too. For he had shown her the Perchorsk archive tapes of previous . . . visitors.

She shuddered, put those pictures firmly from her mind, and examined herself one last time:

Statuesque, she could well have stepped off the cover of one of the West's glossy magazines, but *not* out of the fashion section. Not unless Gypsies were back in fashion! Well, that was a contrivance and she mustn't complain. This wasn't going to be a night out in Paris, or an evening of Californian Chardonnay, sexual innuendo, and telepathic surveillance at the American embassy in Moscow, after all.

But Romany, yes: the clothes at least, if not her looks. An ill-matched combination? Maybe. But on the other hand, the visitor didn't look much like a Gypsy either. He could even be Danish, a fellow countryman! Well, once upon a time. Only his clothes looked Romany. And perhaps his single golden earring. But even that didn't signify a great deal. They were back in fashion for men here in this world, too.

She wore a tasselled jacket of light-brown suede over a leaf-green blouse fastened with a jade clasp, and a flared cotton skirt patterned with autumn leaves. If she were a little less tall, brown-skinned, with black hair and eyes ... perhaps she could be a woman like the ones he had known. And Siggi wondered how many he'd known, and how well. But in any case he was little more than a boy, and she must become his sister, a sympathetic contact in this strange new world.

Stepping into the corridor, Siggi found her escort waiting for her. The young, tired-looking soldier snapped erect, saluted, and shouldered his rifle. It was well past midnight and she could appreciate his weariness. Apart from essential duties, the Perchorsk complex was now as quiet and suffocating as a tomb. Like a vast mausoleum, yes. And for a moment, Siggi could even feel the mountain pressing down on her.

On their way to Nathan's cell, she asked her escort: 'Do you have orders?'

'Only to escort you, Madame, and let you into the prisoner's room. And to wait outside, of course, until you have finished and call for me.'

'That could be most of the night.'

He shrugged and made no answer.

She thought about Nathan. She'd been there when they fed him drugged food and brought him through the Gate. The son – or *a* son – of a man they'd known as the Necroscope. Siggi had read the Keogh files and found their story ... what, fantastic? No, much more than that. The story of a man who could move himself bodily, instantaneously, to any spot on Earth? A teleport, yes, and the first of his kind. Also, he'd talked to the dead, and even had the power to call them up from their graves! And at the end he'd been a vampire, indeed Wamphyri! That was the last time anyone saw him, when he'd disappeared into the Gate riding an American motorcycle.

But it wasn't the first time Keogh had been to Starside. Four years earlier, British E-Branch had sent him there on a mission: to find an agent who'd been lost while spying on Perchorsk. That had been . . . oh, twenty or so years ago? And now this Nathan had come through the Gate, just twenty or so years old. Keogh's son? It seemed reasonable. But it *didn't* seem to be a case of like father, like son. For if he'd inherited his father's powers, there'd be no holding him here. Or anywhere else, for that matter!

Turkur Tzonov considered his arrival coincidental to his plans. But obviously he had to be sure. That in a nutshell was Siggi's mission: find out why he'd come. Was it of his own volition or someone else's? If the latter, what was the nature of his masters, how many of them were there, and when would they be following on behind? Finally, if his answers were satisfactory – if there was no immediate danger or any requirement for extraordinary action – then it would be time to drain him of his knowledge concerning Sunside/Starside preparatory to Tzonov's invasion . . .

They had reached the door to Nathan's room, more properly his cell. In the old days, doors in Perchorsk had all been equipped with locking devices. Following a number of catastrophic accidents and incidents, when too many lives were lost behind locked doors, most of them had been replaced by easier mechanisms. This cell was one of the few remaining rooms with a door that locked. It was also fitted with a small metal panel, like a window, with a catch on the outside.

The soldier had a key to let Siggi in, but as he produced it she said, 'Here, let me.' He held his rifle at the ready as she turned the key in the lock and opened the door. Inside the room, Nathan half-reclined on his bed, clothed and fully awake. He saw Siggi and the soldier, and his eyes narrowed to stare at the gun in the latter's capable hands. But Siggi only smiled at him, shook her head and closed the door behind her, leaving the soldier outside. He at once turned the key in the lock, rapped on the hatch and opened it. 'Madame, will you be all right?'

She looked at his concerned face framed in a small metal square, and said, 'I'm sure that with you out there, all will be well. Now then, close the hatch and please don't bother us again.' However reluctantly, he obeyed her, and as the observation window closed she turned to face Nathan. He was on his feet, nervous as a cat and blinking his startling blue eyes.

She kept smiling, motioned him to sit down, then gave the cell a cursory inspection. A bed, chair, washbasin and chamber pot – so much for accommodation. It might as well be Lubianka in the time of Khrushchev! Then she looked at Nathan.

He was a six-footer, athletic if a little awkward in his movements, shy-looking and yet . . . not innocent. It was what she'd noticed in him before, when she'd seen him on the viewscreens. His eyes, despite being soulful, were also knowing. She crossed to the chair, took it to where he sat on his bed, and sat facing him only a few feet away.

'I'm Siggi,' she said, low-voiced.

He frowned. 'Siggi?'

She nodded and touched her breast. 'Siggi, yes.'

He sighed, as if to say, *What, that again?* Then answered drily, sourly: 'Nathan. Nathan Kiklu.'

'All right,' she said, smiling tightly now, 'I shall try not to be so boring.' And then, without warning, she turned up her full telepathic power and said: *Nathan, I know your mind is shielded. Turkur Tzonov couldn't get through to you, and so your shield must be very strong. Well, my mind is similar, but with me it's deliberate. Now, whether your talent is natural or a*

*contrivance is not my concern at this point, but if
you're not willing to help me I won't be able to help
you.*

At the first unspoken word he had started where he
sat, a small jerk of his shoulders and a tic in the corner
of his eye. That was all; followed immediately by a vain
attempt to hide his surprise behind a blank expression.
But while Siggi had not been expecting his reaction,
still she'd seen it and knew what it must mean. Why,
his mind was like a wall of bulletproof glass made
slippery with a film of oil! Spinning to create its own
centrifugal force and deflect the thoughts of others,
nothing could penetrate or even stick to it. But it didn't
stop Nathan from looking out through it. So much for innocence!

Just why Siggi had tried it she didn't know – a
hunch, that's all – but it had worked. Now, sighing her
wonder and sitting back a little from Nathan, she was
suddenly aware of what she was dealing with here: the
fact that he was from an alien world, and the son of
Harry Keogh, and capable of telepathic reception, all in
one. But then ... what other powers did he have? And
was he as human as Tzonov thought he was?

You're an alien! She couldn't help the thought. *Why,
you could even be Wamphyri!* He could be, yes, hiding
behind this shy, seemingly innocuous facade. He just
could be!

Suddenly Siggi was very cold and trembling. She felt
the short hairs stiffening at the back of her neck;
gooseflesh, not only on her arms, legs and spine but
creeping in her mind, too! This man – this thing? –
could be Wamphyri!

She remembered archive film of a Wamphyri soldier
who had come through the Gate. Perchorsk's defenders,
Russian soldiers on our side of the portal, had blistered

him with their flamethrower and pulped his legs with their automatic rifles, until he'd been brought to his knees ... but only figuratively. For even when he was down, still they hadn't quelled his spirit.

The film rolled again on the screen of Siggi's mind: He'd kneeled there mewling on the gantry in front of the glaring white hell of the Gate, a crippled man for all to see, grey as a corpse and splashed with blood, his own and that of those he'd slaughtered. Yet even as it had dawned on him that this must be the end, so the thing inside him had denied it!

He had looked like a man, but now ...

His mouth yawned open – it opened, opened, opened – oh, impossibly wide! A forked tongue, scarlet, lashed in the cave of his throat. His jaws elongated visibly, making a sound like tearing sailcloth; fleshy lips rolled back in a froth of saliva until they split and spurted blood, revealing crimson gums and jagged, dripping teeth. The entire mouth resembled nothing so much as the pulped, rabidly yawning muzzle of a wolf. But the rest of the face had been as bad if not worse!

The squat nose had broadened out more yet, developing convoluted ridges like the snout of a bat, with moist, quivering nostrils in dark, wrinkled leather. The ears, previously flat to the head, had sprouted coarse hair, growing upward and outward to form red-veined, nervously mobile shapes like fleshy conches. And in this respect, too, the effect was batlike. Or maybe demoniac.

For hell was written in those features and limned in the nightmare expression of that face: a visage which was part bat, part wolf, and all horror! And still it wasn't over.

Before, the eyes had been small, piggish and deep-sunken. Now they were grown to gorged leeches,

*bulging crimson in their sockets. And the teeth ... they
gave new meaning to nightmare. For growing and curving up through the lacerated ribbons of the creature's
gums, those bone knives had so torn his mouth that it
filled with his own blood!*

*As for the rest of his body, that had remained merci-
fully manlike; but through all of his metamorphosis his
ravaged trunk and legs had taken on a dull leaden
gleam, and his entire form had vibrated with an incredible palsy.*

*Then they'd burned him up, hosed him down with
chemical fire, melted him to smoke, steam and stench. It
had been over. It was all over, dissolving like a shadow
in sunlight from the screen of Siggi's mind ... except
for the one thing which she remembered above all
others: that at first, he'd looked just like a man!*

Frozen to her chair. She couldn't move, think, speak.
And Nathan was standing up, reaching for her. He
touched her, held her shoulder, squeezed — but gently!
And now she saw what his whirling shield was composed of: numbers. Nathan's secret mind was hidden
behind an enormous mutating equation! Maths, astonishing maths ... in a man from a largely innumerate
world? All of this was too much; she didn't know
enough about him, didn't know anything! She should
call out for the soldier in the corridor, but there was a
lump in her throat.

His oh-so-gentle touch ... she made to shrink back
from it, but her back was against the back of the steel
chair. And in any case, a moment after he touched her
the numbers vortex had disintegrated into a thousand
shattered fractions, revealing Nathan's thoughts.

I'm NOT *Wamphyri,* he said, emphatically. *The
Wamphyri are my enemies. I'm here because of them,
not as their agent. This is some kind of unjust punish-*

ment, *I think, for a crime I never committed and don't even understand. Do you think I want to be here, in the hell-lands beyond the Starside Gate? I want to be back on Sunside with my young wife . . .*

These were the jumbled thoughts he aimed at Siggi, while behind them she sensed his pain, frustration, and bewilderment. And most of all his loneliness. Suddenly Nathan's hand on her shoulder was warm and very human; she *felt* his humanity coming right through her clothing, and she wasn't cold any more.

She breathed deeply, controlled herself, and said: *I've come here to question you. You come from a terrible place. There's a man who wants to be sure of you. He wants to know your purpose here. He thinks —*

'— I know what the mentalist Turkur Tzonov thinks,' Nathan broke in. 'He's (*ambitious?*) and thinks a great many things, some of which are correct, some incorrect, and others which are simply wrong. He's a (*schemer?*), a would-be warlord, hungry for power. He would examine me, (*subvert?*) me to his cause if possible, put me to use in his schemes. And if he can't, then he'll kill me! Through me, using my (*knowledge?*) of the world beyond the Gate, he would invade and (*conquer?*), not only the Wamphyri of Starside but also Sunside's Szgany, its Travellers! But I *am* Szgany, and I can promise you this: making war with the Travellers would be a grave error of (*judgement?*). And as for going against the Wamphyri — what, knowing as little of them as you do? — that would be a sure sign of insanity!'

From the moment she heard his first spoken words, Siggi had scarcely been able to credit Nathan's fluency in Russian, her own adopted language. And when he'd been uncertain of the words, there he'd filled in by thinking them! Finally she did believe and her mouth fell open. Then:

'Why have you chosen to remain silent?' she breathed. 'I mean, you can speak our tongue! You understand . . . everything!' Her words were so naïve as to sound stupid in her own ears.

He shrugged, but not negligently. 'Our – tongues? – are not dissimilar. And anyway, you are a clever mentalist in your own right. Don't you have a knack with tongues?'

She did, it was true, but not like this!

He read her answer in her mind, and explained, 'That's because you've come to rely too heavily on your mentalism – as a tool of your trade.' His voice was colder as he went on, 'Why trouble yourself with learning a man's tongue, mere words, when it's so much easier to steal his thoughts? Isn't that why you've come here now, to this terrible buried cell, to steal my thoughts for Turkur Tzonov?'

Siggi felt the colour rising to her face under Nathan's steady scrutiny, and said, 'We've all . . . underestimated you.' And immediately she wondered: *Why am I tongue-tied? Why does every word I say to him sound so stupid? What? Am I actually the little sister I was going to pretend to be?* It would be a clever excuse for the warmth she was starting to feel, except Siggi knew that it wasn't the warmth of a sister! And as that realization dawned, so she closed the shutters of her mind and let its mental vapours drift out, obscuring her thoughts. But no need, for Nathan had stopped reading them. As good as his word, he was no mind-spy and certainly no voyeur. Why should he be, when he could simply talk to her?

All of this taking a single second, before he told her: 'No, you have *over*estimated me! Surely you must see – I *know* you can – that I'm not your enemy? What? Only one man, and unarmed? How could I be? I don't mean you any harm, none of you. All I want right now is to get back to my own world, to what was my home before the Wamphyri returned.' Then his face and voice hardened. 'But if or when Tzonov invades Sunside, then I shall be his enemy! As for my silence: it took time to watch, listen, learn. Time to study a new tongue, in (*combination*?) with the minds that think it.'

As he let go of her, backed off a short pace and sat down on his bed, Siggi found herself fascinated anew. Entirely fascinated. Nathan was like no man she'd ever known; of course he was, for he came from a universe which ran parallel to the one we know. But there was more than that to it, a lot more than the fascination of unknown horizons, just waiting to be opened in the depths of his mind. More even than the physical attraction of his young male body, his warmth, the way his eyes spoke soulfully of indefinable yearnings, a past shadowed under the arching wings of nightmare, and an equally uncertain future.

His shield of numbers was down. Siggi could go in but no longer wanted to, not uninvited, and not until he desired it. Whatever his terms, they would be more than acceptable to her. He didn't need his telepathy to read it in her eyes.

'We'll be . . . friends?' he said, offering her a first wan smile. 'Despite Turkur Tzonov?'

'We *are* friends,' she answered, and sighed as if a great weight had been lifted from her shoulders. 'And to hell with Turkur Tzonov! Except —' she frowned. '— He will expect something out of all this.'

Nathan nodded. 'Of course. He'll expect answers, and you shall supply them . . .' He was suddenly thoughtful, withdrawn, subdued. 'But I won't tell you — him — everything, not just yet. No, he won't get all of it until . . . until he brings his machine here.'

Siggi felt her heart sinking like a stone. 'His machine?' Her voice was a whisper. She knew about such a machine, banned now throughout the civilized world, but: 'Turkur hasn't spoken to me about ... about *that!*'

'Nor has he *said* anything to me,' Nathan answered. 'But he has thought it ...'

V

Out of Perchorsk

———————

Siggi had asked him: 'What will you tell me about your-self?'

And Nathan had answered, 'Most of it, but I shall leave out anything which would help Tzonov. It could be argued that anything I tell you will be of some help to him, I know, but in fact there's a great deal that might frighten him off! He would be a fool to ignore the menace of the Wamphyri.'

'You don't know Turkur, despite what you've read in his mind,' she'd told him then. 'And you haven't seen – couldn't possibly imagine – the power of the weapons he commands. How long will it take you to tell me ... everything?'

Again Nathan's expressive shrug. 'How long is a lifetime? I can only tell it as it happened.'

'It would be shorter if I could see it, and it wouldn't exhaust you.'

'In my mind?' He had understood her meaning. 'I suppose so. But still it will take time: most of the night, maybe.'

She'd thought about it, then gone to the door and rapped on the hatch until it opened. 'Give me your key,' she'd told the young soldier. 'Then go to your bed. Your duty is over.'

'My orders are clear,' he'd answered. 'I am to –'

'But I've just changed your orders! This is the way

263

we planned it, Turkur Tzonov and I. So don't interfere with the plans of your superiors. As you can see, the prisoner is completely harmless. Also, I've a gun hidden on my person.' (These things were lies, but she went on anyway): 'In the morning, I shall return the key to Turkur personally. And that's enough of explanations. Now give me the key and I'll continue with my work, and you can go and get a good night's sleep.'

'Madame, I –'

'Or perhaps you'd prefer to explain your disobedience to Tzonov himself, right now, tonight? Maybe you'd like to go and wake him up, so that he can validate what I say?' At which the soldier had handed over the key, saluted and excused himself.

Siggi's actions had been almost automatic; she knew why she'd sent him away but would never have admitted it, consciously or otherwise, not even to herself. She was preparing the way, securing the ground, that was all; she didn't want anyone outside the door, on the other side of that window. It wasn't so much that she wanted Nathan, not yet, but if the night was going to be as long as he thought it was . . .

That had been a little less than three and a half hours ago, and now the two were asleep . . . in each other's arms.

How it had happened, neither of them would ever be sure. But as night stretched out and Perchorsk's energy requirements were reduced, so the room's temperature had fallen by several degrees. Together with their physical inactivity, this hadn't helped matters; soon they had felt the cold and eventually (in order to share their body heat, certainly) they'd sat together on Nathan's bed. Finally it had seemed only natural that Siggi should recline in his arms, and then she'd drawn a blanket up to cover their fully clothed bodies. But when Nathan had reacted to her proximity, she'd known it at once, from which time on their thoughts had gradually turned away from his story to much more intimate things. And then Siggi had known for sure why she sent the guard away.

When her curious hand had discovered him hot and pounding, Nathan had closed his mind, warning her: 'But if I love you, it will be Misha . . .' Of course, for only four or five Earth-days ago he'd been with his young Gypsy wife on Sunside.

'Not if you love me with your body, not your mind.' And she too had called up her mind-smog to obscure her thoughts.

'Even so, still you'll know it. Just as you know it now.'

'But I won't see her face in your mind.' *And what the eye can't see, the mind won't grieve.* 'I'll imagine it's me you're pleasuring. And in a purely physical sense it will be. But you have a need, Nathan, which you can relieve in me.'

'And your need?'

She had taken his hand, guided it to her hardened nipples. 'My need is to satisfy the need in you. This could well be the only chance we'll ever get. And it might be all I'm able to do for you, ever.'

'But you do have your own need?'

'I want you, yes.'

'Because I'm different? Or because you've been ordered to have me?' There had been a certain bitterness in his voice, but he'd stroked her breasts in spite of it. Siggi could hardly be expected to know that she wouldn't be the first woman who had come – or been gift-wrapped and sent – to Nathan.

'Because you are different, probably,' she'd smiled

sadly. 'But "ordered"? To love you? On the contrary, I've been told not to!'

And she had sensed his understanding, and knew that he too was his own man. 'I'm . . . forbidden?'

'Turkur likes to own things,' she had told him. 'Including people. And if he can't own something, still he'll try to deny its . . . its *use,* to others. He would like to own both of us.'

'And this will help set you free?' Her fingertips had felt like small flames, burning where they brushed.

Again her wry smile. 'Hardly that, for I'm in too deep. No, I can't be free. But *inside* I'll be like you: my own person.'

They'd been mainly free of their clothing by then, and when Siggi rolled onto him her breasts were soft, scented in his face. Her woman's juices had prepared the way, and slipping into her was so easy it came almost as a surprise. But as she'd tightened herself to control him, slow him, take charge, then Nathan had seen how expert she was. And then, too, he'd known that she wasn't and never could be Misha.

The first time had been quick, for all her control. But the second was slower, deeper, more knowing. It was as if he reached for her heart, while she in turn tried to swallow him whole. Then, when all too soon it was over and this man from a weird world fell asleep in Siggi's arms and body, she could have cried. For at the last she'd glimpsed herself in his mind, and seen how she glowed there. Not the dark, sweating, sucking thing she'd come to expect – perhaps especially this time – but a haven, a harbour, almost a holy place.

She could have cried because . . . because he might be the one! Oh, it was too early to know, but he *might* be. Except he couldn't be, not ever, because of Misha.

And so Nathan had slept in Siggi's arms as at the

house of an old friend. Then . . . she had wanted to give
him something more than her body, because it might be
her only chance to give him anything, ever. Taking her
jade clasp, she'd placed it in a pocket of his jacket. And
finally, lulled by the steady beat of his heart, in a little
while she, too, had slept . . .

. . . And slept –

– Until Turkur Tzonov woke them up!

Finished with his work, Tzonov had caught up on a
couple of hours' lost sleep until something – some dream
or other – had brought him awake. Siggi's room was
only a few doors from his own; out of curiosity (or
perhaps for some other reason), he'd looked in . . . and
the rest had seemed obvious. What? She was still
working? Right through the night? Ah, but there's work
and there's work! And now, coming here:

'Where's the guard?' His voice was a snarl, his eyes
huge and furious as he dragged her from the bed. His
automatic pistol was trained on Nathan.

Confused by sleep, Siggi tried to think. What time
was it? She glanced at her watch, which was all she
was wearing! A little after 4:30 a.m. In another hour or
so Perchorsk would be waking up. But Tzonov was
already awake, fully awake.

'I *asked* you –' He shook her.

'I *heard* you!' She shouted. 'I . . . I sent him away.'

Tzonov growled low in his throat and nodded. 'Yes,
yes of *course* you did!'

'Out there in the corridor, he was a . . . a *distraction*. I
couldn't work.'

'Work?' Tzonov looked Siggi up and down, sneering
at her nakedness. 'You couldn't . . . *work*? Ha!' He drew
back his hand and slapped her, hard, a backhander
that sent her sprawling.

Nathan was awake now, starting up from the bed. His face was white as chalk, hands reaching. Tzonov turned his gun on him and snarled through clenched teeth: 'Come on, show me how you Travellers fight for your sluts. Give me a reason to blow your guts all over the room!'

Nathan held back, trembling, cold sweat marbling his brow. His eyes were rapt on the Russian's ugly blued-steel pistol, which held him at bay. But if Tzonov had been unarmed . . .

. . . Just this minute risen from sleep and still confused, for the first time Nathan's mind was unguarded, wide open to Turkur Tzonov. Eye-to-eye contact: the Russian read Nathan's angry thoughts and glanced down at the gun in his hand.

'What, this?' In control again, but barely, he knew how close he had come to using it. 'Is this what's stopping you? This and my threat? Oh no, my young friend; I want you alive and kicking! For now, anyway . . .'

Their contact worked in two directions. Once more Nathan saw a monstrous machine in Tzonov's mind – a mechanical vampire, feeding, with himself as its victim! The thing ate his brain with electrical fire, and left his skull an empty shell. But Nathan wasn't alone, for this time Siggi saw it too. Then Tzonov blinked and the picture was gone, and his mind seemed sheathed in ice.

He applied the safety-catch on his gun, flipped back the left-hand drape of his jacket and drove the weapon home in its underarm holster. 'Very well,' he said, 'let's see what you've got if we dispense with –'

But Nathan was already moving – and Siggi was shouting at him, 'Nathan, don't!' Too late.

As Nathan came flying from the bed, Tzonov seemed to back off a pace. But coldly efficient, even robotic in the precision of his movements, at the last moment the Russian stepped to the right, grasped Nathan's left wrist, twisted and leaned back. In mid-flight but descending, Nathan found himself flipped forward in an uncontrolled somersault. And before releasing him, Tzonov used his own body as a pivot and centre of gravity, to add his weight to his victim's impetus.

Nathan hit the vinyl-tiled floor, bounced, rolled, and slammed full-length into the metal wall – and lay still. The 'fight' was over. Tzonov crossed to him, went to one knee and checked his pulse. Then he grunted and looked at Siggi where she was silently cursing and pulling the last of her clothes on. Glaring back at him, she said:

'Well, and have you killed him?'

He shook his bullet head. 'No. I *will* kill him, eventually! But for now he's just winded, dizzy, feeling sick . . .'

'You're the sick one!' She headed for the open door. But Tzonov was there first, thrusting her out into the corridor so hard that she collided with the opposite wall. Then, while she clung there, he took out a duplicate key and secured the door. Siggi saw the key in his hand and clamped her mind tight shut, obscuring its thoughts behind her uniquely misty screen.

Fuck you! she thought again.

She hadn't planned it this way (had she?), but Tzonov had forced the issue. And what he intended doing to Nathan . . . well, it just couldn't be allowed. Siggi told herself that *that* was the real reason why, while Tzonov had been dealing with Nathan and she'd been so hurriedly, breathlessly dressing, she'd left her key on the rim of Nathan's washbasin. It wasn't just the worm turning, the need to take revenge on this grotesque egomaniac bastard and all his cruelties. No, it was a human act, of a kind Turkur Tzonov would never understand.

For she knew now that it wasn't Nathan who was the enemy, the alien here. Not by any means . . .

Something a little more than two and a half hours later, Siggi was in her bed. Her exhaustion was mostly feigned, but not her trembling as she lay there wondering how Tzonov would react to his prisoner's escape. It was unavoidable, something which was bound to erupt at any moment now; in fact she was surprised it was taking so long, unless –

– Was it possible that Nathan had been in such a bad way that he'd just stayed there unconscious on the floor? Perhaps he'd staggered to his bed and collapsed there, and so failed to find the key where she'd left it.

But even as that thought occurred:

Hurried footsteps in the corridor, a muted curse, and a moment later a fist hammering on the door. Then Tzonov's voice demanding that she wake up. Siggi took her time, made sure she looked dishevelled, hoped that her make-up had given her black eye a little extra shine, and that the smoked glasses she wore didn't hide its bruised lower orbit. And belting her dressing-gown, finally she opened the door.

Tzonov was alone. At least that was a mercy. She wasn't about to be arrested. No, that was a stupid thought: how could she have feared that he would dare to charge her with anything? She knew too much about him, and anyway the era of dawn arrests and summary executions was over . . . in the rest of the world at least. But this was Perchorsk, and Tzonov had the power here.

'Siggi.' His voice was harsh, rasping. 'He's escaped!'

'What?' She turned her face away, as if hiding her

eye. In fact she was hiding both of them, making sure that Tzonov couldn't see past the double barrier of dark lenses and mind-smog. 'Who has ... *escaped*, did you say? Nathan!'

'Of course, Nathan! Who else?' He caught her shoulders, forced her to face him – and saw the dark blue bruise under the gold rim of her glasses. His expression changed at once. 'What? Glasses? Something wrong with ... your eyes?'

'No, with my *eye*!' Siggi hissed. 'My left eye, where you struck me! Is your memory so short, then?' She snatched away the glasses – but only for a moment.

'Ah!' He looked staggered. 'But I didn't mean to ... I mean ... did I strike you so hard?'

She covered her eyes, conjured even deeper banks of fog. 'It doesn't matter, not any more. And it isn't important. But Nathan, escaped? How?'

Then ... she let her jaw fall, caused her hand to fly to her mouth. 'The key!' (In time of need, Siggi could be a very good actress.)

'Key?' Tzonov tightened his grip on her shoulders and frowned. 'No, the door was locked. And I had returned my key to the key cabinet. Do you mean the duplicate? But I'd given that to your guard, with orders that ...'

She tore herself loose, ran to where her clothes of the previous night were hanging, frantically searched the jacket pockets. 'I dressed so hurriedly,' she gasped as he followed after her and stood waiting close by, with his fists clenched and the skin over his jaw tight as a drumhead. 'If you hadn't acted like a jealous, egotistical fool ...!'

'You had the key?' Tzonov couldn't believe it, and a moment later neither could she – *as he laughed and slapped his thigh!* 'But I thought ... I thought ...!'

271

Amazingly, his expression was one of relief, and suddenly Siggi knew exactly what he'd thought: that Nathan had his father's powers. That he'd teleported out of his locked room!

'Why are you laughing?' She continued to act it out. 'At me? Of course I had the key. How else was I to let myself out of his cell? But while you were busy ... *throwing* your weight around ...' She hurled her jacket to the floor, stamped on it and burst into tears. False tears, but enough to fool Tzonov. She was only a weak woman, after all. His ego was quite safe. And for the same reason she knew now that he never would have believed that she could *give* the key to Nathan. But now that she was on fairly safe ground again:

'Since then ... why, I've been in such a state that ... that I haven't even *thought* about that bloody key!'

Now Tzonov had someone to blame, chastise, and again his hands tightened on her shoulders. 'Siggi, you're a sick little idiot. You sought to seduce him, yet even now you're not sure that he didn't seduce you. You're assuming you lost the key — but he could well have taken it from you! I should have known better than to let you be alone with him.'

Again she stamped her foot, tore herself free and turned her face away. 'No, I'm not sick! Whatever I did was for you, us, our country. You wanted information, and I got it. Everything I could, anyway. And whatever it took.'

'Ah?' She had Tzonov's attention, if only for the moment. 'He told you things? A lot? Good! But ... why didn't you tell me this before?'

'What?' She glared at him. 'And did you give me even half a chance?'

Tzonov knew that he hadn't. 'Perhaps not. But in any case it will have to keep.' He was fully in control again.

'On the other hand, his escape can't keep. Well, let's see: he's been loose for some two and a half hours, presumably. But a cell is one thing and the complex is another entirely. There's always a guard on the outer doors. And no way out except through those doors. So there's every chance he's still in the place.'

'Where would he go?' She was off the hook and could afford to relax a little. 'He has no friends here.'

Tzonov looked at her sharply. 'The British?'

She acted up to it. 'Yes! He could speak to them.'

'Huh!' Tzonov snorted. 'Well, he could in a fashion, yes.'

'No,' she said, shaking her head. 'Better than that. He's a telepath!' She would have had to tell him eventually, before he found out for himself. So why not now?

'What?'

'It's true. He spoke to me that way, and he's good at it. I would have told you before, if you'd let me before throwing me in here! It's why – it's how – I knew he wanted me.' And before Tzonov could fly into another rage she continued, 'Why, Nathan even told me about what he saw in your mind, Turkur: a machine, and how you planned to use it on him – which is something you never told me . . .' With her last few words, Siggi had even dared to let a disapproving tone creep into her voice.

He avoided her glance. 'I would use it, as a last resort, yes.'

'And leave him brain dead? A vegetable?'

'And leave us with his knowledge, everything!'

'Only as a last resort? You did say that you'd kill him.'

Tzonov was tired of this. 'Get dressed, and quickly. Meet me in the control room.'

'Where are you going?' She followed him to the door.

'To check the security of this damned place. Then to talk to Trask, see if he knows anything about all of this — and how much. If it's nothing, all well and good. And after that, we'll just have to make sure that those two are the very *last* to know anything! Now get dressed. I fancy we're going to be busy . . .'

Tzonov was right: from then on he, at least, was busy.

While Siggi dressed, he organized search parties to work their way through the various levels of the complex; each room and laboratory, every nook and cranny, from the Gate itself to the reception area. Then, as the search commenced, he spoke to and commended the efforts of the prowler-guard who had checked Nathan's cell and found something suspicious in the way he lay there so motionless in his bed. Fetching the key from the control room, the guard had found Nathan's pillows tucked under the blanket in a manner to resemble the human figure. But the door had been locked, so last night's guard must still be in possession of the duplicate key. Without checking that last detail, the prowler-guard had then reported the mystery to Tzonov, but with some small trepidation. There could be a simple explanation, after all. What if the prisoner had been moved?

Tzonov's admiration was boundless. But then —

— He sent for Siggi's guard from the previous night, and threatened and dressed the man down almost to the point of nervous collapse. Following which, when he'd cooled down a little, he had despatched a man to check on Trask and Goodly: were they up and about yet? What was their itinerary for the day, etcetera — his way of finding out their physical and mental condition and perhaps discovering if they knew anything, and how much they knew. (But never a mention from his messenger to them with regard to the alien escapee.) And finally he had spoken to the two-man security guard at the main entrance, one at his post inside the massive doors, the other outside. Their reports corresponded precisely: between midnight and 7:00 a.m. no one had either departed from or entered into the complex . . . at least, no unauthorized persons had done so.

But three supply vehicles had gone out about an hour ago: two heading east for the mainly derelict barracks and military airport at Beresovo, and the third to meet a train at Ukhta in the west . . .

When Siggi met Tzonov in the control room, he was looking sour. Tossing her a parka, he told her: 'Put it on. The weather isn't too good, and we're going out.'

'Where to?' She pulled on the parka and took snow goggles from one of its pockets to replace her tinted glasses.

'I was hoping you could tell me,' Tzonov growled, leading the way from the control room to the entrance bay. 'Let's face it, you were with him long enough! Don't you have any clues? Any idea at all where he might be heading?' Outside the open doors, a driver was ticking over the engine of his half-track vehicle, turning the grey morning atmosphere blue with shimmering diesel fumes. It was starting to snow.

She shook her head. 'Are you sure he's gone out? In this weather, and so far north? Even a trapper or one of the local lumberjacks would find it hard going on foot.'

'I've got teams of men searching every level, the entire complex,' Tzonov answered. 'The first reports are already in. Not a trace of him, and I don't think there's going to be one. No, he has to be out here. I think he stowed away on a supply truck.'

Siggi's throat was dry; her heart was hammering and

275

she must control it, also her breathing. But was it really true? Was Nathan off and running? She hoped so; but *if* so, she had been the instrument of his release! Turkur must be right: she was a madwoman! God, but she must watch her thoughts and actions carefully now! 'A supply truck? Surely the guards would have searched it?'

Tzonov snorted, his breath pluming where he climbed up beside the driver and helped Siggi up alongside. 'There were three trucks,' he answered. 'Two for Beresovo, one for Ukhta. They left before the escape was discovered. As for a search: What? And security around here as slack as hell? Even our own people have been bored to tears – but no more! Siggi, if we don't find this alien, we're in real trouble.'

'But why? And why do you continue to refer to him as an alien? Nathan's as human as you or I, a human mind in a human ... body. He's no plague-bearer. And anyway, we will find him. Of course we will. To him, *this* is the alien world, and we're the aliens. Where can he go? Who will give him shelter?' Even saying these things, asking these questions, she prayed that she was wrong. For her own sake as much as Nathan's.

Tzonov glanced at her as the half-track revved up in a cloud of diesel exhaust gasses and started up the pass along the western flank of the ravine. 'He has only two choices. If he came as a spy, he's now seen as much as he needs to see – of Perchorsk, at least – and must try to get back to his own world. If he is the great telepath you believe him to be, he must know by now that there's a second Gate, and its location. Heading for it, he'll continue to gather information for his Wamphyri masters.' He paused, and then went on:

'That's one scenario. But if he's an outcast or runaway, an "illegal immigrant", as it were, then he can't go back and so must try to hide, fit in with the people around him, merge into our society. Or with any other society that he can reach. That's the danger, Siggi. And as you're surely aware, borders and check posts don't amount to much these days. People come and go as they will.'

'And we can't simply let him do that?' (She wished they could.) 'We can't just let him go, and forget him?'

Now Tzonov's glance was suspicious. 'Have you lost your wits completely? Are you so easily besotted? He is most probably the son of Harry Keogh! The British will find him if we don't. And they'll discover and bring on whatever powers lie latent within him, for their own use! I mean, think about it. Can we afford for our enemies to be in control of another Necroscope? Can we afford that he might lead some British expedition back into his own world ahead of our plans? And just at a time when our country, under our intellectual and political guidance – and funded by the riches of a brand new world – is ready to reassert itself in world affairs? No, of course we can't simply forget him.'

Siggi had known about Nathan's 'choices', of course, and even knew which one he had made, but she wouldn't tell Tzonov. Anything else the Russian wanted to know, but not that. And in any case, Nathan hadn't told her everything, for which she was glad. *What the eye can't see, the mind won't grieve.*

So why was Tzonov heading west? Or was it just instinct? For it would seem that if he was right and Nathan had escaped in one of three trucks, then the fugitive was likely to be heading east. Two out of three would seem the better odds. But in fact Tzonov had probably guessed correctly. If Nathan had used his telepathy to read the destinations of those vehicles in the minds of their drivers, he would have stowed away in the one heading for Ukhta. Ukhta, Moscow, Kiev and Romania, yes, and a cold and lonely two thousand miles journey between, before reaching the underground river that fed the once-blue Danube, the Dunarea, on its way to the Black Sea. Of course, because for Nathan there *was* no other choice but that he head for the Romanian Gate, his one route back to Sunside/Starside and Misha, the girl he'd left there in peril of her very life, or death, or undeath . . .

And now it was time that Siggi told something of these things, too, to Tzonov. It couldn't hurt, not now that he was on the right track anyway and might soon recapture the fugitive. But as Siggi prepared herself to relate Nathan's story:

'The trucks are equipped with radios,' Tzonov mused to himself, gloomily. 'Here in this bloody wilderness, they need them. The drivers probably won't see another human being all along their routes, unless you would describe the local peasants as human beings! Out of the pass, it's two hundred and fifty miles to Ukhta, and forest – and snow – all the way. They'll see a broken-down cart or two, a tractor, the smoke of a logging camp. But if they were to break down, and then a storm came up . . . That's why they need the radios.'

Siggi looked at him. 'You've contacted them, from Perchorsk?'

He shook his head. 'Siggi, this place is the arse-hole of the world! Nothing works here. Contacted them? From the ravine, the complex? That's a laugh. Have you seen the radio room? My God . . . talk about antiques! Also, there's this weird interference, and the snow doesn't help much. The operator got through partially, to the lead truck heading for Beresovo. Enough that the driver was able to clear himself, then stop and check the other vehicle. Which leaves only one: the one that climbed up through this pass an hour and twenty minutes ago.' He looked up at the wide, jagged canyon of light overhead, the firs growing dark on the slopes. 'He's got a good start, our alien.'

'What will you do to him?' She had to speak up, almost shout as the driver dropped a gear to tackle a steep hairpin. Even so, her tone of voice had been unmistakable.

Tzonov's gaze was penetrating, but she kept it out. 'Oh, yes,' he said, nodding thoughtfully. 'But this one really got to you, didn't he, Siggi?' And before she could answer: 'Perhaps you'd better tell me all about him, and about his world. His alien world first, I think.'

At least it would keep her mind busy, off other things. Things she really didn't dare think about. And as the clatter of the engine and the clanking of linked tracks on the frozen metalled surface of the road died down a little, she started to tell it.

'Sunside and Starside,' she said. 'The two halves of a world split down the middle by barrier mountains. Sunside is home to nomadic tribes, Gypsies, travelling folk, except they stopped travelling some twenty years ago after Harry Keogh and his Earth-born son, called The Dweller, destroyed the Wamphyri Lords of Starside. That's as much as Nathan knew about it; he wasn't even born then. But when he was a child of four a handful of vampires returned to Starside. He doesn't know how or where from.

'Again they were destroyed, this time by "fires of hell" that came roaring out of the hell-lands Gate! The other end of the Perchorsk Gate, Turkur. That's what Travellers and the Wamphyri alike call that white-glowing, half-buried portal out on the Starside plain: the hell-lands Gate. Because their legends say it's the gate to hell. And the hellfire that spewed out of it almost seventeen years ago? One of Viktor Luchov's Tokarev missiles? It had to be. A nuclear hell, yes, that was spawned right here in Perchorsk. That was the end of the Wamphyri, or so it seemed. And Nathan grew up on Sunside.

'About the Travellers –'

'– Wait!' Tzonov stopped her. 'Let's see to this first. And you can help.'

They were at the top, the apex of the saddle which formed the Perchorsk Pass. Below them, the ravine was misty in Urals daylight shaded grey from the steady fall of large, soft snowflakes. The cloud ceiling was very nearly total, where only a stray beam of sunlight found its way through on the far south-eastern horizon. They were lucky; even a moderate wind could easily turn this into a blizzard.

The driver had brought his vehicle to a clattering halt; he assisted them in turning back the tarpaulin on the back of the half-track, and manhandling a Norwegian-built snowcat down the ramp of the extended tailgate.

'We're going cross-country,' Tzonov explained. 'Even with snow-chains a truck is limited to twenty-five miles per hour on roads such as these. And no snowploughs before Kozhva. Also, if my judgement of Perchorsk's drivers in general is correct, this one will be stopping every hour or so for cheese and biscuits, black coffee from his thermos, and a sip of vodka. And that's not all, for I'm reliably informed that on this run they normally take a break in Kozhva – to chat with the village girls and post letters! Slack, as I believe I may have hinted previously.' His sarcasm was biting. 'Damn everything! Even in this threatening weather I would have preferred to use the jet-copter, but it isn't back from Moscow.'

He started up the snowcat and helped Siggi mount

and belt-up, then climbed aboard the wide leather saddle in front of her and fixed his own belt. 'The half-track will wait here for us. If we're not back by midday, the driver will go back down and take a meal, then return. We have fuel for two hundred miles, which is about right for a return trip to Kozhva. If we're low I can refuel there. Cross-country, it's only half the distance the truck will have to cover. With luck we'll get into Kozhva half an hour to an hour ahead of our quarry. Meanwhile they'll be trying to contact the driver by radio. Are you ready? Then we'll get underway and you can continue with your story – or rather, with *his* story.'

The snowcat's engine was quiet and very efficient; its skis cut the snow with a low *hiss*, like the outriggers of a trimaran slicing water, where it sped along the narrow white verge of the road down toward the foothills. When they were out of the mountains proper, Tzonov would turn off the road and head northwest for Kozhva through the forests, along the many miles of ruled-line logging tracks. The wraparound windshield gave excellent protection; Siggi was able to continue Nathan's story without shouting.

'The Travellers have very little of science as we know it,' she took up her description of the people of the world beyond the Gate. 'And what they do have is rudimentary, sufficient only to their needs. But like our own Gypsies they're good at making signs, marking forest trails, leaving cryptic messages for others who may follow after. They might have had the beginnings of a technology at some time in their history, but the advent of the Wamphyri put paid to that. Any scientific advances they might have made have been defeated by the constant need to keep moving. Survival is their priority, not science. Now they're five hundred to a thousand years behind us – in some ways.'

And before he could question what Siggi had told him so far, she continued: 'So ... no physics as such, but metaphysics? There seems to be a little of the Wamphyri in all of them. They're not vampires, not even remotely, but there are degrees of what we might term ... what, "tainted blood"? So that what the Wamphyri have in large measure, certain Travellers have inherited down the centuries but to a lesser degree.

'Occasionally a "mentalist" or telepath will show up among them. Or one of them could be a precog like our Mr Goodly, with fleeting visions of the future. Thus, just like Earth's Romany, seers, stargazers and palmists are not uncommon among them. It makes sense that in a world dominated by very real night fears, superstition should be so rife. But there again – and as you and I and all the world's E-Branches are surely aware – parapsychology is not superstition. And neither are the Wamphyri!

'There are degrees of vampire, of which the Wamphyri is/are the ultimate form. But in all their shapes and forms they can only exist on Starside, away from the sunlight. From there they raid on Sunside during its long nights, taking ... food, and captives, back across the barrier range into the shadows of the mountains before ... before the sunrise ...'

Here Siggi lapsed into a reflective silence, causing Tzonov to inquire: 'Well?'

'Um?' She gave herself a shake, which was more a shudder. 'Oh, yes! Well, Nathan told me a great deal about the Wamphyri. And also that you would be a fool to ignore his warning: which is that only a lunatic would attempt to invade Wamphyri territory. He knows our plans, do you see? Plucked from your mind while you were trying to read his!'

'*Huh!*' Tzonov grunted. 'A "taint" of the Wamphyri, do you suppose? Or something he got from his father?'

Despite that Tzonov wasn't able to see her, Siggi shook her head. 'Nathan knows nothing about that. Or rather, he *knew* nothing about it, not for certain, until he read it in Trask's mind. As far as he was concerned his father was Szgany, a Traveller called Hzak Kiklu, who was fatally wounded by a Wamphyri weapon before Nathan was born. He did have certain suspicions, though, which our various thoughts have confirmed. But it does seem to be a pure coincidence that he is the one who has come through the Gate.'

'And how did that come about?'

'It seems to have been his punishment for something, some crime which he couldn't quite specify. But a crime against the Wamphyri! And so he was cast out of his own world into hell – into the hell-lands Gate – from which no one ever returned.'

'Well, that's true enough,' Tzonov answered. 'Except for the other Gate in Romania, it's a one-way system. So . . . tell me more about the Wamphyri. Why do you hesitate?'

Because you can't see in my mind what I saw in his. Nor will you ever, because I'm not going to let you into my mind again. And if you could see what Nathan showed me, then you wouldn't want to see it! But out loud she only said, 'Because it's gruesome.'

'Tell me anyway.'

'Very well . . .' She decided not to elaborate, and after a moment:

'The contagious bite of the vampire is rarely fatal; on the contrary, for after the – what, transfusion? – the victim's blood mutates and his longevity is assured. Or it would be if he were left to develop to his full. But as a fledgling vampire he's now a thrall, *in* thrall to whichever monster occasioned the change in him. And of course, once a man is taken by the plague he can't stay on Sunside but must make his way to the safety of Starside and the aerie of his master.

'In Starside, as a thrall, his fate could be one of many, none of them pleasant. His flesh, blood, even his bones could be required for the "provisioning" of the aerie. Drained of all life-sustaining fluids and truly dead, his body could be dried out, ground down, and mixed with coarse grains as an ingedient of the meal which the Wamphyri Lords feed to their flyers, warriors, and other creatures.

'On the other hand he might find himself cocooned, stored intact, and later changed by the metamorphic skills of his Lord into just such a flyer or warrior – or *part* of one! A creature like the thing which came through the Gate that time, and destroyed a pair of heavily armed, highly sophisticated Soviet aircraft before the Americans shot it out of their airspace. Oh, yes, the Wamphyri can work such . . . what, miracles? Or if not miracles, horrors certainly. For human flesh is like clay to them . . .

'But let's suppose that our specimen thrall is the right stuff. Ah, but then his prospects could be very different! Kept as a true thrall, he might be trained, given the rank of lieutenant, injected with more of his master's evil. And in time – with fifty, a hundred, or five hundred years of longevity guaranteed – why, such a one might even aspire to become Wamphyri in his own right!

'This could occur in several ways. He could inherit his master's "egg" – a weird reproductive seed or self-contained organism, produced in the leechlike body of the vampire Lord's symbiont – or he might even generate his own egg from scratch. Don't ask me how the system

284

works. Nathan himself doesn't know. I can only tell you that a symbiont egg is the *alkahest* or catalyst which will transmute a man into a monster, which will in fact make him Wamphyri!'

She paused to let Tzonov concentrate on controlling the snowcat. There were scattered rifts in the cloud ceiling now. The sky had brightened; it had stopped snowing; the light was much better. They were down into the foothills and Tzonov was turning off the road onto a vast snowslope that swept on for a further fifteen miles or more to the dark-canopied forests and so-called 'pioneer' logging camps. But the Russian's thoughts were bitter, less than patriotic as he scanned the white desolation ahead:

We've been pioneering this region for close on a hundred years now! This should be our Yukon, our Canada, our Norway or Sweden. Old-style Communism was to blame, but in the last quarter century we've learned the lessons of history. Or rather, I have learned them! But in the past I was only the student, and from now on I must be the teacher!

Tzonov's thoughts were so vehement, so determined, that despite Siggi's shielded mind she picked them up. She 'heard' his thoughts and maybe even felt something of his megalomania. Then, shivering a little – perhaps from the cold, too – she shrouded her mind again.

Taking a sweeping downhill course designed to slice the snowfield in a mighty diagonal to the south-west, Tzonov wound up the throttle and let the snowcat skim the drifted snow like a surfer on the swell of a timeless wave. The miles flew by in a hypnotic hiss of skis; the snowcat paralleled an icy, black-pulsing river like a vein in the dead white flesh of the land; soon they were into the woods.

And in a clearing beside a pyramid of logs, there

Tzonov brought his machine to a halt and stepped down to stretch his legs. Siggi dismounted, too, and lit a cigarette. Tzonov, who didn't smoke, cautioned her. 'Is that an American brand? *Huh!* On the one hand we're admonished to clean up our act country-wide, to depollute and let the world breathe, and on the other we're encouraged to ruin our lungs! Now tell me, what good is a healthy land without a healthy people? Well, one day in the not-too-distant future, all such *shit* will be banned! Mark my words.' A mood was on him. His frustrations were starting to spill over.

Another 'vice' of mine that Mr Perfect has never approved of! Siggi thought, but kept it to herself. While out loud: 'I only smoke one or two a day,' she said, 'as I require them, to soothe my nerves. We came down the snowslopes in something of a hurry.'

'Speed has the opposite effect on me,' he growled. 'It's a stimulant. It's as good for me as sex is for you.' His words were harsh, grating, deliberately hurtful.

She still wasn't off the hook. Well, to hell with it! She tossed her head, looked away as he took out a flask and sipped brandy. She glimpsed the flask in the corner of her eye as Tzonov proffered it, but shook her head. And then, quite suddenly, she felt his menace anew and stopped wondering why she was out here, why he'd wanted her to accompany him. She knew it was so that he could keep an eye on her, in more senses than one. No, she wasn't off the hook by a long shot, not yet. And:

'What is it?' she said, still looking away from him.

'Look at me,' he said. She did, and saw his eyes: huge, glassy, staring as if to cut into her flesh. If speed really did work on the Russian like a stimulant, he was still pretty high on it. She saw the bulge in his pants, sluggishly mobile there . . .

'No,' his voice was deep, dark, guttural now, 'don't look at me with those goggles on. Take them off.' That would be the same as taking her clothes off, or much worse. For with Nathan fresh in Siggi's mind, Tzonov would see everything they'd done together. He actually *wanted* to see them together! The bastard wanted to watch Nathan fuck her – to know who had fucked who – wanted to be sure they weren't *both* fucking him!

Siggi stepped back a pace in the silence and the solitude of the woods, and shook her head. 'I don't want you in my mind any more, Turkur. Not ever. There are things in there that are mine alone, private. Oh, we're still in league, far too deeply to pull out and go our own ways, but from this point on it has to be business pure and simple. We have to be partners all the way, and no more Mr Big and Miss Little.'

His face changed. His jaw tightened and his eyes were like mirrors reflecting her mind. But in reality they only reflected her snow goggles, and the swirling mental fog behind them. Then ... he very slowly and very deliberately reached up and removed her goggles, and the first thing he saw was her bruise and the flaring anger in her eyes ...

... And the next thing he *felt* was Siggi's gun in his ribs!

Then, taking back her goggles from his momentarily frozen fingers, she told him, 'And that's something else, Turkur: you must be sure never to hit me again. If you do, then believe me I'll strike back. Perhaps with this –' she aimed her small but spiteful automatic right into his snarling teeth, '– or if not with this, then with whatever else I can lay my hands on. But be sure I *will* strike back!'

She put the goggles back on and continued to face Tzonov down, until gradually he came to terms with it.

287

He had to, for right now there was nothing – not a thing – that he could do about it. But after they had both calmed down a little, and as they mounted the snowcat again, Siggi was nauseated to catch a last whiff of the Russian's mind. And it was just exactly like that: like a bad smell, a mental stench.

For a moment she thought she saw a picture forming in the slime of his mind. A picture of a machine – of *the* machine – the gleaming metal vampire which Nathan had feared. And all of its siphons were sucking on the brain of some poor, shuddering victim.

Except this time its victim wasn't Nathan . . .

VI

Off and Running

Twice they crossed the winding road to Kozhva. On the
first occasion there were faint impressions under the
fresh snow, but on the next the heavy tyre tracks were
black against the white where rubber had stripped
packed snow right down to an ice-sheathed surface and
only a few grey flakes had speckled the glassy tarmac.
Tzonov had an out of date map (but then, he told
himself resignedly, almost everything in the greatly
diminished USS was out of date these days) which he
stopped briefly to look at. And grunting his satisfaction
with their progress at least, he at once set off again.

'We'll be in Kozhva in about forty minutes,' he informed Siggi over his shoulder. 'From this point on I
could just as easily stick with the tracks and catch the
truck on the road. But if we take one more shortcut to
the village, we should be there in time to get a bite to
eat and something hot to drink while we're waiting for
the truck to show up. Meanwhile ... I think we should
put our differences behind us. Why don't you finish
what you were telling me?'

Siggi made it as brief as possible. But in any case,
she could only tell Tzonov what she herself had been
told or shown. She knew that Nathan hadn't revealed
everything, not with complete candour, because certain
scenes from his history had been either very obviously
contrived or else deliberately obscured. For example,

he'd shown Siggi only a glimpse of his mother and the other people he'd grown up with, and done little more than mention the childhood sweetheart who had become his wife.

Also, he had made a number of brief references to a race of near-alien, aboriginal desert dwellers with whom he seemed to have spent a deal of time, but such was his reticence with regard to their society that the few pictures which Siggi had managed to retain were hopelessly confused and without resolution. Other areas were likewise blank, especially with regard to the Szgany in their settled period, and the communities in which they'd dwelled prior to the return of the Wamphyri. As for the rest of it, there wasn't much to tell. She couldn't possibly relive it for Tzonov, as Nathan had done for her.

'Nathan grew up on Sunside,' she began. 'He knew a girl there, Misha, and they had plans. But when he was eighteen the Wamphyri came back yet again. His tribe was attacked and scattered, and his girl taken as a thrall. So he thought, anyway. He took to wandering, became a true Traveller, spent years in the wilderness moving from tribe to tribe. Until he, too, was taken by the Wamphyri.

'His vampire Lord was fascinated by Nathan's light skin and colours, which are rare among Sunside's Szgany. And so he was kept as a sort of pet, and never vampirized. Eventually he escaped and made his way back to Sunside. There ... he discovered his girl, alive and well! They were married. But the Wamphyri pursued him. When he was retaken, his punishment was to be thrown into the Starside Gate. And so he came here ...'

Over his shoulder, Tzonov said, 'But didn't you tell me previously that he couldn't understand his punishment? Isn't there something of an ambiguity here?'

Despite that he couldn't see her, Siggi shrugged. 'If so, it's Nathan's ambiguity, Turkur, not mine. Perhaps there were things he wanted to keep to himself. Is that so strange? Don't we all have little secrets which we would prefer to keep private?' It was going to be a sore point with her for a long time to come.

Tzonov answered with a suspicious grunt, and said: 'Somehow I can't help thinking that there are far too many "little secrets" which this Nathan would like to keep to himself. But I shall discover them soon enough.'

In her own secret mind Siggi thought: *You could be right, of course. But first you'll have to catch him . . .*

They followed a logging trail right into Little Kozhva's main street. Big Kozhva was three miles further on, and this was a logging camp of the same name which employed sawyers, lumberjacks, and other workers from the town. The road passed right through the centre of camp, and according to the people on the street the truck from Perchorsk wasn't in yet.

Tzonov put distance between the snowcat and a giant sawmill whose noise was deafening, and stopped outside a general store issuing food, coffee smells, and a blast of warm air from a roaring log fire in the stone-built fireplace. An area had been set aside for eating; the coffee and 'dogs' were of American blends and manufacture, of course. A handful of customers looked up from their late breakfasts or early lunches as Tzonov ordered coffee, eggs, fried potatoes and onions.

One of the men, a huge, bearded lumberjack, whistled his appreciation as Siggi shrugged out of her parka and sat down with Tzonov at a rough wooden table. In a frontier place like this, she must surely be a sight for sore eyes. Ignoring the other staring faces all about her, Siggi glanced witheringly at the whistler and lit a cigarette. This time Tzonov made no complaint but simply said: 'And now you see what I mean when I talk about such people as sub-human!'

'No, I don't,' she answered. 'These are just men, and men are the same all over the world. But this is a hard place and so these men are grown rough, like the timbers they handle. I find it much harder to understand intelligent, so-called "sophisticated" men, whose bodies may be clean and smooth but whose minds are just as grubby if not worse than these!'

Tzonov scarcely felt slighted. He would never have allowed it to cross his mind that she might be referring to him . . .

Their table gave them a view of the dismal street. Fifteen minutes later the truck arrived and stopped. Tzonov had thought it might. A moment later, the driver came in grinning and slapping his hands together, and found the head of Soviet E-Branch waiting for him. The driver wasn't one of Tzonov's men but he was a soldier; he'd seen Tzonov in Perchorsk and knew that he was a powerful, high-ranking official. He saluted as a matter of course.

And Tzonov was into him in a moment: 'You: what's your name?'

'Lance Corporal Ivanovich – sir!' He was young, burly, flustered under Tzonov's cold, penetrating glare. He wondered what was going on, and what it had to do with him.

Tzonov was looking out into the street; after noting that the canvas at the tailgate was flapping loose, he'd only taken his eyes off the truck for a moment. 'Out!' he snapped. 'Back to your vehicle. Did you stop en-route here? And let me warn you, Ivanovich, it's best not to lie to me.'

'No, sir. Of course not – sir! Yes, I did stop, but only to warm up a little. A minute or two. That's all – sir!'

They stood at the tailgate. 'Open her up,' Tzonov issued his curt instruction. And as the soldier was letting down the tailgate: 'Is your radio on?'

'Yes, sir!'

'Didn't you hear them hailing you? From Perchorsk?'

'The complex? Nothing but static since I left the pass. I think it's the radio to blame. It's on its last legs – sir!'

Tzonov looked into the back of the truck. A spare tarpaulin, coiled ropes, a box of worn-out parts from the Projekt's cranky ventilation system. 'What was your cargo?'

'Just what you see.' Still mystified, the other shrugged. 'I'm on resupply, not delivery. I won't be full until I start back from the railway depot in Ukhta.'

Siggi had finished her coffee and joined them. She, too, looked into the back of the truck. But she saw more in there than Tzonov had seen. He needed eye to eye contact before his talent came into play, but with Siggi ... sometimes it was a lot more than just telepathy. Like now. Why, it was almost as if she could smell Nathan in there! As if she could taste him, feel the rush and whirl of his numbers vortex. He wasn't here now, but he had been, certainly. And even now he wasn't that far away.

Tzonov looked at her. 'Well?'

'Nothing,' she lied.

He turned to the Corporal driver. 'Ivanovich, we're looking for a man, the prisoner we were holding at Perchorsk. It's possible he escaped in this truck. These tailgate lashings were loose. Were they like that when you left the complex? Did you see or hear anything suspicious? Speak up!'

'The tarpaulin was OK when I left Perchorsk,' the soldier answered. 'It probably came loose on its own. I wasn't carrying anything anyway and so had nothing to lose – *sir!*'

Tzonov had been staring straight into the Corporal's eyes and knew that he'd fumbled the lashings in Perchorsk. At least, he knew that the man suspected that he'd fumbled them. It meant absolutely nothing. 'Damn it to *hell!*' he snarled, and turned to Siggi again. And now his eyes were hard and bright as marbles. 'Was he here?'

'No,' she lied again. And her mind-smog swirled, dank and impenetrable.

Whirling away from her and heading for the snowcat, Tzonov only paused to shout back over his shoulder: 'Well, then? Are you coming? For God's sake, let's get out of here!'

'My parka,' she called after him. 'I'll be a moment.'

The young soldier went back inside with her. As he helped Siggi on with her parka, she asked him: 'Where did you stop?'

'About half-way here,' he told her, 'just to warm up, as I said. And also . . .'

'Also?'

'Just outside of town, but very briefly. To let some travellers over the crossing.'

Travellers! The word riveted her. 'Gypsies?'

He nodded. 'They're late this year – or early. It's hard to tell with the travelling folk. They just come and go.' Then, looking worried, he asked her: 'Madame, am I in trouble?'

Siggi only half-heard him. After a moment's silence, she gave herself a mental shake and answered, 'Eh, trouble? No, I shouldn't think so.' And controlling an urge to laugh hysterically, she went outside to Tzonov and the snowcat . . .

*

Standing some two miles to the north of Little Kozhva, a steep-sided knoll of volcanic rock – the plug of a once-mighty caldera – grew up above the forest some hundreds of feet high. The snowcat had skirted its thinly wooded base on the approach to the logging camp. Now, as Siggi and Tzonov headed north for Perchorsk, she asked him: 'How much power does this thing have? Enough to climb that knoll?'

'If I climb gradually, along the contours, and make a complete circuit, yes. Did you want to?'

'The view from up there must be quite marvellous.'

'Very well,' he grunted, however grudgingly. 'It will cost us half an hour, but . . .'

'Are you still worrying about Nathan? But I'm sure that by now they'll have found his hiding-place in the complex, or discovered him half-frozen, trying to climb out of the ravine.'

'Perhaps you're right,' he answered.

By then the clouds were breaking up and wan beams of sunlight were finding their way from the south. They weren't much, but they cheered Tzonov up a little . . .

At the top of the knoll, while Tzonov went off behind a rocky outcrop to relieve himself, Siggi found binoculars in the snowcat's panniers and swept the forested country to the south-west. This was why she'd wanted to come up here: to see if she could catch a glimpse of –

– The travelling folk!

And there they were, the real thing, just as they had been for a hundred, two hundred, five hundred years and more. Romany: pariahs and outcasts, suppressed, persecuted, chased from country to country for all that time. A race apart, yes, yet close and closer to their origins than any other race in the whole world; a party of Gypsies, their half-dozen painted caravans jolting and jingling far beyond the range of audibility, but clear as bells in Siggi's mind as she tried to bring them into focus.

No, she couldn't; they were too far away, three or maybe four miles; running from the winter, heading south. Except ... something the young Corporal had said had stuck in Siggi's memory. Being mobile, and with their knowledge of the seasons, why on earth were they still here? They were a secretive, even esoteric people, true enough, and wherever possible would keep clear of the world's more heavily populated regions; but even so, by now they should be seven hundred miles further south. Down on the shore of the Caspian, in Astrakhan or Baku. Or perhaps the Black Sea, Moldavia ... Romania? Yet here they were, and only now fleeing the rigours of winter.

Siggi looked around, her eyes tracing Tzonov's tracks in the snow. He was nowhere in sight. And again she picked out the thin line of caravans on the fringe of a distant forest. Unlike Tzonov, her talent didn't require eye to eye contact; she could cast her mind like an arrow, if she had a target.

Good luck! she sent. *Run far and fast, Nathan, and never come back.* She didn't for a moment believe he would answer, or even that he could. But ...

... A tendril of numbers touched her consciousness, and at once fastened to her thoughts! Siggi's skin prickled as if she stood close to a giant dynamo. And in her mind:

Goodbye, Siggi. I won't forget you. Nathan's voice, and his unique warmth. But so powerful! And Turkur Tzonov was receptive to strong telepathic signals.

Nathan heard that, too; his carrier probe at once disintegrated; the mental ether was clear again. And just in time, for Tzonov's voice came ringing:

'What do you see? Anything interesting?' The tone of his voice signalled nothing special.

Siggi sighed her relief and called back, 'Smoke from the villages and camps. A flight of birds, geese I think. And some furtive creature in the woods. A dog, perhaps, or a wolf. It's all very cold out there, but it's all very peaceful, too.'

'Do you think so?' He went to the snowcat and started it up. 'Well, my mind is full of vague premonitions. So enough of these sidetracks, let's get back to Perchorsk.'

All the way back Siggi was sad, for now she must keep her mind caged behind bars of her own making. And thinking of Nathan (however much she tried not to think of him), she wondered if he was sad, too . . .

When they arrived back at Perchorsk, Tzonov's 'vague premonitions' quickly assumed tangible form. At the crest of the pass his Platoon Commander was sitting in the half-track's driving seat with the engine already ticking over, waiting patiently for the snowcat's return.

Staff-Sergeant Bruno Krasin was dark-skinned, wiry, long-limbed. Thirtyish, square-jawed and hard-eyed, the blood of his Cossack forefathers still ran strong in him. The son of an old hard-line communist and KGB officer, Krasin was one of Tzonov's most trusted men; indeed, he was the man who would one day lead Tzonov's expeditionary force through the Perchorsk Gate into an alien world. On the way down to the complex he told Tzonov what had transpired in his absence.

'First, our search teams have worked their way through the Projekt scrupulously. They've scoured it just as you ordered, and the visitor isn't here. We've discovered nothing of his whereabouts. Second: it had been snowing in the pass, but not too heavily. So anyone on the run must leave tracks in the fresh snow. You would think so. Yet there was nothing. It's as if he simply disappeared.'

And again Tzonov remembered who was Nathan's father. But Siggi had sworn he didn't have his father's powers. And Nathan had seemed cowed and even despondent in captivity. 'I take it your men are still out searching?'

Krasin nodded. 'I've sent out search parties into all of the neighbouring villages and camps. Also, and despite that we cleared the trucks heading for Beresovo, I've sent a motorcyclist after them to double-check. But in my opinion it's all a waste of time. Something that had to be done, but a waste all the same. I think he had help.'

Tzonov shook his head. 'From here, Perchorsk? Impossible! Who?'

'The British?'

'Oh? How, when they've been kept little short of prisoners themselves? Our agents in the embassies have reported increased esper activity in London, but not around here. And anyway, what could they do?'

Krasin had worked frequently with Soviet E-Branch, providing the muscle behind some of Tzonov's more covert schemes. He vastly admired his talented master, but knew that while Tzonov was a mindspy, he would never make an agent on the ground; that is to say, an espionage agent in the old sense of the word. His talent got in the way; he relied on it too heavily; he couldn't see the wood for the trees. 'The British have known about this place since its early days,' he answered. 'From space, this has to be the most photographed place in the world. They know every track and trail from here north to Vorkuta and south to Sverdlovsk. If they could get a message, or a map, to the visitor . . .'

'He can't even read!' Tzonov exploded.

'But he can see! He's not unintelligent.'

'You told me there are no tracks.' Tzonov's frustrations were mounting.

Siggi cut in: 'He's Szgany, from Sunside. He knows how to cover his tracks. He has avoided the Wamphyri! In the wild, it will be like hunting the Invisible Man.'

'The British!' Tzonov growled. 'This morning I sent a man to wake them up, but I didn't tell them he'd escaped. What, so that they could look for ways to assist him on his way? Anyway, they weren't fit for much of anything. Probably still feeling the effects of the drug ... though by now it should have voided itself.' He frowned, shrugged, continued. 'Apparently they were like zombies! And they didn't appear to know anything. I left a message for them: I have been "called away", but I shall be at their disposal upon my return.'

'But they *are* talented,' Krasin insisted. 'And you yourself have frequently stated that their organization is second to none. Also, they have seen the visitor, spoken to him. And if they haven't helped him in some way, then why were they so eager to leave?'

'*What?*'

'They're out of here.' The other wasn't cowed. 'They came on the invitation of Gustav Turchin, and they invoked his name to get out. They saw Projekt Direktor Vanadze right after you left, and he arranged air transport to Moscow. By then the jet-copter had returned, and of course I had personally supervised the unloading of the machine. No –' he held up a hand, '– the British didn't see it.'

'Vanadze let them go?' Tzonov couldn't believe it.

'How could he prevent it? He asked them to wait until your return, but they would have none of that.

They threatened to speak to Gustav Turchin himself, which turned the trick most admirably. The Premier is like a puppet; his policies tie him inextricably to Western economics; his political survival is entirely dependent upon the USA, United Germany, and the UK. He would have ordered the immediate release of the British, and in the process would have given everyone else hell!'

'They simply flew out of here?' It was getting worse.

The other could only shrug. 'Yes. There was a British Airways Hawk from Moscow to London at 11:45. About now . . . it will be seeking a window into Heathrow. But even if you'd been here, what could you have done? They were guests, not prisoners.'

They were three-quarters of the way to the bottom of the ravine. Two hundred feet below them, the man-made lake of pent water was a sullen, leaden grey. Tiny flyspeck figures in winter white uniforms moved antlike where they searched icy scree slopes. As the half-track slewed onto the ramp to the staging area in front of the Projekt's massive security doors, Tzonov calmed down a little. 'You're absolutely sure they didn't see the machine?'

'I am positive, sir.'

Tzonov took a deep breath. 'Then we must brazen it out.'

Siggi frowned. 'Brazen what out?' In closing her mind to him so completely, she had also denied herself access to Tzonov's thoughts.

'The whole thing is a mess,' Tzonov snapped. 'And we will be the ones who take the blame — unless we turn events to our own advantage. For example: the British espers have gone home in a hurry. Why? Because they've been up to no good here. That will be our story, anyway. So, what have they been up to? Well, we think they may have helped our alien visitor to escape, perhaps by acting upon him like a catalyst until he developed his father's powers. And damn it all –' he slapped the flat of his hand against the half-track's steel door, '– that mightn't be so very far from the truth!'

The doors opened and they drove through. And as the half-track's uproar faded into silence and they dismounted, Tzonov continued to paint his picture of deceit. Ushering Krasin and Siggi to one side, and talking in a lowered tone now, he said: 'How then are we to react? But how *would* we act, if our story were entirely true? We would be outraged, furious! What? Having shown the British every courtesy, they repay us with this ... this *treachery*? Then, as soon as my back is turned, they laugh like hyenas and flee to safety! Perchorsk's staff will back us up; they have seen nothing extraordinary in my treatment of Trask and Goodly. Also, they wouldn't dare go against me.'

'But we did drug those two,' Siggi reminded. 'Maybe that was a mistake.'

'No.' He shook his head. 'I had to get them out of the way. I hoped to move my arsenal, hide it away. Also, we were bringing our visitor in through the Gate; I planned to interrogate him ... oh, a good many things! And all without their interference. *Huh!* Anyway, it's their word against ours. They have no proof. If they dare to bring charges, it will only be as an excuse for fleeing from us when in fact they're running from their own treachery. Of course they are, for their mission is accomplished. They've unleashed an alien creature upon us with powers we don't understand. Ah, but our response ... will be to issue a warrant on this Nathan's life. To all intelligence agents in the field: terminate on sight, and as the Americans are wont to say, "with extreme prejudice!" '

Deep inside, Siggi Dam shuddered. For already it was

as if Tzonov believed his own fictitious but very plausible scenario . . .

A Corporal came into the entrance bay from the direction of the duties and control room. He came to attention in front of Krasin, saluted Tzonov, and took out a slim notepad from a black leather briefcase. 'Sergeant,' he said to Krasin. 'You ordered me to search the rooms which the British occupied. I did so, and found this.'

Krasin examined the pad. 'Blank?'

'It's the light,' the Corporal explained. 'But there are impressions.'

'Well done. You can leave it with me.' Krasin dismissed the man.

In Tzonov's rooms the three examined the notepad under a powerful lamp. The Corporal was quite right; using a soft lead pencil, Tzonov criss-crossed the faint marks until they sprang into sharp relief. Then:

'What?' he frowned. But in another moment his frown faded and was replaced by a look of partial understanding. The drawing was a sign, a sigil: a flat loop with a half twist, in the form of a figure of eight. 'Nathan's earring?'

'More than that,' Siggi breathed. 'That's a Möbius Strip. And there's a connection –' For a moment she could have bitten her tongue, but in the next she reconsidered. What, something as simple as this? A notepad, perhaps incriminating (at least in Turkur Tzonov's eyes), left lying casually in Trask's room where it was certain to be discovered?

'– With Harry Keogh!' Tzonov had caught on to her line of reasoning. 'I remember now. The first time Keogh is known to have used teleportation, he was visiting the tomb of August Ferdinand Möbius in Leipzig. The Grenz Polizei had trapped and surrounded him – but he disappeared! Only to turn up again at the Chateau Bronnitsy, the then E-Branch HQ, and to wreck it!' He turned to Krasin.

'You were right, Bruno, and this doodle tells all. Trask has given himself away. He would employ exactly the same tactics that the British have used before, and send the alien to Leipzig in the hope that his Necroscope father's greatest talent will be reborn there. Except it won't be; on the contrary, it will die there!'

Krasin nodded; he wasn't *au fait* with the Keogh files and records, but Tzonov's enthusiasm for this new clue, this promising development, was infectious. 'And our next step?'

'I'll have to speak to Moscow, Turchin,' Tzonov answered. 'And he will have to give me *carte blanche* in this matter. But I want this Nathan, who or whatever, dead. For after all –' he glanced at Siggi, '– we've already extracted a deal of information from him. We no longer have any use for him and so it's the safest way to conclude the matter. Moreover, it will deny the British any possible use of his services.'

Krasin nodded. 'Meanwhile we'll keep searching, and in an ever-widening circle. Why wait until he gets to Leipzig?'

'Exactly.' Tzonov slapped his shoulder. 'Very well then, let's all of us now agree to act accordingly.'

Siggi was last out of his room. Before leaving she took up the notepad and looked again at the simple telltale sketch. But in the privacy of her own room she smiled a secret smile, and thought: *Well then, Mr Ben Trask, Mr human lie-detector. But just because your talent is to discover lies, that doesn't mean you can't tell one from time to time, eh? Or sketch one? And so you would like to fuck my face, would you? Well, I can forgive you for that, for I know it was only your way of testing me. But if you'll settle for a kiss . . .?*

303

And smiling, she blew a kiss across the empty room . . .

As they passed through customs at Heathrow, Trask and Goodly were met by the spotter Frank Robinson. In his early forties, still Robinson looked no more than twenty-eight or -nine. His freckles gave him a permanent schoolboy look and his hair was blond as ever; he would always seem a 'young' sort of person. His presence at the airport served a dual purpose. One: he was meeting the Head of E-Branch and a colleague off their plane, and two: he was keeping his eyes and mind open for other mindspies. During the last twenty-four hours there had been a lot of unaccustomed esper activity, most of it stemming from the Russian embassy. It had been quite a while since things were as hot as this.

During the drive to HQ, Trask wasted no time asking how the Branch had known he and Goodly were coming home; he automatically assumed they'd know almost as much as he did. But he was interested in the state of play. 'How are we dealing with the Opposition?'

'Diplomatically,' Robinson answered.

Trask knew what he meant: applying pressure to diplomatically immune persons could be difficult. But: 'Would you like to be a little more specific?'

'Well, one of their best telepaths was getting a bit too close for comfort by the time I spotted him. Cheeky sod! He'd booked himself into the hotel downstairs and was listening in from point-blank range! We told our friends in Special Branch about him; they picked him up on a moving traffic offence and planted – er, "found" – some very illegal substances hidden in his car. Tsk-tsk! He's been confined to the embassy while the Minister for Foreign Affairs looks into it. And two more of Tzonov's people have been driving round throwing a screen of static at us morning, noon, and night, trying to scramble our probes. We haven't bothered to counter them; it's good to know where they are and what they're up to, and their efforts have been pretty useless at best. Also, some of our little yellow friends have been showing a lot of interest in us, but since Peking and Moscow aren't in cahoots these days, we've simply let them get on with it. Meanwhile, we're keeping our eyes peeled, so to speak.'

'Huh!' Trask grunted. 'Well, I know I should be reassured, but I'm not. Things feel wrong. We could be under surveillance right now, by gadget if not by ghost.' It was a Branch in-joke. The espers talked of the two sides of espionage: the gadgets of modern day technology, and the ghosts of parapsychology. Except this time Trask wasn't joking but stating a fact. For well over thirty years now, hi-tech electronic surveillance had been one of the world's fastest growing industries.

'The car could be bugged, certainly,' Robinson shrugged. 'But it's something we live with. We can't cover ourselves all of the time.'

'We can try,' Trask told him. 'And this time it's important as never before. So tell me no more for now, and I'll save what I've got until we're home and dry.'

'As you will.' Robinson nodded. 'But at least let me tell you this much: there's a surprise waiting for you at HQ.'

'Good or bad?'

Robinson was negotiating a bend and for a moment couldn't answer. Ian Goodly, precog, was with Trask in the back of the car; he was looking out of his window, saying nothing. Perhaps he was hiding his face, which wore a grin like a Cheshire cat. Finally Robinson answered Trask's question. 'Good or bad? You mean your surprise? Good, I think. Indeed, excellent!'

'We shall see,' Trask grunted. Which was the end of their conversation —

— Until the scanners hidden in the walls of the elevator at E-Branch HQ had cleared them for bugs, and they were on their way up. Then Trask said: 'What's the surprise?'

Robinson grinned. 'I think she'd prefer to speak for herself.' She? Trask wasn't in the mood for games, and was on the point of saying so when the doors hissed open. As they stepped out into familiar surroundings, he heard voices from his office at the end of the corridor where the door stood ajar. One voice was soft and even a little sibilant for all that its owner was a Londoner born and bred: David Chung, who was the acting-Head of Branch in Trask's absence. And the other was female and not quite . . . unfamiliar? Then, quite clearly, Chung said:

'They're here!' Trask and Goodly knew that he could only be referring to them. But who was he talking to? Goodly thought he already knew but would wait and see. They weren't kept waiting, and as 'she' stepped out into the corridor Goodly saw how right he'd been. Sometimes the future was worth reading after all.

Trask saw her, too, and his jaw dropped like a trapdoor. Zek Föener!

Across a distance of a dozen paces, Ben Trask and Zek Föener checked each other out. At first there were differences: they *looked* as different as people do with the passage of time. But stepping cautiously towards each other and as the distance narrowed down, the years and all the changes fell away. Zek . . .

She was still very beautiful. No, Trask made a mental correction, forget the 'still': Zekintha Föener *was* beautiful, as simple as that. She always had been and he guessed she always would be. At five feet nine, she was just an inch shorter than he himself. But a looker: she was something else. Named by her Greek mother after Zante (or more properly Zakinthos, the Mediterranean island where she had been born), Zek was slim, leggy, blonde and blue-eyed. Trask would never forget how she'd looked that time out in the Greek Islands, towards the end of the Janos Ferenczy nightmare; that day on Manolis Papastamos's boat, when they'd gone looking for the white ship, Ferenczy's *Lazarus*, to send her and her vampire crew to hell:

Zek had worn a yellow bikini consisting of very little and leaving nothing at all to the imagination. Just like now, she'd scarcely looked her age but was sleek, tanned, stunning. With her eyes blue as the Aegean, her hair flashing gold, and a smile like a white blaze, everyone had agreed that she was a distraction. It was intended that she should be, a trick she'd learned from a Wamphyri Lady on Starside: that even when men's eyes are wary for other things, still it's relatively easy for a beautiful woman to turn them aside. And not only the eyes of men, but sometimes of monsters, too ...

And that was something else well worth remembering: that quite apart from her wonderful command of telepathy (her father had been an East German parapsychologist), Zek Föener was probably the world's greatest living expert on the Wamphyri source-world. She had actually been there – had lived there for long weeks and months, with both the Travellers and the Wamphyri – and survived the experience on her own until Jazz Simmons had found her, since when they'd never been apart.

Trask returned to the present. Zek must be – some fifty years old now? Not that you'd ever guess it just from looking at her. Strange, but for all that she and Siggi Dam were miles apart, and not alone in their ages, he found it difficult not to compare them. Perhaps it was because Siggi was fresh in his mind, or maybe it was simply that their colours and shapes were alike. But that was a peripheral comparison, lying fuzzy on the edge of his awareness; while the rest of it, seen close-up . . . that was the difference between a fjord and the Côte d'Azure.

Not so simply put, Siggi Dam was flawless and therefore, by human standards, imperfect, while Zek Föener's small flaws were what made her perfect! For example her mouth, whose soft, naturally moist lips were just a fraction too full, and tended to tremble when she was angry. And the uneven jut of her jaw, also when she was upset, which seemed slightly more prominent on the right. Unlike Siggi, and for that matter Turkur Tzonov, too, the two halves of Zek were a long way short of being mirror images, but they did accentuate her humanity. Trask knew which he preferred.

He also knew that all of these thoughts were his alone, that Zek wouldn't betray a trust and read him uninvited. For while the mindspies of E-Branch worked as closely as possible as one body, it was important that they retain their own identities and personalities intact, inviolate. Being a powerful telepath in her own right, Zek would understand that the code of such people made no allowance for casual snooping.

At the other end of the spectrum, however, in the event it became necessary in the performance of their duties (if a colleague's life were under threat, or E-Branch itself endangered), then it might be possible, theoretically at least, to link-up as one Entity, one Talent. It hadn't happened yet, and never would if it meant permanent damage to identity.

Still ... Trask knew how he found Zek, and couldn't help wondering how she found him. Time hadn't been too devastating, but neither had it been quite so kind to Ben Trask.

'Ben,' she finally said, and again looked him up and down. 'Not too much damage, eh?' If he didn't know better ... but he did. She managed a smile; it was wan, half-hearted. Perhaps she was tired.

'I was thinking the same thing –' he answered. '– About myself, I mean! But you ...' He shrugged. 'It's like yesterday.'

'Liar!' Her smile was still wan. 'But a nice try.'

'When did you get in?' They touched hands, hugged however briefly.

'Two hours ago. An early morning flight from Athens.'

'On your own?' Trask raised an eyebrow. David Chung had joined them from Trask's office. He was trying hard to catch Trask's eye across Zek's shoulder. But too late.

Zek didn't look away, didn't even blink. 'Jazz died six weeks ago,' she said, softly. 'Something he'd been fighting a little less than a year.'

Trask squeezed his eyes shut and let out his breath in a slow, painful sigh. 'Oh, Zek! I ...'

He wanted to hold her again but she took a small pace to the rear, and cut him off with: 'Before Jazz died, he said he wished that we'd tidied things up a bit. For Harry's sake, if for no other reason.'

'And that's why you're here?'

She nodded. 'Also, because I thought I might be needed. For almost a week now I've felt that something was going on. I mean, after Harry ... left us, I felt sort of switched off, drained, depressed. But this last five or six days I've felt switched on again. David here has filled in a few blanks for me, but not everything. No, of course not, because I suppose you'll want to clear me.'

'You want to work with us?' It was too good to be true.

Again her nod. 'For now, anyway. Jazz would have wanted me to, certainly.'

Zek's truth registered in Trask's mind. 'You're cleared,' he said. And to Chung, urgently now: 'Where is everyone?'

'In Ops. Working, watching, planning, waiting – for you. We only need your say-so to go in and bring him out.'

Trask said: 'Bring him out? Only as a last resort. Guide him out, that's different.' He looked at Zek again. 'Have you met everyone? Are you fed and watered? Has David looked after you? I mean, I hate to throw you in at the deep end, Zek, but you're right: things are on the move.'

The ice was broken now; its last few slivers were melting away, and Zek's smile was that much brighter. She laughed and said, 'I've had the VIP treatment, but I haven't met everyone, not yet.'

'First, Ian Goodly,' Trask introduced them. 'He's a precog. Ian, I want you to meet . . .'

'. . . Zekintha Föener.' Goodly offered his thin warm hand. 'An incredible asset.'

'She is, yes,' Trask agreed.

But Goodly only glanced at him, and again looked at Zek in that occasionally intense, disturbing way of his, and said, 'No, I meant she will be – and starting right now. Delighted to make your acquaintance, Zek. And don't worry: you're going to get on famously with everyone.'

She took to Goodly immediately, and as they started along the corridor towards Ops, said, 'You read the future?'

'When the future allows it,' he answered, 'and only then when I can't avoid it.' The gloomy expression was back on his face.

'Is it that bad?'

'I'll try to explain it to you some time,' he said. 'Maybe when you're settled in.'

And Trask barely managed to keep from snorting his frustration. It was more of a promise than the precog had made him in twenty years! Well, that wasn't quite true, but he'd never been so ready, willing, and able about it. There again, Trask wasn't Zek Föener . . .

VII

Szgany Ferengi

Introductions took fifteen minutes. The actuality of E-Branch — what its members did, what they were, their various talents — wasn't a problem. Zek simply accepted it at face value, and knew it for a fact. In the old days, at the end of Gregor Borowitz's term as Head of the Opposition, and again during Ivan Gerenko's reign of terror, she had worked for Soviet E-Branch. Better still, she'd been a close friend of the Necroscope and had seen what he could do — and knew what he had been before he left for Starside. Which were qualifications enough.

Then it was time to put them all in the picture. Including Ian Goodly. Things had happened in Perchorsk which Goodly still didn't know about, and Trask wondered how he would take being told about them. On the other hand, perhaps he already knew what Trask would talk about. Things which were plain in Trask's hindsight might very well have been known to Goodly in advance, *before* the event! Working with espers was hell.

Trask got them all seated and walked up and down in front of them for a moment or two to get his thoughts in order. Then, to David Chung: 'What's the chance of the Opposition latching on to any of this?'

'Very small,' Chung answered. 'Things have moved too fast for them. If they'd managed to sneak a couple of good telepaths into London in the last twenty-four hours, maybe then. But they haven't. What talents they do have are small fry, and the best of them has been nailed down in their embassy. They're not even trying to eavesdrop, just slinging a little mental mud about.'

Trask glanced at Zek seated in the front row, cocked his head on one side inquiringly. She put a hand to her brow and closed her eyes, and after a moment nodded and said, 'There's a lot of static about but nothing specific. It's just so much flak. They don't know what to aim at. I think I would know if someone was listening.'

'Right,' said Trask. 'Briefly, then: We went to the Perchorsk Projekt in the Urals to check out a man who had come through the Gate, to find out if he *was* a man. We went because my opposite number, Turkur Tzonov, invited us ... so we thought. But it now turns out we were there mainly because Gustav Turchin had ordered it. Tzonov made the best of a bad situation and used us to his own advantage. His visitor *is* a man, but by no means an ordinary one. And so that you can all stop wondering about it right now: this *isn't* the baby we cared for at Branch HQ that time, who later took his mother to Starside and became The Dweller and a legend there. No, for he was only one of Harry Keogh's sons. And this visitor from the Gate, he's another!

'Now, I'm not a telepath but Nathan – that's his name – spoke to me like that, telepathically, on three separate occasions. It takes a powerful sort of mind to do that, even when the contact is invited, as I invited him. Also, it's true that as espers we naturally accept the existence of diverse talents and so make ourselves more accessible to them. Still, Nathan's talent is something to be reckoned with. He's as good and even better than our very best.

'What we talked about in our first two conversations isn't important, but the last time –' Trask paused and looked at Ian Goodly, who had been listening intently from the first mention of this previously unsuspected contact, '– that was different. It was during last night, or early this morning. Nathan's telepathic "voice" came to me in my sleep, but I sensed it was much more than any ordinary dream. He'd been held a prisoner but had freed himself – don't ask me how! Now he was off and running, heading for Romania and the second Gate, his one route home to Sunside. That's all Nathan's trying to do: get back home again to some unfinished business, which he didn't specify.

'And he needed help. Was there any way I could smooth the way for him, take out any obstacles in his path? Well, perhaps I could, but even so . . .

I told him he'd never make it; if he got as far as what used to be the Romanian border, Tzonov's men would be waiting for him. And Tzonov was only the beginning, for beyond him . . . there is no way Nathan could even get into the resurgence without our help. I told him we had the place guarded, and even a little about the Radujevac Refuge. But at least we're in control out there, so there might be something of a chance eventually. But right now . . . it was out of the question that he might somehow be able to swim or navigate the underground river to the Gate. Quite impossible. No one but Harry Keogh has ever done it, and Nathan doesn't have his father's powers – not yet, anyway.

'How could he have such powers? His people are Travellers, Gypsies. Always on the move to avoid the Wamphyri, they've developed no science as such, no numbers. We know that the Necroscope's thing was a mathematical trick he conjured out of his mind. It was metaphysical maths, Möbius maths, which has nothing at all to do with multiplication tables and slide rules. Nathan has no schooling; his father's numbers are in him, certainly, but they can't find their way out. Not unless he gets some expert help. I told him we might be able to help him that way, and he was interested.

'But he's even more interested in his father, Harry Keogh, a man he never knew. Nathan's only a young man, but all of his life he's had this weird stuff in him, which again he couldn't or wouldn't specify, though I could make a pretty shrewd guess. And he's never known where any of it came from, only the feeling of something incredible waiting just around the corner for him, if only he can get it all together.

'So, I told him a few things about Harry. Not a lot, just enough to illustrate how much we all owed him. And I said that while Harry never got much of a square deal from the living of this world, at least the dead had loved him. So much that they would even get up out of their graves for him! And when Nathan heard that: how much the Great Majority had loved his father, and some of the things they'd done for him . . . that was when I knew I had him!

'But don't think I take any pride in it, and don't get me wrong. I haven't hooked into him like a fish, and I don't intend to play him like one, either. Now that I've met Nathan and know him, I just think he's entitled to some of the breaks that Harry didn't get, that's all. What I'm saying is this: if we do manage to get him out of there, it's for him, not for us. The only satisfaction we'll get out of it is knowing that Tzonov hasn't got him. But after that, it's Nathan's choice.'

Trask let everything he'd said so far sink in, then continued: 'When I woke up this morning I knew our business was done in Perchorsk, and the best thing would be to get out of there and see if we could help

Nathan from outside. And that's what we're doing.'
Again he looked at Goodly but spoke to everyone. 'So
you see, all of this stuff that passed between Nathan
and me is news even to Ian Goodly here, because if I
had told him about it —'

'— Then there'd be another mind to leak it,' Goodly
said, nodding. 'Yes, of course. I understand.'

'Right,' Trask said. 'So now let's talk some more
about Tzonov. Well, Ian and I snooped around in the
Perchorsk Projekt and saw some pretty worrying stuff,
enough that we think Tzonov is going to be a real
problem, and not only to us. He's already ticking like
a political time-bomb in his own country, and Gustav
Turchin's the only one who doesn't seem to hear him
yet. Or we hope he doesn't. But if Turchin's in on it —
well, so much for all the *glasnost* he's been engaging
in.

'For the fact is, Tzonov's got an arsenal at Perchorsk,
and there can only be one reason why. Ian and I saw
the Gate, and we can tell you that it's locked up safer
than the doors on the Bank of England. Just like Nathan,
anything that comes through is going to be trapped and
dealt with at the discretion of the people at this end. So
no need to worry about any sort of invasion from
Starside. But maybe we do need to concern ourselves
about an invasion in the other direction!

'Now here's the problem: how to stop it? How can we
tell Turchin what we suspect if he's in on it? Will he
want to stop it, or will he consider Sunside/Starside a
new Soviet territory ripe for conquest and exploitation?
If the latter, and he lets Tzonov go ahead, how will that
work out for the rest of us? The Russians have made
some pretty big errors in the past, several of which
continue to affect the world even today. Chernobyl and
the Aral Sea are just two examples. But to mess with

something as dangerous as the Gate . . .' Lost for words, Trask shook his head. 'Pandora's box just isn't in the same league!'

David Chung spoke up. 'What will you do?'

Trask shrugged. 'Pass on all we know to our Minister Responsible, and let him take it from there. Eventually it should get back to Turchin, and hopefully he'll be able to deal with it – *if* he's not in on it. And if he is, he won't. Which means that at some time in the future, we might have to deal with it ourselves.'

He hitched himself up on the edge of the briefing podium. 'Right, that's me done for now. There will be a detailed report later, which I expect all of you to read. And now it's your turn. What have you lot been up to?'

Chung stood up. 'I tracked you to Perchorsk, just to keep an eye on you. And incidentally, there's some very heavy Opposition static up there in the Urals!'

'Siggi Dam,' Trask nodded. 'She'll be in my report, too. But I interrupted you; I'm sorry; please go on.'

'This talent, the latent power you felt in Nathan,' Chung continued. 'This "weird stuff", as you named it. It was what I sensed – and Zek, too – even before he was through the Gate. The closer he got to our world, the more we felt his presence. And that's where we hold an ace card over Tzonov. Namely, me!' Chung grinned. 'Tzonov doesn't have a first-rate locator. One or two second-raters, but nothing nearly as good as me. And I have my own crystal ball.' He held up Harry's hairbrush. 'Now that Nathan's through the Gate, it's like this thing has come alive. If it was a lodestone, Nathan would be due north! I can locate – I've *been* locating him – far easier than anything I ever did before.'

Trask's sigh of relief was clearly audible, but: 'I hope you've been careful,' he said in a moment. 'God knows

317

we don't want the Opposition using you as a carrier beam!'

Chung shook his head. 'I've kept my tracking to a minimum, a glance at a time. But I can go to the map board and show you where he is — I mean right now! That's what I was talking about when I said we could bring him out. Under cover of darkness; a stealth helicopter, a team of SAS men, and me; we'd be in and out before the Comrades even knew we . . .'

'. . . Comrades?' Trask held up a hand. 'And that's what *I* meant when I said we could *guide* him out. But go in and snatch him? The way you're talking, anyone would think we're at war! We're not, not even a cold war. In fact with Gustav Turchin in the chair we never had it so good. Which is why we daren't go stirring it up now. But if we can get Nathan closer to the border . . .'

Suddenly Trask couldn't resist it. Shrugging himself down from the podium, he headed for the map board and said, 'Show me where he is.'

Chung beat him to it, got there as the huge screen flickered into life. He held Harry Keogh's old hairbrush tightly in his left hand, reached up his right hand and placed it flat on the screen in an area to the west of the Northern Urals. Then he closed his eyes. A smaller screen inset at the bottom right of the wall screen blurred into grey life, waiting to indicate a specific region. The map overall was sensitive but wouldn't react to Chung's entire palm, only to a finger. And as Chung's brow creased into a tight frown and his eyes screwed yet more tightly shut, so he drew his fingers together until his hand was raised up and only the index finger touched the screen.

'There!' he said.

The inset screen snapped into a clear, detailed chart

of the indicated area, a grid some ten-by-ten miles. Trask pressed the 'hold' button; Chung removed his hand; the small, magnified area on the inset screen defined Nathan's location: an area of woodland, forest trails, frozen marshes.

'So he's somewhere in there,' Trask mused, his eyes rapt on the screen.

'No, not "somewhere".' Chung wasn't known for his modesty in matters such as this. 'He's dead centre.'

In the next moment both men became aware of the perfume of a third person close behind them. Zek Föener. 'David,' she said. 'Ben. Do you remember that time in Rhodes? Harry was in the Carpathians, and we wondered how he was doing?'

The two men looked at each other, then at Zek. And Trask said: 'You want to establish contact?'

'Why not?' She was deadly serious. 'You want to guide him out of there, don't you? And you know that the longer it takes, the greater the danger. Even now his chances are slimming down. So if we can reach him, and if he's willing . . .'

Trask pulled at his chin. The other espers had gathered round, were watching intensely. 'Do it,' Trask said. 'But if you do get through, make it as brief as possible. First establish contact, then we'll work out details which you can relay later.'

Trask had seen all of this before, but it was new to some of the others. Zek closed her hand over Chung's with the hairbrush still in it, and he touched the fingertips of his right hand to the centre of the small screen. Then they closed their eyes, breathed deeply, and concentrated, concentrated . . .

. . . And gasped in unison!

Zek's hand flew from Chung's; both of them staggered back away from the wall screen; Trask caught their

319

arms, steadying them. But when Zek looked at him he saw her expression change from a look of astonishment to one of wonder. And: 'Numbers!' she said. 'He may not know how to use them, but they're part of him anyway. Certainly he knows how to hide behind them.'

'Oh yes, that's him,' Trask said, snatching a breath; and it surprised him, with all of his experience, to discover that he'd actually been holding it!

'But he is hiding,' Zek repeated, 'shielding his mind. And his shield is . . . *very* powerful. If I'm to get through, I shall need help.'

Trask knew what she meant. A group effort, of concentrated will. And as she and Chung stepped closer to the screen, so the espers clustered to them, linked hands and formed a semi-circle with Zek, Chung and Trask at its centre. And now Trask's hand, too, covered those of the telepath Zek, and the locator Chung. And once again Chung made contact with the screen —

— And with Nathan!

But this time they were ready; Zek forced her telepathic probe straight into, and through, the whirling wall of Nathan's numbers vortex. His mind — at first surprised, then afraid — was revealed to her:

Who . . .?

A friend, she sent. *Even as I was your father's friend.*

My father?

The Necroscope, Harry Keogh.

For a single moment the vortex was reinforced; it whirled that much harder, faster, and threatened to hurl her out. But in the next it collapsed, and at its core . . . Nathan was a wondering child. And Zek sighed, for to her touch his mind was the image of his father's in the long ago: warm, vulnerable, innocent. But that had always been the paradox, and never more than at the end. Harry Keogh, vampire, and vulnerable. A Necroscope, who talked to dead people, yet warm. A man with the powers of a destoying angel — even an Angel of Death — but innocent.

He read these things and more, and *knew* that she had known his father. But who was she?

She opened her secret mind. And now it was Nathan's turn to gasp. *Zek!* His astonishment rang in her mind. *Lardis's hell-lander friend! He still speaks of you! You were there, with the Travellers in Sunside! You fought alongside the Szgany in the battle for The Dweller's garden, before I was born!*

She formed a picture for him, of what it had been like. And there was no disguising the fact that she *had* been there, for no one who didn't know the Wamphyri could ever attempt so vivid a description, or conjure such depths of loathing. But then her woman's curiosity took over:

How old are you, Nathan?

He told her.

And now Zek could see it all. *When The Dweller returned Jazz and myself home — when he brought us back here — Harry stayed behind a while, in your world.*

Nathan took it up. *My father, Hzak Kiklu — at least, he was the one I was always led to believe was my father — had been mortally wounded. He was dead. But my mother . . .*

Zek sensed Nathan's confusion, the wound that was opening in him — a feeling of betrayal? — and was quick off the mark to counter it. *Nana Kiklu? Your mother? Still alive and well? But she's an incredibly brave woman, Nathan! Oh, yes, I remember Nana! It was the aftermath; she was lonely and had suffered . . . a lot! But Harry had suffered, too, and in a way he'd lost more than anyone. So they were two of a kind, thrown together by forces beyond their control. Except . . . I'm* sure there was a lot more to it than just that. Zek tried to be as understanding, yet as honest, as circumstances allowed. *They must have fallen in love.*

She could feel Trask's grip tightening on her wrist, and heard his whisper in her ear: 'Get out of there! Don't jeopardize him!'

You've lured me. Nathan was very quiet now, almost accusing. *I have to know everything. And you knew I would . . .*

Nathan, she answered. *You know Trask. His mind is an open book. He reads truth in men. Surely you read the truth in him? You'll come to no harm with us. We won't use you. And from now on I won't intrude upon you again . . . unless you ask me to.*

There was a long pause, and then: *What do you want me to do? Where must I go?*

I'll get back to you soon, Zek told him with a glad sigh. *Please be ready . . .*

That night, the Gypsies made camp in a forest on the edge of a frozen marsh twenty miles east of Kozhva. In the caravan of their old, leathery leader, Nathan was an honoured guest.

From the moment he'd spotted them from his hiding place in the back of the supply vehicle out of Perchorsk (and risked his neck leaping from the truck's tailgate into a bank of snow at the side of the road), Nathan had known that these were his people. They were almost indistinguishable from the Szgany of Sunside. That had come as a shock to him, to find such people here. And an even greater shock to hear their spoken language, which had more of the Sunside tongue in it than the Russian he had been 'learning' in Perchorsk.

Languages were easy for Nathan; matching spoken words to mind-pictures was a simple device, which he'd learned from the desert-dwelling Thyre in their colonies south of Sunside. Thus, almost from his first fumbled conversation with the men of the caravans, understanding had been mutual and friendship inevitable. But he had sensed that meeting up with them was far more than just a matter of good fortune; it had seemed almost predestined, so that now he asked the old chief:

'How did you know?'

The other cocked his head on one side and winked. He was all dark-stained leather, a glint of gold tooth, a plain gold ring in the lobe of his right ear, and more gold on his fingers. But ... no silver? 'Ah, and so you sensed that, did you? That we'd been waiting for you?' The old man chuckled. 'Well, that's my secret. It's why I'm the chief!'

Of course, Nathan could look inside his head if he wanted to, but he wouldn't. That was something else he'd learned from the Thyre: that except in circumstances of mutually agreed intercourse between friends or colleagues, or in times of extreme danger to the community as a whole, the privacy of the individual was ever sacrosanct. A glance might be permissible, acceptable, almost unavoidable, but never the wholesale ransacking of a mind's contents. In a nutshell: it was unseemly to steal the private thoughts of others when simple speech would suffice. A person must always be given the opportunity to *speak* his mind.

It was why Nathan had restricted the use of his telepathy to learning the language of these Travellers. They knew nothing of his mentalism, nor would he enlighten them. For if he should appear too clever, if he knew or understood too much too soon, it could well distance them. And in the event of their rejection – if they were to brand him a thought-thief – eventually he might find himself deprived not only of their friendship

323

but possibly of his liberty, too. Nathan still thought in Sunside/Starside terms, and probably always would.

So he said nothing but simply sat and waited, and was at last rewarded, in some small measure at least, when finally the weathered old chief said, 'There are some strange places in the world, don't you think?'

'I know very little of the world,' Nathan answered after a moment's thought. 'In what way, strange? What places do you mean?'

'Oh, just places.' The old chief shrugged, puffed on his clay pipe, and continued to be vague. He didn't appear concerned about his guest's obvious ignorance, his lack of knowledge generally, or even his occasionally strange manner of expression. 'I'm talking about the old places, you know? The timeless old places. Places the Szgany know – some of the Szgany, anyway – and which they visit from time to time. Places they've always visited.'

Nathan wasn't sure how best to answer that, and so returned to studying his surroundings: The caravan was similar to vehicles he'd seen on Sunside: four wheels, beast-drawn, varnished and painted with intricate, flowing designs. Central to the interior, a wood-burning stove stood on legs which were bolted to the floor; a fire-blackened flue went up through a metal collar to a cowled chimney in the roof. Festooned on the outside with all sorts of pots and pans and other implements that jingled and gonged when it moved, it had a curving roof of varnished boards in place of the waterproofed hides which Nathan was used to. Other than that, and especially here in the forest, he might fancy himself back on Sunside.

But no, it was far too cold for Sunside, and these people were only the descendants of true Travellers. Nathan saw that now – knew that it must be so – and

wondered how long since the first of them had accompanied their banished Wamphyri masters out of Starside
and into these hell-lands. Then they had been thralls
and now were free. So . . . what of their old masters?

'I'm a Ferengi, did you know?' The old man grinned.

Nathan gave a small start. Perhaps his unspoken
question had been answered. On Sunside the name had
been a curse since time immemorial! Of course, for
among the Wamphyri there had always been creatures
of that selfsame ilk. Ferenc, Ferenczy, Ferengi: in all its
forms the name was an evil invocation.

'Vladi Ferengi, aye.' The chief nodded. 'Last of a long,
long line. The very last, for my woman was barren – or
maybe I was!' He grinned and patted the front of his
baggy trousers. 'This firm old friend steamed hot enough
in the romp, but his issue was cold and dead – maybe.
But what does it matter, eh? I have no sons, and that's
the end of it. My people will stop going there. To the
strange places.'

'You mean that you won't be here to lead them
there?' Nathan was curious now.

'That's right. I won't be here to hear the call.'

An idea was beginning to take shape. 'All of this
seems to connect up,' Nathan said. 'You are trying to
explain something which you yourself don't understand,
in the hope that I might understand it for you. And
maybe I do . . . well, some of it. But first you must tell
me: are the Szgany Ferengi an old people? How long
have you been . . . here?'

'My grandfather's great-great-grandfather was a Ferengi, aye,' the old one answered. 'That's as far back as I
care to trace the line. But I've no doubt that *he* would
say the same, if he were here now! How long, you ask?
I've seen the Ferengi device carved in the mountains of
the Khorvaty, which is one of the strange places. But

such a device, eh? And old as the mountains themselves.'

Nathan knew the sigil he referred to; he'd seen it
carved in the timber frame of Vladi's caravan, skilfully
disguised in the intricate but flowing designs that were
painted there: the head of a devil, with crimson eyes,
bifurcate tongue, and grinning jaws that dripped gouts
of blood. He put the picture aside and said, 'The Khorvaty? Do you mean back there? That place in the pass,
Perchorsk, where I . . . came from?'

'Eh? Ah, no! Not there! Only *feelings* there, Nathan,
and recent ones at that: a dozen or two of years at best.
Feelings, my son, which have spawned nothing. I
thought that perhaps this time –' he shrugged, '– but it
was only you.'

Nathan nodded. Things continued to connect, however dubiously. He didn't much care for the connection,
but must pursue it anyway. Perhaps he could accelerate
the process. 'Should I tell you a word, a name?'

The chief raised an eyebrow. 'By all means.'

'Wamphyri!'

It had the desired effect. 'An emissary!' Vladi leaned
forward and grasped Nathan's arm, his astonishing
speed belying his age. 'You *are* from them, their messenger between the worlds! The Old Ferengi is dead – *long
live the Ferengi!* Now quickly, tell me: what message
does he send? And when will he come?'

Nathan saw it all now: Vladi and his people were
descended from Wamphyri supplicants. And suddenly
his skin crawled under the old chief's gaze and touch.
But he mustn't show it; and anyway, it wasn't their
fault. They didn't know, couldn't possibly remember
after all this time, the true nature of the being or beings
they still waited to serve, as their fathers' fathers had
served before them.

Forsaking ethics for a moment, Nathan allowed himself a single glimpse behind the old chief's eyes, and saw:

... The figure of a great man, hands on hips. Toweringly benevolent. And all the world's Travellers at his feet, under his care, prosperous in their gleaming, painted caravans and proudly flying his banner: the devil's head with its crimson eyes, forked tongue, and spattered gouts of blood.

But in the light of the latter ... perhaps Vladi and his people weren't so innocent after all.

'You're waiting for the Ferengi,' Nathan said, but very slowly and carefully. 'I can only tell you this: that he – they – would come if only they could be sure of their reception.' It was true enough, he was sure. But to himself: *Except they believe this place is hell, and I shall never enlighten them!*

'Ahhh!' The old man released Nathan's arm and fell back in his seat against the caravan's side. 'But ... do they think we have forgotten them?' For a moment his huge black eyes were empty, but then they brightened. 'Surely the Ferengi would not send you here without that they could recall you? When and how will you go back – from where will you depart – to reassure the Lords of their glorious reception here?'

Before, Nathan had spoken a half-truth. Now he must lie outright, or at least shape his answer carefully, to disguise his real purpose. But since he'd now associated these supplicant Travellers with the Wamphyri, he shouldn't find too much difficulty in lying. 'There are Gates between worlds,' he said. 'Back in Perchorsk, there was one such, but I may not go back that way. Now tell me: where are the other strange places?'

'Do they wait for you there?' Vladi was excited again. He tapped rapidly upon the side of his veined nose, producing a hollow, drumming sound, and said, 'I know them, these Gates and the strange places which contain them! Only tell me where you would go and we will take you there.'

'Ah, but my route may be circuitous.' (Nathan's turn to be vague.) 'There is information I must gather along the way, before I can go back. You must not question me.'

'Ahhh!' (Again the old chief's sigh.) 'Now we understand each other! But do you see why I was cautious? These things of which we speak, they are not ordinary things.'

Nathan relaxed a little. 'So, the Travelling Folk, you and your people, have waited all these years without number for the Wamphyri – the Ferengi – to return and lead you to greatness. But what of the *Old* Ferengi, who brought you here?'

'Gone.' The other's voice was a sad, empty sigh. 'Turned to dust in their crumbling castles, or stiffened to stones in their unmarked tombs, or burned to ashes in the fires of men. They are no more.'

'Men hunted them down?' Perhaps these hell-lands deserved their name after all: hell for the Wamphyri, at least.

'I won't speak of it!' Vladi shook his head. 'The Szgany Ferengi remain true. When you return you must tell them this: that *we* remember them still, and will always be true to their memory. While I live, at least . . .'

His ancient voice tapered away, and Nathan could see that he was tired. But before he would let him sleep, or sleep himself: 'You still haven't told me how you knew.'

The old man reached up and tapped his nose again, winked, opened the palm of his hand to show its deep etched lines. 'I read things in the lines, in flights of birds, in the mists of the earth. I see things, hear things, know things, which other men can never know! I have ... *feelings!* Voices call to me out of the winds; the planets that travel through the skies direct my travels; the waters of my ears and brain are lured even as the moon lures the tides. And as the Ferengi's true blood of life was in my father, so my father's blood is in me. Ah, for the blood is the life!'

The old chief stood up, turned down the lamp, and in the glow from the stove stepped to his bed beside the door. Nathan went to his own bed, a narrow bench at the back of the caravan, and curled up there. So old Vladi was a seer, a fortune-teller: he read future times ... but he wasn't a mentalist. And Nathan knew that he could leave his mind unguarded, so that Zek could come to him.

Before sleeping, Vladi's whisper reached out to Nathan in the dark: 'About your route. When will you know which path to follow? In the autumn, because I sensed that something was happening in the old places, I instructed my people to lay in food for men and beasts alike, so that we might winter in the caves of the foothills. But now ... it's cold out here in the open, and we may not stay too long.'

'Maybe in the morning,' Nathan answered. 'Come sunup, I'm sure I'll know by then.'

'They will ... speak with you, you think?'

'Someone will, yes.'

'*Ahhh!*'

And to prove it, long after the old chief began to snore, Nathan lay awake, waiting and listening for that someone ...

It was so obvious that Ben Trask wondered why they

hadn't seen it from square one. But having wondered, he'd known the answer to that, too: that mindspies are not spies in the classic sense of the word. David Chung had been pretty close with his suggestion that they go in with a team of specialists. But it wasn't until Trask got in touch with the Minister Responsible, and he in turn spoke to others on a similar level in the Corridors of Power, that everything came together. Chung's sort of specialists wouldn't be required. A different type of specialist was already in place.

For fifteen years now the West had been helping sort out Russia's problems; ever since those three momentous days – the 19th, 20th, and 21st of August, 1991 – when as the result of a bungled coup against the then President Mikhail Gorbachev, old-style Communism had died a well-earned death and signalled the giddy ascent of two hundred and fifty million oppressed people to freedom and a true democracy. But while the mailed fist and the apparatus of the Old State were mainly absent now, the helping hand of the West remained extended, and its influence was never more in evidence.

West of the Urals (only a little more than seventy miles from where David Chung had found Nathan and Zek Föener had contacted him), in the chill, sparsely populated foothills of the Timanskiy Kryazh near Izhma, American geo-satellites had detected evidence of oil and gas fields which might well rival those at Ukhta in the south. Exploratory drilling had started two years ago; satellite predictions had been confirmed; the Anglo-American consortium would collect its very reasonable fee and pull out in two to three years' time as per the contract, leaving other Western outfits to complete the pipeline. And from then on the Russians would pay a royalty or percentage in perpetuity.

Meanwhile the hard-hats were still there, working *in*

situ and resupplied on a regular basis by jet-copter out of Stockholm via Helsinki. Why not from Moscow or Sverdlovsk, or from the long-established fields east of the Urals in Beresovo and Ust'balyk? But if the Soviets had retained that sort of technological capacity or know-how following their industrial, economic and ideological collapse, then the West would never have been allowed in in the first place.

Part of a Western Aid Programme agreed in the early 1990s, the Izhma Projekt was only one of many hundreds of schemes in progress right across the old USSR, from the Black Sea to the Kamchatka Peninsula, and from Novaya Zemlya to Irkutsk. Now a small portion of that huge debt – in the shape of a wanderer from another world – would flow the other way, but with any luck the Russians would never know of the repayment.

Except:

'Maybe our luck just ran out,' Zek said, worriedly.

It was a little after 1:30 a.m. GMT in London, and about 5:00 a.m. local in the woods west of Kozhva, where her call had shocked Nathan from his sleep. She'd kept it short: told him to head due west for Izhma, and what to look for. Then, almost too hurriedly, she'd pulled out. Now Zek's face was drawn, and not only from concentration.

Ben Trask's voice echoed her concern when he asked, 'What is it, Zek?'

'Unless I miss my guess,' she answered, 'there were other minds out there scanning around, looking for Nathan. And one of them was female, and powerful!'

Most of the other Branch members were present, including Ian Goodly. He said, 'That would be Siggi Dam. She's their very best.'

It was hardly reassuring. Likewise Zek's: 'But there

331

was more than just that one. And at least one of the others was a locator, I think. His probe wasn't tele-pathic, anyway.'

The reason they had chosen this hour (the early hours of the morning in the Urals) was a simple matter of human frailty. Espers need sleep as much as other people, and the Opposition's agents no less than anyone else. At five in the morning, people were at a low ebb. There was a flaw in that line of reasoning, of course: namely that Turkur Tzonov would understand the prin-ciple, too. But it had been a calculated risk.

Trask said: 'Do you think they overheard you?'

'Not overheard as such . . . but they might have sensed my presence, just as I sensed theirs.'

Trask looked at a blow-up of the area superimposed on the large screen. 'Terrain?' he queried of no one in particular.

'Fairly flat,' someone spoke up. 'Hard ground and a few woodland trails. Some moorland and frozen marsh, but plenty of cover in bands of dense, boreal forest. Climate? Cold enough to freeze the . . . antlers off an iron elk.' (That last in deference to Zek, Millicent Cleary, and Anna Marie English.)

'But Nathan is hardy,' Zek said. 'A Traveller in the company of his own kind.' She'd taken that from Nathan's mind in a blurred, rushed sequence. 'But I wonder: what on earth were they *doing* up there, those Gypsies?'

'Let's just be thankful they were there,' said Trask. And: 'Weather?'

'Frozen snow on the ground,' the same researcher replied. 'And according to the Finn weather station at Kotka, a lot more of it on the way. But just soft, steady snow. Maybe we should also be thankful that it's not going to be a blizzard! It's due to start in two hours'

332

time and keep going for a day and a half. In any case, the supply plane won't leave Stockholm until it's over.'

'Oh, really?' Trask grunted. 'Well in that case I've got some bad news for the pilot. The first hint of a break in the weather, and he's airborne!' He glanced at Chung. 'And David, I want you to get some sleep. Tomorrow morning you're with me on the first flight to Stockholm. Then, obviously, I want you on that supply plane to Izhma. If our man is coming in out of the cold, I don't want him getting lost.'

Trask looked at the other espers and smothered a yawn. 'As for getting your heads down: with the exception of duties, the same goes for all of you.' He stretched his shoulders and eased his neck. 'I don't know about anyone else, but I'm dead on my feet. Time we called it a day.' And as they started to disperse: 'Thanks for being here, everyone.'

In a matter of minutes he and Zek were alone. 'And especially you,' he told her. 'Thanks for being here.'

'Your coffee is dreadful,' she said. 'But David booked me in at the hotel down below, and theirs is quite good. We could talk about Harry maybe, for a while . . . ?'

Trask looked at her. She looked as tired as he felt, and this was her first time in England. A very capable woman, Zek, but right now she must feel lonely as hell. So did he, come to think of it. But then, he had for most of his life. 'Sure,' he nodded. 'A nightcap would be great.'

They drank coffee in Zek's hotel room (Trask had a small brandy with his), and talked awhile about everything and nothing, until Zek fell asleep fully clothed on her bed. Then Trask pulled a cover over her, put the light off and returned to his easy chair.

And when she gave him a shake it was morning . . .

VIII

Not Quite Hell, and Sheer Hell!

In the uncomfortable, noisy confines of the jet-copter's passenger cabin, Siggi Dam studiously avoided the thoughts of her closest travelling companion and reflected upon the events of the last two days . . .

Back in Perchorsk, Turkur Tzonov had been coldly furious for some thirty-odd hours now. In a way, this had suited Siggi well enough; she had been more than satisfied to steer clear of him. But even on the few occasions when they had come together accidentally, she'd not dared to look into his mind. For some reason (as a result of their showdown, perhaps, or something else which had happened since their trip out to Little Kozhva on the snowcat), Tzonov now demanded the same degree of mental privacy as Siggi herself. He would know it if she attempted to spy on him, and she didn't want to give him any excuse to use similar tactics on her.

Siggi knew how stupid she'd been, and how incredibly fortunate. Stupid in what she had done, and fortunate in that she hadn't been found out. But surely Tzonov's failure to discover her treachery meant that he was stupid in his turn, or at the very least blind. The latter was true, she knew. His egomania blinded him, preventing him from seeing the truth. But if the time should ever come when he did see it . . .

In the evening following their return from Kozhva,

334

esper assistance had arrived from Moscow in the shape of two lesser telepaths and a locator. The latter was a thin-faced, effeminate weasel of a man named Alexei Yefros; Siggi knew him through their work and disliked him intensely. Despite his suspect sexual proclivities (or perhaps because of them) Yefros was a misogynist with an especially ugly sadistic streak. Fully aware of Siggi's telepathic range, still on those several previous occasions when they'd met he had not once attempted to camouflage thoughts which could only be likened to a cesspool. An admirer and close confidant of Turkur Tzonov, he was ruthless, ambitious, and extremely dangerous.

Since the arrival of the espers, Tzonov had kept himself closeted with them in his makeshift operations suite just off the control room. Siggi had not been privy to their conversations, but she did know that Tzonov had spoken at some length to Premier Turchin (or to his presidential adviser, at least), and that he'd been given what amounted to a free hand in the matter of Nathan's pursuit and recapture – with one important exception. Tzonov had wanted authority to bring the fugitive back dead or alive (preferably dead, as Siggi was well aware), but Turchin had insisted that Nathan be taken alive. It was the human rights issue, of course. Gustav Turchin was still cleaning the political mud of a very messy century off Russia's boots, so that the last thing he wanted now was the blood of an innocent on his hands!

The night after Nathan's escape, Siggi had found sleep impossible. Tossing and turning in her bed for long hours at a stretch, only half-sleeping at best, finally she had given it up for a bad job. Rising well before dawn and dressing in her warmest clothing, she'd ventured out into the grey-misted ravine. There, relieved of Perchorsk's claustrophobia and satisfied that

Tzonov and the others were asleep, she'd extended a tentative telepathic probe across the mountains and beyond Kozhva, deep into the woodlands where the Gypsy caravans had been.

The faint, ethereal dreams of loggers, trappers, and villagers, all were there, but she had searched for something else. And she had found it! Like a spiral of mental static from some weird computer mind, briefly (but very briefly), she believed that she had touched upon Nathan's sleeping thoughts — only to discover that someone else was touching them, too! A telepathic mind: feminine, wary, clever, and benevolent. But who? British E-Branch? To Siggi's knowledge there was only one female telepath in British ESPionage: a spinster called Millicent Cleary. But she was sure that this wasn't her. No, for this one was a woman entire, experienced in every sense of the word.

All of this from a mere touch; it said a lot for Siggi's talent, and even more for the talent of the other. For in the selfsame moment that Siggi had become aware of the stranger, so that one had sensed Siggi ... and not *only* Siggi!

Then, made suddenly aware of other talented minds awake and watchful in the night — afraid that they might recognize hers — Siggi had withdrawn her thoughts and returned quickly to her room. And lying there in the dark, with the weight of the mountain once more pressing down on her (but not nearly as heavily as the weight of her fears), she'd wondered:

But if Turkur is using these people out of Moscow in this way, why isn't he using me? Was it her punishment for defying him: temporary exclusion from his schemes? Or would it be more permanent, because he no longer trusted her?

Finally she had slept, but her dreams had been

strange, furtive things in which she was pursued across the ridgy grey landscape of a throbbing, gigantic brain by black-winged inquisitorial thoughts with the piercing eyes, talons, and beaks of carrion crows . . .

. . . And the echoes of their cries (their questions?) were still ringing afar when she started awake. So that with Tzonov and his espers so close, she had wondered: was it perhaps more than just a dream? The invasion of sleeping minds would be common enough practice among espers such as these. And there had been times in Siggi's past when her own duties were such that . . . that she no longer had the right to complain.

That morning, yesterday, Tzonov had been up and about at first light, and his first act had been to cancel the search-parties scheduled for duty in the regions to the east of the pass. But even as he'd ordered the jet-copter made ready for a mission to the west of the mountains, and sought Siggi out to take her with him, so it had started to snow. And heavily.

The flight had been cancelled, (even a routine ascent out of the pass could be hazardous enough without this!) which had served to determine Tzonov's mood for the rest of the day. As for Siggi: she had never been happier to see bad weather. And the snow had stayed, and stayed. Not a blizzard but a continuous fall that blanketed the sky, turned the entire pass white, and forbade absolutely any kind of aerial search or reconnaisance which Tzonov might otherwise contemplate.

As the day had progressed, so Siggi's worries about her standing with the Head of Russia's E-Branch had receded somewhat. With every hour that passed, Nathan was getting farther away, and discovery of her own involvement less likely.

Also, and despite Premier Turchin's orders to the contrary, she knew that if Tzonov did track the fugitive down his men would be just as likely to shoot him as take him prisoner. Later, they would write corroborative reports to show how he had 'resisted arrest' and they had been obliged to use force. On the other hand Tzonov might decide it was best if Nathan disappeared altogether, presumed 'fled to the West'; in which event his riddled body could be dumped into a deep ravine somewhere, and no chance of any blame ever attaching to Turkur Tzonov. Anything, in order to stop Nathan falling into the 'wrong' hands, to prevent his (in any case doubtful) return to Sunside/Starside, or to exact a measure of vengeance in repayment for a bruised ego and a few days of intense embarrassment. But a man's life? It seemed a lot of repayment to Siggi.

She'd tried arguing with herself, tried telling herself that she too would benefit from Nathan's death (for dead men can't, after all, tell tales). But damn it to hell, she'd *known* him however briefly, and been *changed* by knowing him! She would never be able to erase him – the innocence of Nathan's mind – from her memory now. She wouldn't *want* to erase it.

So yesterday had dragged itself relentlessly by; the sky had unloaded its burden, and Siggi's depression had returned to deepen like the snow in the pass . . .

Tzonov had arranged that she have dinner with him and his cronies. Siggi ate very little, kept her thoughts guarded from start to finish, sensed their hostility generally and suffered Alexei Yefros's seething, deviantly carnal glances especially. She could sense the locator's rabid weasel mind loathsomely at work behind his glittering black eyes where they stripped away her clothing, and she shuddered not so much because he wanted her, but for the ways in which he would like to use her.

Finally, the meal had been over and Siggi could flee

back to her room. The day's events had exhausted her, and though she was half afraid of sleep still she had no choice. Mercifully the previous night's dreams (or visitations?) were not recurrent ... at least, not until this morning. That was when she'd discovered that even wide awake, still one may nightmare.

The nightmare was this: that the bad weather was clearing and Tzonov anticipated that by 3:00 p.m. the jet-copter would be cleared for take-off. He and Yefros had a lead on the fugitive and would search for him west of Kozhva, and Siggi would accompany them. Yefros would attempt to locate him (there was this weird aura about him, something numerical, with which he shielded his mind), and Siggi would home in on Yefros's probe for a more positive identification. This shouldn't prove too difficult for her, for as Tzonov delighted in reminding her, she'd already made Nathan's 'acquaintance' ...

Now it was 4:00 p.m. and Kozhva lay to the east more than fifty miles behind them; Tzonov was crammed up front with the pilot and co-pilot, and Siggi shared the passenger cabin with Alexei Yefros. His were the thoughts she studiously avoided, and his the probe she could sense sweeping out from him like ripples on a pool, or some personal psychic asdic, searching for Nathan's fugitive identity.

Yefros was good. Over Kozhva, suddenly he had come alive and pointed out of a window in a direction a little south of west. 'That way! He's there! He throws off equations like a smokescreen, which only serve to give him away!'

But on Sunside (Siggi had thought), *and especially in Starside, in that largely innumerate world of vampires, such numbers would have cloaked him admirably. The Wamphyri home in on fear, sweat, and blood. Nathan's numbers would appear as a screen of mental static to them.* A guess, still it fell only a little short of the mark. But here in this world:

Here it's a traitor (she continued to theorize), *a scent for the hounds, spoor for the hunter.*

Tzonov had been studying his small-scale map, complaining bitterly about its inaccuracies. But in a moment his eyes had narrowed. Fumbling his way back into the passenger cabin, he repeated Yefros: 'West and a little south?' And stabbing a finger at the map. 'You mean the Luza River, Izhma and Sizyabsko? And after that a lot of frozen marshland? Are you sure? But is he just running wild? There's nothing there!'

Yefros had glanced at the map, then stared at it, and his weasel eyes had opened wide. 'Izhma!' he'd gasped then. '*Izhma! The new oil field!*'

'Eh?'

'British and American engineers, Russian workers,' Yefros had continued. 'They're opening the place up. Big news a year or two ago, it promised riches galore. Another fine example of East-West cooperation; like the French hydro-electric scheme on the Volga. Hah! Foreign brains and Russian muscle. It makes me sick! But once a goal is achieved, people forget. The day is coming when we'll kick all of these bastards out, and then it will all be ours.'

'British and Amer ...' Tzonov's mouth had fallen open. 'And they're still there?'

'About all that is there!' Yefros had told him.

Then Tzonov's eyes had bulged as he dug a scrap of paper from his pocket, balled it in his fist and tossed it aside, and Siggi had supposed it was Trask's Möbius Strip sketch. Confirming her suspicion: 'Ahhh – *Trask!*' Tzonov had snarled. 'Damn the smart bastard! A sprat to catch a mackerel!'

Or a 'red' herring? Siggi had kept the thought to herself.

'Damn him to hell!' Tzonov had been furious. 'He threw me off the track, at least until you and the others got here. But do you see? The alien isn't heading for Leipzig or the Romanian Gate. No, he's heading for London, England . . . via Izhma! Or at least, he *thinks* he is.'

Then he'd gone up front to speak to the pilot, and Siggi had been left alone with Yefros. But the locator's mind was on his job; as the jet-copter forged west, he probed ahead; Siggi was able to relax a little and not worry what he was thinking about when his eyes met hers. For a while at least . . .

Fifteen minutes later, Tzonov's shout had reached back from the cockpit: 'We have another aircraft on our screens; on the radio, too. Swedish, and the pilot has just requested permission to land at the Izhma Projekt. He's landing there, right now!'

Siggi had felt things coming to a head. Tzonov was busy; Yefros, too, doing his own thing. She grasped the opportunity of the moment and sent her thoughts speeding ahead. For after all, that was what she was here for, what she was supposed to be doing. But now she felt that she must confirm or deny Tzonov's suspicions, if only to relieve her own tension. Except there was no relief for he was right: Nathan was dead ahead. And not only Nathan but also . . .

'A locator,' Yefros had shouted. 'Chung! I'd know that probe of his anywhere. They're converging, the alien and this British esper dog. Turkur, you're right. That chopper is here to lift our quarry out!'

In the cockpit, Tzonov had cursed and snapped a command at the pilot; vanes tilting forward, the jet-copter had raced west. But too late.

The frontier town of Izhma had blurred by below, and a series of wooden bridges crossing a frozen river. Then marsh and forest; and down in the woods, Siggi had spied Gypsy caravans trundling south. But up ahead ... only two more miles to the Izhma Projekt, its skeletal derricks already clearly visible on the grey horizon. And rising up from a smoky huddle of cabins and construction shacks where the black scar of a pipeline sprawled like a dark metal snake in the woods, a powerful jet-copter with Swedish ID, rapidly gaining altitude.

It had been on the ground for no more than ten to fifteen minutes: scarcely time to unload anything, but more than enough to take on a passenger. Modern and built for speed, the Swede would have no trouble outdistancing its dated Russian counterpart. But in any case, what good would it do to chase it?

Finally the recent past caught up with the present. To Siggi ... it felt so unreal! Things had happened so fast, it came as a genuine shock to realize that she was here – right here and now, with Tzonov and Yefros – holding her breath as Nathan escaped for the second time. She couldn't be mistaken; she *knew* he was aboard the Swedish aircraft. His numbers vortex felt so close it was almost visible in the eye of her mind, swirling like the foreign jet-copter's exhaust as its blades retracted into their housing and its thrusters rotated from the vertical to the horizontal. Then:

'Are we armed?' That was Tzonov, screaming at the pilot. And the pilot looking at him as though he were mad. Of course they weren't armed. This was a military machine, true, but it belonged to E-Branch, not to the Army or Airforce. Its weapon systems had been stripped on handover. Tzonov must know that, surely? He did, but on this occasion he'd actually *wanted* to be wrong!

And if they had been armed? What then?

Siggi felt sick. Tzonov wasn't just a radical but radically insane, she was sure of that now. She looked out through her flexon window and watched the Swedish machine picking up speed, racing west into a lowering sky. And on impulse, opening her mind, she sent after it:

Good luck, Nathan. If the Szgany have a god, I'm sure he will be with you.

All she got back was a whirling confusion of thoughts. No numbers vortex now, for Nathan had other things to think about. In his own world a majority of flying things were creatures to fear, and in this one? For the moment at least, he was no less afraid of the jet-copter. She tried again, and fired one last deep-penetrating thought:

It's all right. You'll be safe now.

Perhaps Nathan heard her; Siggi would never know for sure. But feeling a furtive movement behind her – and noticing what she really ought to have noticed a moment ago, before she sent that final thought – the knowledge fell on her like a peal of thunder that someone else had most certainly heard it!

Tzonov's hand closed over hers on the arm of her chair; his eyes, reflected in the flexon window, bored into hers; his twisted 'smile' was as mad as any she ever saw, as he whispered in her ear, 'And so he'll be safe, will he? Well yes, I suppose *he* will. But what odds? For after all, we'll get what we wanted from him. All you've told me so far, and all you've yet to tell me.'

'But Turkur . . . !' she turned to him.

'Ah, no!' He held up a hand, tut-tutted, turned his glistening, quivering, furiously grinning face away. 'Say nothing, Siggi, not now. Save it for later. I just *know* you're going to have so much more to say later.'

Almost convulsively, she reached inside her parka, but Yefros had come over from his side and was jabbing the muzzle of his gun in her ribs under her right breast. 'Oh yes, please do,' he told her sibilantly. 'It would give me a great deal of pleasure, I assure you.'

Even then, just for a moment, Siggi felt undecided. She knew that any pleasure 'it' might give Yefros the sadist now, would probably be far easier to bear – and over and done with a lot more quickly – than what she might reasonably anticipate from him in Tzonov's threatened 'later'. But finally, releasing her breath in a long sigh, she slumped back and shrank down in her seat. Worse was coming, certainly, but where there's life . . . well, maybe there could be a little hope even now.

Yefros's unpleasantly slim hand was cold and threatening – and lingering – against her flesh, as he carefully reached inside her parka, searched, and took her tiny gun from its secret place between her breasts. And the touch of those fingers, however inarticulate, told far better than words how slim was the element of hope which was all Siggi had left . . .

From the moment he escaped from Perchorsk, Nathan had been a fugitive, but for the last thirty-six hours – ever since Zek Foener contacted him with her instructions – he'd never been more aware of it. For he, too, had sensed the other intelligences which homed-in on her probe; he'd guessed their source and had known they would come after him.

The snow had saved him. He'd seen snow before, albeit infrequently, on those rare occasions when the barrier mountains turned white and even Sunside was bitterly cold through its long, dangerous nights. Twice as a child he'd seen it, and once as a youth, when an avalanche had brought down ten thousand tons of the stuff to strip the mountain naked of trees in a wide swath and fill the gap behind Lardis's knoll almost to its brim. But even that had been nothing compared to this.

The snows of this world seemed to go on forever! And its cold in these northern regions was far worse than that of Starside in the hours before sunup. Nathan was hardy, it was true, but without Vladi and his Travellers he would never have made it. For all that their ancestors had been Wamphyri supplicants (and for all that they themselves *would* be, given the chance), when the parting of the ways had come at last, he knew he was in their debt.

With the last flurry of snow – where densely-grown woods offered Nathan cover to the west, while the route of the Travellers would take them far south to the temperate regions they craved – he and the gnarled Szgany chief had hugged and stood off awhile, saying nothing. Then Nathan had felt ill at ease for what small deceptions he'd been obliged to work. But at the last when Vladi reminded him of his vow – to carry his message of welcome back to the vampire Lords in their own place – then there'd been nothing else for it but to lie again and say that he would.

Beneath the pines the ground was mainly clear. Avoiding the occasional drift, Nathan had headed west until the trees petered out and gave way to frozen marsh. By then the spindly derricks of the Izhma Projekt had been visible, and a strange dull thunder in the sky clearly audible. He had watched in awe and not a little fear as a flying machine came down through the clouds like some giant mosquito, settling towards the huddle of buildings. And because his attention was riveted to it, Nathan had recognized the aircraft as the source of yet another mental probe which, while it was not telepathic, nevertheless served to confirm his location.

Shortly, as he struggled through a deep drift out in the open, a snowcat had come skimming, and this time the source of the probe was riding pillion. David Chung had helped Nathan up behind him; the cat had turned in a circle, sending crisp snow flying; in something less than two minutes the fugitive found himself bundled aboard the jet-copter, which took off without delay.

That had been a little more than seventy-five minutes and seven hundred miles ago; now, crossing the Finnish border west of Lubosalma, Chung breathed easily for the first time in what felt like . . . oh, about three hours. Re-filling his lungs just as gladly, he let himself relax a little.

The passenger cabin was fairly spacious, and even more so in that only Nathan, Chung and the three-man crew were aboard. Trask was waiting in Helsinki where he'd been seeing to documentation and return travel arrangements to London. Now, as Nathan wolfed sandwiches and drank coffee, Chung thought it might be as well to get a relationship going. Lighting a cigarette, he said, 'Zek Föener says you won't find it too hard to understand me. Languages come easy to you. I know you've already spoken to Ben Trask, but most of that was telepathic. Anyway, my name is David Chung.' He held out his right hand, and when Nathan went to clasp his forearm corrected him and showed him a handshake. 'That's how we do it here.'

Nathan at once showed him the Traveller way. 'And that's how we do it on Sunside. Not a lot of difference, is there?'

It stopped Chung dead in his tracks, and Nathan knew it. The most the locator had said to him so far had been when he spoke his name as he helped him aboard the snowcat. Grinning at Chung's expression, he said, 'Zek Föener is right, as you see. I learned a little from Trask, by matching his words to his mind-pictures; but right now in your mind there's only a jumble of words. Most of them seem automatic – instinctive? – and pretty meaningless. They don't much match up with anything. This is nothing new. They are curses!'

'Shit!' Chung said out loud, and then apologized.

'No, I am the one who should . . . apologize?' Nathan *was* still learning after all. 'It's unseemly to look into another man's mind unbidden.'

'You'll do okay in E-Branch,' Chung nodded, returning his grin. 'In any case, you can look all you want. There's nothing in there I'm ashamed of. And if it will help you to get it all together – I mean, to understand . . .'

'It will.'

'. . . Then be my guest. Listen, you'll be debriefed – that is, my people will ask you plenty of questions – in London; I mean back home, where we're going. But until we pick up Trask en route, I'm at your command. Any way I can help, if there's anything you want to know about us, about this world, you just fire away . . . I mean, by all means ask questions.' Despite Nathan's talent and intelligence, obviously it wasn't going to be plain sailing.

They had maybe forty minutes to Helsinki, and Nathan put all of them to good use . . .

They flew in a Sabena jet, executive-class, from Helsinki to Stockholm, and transferred to a British Airways jumbo for the flight into London. Nathan was agog at the size of both airplanes, especially the latter, and at their speed. In-flight, he was fascinated by the food, clothing, hand-luggage (wrist-watches, pens, books, cigarette lighters!) of the other passengers; also by the toilets, the motion picture, headphones, periodic announcements; the provision of drinks, hot food; the view from the windows, everything. Trask had found clothes for him in Helsinki, so that he didn't look out of place. Still, his natural curiosity was that of a child, which *would* have been out of place but for Trask's continuous cautioning. Finally, half-way to London from Stockholm, he settled down and asked Trask to tell him about his father.

As Head of E-Branch, Trask was well equipped for that. Keeping his voice low and starting at the very beginning, he detailed what he knew of Harry Keogh's boyhood up until the time he joined forces with the Branch. Occasionally Nathan would ask a question, but when he stopped Trask glanced at him out of the corner of his eye, and smiled.

It said a great deal for Nathan's new friends: that he felt he could sleep, and safely, in their company . . .

Trask shook him awake just before they landed at Heathrow. The lights had been on in Stockholm when they took off, but now it was full night. Nathan simply couldn't believe the size of the city as seen from the air, and as for its illuminations . . .

'The hell-lands,' he murmured, half to himself.

Trask heard him, and asked: 'Do you really think so?'

Nathan looked at him wide-eyed. 'No,' he said after a moment's pause. 'Not with you people for denizens. Not quite hell, anyway.'

Suddenly Trask's head was full of memories. 'It might have been,' he said, 'if not for your father.' Then, less seriously: 'And maybe it still is. Save it till you've seen the traffic!'

The Minister Responsible was there to whisk them through customs; Nathan was taken to an E-Branch safe house in Slough, whose 'caretakers' were Special Branch heavies and experts in close protection. From now on he would also be in the care of E-Branch agents who would live at the house when he was in residence, never straying more than a thought away. Except he shouldn't expect to be spending too much time there; the safe house was a bolt-hole, nothing more.

During this first visit, Nathan took a bath, shaved, had his hair tidied up; he was equipped with a reasonable wardrobe, supplied with money and extra documentation. Then, to give him something of a background at least, pictures were taken of him laughing, with his arms round a girl he'd never met before and would never see again, and two small children at his feet. The photographs were placed in a leather wallet together with credit cards that wouldn't work and other bits and pieces of false identification and 'authentication', and a wafer-slim calculator powered by light. (Later, en route to E-Branch HQ, David Chung explained the latter's functions; it took Nathan only a moment or two to recognize Ethloi of the Thyre's 'tens system' and learn the values of the alien characters. From which time forward the calculator would be his pride and joy.)

At E-Branch HQ the hour was too late for introductions; Nathan was taken to a room of his own and almost fell into a bed where he could sleep long, soundly, safely. Under normal circumstances there would only be one Duty Officer. Tonight, and for however long it took, there would be four; and, in the hotel down below, a trio of Special Branch plain-clothes officers who now had something extra to think about in addition to discreetly tailing and minding Zek Foener.

But in E-Branch itself while Nathan slept, the four

Duty Officers continued to work steadily through the night, preparing his programme. For tomorrow Nathan would start school. He would learn, the Branch would learn; hopefully both would benefit. As Trask had already made plain, however, their aim wasn't to extract information – not specifically – but to impart it. It was for Nathan, and also for the memory of his father, Harry Keogh. Only a handful of men had ever known him, and even fewer had known him as the Necroscope. But an entire world was in his debt, or even two worlds, and in many ways he'd had a raw deal in both of them. This would be reparation in part, at least . . .

In the small hours of the night, in Perchorsk under the Urals, Siggi Dam had likewise been called upon to make repayment. But in her case Turkur Tzonov was the one to whom account must be made, and Siggi was bankrupt. Moreover, this time the aim was most *definitely* to extract information – and permanently.

Siggi had been awakened in the quietest of all hours, at 2:30 a.m., by the squeal of her door opening after a skeleton key had been turned in its lock. And still believing that this couldn't possibly be happening – that she must be nightmaring – she had sat up in her bed and watched Tzonov, Staff-Sergeant Bruno Krasin, and Alexei Yefros quickly enter the room and move to her bedside. Numb and only half-awake, blinking her eyes in the sudden light, perhaps she'd had just enough time to cringe back from them, moisten her lips, and say, 'What?' before Tzonov covered her mouth and Krasin held her motionless, while Yefros slid a needle into her arm.

That last had woken her up, certainly, when but for Tzonov's hand clamping her mouth she would have screamed. But only for a moment, until the drug began to work. The effect of that had been to put her back to sleep; her body, at least. Following which ... they'd been in such a hurry that they hadn't even paused to close her eyes. And denied all physical command over her limbs, thrown across Krasin's powerful shoulders, Siggi had seen, heard, or otherwise sensed the rest as if it were happening under water, through the liquid lens of some sickly churning submarine kaleidoscope:

Corridor walls flowing by like waves in the apparently slow-motion *jolt ... jolt ... jolt* of Krasin's stride; curved steel wall panels reflecting the ghastly flicker of faulty or shorting neons; an inverted descent through the magmass levels to the core, where the usual knot of technicians and scientists was nowhere in evidence, for Tzonov had either dismissed them or sent them on some clever wild-goose chase. Another descent, down steel ladders in the curved wall of the core and under the white bulge of the sphere Gate itself, to a place where Tzonov opened the cover on a magmass wormhole. He and Yefros sliding feet-first into an alien darkness; and Siggi with a rope round her ankles, hauled along behind and gliding in the smooth bore like some slow toboggan; Krasin bringing up the rear, pushing on her shoulders where he followed head-first.

This was where Tzonov had relocated his arsenal: down in these warped nightmare regions where – for the sake of human sanity – no one ever went these days. Whole sections had been abandoned ever since the time of the original Perchorsk Incident; they had been opened up, briefly, following Harry Keogh's escape to Starside; now they were closed again and would stay that way ... to anyone but a madman and his followers.

Dim lighting flickering into being, and Tzonov and Yefros holding Siggi erect, head lolling, until Krasin could take her from them. Then more jolting motion, and hideous magmass cysts, molds, and other . . . *anomalies* flowing past her frozen field of vision, until they reached —

— The room.

The room of the machine.

It was then that Siggi had wished she were dead. But only her body was dead, and then only temporarily. That could easily change, of course, could easily become permanent. It all depended on how much Tzonov wanted, on how much he intended to leave her. If anything. Her death wish of a moment ago was forgotten; as they strapped her to the table, she no longer desired to die but to live! To live and talk and tell them everything! And she would, only too gladly, without all of this. If only they would listen, and if only she could speak.

'She's drooling,' Krasin said, oddly disgusted.

'Trying to talk, perhaps?' This was Yefros, his voice a trembling, excited whisper. And now, but much too late, Siggi remembered something else about the sadistic locator: that he was an Operator, one of the few men who was qualified to perform what was euphemistically known as 'an operation'.

Siggi put every ounce of non-existent strength into one last twitch of effort — to follow Yefros's movements — and her head flopped loosely to one side. The locator was moving obscene equipment into position, donning a surgical gown and pulling on rubber gloves. There wouldn't be very much blood, but . . . Yefros was fastidious in matters such as this. Siggi screamed, but silently of course. The merest gurgle.

Then a strong hand took her chin and turned her head the other way, and she felt rubber-sheathed brackets clamped into position in the hollows of her cheeks, to hold her head steady. She looked straight up, straight into Turkur Tzonov's magnetic, malignant grey eyes, which peered into and through hers as if they were empty holes in her head.

Until now everything had seemed, what, impersonal? Yes, that was the right word, so much so that it was almost as if it were happening to someone else. On *their* part impersonal, anyway. Siggi was so helpless, they could have done anything to her, used her however they would; but except for what they planned, so far they'd done nothing. Now, however, all of that had changed. Now it came down to Siggi and Tzonov, which made it very personal indeed.

She wanted to curse him – which he knew, of course – but could only plead. She shouted with her mind, when all it required was a whisper. She offered to tell him everything, right now, here, immediately. She was a foolish woman, she knew, and weak. She'd wronged him, and now promised to put it right. From this time forward, she would swear eternal faith to Tzonov, his cause. She *deserved* to be used, abused, and discarded. He could shame her, trample her under, take all she had been or was now to mould to his own design or ruin forever. Physical ruin, yes, but not ... not ... not her *memories* ... not her *mind!* Let her keep that at least. For that was what made her Siggi Dam.

The dome of Tzonov's skull gleamed shiny damp; as he shook his head in a negative response, droplets of sweat gathered and rolled round the orbits of his eyes to drip from his nose. His features, so perfectly balanced, were scarcely human; Siggi saw that clearly now. And his ego was likewise unstable. Capable of withstanding a slap, it could never take a full-blooded punch. And she had delivered a hammerblow! Since when there had been only one course Tzonov could take. And now he would take his revenge.

'Ah, Siggi, Siggi,' he said, shaking his head again and smiling, however mockingly. 'Trusting you was a mistake, and you know how I hate mistakes. But in setting Nathan free, you placed yourself in bondage. Oh, he has escaped to a new world – for the moment, at least – but you? How should I deal with you? By trusting you again, when your treachery is proven? Or should I let your punishment fit the crime? For there would be a wonderful irony in that, don't you see? Nathan goes free, an "innocent" in an alien world, and I control the door, the Gate, into just such a place. The only difference appears to be that you ... that you are not innocent. Not yet. But we can change that ...'

She saw his meaning, and in a moment the numbness of her limbs was matched only by that of her mind. Her brain froze, but not so much that she couldn't feel or at least sense the iciness of the sterile needle probes that slid into her ears through flesh and cartilage.

Then Tzonov took a helmet that trailed a multitude of rainbow wires, the receiver, and let her watch him place it on his head. And still smiling his awful smile, his face slowly withdrew from her line of vision. Someone's thumbs came into view, and closed her eyes as if she were already dead. Then, before the power was switched on, she heard Yefros say:

'It's much like a computer. We don't have to delete it all. Let's start at the beginning. Her birth?'

And Tzonov's answer. 'Let her keep it. We all need to know we were born. It's part of the will to survive. I want her to have that, at least. Without it, she'd be nothing but a bag of plasma. No, she must have something of will, for I want her to run, hide, and to be afraid. I want her to be even more afraid than she is now! As for her childhood: most of that can go. But her sexual awakenings, she should keep them. Siggi was good at that; it might even keep her alive a while, in Star-side!'

And then, scoring her soul like a blunt drill, his laugh! Above all else, even if she remembered *nothing* else, Siggi knew she would always remember that. Tzonov's laugh: cruel, malevolent, vindictive. It would ring in the achingly empty corridors of her mind forever.

Following which, darkness. For that was when they switched on the power, and began down-loading her brain . . .

PART FOUR

The Rest of Nestor's Story

I

Nestor, Necromancer!

Hunting on Sunside

Two years earlier in time, and an entire dimension away in parallel space:

The vampire Lord Nestor's first lieutenant, called Zahar (once Zahar Sucksthrall), coaxed all speed from his small and singularly burdened mount and headed for the barrier mountains. His mission was of the greatest possible urgency, for even now the sun was rising up beyond the gold-tipped crags, slowly but surely climbing to the highest point in its low but deadly arc. Deadly to all vampires, to the Wamphyri themselves, and certainly to their lieutenants.

Already sunlight came spilling through several of the high passes, glancing from the tallest peaks, permeating Starside's gloomy upper atmosphere and banishing the stars; except those that burned over the Icelands far to the north. On high, even the sinister Northstar, motionless where it stood at its zenith over Wrathstack the last aerie, was little more than a glimmer now. And when the sun was at its highest, shining on Wrathspire itself, then the Northstar would fade entirely from view.

By then Zahar must be on his way back, or better still already back, safe within Suckscar's massive walls and halls and labyrinthine ways. Oh, he would come to no harm so long as he kept himself and his mount out of the sun's lethal glare, but the knowledge itself – that spears of sunlight would soon stab through the mists of Starside to sear on Wratha's turrets and spires – was sufficient to speed him on his way. For when the sun is risen, the Wamphyri and theirs are cowards all. And if they were not, then they would be dead. Just as the 'Lady' Carmen would soon be dead. But the true death, not undeath.

And so Zahar shivered as he landed in a writhing ground mist, bundled Carmen down from the flyer's back, tossed her over his shoulder and climbed a scree-littered saddle between spurs; until at the top he saw the southern rim aglimmer with yellow fire, but not yet awash in it. And pegging her out on a mound of stony earth – hammering in the ironwood pegs left-handed, for his right hand and arm were still painful from the process of metamorphic healing, which as yet was far from complete – and making fast her wrists and ankles with strips of tough leather, he shivered again and even jerked to his feet on two occasions, turning in a complete circle and gazing all about. For it had seemed to him that while he worked, someone had watched: a sensation he'd known often enough before, but only when Vasagi the Suck was alive.

Vasagi: master of mime, metamorphism, and telepathy alike. Except the Suck was dead now, and Nestor the new Lord of Suckscar ... yet still Zahar shivered. Perhaps he sensed the uneasy vampire spirit of his old master – Vasagi's ghost, as it were – wandering restlessly abroad in the mountains, waiting fearfully for the sun, doomed for eternity to steam into mist with each recurrent sunup yet to come ...

Finally Zahar was done and the undead corpse of Carmen all tied down, and not a moment to spare. Golden fire was creeping on the south-facing crags, setting the peaks ablaze, staining the saddle a poisonous yellow as the sun, as yet unseen, swung slowly east. And Zahar knew that if he did see that fiery orb, then he would see no more. It was time to be gone.

Again the feeling came that someone or something observed him, but this time in his haste Zahar ignored it and ran back to his flyer. A moment more and he'd launched ... a gentle glide, down and out over the boulder plains. But behind him he could almost hear the sun's golden claws scrabbling on the rocks, and feel the yellow beast's breath turning the air to acid. And his terror of burning was so great that he never once glanced back but sat hunched in the saddle, eyes staring straight ahead, as he sped like an arrow for Wrathstack.

While behind him, between the spurs where the rim of sunlight crept ever closer to Carmen's feet, and the vampire stuff in her finally recognized the peril and brought her starting, then screaming awake from undeath to sure death –

– Something *other* than sunlight came creeping, like a shadow from the shadows of the crags! A thing in a cloak and mask of cloth, with holes cut for its yellow-flaring eyes. A thing that took up a rock and broke the ironwood pegs, helped Carmen up and led her staggering, sobbing from the sun's sighing encroachment. And up over the dark rim of the saddle the thing led her, and down a scree slope into the permanent darkness and safety of a north-facing crevice in the rocks.

As they went, so she cried out: 'What ...? Who ...?' For as yet she was like a lost child, with little or no understanding of her whereabouts and circumstances, except that she was a changeling whose change – whose very existence – had almost been terminated.

But the one in the cloak and mask merely hushed her

and replied: *Quiet, now, Carmen, all is not lost. As was my fate, so is yours. Yet we have both escaped it. We are banished now, for the moment, and sent out of our rightful places. But still we're alive, you and I; we'll live on and grow strong, and one day return. We'll return for our revenge, which will be sweet, I promise you! Trust me. I know the way.*

And gasping, clutching her terror-parched throat, fainting in his arms in the darkness of their refuge, she knew that it was true, that if anyone knew the way it was this one whom she had thought dead and gone.

Oh, she had been glad enough then that he was no more, that the handsome Lord Nestor had come to take his place. But not as glad as she was now that he was back, not when it meant life to her. Both glad and terrified at one and the same time. For despite an awful, hideous alteration, she could not deny but that this was her old master. She'd guessed it as soon as she heard his mental voice, and now knew it definitely as he took off his mask and tossed it down.

But his face! *His mangled, maniac face!*

And then she knew no more, for a while at least . . .

All of which lay two long years in the past, and only part of it known to Nestor (and then erroneously) where he lay healing and dreaming under the bank of the river in Sunside.

And as his metamorphic vampire flesh expelled the last few silver pellets of Szgany shot and the last drop of yellow pus, and the small wounds knitted over, so his dreams switched from the vacant meanderings of subconscious psyche to a more positive theme, when he lived again the life he'd known in Suckscar in his early days as Nestor of the Wamphyri . . .

*

Time had passed since Nestor's ascension – six months, then nine – and the might-have-been 'Lady' Carmen was all but forgotten. But the young Lord Nestor's awful talent, which he had discovered through her, was not. Despite that it repulsed him, it also fascinated him, so that he was driven to experiment. For he was a necromancer with the power to question the dead, and he was the only one in all Wrathstack who could do it. It made him equal, perhaps even superior, to the rest of them.

But they all had their various quirks and talents, if 'talent' may adequately describe Wamphyri mutations, anomalies, and aberrations. Wran with his rages, which gave him the strength of three; his brother Spiro, who constantly practised to achieve his father's killing eye, though with no noticeable success so far; Gorvi, whose guile was such that he would even cheat himself, if that were at all possible. And of course the Lady Wratha with her mentalism and mind-cloaking technique, so that she was able to read the thoughts of the others while yet keeping her own to herself – mainly. Even the dog-Lord, with his lycanthropy, which made him look even more like some monstrous wolf when he went off hunting on Sunside.

Yet Nestor's talent was . . . different.

Word of it got out (this was hardly surprising; Wratha had spies everywhere, in all of the manses), and within a year everyone in Wrathstack knew that Nestor was a necromancer. Meanwhile, Canker Canison had become a frequent visitor to Suckscar, and his and Nestor's friendship had developed.

'Useful, is it, this weird talent of yours?' Canker growled one evening, when at last the sun was off the peaks.

'It probably will be,' Nestor answered.

They were sitting in one of Nestor's private rooms, a place that looked south to the barrier range. He liked to sit here at this hour, watching the peaks turn from gold to grey. He would even sit here in the predawn hours, and witness the reverse. But on those occasions, long before the first true rays came stabbing through, then the curtains would be drawn and Nestor gone off to other, safer places.

'But just exactly *how* do you use it?' Canker was curious. 'How are you using it now, I mean?'

Nestor shrugged. 'At present, I merely ... experiment.'

'You talk to dead men? And did it happen just like that? Suddenly you could talk to them?'

'Ah ... no,' Nestor answered. 'The first time, one of the dead talked to me. Except she was undead. Since when ... well, the dead would not speak to me at all, if they had a choice.'

'She was undead, you say?' Canker frowned and his red eyebrows crushed together over his snout. 'Then how could you be certain of your talent? The undead are not truly dead.'

'This was a thrall,' Nestor replied. 'She was a mere vampire, not yet Wamphyri. At the time ... I was inexperienced and had taken too much from her. But even so she would only become Wamphyri if I allowed it, which I did not. She had no mentalism as such, or should not have had it, and yet she spoke to me in my mind. She was *dead*, Canker, but when I touched her she knew me and named me for her murderer! In which she was correct, of course, for I could not suffer her to live.'

'And after that?'

'I had her destroyed: scorched at sunup on the high crags, which put an end to her. What's more, it put an end to what was left in me of pity. And it was only then that I became Wamphyri in the fullest sense. For in our hearts we are cold creatures, Canker, and I was not cold – not completely – until then.'

'We're not so cold,' Canker argued. 'Indeed, we can be hot as a furnace at times! But we know how to do what must be done, and that without a deal of fuss. We are survivors, Nestor!'

'Without emotion, feeling, purpose? What use to survive as a piece of stone?'

'This is your leech arguing,' Canker coughed. 'It can only be. You are playing word games, and your parasite directs their course. For as you must know by now, when the mood is on us we argue just for the sake of it, like now. But emotionless? Purposeless? The Wamphyri? Is that what you're saying? Then you don't know the half of it! But I believe I do know what's wrong with you, my lad! Why, you haven't given yourself a chance! You think you've seen it all. "And is that all there is to it?" you ask? "To slake my thirst on blood forever and a day, and grow no older or wiser but live like some bloated leech in a pool?" Aha! But Canker has the answer.'

'We were talking about necromancy,' Nestor sighed. 'Not my malaise.'

'Malaise, aye,' the dog-Lord barked. 'The very word! But you were morbid enough before, and now this necromancy? What, to talk to dead things? Huh! I see no sense in it. What can they tell you anyway? How to survive? No, for they failed to survive. How to make merry? No, for they have lost the art of laughter. How to love – or lust? What, with parts all rotted away? Now tell me, what do you get from it? And if the answer is nothing, then I say let the dead alone and instead learn how to live!'

365

'What do I get from it?'

'What can they *tell* you that you don't already know? For after all you've outlived them, haven't you?'

Nestor slowly shook his head and said, 'But it isn't like that. Now listen, and I'll try to tell you. The last time I was on Sunside, after the raid, I sensed the freshly dead trembling where they lay. What's more, I sensed that the ancient dead – who had passed on years before – were trembling, too. And all of them knowing me and going in fear of me.'

'But of *what* do they go in fear?' Canker flapped his great hands.

'In fear of my art.'

'To talk to them?'

Nestor looked away. 'To torture them . . .'

'Eh?' Canker sat up straighter.

'The dead don't talk to me of their own free will,' Nestor explained at last. 'They have to be made to do it.'

'You make them talk to you?'

'It is my . . . my art, yes.'

'By torturing them?' Canker goggled.

'Ever since that first time, yes. But don't you see? Carmen couldn't have talked to me at all, if I wasn't a necromancer.'

'Carmen?'

'That was her name. One of the girls that the Killglance brothers tried to steal away that time. Surely you remember? Better for her if they had! Since when the dead have avoided me, but they can't avoid my art.'

Canker sprang erect. 'I have to see it for myself! On Sunside, yes, in just a few hours' time. We'll hunt together, and afterwards . . . you can show me how it's done.'

'I can show you it, certainly, but not how it's done,' Nestor told him.

'Eh?'

'You won't learn anything from it. What I do is not mentalism, not as you know it. You'll be able to hear me talking to them if I ask my questions out loud, certainly, but you'll never hear their answers. These are *dead* minds, Canker!'

'Very well ...' The other gave a shrug, pretended to understand. 'But at least I'll see you ... at work, eh?'

'Oh?' Nestor looked sideways at him. 'And who's the morbid one now, Canker?'

'Morbid? Never! Eager for new experiences – always! Except ... tell me this: how may one torture a dead, unfeeling man?'

'*That* is my art,' Nestor answered. 'When I touch them, they do feel it. They hear my words, which no one else can hear, not even my lieutenants; they feel my hands on them, the tearing of my nails; they know my threats are real. And as for what they tell me ...'

'Ah! The crux of the matter,' Canker cried. 'Well, then, what do they tell you?'

'Listen,' said Nestor, 'for there's that which you should know. Death ... isn't like that.' His voice was suddenly faraway, dreamy.

'Eh? Not like what?'

'Not like you think. You think that death's the end, but it isn't. They go on.'

'The dead go on?' Canker gave a snort. 'Hell, no! They go down in the ground, or onto a funeral pyre, or into the grinders for the provisioning. On Sunside they even go to waste, but that's as far as they go. And here in the last aerie there's no waste at all. If that's what you meant by going on, then I have to agree. They go on in the bellies of our beasts, to fuel them in the flying and the fighting!'

'You are talking about their bodies,' Nestor replied,

367

his voice becoming firm again. 'But I'm talking about their minds. Their *minds* go on, Canker. And so for as long as there's something of body left to touch and torture, and mind which I may speak to, I can communicate with them. The Grand Inquisitor, who overcomes Death Himself!'

Canker scowled, sniffed like the great red hound he was, shook his head. 'But again I say, what use to –'

'– I'll tell you what use,' Nestor cut him off. 'What a man did in life, he continues to do when he's dead. Not physically but in his mind! The lover loves, not with his wasted lich body, no, but *in his mind*! And he dreams of all the ways he never loved, even though it's too late to try them. And the builder? Why, he continues to build, not of stone or stick or sod but airy thoughts! And he dreams of excellent houses and cities which can never be built, because no one knows what's in his dead mind. And what of the thinkers who look outward to the stars and wonder? Now they have been given a gift of time, with nothing to do but study the wheeling of the spheres, and dream of other suns and worlds beyond this one. Then there are the hunters and weapon-makers. They hunt still, and forge their weapons as of old. They devise new traps for the beasts of the wild, superior in every way to the ones we use. And the weapons in their mental workshops are keener far, while ours are often blunt, clumsy, and turn to rust too quickly.' Nestor paused, and in a moment continued:

'And you ask what use? Very well, I'll tell you what use. Whatever a man was or did in life – whatever secrets he knew then, and anything he's learned since, from the teeming dead; whatever new thoughts he has thought, or ancient schemes he's schemed – I can know it all, by means of my art!'

Canker was astonished. 'Whatever he's learned *since*?

But how can he learn anything once he's dead? I mean, from whom may he learn it?'

'Ah!' said Nestor. 'And that is something else that fascinates me. For just as we communicate with each other, so do the dead converse. They talk to each other in their graves and resting places, and their thoughts go out to all the dead without any man ever knowing or even suspecting them – except me. For I am a necromancer. But when they know I'm near, then they fall silent, for they fear my art. And they stay silent, until I touch them . . .'

Nestor's voice had sunk so low and turned so cold that Canker shivered . . . then gave himself a shake. 'But you must demonstrate! Tonight, on Sunside. We hunt together, agreed?'

'As you will,' answered Nestor.

'And so you're loathed by liches, eh?' Canker scratched at his too-long jaw. 'Which is enough in itself to earn you a name.'

'A name? But I already have a name.'

'*Pah!* Nestor? What is that for a name? Good for a first name, aye. But as for your second – Lichloathe! That's it: the necromancer Lord Nestor Lichloathe, of Lichscar!'

'No!' said Nestor at once. 'I mean, yes to the giving of names, but no to changing them. For I'm used to Suckscar now. Let it suffice.'

'So be it.' Canker shrugged. 'Now I get me down into Mangemanse to work on my instrument. Several hours to go, I think, before we'll need to prepare for the raid. Then it's off to Sunside, where with any luck I'll witness this weird wonder that you work. Except, before I go . . .'

'Yes?'

'Earlier you mentioned your malaise.' Canker seemed anxious. He was genuinely fond of Nestor.

369

Nestor's turn to shrug. 'I played a word game. It meant nothing.'

'No,' said Canker. 'Everything means something. Now tell me: are you getting enough of women?'

'There are lovely girl thralls in my manse, yes,' Nestor answered.

'And how do you feed yourself?'

'The same as you. I don't like it red so much, except for when I drink on Sunside. Apart from that I have good meat and wine, and occasionally a little fruit.'

'And blood? Only on Sunside? You don't use your thralls? But you should, Nestor, you should! For what are they after all but vessels? And never forget: the blood is the life!'

'When I sleep, then I drink . . . occasionally.'

'But carefully, eh? That Carmen incident taught you a lesson, it seems.'

'Perhaps it did,' said Nestor.

'Huh!' the dog-Lord grunted. 'Then what is this malaise? Do you know its source?'

'No,' Nestor lied . . .

. . . And feeling Canker's thoughts nibbling at his own, he changed the subject. 'So tell me, my friend, how goes it with your moon music? A whole year gone by, and still you're hard at it.'

Canker was distracted from his own line of questioning. 'My music? My instrument? Hard at it? Too true! This music is no easy thing. But it comes, it comes. Have you not heard me, in the sunup when the others are fast asleep? Surely you recognized the tune you gave me?'

'I've heard you,' Nestor nodded wryly, 'and I've no doubt that Wratha and the others have, too, when we *should* have been asleep! As for knowing your tune: I knew it, vaguely.'

'Oh – hah-*ha*!' Canker capered wildly, threw back his head and laughed. 'And have I disturbed you, then? Good, excellent! Not so good that I have ruined your sleep – no, of course not, never that – but wonderful if I've managed to disturb the rest of them. It's my image, you see. For I'm a madman and mischiefmaker. We have to keep up appearances.'

Nestor managed a grin. 'Well then, away with you and practise. Later we'll fly out and do a little raiding on Sunside – but just the two of us, for as yet I'm jealous of this talent of mine and guard it well. And later, we'll seek out some old Szgany burial place, where you shall see what you shall see.'

'Agreed!' Canker yelped, as Nestor patted him fondly on his furred and sloping back. And then the necromancer saw him out of Suckscar, accompanying the dog-Lord until at the last he loped out of sight, down and around the spiralling stairwell that descended into Mangemanse.

But as soon as Canker was gone –

– Nestor returned to his brooding, to his ... malaise? And indeed he knew its source. Somewhere in the world – far away, perhaps, but there nevertheless – his olden enemy out of Sunside lived on. That was the source of his disquiet. He *knew* that his enemy was alive just as surely as he recognized the pattern of the numbers vortex swirling in his head, that whirlwind rush of metaphysical symbols which was his enemy's cloaking device, with which he kept his secret mind shielded. It rarely bothered Nestor in the dark of night, when he was up and prowling, or hunting on Sunside, or running Suckscar to his own design; but during the fear-fraught hours of seething sunlight on the barrier mountains, when Wrathstack slept and the furnace sun's bright and lethal rays burned on the Lady Wratha's highest turrets and towers – then he felt it.

At first it would be in his dreams, which in themselves were a swirl of misty unmemory, or half-memory, of things he really did not *wish* to remember; but coming awake and as his dreams faded to wraiths, still the hated numbers vortex would linger on. Faint, ah, faint, but real for all that. And lying awake in his bed with his sleeping vampire women, as the cold sweat beaded his flesh and his nerves jangled with each smallest creak of a baffle or wailing of wind beyond his windows, then he would know that his olden enemy lived on. Moreover, he also knew that while for the moment that enemy was far removed, one day he would surely return . . .

In a way he dreaded that day, without knowing why, but in another way he longed for it. For he would never be free of the numbers vortex until he was free of his enemy, who and whatever he was.

But that was only one source of Nestor's malaise, and the truth of it was that there was another. A need – a gap, a void in his existence – which required filling. For Canker had been partly right to question him about women. But there was a *certain* woman he had not questioned him about, because he had not known. Only Nestor himself knew, and he was loath to admit it. For after all, she'd made a fool of him once already.

And yet . . . in his dreams, all too frequently, she seemed to call to him, and he felt her lure even in his waking hours; so that occasionally, musing, he would find himself (if only in his mind, in the eye of his memory) up there again on Wrathspire's roof, his lips on hers and her breast in his hand.

A malaise? No, it was the lingering after-images of dreams such as these that distracted him. The conflict of his desires. On the one hand, revenge on his enemy. And on the other, Wratha the Risen: the thought of their steam rising up from a bed made sodden by their juices . . .

That same sundown, an hour after the sun's true setting – when the ethereal fan of pink and golden spokes which was its aftermath wheeled in the sky over Sunside and melted to an amethyst glow, and the night crept in, and stars clustered like nuggets of ice frozen in their eternal configurations, and the Icelands aurora fluttered its banners across all the northern skies – then the Wamphyri flew to Sunside. Not only Nestor Lichloathe and Canker Canison, but all of them.

Taking their senior men with them and leaving lesser lieutenants and thralls in charge of their manses, they set out from Wrathstack to raid on the Szgany. They left in the space of the same hour but in small parties, not en masse; the time lay well in the past when they had worked as a single unit under Wratha.

Nor were their parties uniform: the Guile's lot flew south and a little east, and was composed of Gorvi himself, three lieutenants and two small aerial warriors. The Killglance brothers headed due south, and took only their chief lieutenants along with them; they would seek their prey in roughly the same area where Wran and Vasagi the Suck had fought their unequal duel. And the Lady Wratha flew westwards with only two of her men, and used the glaring hell-lands Gate as her marker where she sped for the soaring spires and plateaus which were her favourite vantage points, from which she would choose her target.

As for Canker and Nestor: they made for the great pass a little to the east of the hemisphere Gate, a dog-leg gorge that split the barrier mountains to their roots, passing north to south right through them. If they were fortunate enough to recruit a handful of thralls beyond the pass, then their victims would find it an easy route to follow home to the last aerie.

And gliding on a tail-wind, they conversed as they went:

An even, two-way split, Canker grunted in Nestor's mind. *We work together and share the spoils equally.*

Of course. The other agreed, but with this rider: *And if there are women, we split them equally, too.*

Split them? Indeed I will! the dog-Lord laughed obscenely for a moment, then sobered. *But yes, I understand, and I'm more than pleased with that arrangement. Damn, I have a few too many bitches in Mangemanse already! And when I'm away, like now, all they can do is squabble. They fight for my affections, Nestor.*

Nestor doubted it but said nothing. More likely Canker's women fought to determine who would stay out of his bed! (This was a thought which the necromancer kept to himself.) But forget Mangemanse, for the fact of it was that Suckscar did go a little short on women, and Nestor had lieutenants and thralls other than himself to consider. For if a man is not happy he will scheme and plot, eventually get himself in serious, even terminal trouble, and so deplete the aerie. On the other hand, genuine happiness as such is scarcely the province of vampire thralls, but ... at least their loads might be made a little easier to bear.

This last thought had escaped him and been picked up by Canker. 'Too true!' the dog-Lord called through the blustery air, slicing it with his bark. 'You have to keep them happy. For you can be sure there are those among 'em who'll be lusting after your women even now – aye, and lusting after Suckscar, too! There must be, else nothing would ever change and no one ever ascend.'

Nestor nodded and answered grimly, 'Indeed, for it's the getting there that counts.'

'Right!' Canker howled. 'And without new blood — among the Wamphyri, I mean — we'd all stagnate and become doddering old cripples like the lot we left behind in Turgosheim.'

'You must tell me about them some time,' Nestor answered. 'The full story. But for now . . . let's keep the noise down. A few more miles and we're through the pass, so from here on in silence is the order of the day.'

As you will. Canker fell silent a moment. Until: *Ah! But can't you just smell 'em from here, Nestor? Szgany! Meat on the hoof — sweet blood, hot and surging — young breasts and buttocks and cunt galore! Me? Why, I'll risk the odd crossbow bolt any old time, to fire a few shots from my own weapon.*

Your 'image'? Nestor's sarcasm dripped, but Canker chose to ignore it.

No lad, not this time, he answered. *Not my image but my lust. I want to be into a fresh, untainted woman. Or several!*

You're a lech, said Nestor, but without malice. *A satyr.*

Not a bit of it, Canker grinned across at him. *I'm Wamphyri! And so are you . . .*

The Sunside end of the pass was in sight, and beyond it a far horizon still stained with strips of dying colour: dun orange, a pale, dirty yellow, and amethyst. Nestor and Canker ordered their flyers up, up, until they rode with a knot of dark clouds scudding south. Should they be seen from the ground, they'd be just two more clouds chasing the fallen sun.

Now the hunt was on, for down below was Szgany territory. And as Nestor led the way and sped out with the clouds over the forest, so Canker inquired: *And just where do you think you're taking me? Man, these woods are dense, and the Szgany know them a damn sight better than we do! We should stick to the fringes, look for their fires. And where in hell do we land? And having landed, from where do we launch? I mean, I know you're no novice, that you've done all this before, but you're listening to the voice of real experience here. Seventy years of it. And I tell you we should —*

— *Shhh!* Nestor hushed him. *Let me think. It's this way, if my memory serves me right. Aye, this way!*

What is this way? Canker demanded.

Meat on the hoof, Nestor told him. *And everything else you mentioned. A woman for you — neither virginal nor young, but untainted certainly — and another for me. And the blood of a good strong man to boot. You can have both the man and his wife, and I shall have their daughter. Not the best of thralls, be sure, but there's always the provisioning.*

You know this for a certainty? Canker was eager now. *That these people are here, I mean?* But he could tell that indeed Nestor knew it for a certainty.

I know it. Down there, maybe four, five miles ahead, a cabin in the woods, all secret and hidden away. Their fire is out by now but its smoke will linger a while. In a minute or two you'll sniff it out with that great wolf's snout of yours. That is, now that you know it's there to be sniffed.

Huh! Canker grunted in Nestor's mind, and complained: *But the wind's in the wrong direction! Still, if there's smoke to be smelled, be sure that Canker will smell it!*

Ahead, a river uncoiled from the night like a silver snake glinting in the starlight. And Nestor remembered a time when he had very nearly drowned in that same river. Only Brad Berea had saved him, and returned him to life in the warmth and security of his cabin in the woods. Except ... Brad had been unkind to him, too, at times, and his wife Irma was often surly and grudging; she'd even begrudged Nestor his food, despite that he'd hunted for all of them. Only Glina had truly felt for Nestor, and they had been lovers a while.

Well, they'd shared sex, at least. But love? No, for Nestor already had a love ... or would have had if his olden, forgotten enemy had not stolen her away. But Glina would make a good bed-warmer in Suckscar, be sure, and certainly she could teach some of the other women in Nestor's harem how to relieve a man of his juices.

There was no pity in Nestor now. In fact, it puzzled him why he'd held off all this time, knowing where the Bereas were and all. Perhaps it was that for a while he *had* felt something of pity – for Glina at least, if not for her parents. But that was then and this was now, and pity and all such emotions were Szgany failings, not Wamphyri.

Smoke! Canker cried in Nestor's mind. *A whiff of it, anyway, lingering on from the evening meal. Aye, and food smells, too, from the same source. Nestor, we've passed over them!*

I know it, Nestor replied. *Now then, search for a knoll or cliff. That's where we'll land, and from there go on afoot.*

Keen Wamphyri eyes scanned the night, and Canker sent his wolf senses vibrating outwards from him like the unheard locating call of a bat into the darkness. And:

Over there, to the west. He leaned his flyer westwards. *A knoll, mainly bald, rising out of the woods. It should suit our purpose.*

I remember it, Nestor answered. *I've hunted there upon a time. Rabbits and the occasional goat.*

Ah, but rarer meat tonight! Canker chuckled. And in the next moment he was businesslike again: *Very well, let's be at it . . .*

Wamphyri senses guiding them safely down, they landed on the knoll in a swirling ground mist and settled to the rounded summit in twin slithers of sliding scree and crushed creepers. And leaving their beasts nodding there, but with easy access to flight, they descended the knoll by its eastern face.

Then a short, silent, gliding trip through the gloom of the woods, Nestor moving like a shadow, tree to tree, and Canker loping, leaning forwards, stepping so light that never a twig was broken. A mile and a half, and:

We're there. Nestor's mental voice was like a waft of cold air in Canker's mind. And the dog-Lord thought, but to himself:

How this one has advanced in just one short year, before answering: *Where are we? Where?*

This path. It leads from the river to the cabin. The cabin of Brad Berea, his wife and daughter. But remember: Glina Berea is mine. Before . . . I was hers. This time it will be different. She'll be mine always, in Suckscar. And unlike the others, who suffer me because I am their Lord, I fancy Glina will love me, because I am a man. And I'll give her power in my manse, once she's a vampire.

They followed the path to the cabin of the Bereas, all shaded under great trees and lost in a tangle of bracken and roots. No light showed through the woven shutters on the windows, but Nestor knew that a small shaded lamp would be burning inside; also knew there was a bolthole to the rear: a tunnel cut through the roots of an ancient, fallen ironwood.

Give me a moment to make my way to the back, he told the dog-Lord. *There is a secret door. Inside, the girl Glina has a bed against the back wall, behind a curtain. She sleeps only a step away from the bolthole. But when you go in the front here, let her run ... be sure she won't run far, for I'll be waiting. Look for a ladder which climbs to a bed under the roof. That's where Brad and Irma will be. They are yours. But careful, the man's a good shot and keeps a powerful crossbow to hand both day and night.*

Thanks for the warning. Canker's answer was a mental grunt. *But you need not worry for me. I can smell them up there even now, and what they're doing. The girl smells a little sweeter, true, but we have a deal.*

Good, said Nestor, and swiftly disappeared into darkness.

Canker gave him a count of twelve, then loped to the door, put his great shoulder to it, and smashed right through. Torn from leather hinges in a tangle of shattered withes, the door fell to the hard-packed floor inside. Canker's glaring scarlet eyes took in everything at a glance: a curtain hanging open a crack at the rear of the cabin ... frightened eyes peering as the shade was snatched from a lamp ... then the billowing of the curtains as the girl fled. And because his vampire senses were alert as never before, he even heard her faint gasp of horror before she bundled herself into the bolthole.

While from up above:

The smell of sex had been replaced – by the acrid stench of fear! Brad Berea's voice was hoarse, calling: 'Glina! What is it?' His bearded face – eyes wide and staring, mouth agape as in a yawn – peered down from the platform under the roof.

'Nothing much,' Canker snarled at him. 'Only me!'

Brad's face disappeared; in a moment he was back, swinging his legs down onto the upper rungs of the ladder, hanging there as he aimed a crossbow at the spot where Canker had been. But Canker was no longer there. Instead he had stepped to the foot of the ladder, where now he swept his arm like a knife through its brittle wooden legs, bringing the whole contraption crashing down. And Brad came with it.

As Brad smashed down among the ladder's ruins, Canker kicked the crossbow from his nerveless fingers and sent it clattering across the floor. And: 'Ho!' cried the dog-Lord. 'And would you shoot a poor old wolf like me? Shame on you!' He caught Brad under the arm and dragged the dazed man to his feet. Brad struggled a little then, and Canker felt his great strength. Nestor had been right: this burly barrel of a man would make a good strong vampire thrall. And so, before Brad could recover further: Canker bit him, sinking elongated ivory fangs deep into his neck. Brad choked something out, a word, inarticulate, and writhed in Canker's grip like a crippled snake. Until the dog-Lord crashed a fist into his ear and stilled his struggles.

Then:

'Brad!' A shriek went up. Canker glanced overhead, saw a woman's terrified face gazing back at him. And:

'Madame,' Canker bowed grotesquely, 'your husband is mine now – and so are you.'

He let Brad crumple to the earthen floor, crouched down a little, leapt high and caught the edge of the platform. And dragging himself up, he saw Irma where she had fallen back onto a pallet bed. Her hand covered her mouth and her eyes were wide as windows. She would be thirty-eight or nine, but was still in fine fettle. Especially he noted her breasts, in the brief moment before she snatched up a coarse sheet. They were large and loose, Irma Berea's breasts, and Canker liked them.

'Ah ... ah ... ah!' she gasped, as his hand found his belt and loosened it, and his red eyes seemed to drip like candles. And: 'Ah ... *ahhh!*' she half-panted, half-gasped again, as she saw him revealed.

'Oh, indeed,' Canker gurglingly, greedily agreed, advancing on her and tearing the blanket away, and reaching for her body. And as Irma's cries tore the silence of the night, so the dog-Lord repeated her gasp over and over and over again, filling her head and her body with the sound of his panting, and with more than just sound:

'Ahhh ... ahhh ... ahhh ... ahhh ... *ahhhhhh!*'

II

Nestor's Art

Glina Berea crouched low, the hair of her head brushed by roots dangling through the soil of the ceiling, her fingers occasionally scrabbling at the stone-paved floor of the bolthole tunnel, panting as she fled through the fallen ironwood's dead root system to the secret exit. Out there the deep dark woods, which she knew like the back of her hand; clouds covering the moon, holding back its light; an owl hooting sleepily in the distance. She could escape, flee into the woods to one of the many hiding places she knew there. But as Glina passed through the disguised outer door and let it swing back on its hinges, her thoughts were not so much for herself as for the fate of her mother, father, and ... and one other.

If only she'd had time to —

'— Time to what, Glina?'

Barefoot, she skidded to a halt in wet leaf-mould and saw a shadow grow up beside her out of the gloom; but a shadow that knew her name. An even darker blot in the dark of the night, it flowed upon her, towering huge as if to crush her with its awesome power and presence. But ...

... That voice. Didn't she know that voice?

'And so you do remember,' the shadow sighed with its deep, dark, tantalizing voice, and moved closer still. And again she thought:

382

That voice! Can it possibly be? If so, then he had chosen the worst possible time to return. And why was he so still, so very silent?

As hoarse shouts and a crashing sound erupted from the cabin, and a muted squawking like throttled chickens but in her father's choked voice – and moments later her mother's fearful screaming – so Glina realized that the worst of her fears had been utterly selfish: that she would be left on her own. But now, if this stranger really was him ...

Heart fluttering, scarcely breathing, she reached out a trembling hand and touched his arm – and in that same instant the clouds cleared the moon. Pallid light struck through overhanging branches down into the small clearing, and Glina saw that it was indeed Nestor. He stood there with his eyes half-shuttered, handsome as hell, dark in a cloak the colour of night. And clasping his arm, she gasped. 'Nestor! It *is* you! But come, we must run, hide. The Wamphyri are here!'

'I know,' he said, in that sepulchral voice which was his and yet not his.

Then ... he opened his eyes wider and she saw their scarlet glow, the convolutions of his vampire nose, and the white gleam of his teeth. And she knew that it wasn't only his voice which was him and yet not him. 'Nestor!' Her jaw fell open and she half-swooned into his arms.

But: 'Ah, no,' he told her, gathering her up. 'Not simply Nestor, Glina, not any more. For from now on you must call me Lord.'

As his needle teeth struck into the fluttering veins of her neck, so she succumbed more fully to her faint ...

Glina woke up and thought that she was burning: the roaring, leaping flames, the yellow glare, the wall of heat! But it was only her home that was burning. She saw it through the spread legs of the two who stood there, arms akimbo, apparently admiring their work. Then . . . her heart leapt within her breast. The cabin!

'My bairn!' she cried, struggling to sit up. 'You're burning my bairn!' And shrieking like a madwoman — which in that moment she was — she reached up and clawed at Nestor's legs. But she could only loll there against him, too spent to drag herself upright.

He shook his leg and, as her words sank in, made to thrust her away from him. 'Bairn, Glina? What bairn?'

'Barn, did she say?' Canker scowled at her. 'No barn that, but a cabin! Or it was.'

'My . . . my *child!*' Glina sobbed, swaying like a stricken animal on all fours, and crawling towards the fire. 'My poor burned child!' But only half-way there the roof caved in and the flames were fanned outwards, threatening to engulf her. Even so, she would have crawled on if Nestor had not stepped forward, grabbed her up, dragged her back from the inferno.

'What child, Glina?' His face was an impenetrable, almost emotionless mask in the firelight; unlike Canker's, which was still swollen with lust and power. 'You had no child.'

'Oh, but I did!' Her voice was a babble, a crazed shriek. 'Sixteen sunups ago . . . *your* child, Nestor, you black-hearted beast! He's in there,' she pointed a madly shaking hand at the blazing cabin, 'hidden in the wall in his crib. We prayed that if the Wamphyri came, they would fail to find him. And you did fail. But how could I know you'd burn the cabin? And so it's your own son that you've burned, you damned *vampire!*'

'I . . . I fathered a son?' Something of life had come into Nestor's face, which didn't look quite so soulless. But in the next moment the cold and the dark were back. What was done was done. Despite that it had not been done deliberately, still it was done. And anyway, Nestor wanted no bloodsons. Not yet.

He released Glina who at once fell wailing to the earth at his feet and began beating her fists into the dirt. Until suddenly she stopped, glared up at Nestor and spat: 'And my mother? And my poor father, too? Did you also burn them alive?'

Canker stepped forward and glared at her where she sprawled. She was homely at best, with brown lustreless hair, nose a little too sharp, heavy buttocks, and breasts too large and pendulous despite her youth. Canker couldn't see what Nestor wanted with her, him being so handsome and all.

'You, Glina,' he snarled at her. 'Your mother and father are alive. They lie sleeping in the grass, safe from the fire but burning from a different heat now that the fever of my bite courses through their veins. Rising up before the dawn, they'll head for Starside to be mine in Mangemanse.' And to Nestor:

Does she speak the truth? Have you known her before? Well, obviously you have, else how could you find your way back here? But a child? Your child?

She speaks the truth, Nestor answered. *Can't you read it in her mind?*

I read hatred in her mind! Canker answered at once. *And a longing for death ... or better still, revenge! Ah, but she has strength, this one! She's awake well before her time, and she squawks too much. You want my advice? Put an end to her, and now. Or if you wish, I'll do it for you ...* He made as if to grab Glina's hair, but the other put himself in the way.

The threat to her child woke her up, Nestor told him. *Else my bite would have kept her down. But ... she is strong, yes, and will take command of all my women in Suckscar.*

Canker shook his great wolf's head. *My friend, you're making a mistake.*

Then it's my mistake.

'Kill me!' Glina cried. 'I don't want to be a vampire. I don't want to live in a cold aerie on Starside. Not without my bairn. Not without our baby, Nestor!'

The cabin was now a gutted shell, a red-roaring bonfire like a livid skull, whose blackened window eyes gushed smoke and flames. Nothing was alive in there, not possibly, but it seemed to Glina that she heard a baby's crying in every lick of fire and *whoosh* of falling timbers. And when finally she knew that it was over, then she sank down again to the earth and cried a little, and quickly rocked herself to sleep.

'*Now* my bite works on her,' Nestor said, satisfied.

'You should strike 'em in the ear, as I do,' the dog-Lord grunted, swatting the air with his fist. 'Knock them down and they stay down, and the fever burns that much faster.'

Nestor shook his head. 'No, for that way you'll lose some by breaking their skulls. And I prefer thralls, not idiots!'

'*Huh!*' the other snorted. 'Skulls mend. Most of them.'

But a mood was on Nestor now, and it was not the mood for argument. 'Have it your own way,' he muttered. And stooping to pick Glina up, he tossed her over his shoulder and headed for the knoll.

'Can't she make her own way, like her mother and father?' Canker called after him.

'I have my needs, much like you,' Nestor answered, without looking back. 'Some of which are immediate and may not be kept waiting. But I want her awake. Strange as it may seem to you, this girl knew how to satisfy me, upon a time.' And to himself: *Indeed, she was my teacher and mistress, when I knew nothing.*

Behind him, Canker went down on one knee in the grass and put his hands on the foreheads of his new thralls. And: *Come to me*, he told them in their sleep, *in Mangemanse. And if any man or woman shall say to you, 'you are mine,' then tell him, or her, that you belong to Canker Canison. For the other vampire Lords – aye, and a certain Lady, too – they are as nothing to me! But only fail to answer my call, then be sure I'll seek you out wherever you have been stolen away, and eat your living hearts . . . and your seducer's, too! So be it!*

Following which he loped swiftly after Nestor, to catch up with him . . .

Only an hour or so into sundown, and already we're three fine thralls better off, Canker chortled in Nestor's mind when they had been aloft for some little time.

And more thralls to go, I fancy, the other answered, training his concentration on the terrain below as they winged back towards the barrier mountains. *Can't you sense them?*

'What?' Canker burst out, staring across the gulf at him.

The air was still now and they flew only a little distance apart, so that shouting was unnecessary. But the dog-Lord was annoyed; his senses were perhaps superior to all others of his ilk; what could Nestor have sensed that he did not? More smoke, furtive movement in the night, the frightened thoughts of Travellers seeking a hiding place till sunup? If so, then why did Canker sense nothing? Ah, but this Nestor was a curious one: an enigma! And Canker was fascinated by him.

I sense . . . thoughts, said Nestor. *And I sense . . . whispers! Hushed, cautious words spoken in the dead of night. Someone hides – perhaps a good many some-ones – and they know we are here.*

Hah! Maybe they saw us limned against the moon, said Canker, at once falling into his mental mode. Or they've spied us darting out from the edge of the cloud. And then, in admiration of his young friend: *You've come on faster than even I suspected, Nestor, and I have always known that you'd be great! Now then, where are these secretive whisperers in the night?*

Those three knolls there, at the edge of the woods. Nestor pointed. *Between them, a wooded triangle. And central, a rocky outcrop weathered to a dome.*

I see it! Canker grew excited.

Down there, that's where they are. They are some-where ... down there. But a moment later: *Ah! And now they guard their minds! They've sensed me listen-ing in on them.*

Canker was puzzled. *What, Travellers? Mentalists among the Szgany? Several of them? Well, and it's not unheard of, I suppose. But together? In a bunch?*

Nestor was silent – too silent, now – and Canker sensed the darkness in him like a shroud for his shriv-elled soul. But there was something of awe, too, the sudden recognition or acceptance of knowledge which had been absent just a moment ago. *What is it, Nestor?*

Still the other was silent, listening ...

Nestor?

And at last he snapped out of it. *They are not ... they're not what I thought they were.*

Not Szgany?

Oh, yes, they're Szgany. Or they were ...

Were? Canker scowled, finally admitted defeat, and barked out loud: 'What in all Turgosheim and Starside together are you talking about? Give me a clue, can't you?'

If he had thought to galvanize Nestor he was mistaken. For now the other was quieter still and his mind even darker as he guided his flyer into a swooping glide towards the cluster of knolls. Following him down, the dog-Lord demanded: *Well?*

And at last Nestor answered him. *These are the dead of the Szgany, Canker. Which is why you failed to detect them. I realize that now, that these are dead men in their graves: tattered leather and fretted bone, or ashes in small urns, all gathered together in one place around that mortuary rock.*

Ah! Canker's mental gasp. *An ancient Traveller graveyard! Your art ... you sniffed them out!*

But barely before they sniffed me out! For they smell me as the forest creatures smell a fire: with vast amaze and fear. Except it's my talent sets fire to their old bones! Then, since they can't run from me, they try to shut me out; they fall silent and wait for me to go away. But this time I'm not going to. Not for a little while, anyway. And you, Canker? You wanted to see me demonstrate my art? Well now's your chance.

I cannot contain myself, the dog-thing admitted. *What? A man who pursues his prey even beyond death? You'll be a legend yet!*

They landed on the rim of the central outcrop and climbed carefully down. At its base, uncounted years had weathered the yellow sandstone into a series of shallow cavelets useless as hiding places for living Szgany, but more than sufficient for their dead. Which was exactly what they found:

A mortuary, as Nestor had guessed – or known.

In all the cavelets, niches had been carved in the walls where urn after urn reposed in the echoing rock. Entire families had been burned and interred here, as each member in his turn died; but that had been in the years of the Old Wamphyri, who were no more. It had been in the merciless years of the vampire, when the only safe way was to burn the dead. Since when there'd been some eighteen years of peace – broken only once – before Wratha came with her renegades out of Turgosheim. And in those eighteen years men had commenced to bury their fellows again, returning soil to soil. Or to wrap them in oil-soaked cloths and deposit them on ledges in dry places, where their descendants might visit from time to time and perhaps even talk to them. Except, of course, the dead could not talk back. Not to just anyone . . .

This was just such a place. In the deepest, driest caves, ledges had been cut in the walls which housed complete carcasses, the mummies of old Szgany chiefs. None of the corpses was recent, and some must have lain here for – oh, the full eighteen years, by Nestor's reckoning – since the earliest days of Traveller freedom. But he did not want to inquire of one who had been dead too long. No, he wanted one more recently dead – say ten to twelve years – because he had a question for him which went back to his own unremembered childhood. Indeed, it concerned one of the few memories he still retained from the olden times before he'd been hurt and . . . and before he had forgotten things; before he became Wamphyri. And so he chose a cadaver which had only journeyed midway down the long, lingering road of dusty decomposition, and went to him where he lay upon his sandstone ledge.

Then, as Nestor drew near, so the old one began to tremble. Not visibly – of course not – but in his deadspeak mind.

'He knows me!' said Nestor, his voice the merest whisper, echoing away and back. 'He knows me for what I am.'

It was blacker than night in the cave, but this was of no consequence to Wamphyri sight and senses. The Lords Nestor and Canker could see as well – and indeed better – than in broad daylight. For daylight is bred of the sun, and nothing of the sun is of benefit to the Wamphyri. Except that men live in it.

Canker Canison stood to one side of Nestor and back a pace, watching. He saw how Nestor's hands trembled as he reached out and placed them upon the mummified forehead and sunken chest of the one who was no more. And it was hard for Canker to believe that anything of sentience remained in the tattered, withered husk which Nestor touched. But:

Do you hear me, old Chief? Nestor queried. But Canker heard nothing – not even a whisper – for this was not mentalism but deadspeak. *Do you feel my hands upon you? I know you do, for I can sense your mind clamped shut like a trap on a bear's leg, and though your body can't move, still your trembling is like a fever in you. And yet I say to you, you need not fear me.*

'Well?' Canker grunted from behind. For to the dog-Lord's mind it seemed that nothing was happening. 'What now?'

Nestor turned his head and looked into Canker's wolfish eyes, their blood-hued orbs and tiny pinprick pupils, yellow as his mistress moon. 'Be quiet! Let me make contact with him. For until I do you'll hear nothing, see nothing.'

'Then what is this for a demonstration?' the other seemed affronted. 'How can I know what passes between you, if indeed anything passes between you?'

'Either be quiet,' Nestor snapped, 'or go and leave me on my own here! There's that which I need to know from this one.'

'Huh!' But the other fell silent.

I ask you one last time to speak to me, Nestor told the cadaver. *I want to know who you were, and I want to know what you heard, felt, saw, one morning in that time before you died, when the fleeing clouds glowed red, and the billowing belly of one cloud in particular – a great white nodding mushroom of a cloud – burned crimson over Starside. Do you remember? I know you do: when there was thunder in the air and earth alike, and warm unseasonal winds came rushing through the passes from the north. And I repeat: you have nothing to fear from me, not if you tell me these things as best you remember them. But if you do not . . .* Thus the monstrous threat (for all that it was unspoken) was issued.

In Nestor's mind, conjured there by his own questioning, a scene from childhood opened up. He knew it of old, but never as vivid as this: a true memory, as if some lesion had finally repaired itself in the damaged whorl of his brain, adding colour and definition to previously misty monochrome pictures out of the past. And because Nestor's thoughts were deadspeak, the pictures were seen by the extinct Szgany chieftain, too:

The barrier mountains as viewed from Sunside; a thin morning mist drifting through crags which were silver-grey, because the sun had not yet discovered them. A glade hidden deep in the forest, mist-damp, all green leaves and dark green shade, where the birds had barely commenced their dawn chorus before lapsing into abrupt silence; for suddenly the earth underfoot had given itself a mighty slap and a shake, and a sheet of pulsing, dazzling white light had turned the mountains to a black silhouette. Then:

Webs of white lightning leaping and coruscating between the clouds over Starside, clouds which at once

*fled outwards from a certain spot in the white-pulsing
sky. And the fleeing clouds all red in their underbellies,
reflecting unseen fires. While bloating like some gigantic, loathsome mushroom in the cleared central space —*

*— A great grey cloud on an upwards-thrusting pillar
or stalk of fire and smoke, growing up behind the
mountains and swaying there; its puffball head all
roiling and churning from within, displaying the madly
blazing fires at its red and yellow heart!*

Nestor saw these things through the eyes of memory,
which were also the eyes of a badly frightened four-
year-old child, namely himself. But now as a man he
knew for a fact that whatever the memory signified, it
had happened; and also knew that it was important to
him. He had woken up there in that forest glade, and
cried out into the dawn. Something had brought him
awake to witness the lightnings, the fires in the sky
and the roiling mushroom cloud. But what? Whatever it
had been, it had sent him tottering, crying to his mother
(his dear mother! But who had she been, and where
was she now? And anyway, what difference did it
make, for he was Wamphyri?) to be crushed in her
arms and comforted. And it had caused him to ask her
a question which had no apparent source, one to which
he'd received no satisfactory answer:

'Is my daddy ... is he dead?'

But even though he no longer remembered his mother
— not a single detail — he recalled how quiet she had
gone, and how her heart had fluttered as she held him
against her breast ...

All of which was deadspeak, and so passed from
Nestor's mind into the mind of the old Szgany chief.
And the old chief was trembling again, no less than the
necromancer's forgotten mother on that morning of
mornings; but still he said nothing. Until:

393

Well? Nestor asked him again. *And will you remain silent forever? I think not. You know what I am, the nature of my art, for even now you can feel my hands resting oh so lightly upon your dead flesh. When I touch you – whatever I choose to do to you – you will feel it. If I were to break off one of your dry and crumbling fingers, you would feel the pain of it even as if you were alive. And if I were to dig into your wormy chest and squeeze your heart, it would be like a second dying . . . except you are already dead, and so I could do it over and over again. You know I speak the truth, and now it's your turn to speak the truth. You saw the pictures in my mind, memories from my childhood? Yes, I'm sure you did. I want to know what they signify, and I want you to tell me . . . now!* He took the skeletal hand of the chief carefully in his own powerful vampire hand, and blew the dust of the cave from the crumbling flesh and white bone knuckles. And:

I . . . I may not speak to you! The chief's voice was pitiful in its terror.

You are forbidden to speak to me? Nestor stroked the hand and gently eased the fused fingers apart from one another.

You are a vile necromancer! The dead will forsake me to darkness and loneliness forever if I breathe a single word to you.

But you have already breathed a good many words, Nestor replied.

'Speak up!' Canker rumbled from behind. 'What's all this muttering?'

'Ah!' Nestor was startled for a moment. But then: 'Muttering? Was I? Then be quiet and I'll speak out loud for you. It will make no difference now that we're in contact, myself and this wormy old thing.' And to the chief:

'So. You are unwilling, and I am impatient. Indeed, my patience is at an end!' And with one hand upon the corpse's brow, he used the other to crumble two of its desiccated fingers into dust! Behind Nestor, Canker gawped and gasped his delight.

And now the old chief was no longer unwilling. Perhaps he had not believed it himself: that Nestor could hurt him even as if he were alive. But *now* he believed it. Part of his hand had been crushed into dust, and the pain had been real. It was the necromancer's art: that the dead could sense him near, hear him when he spoke to them, feel him when he touched them – or when he did other things to them.

And in Nestor's weird mind the dead old man was screaming, for he'd felt his fingers pulped as beneath a falling boulder! They were dust and brittle bones, but when Nestor had crushed them they'd been as flesh again.

For a while Nestor listened to the old chief's screaming, and to the absolute silence of the rest of the dead where they were scattered about. Their silence, their fear, and their hatred. It made him feel powerful, especially their hatred. He *was* powerful, for he was the necromancer Lord Nestor Lichloathe of the Wamphyri! But he was truly impatient now and desired to be up and away; away from this dead place and all its dead inhabitants, up into the night sky and searching for the living. For it's blood which is the life, not dust.

Now he sighed a false sigh and arched his hand on the old chief's chest, until his blunt, powerful fingernails formed a bridge there. Only give a push ... his hand would sink through rotten cloth and wormy flesh into the very soul of the one who lay there incapable of movement. And if the old chief had not had faith in Nestor's talent before, certainly he believed in it now, especially knowing what was in the necromancer's mind.

Wait! He cried, his deadspeak voice broken like an old pot. *I will speak! I'll tell you everything you desire to know: the meaning of these things which you have remembered, how I myself rememember them and what they meant to me. Indeed, I think they may be the reason I died before my time . . .*

Nestor was fascinated. 'Say on – but first you'd best tell me your name. For it seems improper to share this mutual event from the past of both our lives, without that we've first been introduced. And after all, you *know* who I am, but I've not yet had the pleasure.'

Must I t-tell you my n-n-name? The other's voice shivered, almost as if it would fly into shards.

'Oh, yes. For if you lie to me . . . I'm sure that your sons and daughters and their children are still abroad in the world of the living. So that even whcn I've finished with you, there shall always be other fish to fry – *if* you have lied to me!'

My sons? The old man was distraught; Nestor could almost sense him wringing his hands, though of course he lay motionless on his shelf. *And . . . and their sons?*

The necromancer merely shrugged. 'I am a vampire – indeed a Lord of vampires, Wamphyri – and prey upon the living. But tell me the truth and you and yours are safe. I'll not bother them . . . I swear it.' Nestor's voice was the soul (or soullessness) of sarcasm.

You swear it? You? And should I believe you?

'Do you have a choice?' Nestor smiled with his voice . . . and then stopped smiling. 'Enough! Let's have done with this now. Should I squeeze your heart, until all of the worms that are in it are pulp?' He pressed down lightly, until the nails of his hand cut through the mouldy cloth of the other's shroud.

No! No! The old chief gasped his deadspeak denial. *Only hold off, necromancer, and I shall tell you all.* And without further pause, he did:

I am – I was – Agon Mitrea, son of Lexandru, and like my father before me I led the Szgany Mitrea through fifteen years of Wamphyri oppression; also through the balmy years of peace. Until they came again, briefly, out of the Icelands, but only to be destroyed at the hell-lands Gate. And that is the time and the event which you have remembered from your childhood. I cannot be mistaken.

'What? The destruction of the Old Wamphyri?' Nestor's fascination grew by leaps and bounds.

Indeed, the corpse gave a motionless deadspeak nod. *After that, gradually the Szgany stopped travelling, most of us, to make our lives in towns and settled camps. But following the fire in the sky, the thunder in the earth, the DOOM across the mountains in Starside, I had only three years left. And I will tell you about it:*

That morning of which you speak – it must be fifteen or sixteen years ago now – I witnessed that same awesome wonder exactly as you did, though I suspect I was very much closer to its source than you were; too close, in fact. The pulsing white light, a great sheet of it that threw the mountains into silhouette and burned like naked fire on the ball of the eye; the crack! – sharp as a stone split by the heat of a furnace – followed by a dull rumble of continuous thunder in air and earth alike; the web-like lightnings and fleeing clouds, all red and flickering in their underbellies. And then that monstrous mushroom ball, growing taller than the mountains themselves, climbing higher and higher, with the fires of its guts all spilling out from its heart!

Nestor saw it all in the dead man's mind just as he himself had described it, but closer and from a different angle. And now he said: 'You say you were closer than I was — much too close, in fact — but where were you exactly, and what do you mean, too close?'

In those days my people lived only a few miles from this very spot, this ancient Szgany burial place, Agon answered at once, for he was well under Nestor's control now. *We dwelled in a settled camp west of the great pass through the barrier mountains. That morning I was out with . . . with my sons —*

— But in the next moment, realizing what he had said or given away, Agon paused in shock, as if he'd suddenly clapped a hand to his mouth.

Nestor smiled and said, 'Ah, and so you do have sons? Now I can be sure you'll tell me the whole truth. But go on: you were out that morning with your sons . . .?'

Out h-hunting with them, y-yes, old Agon continued, wishing it were possible to die again, right now; which he would gladly do, if only it would put him and his beyond the reach of this fiend. *We were up before dawn; the rabbits come out in the dawn, likewise the deer and wild pigs. There are good hunting grounds in the eastern foothills, beyond the mouth of the pass. We had been there and were on our way back, loaded down by the weight of good meat; all Sunside on our left hand, a glorious sun just breaking free of the horizon, and the mouth of the pass on our right . . .*

. . . And that was when it happened — when the fading stars were blotted out entirely, and all the sky over Starside turned blinding white! We were blinded, if only for a moment, or seconds at most. We staggered and stumbled as the earth trembled, and some of us even fell to the ground to hug it. Ah, but they were the lucky ones! They were shielded from what came next. For even as the clouds burned red and began their

panic flight, so a hot wind from hell blew through the pass from Starside. And there was sulphur and stench and burning in it, and most likely poison, too. No, I am certain – there was poison!

I smelled it, breathed it in, felt it burning on my face. A wind out of Starside ... but warm? I didn't know what to make of it. It was the breath of hell, or the exhaust of the weapons of hell at least; or possibly, but I doubt it, the awful stench of a vampire wizard's experiment, which had rebounded and destroyed them all at a stroke ... And as if he were out of breath (this man who had not breathed in all of thirteen years), Agon Mitrea at last fell silent ...

Until in a little while Nestor told him: 'Not all of the Wamphyri were destroyed. The Old Wamphyri, aye, but not those who inhabit the last aerie now. For far in the east, beyond a great red desert wasteland, the lands have been ruled by vampire Lords from time immemorial until the present day. Their place is called Turgosheim, which is the source of –'

– Of this most recent ... infestation! Agon finished it for him, his deadspeak voice filled with loathing.

Now it was Nestor's turn to fall silent a moment, and to tilt his head slowly on one side. And how his eyes burned red in the darkness of the cave as he gazed down on the corpse of the old chief and repeated his final word out loud: 'Infestation? What, like lice, do you mean? You are very ... frank, Agon Mitrea, son of Lexandru.'

I could not hide my feelings about you and your like even if I tried, the other answered, bitterly now. *No, not even if you make me pay for it!*

'No need for payment,' Nestor told him. 'Not yet ...'

Then what else do you want from me?

'Tell me about this poison,' Nestor said. 'For obviously

399

you believe that is what you died of just three years later.'

There were rumours, theories, wild guesses about it. Agon Mitrea gave a careless deadspeak shrug. He was sure the Great Majority would want nothing more to do with him now, not after he had spoken to a necromancer. And exiled to eternal darkness, denied the comradeship of the teeming dead, what good would this monotonous non-existence of his be to him then? The Szgany are not without their so-called 'wise men', seers and thinkers, he finally continued. Some had it that the Old Wamphyri, led by Shaitan the Unborn himself, had been wizards who called up one too many demons out of the earth. They said that the poisonous mushroom cloud must have been one such demon. But as I've told you already, I doubt it. Be that as it may, its poison spread like wildfire on Starside. The stony ground there was said to shine at night, and whatever was in that shine, it killed off the cavern trogs in their hundreds and produced as many grotesque mutations among them!

'A foxfire?' Nestor was curious now, for he'd seen just such a plume of shining earth on Starside, like a finger five miles long, pointing north from the glaring hell-lands Gate. Also, there were traces of that same luminescence in the foothills and along the base of the mountains to the west, where the trogs dwelled in their dank caverns.

Like a foxfire, yes. But foxfire is the glow of rottenness, and this was the glow of death!

'Explain.'

There's nothing much to explain. Again the old chief's shrug. Those men with me in the mouth of the pass: by sundown their hair was falling out; their gums and fingernails bled; their faces turned white where they'd *gazed into the hot wind through the pass. And none of them fathered children from that day to this. Several died, of which ... I was one. As for the ones who stumbled and fell down in the heather or behind boulders when the earth shook — yes, and mercifully my sons were among them — they suffered very little. Only a sickness, a malaise, which wore off in time.*

'Enough!' Canker barked from behind Nestor. 'I can't make head or tail of it. Oh, I believe that you speak to him and he answers you, but it makes no sense to me for I hear only you. Therefore I waste my time here. And I fancy you waste yours, too. Now, are you coming — or do I go on alone, and see you later back in Wrathstack?'

Nestor looked at Canker, then at the lich of Agon Mitrea. He had no more questions for the old chief, and like the dog-Lord he had had enough of corpses for one night. He turned to follow Canker where already he was loping towards the exit ... then paused and slowly turned back. And: *But I have not said my farewells.* He used his deadspeak.

Say nothing, but simply go! Agon shuddered his relief.

Except —

— At the start of their question and answer session, the old chief had not been very forthcoming. That had been a mistake on his part, from which the teeming dead might learn something. And later, Agon had been ... frank. Indeed he had been too frank. Despite Nestor's recognition of the fact that the louse and the vampire are two of a kind, which is to say bloodsuckers, still he'd not cared for the old man's comparison. So that now Nestor thought to himself: *this Agon really should be taught a lesson.* And drawing back his lips from his teeth in a snarl, and grasping the corpse's elbow and upper arm, suddenly and without warning he gave a twist and a wrench, and tore the limb free of its rotting shoulder! Shreds of tattered black flesh hung down from the gaping socket and fat white graveworms wriggled where the dismembered arm flopped to the dusty floor. Then, as Agon's mind yawned open like an incorporeal mouth to issue a scream of denial, so Nestor coughed up phlegm and spat it into his empty eyesockets, and bayed with laughter as the old chief recoiled from it without moving the merest fraction of an inch.

Following which, smiling in his morbid fashion, Nestor set out after Canker. And as behind him the violated corpse issued peal after peal of silent, resounding shrieks — and the teeming dead in their urns and on their ledges cried out for pity — finally Nestor Lichloathe knew that he had earned his name in full.

And he was glad . . .

III

After the Hunt: Nestor and Glina

A little over three hours later, after resting their flyers a while in the foothills of the barrier mountains, and having then launched skywards to fly with the clouds once more, Nestor and Canker's vampire senses simultaneously picked up strong Szgany vibrations. Landing at the edge of dense woodlands six miles west of the great pass, they found warm embers in a dead fire.

Then, going to all fours and sniffing in a wide circle all about, like a great hound or the dog-thing that he was, Canker soon picked up the scent; and with Nestor following on close behind, he began tracking his prey along the overgrown forest paths. In less than half an hour they had found the Traveller group: two young men, two young women, a twelve-year-old girl and an infant.

They had split into two family groups and slept beneath oiled leather awnings roped to the lower branches of trees in a natural clearing. And they were bundled up in cured furs on beds of bracken when Canker and Nestor came upon them.

Now this is more to my liking! The dog-Lord coughed in Nestor's mind where they stood like wraiths wrapped in a mist of their own making, looking down on the sleeping faces of the group. *Aye, this is the 'stuff: it's exactly what I had in mind! A man each, a woman each – this sweet girl-child with her sex unexplored, tight as* a mouse's earhole, to open up and fill on the one hand, bite into and drain to the dregs on the other — and an infant for roasting in the mountains when we're feeling peckish, before we fly back to Starside! And come sunup, four brand new thralls in our manses in Wrathstack! This will have been a night and a half, and time for a lot more business yet. Hah! But we make a good team, you and I.

The infant lives, Nestor answered.

Of course he does, Canker agreed. For now.

No, he is to remain alive, untouched, untainted.

What? But he'll be succulent! And without these adults — with them as thralls in Wrathstack — what chance does he have anyway?

Plenty of chances, in Suckscar.

You'll give him to that dumpling Glina? In place of the one she lost? Canker's mind was shrewd when he desired it to be.

Aye. It sometimes works with wolves. Without the infant we deprived her of she might hate me, and I want her to love me.

You put a lot of store by that girl. Is she that good?

She was good to me, upon a time. I ... have my reasons. Let it be ...

So be it, Canker shrugged. The child lives. In which case, the young girl is mine.

Will you keep her?

No, but I'll be into her! And I'll drink what's left when I'm done!

Nestor scowled and said: Fox, dog, wolf? Maybe there's something of the pig in you, too! She's a mere child, Canker! But in fact he knew that she was only meat, or would be soon. And anyway, he didn't really care one way or the other. Yet in the back of his mind, in the ever shrinking human part of him, perhaps something shrieked its abhorrence even now; but if so its cries were weak and went unheard.

As for what Nestor had said to the dog-Lord, which must surely be seen as an insult:

Nestor could say *anything* to him, even things which would get other men killed. Usually Canker would grunt and turn away, to show his disapproval if Nestor's words had cut him; but this time he was satisfied to laugh in his fashion. *A child, you say? Well I say she's a she! And she'll be good and tight!*

His laughter died away in Nestor's mind, to be replaced by cold cunning, insatiable lust, and purest evil. Then, with his eyes blazing like fires as his fangs commenced to lengthen and salivate, Canker went into a crouch over his intended victims and growled in Nestor's mind: *When you are ready, just say the word.*

Nestor was ready. 'Now!' he said out loud.

They had hung their gauntlets from branches, to be picked up later when all was done. There had seemed little or no requirement for serious weaponry on this occasion. Now they reached down together, gripped the men by their throats and drew them swiftly from their beds. Canker's was very young; the dog-Lord nipped him in the neck, delivered a stunning blow to the side of his head, tossed him aside and reached greedily for his suddenly screaming woman.

Nestor slammed his man against the bole of the tree and, as the wind was knocked out of him and he opened his mouth to cry his shock and terror, pinned him there by driving the six-inch blade of his knife through his gasping mouth and right cheek, deep into the bark and tough timber core. Conscious for now, the man stood there naked and shivering, slopping blood and saliva, gurgling where he clung to the tree to keep from falling and ripping his face wide open. He tried once to free the knife, despite the incredible pain it caused him, but only half-awake and weak from shock and horror – and Nestor having driven the knife home with a vampire's enormous strength – it was a wasted effort.

Meanwhile, Nestor reached down again into the bundle of furs, but his attack on the man had taken time and given the woman a breathing space. She was already on her feet and running.

'After her, lad!' Canker cried, from where he'd tossed his victim face-down across a fallen tree trunk, mounted her from the rear and was hammering into her while she howled the agony of her violated flesh. 'Ah, the thrill of the chase is – ah, *ahh!* – good,' he panted, 'but the rewards are so much better! Except you mustn't forget – ah, ahh, *ahhh!* – leave the girl-child to me. For I'll not be – *ahhh!* – I'll not be too long here.'

The girl, who had been sleeping a little apart from Canker's targeted group, was also running; her long, slim white legs flashed in blue starlight as she sped barefoot into the forest. Nestor noted which direction the youngster took, passed the information to the dog-Lord in a single instantaneous thought, then hurried after the woman and quickly caught up with her.

Panting, whining deep in her throat like a trapped animal, she found her way blocked by thorn bushes, spun on her heel and saw Nestor coming ... and rushed straight at him! Taken by surprise, indeed astonished, for a moment he stood stock still – until he saw the starlight glinting on the knife in her hand! And that hand even now arcing towards him. Ducking to one side, he felt the keen blade slicing into his arm: cold metal wetted on blood, cutting skin, muscle, metamorphic vampire sinew.

Furious, snarling – controlling his pain as only a Lord of the Wamphyri can – Nestor struck at the woman's knife arm and felt it break like a twig. And as she cried her agony he clouted her on the head in the manner prescribed by the dog-Lord. Felled, she at once slumped to the forest floor.

While from some little distance away:

'A-ha!' came Canker's bark of triumph, and a moment later the wail of the waif. For the dog-thing had pursued and caught the small girl. And of course Nestor knew what he would do with her. But that was the way of it; the Wamphyri have their needs, and Canker's needs were . . . often prodigious. And after all, the blood *is* the life, and young blood is the sweetest.

Briefly, curiously, Nestor found himself wondering whether Canker would drink before or after he'd used her . . . or during? But in any case the girl was as good as ruined; she would be a vampire in Mangemanse, if the dog-Lord left her enough strength to make it through the pass before the dawn . . .

The infant's extra weight was negligible. Bundled up at the rear of Nestor's saddle behind Glina's slumped form, it cried out once or twice during the blustery ascent on the night thermals, but that was all. Yet its cries were sufficient to cause Glina to stir and moan in her vampire sleep.

Sensing that she would soon wake up, and again before her time, Nestor decided to test his theory. If Glina took to the child – and if the merest spark of her old love for him could yet be rekindled – then he would carry her to Suckscar, to be his thrall and warm his bed. If not . . . perhaps he would still take her to Suckscar. There was always the provisioning.

'What now?' Canker called across to him, breaking his train of thought. 'What say we settle in the heights and rest awhile, and scan for Szgany fires and such?'

'Not me,' Nestor called back. 'I'll stop while I'm ahead. You carry on if you wish, and I'll see you back in Wrathstack. Me, I've had more than enough for one night. My flyer's weary. I'll take a break in the heights, aye, but then I'm on my way back.'

Canker looked across at him and grinned lewdly, shrewdly. 'Your mind's an open door, Nestor. You never even sniffed that girl back there, or touched Glina for that matter. But now at last your juices are working. You want her, but you're being coy about it. Well, that's fair enough. Have it your own way. Canker's not the one to stay where he's not wanted. And anyway, you're right: enough's enough for one night. I have work aplenty in Mangemanse. I want to get back early and see what my lads are up to . . . and my lasses! And then there's my moon music . . .'

'Farewell, then,' Nestor told him.

And Canker threw back his head and yipped, then sped for a gap between the peaks and was soon lost from sight . . .

Nestor landed his flyer in the thin soil of a saddle between jutting granite outcrops. Situated at a slightly higher altitude than the Sunside treeline, the hollow was thickly clad in purple night-blooming heather, which gave the place a cloying, sickly-sweet smell.

He lifted Glina down from his saddle and saw how cold and trembly she was. Well, and she would soon become accustomed to that; only the most extreme sub-zero temperatures will seriously incapacitate a vampire. But for the moment . . . they might as well be comfortable, at least.

And so he took down the infant child, wrapped him in his own soft leather jacket and laid him to one side, then spread the cured fur in which the child had been bundled and placed Glina upon it. Which was when she woke up.

'What? Who?' She struggled to sit up a little way, then fell back, to lie there wrapped in dark fur, pale and dishevelled in the starlight. She looked, and was, a captive thing, a thrall, not only physically but mentally, too; or she would be soon. Which excited him and made him want to use her. But he would not take her by force, for he wanted her to come to him as she had used to. If she wouldn't, then he would find another use for her. She was only flesh and blood.

She had been watching him for some time, until finally: 'You ...' she said. But her voice was dead, empty.

He took the child to her, showed her his face.

'My baby?' Suddenly Glina's voice was a whisper of hope; she couldn't believe it; she reached for the child ... and saw that he was not hers.

'No,' said Nestor, shaking his head. 'He's not yours. But he can be, if you want him.' He covered the baby again and put him to one side, in the heather.

'You burned my baby,' she said, her voice cold again. 'And now you would give me this one? Some other poor mother's loss?'

'I didn't burn your child.' Nestor lied easily, for lying is the natural province of vampires. 'It was the dog-Lord, Canker Canison. He burned your cabin. In any case, we didn't know there was an infant in there.'

'But my baby burned nevertheless. And you, Nestor? What do you care? You are a vampire!'

He shrugged. 'It was my destiny. To be Wamphyri. Didn't I always tell you I was the Lord Nestor? Well, and now I am.'

Suddenly Glina was sobbing: deep, wracking, painful sobs.

He sat down with her and put an arm round her shuddering shoulders. 'Tears change nothing.'

Amazingly, she snuggled up to him ... or perhaps not amazingly. She was after all his thrall, and Nestor was her master. Also, he now felt a power in himself, a talent which he had not used before, because he'd not been aware of it; had not needed to know it. And his eyes were hypnotic and his voice languorous when he said, 'Aye we sat together many a time, you and I, in your father's cabin when they were abed. And sometimes we'd go down to the river, too . . .'

Conscious of her flesh, he opened the furs a little until his hand could steal inside to weigh her breasts. Just as in that other time. And again she softened and snuggled closer, and said, 'You don't know how many times I've cried myself to sleep and longed for your return. But not like this. Nestor, what will become of me? Will you make me a vampire, too?'

'But it's done,' he said, with another shrug. 'My mark is on you. It's the mark of that which governs me and could be no other way. As to what will become of you: we'll fly to Wrathstack, the last aerie, if you wish it. And the child, too.'

'And if I do not wish it?'

'Then you must make your own way, for you can't dwell on Sunside now.'

'Then I have no choice.'

'You loved me, upon a time,' he said, his hands insistent now.

In their turn, her hands found his member standing erect and jerking. She lay back, sighed, threw open her blanket of fur. 'How I have wanted you! And even now, when I should hate you, still I want you.' It was his vampire stuff in her. From time to time she would hate him, look back on what she'd lost and hate him. But when he called to her she would always come, and she would never be free from his fascination.

'You were like no other,' he answered, throwing off his clothes, 'because you loved me and gave your all. Now, in Suckscar, they only give to fill my needs, because they desire to please me. But ... it rarely pleases me.'

And he entered her like never before, and his metamorphic flesh filled her and brought her shuddering to an instant orgasm – and another – and another! Until she cried out for him to stop, for she felt that she couldn't stand one more. But he gave it to her anyway. And because her sex was bruised, Nestor took her in her mouth and in her exit, and was well-received in both. And for him it was like it had never been in Suckscar.

As for Glina: she'd never in her wildest dreams imagined it could be like this with any man; and of course it couldn't, for Nestor was much more than a man. He was Wamphyri! And what woman will ever go lusting after men, once she has had a vampire ... or after he has had her?

Upon a time (it seemed an age) Glina had seduced him. Now she, in turn, was seduced. By his voice, his eyes, his hands, his body. She was (of course) enthralled. And she knew that if she couldn't have him – have this, which he had showed her – then she would destroy herself utterly. And so she determined that she *would* have it, and be his mistress in Suckscar.

But what Glina didn't know was this: that of all his mistresses she would only be one.

And what Nestor didn't know and never discovered was this: that Wratha the Risen had seen him with Glina ...

Wratha's raid on Sunside had been disastrous.

411

Plotted in anger and badly executed as a result, the outcome had been no better than last time. For the previous raid had also been against ruined Settlement, and it had worked out expensive indeed: she had lost one lieutenant dead and another seriously wounded, a newly-weened flyer destroyed, and a small aerial warrior decoyed, brought down, deflated and burned. As a result of which Wrathspire had been depleted and Wratha the Risen had vowed revenge on the Szgany Lidesci, whose name had become a curse throughout Wrathstack in its entirety.

For Wratha wasn't the only one who had been frustrated in her attempts to raid on Settlement. The other Lords were in the same fix; try as they might, they could never go anywhere near the place with impunity but suffered losses at every turn. For the erstwhile inhabitants of Settlement — a town which Wratha and her renegades, as they'd termed themselves then, had tried to destroy on their very first excursion out of the last aerie — had proved a difficult lot to cow. Indeed difficult wasn't the word for it: they were impossible!

Fighters born, their leader was a man who seemed as crafty and merciless as the Wamphyri themselves. His name was Lardis Lidesci, which was also a curse on Wratha's lips. He set traps for flyers, decoys for warriors, and had crossbows and devastating explosive weapons which fired lethal silver pellets to penetrate and poison vampire flesh.

And tonight's raid? Another flyer pierced through its neck with a bolt from a giant crossbow; its lieutenant rider knocked out of his saddle and doubtless dealt with by the defenders of that tottering, derelict pile; the flyer itself shrilling like the wind off the Icelands in Wrathspire's turrets, raining its vital fluids, finally crashing in the Sunside foothills ... a total loss. And never a captive taken, nor a single changeling thrall who ever made it out of the region to come shambling and mewling over the boulder plains before sunup, and nothing to show for this humiliation except perhaps in Wratha's vampire heart: her absolute determination that one day she'd bring the Szgany Lidesci — Lardis included, *especially* him — to their knees!

As for Settlement itself:

The town stood (or slumped, now) at the base of Sunside's foothills some eighty-odd miles west of the great pass. It had been a thriving community when Wratha and the others came fleeing here out of the east from Turgosheim beyond the Great Red Waste. But flying out from the last aerie on that initial raid, they'd first hit Twin Fords, a neighbouring town, then Settlement, and reduced them to so much rubble. It should have been total victory, followed by utter subjugation of the Szgany and eventually a free run of Sunside such as that enjoyed by Vormulac Unsleep and his vampire colleagues in Turgosheim. It *should* have been like that, but wasn't. For during the course of those vicious preemptive strikes, Wratha and her raiders had themselves been taken by surprise — when the humans hit back!

In Turgosheim's Sunside it had been very different. There the Szgany were docile, cowed, supplicant creatures. Sullenly but without any real objection, they had given to the Wamphyri and would never dare refuse them or even hint at fighting back. So that Turgosheim's Lords had been able to use Sunside and its inhabitants like a vast larder to plunder at will, and had even operated a tithe-system designed to ensure a fair split of the spoils; not only of human spoils, but of all good things out of Sunside. For there in the east even the so-called 'free' men of the Szgany spun cloth and forged for their masters; they fashioned their clothes and weapons for them; they farmed, hunted and gathered for them ... and they bred for them, of course.

But the Wamphyri of Turgosheim had been greedy, destructive masters; to a man, they'd lived for today without a thought for tomorrow. And over the course of hundreds of years Wamphyri depredations had cut Szgany stock to the bone, until the inhabitants of Turgosheim's Sunside had been little more than grubby animals. They were human, but had been debased almost to extinction as members of that race. And if blood is truly the life, theirs was a trickle thin as water, growing thinner with each new tithe.

It was just one of several reasons why Wratha and the others had fled out of Turgosheim in the first place: so that they might give free rein to Wamphyri passions in pastures new. But there were other reasons, too. There had seemed no future in Turgosheim, where the upper echelon was so firmly ensconced as to be irremovable, while the lower orders were falling into a gradual decline, just like the people they victimized.

But far to the west:

Rumours had told of a vast and sprawling land of plenty, of milk and honey and rich red blood! And these were rumours which the Lady Wratha couldn't ignore. Determined to discover the truth of it for herself, also to escape from Turgosheim's claustrophobic constraints, she had drawn together a crew of malcontents much like herself: Vasagi the Suck, Wran the Rage and his brother Spiro Killglance, Gorvi the Guile, and Canker Canison; and all of them had commenced in secret to make flyers and forbidden aerial warriors like none seen before, all with stamina enough to carry them and their makers over the Great Red Waste into the west.

So they had arrived here with their lieutenants some eighteen months ago, and had at once begun raiding on

Sunside to improve their lot in the last aerie of the Wamphyri. At first they had worked as a team, but that hadn't lasted. Arguments had split them up; old scars had started itching anew; old scores still required settling. That was why Wran and Vasagi had fought their duel on Sunside, from which only Wran had returned. But other feuds were in the offing, Wratha was sure. Vasagi had been an ally of sorts, and now he was no more. And for all that Wratha was strong and her manse secure, still she knew that she was a woman while the others were all men. Well, men of sorts . . .

It had been to strengthen her hand − and also to avenge herself − that Wratha had launched this latest raid on Settlement; she'd needed strong Lidesci blood for her men and beasts, and a handful of Lidesci thralls wouldn't go amiss in Wrathspire, either. Failing, and finding herself depleted yet again, she'd ordered her creatures home while she herself rode a high wild wind and raged into the night. And anyone who had seen her would know why men were careful in their dealings with the Lady Wratha. Except no one had seen her.

But as Wratha had calmed herself and descended from the turbulence of upper air to float on the blustery thermals over the high crags, she had seen Nestor and Glina. Then, using her mentalism to explore Nestor's mind − knowing what he was doing and how he was enjoying it − she'd barely been able to control a second bout of furious raging. Nestor was with some chit out of Sunside, some Szgany slut, filling her to brimming. He was with . . . a mere girl, when he could have been with Wratha!

Withdrawing from the lurid churning and throbbing of his mind (but carefully, so that he would never suspect she'd been there) at first she turned her flyer's head towards the highest peaks and Starside. But in another moment, gritting her teeth and giving a vicious jerk on the reins, she turned back. And in the dark and seething quagmire of her undead mind, only one thought now:

This ... this *Nestor!* And despite herself, she had to know more about him and the way he was with women.

Landing her flyer some hundred yards away, knowing that the wind's bluster would cover the slither of scree as the hovering beast touched down, Wratha dismounted and hurried to the saddle where she'd seen them together in the heather. And keeping her mind tightly guarded, peering through a gap where jagged fangs of rock leaned together, she spied upon the ... the lovers?

And how many times had she spied on him from her high windows, going out upon his flyer to practise? And how often had she insinuated herself into his mind, watching him at work and at play? He had his women – of course he did: he was Wamphyri! – but he rarely enjoyed them. Indeed, he was with them much as Wratha was with her love-thralls: utterly bored. She'd sent out thoughts to lure him when he was asleep; she'd planted pictures of herself in his mind, and she had used her vampire art to beguile and fascinate him ... to no avail, for he was naïve. Not naïve as a man, no, but as a Lord of the Wamphyri, certainly.

And oh, this fine young body, this oh so *beautiful* body, all muscle and fire and energy – all wasted on such as this! Wratha could laugh, but instead felt like crying ... and was at once outraged by the very idea. What, Wratha the Risen, bawling over a man like some Sunside peasant girl? At her age and with all of her experience? No man – not one, *none* of them – had ever been worth the effort. But this one ... could it be that he was? But no, he wasn't, it was just the way he enjoyed coupling with this slut. It was his pleasure. It was the tingle she had felt in his blood. It was that he *wasn't* making love to Wratha!

There, it was out: she fancied him. No, she actually lusted after him! Before, there had been plenty of time; she had known that Nestor would come to her eventually; following which she would soon tire of him and send him away. But now ...

... Time had run out. He had not come to her. He had taken a woman who pleased him. A dull, stupid, even plain Szgany bitch, but she *pleased* him! And Wratha felt pangs she had never known before, which might be the acid burn of jealousy, or possibly the bittersweet sting of ... love? Yes, perhaps even that. But true love was so rare among the Wamphyri it was almost unheard of. And yet Wratha had heard of it, had even seen it for herself.

Back in Turgosheim the great Lord Vormulac Taintspore, called Unsleep, was *still* in love, despite that his lady had died seventy and more years ago, and he had not slept for all of that time. Such was Vormulac's devotion that he'd kept his manse, melancholy Vormspire, like a mausoleum to her memory.

Then there had been Karl the Crag's love for Wratha, which had destroyed him in the end. It had to, for she'd been ambitious then as she was now, and with Karl in the way could never have ascended into the circle of Ladies. But instances such as this were rare, indeed singular.

And with all of these thoughts and plenty of others in her head she watched them coupling, and with every jerk of Nestor's buttocks or gasp of joy or sweetest pain from Glina, her eyes protruded a little more from her head and the figured bone scarp upon her brow burned crimson from their glare. Wratha saw the ways he took her, the sheer inexhaustible power of the need driving him on, and knew that no man – not even Karl the Crag – had ever taken her like this.

It was his youth and his passion and his lust, and it was every erotic dream he had ever dreamed; all of it bursting out of him now, amplified by his vampire leech to previously inaccessible, undreamed heights. And:

If he is not careful, Wratha thought, *he might easily fuck that girl to death!* (Ah, but Nestor knew what that would mean, and it was not a mistake he'd make twice.)

Wratha's nipples were hard as callouses yet sensitive as open sores where almost unconsciously she squeezed them through her robe, and she felt the bud of her sex stiffening to a small finger as her hand stole down to her mass of black ringlets and into the cleft of love. And Wratha the Risen – even the Lady Wratha herself – stood trembling, panting and masturbating as she watched Nestor shudder to a climax, the way his seed spurted from the corners of Glina's mouth.

Then, it was over. Nestor fell back and lay sprawled on the heather; Glina took up an infant, hugged it to her bruised breasts, covered herself and the child with furs and curled up to sleep. They were like young animals, making love until they were exhausted and then sleeping it off. And suddenly the Lady Wratha was exhausted, too. She had brought herself to orgasm, right along with Nestor, but all it had left in her was a dull ache, by no means the relief which had blossomed like a weird night orchid in his mind and body.

Again Wratha felt like crying, the furious sting of tears trying to be shed, and again she detested herself for it; but the reflected blaze of her eyes under their scarp of bone was lacklustre now, like a lamp turned low. And so, before vastly enhanced Wamphyri emotions could make a fool of her entirely, she backed out of her hiding-place, returned to her flyer and launched for Wrathstack.

But even as she climbed aloft and sped for that last lone fang of rock against its backdrop of diamond stars, blue-sheen horizon and shifting, sighing auroral curtain, Wratha knew in her heart that nothing would be quite the same from this time forward. Because for the very first time in her too-long life and undeath, she was sure that she actually did have a heart after all . . .

In Suckscar that sundown (a 'night' which lasted as long as three days in an unsuspected world beyond the so-called hell-lands Gate), Nestor made Glina his first woman. But first he waited until the fever had gone out of her and her eyes took on that unmistakable feral look.

And the fact of it was, her vampirism enhanced her; not to the fantastic extent of Wamphyri enhancement and metamorphism, but it did lend her a certain elegance of motion in place of the clumsiness she'd displayed before, and a sort of sensual intelligence or self-awareness which her master found disconcerting in a girl who had been so dull. She was his thrall now – a vampire, yes – but paradoxically, there seemed a lot more of the Gypsy in her, too, than was previously apparent. His bite – which changed other women into blood-lusting creatures, none of whom could ever be trusted entirely, certainly not in their instincts and thoughts – had changed a mainly naïve girl more truly into a woman. She had been, in Canker Canison's eyes, 'a dumpling'; she still was, but was now more nearly edible.

Conducting her through Suckscar, and making

known to his males the role she would play in the manse, Nestor fancied that his lieutenants and senior thralls found the swivel of her more than ample hips attractive, her glance alluring. But it could be that they desired to keep on her good side, because she was a favourite of their master and would now control the comings and goings of all the other women.

Finally he introduced her to his female thralls, each by name, and told them that from now on she would be in charge of their work roster, overseeing all of their duties. Glina's word would be law among them; let anyone complain, make difficulties or put obstacles in her way, she would report that fact to Nestor and he would know how to correct the situation. But all of his thralls knew him now, how he meant what he said, and none of them were about to make difficulties.

Then, while Glina familiarized herself with her new duties, he went alone to his senior thralls and lieutenants and warned them off. What the dog-Lord had said to him, or hinted, about the more ambitious of his men lusting after power and position, had struck a chord. Perhaps he had allowed too much freedom in Suckscar, and the reins must now be tightened; his lieutenants were the first to feel his telepathic scrutiny.

But Zahar and Grig had learned their lessons well; they harboured no real ambitions in respect of Suckscar, nor did they seek to seduce Nestor's women. What? Was it likely they would cross a man who could torture them alive, then torture them dead? No, for they knew that Nestor was a necromancer.

As for his lesser male thralls:

His message to them was simple. Glina was now the first of his women in Suckscar. She *was* his. If any man so much as looked at her lustfully, Nestor would first feed his parts to a warrior, then feed *him*, slowly and feet first, into the meal grinders. And since these were simple thralls, he had allowed Glina to be in attendance when he instructed them in this fashion, so that she took it that indeed he valued her beyond all the other women. And her step grew a little lighter by virtue of that fact.

She was given her own rooms directly beneath Nestor's in an excavated area under the sweeping stairs to his apartments, with a narrow spiral staircase that climbed up to an annexe off his bedchamber, and even had an older woman assigned to her to clean her rooms and mind the child. So that Glina's lot was in every respect superior to any other woman's in all Suckscar. And so she took up her new life and duties, and quickly learned all that was required of her ... at least with regard to her mundane responsibilities, within the manse.

Then, before the next sundown as she lay in her bed and wondered about Nestor where he slept somewhere overhead, suddenly she heard his call, or felt it, and knew that he wanted her. And climbing the spiral staircase to his chambers, she entered his bedroom ...

... Only to discover that two others were there before her!

Nestor saw the look on her face and quickly cautioned her: 'Say nothing. Do not offend me or mine. These girls are here to be instructed – by you! For although they are beautiful, they have forgotten the part which made them innocent and beguiling women. For there is innocence even in sex, but there is no satisfaction in sex with such as these, whose nature it is to be promiscuous. That is why you are here: to teach them the art of innocence, naïvety.'

She was bewildered. 'But I don't have that art.'

'But you do, for you satisfy me. And when they have

421

learned it from you, then part of my life at least shall be complete.'

'You want me to show them how to –?'

'– Yes,' he cut her short. 'I want you to show them everything, Glina, while you still can. For as yet you're more woman than vampire, and I have been bored in my bed for far too long. My needs are not well served here.'

Now at last she saw her true position in Suckscar. But she was his thrall and must obey. And she did.

And so the last flickering spark which yet remained in Glina Berea, which might even have been rekindled into love of sorts, however dark and strange, died in her that time. For she knew that whatever course her life took from this point forward, she would never forget the events which had befallen her: the fact that she was now a vampire, the similar fate of her mother and father, residents now in Mangemanse, the monstrous burning of her child.

Probably, the time would never come when she might take her revenge. But if it ever did –

– Then she *would* take it . . .

IV

Wratha's Vow – Gorvi's Proposition

In the heights of Wrathspire, Wratha the Risen brooded.
Like a great black cloud she brooded, roiling and rumbling and constantly threatening rain. Except the Lady
Wratha's rain burned like acid! Six months and more
she had been this way, while her thralls went in fear of
their lives. Plainly she was distracted and they had
learned to leave her that way. Only break into her train
of thoughts and draw her back to reality, however
briefly ... all hell would break loose! She would fly into
a rage, hurl abuse and other things, and rush through
the manse like a lunatic storm, bowling everything over
in her passing and issuing the direst threats left, right
and centre, at all and sundry.

For Wratha had a great many things on her mind,
which demanded her utmost concentration and mental
co-ordination; or so she was given to excuse herself –
which in itself was strange, for as a Lady of the
Wamphyri she scarcely required to make excuse for anything! But it was obvious that in fact her co-ordination
was in tatters and her concentration non-existent. Something, it seemed, was stretching the Lady's nerves to
breaking.

She had lost all interest in the administration of
Wrathspire, so that her lieutenants had never known
such freedom in the running of the place. No domestic
problem or dispute could be permitted to disturb her,

no slightest whisper or unaccustomed jangle of sound, no unexpected footfall. She fell behind in her self-allotted duties (mainly the all-important overseeing of the aerie itself), and the orders-group meetings which had always been such a regular feature of life in Wrathspire became fewer and fewer, until they ceased entirely.

Her males – almost all of them, from the lowliest novice to the most senior lieutenant – began to take advantage; likewise her vampire women. Lustful affairs, which Wratha had kept to a minimum for all that she knew her thralls must amuse themselves as best they could, swiftly gathered impetus; schedules suffered as a direct result; Wratha scarcely noticed.

Her love thralls could not satisfy her; when the best of them failed her, she murdered him in her bed. And the others grew thin.

The aerie quickly went to pieces. Grotesque siphoneers in their discreetly curtained niches developed sores and parasitic infestations, and the water they drew up from Guilesump's wells became less than pure, because their wayward keeper serviced a woman instead of the flaccidly insensate creatures in his keep. Foetal warriors waxing in their vats went untended, and one of them even slumped, expired and eventually stank, because no one saw fit to drain the huge corpse of its corruptible wastes and morbid fluids. Cooks in their kitchens made do with what little was available, but the manse's fare was less than satisfactory. Pantries and cold-storage rooms stood empty, likewise the granaries. Flyers went mewling hungry, and in the raids on Sunside were wont to grow weary and unreliable.

And through all of this, apparently unaware, Wratha merely brooded . . .

But during the long days when the rest of the stack slept, then she would sit up and send her thoughts down into Suckscar, to worm their way into Nestor's dreaming mind. Before, this had been little more than an amusement: it had titillated Wratha to read his sleeping thoughts (or occasionally, when he was with a woman, his lustfully active thoughts; but rarely, because more often than not his women bored him, which pleased her). But now . . . it was no longer an amusement but an agony, and the Szgany girl Glina was the source of Wratha's pain. For she had known Nestor as a man, while Wratha had not.

She was an artless shad at best, this Glina, yet apparently there was one art which she had mastered: the pleasuring of the necromancer Lord Nestor Lichloathe of the Wamphyri; mastered it to such an extent that Suckscar's new Lord even required her to instruct his other women in order that they, too, might satisfy him. Except they were mainly incapable of instruction, for they had long since lost what Glina retained: that very artlessness which Wratha so despised!

It *was* that she was naïve, or pretended to be because it pleased him. Her sex was always fresh, quivering, half-afraid, yet full of longing. She was a woman but continued to play the girl, the innocent, so that her Lord would need no other. For when he was with her he was the untried youth again, jerking erect as he stroked her teats or bruised them in his passion.

It was as if he remembered a time when love – human love, Szgany love – had been something other than lust and was trying to recapture it. Or . . . perhaps it was that he remembered some other *lover*, not this Glina, and was trying to recapture her!

And as soon as that thought came to Wratha, then she knew she was on the right track. For it made sense out of a paradox: how Nestor could fancy – and continue to fancy – this merely homely creature when he was surrounded by girls of Vasagi the Suck's choice; for Vasagi had installed most of the women who dwelled now in Suckscar, and for all that he'd been a monster in his own right, the Suck had had an eye for beauty. But the difference was this: that Glina had actually loved Nestor upon a time. And for all that she had been a novice herself, still she had taught him all he knew. Now ... he knew other things, but still he remembered how it had been with Glina. While his brain may have forgotten much of his past, his body continued to remember. And not only Glina, but someone before her.

Oh, Wratha knew their history well enough; she'd stolen it right out of their minds! She knew that Glina had been Nestor's Sunside lover, for she had seen pictures from his past replayed a dozen times in the eye of his mind. But more than this, she knew there was a fury in him when he made love to Glina, which he would rather expend on this unknown Other. Some unrequited love out of his unremembered past? It could only be ...

Whoever she was, this Other, it seemed to Wratha she was worthy of serious consideration; for if Nestor Lichloathe had found and brought back Glina out of Sunside – and out of his more recent past – then one day he might also find and bring back the Other, too, from a yet more distant period. And what then? All of Wratha's plans gone up in smoke? No, not at all, for by then Nestor would belong to Wratha!

As for this Glina: what was she? Simple: she was nothing! What, this ungainly Szgany peasant? She was a flame that would soon flicker and die; a piece of tarnished property, a tool to be used, blunted, and eventually discarded. Ah, but if or when Wratha should ever set eyes on this Other, be sure she would know

426

how best to deal with her! And she would deal with her, most certainly.

It was her vow . . .

In that same six-month period of twenty-six sunups, Nestor's fame or infamy as a necromancer had spread through all of the stack. In every manse from Guilesump to Wrathspire, his talent was the subject of gossip and speculation. The former among the lieutenants of the Wamphyri and lesser thralls, and the latter among the vampire Lords themselves.

Canker Canison was mainly to blame for spreading the word. Pleased to call himself Nestor's friend, he was 'proud' of the comparative newcomer and desired to see him elevated among his peers. For the dog-Lord had the dubious gift of scrying future times, and he had foreseen that Nestor's talent would make him very powerful, a force to be reckoned with in the last aerie.

And Canker was right.

Late one sundown after a full night's raiding on Sunside, when the Lady and all the Lords were safely returned to their various manses, the lieutenant Grig Lichloathe made report to Nestor in the quiet room where he rested from his bloody work. There the Lord of Suckscar stretched out in a huge wickerwork chair, sipped coarse Szgany wine and watched the grey glimmer of a false dawn creeping on the distant crags. Nestor was reluctant to go to his bed because for months his dreams had been made wretched by recurrent erotic visions . . . mainly of Wratha the Risen. Over and over he would revisit Wrathspire's roof to play out that scene where Wratha had fallen into his arms, but only to escape from him when she felt his surging ardour.

And when he started awake from dreams such as

this, all drenched in sweat and whining his frustration – and with the soft curve of Wratha's breast still warm in his tingling palm – then Nestor would put aside all thoughts of his other women, Glina included, as if they were nothing. For he knew now what he wanted, if not how to get it. Also, he was prideful. Wratha had made a fool of him once, and Nestor wasn't about to let it happen again.

The trouble with Wratha the Risen was this: she liked to toy with her men, and all the men of Wrathstack knew it. Still, Wran Killglance would have her if he could, and Gorvi the Guile if he thought it would strengthen his hand. As for Canker Canison: the dog-thing had openly admitted that he would swap half of the whelps in Mangemanse – even his own flesh and blood – for just one good ride on Wratha! But there was her reputation to consider, which was that of a certain spider: the sort that lures a male with her sex before she devours him! How may one mate with a maneater? With a great deal of care, the Lord of Suckscar was sure . . .

These were some of the necromancer's thoughts as his man Grig Lichloathe approached, bowed, and shuffled his feet until he had his master's attention. And finally: 'What is it?' Nestor spoke softly, as was now his wont.

'A flyer has landed in the main bay, Lord,' Grig answered. 'Turgis Gorvisman is here with a message from his master.'

'From Gorvi?' Nestor lifted an eyebrow. 'And have you left the lieutenant waiting?'

'Yes, Lord.'

Nestor stood up. 'Then take me to him. Let's see what's on the Lord of Guilesump's mind.'

In a walled staging area over the landing-bay, Turgis

Gorvisman prowled to and fro, three paces this way and three back, between six of Nestor's senior thralls. They were armed and he was not. It would not have been seemly – indeed, it would not have been allowed – to bring a gauntlet into another's manse. A huge man as most lieutenants were, Turgis's message was brief and his voice a fair imitation of the rumbling growl of a Sunside bear as he said: 'Lord Nestor of Suckscar, my master Gorvi the Guile proposes a meeting with you. He would discuss business: a matter of mutual interest, which might possibly lead to huge profits for both of you.'

'Indeed,' Nestor answered, inclining his head. 'And the nature of this . . . business?'

The other shrugged, and growled wryly: '*Hah!* That will be the night, when Gorvi the Guile shares his thoughts with lieutenants or lesser persons! But this much I know: my master has heard it rumoured that you are a necromancer, with the power to talk to dead men.'

Nestor nodded. 'He wishes to avail himself of my talent, then. And where will this meeting take place?'

'In Guilesump, naturally.'

But: 'Ah, no!' Nestor shook his head, and smiled a slow, knowing smile. 'If at all, it will take place here, in Suckscar.'

'I very much doubt it,' said the other. 'For the Guile seldom leaves his manse except to raid on Sunside, or when he inspects his creatures where they prowl abroad near the foot of the stack. He prefers accustomed places, in order to maintain a measure of control. He takes no chances.'

'In this we are not dissimilar,' Nestor replied. 'Now go back and tell your master that I'll meet him an hour from now out on the boulder plains, due north of

Wrathstack and just a mile from its foot. In fact, we'll meet in the shadow of the stack itself.'

'At sunup?' The lieutenant's gaze went out over the wall and across the mighty gulf of air, high over Starside to the barrier mountains.

'The sun never shines on the boulder plains, fool,' Nestor retorted, but quietly. 'Anyway, we'll be meeting in the shadow of the stack, as I said.'

'I heard and understood you,' the other answered. 'But I also know that Gorvi hates to be abroad when the sun rises over Sunside. It is his nature.'

Nestor turned away. 'It is the nature of each and every one of us, to fear the sun,' he said. 'Also, it's our nature to argue, and to have our own way. Gorvi desires to talk business with me; very well, I've named the place and time. Just the two of us. No gauntlets, lieutenants or warriors. If this is satisfactory, he'll be there. If not . . .'

He made to go back inside.

'I can only tell him what you have said,' Turgis nodded, and started down a ladder to the landing-bay. 'Who knows, he might even agree.'

Nestor paused and glanced over his shoulder, and stared into Turgis's eyes before he disappeared from view. 'Those are the arrangements,' he said. 'If Gorvi doesn't like them, he can wait a six-month before approaching me again. Time is in short supply. I can think of better ways to waste it than in arguing meeting places with Gorvi the Guile.'

'So be it,' the other's answer came back to him.

And in a little while, Turgis Gorvisman launched out and down from Suckscar . . .

Gorvi was there. Nestor had watched from a north-facing window and had seen the Guile speed out upon a flyer. Only Gorvi could look like that: a great evil scarecrow of a man hunched in the saddle, his cloak flapping like the wings of a huge black bat. The other Lords were sinister, naturally, but Gorvi the Guile was sinister.

And with certain reservations, Nestor had sped after him.

For of course, Gorvi had been the one who would have made trouble for Nestor when first he came here out of Sunside. And it was Gorvi who had suggested a trial period, following which Nestor would either be accepted ... or dropped. Probably from a very great height!

Well, it hadn't come to that, but neither had Nestor forgotten. And now the Guile wanted something from him. All well and good — but nothing for nothing, be sure.

Nestor landed his flyer on a shale hillock some seventy yards from where Gorvi stood beside his own beast. Dismounting, he glanced all about, and turned his eyes on Wrathstack a mile away. Possibly they had been seen flying out and were even now spied upon. He felt the shields go up in Gorvi's mind and applied his own. Their thoughts were now guarded.

And striding out towards each other, they and their long shadows soon came together in the greater shadow of the last aerie. They looked at each other a moment or two: Gorvi tall, slender, with the dome of his skull-head shaven except for a single central lock with a knot hanging to the rear; dressed in black, as always, so that the contrast of his sallow flesh made him look fresh-risen from death; and his eyes so deeply sunken they were little more than crimson jewel glimmers in their black orbits, yet shifty for all that. And Nestor: not quite so tall but well fleshed-out and handsome as hell, and open as a door left banging in the wind . . . or open by Wamphyri standards, at least. Then:

'Well?' said Nestor. 'And do you have business with me? Or is it that you've decided I didn't quite "get there" after all, and now you'd like to throw me out to fend for myself in the stumps of the fallen stacks and scramble for a living in the scree and the rubble of Starside?' And he laughed a quiet, humourless laugh. 'Ah, but that will be the day, Gorvi!'

'That's all over and done with.' Gorvi's voice was oily as ever as he held up a slender but wickedly taloned hand in a gesture intended as placatory.

'Forgotten by you, perhaps,' Nestor answered in his quiet fashion.

Gorvi threw up his hands. 'I came out here against my best instincts to meet you as a friend, a colleague, even a partner! Now tell me: how may I make known to you the details of the . . . the matter in hand, if you insist on scowling, carping and mulling over ancient, best-forgotten scores? Anyway, what are you complaining about? You did "get there" in the end, didn't you? What? And if I had not set a limit on your ascension, can you honestly believe that the others would not have done so?'

Nestor smiled his slow, cold smile and said: 'Don't waste my time, Gorvi. Why don't you get to the point? What is it you want from me? Who do you want me to . . . examine?'

The Guile tried not to look too surprised, but Nestor saw how his eyes narrowed. And eventually, carefully, Gorvi said: 'But you've been talking to my man, Turgis.'

'Isn't that why you sent him to me?' Nestor raised an eyebrow. 'Perhaps you should have cut his tongue out, and sent him to me dumb! Turgis told me nothing – except that you were interested in my necromancy. That was enough.'

'Huh!' Gorvi snorted. 'And they call *me* the Guile!' But in a little while: 'Very well, I do have a man – or the body of a man – who has or did have secrets. And yes, it would be in my interest to know the things he knew. Indeed I would give a lot to know them. Even so much as half of the profits.'

'An even split?'

Gorvi nodded.

'But of what?'

'Knowledge! Flesh and blood! Red revenge! Women for your bed! And sly, taunting laughter on our lips when the others see what we've achieved! All of these things and more.' Gorvi grinned to show his needle teeth and crimson gums. 'Well, what do you say?'

'I say you've told me nothing, as yet.'

'Very well,' said Gorvi. 'Now hear my story. Almost two years ago, when first Wratha led us here out of the east, our first raids on Sunside were against a pair of Szgany townships named Twin Fords and Settlement. And that was when we first learned that there are Szgany and Szgany. In Turgosheim's Sunside, for over a hundred years, our prey had given us no real trouble. But here they fought back! We lost flyers and men that night, which we could scarcely afford. Indeed, we lost almost *all* of our lieutenants. And we vowed revenge!

'The first of our losses happened in Twin Fords, and we Lords were lucky that we weren't among them! The men of Twin Fords – some of them at least – knew what they were doing; they'd had dealings with vampires before. They had crossbows, which had been forbidden in the east since Turgo Zolte's time. Tipped with silver and steeped in kneblasch, their bolts were of ironwood. Also, they wore long knives in their belts and were equipped with sharp wooden stakes!

'Vasagi the Suck took a bolt in the side, but to him it

was little more than a scratch. And in any case, Vasagi was a master of metamorphism; he would quickly shed the poisoned flesh and replenish himself. The fact that he'd been shot at all, however, had come as something of a shock. And as I said, the rest of us were lucky. We were lucky, aye, but as for our lads ... the majority of our lieutenants went down and stayed down.

'Ah, but didn't we make them pay for it? You can be sure we did! We wrecked their town, ordered our warriors down onto their houses to crush them flat, made as many changeling vampire thralls as we could, and instructed them to report to us with all their goods in Starside before the dawn. Canker Canison ravaged with a vengeance; the Killglance twins raged like the madmen they are, naturally; and the Lady Wratha ... well, she was wrathful! As for the town: we'd turned it to a shambles and it was the beginning of the end for Twin Fords. But it hadn't even started yet for Settlement ...

'That first town was serious work. It had been necessary to recruit thralls and lieutenants, have them fill our manses with all the good things out of Sunside, and set them to work for us in Wrathstack the last aerie, to make it liveable. And despite our losses, in the main we'd been successful. Szgany losses were far greater, and what are a few lieutenants after all? Still, it *had* been serious work. But Settlement would be for fun. So we thought ...

'It was Wratha's idea. She must have thought: "Now that my dogs have done their work, maybe it's time I let them off the leash a little." For we were Wratha's renegades then, do you see? And we might have been even now, if she wasn't such a thief. But that woman ... for every four we recruited, she stole one away! That's what broke us up, and that's the way we've stayed. Oh, each of us has a part to play in the maintenance of the stack — *huh!* And some play a greater part than others, too! — but as for the rest of it, we're on our own. But there, I've strayed a little from my story.

'So, Wratha rewarded us by turning us loose on the second Szgany town, this veritable fortress of a place called Settlement. Well, she and the others were straight into it, no warning and no quarter given. But as for myself . . . right from the start I hadn't liked the look of it. Especially not after the trouble we'd had in Twin Fords.

'Now, Settlement stands in the mid-west, directly below the foothills at the edge of the forest. The entire town is housed within a massive timber stockade with watchtowers and four huge gates, and giant crossbows mounted on the battlements . . .' Gorvi paused and frowned.

'But . . . why do I concern myself to tell you all of this? Surely you must know something of Settlement from your Szgany days?' A moment more and he snapped his thin fingers. 'Ah, no! I remember now: you have no memory before the time of Wran and Vasagi's duel.

'A pity, for if you had, perhaps you would also have the answers to my questions . . . without that you must torture the dead for them!'

Nestor shrugged. 'I still don't know what your questions are.'

'I'll get to it,' Gorvi told him. And after a moment:

'That first night, after Twin Fords, I let the others go ahead and raid on Settlement while I settled for smaller prey. There was a house on a knoll in the foothills, overlooking the town. I had seen its lights, however briefly, from on high. But as we stationed our aerial warriors windward of the town behind a jut of crags, landed our flyers in the hills and called up a mist, so

435

the lights were extinguished. It made me suspect that just like the people of Twin Fords, these Settlement folk had also had dealings with vampires. All the more reason to steer clear of the town . . .

'Well, I'll cut a long story short. While Wratha and the others fell on the town, I made straight for the place on the knoll. And without pause I landed my flyer on top of the house and crushed it, then looked for survivors in the rubble. There was no one there. But scanning all about, I discovered a woman hiding in a stand of trees behind the broken house. She knew I had spotted her, made a run for it and ran right into me! She was mature, good-looking, and had a fine body on her. I would have struck her down at once, there and then – taken her for my thrall, and taken her, too – if not for an interruption.

'A youth, no older than you yourself, Nestor, had come up from the town. He was the woman's son, surely. And he attacked me! One man, or callow youth, and he dared to attack Gorvi the Guile! It was astonishing. Ah, but he had a knife! The blade of his weapon was coated with deadly silver, which burned me where it glanced off my ribs and sliced my forearm. And meanwhile the woman had found a hatchet!

'Somehow I had been unarmed, my gauntlet had slipped from my bloodied forearm. And these people . . . how they could fight! The one with a knife and the other with her axe! Suddenly I was in trouble, and so called out to my flyer: "Roll on them, crush them!"

'The clumsy beast made to obey me. Thrusting itself out of the shambles of the house, it struck the woman with a wing tip and knocked her over the rim of the knoll in its steepest part. She disappeared with a cry into darkness. That left the youth, and a single clout stunned him.

'But I was wounded and that concerned me. Cut with silver, my ribs and arm would take a while in the healing. The hunt was over where I was concerned. I drank from the lad, only a little but enough, bundled him into my flyer's pouch and launched for Starside and Guilesump.

'So my captive became a common thrall, and went about his menial tasks for a month or two in the basement levels of the last aerie. But later, when it became clear how extraordinary were these Settlement folk – like thorns in Wamphyri flesh – then I considered him again.

'The trouble with the Szgany Lidesci is this: they have a superb leader, a man called Lardis. Thralls taken from other towns and camps have informed us that Lardis was a young chief in the old days, in the time of the Old Wamphyri. Now he is an old chief, and so much wiser. No one knows our ways better than he does, and no one is better trained and equipped to kill us! Indeed, that's his vow: to destroy the Wamphyri utterly, every last one of us. But he won't, because he can't. And even if he could, we would destroy him first.

'But ... how may we go about it? What are his weaknesses? Apparently, he has none! And his strengths? Well, to start with he has Settlement. Yes, it's still there! However much we tried to destroy the town during those early nights, in the long days that followed Lardis would build it up again. Except the houses are now traps for flyers and sometimes warriors, and there are twice as many crossbows on the stockade wall. So now Settlement exists solely as a lure for unwary vampires, and you could be forgiven for asking: why don't we simply avoid it? But to know that there are men there – and probably women, too – through the long dark nights, is in itself a lure! It is as if Lardis were flaunting himself, saying "Come and get me!" And oh, we would dearly love to.

'For there's good rich fighting blood in these Lidescis, Nestor. Good lieutenants in the making, good strong women for the loving, good flesh for the fashioning. And apart from all that, there's revenge! For do you know, while we got thralls out of Twin Fords that first night, we got nothing out of Settlement but a bad taste in our mouths! Well, our get amounted to a handful at best. And of course there was this Jason, which I took from the house on the knoll. But damn few thralls out of Settlement, and that's how it stands to this day. This Lardis Lidesci, he hunts changelings down with a will, and burns them before they can make it across the barrier mountains. So that now he's as much a legend as we are!' Gorvi paused again, and glanced sideways at Nestor's face in an attempt to gauge his thoughts . . . then looked again, more sharply.

And: 'Is something the matter?' Gorvi queried. For a peculiar, faraway look had come over Nestor's face, and he'd turned his head and eyes to gaze towards the south-west. In the direction of Settlement, in fact.

'Jason, did you say?' Nestor's voice had also undergone a change; it was uncertain, faltering. Blinking his scarlet eyes, he stroked his temples and issued a small moan, as if he felt a pain. 'This one you took from the house on the knoll – Jason?'

'Aye,' Gorvi nodded, frowning now. 'What of it?'

And again the look of pain on Nestor's face. But not truly a physical pain. Merely that of remembering. Then . . . it came to him in a flash! And: 'Jason Lidesci,' he said. 'Lardis Lidesci's son! That house you destroyed on the knoll: it was the Old Lidesci's place. You had your greatest enemy's son in the palm of your hand, and you didn't even know it!'

438

'What?' Gorvi's mouth gaped open. 'Are you sure? *How* can you be sure?'

'Because ... because I knew him,' Nestor answered. 'Jason, the house on the knoll, the town, everything! As you described it, so I remembered it. Some of it, I think.' But already the dazed look had crept back onto his face. He groaned, clenched his teeth, and slammed a fist like a rock into the palm of his hand, then cursed and turned away. 'It comes and it goes. One minute I see ... things, and the next they're forgotten.'

'Our greatest enemy's son!' Gorvi clapped a hand to his pallid forehead. 'I might have known it! He was trouble from the very start! Surly, difficult and defiant. And when I sent for him, to question him about the Szgany Lidesci – that is, after they had become important to us – then he tried to make his escape from Guilesump and set out over the boulder plains for Sunside. Which would have been the end of him, of course, for the sun would have done for him. Except it didn't come to that.

'I have warriors who guard the stack from ground attack. They drove him back and my lieutenants went to pick him up. No such luck! He dodged them, came back to Wrathstack and commenced to climb it by an exterior route. It was the worst possible move; on the approach to Madmanse the climb peters out, and the face leans into an overhang. But why did he climb? To what end? He would either fall or be retaken by a flyer, and he would be mine dead or alive. Well, I was soon to learn why he made for the heights. It was because he *intended* to kill himself!

'Such is the fighting spirit of these people. Rather than divulge the secrets of the Szgany Lidesci, this Jason – Lardis's son, you say? – would climb up to a high place and throw himself down. And that's exactly what he did. Moreover, he had a sliver of ironwood with him which he held against his heart. When he crashed down it was driven into him and that was the end. For after all, even a vampire is only flesh and blood . . .

'He had fallen some one hundred and eighty feet onto a wide ledge and was dead in the instant he hit. I left him there as a warning to others. But as you know, Starside's air is sharp and desiccating. Things rarely rot here but shrivel and mummify. As we are wont to say, dead men "stiffen to stones". There are no carrion-eating birds here, and there was no way up to the body for my bulky earth-bound warriors, which might otherwise devour it. So . . . I left him there. Until a few hours ago.

'For recently I have heard it rumoured that you have the skills of a necromancer and torture dead men for their secrets. And that's why I've come here, against my better instincts, out onto the boulder plains at sunup to talk to you. I want you to talk to him, and discover the secrets of the Szgany Lidesci!'

Nestor was almost himself again. 'What secrets, exactly?'

'Why, is it not obvious?' Gorvi raised his eyebrows. 'Now listen. The reason this Lardis and his people are such a nuisance to us is simple: by daylight they're up and about setting traps and such in Settlement and the regions around, and then by night they vanish into their hiding places which we haven't yet found. What I want to know – or rather what we, you and I, need to know – is this: where do they go to, and where and when are they at their most vulnerable? As soon as we discover these things, then we shall raid on them with as much force as we can muster and make them ours. For once they're scattered, then they're finished. We can pick them off at our leisure.'

'It would appear to make sense,' Nestor nodded. 'But tell me: just where would you have me perform my ... *examination* of this Jason Lidesci?' In his weird and damaged mind, all memories of Settlement in a previous time had faded away again, but he felt the place had strong connections with his old, unknown enemy. With him and with someone Nestor had loved very dearly, who had betrayed him in favour of that same old adversary.

But Settlement? Had his betrayal – and the damage to his mind, which had robbed him of his past – had it really happened there? So far in his raiding on Sunside, Nestor had avoided Settlement. He'd told himself it was out of respect for those same fierce Travellers which Gorvi had mentioned, the Lidescis. And indeed their name seemed far too familiar on his tongue. Only speak it ... visions would pass like the streaks of shooting stars across his mind. Not memories as such, but monochrome scenes – bursts of white light and black silhouette, burning like after-images on his scarlet retinas – of mighty stockade walls and towers, with foothills looming on the one hand and dark forests on the other. But then there would be pain – in his brain, his very mind – and the scenes would shatter into fragments like a piece of slate broken against a boulder.

These uneasy thoughts of Nestor's had taken but a moment, by which time Gorvi had answered, 'Where will you examine him? Why, in Guilesump, where else? For that's where Jason's body is. I have his body, and you have the talent.'

Nestor looked at him. 'You'd have me enter your manse of my own free will? Ah, no. I prefer a neutral place.'

Gorvi scowled. 'Where then?'

Nestor thought about it. 'In the glare of the hell-lands

Gate, in the first hour of the next sundown ...' He paused and thought again. 'No, better than that, we'll wait until all of the others have gone off raiding on Sunside. Then, you'll fly to the Gate alone – well, with a dead man for company – and I shall follow on behind. And we'll see what we'll see.'

Gorvi shook his head, looked puzzled, but finally agreed. 'So be it.'

Following which there was nothing else to say or do. And shortly thereafter in the sky over Starside, twin manta shapes pulsed and scudded with the clouds for Wrathstack ...

In fact it was three hours after true sundown before the rest of the inhabitants of the last aerie had departed Wrathstack to go raiding on Sunside, but Gorvi was patient and Nestor had all the time in the world. For if the truth were known, the necromancer was not sure he wanted to know Jason Lidesci's secrets after all; he was perhaps afraid that he would learn too much.

But Gorvi flew out as prearranged, and Nestor followed on. And just within the glare of the hell-lands Gate, they gentled their flyers to earth and Gorvi got down the long blanket roll from his beast's side. Opening it, he beckoned Nestor closer.

As the Guile had forewarned, the lich was a broken, shrivelled thing. Its contorted face told Nestor nothing: it could be anyone's face. It had been badly battered in the fall from Guilesump and had dried like a papery wasp's nest, all crumbling and flaky. And the body and limbs were no better. Most of the bones were broken, and some protruded like white kindling as from the makings of a fire.

'How long had he laid there, on that ledge?' Nestor inquired.

'Two years,' the other shrugged, 'but not uselessly. Whenever I had a difficult thrall — it happens occasionally — I would take him to a high window and let him look down on this one, and ask him if he could walk upon the air like the Wamphyri. For as you must know, we Lords can fly when we must, but common thralls and lieutenants can't. The sight of this Jason all crumpled there would usually bring them to their senses. And if not . . . there were always other ways.'

'Two years,' Nestor repeated him. 'You must be right: the air of Starside is sterile, bloodless. It's as if we've sucked the life right out of the place!'

'Not us but the barrier mountains.' Again Gorvi's shrug. 'Where there's no light there's little or no life. But there's always undeath.'

'This is a mummy,' said Nestor. He gazed down on the shattered body, though as yet he had not touched it.

'Are you saying you can't do it?' The Guile stared hard at him, then at the crumbling corpse. 'Is he too far gone?'

Nestor looked at him, blinked, and smiled a very terrible smile. 'No, not at all,' he answered. 'If he were ashes in an urn, still I could talk to him. Indeed, he's listening to me even now.' His voice had fallen to a whisper, a dry throaty rustling.

'Eh?' Gorvi's jaw dropped.

'Oh, yes.' Nestor uttered a strange, sad sigh. 'And can't you see? He's trembling, too.'

The Guile took a pace back from the necromancer, who might just be a madman. 'Trembling? But . . . I see nothing!'

The other went down on his knees. And: 'Seeing,' he said, 'is not the art. Ah, but to *feel* him trembling, and to know it for a fact — that is the true art.'

And smiling again, he reached out his hands to the shuddering corpse of Jason Lidesci . . .

443

Conversation with a Corpse – Nestor and Wratha: The Assignation

Gorvi the Guile was suddenly aware of a change in the psychic aether, the atmosphere, the very aura of the place. Starside in the vicinity of the Gate was a strange region: what with the blindly vacant glare of the dazzling white hemisphere portal, like an immense eye in its crater socket, lighting up the sterile soil, blackened boulders and fused slag all about; and the riddled condition of the blasted earth and rock around the crater itself, as if a nest of giant worms had burrowed there; and that weird plume of softly pulsating luminescence reaching out from the Gate to point north like some dumbly accusing foxfire finger. All of these things, plus the reason for his being here, had given Gorvi an unaccustomed feeling of foreboding. But he suspected that this new sensation, this tingle of awareness (but of what?) on the periphery of his vampire senses, was something other, greater, than any chance combination of location and circumstance.

More sensitive to sinister influences than Canker Canison, the Guile sensed the flow of ... *something*, between Nestor and the lich. And as the necromancer's hands came down on the corpse's crushed brow and shrunken chest, so that unknown something increased tenfold. In that same instant, Gorvi came to believe in

Nestor's talent; he was satisfied that the youth could actually converse with one who was no more. And perhaps hoping to eavesdrop on what passed between them, the living and the dead alike, he moved a little closer. But Nestor's words were deadspeak, which the living cannot hear, as he said:

Jason Lidesci, badly broken though you are – unrecognizable, and forgotten by me as all of my past with the Szgany is forgotten – still I know who you are. And I know that upon a time I knew you as you were. Now I want to know you again.

The other said nothing, but Nestor felt him exerting his will and strengthening his resolve – to continue to say nothing.

Ah! But that won't work. I know how strong you are. Gorvi has told me how you hurled yourself down from Guilesump before you would talk to him, because you thought you could only die once. Well, that was true enough then. But through me you can feel the pain of death over and over again, as often – or as seldom – as you yourself will it. Or as often as I will it . . .

But even though Nestor let the pause stretch itself into a monstrous threat, all he felt was a further strengthening of the other's will. And he found it amazing that for one who was dead, this Jason could be so strong. Well, strong for the moment . . . but for how much longer?

In fact, it wasn't so much Jason's strength that Nestor sensed but his strong inclination to disbelieve. For like certain others of the teeming dead when the necromancer first spoke to them, he also doubted this vampire Lord's talent. After all, Jason had neither seen, felt, touched nor tasted anything since the moment he'd launched himself on his fatal dive from Guilesump's mist-slick wall. He had not even been aware of the grit

445

and pebbles which had hammered themselves into his broken skull and limbs when he struck home, or the wind's bluster about his ledge, or the tiny bats which flitted close to inspect his desiccated body, then flew off chittering into the gloom. Only the eternal darkness and loneliness had touched him, and the only taste he'd known was the bitter bile of frustration: that he was dead while such as Nestor, Gorvi, and the rest of the Wamphyri lived on to plague his people.

So why should he now believe that Nestor Lichloathe could touch him, hurt him, cause him pain? What *was* pain anyway but the shrieking of tortured nerves or ligaments, or the bubbling up of morbid fluids in a sick body? And how may one even begin to feel it in nerves and muscles and veins which have cast off life and stiffened to knots of leathery gristle, or in fluids leeched off by the sucking winds, turned to vapour and blown away?

But on the other hand:

Jason had died a vampire, but knowing *how* he had died and why, the dead had come to accept him. While his other senses were sadly defunct, at least he could hear the Great Majority when they talked to him. But *only* them, until now. And from them he'd heard a good many things. Oh, he knew that the teeming dead believed in Nestor's powers; for he'd heard them time and again whispering in their graves, terrified that sooner or later the monster would come for them. Why, there were even those among them who swore that they'd already suffered at his hands. But Jason found it hard to credit.

Except ... what of Nestor's deadspeak, which Jason heard as plain as the voices of the Great Majority? It was one thing for the dead to use that metaphysical medium, but a *living* creature? And that was the reason why he feared Nestor and hated the sound of his deadspeak voice. For the vampire Lord was not dead but very much alive; he had a leech; he *was* Wamphyri, yet he too was gifted with deadspeak. And if he had that . . . what else did he have? It was this which made Jason tremble.

All of these thoughts were his, which he fought hard to keep to himself. But finally Nestor smiled his terrible smile; for concentrating on Jason's corpse, directing all of his necromancer's powers at the lich, at last he'd broken in on his victim's thoughts and heard or sensed that last fearful query. And knowing that the dead man would hear him, he repeated his question out loud:

'What else do I have? Is that what you want to know? Well, perhaps it's time I showed you.'

Without further pause he took his hand from Jason's forehead, caught a papery eyelid between finger and thumb, and tore it free as easily as tearing the fragile wing of a moth! It was nothing — oh, a dreadful act, certainly: to defile a corpse — but nothing that required any real effort. To have done it to a living man would have been something else. That *would* involve a measure of resistance and a guaranteed response. But not from a dead man, surely. For the dead don't feel pain . . . do they?

Well, and now Nestor's victim knew the folly in that line of reasoning. For Nestor *was* a necromancer, and Jason did feel it! Felt the blood spurt, the red ruin of his face, the impossible agony of that previously insensitive but now highly *sensitized* part torn away like a piece of bread from a loaf. Felt it and screamed, screamed, screamed!

And: 'Ah!' Nestor sighed. 'So you have a voice after all. I was beginning to think you were dumb. But no, you're merely stupid.'

Gradually Jason's sobbing shrieks subsided, became gasps of shock, horror, and finally petered out. Now it was as if he were a man holding his breath and hiding in the dark, but one who knew that his adversary could see in the dark and knew his every move. Yet still he was reticent and Nestor felt not only pain but defiance in him.

'Must I hurt you again?'

No! the other's gasp of terror was as real as from a living throat. *You are right: I am that Jason you knew in Settlement. I was taken on the night of the first raid, and it seems that you were, too. But you submitted, obviously, and I didn't. Well, as a child you always played at being Wamphyri. It's possible that some might even believe you're the fortunate one. As for me, I don't think so. Even dead and miserable, still I prefer it to the living death which is vampirism. For me there is no hell ... except the one which you vampires have created to inhabit!*

'Well said,' Nestor nodded. 'You have a way with words, for all that a great many of them are wasted and others ill-advised. As for hell: there's a hell for every man, be sure. Didn't I just show you a small corner of yours? But let it be. I think I would prefer it if you simply answered my questions, rather than spouting your defiance and loathing. Do you agree? If not, there are other parts you can lose.' He tugged tentatively at the tattered web of what had been Jason's left ear.

Again the other's gasp, and: *No! No! Only ask your questions. And if I know the answers, I will tell you.*

'All of the answers?'

As much as I know. But still there was an edge of sullen defiance in Jason's deadspeak voice. Nestor shrugged. He would see what he would see.

'And so you knew me in Settlement. Very well, tell me my history.'

The other was puzzled. *What? I should tell you what you already know?*

'No, only what I have forgotten. For you see, I have no memory prior to this. Well, some few fragments of memory: of being wounded, a near-drowning, a life in a cabin in the forest, finally of becoming Wamphyri. But of my childhood and my youth, nothing. You are now my memory, or will be. But first tell me this: when I spoke to you, you knew who I was without that I first told you. How?'

Because there was only one creature you could possibly be, Jason answered, *for you are one of a kind. You are of the living — a sort of life, anyway — yet speak the language of the dead, and they fear you for both your voice and for your touch. I learned your name from them, the teeming dead, only to discover that I had known it long before that. For you are the necromancer Lord Nestor Lichloathe of the Wamphyri, once Nestor Kiklu of the Szgany Lidesci. And we grew up together, in Settlement. Better if we had died together, too.*

It was more or less as Nestor had expected. Except:

'We ... grew up together?' He frowned. 'I have no recollection of that...' But in fact in the back of his mind, a far faint scene was already glowing a little brighter: a picture of forest paths and glades, and children, three of them, laughing at their play. Two boys ... and a girl, they were perhaps ten or eleven years old. But the scene was viewed through the eyes of a fourth child, which Nestor supposed could only be himself. Out of focus, the picture jogged Nestor's memory a little, but not enough. Also, because of the current damage to the corpse of Jason Lidesci, Nestor had not managed to identify him as a member of the small group. And so:

'Let me see you as you were,' he demanded of the

trembling lich. And at once, despite that Jason did his best to stop it, a reflex picture of himself as a child was mirrored in the eye of his mind; which Nestor saw, of course. And now he knew that indeed Jason had been one of the children in the forest scene. But the other two?

'Did you see those children in my mind?'

Yes.

'What were their names?'

What? And have you also forgotten them? But they were your closest . . .

Nestor sighed a false sigh and grasped the other's lolling bottom jaw. He twisted it just a little, until brittle flesh at the right-hand corner of the corpse's mouth began to tear like paper. Which was more than enough for Jason Lidesci. For to him it seemed that something was ripping his face apart!

Ah, no! My face! He relapsed into racking sobs.

'The other two?'

Misha! Jason screamed aloud. *The girl was Misha Zanesti!* And sobbing brokenly, gasping his deadspeak agony, he hurriedly went on: *As for the boy, he was . . . he was Nathan. But do what you will to me, Nestor, I can't believe you've forgotten him!*

'Misha? Her name was . . . Misha?' Nestor's voice was suddenly changed. Previously a whisper, now it was harsh, choked. And with his eyes bulging as his lips quivered back from fanglike teeth, he snatched away his hands from the dead man.

Just how often had the necromancer woken up from angry, fretful, fading dreams with this very name on his lips, without knowing the meaning of it? Often enough, aye. But now he believed he did know. And slow as flabby bubbles in a swamp, gurgling up from his damaged memory, another picture formed: a wooded river bank, and the children as before. Except they seemed a little older now, and this time there were just the two of them . . .

. . . Nathan and Misha.

And Nestor a silent, stunned observer now, just as he had been then:

The children at a bend in the river, where the rippling shallows had formed a beach of yellow sand and white shingle. Nathan sitting on a rock, with the woods as a backdrop; Misha swimming, laughing, taunting the boy on the bank. She stood there naked and posturing, beckoning, daring him to join her in the river. Sunlight shimmered on her brown pixie body, highlighting her barely formed breasts, glinting on jewel droplets of river water in the thin black cobweb of her pubic triangle. Not quite a child, Misha, but not yet a woman, she was all innocence (or not-quite-innocence), where she showed herself to this Nathan.

And Nestor felt about her now as he had felt then: that he wanted her, yet at the same time despised her for her naïvety: that she'd never recognized his feelings. In those early days he would not have known what to do with her anyway, but still he'd wanted her, even though her heart belonged to someone else. He knew it from a tearing inside, as if someone had squeezed his guts: that Misha had belonged to Nathan. And he wondered:

Is this really the one, the child, girl, woman who later betrayed me? Was it Misha who spurned his love, in that time when he'd been capable of true love? But pointless to merely wonder, for he knew. And he also knew with whom she had betrayed him.

For Nathan was ankle deep in water now, throwing off his clothes, laughing as he rough-and-tumbled her in the shallows. Their bodies touching, not yet intimately, more like siblings. But Nestor knew that the intimacy would come later; even years later, by which time it would be too late for him.

And so it was this Nathan who was his olden enemy; but an adversary of long-standing, who it now appeared had even been Nestor's rival in a mainly unremembered childhood!

'His face,' Nestor rasped, as the scene in his mind faded to a misty shimmer, then vanished entirely. 'You, Jason: show me what he looked like the last time you saw him.'

That was the night of the raid, the other brokenly replied, knowing that he was beaten and how useless and painful it would be to speak anything other than the truth. *All three of us had been to Starside with my father on his annual trek, and we were just home. It was the last time I saw Nathan, and the last time I saw you. Indeed it was the last time I saw anyone from Settlement, or anyone else entirely human, ever again.*

Nestor's patience was running thin. He had asked for one clearly defined thing, and had been fobbed off with something else entirely. Obviously this Jason was exactly as Gorvi had reported him: surly, difficult, defiant even now. What's more, it could be his screams had been louder than warranted by the amount of pain inflicted. In any case, Nestor had had enough.

'It seems to me you're deliberately slowing this down,' he snarled, reaching out again and grasping the corpse's dangling, almost weightless arm. 'Wherefore, I'll say this only one more time: show me his *face!*'

Yes! Yes! Jason was terrified, and real terror now, leaving no further doubt in Nestor's black heart but that at last he would get the truth. But just to be absolutely certain ... he tugged on the arm until it almost came loose at the elbow! Which was the absolute end of Jason's reticence, if there had actually been any in the first place.

There are screams and there are screams. Jason Lidesci's silent deadspeak screams that hideous night reached out in all directions. They echoed across the barren boulder plains, reverberated in the passes, flowed up and over the mountains into Sunside. The dead in all their many places heard him, and knew what was his torment ... and could not offer a word of comfort, in case Nestor heard them and came to investigate. Filled with the most awful, impossible agony as he felt his flesh tear and his bones come loose at the joint, Jason's screams were such as to *wake* the dead, except they dared not wake. For a necromancer was among them.

'His face!' Nestor demanded yet again, and twisted the arm one last time, without giving his victim a chance to recover. And when at last Jason's shrieking and sobbing subsided, finally Nestor's order was obeyed.

A face – Nathan's face, Nestor's olden enemy's face, his Great Enemy's face – came floating up from the pulsing red and black pit of pain which was Jason's mind, and firmed into being where the necromancer could see it.

And he knew it!

Blond hair, blue eyes, and pale as can be. Handsome in a sad, shy sort of way. Szgany, and yet not Szgany. And suddenly Nestor remembered how sometimes he'd been ashamed to call Nathan his ... to call him ... his ... his ... *his* ...

His mind went blank, numb, rigid as the rock of the mountains themselves.

But Jason's mind – apart from his unspeakable agony, or perhaps because of it – was suddenly crystal clear.

For looking in on Nestor's deadspeak thoughts, he knew what the necromancer had searched for ... and also the mind-warping shock of what he'd discovered. And:

Oh, yes, he sobbed in Nestor's mind. *You are correct. And while you championed him as a boy, later there were times when you wouldn't even accept him. Now you know why I couldn't believe you had forgotten him. For indeed that face I showed you was the face of Nathan Kiklu. A far better man than you, Nestor, for all that he was your twin brother!*

Nestor jerked to his feet, recoiled from the truth of it like a startled deer. He who had been the torturer was now in turn tormented. His Great Enemy was his brother? Not identical, no, but Nathan and Nestor Kiklu? The same flesh? From the same womb? They had been Szgany together: Nestor, Misha, Nathan and Jason. As children, they'd played, laughed and cried together. And indeed in those childhood days Nestor had played at being a vampire Lord. But that was before he became Lord Nestor of the Wamphyri.

And so for the very briefest of moments Nestor was reunited with his past, until his vampire saw the danger in it and worked to erase the error. The metamorphic synapses which had welded in that moment of memory came apart again, and Nestor came apart, too, from what human impulses had started to galvanize him.

His thoughts were deadspeak, and Jason Lidesci had known them. *For a moment I saw you again, Nestor,* he said. *The real you. Ah, but you're Wamphyri now, and the real you no longer exists. Or if it does, then it's only to serve the beast in you.*

Nestor pointed a trembling hand at the corpse, and said to Gorvi: 'Take that away! Do what you will with it! Destroy it!'

'What?' Gorvi was astonished. Silent until now, he'd been patient and seen this pantomime out to its end: Nestor speaking to a corpse, and emptiness for answers. Oh, there'd been an atmosphere of sorts, something in the air, but nothing of any real substance. And now this: the so-called 'necromancer' trembling like a girl, apparently afraid of a dead man. 'But you've learned nothing!'

'I've learned enough!' Nestor turned on him. 'Perhaps too much. Old hatreds are awakened; a mischief I had thought was forgotten returns to plague me; memories come and go, which I am better off without . . . I think.'

'But what of the Szgany Lidesci?' Gorvi was outraged. 'We had a deal!' His face was suddenly twisted with suspicion. 'Or perhaps you've reneged, learned what it suits you to know and keep to yourself, and you're now backing down.'

'Fool!' Nestor spat at him. 'The Szgany Lidesci? Settlement? But when I go raiding on Sunside, it's a *habit* of mine to land on the crags over the foothills and look down on that battered fortress of a town. And when I do I know the place, I remember it, however briefly! But attack it? Attack them, the Szgany Lidesci? No, never! Or at least, not yet. Not until He returns.'

'He?' Gorvi was mystified.

'An old adversary, my Great Enemy. He . . . *stole* something which was mine . . .' Nestor hesitated a moment, frowned, stroked his aching brow, then continued. 'I think . . . I think he stole a *woman* from me, Szgany, a girl of Settlement, and ran away. If she lives there still, with the Lidescis, I'm sure that one day she'll lure him back as the moon lures Canker Canison. But only let her die in some ill-conceived raid, where our losses may be greater than those of the Szgany, and then he'll have no reason to return and I could lose him forever. Aye, and my red revenge gone with him!'

'A woman?' Gorvi was tired of this now. It wasn't going his way at all, and that was too bad. 'Are you letting some Szgany slut eat at you? Is that what this is all about? Some ancient rivalry? But the past is the past, Nestor. We live for today, and for tomorrow, and for as long as we live! The past is dead and gone but the undead go on forever, or as long as blood allows.'

'Enough!' Nestor growled. 'I have a course to run. The dog-Lord has told me that it's a devious thing to read the future, for while events are set, the manner of their occurring is not. Well, I fancy that for me there's a certain danger in reading the past. If I was meant to know it I wouldn't have forgotten it in the first place. When the time is right, then I'll know how it was. This lich — this Jason Lidesci — is a link with things which could change me. And I prefer to remain as I am. For now, at least. So do what you will, but I'm finished here. I'll call my men, Zahar and Grig, who are waiting to go hunting on Sunside.'

'We had a deal!' Gorvi stormed again.

'And now it's broken!' Nestor snarled. 'Challenge me if you will, to a duel on Sunside.'

'Don't tempt me, pup!' Gorvi shrank back, but Nestor read the treachery in his heart. And also his secret mind. The Guile had taken no chances: there were men of his here even now!

They came from behind the glaring hemisphere of the Gate, a pair of bulky, leather-clad lieutenants. Against Gorvi alone, Nestor had a chance. But against the three of them? He glanced towards his flyer, but Gorvi's lads were already putting themselves in the way. They wore gauntlets, and one of them tossed a third gauntlet to his evilly grinning master.

Nestor said, 'So. And this was how it would be. I was to rob this lich of his secrets, so that you could murder

456

me and take them for your own. You were against me from the first.'

Gorvi took a sly, flowing pace forward, and his voice was oily, dangerous as he said: 'What, and did you think they named me the Guile for nothing?'

Before they could close in on him, Nestor turned and ran. But only for a moment. For suddenly there came the dull, heavy throbbing of propulsors as a black-pulsing shadow flowed over the boulder plains. An aerial warrior, one of Nestor's creatures, performed a slow, low circle. While in the sky directly overhead, a pair of flyers formed their wings into air-traps and settled towards a landing. In their saddles, gazing down, Grig and Zahar Lichloathe looked fair set to fight.

Now Nestor turned to face Gorvi, calling out to him in a low voice:

'I know *exactly* why they call you the Guile: because you are sly, devious, and secretive. That's why I, too, came prepared. And do you still want to fight, now that the odds are on my side? Then go right ahead. But think on this: if you lose your life, it won't be the end. For we'll meet again, in Suckscar. And you won't be so secretive then – I guarantee it!'

Gorvi called off his men and waved them back to their flyers where they were hidden away to the rear of the hell-lands Gate. And as he climbed into his own saddle:

'We are no longer friends, Lichloathe,' he called out.

Nestor snorted and answered, 'We never were. What? Should I have you for a friend when many a trustworthy scorpion goes wanting? Back to your dungeons, Gorvi, and scheme some better schemes.' And to his lieutenants:

Stay aloft. We head for Sunside. In the forest just a mile south of Twin Fords there's a Szgany hiding place.

I've sensed it before. Sometimes they use it, others they don't. Well, and if they're in tonight, we'll have them. As for his warrior:

You, creature . . . go home. Back to your pen. On my return, there'll be a tidbit or two.

And as the loathsome construct turned and fired its propulsors for Wrathstack, so the necromancer mounted up and in a little while was airborne with his lieutenants. Then, wheeling their beasts in a star-spattered sky, all three set course for the great pass and the sweet red fruits of Sunside . . .

. . . Except the night was anything but fruitful.

Those vibrations which Nestor had sensed during previous hunting trips turned out to be the lure for an as yet untried Szgany ambush routine, and he and his lieutenants almost became its first victims. Landing at a suitable site in the forest and heading for the source of the vibrations – the fading smell of cooking, the scent of Szgany flesh and blood, the body-heat of humanity, and their dreams, and the night whispers of those who were awake and stood guard – the first Nestor was aware of the trap was when Grig took a bolt in his shoulder too close to his heart, which knocked him off his feet and robbed him of most of his strength, and Zahar yelled a warning that would awaken the entire forest. Following which the Szgany were everywhere.

Obviously this was one Traveller group which had learned from the example of Lardis Lidesci and his people.

Nestor and Zahar were fortunate indeed. Kneblasch-soaked, silver-tipped crossbow bolts came within an inch; a great tree, sawn through at its base and held in place with guy-ropes, came crashing down, its lopped-off branches sharpened to stakes that hammered into the forest loam; nets weighted with silver hissed down out of the treetops, and a fine mist of reeking kneblasch oil fell like a poisonous rain from on high. Then:

An ambusher fired the underbrush! Catching at the greasy shrubbery, flames leapt rapidly from branch to branch. A ring of fire was formed which trapped the three, turned night into day and robbed them of their night-vision advantage.

Dragging Grig behind them, and slicing through a tangle of nets with their gauntlets, Nestor and Zahar fled. And Grig was lucky, too, because another Lord might well have left him to his fate. But Nestor had only the two lieutenants and could scarcely afford to lose one of them. It was as simple as that and nothing of loyalty in it; a vampire, especially a Lord of the Wamphyri, worries about his own life first. Indeed that's *all* he worries about.

All three were scorched, sickened by the kneblasch, humiliated by the outcome: to have been routed by a handful of men! For Nestor it was maddening, infuriating – and worse to come when they got back to their flyers.

Grig's mount was finished. Flopping like a crippled moth on its underbelly, where more than half of its thrusting limbs had been sliced through with machetes, the creature made sounds like a mewling infant. Blinded by burning tar – with its manta wings still smouldering where the same substance had made great black holes in them – it lolled there, cried its bewilderment, nodded its scorched and blackened head.

Nestor's flyer had also suffered; stabbed several times in the neck before it had rolled on its attacker to crush him, it leaked its fluids and was barely airworthy. If he could fly it back to Suckscar in one piece, the beast would heal in time. But it was a big if. Only Zahar's creature was one hundred per cent fit, for it had learned from the trials of the others and had rolled on its two attackers before they could do any real damage. Their crushed bodies were a mess beneath the creature, where gore and guts had erupted from gaping mouths and other orifices.

Less than an hour ago, Nestor and his men had landed on a gently sloping, wooded hillside which would normally make a good, easy launching site. Now, angry, confused and in haste, they made a less-than-graceful exit. Zahar had taken Grig up behind him on his good flyer, while Nestor rode alone on his weakened beast. But their sliding, slithering, bone-jolting launch was much less than satisfactory, and they left a wide swath of flattened bushes in their wake. All of which served to fuel Nestor's fury.

No sooner were they safely aloft than he ordered Zahar home and followed on awhile before landing on a south-facing plateau in the barrier mountains. There he rubbed spittle into his flyer's wounds to hasten the healing, then let the beast rest and settle down while he stood on the rim, gazed down on Sunside, and considered the events of the last few hours. And as his anger cooled he recognized the truth of it: that they had been disastrous events, all of them.

First, the loss of a useful flyer, not easy to replace. Second, his man Grig was badly wounded and wouldn't be good for anything for several sundowns. And third, Gorvi the Guile was now his sworn enemy, and without doubt would try to make trouble for him. (Well, nothing much changed there, at least!) But as for the rest: a great deal lost for no gain whatsoever. Nestor's frustration was vast, and not only as a result of tonight's shambles. For in the back of his mind – but ready to surface at a moment's notice – there was his frustration in respect of . . .

. . . The Lady Wratha!

She was here! She had heard his thoughts! She was smiling at him, in his mind! Her superior mentalism! He had let himself be seen for what he was: a lovesick child! (*The warm, silky feel of her hard nipples and soft breasts, which whenever he thought of her set the palm of his hand tingling just as it had tingled that night on the roof of Wrathspire.*) Except he could see now how easy it would have been for her to put it there, to insert such a vision into his inexperienced mind.

But if she had wanted him to think of her that way —

— Then perhaps she had *wanted* him!

'Inexperienced, aye,' she said, stepping out from behind a teetering boulder. 'That you are. While I have all the experience of a hundred years. So don't feel too badly about it, my handsome Lord Nestor. For I tell you this: if I had tormented the others in the same way, why, they would have fallen into my arms in a day and a night!"

'Why are you here?' He felt stupid and naïve even asking it. She was here to taunt him, of course. Because she knew now that she had him. Or . . . was she here to claim her prize?

'Neither one.' She shook her head. 'The prize is yours, Nestor. To claim at sunup in Wrathspire, when I go to my bed. Or in Suckscar, if that's how you will have it. Nor do I wish to "have" you, but that we shall have each other. Perhaps you would have come to me before, or me to you, except you brought a mistress out of Sunside. And are you satisfied? Has she been enough? Ah, I doubt it! For a little while, maybe, but you are Wamphyri now, Nestor. And yet you are a strange one, too, for there are things in your past which cling even now, and you still remember the true art.'

'The true art?' He even *felt* like a child in front of her.

'Of love. For the Wamphyri feel only lust.'

'Including yourself?'

'You can only have what I have to give.' She moved closer.

And like a fool he stepped back a pace and said, 'But you offered it before, and then refused.'

'Think back,' she said. 'I made no offer. Since when is a kiss a licence to rape? You would have taken me by force, which no man ever did. For all that I wanted you, that was something I couldn't allow.'

He frowned. 'But if you don't know this "true art", as you call it — if you can't experience Szgany love as they know it now, and as I seem to remember it — what difference will our being together make? You have asked: am I, Nestor, satisfied? But I ask: can I be satisfied? Is it any longer possible? For as you've pointed out, I am Wamphyri.'

'Why don't we find out?' And she took another flowing pace towards him. But this time he stood still.

She was clad in leather splashed with blood, but wore no gauntlet. Suddenly he thought again about her being here, and wondered: Is she alone? While out loud, again he asked her:

'Just why did you come here?'

'I am alone, yes,' she answered. 'We had a good raid for once and recruited seven thralls, and as many again will trek for Starside before the sun is risen. But flying back to Wrathspire I saw you here and sensed your thoughts; easy, because I am used to them. And because I felt your pain, anger and frustration, I knew it was time. So I ordered my people on and came to you.

'For while I've waited, I have also watched you, Nestor. In some ways you found the metamorphosis from man to Wamphyri easy, while in others it was difficult. But if you think your trials have been hard,

462

then what of mine? I have known frustration, too, and my manse has suffered as a result. All needs putting to rights, and I must see to it. I have heard the odd whisper circulating about the quality of my water, and other ... *conditions* in my manse, which have caused certain Lords to chuckle behind my back. And I, too, shall whisper and chuckle, when I call for him whose duty it was to see to my siphoneers. And as for those who keep watch over my war-beasts, waxing in their vats ... *they* have waxed enough. Time that they waned a little. Moreover, there have been affairs in Wrathspire which I never sanctioned.

'Oh, a good many of my manse's "affairs" require resolution, but not before my own needs are served. For such as they are, they allow me no peace of mind ...'

Her eyes gazed into his a moment, searchingly, before she repeated: 'My needs, aye. And ... yours?'

He closed with her, reached for her ... and she placed a hand upon his chest, holding him back. But seeing the angry thought which instantly flashed across his mind: 'Ah, no, my handsome young Lord,' she smiled. 'I've learned my lesson and will not torment you again. For the last time cost me too *much* time. But don't be impatient and try to remember: I am the Lady Wratha. This is neither the time nor the place for love ... or for lust.'

'When, then? And where?' His throat was so tight it very nearly choked him, so that his words came out a husky gasp.

'We are neighbours,' she answered, her own voice falling to a whisper, a promise. 'Only climb to Wrathspire in the hour before sunup. Neither man nor creature shall bar the way.'

'I ... want you,' he said, and yet again felt foolish.

'Then come to me,' she told him. And as she walked

away, pausing only once to look back and smile, Nestor found himself trembling like a young boy.

Following which, from time to time until the next sunup, he would tremble a great deal and feel that accustomed tingle in his palm. But he would also know that Wratha had not put it there. She had no need to.

Not any longer . . .

When Canker Canison returned out of Sunside, Nestor went down into Mangemanse to ask him about Wratha. Previously, he'd heard a good many things about her but now wanted it in more detail or from a source which was trustworthy. The dog-Lord told him her story, what he knew of it, but paused before finishing and said:

'Ah! You would go to her! A liaison! I have seen through your inquiry! What, but you are fortunate! You have so much to learn, and Wratha has so very much to teach you. Now tell me: when will you see her?'

'Between you and me?'

'Of course!' the other barked. 'Do you think I'd betray you? I am excited, that's all, and in spirit I'll be with you. Ah, but if only I could be with you in bed! That Wratha . . .'

Nestor rubbed his chin to keep from grinning, for the delight which Canker showed for him was both genuine and infectious. 'In the hour before sunup,' he said. 'Then I climb to Wrathspire.'

Canker's long bottom jaw fell open, and his mood changed in a moment. 'The hour before sunup?'

Nestor nodded. 'Something amiss?'

'No, no . . .' The other shook his head, looked worried, then changed his mind and nodded. 'Yes, yes! Something could be very much amiss. It's all in the nature of Wratha's ascension . . .'

'Well, say on.'

'She murdered Karl the Crag . . .' Again a pause.

'. . . Must I drag it out of you?'

'Now listen to me,' Canker growled low in his throat. 'In Wrathspire at sunup, the sun shines through several windows. Or it would if they weren't kept heavily draped.'

'So?'

'It is the pattern I don't like, for it was the same upon a time in Cragspire in Turgosheim, where Karl the Crag was master. And he would be to this day, if not for Wratha.'

'How did she murder him?' Nestor tried to be patient.

'It's hearsay, of course.'

'Will you tell me, or won't you?' The necromancer's patience was all used up.

'She got him drunk!' Canker barked. 'She exhausted him with her sex, bound him to a bed and opened the curtains! She let the sun shine directly in upon him. She decked the walls with bronze shields burnished to mirror brightness, all concentrating the sunlight on Karl in his stupor, while she stood safe in the shadows. It didn't take too long. Karl fried and his leech deserted him. But in the brilliant light it, too, was finished. And as Karl's parasite blackened and smoked, so Wratha closed the curtains. The leech issued its egg – one last chance for continuity, a final throw at reproduction – and Wratha made it welcome! She had been a vampire thrall, Karl's mistress, and now was Mistress of Cragspire, soon to be Wrathspire. So she ascended . . .'

'A pattern, you said.' Nestor was thoughtful. 'But if she planned any such fate for me, what would she gain from it? That time in Turgosheim it was her ascension. But here she is risen! Also, forewarned is forearmed. She'll not get me drunk so very easily, believe it! And

465

I'll make sure to stay well away from any south-facing windows.'

Canker was astonished. 'Still you'll go? Despite what I've told you?'

Nestor looked at him, looked away, shrugged. And finally: 'I've been Wamphyri for something less than two years now,' he said. 'But before that I was Szgany, and of the Lidesci clan at that. They are a hot-blooded people, as you know, and my parasite has turned up the heat tenfold. Will I go, you ask . . .? Now tell me, my friend, would you?'

Nostrils gaping suspiciously, Canker sniffed the air. His great furry wolf's ears, with their dangling lobes fretted into a sickle-moon sigil, twitched this way and that as if intent on distant sounds or thoughts. Finally he fell to all fours, threw back his head and howled. And his ribbed throat throbbed as its eerie ululations echoed through all of Mangemanse. But as they died away . . .

A trickle of saliva dribbled from the corner of the dog-Lord's panting, soft leathery mouth. And looking up at Nestor, he whined and said, 'Lord Lichloathe, my lad – but how could I possibly resist it?'

VI

Nestor and Wratha: Their Joining

When Nestor got back up into Suckscar, he found Zahar waiting for him with a surprise. Wratha had sent him down a present of three Szgany males from the night's raid. There was a youth, a grown man and a greypate. For all his pride, Nestor was hardly the one to refuse them; not now that the get out of Sunside had grown so small. He did note, however, that they were all males, which Wratha must surely prefer to keep. But on the other hand and in the current circumstances, he could see why she wouldn't want to send him women fresh out of Sunside . . .

As for sending him *any* token of her esteem at all – especially one of precious flesh and blood – that was completely unheard of, and Zahar was at a loss to understand it. 'Is the Lady in your debt, Lord?' he finally found courage to inquire. And indeed, in respect of Wratha's spying on Nestor – her interference with his dreams, and what all – perhaps she could be said to be in his debt at that. Whether or no, he looked Zahar square in the eye and answered:

'She could be, eventually . . .' And on afterthought, 'Let's just say that she and I have business together.' But the truth of it was that he fancied he might end up in *her* debt – if he had gauged the situation correctly. Canker had told him how much she could teach him; again Nestor must put his pride aside and allow himself

467

to be taught; if he could match her even part of the way
... there might yet be revelations on both sides. His
vampire women in Suckscar had already shown him
more than most men learn in a lifetime.

But then of course there was the dog-Lord's warning
too, which, if he was right, might well prove lethally
dangerous. And in that case this 'gift' was simply a
clever garnish hiding the poison on the meat under-
neath. But being offered food and actually eating it are
two different things entirely. Nestor must simply wait
and see how hungry he would get.

And meanwhile:

Using his virulent bite, taking sustenance from his
new thralls and at the same time imparting to them,
Nestor indoctrinated both of the younger men into his
household; they were his now. He sent the youngest to
attend Grig; he was to care for the wounded lieutenant
and, when he was fully recovered, become his appren-
tice. There would be plenty of work for the more mature
man: tunnels to be dug, quarters enlarged and pens to
be cleaned; he would go onto Suckscar's work roster.

As for the greypate: Nestor didn't even give him a
second thought. He was for Suckscar's provisioning.
Meat for the communal dining tables of the common
thralls, and crushed bone for flyer- and warrior-meal,
both were hard to come by and getting harder. Sooner
or later there must be a reckoning, a reassessment.
There had to be easier ways to collect the fruits of
Sunside than by raiding; perhaps he would speak to
Wratha about it ... later. For if she could afford to send
him thralls out of her own get, it must be that she was
doing better than him. So it was possible he'd have
'business' with her after all ...

The administration of Suckscar claimed Nestor's attention well into Starside's long night. Before he knew it there were only a few hours left to sunup. Instructing Zahar to wake him when the peaks of the barrier mountains turned from ash-grey to a leaden glimmer, he went to his bed. But three hours before the dawn, when Zahar was still about his duties, he came awake of his own accord.

For once he had not dreamed, but he had tossed and turned and sweated a cold, vampire sweat. It was his leech; his parasite knew his emotions and sensed the danger in them; it caused him to see all sorts of perils in the course which he'd set for himself. But as the time drew closer Nestor saw only one thing, and he drove all niggling doubts from his mind. For what he had said to Canker was undeniably true: Wratha *was* risen; she occupied the grandest manse in the entire stack; she had little or nothing to gain from seducing him only to murder him. Wherefore it must be that she fancied him. As simple as that. And for his own part, Nestor could scarcely imagine anything more delicious than to go with her to her bed. Whether or not the excitement would last remained to be seen, but as in each and every 'love' affair, the excitement itself was enough for now.

Rising up, he bathed thoroughly and breakfasted. It was hardly the hour for it, but he felt he should fuel himself on a little something at least. Sunside honey, coarse bread, fresh milk from his udderlings (some of which were once women, others which were still shads, but all of them grown huge through various metamorphic processes), and just a morsel of meat, sweet rabbit from Suckscar's farm. He still had no real appreciation of manflesh, except in the liquid which is the life: blood.

Then he threw off his robe and got dressed in his

finest, softest leathers, following which there was little more than an hour left to wait. Prowling his rooms to and fro, he knew what an ardent young lover he must seem to anyone who saw him like this. But no one did see him, except –

– Glina!

She had come up through her spiral staircase and stood in a curtained archway watching him. And Nestor had been so lost in his own thoughts that he had not noticed her. But now:

'Yes, what is it?' And he was surprised to recognize an edge in his voice, as if he were hiding something – as if he, Lord Nestor Lichloathe, should require to hide anything from a common vampire thrall such as Glina!

'I ... I thought I heard you call me,' she answered. And he knew it was a lie.

'You came to spy on me.' His voice was quiet, which signalled danger.

'On you, Nestor?' She'd been familiar with him right from the start; when they were together in his bed, he even demanded it. 'Why would I spy? All there is to know about you, I already know. Except why you went to your bed so early, and why you're up already and dressed. Perhaps you have an appointment?'

'Do you question me?' He frowned. 'Do you dare?' His voice was still low, but harsher now. 'Who have you been speaking to, Zahar?'

'I have not seen Zahar for a day and a half. Is something wrong?' Her voice was full of a genuine concern.

Nestor's frown lifted, but slowly. Finally he sighed and shook his head. 'Nothing is wrong. Go now.'

'You do not ... want me?'

'Not now,' (and probably not ever again; for already she palled, without that he'd even been to Wratha as yet). 'Later, possibly.' (But only possibly.)

She looked a little sad, hung her head, and nodded. 'So be it.' And drawing the curtains behind her, she descended her spiral stairwell. But strangely, Nestor felt a lump enter his throat, causing him to call out: 'How fares the little one?'

The footsteps paused and her answer came back: 'He is as well as can be. Would you see him? Should I bring him to you?'

'Not now,' he said again. 'Perhaps later . . .' But in truth he had no interest in the child and occasionally wondered: *What is this human baby doing in Suckscar anyway?* It were better if he'd taken Canker Canison's advice that time, killed her out of hand and let the dog-Lord breakfast on the infant. Except Glina had had her uses then. And perhaps she would again. She was as good and better in his bed than any of the others, anyway . . .

By the time he had thought these thoughts, she was gone.

But when he went up by a narrow, cobwebbed, disused route into Wrathspire, she was watching him from a shadowy niche. And she knew there was only one place he could be going.

And so Glina continued to know all there was to know about Nestor Lichloathe . . .

Wratha had promised the way would be easy, but Nestor couldn't believe how easy. Neither common thrall, lieutenant nor warrior guarded the route from Suckscar to Wrathspire. From the pens in the rear of Wratha's landing bays, he heard the subdued mewling of flyers; in the level above he was aware of a distant clamour and the frantic clanking of chains, as if some creature knew of an intruder and hurled itself about in a pointless frenzy; in the next level a shadow was glimpsed just the once, which silently, discreetly retreated and vanished.

It was *that* easy.

True, Nestor had kept well away from the main passageways and staircases, so that his route had been circuitous; also a fact that as dawn approached, Wrathspire's vampire inhabitants would be taking to their beds, all except for a skeleton staff and watch. But apart from the aforementioned and entirely acceptable exceptions – the mewling flyers, the distant protests of some fearsome guardian, and the fleeting presence of a very discreet shadow – he'd neither seen nor heard anything to inspire fear or flight.

Then, as he approached the penultimate level, he was met by a beautiful vampire girl who bowed and told him she was Wratha's handmaiden, here to escort him to her mistress. Her dress was thin and deep-cut between her pointed breasts, which showed in all their ripeness when she bowed. She was very shapely: as comely and desirable – perhaps even more desirable – as any of his own women, Nestor thought. And as he followed her, she glanced back at him coyly and said:

'My Lady trusts you met with no obstacle on your way up?'

'None.' He shook his head. 'I came by an indirect route. I am discreet.'

'I know my Lady would appreciate that,' she answered. 'But had you chosen even the most direct route, it would make little or no difference. Wratha makes you welcome here. As for discretion, my Lady gives orders which are obeyed. When she instructs her thralls, "in this or that hour you will all be in your beds ... nothing will stir ... I am not to be disturbed", then the only indiscretion would be to disobey her.'

'I see,' Nestor answered.

He followed her up a narrow staircase, a steeply rising tunnel hewn through solid rock. The light was dim but it made no difference; their vampire eyes saw clear as day. And since she led the way and her dress was short, he saw her nakedness beneath. At the top of the stairs was a landing and a niche, where chains hung empty from the rear wall. Normally a guardian warrior would be stationed here.

They entered a narrow tunnel, and where the way was narrowest she flattened herself to the wall. 'You may pass,' she told him, smiling in her eerie fashion. 'At the end of the passage you'll enter a junction with several tunnels leading off, one of which is marked with my Lady's sigil.'

He made to pass her front-to-front, and her hand at once fell to his member to stroke and clutch it. Fixed there, astonished, he watched as she used her free hand to part her dress so that her breasts lolled free. Then:

'What? And is this your idea of discretion?' he husked, brushing by her at last. 'What would your mistress say to this, I wonder?' But for all that his words were a threat, still he was tempted. His blood was up and his member jumped and jerked in her hand even through his leathers. His eyes were drawn to her breasts, too, which looked delicious, so that it was hard not to reach for them.

But before he could move to do so, the girl released him, laughed and repeated: 'My only indiscretion would have been to disobey her! For if you had come to her with anything less than passion, it would not be enough. Many men would be unmanned by the prospect of entering another's manse, unarmed and entirely vulnerable. After all, the way is dark and dire, and you could have met with monsters! Your ... ardour might have suffered as a result. In which case I would ask you to turn back here and now, go away and wait for a better time. Ah, but it is obvious that the Lord Nestor is no such faintheart! Indeed you are ... what, ready? And so is my Lady Wratha.'

Following which she put her breasts away, turned her back on him and ran back the way they'd come, leaving Nestor to wonder: *What was all of that about? More garnish for the poisoned meat?*

In any case, too late now but to carry on and taste it ...

As Nestor entered Wratha's private chambers, it was at once apparent that these were a Lady's quarters. He *knew* they were, of course, but even if he'd been ignorant of that fact ...

... There were mirrors here, for a start: plates of gold hammered flat and polished to a high sheen, which gave warmth and life to his reflected features even though they were cold and lacked the spark that sets common humanity apart. He would have known from the mirrors alone that this was a Lady's manse, for only an extremely vain Lord would adorn his walls with such as these; and even then, given the greatest possible vanity, it could never compensate for the awareness of lack of soul which was the true message that Wratha's mirrors imparted. No, mirrors were an abomination, which since time immemorial had been used by the Szgany of Sunside to reflect lethal sunlight into the faces of their Starside enemies. But apparently Wratha had risen above such things; she was *pleased* to see herself as she really was ... however she was.

Well, and now Nestor, too, could look upon his own face again, examining it in full for the first time since leaving ... since he became Wamphyri. And what he saw *was* a tall and handsome Lord, albeit a Lord who wondered at his own temerity, that he'd come here of his own free will where wiser men than he might fear to tread.

But as he looked at himself, it seemed he saw something else. And for all that he knew he was host to a vampire leech, still he did not like the corrugations which made his skin reptilian, and the cobra's hood which suddenly shielded his brow and eyes. These things were illusion, he knew, and engendered of his own mind; but still he preferred the looks of the man to that of the thing which governed him.

Turning abruptly from the mirror, he took in at a glance this anteroom which he'd entered through a narrow archway hung with bat-fur drapes. It would appear to be Wratha's dressing-room, where she tended her looks in private. There was a stone washbasin, carved ironwood shelves for powders, perfumes and oils, and several niches cut back into the walls where various garments were kept on bone hangers. The Lady Wratha did not go wanting for clothes.

Her undergarments were of best quality Szgany lace; outer clothing was generally of soft leathers and skins; dresses were bat-fur, or the soft white hide of young albino bears. Wratha's boots were of good shad-leather hand-tooled by Szgany craftsmen; the soles of her slippers were of flexible white cartilage fitted with leather thongs; a number of curved, intricately carved scarps of bone (the shields which she wore upon her brow to disguise the rare but disturbing disorder of the eyes which transformed her whenever she gave sway to ungovernable rages or furious emotions) had been fashioned to be ornamental rather than functional. There were earrings, bangles and anklets, pendants and brooches, mostly in common gold . . .

Nestor saw all of these things and the thought

occurred: *But with so many items here, what can she be wearing now?*

Nothing! came back the answer, and her low, unmistakable laughter tinkling in his mind. *Why don't you come through? Do you find my clothes so fascinating, then? If so, then what of my nakedness?*

Apart from the tunnel or passageway by which he'd entered, there was only one exit. And holding his breath (though why he could never have said, for nothing in the world could make him back off now), Nestor passed through more ropes of bat-fur into Wratha's bedchamber. And there he found her, clad as foretold in nothing – but foam and water!

She was in her bath!

'But as you see, there's plenty of room for two.' Wratha smiled, and Nestor had never seen anything more seductive.

His fate was now entirely in her hands. Right now, without delay, she could call her lieutenants or guardian warriors, and that would be the end of the necromancer Lord Nestor Lichloathe of the Wamphyri. He knew it and she knew it. But they both knew that this was not her purpose and could never be so long as the One Big Question remained unanswered. For there was something else they must know, which knowledge would be carnal: the culmination of that consuming attraction which had been growing between them since the morning Wran the Rage gave Nestor Vasagi's egg and brought him out of Sunside.

He took a pace towards her huge bath – at least six and a half feet square where it had been cut into the floor, and finished at the rim with glazed Szgany tiles – and behind him as he paused, his leather jacket fell to the coarse-woven carpet. Wratha was a mass of milky bubbles; opaque, they hid her loveliness from view.

Another pace, and his shirt was left behind. She lifted up her milk-white arms to him, and Nestor's breathing went hoarse and ragged as the upper halves of her breasts bobbed on the water and dripped foam.

'Can you do this?' she said. Her eyes, scarlet just a moment ago, were dark now and Gypsyish. 'Metamorphism,' she told him. 'It is draining but sometimes worth it; worth it here and now, for I know there's still a lot of Szgany in you. You want innocence, Nestor, and as you will see, Wratha can be innocent if needs be.'

He took a third pace towards her, and now he was as naked as the Lady herself.

'But you don't know that,' she taunted, again reading his mind. 'Perhaps beneath the foam, I'm wearing some gauzy shift.' She laughed again, stared pointedly at his throbbing, jerking manliness, and licked her scarlet lips. And her eyes were full of him.

'Then I'll go through it,' he husked, as if he were driving the words through the crusts of his dry throat.

'You are dry,' she said. 'But see, there's a measure of good Szgany wine here.' Reaching out, she touched a stone jug and golden goblets where they stood on the tiled rim.

He was at the edge and saw a step just under the surface where Wratha's wavelets disturbed the water. Swallowing hard, he answered, 'I know what I want to drink, and from which dark well.'

And now the Lady's voice was as husky and drunk with lust as Nestor's own, as she told him: 'I know your come will be as sweet as your fine firm body. And so we'll drink together.'

As he stepped down into the bath and reached for her, the water and foam swirled round his rubbery knees. But Wratha held back, breathless as she instructed him: 'Bathe me, and I shall bathe you. To touch

477

is allowed, but nothing more for now. We'll make all parts clean as never before, before we dirty them.'

'I want you now.' His voice was a growl.

'Don't spoil it, Nestor.' She shook her head. 'In times to come we'll fuck in this bath a hundred times, I know it. But as for now ... my bed is waiting. What, and would you drink froth and bubbles along with my juices? But when we've bathed you'll be so much harder, and I shall be so much softer ...'

They bathed each other, and Nestor thought it was probably the cleanest he'd ever been. She lingered over him, and he over her, and nothing to interfere with or stay their hands except the soft water and honeyed soap. So that when at last she kissed his swaying, burning tip, but briefly, stood up and wrapped herself in a towel, he knew that she'd been right. His rod had never been so hard, and she had never been so open to any man.

Towelling themselves dry and barely able to keep from continuing their fondling, they moved to her bed. High and wide — built of great heavy slates, with the top layer hollowed in the middle to take a fur-stuffed mattress — it was massive. Wooden steps led up on one side, which Wratha climbed to turn back a soft bearskin blanket. And dropping her towel, she turned and showed herself to him where he followed. After that ...

... It was delirium!

Human beings can never experience the *full*, unfettered violence and animal sex of the Wamphyri and live. But Wratha and Nestor were no longer human. They *were* Wamphyri!

And so for five long hours they did all and more to each other than ever man and woman had done before, except maybe for one other affair long, long ago (and in this very bed at that), or in the depths of drugged and frenzied fever dreams, or the dungeons of torturers. So that at last Nestor was satisfied.

And perhaps surprisingly – to her surprise, at least – so was the Lady Wratha . . .

Later they talked.

'Was I innocent enough for you?' Wratha lay spread-eagled beneath the bearskin blanket, one lovely leg protruding, her jet black hair damp and gleaming, releasing coils of scented vapour from her heat.

'Look at you.' Nestor smiled a wry, drained smile. 'With that wanton sprawl of yours, and those knowing eyes? Even when you made your eyes dark, they were scarcely innocent! Have you ever *been* innocent, Wratha? I know your story; I heard it from the dog-Lord, who is my friend.'

'Well,' she shrugged, 'and Canker's right. No, I've known nothing of innocence, not ever. I would have liked to, but life as a Szgany girl in Turgosheim's Sunside one hundred years ago . . . was not the best environment in which to learn it. We were slaves to the Wamphyri from birth. But at least I kept myself to myself until they took me. Even so, it wasn't so much that I was innocent but clever. And I've stayed clever.'

She propped herself on one elbow. 'Very well, so I was not the sweet and shuddering, untried Gypsy flesh you so admire or lust after. But I tried to be.'

'If I had not known,' he told her truthfully, 'then you would have fooled me. When you tightened on me, you could have been a young girl, certainly. And when you cried out, it was as if you were a virgin. But you exude . . . womanhood! You are hot and exciting. There is no disguising that.'

'So I was not *everything* you wanted?'

'You are the most beautiful creature in Wrathstack,'

he told her. 'If you are not everything I could want, then where can I find it? No, you are everything. You were everything. I won't be able to go to my bed again in Suckscar without wishing I were here with you.' He touched her breasts, and her nipples instantly hardened between his fingers. It wasn't metamorphism, simply her natural reaction to his caress. And when her slender hand fell on him, Nestor too reacted, despite that he'd thought he was drained.

'I'll tell you something,' she said, looking deep into his eyes. 'And this is the whole truth: I never gave myself to any man before. Not even Karl the Crag, who was my "master". Oh, he took me, aye, and believed that I enjoyed it. Indeed, he "knew" that I loved him! But in fact I loathed him. Following which I suffered the sleep, but worse than any gone before. I was buried alive, Nestor, and no one was ever more frightened! I still start awake, cold and clammy in my bed, as if it were the rock tomb in which I became a vampire . . .

'Since when . . . I've had men be sure, but I never gave myself to one. Not as I've given myself to you. Oh, I tried a Lord or two in Turgosheim — the bravest of a sorry bunch — but only to discover that the sap had gone out of them. Maybe they'll get it back one day, but not until they pursue me out of that pesthole gorge and return to the true life. Not until they learn how to live again, and lust, and drown themselves in blood! That's what I wanted and it's why I fled: to return to the old ways and turn this western Sunside into a vast and sprawling charnel-house, and make my men and warriors strong! I would have had it, too, if this gang of grumbling renegades who inhabit my stack hadn't turned on me.'

'You stole their thralls,' Nestor pointed out. 'Even from the first raid on Twin Fords, you were a thief.'

'I took what was rightfully mine!' she cried, drawing back from him a little. 'I was their leader, and a good one. But Wran and Spiro, they are madmen who have no reason and so won't listen to it. As for Gorvi, his instincts are so inbred he cannot think except in ever-tightening spirals: to plot and scheme and work to his own devious designs. Vasagi the Suck, however ugly, was the only clever one among them; I had hoped he would kill Wran, so that I could draw the others back into one body, but it was not to be. Vasagi is no more, and we are still divided. As for Canker Canison, what can I say? His father went baying mad, and it seems to me that the dog-Lord follows a like pattern! That damned bone *thing*, that instrument he plays, whose so-called "music" blares out even here: to lure his silver mistress down from the moon, indeed! *Bah!* It was a mismatched batch I chose to bring with me out of Turgosheim ...'

She paused, and in a moment: 'But there, it seems I've strayed a little from my theme, which was innocence.'

'And was I innocent?' he asked her.

'You want me to say no,' she told him. 'But in fact you were. Not naïve, but innocent, aye. Because you have not had a woman before me. A Szgany girl or girls, maybe, and a handful of vampire thralls, but never a woman. And anyway, there is no other woman like Wratha.'

No, not like you, he kept the thought to himself. *But one I wanted, who was ... what, stolen from me? One day I'll teach her all I've learned, even what I've learned from you. It may kill her – with pleasure, or pain, whatever – but at least I shall know her at last. And she'll know what she's missed, that she could have been my Lady in Suckscar.* And a fleeting picture of a girl, standing in a river's shallows, sun-splashed and dripping water, crossed briefly over his mind. But all hidden from Wratha.

'Are we unique, then?' he asked out loud. 'Vampires, and yet true lovers? Are we forever for each other, or is this a fleeting thing?'

'It will last as long as it lasts,' she answered. 'I ask only one thing.'

'That I'm faithful? But how? I'm Wamphyri!'

'No, not that.' She shook her head. 'But that if we part, or when, then that we go our separate ways with honour. Neither bitterness nor treachery of any sort. When it's done it's done, and that is all.'

'Agreed. And until then?'

'That we're lovers, and allies.'

'We are lovers,' he answered. 'But allies? Against what? To what end?'

'The hunting goes badly.'

'For you, too? And yet you sent me three good ones. Well, two good ones, and a third for my manse's provisioning.'

'It was my token, my promise. I gave to you, so that you would know you could give to me – safely, without fear – and you have. And I appreciate it. I didn't know how much I needed a strong man by my side, and in my bed. But indeed the get out of Sunside grows smaller. If we can work together as lovers, then surely we can work together against the Szgany?'

'I had intended speaking to you on that very theme,' he answered in her conch-like ear, for Wratha had crept back into his arms. 'Something must be done, for the stack suffers. We all suffer alike.'

'But the others are incapable of helping themselves,' she nodded. 'Because they're stupid and selfish, and can't see past their own noses. They're like Szgany fishermen who quarrel over a stretch of river: one man can't handle the nets alone, and so all lose out. But the two of us – working together, as a team – we can grow strong. For there are plenty of fish in Sunside, Nestor. It's just that as individuals we're inefficient. And so I say it again: we can do it together, you and I.'

'The three of us.' Nestor held her closer, let his hand reach down the curve of her back to the valley of her buttocks.

'Three?'

'Canker is strong, and cleverer than you think. Forget his music and his moon madness; that is only one thing, and anyway he's not so mad. I've learned a lot from him.'

'It's true he makes good monsters.' She took his stirring male cluster in the palm of her hand, gently revolving and jiggling his parts. 'Will he be amenable?'

'He loves me like a son,' Nestor answered, lowering his head to draw a stiffened nipple into his mouth. Then, withdrawing, he frowned and said: 'But on the other hand, Gorvi hates me.'

'He hates all of us,' she answered. And sighed. 'Ah, what it is to be young!'

'Eh?'

'Your rod is pulsing again. I can't believe it!'

He chuckled darkly. 'Oh, it's my body, Wratha – but it's my vampire's lust! And the Wamphyri are inexhaustible.'

And reaching down between her coarse dark curls, he found her bud and triggered it. Her leg went over him at once, drawing him closer. But as if to deny her resurgent need, she said, urgently: 'It's important we talk – and now. There'll be time enough to satisfy our other needs later.' And in a voice on the edge of trembling: 'As if we hadn't already done so!'

'One mouth says one thing,' Nestor husked, 'and the

other denies it. The mouth in your face is wise and speaks prudently, but the one between your thighs is greedy and mindless of all but pleasure. When they speak together, as now, all is confusion.'

'A Szgany saying?'

'Probably.'

'Then here's another: a stiff prick has no conscience.'

'And a soft wet cunt is deep as a swamp, and just as hard to escape from.'

Another moment and he would be in her again; she pulled apart from him and shook her head: 'We must talk!'

He sighed and rolled over onto his back. 'Very well, say on. But work my meat a moment. The throbbing is delicious.'

'You are insatiable!' she laughed, grasping him.

'Not me – my vampire!' was his excuse.

'Now listen,' she said. 'If we three work together, then Wran, Spiro and Gorvi will doubtless join forces too. And that is all to the good.'

'How so?'

'Because they will then put aside their differences and ready themselves for what they'll see as inevitable battle. I *want* them to be prepared, for I have seen what they have not: that eventually Vormulac and the others will come bursting out of Turgosheim to wage war ... against me, Wrathstack, the last aerie! For in Turgosheim's Sunside the blood grows thin, while here it's still hot and red. Vormulac knows that's why I came here in the first place: to better myself, to grow strong. He doesn't know if I'm successful, but he daren't take the chance that I'm not. And so he must come, eventually, unless he's even weaker than my estimate! He *must*, for he'll fear that I'm building an army to return and attack him! And so when war comes it won't be between us renegades but two great armies: Vormulac's and Wratha's. Oh, Gorvi, Wran and Spiro will know which side to take! For they'd get short shrift from the invaders.'

Nestor was thoughtful. 'Canker has been a mine of information. He's told me a lot about Turgosheim. There are so many Lords . . . and what if they all come together?'

'I'm sure they will.'

'Then how can we win?'

'Because this is home territory. And by then we'll be an army in our own right. Far easier to defend than attack, Nestor. And remember: they'll be exhausted from their long flight. But we'll be fresh. And our familiar bats will bring us warning well in advance. Indeed, even now and ever since I first settled here, I have had my creatures stationed in the eastern ranges of the barrier mountains, watching and waiting.'

'But if we in Wrathstack are positively divided, so that we can't even work together in peace, how will we make out in war?'

Wratha shrugged. 'We're not so divided. We three – you, me and Canker – have the top levels of the stack, while Gorvi and the brothers Killglance have the bottom. If Wran denies me gas from his beasts, I deny him water from my siphoneers. Insofar as the proper maintenance of the stack is concerned, that's how it works; we need each other this much at least.'

'Have you talked to the others about this invasion you're sure will come?'

'In the early days, often. And they listened to me, then. Since when they've grown lax. We all have, for various reasons. There were easy pickings at first, until this Lardis found his feet and the other tribes started to follow suit. Aye, the living was easy, and we lost something of our impetus.'

'Then how will you get it back?'

'Oh, I know the way. When you, me and the dog-Lord start working together, and when the others see our get, then they'll unite as stated. And when they see our new monsters? Our aerial warriors and fighting creatures? And when we make gas chambers and fashion our own beasts? And when we double and redouble the numbers of our lieutenants? *Hah!* They'll do the same. We shall *cause* them to gear themselves for war. We shall be their inspiration!'

Nestor nodded. 'The entire stack will benefit and be that much stronger.'

'Exactly! Even as you are strong.' She got down in the bed and trapped him between her breasts, gentling his bruised, jerking shaft, then took him in her mouth and entered his tip with the sharp points of her split tongue.

'Wait!' Nestor groaned, inverting himself and burying his face in her core. And:

Together? she whispered in his mind, feeling his imminent explosion – and her own – as she drew him into her throat.

Together, he answered, sucking on her elongated clitoris like a calf on an udder. So that in a very little while they both drew milk.

And revelling in each other's juices, the thought occurred to both of them together: that if the blood was the life, then surely the milk was its spice . . .

They slept long and long, but Wratha was first to come awake. Then, stroking him where he lay on his back, listening to his heartbeat, his breathing, and feeling the slow rise and fall of his massive chest, she wondered again: love?

Was it possible, between vampires? Between members of the Wamphyri? She knew it *had* happened to others, yes, but to Wratha? What if the feelings she felt now deep inside were merely fleeting, insubstantial things? Well, so be it. Ah, but what if Nestor's feelings were the same? One thing for the Lady Wratha to reject a lover, but to *be* rejected?

He was moaning in his sleep, tossing and turning a little, perhaps beginning to come awake. She had never stayed with him before, in his mind, to the point of waking. Previously, she'd entered and inserted her erotic pictures – dreams of herself, the two of them together, as now they had been together – and departed. Or on occasion she'd spied on his own lustful dreaming to discover his preferences. But now . . .

. . . What was it that disturbed him?

She glanced into his mind – but too late! He was coming awake, right now.

And all she got was a single word, a name, but a name that glowed in his mind like an iron in a fire: Misha.

A girl's name . . .

And Wratha wondered: *Is this the unknown Other? Nestor's unrequited love out of Sunside?* But no need to wonder, for she knew it was.

He yawned and sat up. 'Wratha?' He looked at her, reached for her – but she was up and out of bed, slipping into a robe. 'Wratha? Is something wrong?'

He was sleepy, but perhaps he'd glimpsed her eyes.

'Wrong?' she almost ran into her dressing-room. 'Why, no. What could be wrong?' But in her mirrors the Lady saw what was wrong. And fitting a curved bone scarp to her brow, turquoise earrings in the lobes of her conch ears, and sapphire discs to her cheeks, she sought to disguise the evidence of her wrath: the way her eyes bulged, and their crimson, hell-fire glare!

Misha!

It took all of five minutes to lock the name out of her head. And another five to cool the incredible fires racing in her vampire blood. And: *Love?* she wondered again, but kept the thought to herself. *Or should it be hate?* Or was the dividing line between the two too narrow?

But she knew the name of that dividing line well enough.

It was jealousy!

VII

Wratha's New Raiders

That the dog-Lord Canker Canison was crazy in his fashion, and deranged as any feral creature who falls under the influence of the full and hurtling moon, was not to be denied; but as Nestor had pointed out to his vampire lover in her bed, at other times and in other ways Canker was sane as could be and might even be considered wise. As now, for instance.

For when it came to a choice of allies, the Lord of Mangemanse had neither time nor kind words for Wran and Spiro Killglance, his closest neighbours, and he was equally disdainful of Gorvi the Guile down in the aerie's shadowy sump. But sane or crazy, the overriding factor in his decision was this: that the necromancer Lord Nestor Lichloathe had seen fit to join up with Wratha in her scheming, and if it was good enough for him it was good enough for Canker. Such was the dog-Lord's affection for his young friend, let Nestor merely suggest something ... it was done.

At a meeting in Wrathspire, the three devised a strategy: tactics of a sort against the Szgany. And in the next sundown, taking their warriors, lieutenants, and even aspirant lieutenants with them, they put it into practice and went raiding en masse on Sunside.

And it was a raid to remember!

Wratha had no knowledge of warfare, and neither Canker nor Nestor was any better equipped. And so their plan was simple: one party to flush the Szgany out; one to form a gantlet like a net, wide at the entrance and narrowing to a tight neck; and a third lying in ambush, to block any escape and turn the prey back into the killing zone.

How it worked:

The three and their forces crossed the barrier mountains just an hour after the true sundown. Their crossing point lay midway between the hell-lands Gate on Starside and Settlement on Sunside, which is to say some forty miles west of the Starside mouth of the Great Pass. Then, while Canker and his pack landed, rested up and waited in the higher Sunside foothills, Nestor, Wratha and theirs split into two groups and headed out across the Sunside forest belt. Wratha angled west while Nestor skewed east, so that when they straightened out to fly parallel they were perhaps two miles apart. And staying well below the clouds, they knew they would be amply visible, and the rumble and sputter of their warriors plainly audible to Szgany on the ground.

Any Traveller groups directly beneath the two aerial parties would go to earth, freeze, suffer the gut-wrenching stench of warrior exhaust gasses settling from the night sky, and wait for the terror on high to pass. But as soon as they thought it was safe to move, then they'd break cover, split up, seek safer hiding places. Some would be lucky and relocate themselves outside the entrapment zone, but others less fortunate would run inwards and right into it . . .

Along the route south – as the twin clouds of ill-omen which were Wratha, Nestor and their parties pulsed like a two-pronged pestilence in the sky – they ordered down warriors or the occasional flyer and rider, to occupy vantage points in the forest and find

490

themselves good relaunching sites, thus forming a gantlet. And so the net extended itself south.

Four or five miles out over the forest, the two parties performed an aerial pincer movement and joined up in one body. Then, except for Nestor and Wratha themselves, and their first lieutenants, the remaining flyers landed their riders without touching down, and lifted off with empty saddles. And while on high the Lord and Lady turned their mounts about-face and flew north down the centre of the gantlet, so their thralls on the ground began forging through the woods for the barrier mountains, ensuring that they made as much noise as possible along the way.

Within the gantlet, panicking Szgany groups were driven in the same direction, by the bellowing of vampire thralls to the rear and the hissing of monsters on the flanks. The night seemed filled with menace: nodding flyers and belching, amorphous, armour-plated warriors were everywhere, and strutting lieutenants were wont to loom large out of the darkness.

Meanwhile –

– Canker and his pack had come down from the foothills to set up their ambush in the bottleneck, among boulders and rocky outcrops where some ancient upheaval had shattered the forest's floor. And while he waited, so the dog-Lord conjured a thin vampire mist from his own body, and called up a ground mist out of the earth to swirl all about and give his forces cover . . .

While returning out of the south:

Wratha and Nestor, performing low, lazy, north-drifting circles overhead, used their mentalism to order men and monsters in from the flanks, tightening the net. The trapped Szgany parties fled north, began to meet up with each other and shoal like panicked fish. Colliding, they milled left and right, met up with nightmares in both directions, and so continued to run ragged and panting along the one safe-seeming route. But after four and a half miles of forest they were on their last legs.

They saw flyers descending out of the night sky and were terrified; the flyers had no riders, but the trapped Travellers couldn't know that. Warriors trampled, hissed and roared in the undergrowth; the black shadows of manta shapes flowed silently over starlit glades; vampire voices shouted orders.

While from on high, Wratha sent to Canker: *Now!*

And Nestor, to the small encircling force of thralls and lieutenants on the ground: *Now!*

Then, as the carnage commenced, so he and Wratha descended, landed their beasts, and joined in the free-for-all. But it was a short-lived affair. Something less than forty Travellers – men, women, and children – had been caught in the vampire net; seeing there was no way out, a handful of them tried to fight back.

The men had crossbows. Silver-tipped, kneblasch-soaked bolts zipped in the dark, most of them uselessly; razor-honed machetes flashed in starlight, but the arms which wielded them contained neither strength nor hope; ironwood stakes sharpened to needle points were grasped in slippery, trembling fists. Against powerful vampire thralls, leather-clad lieutenants, the Wamphyri themselves – against gauntlets, night-seeing eyes and metamorphic flesh – they were as nothing. The Szgany were utterly exhausted; the lingering stench of warriors sickened them; their aim was off.

Canker's thralls – his 'hounds' – rounded them up. Loping among them like one of their own wolves, they scarcely saw the dog-Lord himself until they felt his bite in arm or thigh, or he reared up to snarl and spray saliva, and smash his fist stunningly into the side of a victim's head. Anyone seen to be carrying a crossbow

... was a dead man. Canker's, Nestor's and Wratha's gauntlets seemed painted scarlet. Women and children were herded to one side, but men were knocked down and vampirized at once.

Two minutes, three, and it was all over.

Eight men, one woman and two thralls had died in the fray, both of the latter with bolts dead centre in their hearts. One of Wratha's senior lieutenants had suffered machete slashes to his chest and shoulder; his leathers had protected him; he was on his feet and would survive. Two of the dog-Lord's 'hounds' had been stabbed with ironwood stakes, but not deeply.

Of the twenty-seven Szgany survivors, thirteen were men or boys, and three of these were greypates. Since the old men had little or no value except as meat, Wratha ordered their immediate execution. Their bodies, along with the other dead, went to fuel the warriors. The rest of the males, those who had not yet been recruited in the accustomed fashion, were now bled. Wratha and the Lords claimed the first of these bloody fruits, naturally, followed by their lieutenants and thralls.

Most of the men thus infected fell at once into their vampire sleep; those who did not were ordered into the mountains, to cross into Starside before sunup. Then it was the turn of the fourteen women and girls.

These had been split into three fairly balanced groups, two fives and a four. The Lady Wratha took the smallest share of the get in females and turned her senior and junior lieutenants loose on the shivering, ragged quartet. There's more than one way to vampirize a woman, and her men had done exceedingly well this night. It was Wratha's idea of a small reward.

Watching the mass rape — the swift and merciless shredding of garments, the naked, cringing girl-flesh, the twining, spastically jerking limbs and thrusting of tightly knotted buttocks, and all the mauling, gasping and sobbing – Nestor had to admire Wratha's style; her men would remember and be grateful. Learning from it, he set his own lads loose on his get of five, and stood close to Wratha where each of them recognized the other's excitement. And looking forward to their time together, they knew how good it was going to be in Wratha's bed at sunup.

As for Canker: where women were concerned, no mere thrall came before him! He took each of his five in turn, and rapidly, but saved himself for the last one, a girl of no more than fifteen years, who he took from the rear like the dog he was. And finishing with each he tossed them to his men, howling: 'Don't let them go wanting, lads! Let them know what is their lot, in Mangemanse!'

In a little while it was over. The worst of the raping at least . . .

Then Canker's lieutenants built a fire and the two sweetest, youngest children were butchered for roasting. It was by way of a celebration. Shortly, the vampire thralls sat around in red-flickering light and ate smoking flesh, while those of them who still had the urge and the wherewithal dragged half-stunned women away into the bushes to shag them.

Then to the final count, when it was calculated that the total remaining get was twenty-two, five of which were already en route across the mountains for Starside and the last aerie. Most of the females would go on the backs of flyers, and the rest would follow on foot. All of them should make it. Wratha would claim eight all told, and seven each to Nestor and Canker. It had been an excellent raid, and as yet only seven or eight hours into sundown.

'What now?' Nestor asked Wratha where she sat by the fire, her scarlet eyes made golden by its glow.

'Now?' She looked up at him and her gaze might almost be vacant. But then in a moment the glow beneath her scarp blazed up brighter, and her voice more animated as she answered: 'Now we unload this lot in our manses . . . and then we come back for more!'

'What, tonight?'

'Why not? We've been asleep for far too long, all of us. And if my plan to galvanize the stack is to work, then we need to show Gorvi, Wran and Spiro that we mean business. Can't you just see their eyes popping when they see this lot? They'll be over here as quick as it takes to tell, trying their damnedest to catch up with us. And I want them to! If I can't make them work with me, then let them think they're working against me, just as long as it's to the same end. For you'd better believe me, Nestor, time is running out. I feel it in the wind out of the east: Turgosheim is stirring and it won't be long now.'

'In which case,' he took her hand and helped her up, 'if we've armies to make, then we'd best be at it.'

They broke camp, mounted up, and launched into the night. And sated for the moment they headed for Starside and the last aerie . . .

Four hours later they struck again, this time five miles east of the Great Pass and on the edge of the forest belt. And this time, too, a different tactic. Leaving Nestor in the foothills, Canker and Wratha used their parties to form an arc two miles across and cutting a mile deep into the forest. Dropping down from their flyers but leaving them airborne along with the warriors, they then tightened the arc in the direction of Nestor. The warriors flew to and fro over the catchment area, filling it with their gasses and destroying the will of any Travellers caught in the trap.

And it worked. Driven north as the vampire net closed, the Szgany fled straight into the arms of Nestor and his party. The catch was smaller than before but still considerable: six males, four women, and five children. Two elders crippled with rheumatism were killed out of hand and divided between the warriors; the four youngest were put to death and taken for meat; the remaining get was split three ways to be flown back to the last aerie. And at that Wratha called it a night.

Back in Wrathspire, they met to talk and count coup. And Canker was jubilant:

'Ten! I can't believe it! In my vats, I've a warrior waxing which I intended to terminate for lack of stuff, but now I can bring him along. There are fresh women for my pups, several of whom have gone without. I was even thinning down my manse's workforce, in order to satisfy the requirements of the kitchens and the provisioning. But now my rosters are filled again, and even muscle to spare. What a night!'

'We've done well,' Wratha nodded. She had changed into lounging clothes: a thin sheath that fitted her gorgeous body like a glove, slippers, a jewelled scarp upon her brow. Every inch a beautiful 'girl', it was hard to believe that she had survived a hundred years and more. The blood is the life . . .

They were in Wrathspire's great hall, gathered round a blazing fire and sipping wine. It should have been a celebration, but Nestor was frowning. He had something on his mind, which caused him to display his irritation and frustration.

'Out with it,' Wratha said after a while, and he looked up in something of surprise.

'Is it that obvious?'

'Your dissatisfaction?' Canker barked. 'Aye, it is.'

'Then I'll explain,' Nestor nodded. And to Wratha: 'You see, Lady, you are not the only one who can think and plot for the future; I also have a mind. Very well, so tonight we were successful – to an extent. We've replenished our manses, with blood and meat and good strong working muscle, no doubt about that. But an aerie needs more than that. Canker has explained to me that in Turgosheim the Wamphyri were excessive in their requirements, depleting their Sunside prey to the point of decimation. Why, you almost committed the ultimate folly: to wipe out the Szgany, whose blood was your source of life. That was the main reason why you fled here in the first place: to find the makings for expansion, which were lacking in Turgosheim.'

'All true,' Wratha agreed.

'And yet now, here in the west, we pursue the same course as before!'

Canker snorted. '*Hah!* But impossible to deplete this Sunside to that extent! There are thousands of them out there!'

'Not impossible.' Nestor shook a finger at him. 'And anyway, that's not the point.'

'Then what is the point?' Wratha was genuinely curious, for it was quite obvious that this was not just Nestor being argumentative in the manner of the Wamphyri.

He leaned back in his chair, away from the fire, and said: 'Now tell me: how many of our western Szgany tribes are supplicant? Oh, in Turgosheim's Sunside, all of them, I know. But how many here?'

'One,' Canker answered it for him. 'They are two hundred and eighty strong and live in a town fifteen miles east of the Great Pass, between the foothills and the forest. They work in metals and are good at making and mending gauntlets. But they are few in number, as stated, and so we take only their goods, not their lives. Their fathers and grandfathers were supplicant in the old times, before we came here, and it appears the weakness was bred into them. They supply us with honey, grain, nuts and fruits, beasts and preserved meat, wine and materials for our clothes, and metal tools for our thralls.'

'Exactly,' said Nestor. 'One small township, and we Lords and Lady take a regular tithe of them and divide it five ways: between Guilesump, Madmanse, Mangemanse, Suckscar and Wrathspire. Except I don't know if you've noticed, but each time we collect, the takings are that much smaller! Honey grows scarce and the granaries are close to empty; our flyers go hungry. So tonight we fed our warriors ... ah, yes! But when was the *last* time they had it red? To simply exist is not enough.'

Wratha said nothing. She was beginning to see his point.

He looked at her again. 'Now, Wratha: you've said we must build an army. Good! I agree. But of what? Why, we barely have the means to satisfy our individual needs as they are, without that we feed entire armies! What we need are more supplicant Szgany tribes. If *all* of Sunside were in our grasp, to use as we desire, then we would be unconquerable! As for Vormulac and the rest of your "friends" in the east: let 'em come!'

She stood up, put her hands behind her back, walked this way and that before the fire. 'You are right. And we could do it, too — bring all of the Szgany tribes to heel, as in Turgosheim — but for one thing.'

'Oh?'

'Lardis Lidesci!' The name fell from her lips like acid.

'I know what you mean,' said Nestor. 'And did you

know, *I* was a Lidesci, upon a time – not related by blood, no, but of that tribe? And I dwelled in Settlement.'

'Huh!' She snarled. 'Settlement! And how may we quell the Szgany – herd them, pen them, put them to work, *milk* them! – when this Lardis sets such an example? He's clever as a fox; he controls superior killing weapons; and his territory – yes, *his* territory, damn his rancid Gypsy heart! – is one enormous trap ... *for the Wamphyri!* Indeed, the only difference between him and us is this: we must fly out from Starside into Sunside to kill, while he stays home and does it! Kills *us*, or would if he got the chance! And certainly he has killed our lieutenants, warriors, flyers and what all. Moreover, the rest of the Szgany are following suit. Lardis has given them heart; he shows them the way; why, it's even dangerous to go anywhere *near* him!' Too furious to go on, she fell silent.

Canker scratched his long bottom jaw and said: 'Then all seems simple to me ... well, the solution, if not the means of execution. We have to raid on Settlement, find this man and do away with him. We have to crush his people, their will, and of all the Szgany bring *them* to heel first. Following which, any other resistance will soon collapse.'

'Agreed,' said Wratha. 'But how?'

'Wait!' Nestor got to his feet, and faced her across the hearth. 'Are you now considering a raid on Settlement, the Lidescis?' He had to turn her from it. If Misha was there, among the Szgany Lidesci, then he must wait until his olden enemy – his Great Enemy, his brother – returned to claim her. But these were thoughts which he guarded closely and kept to himself.

'I've *always* considered it,' Wratha answered, her girlish face twisting into something else entirely. 'And

I've tried it, with disastrous results! Now I want revenge, for all they have destroyed which was mine, and for all of my frustration!'

'And you'll have it,' he said, 'but not now. Shortly, but not now.'

'When, then?'

'When we're strong enough. When we're so strong that all the traps and lures, shotguns and giant crossbows, silver and kneblasch and everything else they can throw at us just won't be enough! That's when.' *And when Nathan returns, to be with the one he stole from me.*

Canker's turn to be curious. 'Shotguns?'

Nestor blinked, frowned, shook his head and closed his eyes for a moment. 'A ... a memory, I think, from my past, my time among them. Shotguns, aye. Their weapons which fire pellets of silver. Weapons out of ... another world? But I ... I can't remember more than that. Let it be.' His furrowed forehead cleared.

Wratha waited until she was sure he was himself again, then asked: 'And how do you suggest we go about making more supplicant tribes? These people were settled when first we came here, town dwellers in the main. But now they're Travellers as in the old days. Or, like this Lardis Lidesci and his lot, they inhabit crumbling old towns by day, and sneak into their hidy-holes at night.'

Nestor nodded. 'This is how I see it,' he said. 'We send our metal-working friends as messengers out into the woods and along the old Szgany trails, to carry our promise abroad: good will and long life to any Szgany tribe or group who will work for us on Sunside. They will be required to pay us a tithe in all of their good things, in return for which we'll spare them, even as we spare the metal-workers. In their new security, they can

500

then settle down again in permanent camps and towns. They shall hunt, gather, farm for us, as in Turgosheim. Except we shall stick to our promise and not take flesh and blood. But any who don't see fit to work for us –' he shrugged, '– they are fair game.'

'Fine,' Canker growled. 'And just suppose we do manage to set up a system of tithe-paying Szgany camps. How do we protect them from Wran and the others?'

'They'll set up their own,' Nestor answered. 'If they hit our supplicants, we hit theirs. It's as simple as that. As for following Lardis's example: he is in the west while our metal-workers dwell in the east. It seems unlikely that the methods of the Lidescis have spread so far abroad.'

'It might work at that,' Wratha mused. 'And in any case, anything is better than inactivity. Very well, we'll try it. The night is still young. What say we attend to our new recruits, get a little rest, then fly out to see our supplicant gantlet-makers and give them our instructions?'

Canker didn't seem too happy with this arrangement, but: 'Very well,' he growled. 'But will it take all of us? I've not yet had the chance to properly ... explore the night's get. My new females interest me. I have my needs, as well you know.'

'We're all in the same position,' Nestor told him. 'All of our new people require proper indoctrination. And you ... how much time do you need for the rutting anyway?'

Canker grinned. And: 'Damn you, Nestor!' he said, but without malice. 'You read me as well as you read one of your dead people!'

'We're in this together,' Wratha said, 'and so we must see it through together. Six hours before dawn we set out, just we three and a couple of lads apiece, and a warrior each to act as guard dogs.'

As they prepared to go their separate ways, Canker said: 'I can't wait to see Wran's face when he hears of our success this night!'

And Wratha told him, 'He has already heard it.' She smiled a wicked smile, then tilted her chin and looked demure. 'Surely you know I have spies in all the manses . . ; well, no longer in Suckscar and Mangemanse, not now that we're colleagues. But in Guilesump and Madmanse, certainly. I instructed certain persons in my employ to watch our movements very closely, and to report them to their supposed masters. Spies are not only useful for picking up information, but also for spreading it abroad. Wran and Spiro know what we've done tonight, aye, and so does Gorvi the Guile. And it's my guess they're together even now, making plans of their own to bring them up to par. Except we have the lead, and so they must work hard at it.'

Canker and Nestor grinned and made for an exit, and Wratha called after them, 'Until later.' But in Nestor's mind: *not too much later. See to your new thralls and return. I'll have a hot bath waiting, and something even hotter!*

She knew it was a promise he couldn't resist . . .

For the next four months all went as planned, or as nearly as possible. Supplicant camps proved hard to get started, and at first were made up of very small Szgany groups. But once they were established and uneasy contact with the vampire Lords and Lady had been made – when the first tithes were taken, and no blood spilled – the idea caught on. For the Szgany east of the pass were tired of running. They knew that the cowardly metal-working Wamphyri supplicants lived comparatively easy lives (at least that they were safe and settled, not wandering in the wilderness or starving in foothill caverns), and like them they were now prepared to pay for protection – so long as the tithe was of goods, not flesh and blood. It was hardly a satisfactory existence, but at least it was bearable and a life of sorts. It had to be better than living in constant fear of vampire raids, of being eaten or enslaved and dragged into Sunside as meat on the hoof.

Gorvi and the Killglance brothers had been quick to take up the challenge. That was how they saw Wratha's new alliance with Nestor and Canker: as a challenge, of course. Despite that the Lady claimed her group's activities were purely defensive – which well they might be, for the possibility of an invasion out of Turgosheim was by no means negligible – still this full-speed build-up of muscle was very worrying to them. What if no outside threat materialized? How then would Wratha and her allies use their warriors and men at arms? To annex the rest of the stack? Possibly.

But while Gorvi, Wran and Spiro joined forces, they drew the line at setting up tithe-camps of their own. It was easier and faster to concentrate their existing forces in mass attacks on Sunside, as Wratha had done at first, to fill their manses with lieutenants, thralls, warriors and flyers, and generally bring themselves to battle-worthiness. And because the Lady's forces were for the moment superior, the ulterior triad must grit its teeth and hold off from raiding on her new supplicant camps. But the toll they took on the rest of the Travellers, especially in the regions west of the pass, was massive.

And so the last aerie was filled with life of sorts, and Wratha was satisfied – to a point. But there remained several thorns in her side, which she could neither salve nor remove. The sharpest of these was Nestor

Lichloathe's refusal to raid on Settlement. Wratha had guessed the reason (that Misha, his unrequited love, was there, which he would not jeopardize), but without knowing Nestor's real motive: that he was waiting for his Great Enemy to return out of far places to claim her in his own right. Then he would make his move, and claim *both* of them . . .

When they were not raiding, collecting tithe, seeing to the administration of their manses, Nestor and Wratha spent most of their time together. It was a mutual fascination, and one that waxed rather than waned. When she was on her own, Wratha found herself thinking of Nestor – always. Since he was now accessible, she'd mainly given up her mental invasions of his privacy, but she could never give up her consuming preoccupation with the *thought* of him: his beautiful young body, his sexual energy, and his determination – which rivalled her own – to be a leader among men, even among the Wamphyri. That might become a problem one day, for there can only be one leader of leaders. But that day was still a long way off. A joint bone-throne, maybe?

In which case, obviously Wratha's love-thralls would have to go. Except . . . they already had! Where Wrathspire was concerned they were less than drones now. Why, she hadn't taken a man – any kind of man – since that first time with Nestor! She'd not needed to, for she was satisfied in that respect as never before. And of course, he would have to give up his vampire women. But there again, it appeared he'd already chosen that course for himself. He no longer so much as looked at his female thralls; even his old flame out of Sunside, Glina, with her supposed 'innocent' sex, had been unable to tempt him. On those few occasions when

Wratha had spied on him out of habit, she had seen that he now kept to himself, except for herself.

So, she no longer had any rivals here in the last aerie. But in Sunside . . .?

Towards the end of that same four-month period of great activity and productivity, one sunup in the twilight hours before night:

Nestor and Wratha had taken a meal together in the Lady's apartments. They'd shared common but satisfying fare: suckling pig roasted on a spit over glowing ironwood embers, and sliced Sunside fruits in aromatic Szgany brandy; all washed down with a peppery wine. Then they'd made love and slept wrapped in each other's arms awhile, and had woken up to find themselves making love again! Afterwards, Wratha had made a last attempt to bring Nestor round to her way of thinking and convince him that they and Canker should now launch a massive joint attack on Settlement — ostensibly to bring down Lardis Lidesci. Being Nestor, of course he'd once again refused to be swayed.

Now, while she felt frustrated within herself, paradoxically the Lady felt nothing of anger towards Nestor. How could she *possibly* be angry with him, her lover, the young and handsome Lord Nestor Lichloathe of Suckscar? So that she issued a wry, silent snort and wondered:

Ah, but then again, how can a Lady of the Wamphyri possibly feel so . . . so what? So soft? So hurt? So much like some common Szgany slut on Sunside? So . . . jealous? But jealous of what? An unknown girl out of his past, even out of his mind? Some figment of his impaired memory? Why, for all I know this Misha is a hag — or dead even — or someone Nestor would find unworthy now that he is Wamphyri!

But for all her attempts to apply cold logic to her confused emotions, still the Lady paced the floor of her bedroom, to and fro while her lover lay sleeping in her great bed. And glancing sideways at him from time to time, she considered her options; or rather her . . . her what? Her plight? That she was in love with him?

Was it love, she wondered yet again, for maybe the hundredth time? Certainly something was wrong with her. It wasn't simply that he was always on her mind. No, for more than just a thought, Nestor was in her eyes, her nostrils, her ears and mouth; and Wratha knew that she could *never* have enough of him in her body!

When they were apart:

She could *taste* him on the sensitive buds of her forked tongue. She could *smell* him – the pungent odour of his body, sweat, parts – like the scent of some weird Sunside orchid. She could *feel* him driving into her core, and see his face above her face: how his mouth fell open and his eyes closed, the perspiration forming on his brow in the instant that he fired his juices into her. And she could feel the hot splash of those juices, too, laving her insides: the way his sperm lived in her, tens of thousands of mindless minuscule lives . . . until her parasite leech released its own juices, like an acid to burn these tiny intruders.

Of course, that last didn't have to be. She could will it otherwise if she so desired. She could still her leech and let Nestor's seed live, and bring forth a child. But for what? She required no bloodsons, to grow up into men who would covet her manse and position. And yet . . . it would be an experience, to produce a child out of Nestor's seed and her egg – her *human* egg, of course . . .

Hah! But wasn't that just the trouble? Thinking of

Nestor, she even *thought* like a woman ... like the common Szgany women of Sunside ...

... Like this Misha?

And had she wanted his children, too?

That last thought increased Wratha's frustration four-fold and even made her feel angry towards him! She whirled towards her great raised bed ... and saw that he was stirring. She had thought he was asleep, but what if he'd been merely drowsing? Had he been listening in on her thoughts? Was he even now?

She shielded them at once! Her pride ... Nestor must never know how deeply he ... the strength of ... he must *never* know! For such knowledge would make him strong and Wratha weak.

He groaned and raised himself up a little on one elbow, and she forced a smile and said, 'Oh? Awake at last, are you? And nothing stirring? Well, that makes a change! If I didn't know you were Wamphyri, I might suppose you were merely human after all! But see, I've brought a little wine.'

She poured smoky Szgany wine from a jug into a goblet and took it to him. And at the top of the wooden steps she kneeled beside him where he lay naked and spreadeagled.

As he took the goblet and slaked his thirst, she tilted her head on one side, smiled again (but softly this time, and almost as naturally as the girl she pretended to be) and said: 'Look at you, Nestor, all sated and sprawled there defenceless as a child. Why, I could have poisoned that wine with grains of silver! While you were sleeping, I could have anointed you with oil of kneblasch, or plunged a silver dagger into your heart. Even now I could call one of my guardian creatures to slurp your soft flesh. Is it that you've no fear, or simply that you love and trust me?'

'It could be all three of those things,' he answered with a grin, 'or none of them. But mainly it's that I can't get up off my backside!' And only half-mockingly he added: 'What, and do you intend to kill me, then? As you killed Karl the Crag in your bed in Cragspire? If so, then do it now while I'm happy.'

'Karl was my master,' she answered, frowning. 'Or thought he was. But he was *not* my lover. I've never had a lover, until you.' She reached out and gentled his flaccid, lifeless parts. They were bruised, but what is that to a vampire Lord? Then, still frowning, she said: 'But . . . happy? Did you say happy?'

She found it odd that he would use such a word, for vampires were rarely, if ever, happy. Happiness . . . just wasn't part of their landscape. Wratha must put it down to the fact that he wasn't long Wamphyri, and still occasionally thought in Szgany terms. Oh, the Wamphyri knew well enough how to enjoy: how to revel in scarlet extravagance, and glut themselves with their excesses; how to laugh and roister, thrill and exult, usually at the expense and the pain of their victims. Certainly they understood pleasure: the gratification of their enhanced appetites and lusts in feasting, drinking and fornication – but again and always at the expense of others.

Indeed, that was their only 'happiness': the outrage and agony of common humanity. But Wratha suspected that Nestor had meant the true happiness, which astonished her. So that again she asked him:

'And are you . . . *happy*, Nestor?'

'I think so.' He clasped her to him. 'I have all that a man needs, and in you more than *any* man could ever need! What more is there? Unless there's some special delight which you haven't yet shown me.'

Holding her like that, with his chin over her shoulder,

Nestor's face was hidden. Wratha suspected that he hid it deliberately; also his feelings, his true thoughts: that indeed there was something more. But not something which she could give him. And scanning his mind – and meeting with a blank wall – her suspicion seemed confirmed.

Turning her face away so as not to show her disappointment, she pushed him away, hurried down the steps and passed through into her dressing-room. Dressing, she heard him call out: 'Wratha? Is there something?' What's more, she felt *his* querying probe in *her* mind and immediately brought down mental shutters to close him out.

'No, nothing,' she called back to him. 'But night falls fast and we've business to attend to.' What she really meant was that *she* had business to attend to.

On Sunside.

Killing business . . .

VIII

Wratha's Rout – Glina's End

Wratha's orders were simple: put the women to death, all of them.

Not ravish them, or stun them and drink from the scarlet streams of their hearts, or by any other means molest and vampirize them, but simply kill them out of hand – dead! *All* of the women, the girls, even the smallest infant females of the Szgany Lidesci wherever they were found. And not just for the duration of this raid, but in all future raids, too.

For if there were no women, Wratha told herself contrarily (for of course she knew her real purpose in ordering this enormous atrocity), then eventually there would be no children; and without children the troublesome Lidescis would fade away and vanish in a single generation. Which is not a long time to one who has lived as long and remained as young as Wratha the Risen, or at least young in appearance. It was her way of making logical an entirely illogical command. For if the same rules were applied in all of Sunside, then Nestor's prognosis would come true and it would be Turgosheim all over again.

But the truth of it was that her order would only apply here, in Lidesci territory, and her reason for issuing it was likewise simple: pure (or impure) jealousy, with perhaps a jot of vengeance thrown in for good measure, to cover her previous losses. Mainly the Lady was jealous of a past in which she had no part, and of a supposed love which she could not even begin to understand. For she had never known love – not as a common woman – until Nestor, and feared that she might never know it again. Savagely territorial, the Wamphyri do not give up their possessions easily. And Lord Nestor of Suckscar now belonged to Wratha the Risen, though not as much as Wratha belonged to him.

Rivalry? For Nestor's love, his lust? Not in Wrath-stack, not any longer. For he was well and truly seduced, and Wratha even more so, indeed completely besotted. But in Sunside, possibly. Or impossibly, when her will was done. And with regard to the Lady Wratha's will, and to orders, there was one other command which she issued:

If any man should discover a Misha among the Szgany Lidesci's women, he was to bring her at once, unharmed in any way, to Wratha. Then she would be harmed, be sure, but not before the Lady had examined her most minutely, to discover Nestor's preferences in women generally, and that which he most fancied in Misha specifically. Following which . . . Wratha would eat her living, smoking heart, and feed the rest of her to the frenzied warriors.

Which was the circuitous route by which the Lady's lieutenants finally came to understand that it was an unknown girl, a mysterious Misha, who was the real reason why their Lady mustered her men- and monsters-at-arms in the early twilight, and waited impatiently for the last golden streak to fade from the peaks of the barrier mountains before launching them south for Sunside, Settlement, and infamous Lidesci territory.

And all of this while most of the stack's inhabitants lay asleep.

But not all of them . . .

*

Nestor stood alone with his thoughts, gazing from a window in his south-facing room of repose. As usual, his eyes rested on the grey peaks of the craggy barrier mountains way beyond the distantly pulsating glow-worm of the hell-lands Gate. There in the south-west, beyond the high scarps and plateaus, and across the foothills, at the edge of the forest, lay the once-bustling township of Settlement. And somewhere in the wilderness around that battered pile of a place – in the dark woods or cavern-riddled cliffs, or in the hollow roots of the mountains themselves – the Szgany Lidesci had their hiding places to which they retreated at fall of night.

But of all the Wamphyri in the last aerie, Nestor was the only one who actually *knew* the location of their principal refuge. It had come to him in Wratha's bed, as she had tried to convince him to raid on Settlement. A fleeting vision out of the past, from his forgotten childhood and youth: of a great hollow boulder, almost a small mountain in its own right, in the Sunside foothills. And its name was Sanctuary Rock!

A fleeting vision, aye, but one which Nestor had wanted to retain, which he'd assigned to his currently *perfect* memory before closing his thoughts on it, to keep it safe in his secret mind. This was the essence of the secrecy which Wratha had sensed in him: not thoughts of Misha, but of Sanctuary Rock in the foot-hills – that honeycombed boulder, that maze of caves, burrows, pitfalls and gantlets – where it backed up massively into the roots of the barrier mountains. The future refuge of his Great Enemy when at last he returned. But only let Wratha discover it first ... and all dreams of vengeance were flown right out the window –

– Even as Wratha herself was now flown!

Nestor gave a start, stared, then glared south-west. It was Wratha, aye ... and her entire entourage – Wrathspire's not inconsiderable army – even now on their way to Sunside! But without him? Without Canker? What was she up to?

Wratha, her six lieutenants, twice as many apprentices, and four warriors, two of them only recently waxed, all spurting or pulsing south under throbbing gas-bladders and vibrating manta wings; and all attired for battle. Even from here, Nestor could clearly see the sheen of starlight on blue-green armoured scales and part-sheathed claws; the bright gleam of gauntlets and polished black leather jerkins.

And he knew, of course, where she was going. But he didn't know why. He could only suppose it was to bring down Lardis and destroy the Szgany Lidesci: Wratha's stubborn pride, aye. Since Nestor had seen fit to deny her his aid at this time, she'd do the job herself and put *him* to shame!

But if by chance she were successful and struck devastating blows against Lardis and Settlement, and perhaps went on to find Sanctuary Rock ...?

What of Misha then? Much more importantly, what of Nestor's olden enemy, his Great Enemy, his treacherous brother? Would he *ever* return, if the Szgany Lidesci were no more?

From somewhere came the wail of a child: Glina's adopted brat, which Nestor had brought out of Sunside.

Glina: *hah!* Canker had been right: it had been a mistake to bring her into Suckscar. Fair and considerate in her managing of the rosters, she had grown too strong. All of the women liked her, and since she controlled them and their duties, Nestor's lieutenants and thralls liked her, too! She could match them up and cater for their affairs to order, or for favours. He had given her too much power.

And that child, that entirely human toddler in Suckscar: what of him? For all that he was sweet meat – fair game, and pure and innocent as only a child can be – the bloodlusting vampires of the manse handled him as if he were of their master's flesh, Nestor's own son, his bloodson! Was that Glina's idea – that one day this brat would get her master's egg and become a Lord in his own right?

Well if that was what she thought, she could think again. Suckscar was only the beginning; and after that, all of Wrathstack, soon to be Lichspire. Then Sunside in its entirety, and all of Starside, too, including the blackened, exploded stumps of the fallen aeries, those that were still habitable. And – and then what? Turgosheim in the east? Why not?

But – with Wratha at his side?

Well, she'd be at his side to start with, anyway . . .

But there was only one real destiny for the necromancer Lord Nestor Lichloathe of the Wamphyri: unopposed Emperor of a sprawling Vampire Dynasty, not only here in the west but across the Great Red Waste, too, and further still, in whatever lands might be discovered! Except . . . his revenge on his Great Enemy must come first. But not if Wratha ruined it by destroying the Szgany Lidesci.

He must stop her!

Nestor turned from the window in haste, and saw the dog-Lord watching him from the doorway. And: 'No need to stop her,' Canker barked, having read Nestor's last thought right out of his head; which was not difficult, for it had been a forceful projection. 'Not unless you'd save her from disaster. Myself, I think it were better Wratha learns her lesson here and now:

514

that together we're strong, and divided we fall.' He loped to Nestor's side, looked out of the window, saw what Nestor had seen.

Canker had been escorted here by Zahar, which was scarcely necessary; everyone in Suckscar, and Mangemanse, too, was aware of Nestor's and Canker's friendship. It was simply a custom (or precaution?) of the aerie: that any and all visitors should be escorted, even when they were expected.

Nestor caught Zahar's eye. 'Go, alert your colleagues. We ride out within the hour. But prepare my flyer at once, for I might go on ahead.'

And after Zahar had gone, Nestor turned to Canker: 'Disaster? For Wratha? What do you mean?'

'I scry on future times,' the dog-Lord answered. 'A dodgy business at best! But sometimes when I dream, I can't help the things I see. Wratha isn't going to have an easy time of it on Sunside. She goes against the Lidescis, am I correct? I thought so. And they're waiting for her, be sure. That's why I came to see you. To warn you against accompanying her.'

'You saw me in your dream?' Nestor knew that the other's scrying was true. In many small ways, he'd had the proof of it often enough.

'Neither you nor myself,' Canker answered. 'But I came up anyway, in order to be sure.'

'Will she be hurt?'

'Only her pride. But she'll suffer losses, aye. How would you have stopped her, anyway?'

'I would first try to reach her mind, from an outside balcony, maybe. And if that failed fly after her, to catch her in the heights over Settlement . . .' And realizing his error: 'Or if not there, wherever she makes pause to breathe her mist.' He quickly covered up.

'No.' Canker shook his head, sending his red hair

flying. 'No "wherever". Settlement will do fine. But tell me this: are you also a viewer of times, and since when? Did you also read the future in a dream, and see the troubles waiting for Wratha at the end of her flight? Why would you want to stop her? For our sake because she's an ally; for your own sake, because you are into her and would miss it if she were slain; or was it . . . for some other reason? Ah, but you never have raided on Settlement, have you?'

The dog-Lord wasn't smiling. He was missing something here and knew it. But what? Something important? He reached out an instinctive mental probe to brush up against Nestor's mind.

'Would you steal my thoughts?' the necromancer snapped.

Canker backed off, shrugged, whined a little. 'Habit, Nestor. Forgive me.'

'I don't want any harm to come to her,' Nestor said. *Well, not yet. Not until she's united the stack. For if there really is a threat from the east, we may well need the Lady Wratha and her dubious qualities. Certainly we'll need her men-at-arms and warriors! But after that . . . there are other women in the world.* At which he finally recognized the truth: that his lust was all but burned out of him and he did not 'love' the Lady after all. A full-fledged Lord of the Wamphyri, he didn't love or need anyone. Especially a liar like Wratha. For the fact of it was that she *was* a great liar, in her body if not her tongue. Nestor had mistaken experience for truth, had been willing to believe that what she gave him was new and true. But it wasn't: it was old and false, even as old and false as Wratha herself. A hag was lurking there under the sweet girl-flesh. He knew it for certain now. He always had known it, from their first encounter on the roof. How could she expect love?

516

Why, Wratha had sucked men to death – with *both* mouths!

And as for sex, Nestor was right on that point, too: there *were* plenty of other women in the world . . .

. . . And one especially, in Sunside? Hiding in some hole in the ground, with the Lidescis?

But all of this unspoken and locked in his secret mind, so that Canker couldn't hear it.

'Too late now, in any case,' the dog-thing barked. 'She's well away. Something has angered her and she'll take it out on the Lidescis if she can. Well, and good luck to her. For she'll need it, be sure. I saw thunder and lightning, Nestor – explosions red, green and orange! Aye, and I heard the death-screams of men, flyers and warriors alike – vampire screams, which are different from those of common men. For while a man's screams don't last too long, those of a vampire go on and on and on . . .'

Nestor was calmer now, thoughtful. 'And yet you say she'll suffer no harm?'

'Not personally, no. Losses among her lads and creatures, certainly.'

'Then let it be. You're probably right: a lesson learned. After this, perhaps she'll leave the Szgany Lidesci alone.'

'What is it with you and them?'

'Something . . . old.' Nestor looked away.

'An old scar, still itching?'

'Yes.'

'Say no more. You are my brother. I understand.' And Canker put an arm round the other's shoulder.

'Let's see how it works out for her,' Nestor said. 'What was it we had scheduled for tonight, anyway? Tithe-collecting east of the pass? Well, our lieutenants are capable lads. They can tend to that. What say you and I go spy on Wratha, eh? See what she's up to, and what befalls her. We can observe her and her works from the foothills over . . .'

But this time Canker was quicker off the mark. 'Over Settlement, aye,' he nodded. 'Very well, I go to prepare . . .'

And Canker had been right.

Less than an hour and a half later, he and Nestor landed their flyers in the foothills over Settlement. And down there, it was much as the dog-Lord had said it would be.

Wratha had called up a mist to send rolling in through the battered gates and shattered stockade fence of the ruined town. Then she'd surrounded the place as best she might with her lieutenants and thralls, probably three men to a side, outside the gates, to deal with any fleeing humans. Overhead, no more than midges at this distance, the Lady herself and her six remaining men-at-arms rode their flyers and commanded the warriors.

Her two mature fighting creatures were already down inside the fortress walls, battling in the mist (though with what was hard to say, for Wratha's mist was a good one). In the still of the night, however, with their enhanced Wamphyri senses, Nestor and Canker were not at pains to *hear* the sounds of battle: the snapping of timbers and crashing of collapsing houses; a thrumming and whistling, as of huge projectiles in flight; the awesome belching and growling of furious warriors at work. And in a little while they more than heard it.

'But where's the thunder and lightning?' Nestor had voiced his query just a moment ago, so that it still hung in the air like some weird invocation when the answer came . . . from below!

And: 'But there – ah, *there!* – is the thunder I promised you!' The dog-Lord whined and panted; and both of them started massively at the new sights and sounds from besieged, embattled Settlement.

A ball of fire, green at first but expanding through yellow and orange to a red glare, bloomed like a giant's torch in the centre of the town. Something writhed in the heat and the smoke as the mist was thrown back: a warrior, coiling like a crippled snake as it burned! Then the bellowing and belching was drowned out by the blast of a terrific explosion, whose echoes bounced up into the mountains to ricochet between the peaks, then down again to the dumbstruck vampire Lords where they gazed in astonishment on the scene below.

Amplified in the vacuum left by the explosion, the challenging battlecries of an uninjured warrior continued unabated, while those of its stricken twin had turned to shrieks of purest agony! Down there in the ruddy night, someone or ones must be throwing oil on the thing in its death throes; fires blazed up sporadically all around the area of the original explosion; the gigantic writhing continued, but frenziedly now.

Battle was truly joined, and no stopping it. And as the Lady's flyers descended towards the town, black motes against the flickering illumination of various fires where they broke out upon the ground, so the sky over Settlement came bursting alive with sputtering, brilliant blue and emerald-green trails of fire, like shooting stars fired from the walls of the town.

'And *there* is my lightning!' said Canker.

A flyer was hit, became a green and yellow fireball full of black, tumbling debris! Other flyers panicked, skewing this way and that and even colliding. The amazed, outraged cries of stunned lieutenants came echoing up on the stench and turbulence of furious explosions and sulphur thermals. A faulty, shrilly whistling, madly cartwheeling projectile exploded as it struck another flyer in the root of a manta wing, causing the blazing, mewling beast to go spirallng down to a fiery doom. Its lieutenant rider went with it, burning and screaming all the way.

'She's being blown out of the sky!' Nestor whispered, to no one in particular.

'Just as I foresaw it,' Canker nodded grimly. 'We all knew that this Lardis was testing new weapons – we saw evidence of it while raiding on the borders of his territories: incredible thunderclaps and flying fires – but this is simply . . .'

'. . . Fantastic!' Nestor finished it for him. And, a moment later: 'Look. She's finished.'

It was true. Wratha's pride had taken another beating, but even she knew when it was time to call it a night. Her flyers were rising up through a fusilade of searing fireballs, and on the ground a part-blazing warrior seemed hard put to get aloft. Finally it succeeded, and the speed of its rumbling ascent put out the fires in its flanks. But at least one of its flotation bladders exploded as it listed into the sky. As for the other, less fortunate creature: it was nothing but a mass of shuddering, steaming meat, gouting fire, smoke and sickening stench now.

And outside the walls, rising from the woods and the lower slopes of the foothills, more flyers made hastily, erratically aloft, swerving to avoid the bolts of giant crossbows and the rockets of jubilant defenders. It was a rout!

'So much for raiding on Lidesci territory!' Canker growled low in his throat.

Nestor nodded. And to himself: *In force, openly, a dangerous game, aye. But covertly, at the right time and in the right place? Sanctuary Rock, for instance . . .*

'If she comes this way she'll see us.' Canker was nervous.

'Let her!' Nestor spat into the scree. 'Let her know that *we* know what a fool she's made of herself!'

'Ah!' said Canker. 'But you haven't seen Wratha in a fury, have you?'

'Then it's time I did.'

'Might I suggest some other time?'

'Why not now?'

'Because she has warriors with her – some of which remain whole and fighting fit – and we don't! Be advised, Nestor: do not taunt her now. Oh, she'd probably miss you later, but much *too* late for Nestor Lichloathe and Canker Canison! Me, I say we launch and make ourselves scarce.'

Nestor was reluctant, but just this once Canker had it his way . . .

When Nestor's and Canker's lieutenants were returned from the tithe-gathering, Nestor sent for Zahar and asked him:

'How did it go?'

'Well, Lord. Honey, grain, meat and wine. And you? Flesh?'

Nestor shook his head. 'That wasn't our purpose. And don't ask me what our purpose was. As to why I've called you here: I have work for you.'

'Only instruct me, Lord. What is it you wish?'

'It's Glina. I want her replaced, both in her quarters and in her duties.'

Zahar was taken aback but tried not to show it. He shrugged and said, 'Glina has worked well. Now she reaps her reward. You *will* reward her, Lord? With an easier routine, perhaps? So that she may devote more time to the babe?'

Nestor sighed. 'You are devious, Zahar. All of you are devious. No, I will not reward her. She goes on the work roster. Choose a woman – the most attractive of my women – to replace her. I'm weary of Glina climbing the spiral stairs. I have not had her in my bed for . . . oh, a long time. Nor will I have her there again. From now on she works with the rest of them, and just as hard. As for the child: I've no use for a human child in Suckscar. See to it . . .'

Zahar couldn't suppress a gasp. He fought to maintain something of his equilibrium. 'You mean, return him to Sunside?'

'The choice is yours,' Nestor told him, coldly. 'Sunside or the provisioning. I have no interest in the matter. Go to Glina now and tell her, and by sunup let it be as I have ordered it.'

'You won't tell her yourself?' This was brave of Zahar.

'Are you saying I fear her?' Nestor looked at him, raised a sardonic eyebrow. 'No, I'm simply *sick* of her – and of all men and creatures who question me! Perhaps you fear her, eh? Or do you simply fear the change, when you won't find it so easy to conduct your affairs.'

'My . . . affairs, Lord?'

'Your own and the affairs of all the others, too.' Nestor's voice was very quiet, very dangerous now. 'Do you think I don't know how she *arranges* things for you?'

And now Zahar was very brave. 'But all to Suckscar's benefit, Lord.'

'There is only one creature in my manse which is entirely to Suckscar's benefit,' Nestor told him, in little more than a whisper. 'And I am it! But while I cannot be replaced, all else can and will be if I see fit. Now go, and be sure you carry out my orders.'

'Yes, Lord.' And only too glad to be out of his master's presence, Zahar retreated.

It was the same sundown. Wratha had been back from her disastrous raid on Settlement for some time, but never a word out of Wrathspire. Doubtless she licked her wounds.

While down in Suckscar:

Nestor was now Wamphyri in the fullest sense of the word. He was enormously powerful, the Lord of a mighty manse, a necromancer who read the minds of men dead in their graves, and also ... Wratha's lover? As to that last: things could change. For as the Lady herself would be the first to admit, she was after all only a woman, no matter how high she had risen.

Ambitious? Oh, she was that, all right! But what of Nestor's own ambitions? He supposed they must clash eventually. It seemed unavoidable. Meanwhile, well, he would make the best of it. It wouldn't be too hard. Certainly Wratha knew how to satisfy his lust.

But there's lust and there's lust, which in a man is not always for the body of a woman. Nestor's lust for revenge was powerful. Revenge on his Great Enemy, and on the girl who had betrayed him. That must come first. But afterwards –

– He considered the rest of the stack. Canker first.

The dog-thing was not a problem. It was as if he followed Nestor to heel, like a tame wolf. He would make a fine, trustworthy lieutenant when the time came.

Then he gave thought to Wran and Spiro. They, too, might be brought to heel. Wratha had done it, upon a time. Oh, they had slipped their leashes eventually, but that was because in bringing them here she had freed them from the tyrannous restrictions of Turgosheim.

They had seen no point in trading one tyranny for another, one ruthless leader for a yet more ruthless priestess. The Killglance brothers were Lords after all, and Wratha only a Lady . . .

But Spiro:

Nestor had heard how he continued to practise his killing eye. And with some success at last.

On Sunside, during a raid, the brothers had got in trouble. Ambushed by desperate Travellers, they'd been obliged to fight hand to hand. Spiro had got his gauntlet stuck in the skull of a man, so that it was wrenched from his hand. Then, as another human attacked him with a machete, he'd tried to use his killing eye. And at last his father's talent was seen to have been passed down to him! The metaphysical blast from his evil vampire eyes had been sufficient to burst his victim's heart, rupture all of his vital organs, stop him dead — literally!

So that now, while Wran had his rages (which were terrible in their own right), his brother had the killing eye of Eygor Killglance. But, of course, men were only weak and the Wamphyri were strong. Nestor did not for a moment believe that Spiro's murderous glance could affect him, or any of the stack's vampires for that matter. Still, the weird talent of Spiro Killglance would be worth watching out for.

Finally Gorvi:

The Guile would not be difficult to sway, not when all of the others were seen to toe the line. But Nestor knew that he would always have to watch him. Gorvi must never be placed in a position of trust. Indeed, it were better if he occupied no position at all — except perhaps a very deep hole somewhere out on the boulder plains . . .

Nestor had got so far with his thoughts — his plans?

– for the future, when Grig came to him with a message from the Lady Wratha. It was a simple thing: 'Come.'

Grig delivered it and stood grinning.

Usually Nestor would laugh along with him, for his lieutenants knew well enough what this kind of invitation from Wratha signified. But tonight he scowled, and Grig quickly changed his expression. 'Lord?'

'Is her messenger still here?'

'In the upper corridor where it leads to her landing bays. I left him there, watched over by a guardian.'

'Go to him,' Nestor said. 'And tell him to tell her . . . no!'

Grig gawped. 'Simply that?'

Nestor shrugged. 'She asked for me with a single word. And that's how I choose to deny her.'

Grig backed away, turned to go, and Nestor stopped him with another single word. 'Wait.'

'Yes, Lord?'

'From now on never smile in my presence unless I smile. Do not grin unless I grin. And don't laugh, ever.'

'No, Lord.'

'And don't forget,' Nestor warned. 'For if you do . . . it's difficult to smile without lips.'

Grig fled . . .

The night passed, however slowly. There were no more 'commands' from Wratha that Nestor attend her, though on two occasions he sensed her mental groping at the edge of his awareness. He was strong now and knew how to shut her out. He did so.

The aerie was unusually quiet – not only Suckscar but the entire stack top to bottom – like the quiet on Sunside before a storm. Nestor sensed his colony of giant bats stirring in their cavern niches and felt ill at ease without knowing the source of his disquiet. He saw to the manse's administration, then prepared for bed.

He did not see Glina, or hear the customary wailing of her adopted child. Obviously Zahar had been diligent in carrying out his orders.

Nestor felt lonely. He called for a girl, took her to his bed. She tried hard to please her master but ... was cold. No, not cold, but after Wratha there was no real fire in her. Nestor sent her away.

He slept ...

... And dreamed of the numbers vortex. Of that, and of other – things.

Nestor's dreams were usually scarlet, as are the dreams of all the Wamphyri. But this time there was no blood. Instead, he dreamed of a bloodless war, of a battle with the dead, and Nestor Lichloathe the only living creature on all the battlefield!

He fought alone, with neither men nor monsters to support him but only his clogged, stinking gauntlet, against a teeming legion of the dead whose crumbling, rotting bodies stood erect again as quickly as he cut them down! And despite that it was a hopeless task (for who may kill the dead?) still he willed himself to fight through them to get to That which they protected, the Thing which commanded them, his Great Enemy from times all but forgotten except in brief flashes of tantalizing memory.

Finally, when he stood panting from his exertions upon a mound of soul-heaving corruption – human debris whose pieces yet clutched and clawed at him to pull him down – at last the mind-refuge of Nestor's hated opponent materialized: a rearing, nodding cone like a tornado of rapidly mutating equations! The numbers vortex!

And within the rush and swirl of the tornado, half-

hidden in the uproar of mad mathematical eruptions, Nestor saw the infinitely sad, face of a yellow-haired, blue-eyed giant; made sad, perhaps, by the almost sacrificial mutilation and slaughter of his teeming dead army. But not by that alone.

For it was as if Nestor saw behind those plaintive sapphire eyes right into his enemy's soul; and strangely, inexplicably, he knew that the giant felt for him, knew that his Great Enemy was sorry ... for his brother, Nestor Lichloathe!

At which a hand fell on his shoulder and he came starting awake!

And it was sunup.

Zahar was there, backing away as Nestor shot bolt upright in his tumbled bed. And the Lord of Suckscar was damp with cold sweat, panting for air as he adjusted to being awake. Then:

'What is it?' he demanded, as finally he knew his whereabouts and took a grip on himself.

'It is Glina, Lord.' Zahar's face was pale even for a vampire.

'What of her?'

'I told her your intentions, your orders, with regard to herself and the child. She set to making her quarters clean and asked me to return in an hour. But when I went back she was not there. Neither Glina nor the baby.'

'Fled? But how?' Nestor got up, got dressed.

Zahar shook his head, sadly Nestor thought. 'No, not fled. In hiding. Waiting for sunup.'

'Explain.'

'I searched the manse but couldn't find her. She couldn't go up into Wrathspire, or down into Mangemanse, and so must be here. But Suckscar is vast, as well you know, and Glina is familiar with every nook and cranny. Also ... a good many of your people owe her favours, Lord. Perhaps someone had hidden Glina away, just for a few hours. I hesitate to suggest it, but that is how it ... how it begins to ...' And he paused with the accusation only half-spoken.

'Go on,' Nestor told him. 'I know what you would say: that Glina has friends. Difficult, between vampires, yes. And yet I, too, have one friend at least.'

Zahar nodded eagerly, and said: 'Two, Lord, if you'll only include me.' And he quickly continued, 'I knew she must reveal herself eventually, knew she must come out if only to eat or to feed the child. Well, and finally she has come out, but as you see, not until the sun is up.'

'Where is she?'

'She has climbed by an external route, up onto the south-facing wall of Wrathspire.'

'And the child?'

'He is with her.'

Suicide, it could only be. And the infant? Far better to let him die now – swiftly, surely, and too young to know that he'd even lived – than take a chance he might go to the provisioning. So thought Glina. And Nestor knew she'd thought it.

'Take me to where I can see her, talk to her.'

'Yes, Lord. But ... you've slept long and long. The sun is well up. I fear we'll be too late.'

In any case, they went. And on their way: 'What is it you would say to her, Lord?' Zahar was curious. 'Is it that you'll try to bring her down?'

Nestor glanced at him once only, with eyes that blazed up in his face like hell's own fires. And: 'No,' he answered. 'Let her stay there and wait for the sun to strike. I have only one thing to say to Glina, and it's this: goodbye!'

And from then to Wratha's landing-bays, silence accompanied them the rest of the way ...

*

Wratha was there, too, with several of her lieutenants. Some of her men would climb up after Glina, but the Lady stopped them. 'No, let's wait and see what this silly woman will do. For it's hard to believe she'd deliberately burn herself – not for the love of any man.' And she glanced sideways at Nestor.

And moving closer to him, smiling – yet hissing like some venomous snake in his mind – she asked: *Why did you not come to me?*

Seeing Wratha again, seemingly demure and recovered from the ravages of her Settlement battle – gorgeous in a revealing gown, and utterly edible – and knowing he could be in her even now, Nestor's lust flooded his veins to heat his blood as hotly as ever.

Because I had things to do, he lied.

Such as?

Removing this one from office, and sending her away from me.

Then she is here because of you?

Yes, he answered, mainly out of Wamphyri vanity. *And also because I would send her adopted brat back to Sunside – or to the provisioning.*

Oh? But I had heard rumours that he was your adopted son, too.

So much for rumours, Nestor answered.

They might have conversed further, but at that point a sigh went up from Zahar and the other lieutenants and thralls where they craned their necks to look up at the soaring south-facing wall of Wrathspire. Their viewpoint was from a walled, natural promontory or broad balcony over Wratha's main landing-bay, whose elevation was some sixty feet short of the bleached-white upper levels. Up there, along a line so regular it might even be a fault in the aerie's rock face, the natural features of fissured chimneys and ledges, and vampire constructed buttresses, windows and cartilage catwalks, turned abruptly from a weathered grey colour to an almost crystalline white, and the very rock itself seemed calcined with fire.

And indeed it had been, for this was the sun's demarcation line, above which the uppermost levels of the last aerie had been bleached white through centuries and even millennia of purifying sunlight. For when the solar furnace rose to its highest point over Sunside and blazed through the high peaks and passes, this was where its brilliant rays alighted, like a false halo to blister the corrupt head of the stack.

Up there on a ledge, to which she'd scrambled from a cartilage catwalk where it petered out, Glina hugged a small bundle to her breast and crouched in the shade of a shallow niche. But it was too shallow, that niche, and would not save her when the sun crept beyond the peaks and its rays swept from east to west across the face of Wrathstack.

Which was why Zahar and the others had issued their massed sigh, for even now the eastern corners of the upper spires were turning to glowing, blinding gold, as a seething vertical tide inched across the stone towards Glina in her crevice. She saw it too, and knew it was her time. Then –

– She stepped out upon the ledge, and lowered her feral eyes upon Wratha, Nestor, Zahar and the rest. But mainly Glina gazed at Nestor with eyes yellow as the brightening light they reflected, so that he could feel them burning on him.

And Wratha frowned delicately and said, 'She hates you.'

To which he replied, 'She has good reason.' But his voice was cracked and dry.

At which juncture – a strange thing! For suddenly

Nestor wanted to cry out, to warn Glina of the sun's approach, command her to come down, find a window, creep in out of danger. He had thought that compassion and all such feeble human emotions were dead in him and flown forever, but now seemed unsure. A certain poignancy, a gnawing frustration, chewed at his insides. Guilt? In a Lord of the Wamphyri? Ridiculous! And yet . . .

. . . What *was* Glina after all but a harmless creature he'd stolen out of Sunside? What had she done to deserve an end such as this? But if she'd done nothing it was because she *was* nothing. Just a stupid Szgany bitch, a snap of the fingers. So why should he worry over her fate?

Wratha had heard him. *Exactly, she's nothing. Why concern yourself? Because she was your first? But think: Wratha is your last! And is there any comparison? Between me and any Traveller shad? If so, then go to some other's bed when your work is done. But be sure if you do that I won't call for you again!* A threat of sorts, but he sensed an edge of desperation in it. Whatever they had had together, Wratha clung to it still. It gave Nestor power over her, which he would test eventually. But for the moment —

— He made no answer, mainly because he was watching Glina; also watching the sun, or rather its seething, sighing, cleansing ray lighting up the face of Wrathspire as it drew close to the woman on her ledge. But much too late to do anything now. She was doomed.

Another sigh went up from the assembled vampires. It was strange: a sigh of horror from such as these! But this would be their doom, too, if ever the sun should find them out.

As a life nears its end, time speeds up. Nestor couldn't remember who had said that: an old man, he believed, on Sunside, probably. Just another fragment from his forgotten past fitting itself into place. But as for what it meant:

A man's youth lasts forever, or seems to. But as he gets older, so the years get shorter. And his last few hours? They must fly like seconds. The same goes for women, of course. As for Glina, she was already down to those seconds. Five, four, three, two, one ... and then no more.

At the end, the sun scythed across her in a rush!

She felt its deadly light on her face, in her eyes!

Her shoulders had been slumped, as in defeat, but now she snapped erect on her ledge. And as the first tendril of smoke puffed up in her hair, she looked one last time down on Nestor, and hurled the baby towards him!

It fell short, and went without a cry fluttering into the abyss. It seemed to drift on the air, but in fact fell like a stone. And was gone ...

Then Glina cried out, but just the once.

She lifted up her arms to embrace the sun. Her face blackened in a moment and her shift billowed up from the steam and stench rising beneath it. Her hair burst into flames, and her shift followed suit. Yellow fire, almost invisible in the sunlight, enveloped her.

For a moment more she stood there — like a human torch, a sacrifice to the sun — then crumpled to her knees and toppled forward into eternity ...

'Gone,' said Wratha with some satisfaction. And silently, to herself: *An old flame, blazing to the end, finally consumed by its own fire. And all her 'innocence' gone with her.*

She turned to Nestor, but he was no longer there. Instead, she saw him descending from the promontory to the landing-bay, heading for Suckscar with Zahar. *Nestor!* she called after him.

Later, he answered, without looking back. For he knew he had power over her. But he also had power over the dead, and now there was one among them who he must speak to . . .

He had her burned, blackened, broken body brought up, and in the privacy of his room of repose he approached her. But before he could even touch her:

You are cursed, Nestor, she told him, in a totally emotionless deadspeak voice, freed now from all the agony of death but remembering it well enough. *You are all cursed, of course, but you especially.*

He held back and said: 'When I brought you up here from the rubble and the scree, my only thought was to . . . comfort you?' Oddly, it was the truth, but even Nestor could see the cynicism in it now.

She laughed a laugh empty as space. *Not so, Nestor. It was to beg my forgiveness! Except you are Wamphyri and don't know how. And anyway I do not, will not, cannot forgive you. Will you make me? Oh, I know you have the power. But though I may say the words, you know I'll recant them in the very moment they are spoken. And what difference would it make? You are cursed. Not by me alone, but by all the dead!*

At which the vampire in him rose up. 'So be it! What? And should I fear the dead? On the contrary: they fear me. Hah!'

But after a moment, she told him: *For now, perhaps. But in the end? You should never forget, Nestor, that all things have a beginning and an end. And as for the teeming dead: I think you should fear them, yesss . . .*

He suspected it would be the last thing she ever said to him and felt a momentary panic. 'Explain yourself.'

But she was silent.

Then he called for Zahar, and told him: 'In the twilight

before sundown, bury her in the Starside foothills above the hell-lands Gate. Find a crevice in the rocks, and wall her up. But don't tell me where you put her, for she's forgotten now and should stay that way.'

And to himself, in a fashion similar to Wratha's short and cynical eulogy:

Forgotten, aye – and all her curses with her!

But do curses die as easily as women? Even vampire women, in the right circumstances? And even the Wamphyri, when their time is come?

Somehow, Nestor doubted it . . .

IX

Return of the Enemy – Nestor's Revenge –
Canker's Moon-mistress

Gradually, achingly, Nestor came awake. But not to his soft bed and the comforts of some vampire girl's breasts and buttocks in Suckscar. And yet his first thought was this: *My life as a Lord has made me soft!* Which was a contradiction in itself, for as a Lord of the Wamphyri Nestor was hard as never before; both physically and mentally hard, with little or nothing of human emotion left in him, and certainly nothing of the frailty of human flesh.

But even the metamorphic flesh of a vampire has its weaknesses, such as sunlight, silver, kneblasch, and the sharp and splintery point of a hardwood stake; and, of course, a certain disease – a destroyer of the flesh itself, that causes it to slough away in lifeless pieces – which men have named leprosy and vampires avoid as surely as sunlight! For where the latter may be mercifully swift, the former is tortuously slow, irrevocable and utterly merciless. The hundred year death . . .

Nestor came more surely awake, and at first was surprised by a discomfort so great it was pain. Then he remembered where he was; and the damp grit in the corner of his mouth, the small pebbles pressed into his face, and the earthy smell of a riverside cave confirmed it: his location and predicament both.

He broke fragile scabs in the corners of his eyes as he forced them painfully, shrinkingly open, ready for the bright and deadly dazzle which might await them even now. But no, he was safe; his sleep had been a long one — of exhaustion, recuperation, replenishment — from which the setting sun and his vampire nature had finally called him awake.

For outside, beyond the low, frowning mouth of his refuge, the gurgling river was a leaden grey and showed nothing of reflected sparkle. It was the twilight before sundown, which in a few more hours would turn to night . . . his time.

He sat up — but too swiftly, abruptly — which caused him yet more pain. Indeed, it seemed there were several small hurts in his body unremembered from this morning, which only now made themselves apparent: a lump inside the knob of his left shoulder, where he'd broken his collarbone in the crash; lower ribs which were bruised, aching and possibly broken; massive bruising covering all the left side of his body, hip and thigh. Ah, but *that* had been a tumble!

As for his face and eyes: they were healing, and rapidly. And Nestor knew it was the swift metamorphic reconstruction or revitalization of damaged parts which hurt him so. His vampire flesh had expelled those pellets of silver which the lepers in their colony had missed; his cracked and broken bones were fusing even now, so that soon they'd be stronger than the original material; the ravaged flesh of his face was sealing itself with scar tissue which eventually he could keep or shed to suit himself. (Probably he would keep it, if it was not too unsightly, as a reminder of the debt owed him by the Szgany Lidesci.)

The Lidescis . . . the name was like bile in Nestor's mouth. Perhaps it would have been better after all to let

Wratha talk him into a massed raid upon them: himself, the dog-Lord, Wratha and all their forces. If he had not been so stubborn – if he'd told his colleagues his secret, showed them Sanctuary Rock and led them in the battle to take it – things wouldn't have come to such a pass. But as it was . . .

. . . What of this Nathan – his Great Enemy, the master of the numbers vortex, his unknown *brother* – now? And what of the bitch Misha, who had betrayed Nestor in a world largely forgotten? For those two were the real cause of his current fix, and the hell of it was that even now he didn't know the outcome of his plan to trap and dispose of them: whether it had worked in whole or in part, or whether it had been a total failure.

Only Nestor's lieutenant, Zahar Lichloathe, once Sucksthrall, could tell him that. And Zahar was in Suckscar, if he lived at all! But however things had gone, from Nestor's current point of view they'd gone disastrously wrong! Yet on the other hand . . . perhaps it wasn't so terrible after all. For as he put out tentative vampire probes into the evening all about, and as he employed enhanced Wamphyri senses to *listen* and *smell* and *feel* the mental aether, nowhere could he detect the numbers vortex or even a trace of it. For the first time in as long as Nestor could remember, his mind seemed completely clear of it.

As he gingerly fingered his torn but mending face, brushed tiny pebbles and grit from his hair and prepared to go out into the lengthening shadows of twilight where the birds of the forest were hushed as they settled for night, Nestor thought back on the recent events leading to this present moment . . .

. . . After Glina had cursed him (a curse that echoed even now in Nestor's memory like a weird invocation, and one which seemed to be working at that!) and following immediately upon her subsequent suicide:

Though he had resisted temptation until three-quarters of the way through sunup, eventually the lure of Wratha's vampire body had sufficed to draw Nestor up into her manse even as the water from Gorvi's wells was drawn by her siphoneers. And despairing of what he had seen as a human failing and weakness, still he'd gone to her.

But ... it had not been the same. For Wratha it may have been, but not for Nestor. For he'd felt his dominance and had known that Wratha loved him, or that her feelings for him were a vampire's equivalent of love. And the knowledge of *her* weakness in this respect had become his strength! Afterwards, when they had slept, then he'd dreamed again: of the numbers vortex, of course, and the One who hid in its heart, his hated brother, Nathan. But finally starting awake, Nestor had known that *this* dream had been different from any other.

For even when he was fully conscious, something of it had stayed with him, niggling there at the back of his changeling mind — that maddening, meaningless swirl of mutating numbers! Oh, it was faint in the sighing of the fading sunlight on the mountains, yes, but it emanated from Sunside and Lidesci territory nevertheless. And it was real. No longer a memory but a fact; absent for so long and only now returned, but *actually* returned ...

Returned ...

The thought of that — of his Great Enemy, returned — had made Nestor's vampire flesh tingle. And Misha, his stolen love? Was she, too, out there even now, together with *him*? Were they lovers again, plotting against Nestor anew as once before they had plotted in an earlier existence?

And he had 'known' that the answer to all of these inward-directed questions was *yes!*

And he had also known what he must do about it . . .

Back down in Suckscar, hearing Canker Canison singing to a pale, sunlit moon from some north-facing balcony in Mangemanse, Nestor had sought him out for his advice. And the oneiromantist dog-Lord had read his dream for him and looked into his future, but not without a warning: that the future is a devious thing.

'The danger lies not so much in reading what will be,' Canker had told him, 'but in trying to alter it. The future is no less inviolable than the past. What *has* been is fixed that way forever. And what *will* be . . . will be!'

Still Nestor had wanted to know: 'And for me?'

For answer, falling to all fours, Canker had tilted back his head and howled his misery! Then, springing upright again, he had clutched Nestor to him; and in the next moment his growl had been very deep and far too ominous as he said: 'Perhaps it would be best if you took me with you, my friend.'

'Took you with me?'

'To Sunside in the twilight, where you'll do your best to scratch this itchy old scar of yours. For it seems to me you'll be staying there a while, whether you want to or not. And a day on Sunside is death, as well you know . . .' Then the dog-Lord had brightened. 'Yes, that's it! I'll go with you! For that's the way I saw it: that you were not alone.'

'I never intended to be,' Nestor had answered, shaking his head. 'But I'll not jeopardize you, for it isn't your problem. No, I'll take Zahar along. And that way this future you've seen won't be changed. Except . . . I don't yet know what you saw.'

'I saw trouble, fire, pain and torment,' Canker answered. 'I saw brothers – twins and yet not twins – one of them hurt, damaged, perhaps permanently, and the other sent far, far away. Only don't ask me which brother was which. And as for changing the future: don't trouble yourself. For as I told you, it may *not* be changed. Nor will it be denied.'

And Canker had stood there whining, perhaps even crying in his way, as Nestor returned thoughtfully to Suckscar . . .

Then, almost too soon, it had been the twilight before sundown, and the grey peaks of the barrier mountains had beckoned Nestor as never before. He had felt lured by them where they turned to blue ash under a hurtling moon and ice-chip stars; lured by the peaks . . . and by the numbers vortex both! For instead of fading as of old, now the vortex had waxed in Nestor's head to a living power, whirling like a dust-devil in his enhanced Wamphyri mind, so that he had been doubly sure that his Great Enemy was back.

And before the rest of the aerie was fully awake, Nestor and Zahar had saddled manta-winged mounts and flown to Sunside; so that by the time Canker had changed his mind about changing the future and rushed up from Mangemanse to restrain Nestor – and before Wratha had yawned three times, frowned and sent out a vampire probe to seek him out and discover the reason for his absence from her bed – it was already too late.

Resting a while in the barrier mountains, Nestor and Zahar had gazed down on Sunside. And by virtue of the numbers vortex, Nestor had known that his Great Enemy was down there even now. Except this time he could find him, by *following* that trail of alien numbers which rushed faster and faster, ever more maddeningly through his head. At long last he would track the maelstrom to its source and destroy it – destroy *him* – forever!

And Misha, if she was with him? She would be stolen away into Starside, to be Nestor's thrall in Suckscar. All of which had been explained to Zahar, so that Nestor need only caution him:

'If aught befalls me, my enemy must not go free. No, for I can't bear the thought of that! If I'm destined for hell, I want to know that he got there before me, or that he's following close behind. These are my instructions:

'He is mine and you shall take the girl. If all goes well we head home at once. But if I come to grief my order is this: drop the girl and take him! Do you understand?'

Zahar had understood, and also Nestor's next instruction: that his enemy was to be tossed alive into the hell-lands Gate on Starside!

Then they had mounted up, and Nestor had told Zahar: 'Now follow close behind and I'll take you to them.' And he had. Up until which time, all had gone as planned. But from then on . . .

All had gone astray.

Oddly enough, Nestor remembered very little of it, other than that he'd followed the numbers vortex to its source, and discovered his prey heading west for Sanctuary Rock; the two of them together, of course. After that it should have been the very simplest thing: a Lord of the Wamphyri and his lieutenant, both of them mounted upon flyers, against a pair of Szgany lovers wandering in the twilight like lost waifs?

He had seen them from on high and could not fail to note the travois which they hauled behind them, weighted with their few worldly goods. And he'd known what that travois signified: that they were recently wed, and were even now returning from their nuptials. Well, what odds? Nathan had had Misha before, Nestor was sure, and it made little or no difference now. But it infuriated him nevertheless. And worse, it distracted him.

He saw man and mate, but failed to see the *other* who was there, their possible salvation. That other who carried a shotgun, which Nestor remembered as being 'a weapon out of another world'.

Then, as the hunters descended through a thin mist under vibrating, membranous manta wings arched into air traps, the pair on the ground had seen them! Leaving the travois behind, they'd split up and scrambled in opposite directions. Acting on Nestor's instructions, Zahar had gone after the girl while his master pursued Nathan. But in the milky swirl of a deepening mist, still Nestor had failed to appreciate the presence of a third Traveller. Until –

– Twin flashes of light, matched by a double-barrelled blast of sound! By which time it had been too late. Nestor's flyer was hit in the face; indeed half of its face had been blown away, and the wonder was that the beast had managed to stay aloft. But that hadn't been the end of it. There'd been more gunfire, this time directed at Nestor himself.

The agony of those tiny, poisonous silver pellets chewing deep into his metamorphic flesh! Almost unseated, somehow Nestor had managed to hang on. And reeling sightless in the saddle, his face a raw red mess and consciousness slipping as he fought to command his crippled flyer up, away, and back to Starside, again he'd remembered Glina's curse and Canker's warning.

Following which he remembered very little:

A long low glide, and his inability to impress himself on his mount's mind. The gradually declining beat of the flyer's manta wings; its agonized mewling; the way it tilted first to the left, then to the right, its balance upset by the silver shot in its tiny brain. Unable to find the strength to climb, disorientated, dying, the beast had headed out over the Sunside forest . . . and crashed there.

The crash! The whiplash as he was hurled from the flyer's back. His body somersaulting, smashing against the bole of a great tree, falling through branches which snapped under his weight, down to the forest's floor. And the darkness . . .

Then:

Ministering hands? Kindness? Ointments and bandages, to assist in the healing process which Nestor's leech had already commenced. And brief bouts of consciousness. And the occasional wishful thought that perhaps Wratha had found him crashed and brought him back to the last aerie. But she hadn't.

No, for the lepers had found him!

His hag-ridden, blundering, half-blind escape from their colony in the predawn light, and the knowledge etched in acid on his vampire mind that he had been in their hands, in their care, and breathing their air for the greater part of a long Sunside night!

Lepers!

Leprosy!

The Great Bane of the Wamphyri!

Nestor snapped out of it . . . and found himself stripped naked, scrubbing himself in the river, scrubbing the feel, the smell, the taint and even the knowledge of leprosy out his body, his brain, his very existence. Except the knowledge was there forever, and he knew it. What had been could not be altered.

Shivering, he went to the riverbank and dressed himself in his soiled clothes, and thought: *It is contagious, but not inevitable. Also, I'm aware of the danger, and so is my leech.*

Within him, he knew that his parasite was working to discover and destroy anything of leprosy – anything alien at all – which it might find in his body and blood.

But he knew, too, that it had already tasked itself to produce an antidote to the poison of the silver shot; also, that it worked hard to replace the tissues damaged by the shotgun blast and his crash both. In short, he knew that his leech was overburdened.

But he must put it out of his mind. A man might live with lepers for years and remain free of the taint, and he had been with them for one night only. (*What, with his torn flesh, open and inviting of contagion? And them feeding him, touching him, breathing on him?*)

Damn . . . it . . . to . . . hell!

Nestor gritted his teeth, shook his head furiously, gazed north through bloodshot, blood-red eyes and glimpsed the first stars of night glittering over the barrier mountains. And high over the last aerie, the Northstar like some frozen blue jewel, calling to him as once before it had called.

But the ice-chip stars were blurred, twin-imaged, and his damaged eyes filled with tears, of pain and frustration, as he tried in vain to fix those celestial gems in their orbits. All to no avail. It was useless; the healing could not be hastened but must take its own time; he must rely on his darker vampire senses to see him through the woods and across the mountains.

Well, and that was something which Nestor had done before, too, with nothing to rely upon but the damaged mind and memory of a dull Szgany youth, and when all he had known was what he *wanted* to be. And now that he was? It should be easy.

So he set off north, and gradually his aches and pains settled to a dull background throbbing, and his at first cautious tread took on pace, rhythm and the easy flow of the vampire to eat up the miles.

As before, the Northstar was his pharos; it guided him along the shortest route, though naturally he followed trails old and new where they were available, just so long as they pointed in roughly the right direction. And in the deepening night Nestor was in no great hurry, for the night was his friend and he was Wamphyri and inexhaustible . . .

. . . And hungry.

In a little while he knew his whereabouts: the woods some three miles south and one east of Settlement. Upon a time he'd played here as a child, and hunted here as a youth. The memory came and went, insubstantial as a tendril of ground mist, evaporating in his mind. His childhood and youth were forgotten in a moment, but instinctively, still he knew where he was. Four miles and he'd be into the foothills. And all the long Sunside night spread before him, through which he'd climb the barrier mountains to safety long before the sun was up.

Except he knew now that Wamphyri 'inexhaustibility' was a fable; his travails had taken it out of him; despite his long sleep he *was* beginning to tire . . . and he was still hungry.

In a hundred years' time – ah, but it would have been so easy! To find a point of elevation, spread his stretchy Wamphyri flesh into an airfoil, fly and glide home to Starside. But Lord though he was, in that respect Nestor was still immature. He had progressed, yes, but not yet to that point. Not yet to the extent of that incredible skill or art. Indeed, as of yet he'd not seen a one of the Lords of Wrathstack in actual, physical, unassisted flight, though Canker had sworn that they all could do it, if or when necessary.

But flight! Just think of it: to launch oneself and drift aloft on the night winds! Nestor inclined his head and glanced longingly at the star-shot sky –

– And saw *manta shapes gliding up there!*

At first his thoughts were chaotic:

What, a search-party? Had Zahar or Wratha organized lieutenants and thralls to come across the mountains and look for him? Well, Wratha perhaps ... but Zahar? It seemed unlikely. Despite that Nestor had sworn he'd be back, his man Zahar must see this as his chance for ascendancy. Just how he would manage it was hard to say: Zahar had no egg and he wasn't long a vampire himself. But it was a chance, certainly.

Wratha, then?

Nestor sent a probe skyward, and saw that it wasn't Wratha. Indeed the riders on high were the last people he had wanted to see, and certainly they were the last he'd want to discover him here: the Killglance brothers, Wran and Spiro! They and a small party of hunters were circling overhead, gradually descending. But even as he watched, the descent became a swoop: like the plummet of hawks stooping to their prey.

Nestor's vampire senses had been sharpened by the presence of danger on high; now from the north-west, he heard the crashing of underbrush; even at this distance the hoarse panting of fleeing Szgany was plainly audible. The brothers had found a party of Travellers, and very shortly the night would turn to rack and ruin, fire and blood. Nestor's heartbeat picked up and his own blood surged at the thought of it.

He had been lucky. If the marauders weren't so intent upon the hunt, they must surely have sensed his probe. And he could be fairly sure how the Lords of Madmanse would have dealt with him: not necessarily a quick death, but one from which there'd be no returning. The sword, the stake, the cleansing fire.

Of course, for who would there be to witness it, and who later to accuse? None but the brothers themselves, and their thralls. And Nestor was without a doubt their enemy, who sided with Wratha and the dog-Lord to make Wrathstack's upper half a fortress in its own right, and leave the others to their fate. Get rid of him and Wratha would be that much weaker, and the brothers that much stronger.

Yes, he'd been lucky. And his luck was holding. Someone – a Traveller, obviously, from his crashing, stumbling, blundering flight – was heading his way. Flushed out by the Madmanse twins, sweet salty sustenance was on its way, rushing straight into Nestor's waiting arms.

He melted into the cover of tree-cast shadows, breathed a vampire mist, let his dark Wamphyri senses drift out from him to meet and explore whoever it was that fled in his direction. And there were two of them: a man and a woman. Sufficient for *all* of his needs.

Nestor let them come, and now their approach was that much more cautious. Not because of him, no, for they had no knowledge of him. Because of the *sounds* from the deep forest at their backs: the hoarse, desperate shouting of fearful men; shrill, feminine cries of terror; and the coarse pitiless laughter of their pursuers and tormentors. But all from some distance away, and this pair thought that they'd escaped it. So that now they crept in the night like mice, and tried as best they might to still the thudding of their hearts, to quiet the panting of their ragged breath.

But Nestor heard everything, and waited . . .

And eventually they came.

Then –

– He stepped out of his own mist and confronted them! The shock was so great that the woman – no, she was only a girl – simply fainted away. As for the youth: his jaw fell open and he lifted an arm and hand, perhaps defensively . . . except his hand contained a crossbow!

Nestor leaned to one side as a bolt whirred too close to his ear, and he struck at the other's extended wrist with the flat of a hand as hard and as heavy as wood. The youth's wrist broke but he made no sound, for Nestor's free fist had already crashed into his face. His jaw disintegrated and his teeth collapsed inwards, driven into the back of his throat by Nestor's thorny knuckles. Gagging, he flew backwards and slumped against the bole of a tree. Nestor followed up and drove his right fist *into* the other's chest, crushing his fluttering heart, nipping its pipes, tearing it from his body while still it palpitated in his hand.

Thus it was done, and all so silently.

And holding the still-shuddering corpse of his victim upright against the tree, Nestor slaked his thirst and satisfied his hunger there and then.

Or one of his hungers, at least . . .

In a little while the girl stirred and uttered a low moan. And when her eyes flickered open Nestor was there kneeling beside her, looking into her face. Her mouth flew open in what started as a scream but quickly gurgled into silence. For his hand was at her throat, tightening, and the look on his deeply scarred, savagely lustful vampire face was a warning in itself: *don't!*

Then she looked beyond him, up through the canopy of the trees, to see clouds scudding against a backdrop of cold blue-glittering stars. She was seated with her back to the leaning bole of a tree, and she was naked to the waist where her upper clothing had been torn from her in strips, like rind dangling from a ripe fruit.

In that same moment she knew that this wasn't just a bad dream; she remembered where she was, who she'd been with, and what had happened. Her eyes opened wide, glancing this way and that in the starlight, until they found her lover ... slumped close beside her at the bole of the same tree! Slumped, almost crumpled there, and bloody as a freshly slaughtered beast.

Then she turned her searing, accusing gaze on Nestor again, saw the look on his face and knew what it meant. That he wanted her and would have her. Similarly, he knew what *her* look meant: that she would kill him if she could or cause him to be killed, and never mind the consequences. He knew she'd scream her lungs out if he gave her the chance, and also how easy it would be to squeeze a little harder and finish it. Except ... he wanted her conscious. Or conscious at first, at least.

From the darkness of the near-distant forest, the sounds of Wran and Spiro's raiding party about their business had settled down to a chorus of sobbing, pleading female voices, the occasional shriek of agony or infrequent burst of guttural laughter. Knowing what these sounds signified, that by now the Killglance brothers and their lieutenants were enjoying the women they had captured, Nestor's vampire passions were inflamed and his blood sang in his veins as he felt his own need growing by leaps and bounds. He would do the same, right here and now, immediately, but knew that if the girl cried out she would surely be heard.

If she cried out ...

Coming slowly to his feet, but never for a moment relaxing his grip on her throat, he looked down on her gazing up at him. Despite that her face was grimy, streaked with tears, and bore the bruises and scratches of her panic flight through the night forest, still she was beautiful, or would be in the right circumstances.

As he continued to straighten his legs and stand up, Nestor released his rigid rod from his trousers and let it stroke upwards through the central indentation of her rib cage, then between her firm, quivering breasts.

Her beautiful breasts ... her shivering shoulders, gleaming like marble in the night ... her pulsing throat. The *depth* of her throat. But her face was turning blue from the pressure of his iron fingers. And gradually, as she began to choke, so he released his grip on her windpipe.

Instantly her mouth gaped open and she drew massively on the night air. Nestor knew that when she expelled that breath it would be in the form of a piercing shriek, which was something he simply couldn't allow.

Ramming himself forward into her mouth, he reached down to trap her hands where they flew to his vulnerable parts. And concentrating on his metamorphic flesh as it surged into her throat, he filled her as so often he'd filled the Lady Wratha; except Wratha was Wamphyri and had wanted it, and could take it.

In his awful ecstasy, Nestor's metamorphism was that of a Lord full-fledged. He extended into his unknown victim like lava in a volcanic, subterranean sump, filling every available space. Sex was his purpose, but his leech's need was sustenance – a direct flow into Nestor's own stream – to supplement the nutrition he'd had from the young man. Within the girl's writhing body, Nestor's flesh put out small hooks to hold itself in position, and needle-like siphons to pierce her innermost veins and arteries, drawing off her life-force while yet it remained.

But it didn't remain for long.

As her hands went limp in his, Nestor released them and reached for her breasts, and squeezed them as if to force her juices – and his own – to flow that much faster. Except the flow was already ebbing as she gave up the unequal struggle.

The knowledge that she was dying, that he had

devoured her life, incensed Nestor even further. Moaning the sweet agony of his relief — shuddering head to toe, crushing the girl's upper body to the tree — he reached climax and ejaculated in a series of long bursts. Then it was over, and in a little while he began to shrink back into himself and withdraw . . .

After that, Nestor would have skirted the hunting party out of Madmanse and continued his trek without delay, but there was a matter of great importance which he must see to first. His male victim was most certainly dead, and the true death at that: Nestor had ruined his face and ripped out his heart! But the girl was whole. She'd been depleted, but her body was intact and quite incorruptible. For as well as taking, Nestor had given far too much of himself. In short she was undead, a vampire, and with copious amounts of Nestor's seed in her she could very well become Wamphyri.

Or she might have become Wamphyri . . .

Nestor took up the youth's crossbow, found a second bolt beneath the tiller, and discovered a third in a narrow sheath sewn into the dead man's jacket along the seam of the forearm; both of which he sent plunging into the girl's heart at point-blank range, pinning her to the tree. Now she would not wake up from her undead sleep but simply rot here, unless Travellers found her first and burned her. Long before then, however, the sun would be up, when anything of the vampire left alive in her would likewise die.

And without another moment's thought for her, or a word said over her, Nestor set out north again and skirted the continuing sounds of savage celebration where they echoed in the depths of the violated forest. Once, through the trees, he saw the flickering yellow flames of a campfire dancing in a clearing, and several nodding grey ghost shapes which could only be the silhouettes of flyers; but striding out and stronger now, he soon left all of that far behind . . .

Without further incident, Nestor came at last to the foothills and commenced climbing, and one-third of the way through Sunside's three-day 'night' found himself almost up into the hard rock outcrops, scree-covered saddles, and sheer cliff faces of the barrier mountains themselves.

Now the going was harder but Nestor was undeterred. With something over forty hours to go before sunup, he would be up into the peaks, safely through the high passes, and down into the shadows of Starside before the searing sunlight could discover and devour him. He slept once, briefly, in a cleft in the base of a cliff – and woke up thinking that he'd overslept and the sun was already up!

But it wasn't. Though the evilly glittering Northstar was hidden now by the wall of the mountains, the rest of the stars shone cold and bright as ever overhead, and the long night was only half-way through.

Twice as he climbed he saw signs of Wamphyri activity. On the first occasion, a handful of heavily burdened manta shapes pulsed wearily overhead on a course for Starside. This would be the Killglance brothers; having slept off their orgy of blood-letting and red rape, they'd be on their way back to Madmanse.

The second time it was a mist that drew Nestor's attention: a vampire mist, rolling like a soft, shallow white lake through the once thronging thoroughfares in the deserted ruins of Twin Fords far below. It could be Gorvi the Guile down there (for he was a crafty mistmaker), or the dog-Lord, even the Lady Wratha herself, but Nestor made no inquiry. Up here in the heights he was vulnerable and wanted no enemy coming to investigate his presence. But if it *was* Gorvi down there, hunting on his own for once, and separate from the Killglance brothers —

— Perhaps there'd been a falling out between them. Nestor hoped so.

Even as he looked down, a fire sprang into being in the old town's centre where a house went up in flames. Doubtless a celebration was in progress. So Twin Fords hadn't been deserted after all. Not tonight, at least. But tomorrow it would be, most certainly . . .

With the first flush of a false dawn staining the southern horizon, Nestor made his way wearily through a high pass to cross the dividing line between Sunside and Starside. An invisible demarcation, it was the halfway point where Sunside disappeared from view, even the horizon. And in the Stygian shadows of the Starside peaks, at last he felt safe.

So he returned into Starside, and emerged from the pass to gaze down on the barren boulder plains. In the north-east, way beyond the hell-lands Gate, the last aerie of the Wamphyri was alive (or undead) even now; from here it was invisible, except perhaps as a series of faintly twinkling lights in the dusky-blue distance. As for the glaring hemisphere Gate: that lay in the foothills around the curve of the mountains, which kept it hidden from view.

Nestor found a flat-topped boulder and sat himself down. He was tired and would rest a while, perhaps even sleep. But first he must at least attempt to make contact. In Wrathstack, the Lords, Lady, and all their lieutenants and thralls would be making ready for the long day. Wratha would be drawing her bat-fur curtains in the higher towers and turrets and south-facing windows of Wrathspire; Canker would be out on a Mangemanse balcony somewhere, singing a last sad song to the blind, uncaring moon; down in Suckscar, Zahar would be wondering what was become of his master. Those without duties would be taking to their beds, while the shift-workers and watchmen would be up and about, seeing to the maintenance and security of the five great manses.

Despite that Nestor's eyelids weighed as heavy as lead, he stared into the north-east at that perhaps imaginary twinkle of lights, projected his Wamphyri thoughts at a mental picture of Zahar in Suckscar – and was immediately rewarded as his probe found not one but three receptive targets! Zahar, Wratha, and Canker: all of them at various windows in their various levels, all gazing into the south-west and thinking of Nestor.

Zahar's emotions were mixed, his thoughts confused, as his mind met that of his master. He couldn't send without Nestor's aid but was his master's true thrall and received his thoughts well enough. And when Nestor's probe touched him, it was as if Nestor himself stood there, saying: *You, Zahar, come to me!*

'Nestor!' Zahar whispered.

The Lord Nestor, to you! Now come at once, to the barrier mountains. And bring an extra flyer.

'But . . . you're back!'

And didn't I say I would be? Now hurry, for I'm ready for the comforts of Suckscar. And Zahar . . .

'Yes, Lord?'

My Great Enemy. Is he . . . ?

'On his way to hell, Lord, aye!' Zahar was in command of himself once more. 'Or perhaps he's there already. For it has been a while now.'

Good! Now get out here with that flyer, and I shall guide you to where I wait.

And: *Nestor!* (This from a delighted Canker.) *But where are you?*

The barrier mountains, perhaps a mile or two east of Twin Fords, but on our side of the range. An hour and a half, maybe two hours, and Zahar will pick me up. I'll be back in the last aerie before the peaks turn from grey to gold!

But in one piece?

Yes ... Well, almost.

I'm coming, too! Canker yelped in his mind.

And: *Nestor!* (This from a concerned, even wrathful Wratha.) *Are you hurt?*

He let her wait a while, then replied: *Nothing that won't mend.*

Damn you! What you've put us through. And all for ... for a woman!

Ah, and so you have spied upon my mind! Nestor accused. *But you are wrong, Wratha. No, it wasn't for a woman but revenge! I don't want the girl, just as long as he doesn't have her.*

He? Him? Who do you mean?

That's my business. Or it was. Now ... it's finished. But Wratha, listen to me: I'll make it up to you. From now on, any time you want to raid on Lidesci territory – you, me, and Canker – I'm with you. For you see, it really doesn't matter now. Nothing matters now ...

And indeed it was as if a mighty weight had been lifted from his shoulders.

After a while she said: *I shall expect to see you soon, in Wrathspire.*

To which he answered: *Expectations are fine, and sometimes they even come true.*

Then he lay on his back in a patch of crumbly, desiccated heather, and in a minute or two was asleep ...

*

Nestor slept for well over an hour. He only woke up when he felt the presence of other minds searching for him and closing with his location. Then, using Wamphyri mentalism to guide his rescuers in – issuing topographic directions and an occasional correction to their course – he watched them come gliding diagonally across the foothills and pulsing into the heights; until they drew level with him, spied him in the rocky saddle where he waited, and sought safe landing sites close by. Zahar and a riderless flyer were first down, with Canker following behind.

When they were safely down and dismounted, Nestor went to them. 'Well done,' he told Zahar cursorily, before turning to Canker.

The dog-Lord bayed like the great hound that he was, gathered Nestor up in his arms, and growled: 'But I have *worried* over you!' His scarlet eyes with their yellow pupils narrowed as they inspected Nestor's facial ravages. 'Not without cause, it seems.'

Nestor held him off and shrugged. 'A few scars? They are nothing. I may even wear them as a trophy. Aye, for it seems I've won, Canker. It seems I've won!' And sharply, to Zahar:

'You're sure?'

'About your enemy?' Nestor's lieutenant snapped alert. 'I brought him awake in the moment before I tossed him into the Gate. Oh, he knew where he was going, all right – to hell!'

'*Huh!*' Canker growled, as Nestor relaxed and smiled a grim smile. 'Well, perhaps one day you'll tell me what this was all about! Meanwhile, what are we doing here? For if you'll take a look back there...' Their eyes turned in the direction of his pointing hand.

Behind them, rising up from the unseen valleys and forests in a haze of golden dust motes, dawn proclaimed itself. It was daubed pink and yellow on the underbellies of Sunside's drifting clouds, and painted amethyst on the curving southern rim of the star-shot, blue-black atmosphere. It was given voice in the startled songs of mountain birds, and echoed in a soughing wind as thermals commenced to rise and draw cold air out of the dark vault of Starside.

They mounted up and launched into the dawn wind, set their course east and a little to the north, to take them home to the last aerie. But in something less than an hour, as they glided down across the Starside foothills and passed low over the hell-lands Gate . . .

. . . A diversion!

What?! Nestor and the dog-Lord issued their mental question-exclamations almost in unison, while Zahar said nothing but simply stared down in astonishment and fascination at the glaring white dome of the Gate *. . . and at the figure which even now stepped down from its crater rim, to go stumbling and teetering out across the boulder plain!*

A woman? Nestor hissed. *But human? Here?*

And Canker, gawping: *Some Traveller woman, do you think? Taken on Sunside in the night, in thrall to Gorvi or the Killglance brothers, and left to find her own way home to the last aerie? But . . . would they really leave a creature as beautiful as this to the perils of beasts and mountain passes? It seems scarcely possible!*

Hauling on their reins, they brought their flyers round in a tight semicircle and commanded them to sideslip this way and that, settling to the sterile boulder plain like flat pebbles to the bottom of a pool. And glancing at Canker as they landed, Nestor saw that the dog-Lord was transfixed, his long jaw hanging loose as his eyes soaked up the sight of the girl from the Gate.

'A creature as beautiful as this,' Canker had said. And indeed she was beautiful ... and her colours totally alien! Nestor couldn't say if he'd seen such colours before, or even if they'd existed ... in a woman. But in a man? What of his Great Enemy, Nathan, gone now into another world? Hadn't his colours been much the same? And hadn't he always dreamed of a place where they would fit, where he would be accepted? Somehow Nestor knew that he had. Maybe they were all the same in that far strange world, that alien hell, even as the Szgany were the same in Sunside. Or perhaps this was just some weird and wonderful coincidence.

For the woman from the Gate was a statuesque, unheard-of silvery blonde, and her eyes were blue as the sky's vault on a clear day! Her skin was pale, unblemished, perfect; likewise her features. Long-limbed, her flesh was firm beneath undergarments of sheer silk, which were clearly visible under the swirl and waft of a gown wispy as butterfly wings. Less than opaque, the garment floated as if fashioned of shimmery silver cobwebs!

She had seen them falling out of the sky, landing and dismounting. Now she ran from them and a wailing cry, like that of a frightened infant, came back to them. Canker immediately went to all fours and was after her in a series of leaps and bounds. But catching up with her, strangely ... he held back! The dog-Lord and alien woman faced each other; she put up hands formed into claws, with sharp, scarlet nails, and snarled at him; he stood there upright, stalled and astonished, jaw lolling open.

The tableau remained frozen until Nestor and Zahar came on the scene. Then:

'Keep *back!*' Canker growled, whirling on the pair as

they approached; and Nestor had never heard so clear a threat in any voice! But from the dog-Lord? He couldn't believe it. Yet Canker's muzzle dripped saliva, his fangs were sharp as bone knives where the soft, shiny black leather of his mouth was drawn back and wrinkled, and his eyes glared a savagery completely out of character — at least where Nestor was concerned.

'What is it, my friend?' Nestor's own voice was as calm and hushed as ever; which was as well, for it brought the other to his senses.

'Eh?' Canker shook his head as if to clear it, glanced at Nestor and Zahar, and returned his gaze to the girl. She looked into the cores of his piercing animal eyes, shrank from him and hissed like a wild creature, spitting her terror. But as Canker took a step towards her and loomed close, she knew his overwhelming power and submitted to it. She stood up straight, arms by her sides, trembling in all her limbs. Then her eyes rolled up and she would have crumpled to the hard earth; except the dog-Lord swept her up, but oh so *gently*, into his great arms!

And turning to Nestor: 'Eh?' he said again. 'But isn't it obvious what — *who* — she is?'

'No.' Nestor shook his head, stared hard at the girl in the other's arms. 'Not at all obvious. For I've never seen anything like her.'

'But *I* have!' Canker barked. 'Often, in my dreams! Didn't I describe her well enough? I know I did. Only turn your eyes to the sky, Nestor, if you would know her heavenly origin. Up there, the hurtling moon! For she is my silver moon-mistress!'

Nestor glanced at the sky, the tumbling moon, then stared his amaze at Canker. 'Your . . .?'

'Aye, at last!' The dog-Lord was triumphant. 'I called

her down with my moon music, and goddess that she is
– of her own free will – she came through hell itself, to
be by my side in Mangemanse!'

PART FIVE

Discovering Harry

I

Harry's Room Revisited

Nathan Keogh was far from innumerate, not any longer, but he was illiterate. The Szgany of Sunside had been good at making signs, but not at writing. Indeed they had no writing as such. Which was why he frowned at the menu which Ben Trask had handed him just a moment ago and shook his head apologetically. 'I'll have . . . whatever you're having,' he told his mentor-in-chief, simply. Yet the look which he gave the older man was anything but simple. If anything it was an accusation, but not in connection with ordering lunch in an Indian restaurant in London.

Trask hadn't intended to embarrass his protégé. 'Ah! I'm sorry.' He held up his hands a moment, then let them fall despondently. And smiling wryly he said, 'I wasn't thinking.'

'Yes, you were,' the other nodded. 'You were thinking how strange I am: untutored, often gauche — by your standards, at least — and rather primitive. Yet at the same time a potential superman, a fantastic weapon. And that's how you'd like to use me, as Tzonov would have used me before you: as a weapon!'

'But I wasn't —' Trask the human lie-detector started to deny it — and stopped. Looking into Nathan's eyes, even without looking into them, he knew that the other spoke the truth. He *had* been thinking it, if only for a moment. But not quite the way Nathan had believed. 'Not like Tzonov would have used you, no,' he said.

'Oh?'

'If you were going to read my mind anyway, you might have at least followed through,' Trask told him. 'It's like reading the first pages of a book, or a chapter out of the middle: you didn't get the whole story.'

'And what is the whole story?'

'You *would* make a fantastic weapon, yes,' Trask nodded. 'I was thinking that. And I would "use you", if that's the way you choose to see it. Not for myself, Nathan, but to save an entire world, or both of our worlds if it should come to that.' He sat back in his chair. 'Very well, you want to read my mind. I have no problem with that. Go right ahead, and welcome to it. See if I'm telling you the truth.' Trask's hypnotic implant was still in place, but he wasn't using it. He hadn't used it since Perchorsk five days ago.

Nathan looked into Trask's eyes a moment and felt tempted to scan his mind again, however briefly. Then his face coloured up and he looked away. Trask thought he knew what the red flush signified: shame. The espers didn't spy on each other and Nathan knew it. But he also knew that Trask had told him the truth, and that in any case the way Trask would or would not use him had nothing to do with his problem.

Nathan's problem was not that he didn't trust Trask or his team of mindspies – he'd checked them all out and knew that he could, with his life – but simply that things weren't moving fast enough for him. It was his mounting frustration. The novelty had worn off and in just a few days he was heartily sick of what seemed to him an entirely sick world. All he wanted now – and *right* now – was to get back to Sunside. But Trask had told him it just couldn't be.

Trask knew there was a problem, too. Nathan hadn't spoken about it as yet, but it was there. Trask could play a guessing game with him, he supposed, and when he hit the right question read the truth of Nathan's answer in his expression, but that wasn't Trask's way. Anyway, he believed he already knew what Nathan's trouble was. 'You're homesick,' he said. 'And you're taking it out on your friends.'

Trask had used a new word but its meaning was perfectly obvious. 'Oh?' Nathan answered. 'And wouldn't you be ... what, homesick? In a strange world, dressed in strange clothes, eating strange food and putting your trust – your entire life – in the hands of strangers? A world you always thought of as a sort of hell, and the more you get to know about it, the more likely it seems you were right! A world where you own nothing except what's been given to you, where you don't know anything except what you're told, and where you can't go anywhere unless you're taken. This world of yours has so many wonders ... and so many horrors! Why, you people don't even understand its ailments yourselves! It astonishes me that madness isn't rife, and I've only seen a small part of it. Homesick? Yes, I am. I have a wife on Sunside ... maybe. But Sunside is a whole world away, and I don't even know if she lived through the attack. By now, she could be in thrall to some vampire Lord in Starside.' But he didn't say that the Lord would probably be his own brother, a vampire in his own right.

'Homesick for a vampire world,' Trask said, trying hard to understand. Oh, he understood the loneliness, but not the rest of it. Instead of feeling ... well, alone, yes, but safe, like a refugee, Nathan felt like an outcast. And despite the living nightmares which dwelled in Starside and called themselves Wamphyri, still he wanted to go home.

'I can't help reading you,' Nathan said, looking directly into Trask's eyes. 'Not when you're coming across so clear. Yes I *still* want to go home! Homesick? I suppose so, but that's not all it is. I'm not sure what it is, except that somehow I might have the answer. I think it's in me: the answer to all of this, the final destruction of the Wamphyri. A weapon? Yes, possibly, but in order to destroy the enemy you have to take your weapons to him. You can't hide from him in alien worlds.'

That had been pretty eloquent, Trask thought, from someone who just one short week ago didn't understand a word of English. He tried to think of something to say that wouldn't sound trite and was saved by the approach of a small, waddling, gap-toothed waiter. 'Are you ready to order, sir?'

'Onion bhaji starters for two,' Trask told him. 'And a main course of chicken biriani. Also for two. Oh, and two beers.'

They were in a place just off Oxford Street. It was a down-to-earth place, hardly *haute cuisine*, but Trask didn't eat high class, not if he could avoid it. It just wasn't his thing: collages in brightly coloured soup, raw vegetables and half-cooked fish didn't turn him on. And he didn't think Nathan would respond to it either.

'But you're doing so well,' he said. 'You've been with us, what, four days? Just four days,' he nodded, 'and already you fit right in. And you're learning, Nathan. We're teaching you all we can . . .'

'. . . And learning from me?' Nathan was disarmingly frank.

Trask nodded. 'Yes, of course we are. How you feel about Sunside is how we feel about our world. And narrowing it down a little, it's how we feel about our different cultures, east and west. Just as you have enemies in Starside, so we have potential enemies in the east. You know one of them, Nathan, and you discovered his intentions: to infiltrate your world as an aggressor. But if he succeeds . . . your world is only the first. Next comes our world, which he'll overthrow using whatever resources he wins in Sunside/Starside. So you see it's as simple as that. We need to know about your world in order to counter his aggression, if it should ever come to that.'

Nathan nodded. 'I think I understand all of that. But now you have to understand. One of the first things they showed me in your headquarters was film of your history. It was very . . . *condensed*? Yes, but it was very – *graphic?* – too. And I keep thinking about it. Your wars have been devastating! And one of the worst things about them is that you don't just fight them on your own and your enemy's territory but on – *neutral?* – ground too. And you leave the scars of your battles behind. As your weapons got better, the scars they left got bigger. Don't forget, Ben, that I've seen the result of one of your weapons used on Starside. It was bad enough there, but if it had been Sunside . . .' He shook his head.

'Not one of ours,' Trask told him. 'Theirs.'

'Does it really matter?'

Trask thought about it a moment. But there was only one truth and he knew it. 'If Tzonov investigates, invades, tries to plunder your world, we'll do our damnedest to stop him. Oh, we'll try to stop him here first, thwart his plans as best we can. But if we can't . . . he's not the only one with a gateway into Sunside/ Starside.'

Nathan's face was suddenly very pale, sad. 'So, despite all my arguments and everything you told me – that you only wanted to help me – still you will take your weapons, and men who can use them, an army however small, into Sunside?'

'Against Tzonov – if it's necessary that we go against him – yes.' Trask wasn't going to lie; even if he did Nathan would know it sooner or later, and he wouldn't forgive him for it.

'Then you are as mad as he is!'

'Not mad, dedicated.'

'And is Tzonov dedicated, too?'

'But to himself,' Trask nodded. 'To his own ideals. While our dedication is to freedom.'

'Your freedom. Not the freedom of the Travellers.'

'The freedom of all men, Nathan. If this thing starts, and when it's all over, your world can still be yours. But without your help it might not be. You might lose it to Turkur Tzonov and others just like him.'

'Possibly.' Nathan looked doubtful, worried. 'But on the other hand I see a very different . . . what, *scenario*? And I wonder: have you even considered that Sunside/Starside might end up *belonging* to the Wamphyri in its entirety?' Just for a moment, the expression on Nathan's face was so like his father's had used to be – innocent, bemused, and lonely, yet paradoxically cold, knowing, enigmatic – that Trask actually saw Harry Keogh sitting there. But only for a moment, for in the next his laughter was forced, harsh, even sardonic. Until he was through and quietly said:

'I tell you one more time: you, your people, Turkur Tzonov – *anyone* of this world who would venture into mine knowing so little about it – you are all mad! The Wamphyri will eat you. I mean they will simply – literally? – *eat* you!' He was still trying out new words. 'Yes, literally. And very definitely . . .'

Again he reminded Trask of his father; his conviction was that concentrated, his warning that clear. Harry

Keogh, yes, as Keenan Gormley had first known him, before the Necroscope developed his powers to their full. But Trask must be slipping: here Nathan had presented him with yet another opportunity to learn more about the Wamphyri, and he'd almost let it go.

'You've seen film of our weapons of war, which make Lardis Lidesci's shotguns look like toys, and yet you still think the Wamphyri can triumph?'

Outside the plate-glass window a tourist bus passed slowly in heavy midday traffic. 'Do you see that ... vehicle?' Nathan indicated the bus. 'In Turgosheim I saw one of Vormulac's aerial warriors – a creature freshly waxed in his vats, twice the size of that vehicle, armoured like one of your tanks and weaponed tip-to-tail – go crashing into the gorge. It was a training flight and the warrior had ... design faults? But when this monster hit the bottom, the force of the crash was such that it tore chunks of stone out of the turrets of a lesser manse. And even the chunks were as big as that vehicle!'

Trask shrugged, but not carelessly. 'You've seen our tanks, then. And their firepower? Now tell me: do you really think a warrior creature could stand up to a machine such as that?'

'No.' Nathan shook his head. 'Not even the most ferocious of them, for even they are only flesh and blood. I don't think so and I didn't say so. But now you tell me something: if you can't get me through this Romanian Gate, how can you possibly hope to get a tank through?'

Trask grinned, but again without malice, and said: 'You haven't seen all of our films, then. Nathan, we've got tank-killing weapons that can be fired by single soldiers as easily as you fire a crossbow! One good shot can take out an entire tank. And as for a warrior:

they'd just blow it in half! And these are weapons which we *can* take through!'

'But not me?'

'Not yet.'

'Why not?'

Trask sighed. 'I thought I'd explained something of that in Perchorsk, and again on your first day at E-Branch HQ. We haven't even *seen* the Romanian Gate yet, Nathan! Oh, we know it's there . . . your father used it once, to enter into Starside. But so far he's the only human being who ever did.'

'You did explain it to me, yes,' Nathan answered. 'Maybe I wasn't paying too much attention. There was a lot going on. Please tell me again.'

Their food arrived. While Trask talked, Nathan tried his starter course, found it delicious, ate with gusto. His beer was also good but he sipped cautiously; Trask had warned him of its potency; Nathan wanted to keep a clear head.

'The Gate is up an underground river which empties into the Danube,' Trask began. 'Shortly after your father discovered it, Romania overthrew its government and opened its borders. Communism was on the point of collapse. Conditions in that country were dreadful! Many of the people lived like animals, all as a result of political corruption . . .' He paused. 'Are you getting all of this?'

'Yes,' Nathan nodded. 'I hope you don't mind, but –'

'– You're matching my thoughts to my words?'

'If it's permitted.'

'It is. I don't have anything to hide.'

'Then go on.'

Trask went on:

'The Western World was asked to help. Not only in Romania but in all of the old USSR's satellite countries.

The West had the power, the knowhow, the wealth which our democratic systems had created, while the USSR and friends were bankrupt not only of ideologies but also of hard cash. That is to say, they were incapable of further expansion or interference in the affairs of lesser states; they were no longer a threat; they had nothing with which to bargain. They could only beg.

'If the boot had been on the other foot, doubtless they'd have rolled over us. But it's as I've been telling you: here in the West we believe in the freedom of all men. So we helped them out, and we've been doing so ever since.

'The children of Romania had suffered especially badly. So ... we built a Refuge for them; I mean *we*, E-Branch, with our government's blessing of course. And we built it over the mouth of the Romanian tributary, using the force of the resurgent water to drive our turbines. It was a place of safety, a hospital, a school — and a trap, a filter, a dragnet!

'The water coming out of that underground river was all channelled through a screening system which would isolate any ... solids. It was our way of ensuring that we weren't going to have any more "visitors" from your world, Nathan. For you see, that Romanian river had been the source of vampirism in this world for as long as men can remember. But from now on, nothing bigger than a small fish would ever get out into the Danube.

'So what we had was this: two Gates, one under the Urals in Perchorsk, and one buried deep underground in Romania. You know about Perchorsk through personal experience, and now you know about the other Gate. The Russians looked after the one, kept it secure, took precautions against any Wamphyri contamination which might come out of Starside. And we looked after the place in Romania. The only difference was this: that they had access to their Gate, while ours was beyond our reach.

'So how did Harry Keogh, your father, reach it? Well —'

'— This much I know,' Nathan cut him off. And now he did the talking while Trask ate. 'It was in Tzonov's mind in Perchorsk. Something my father could do, which Tzonov feared. And he wondered if I had it, too. Also, it has been in the mind of almost all of your mentalists, your espers. Including you, Ben. Something called the Möbius Continuum. My father used it as a means of . . . of going to places.'

Trask paused with a forkful of food half-way to his mouth, and said, 'He could use it to go almost anywhere in this universe! Certainly in this world. But Sunside/ Starside is another universe expanding parallel to this one, and Harry didn't know how to use the Möbius Continuum to bridge the gap. Möbius himself didn't know that. Only one man did: your brother, called The Dweller in your world. Harry Keogh told us that much when finally he returned to us. But about The Dweller himself . . . we really don't know very much — except that in the end both he and Harry were Wamphyri. And maybe The Dweller still is.'

Yes, Nathan thought, and now I have another brother who is also Wamphyri, but the thought was entirely his own. While out loud:

'No.' He shook his head. 'The Dweller is no more. And my father's dead, too. I remember Lardis talking about it. It was a weapon out of Perchorsk that killed them: "a breath of hell"! It also killed off the rest of the old Wamphyri, as they were at that time. But the new Wamphyri . . . they are different.'

'How, different?'

'They're clever.' Nathan thought of Maglore of Runemanse, and automatically touched the golden sigil in his ear. 'They're more devious, more devilish! They pretend civilization, *sophistication*? But that only makes them worse.'

'I know what you mean,' Trask nodded. 'In this world, some years ago, we had a man called Hitler. He was civilized, "sophisticated", too — as were his ideologies, his machines of destruction, and the genocide which he would have turned loose on the majority of the human race!'

'What happened to him?'

'We killed him, and his army. But his ideas ... are taking a little longer. We are winning, though. In this world, anyway. And we can win in yours, too.'

'Not if you can't reach it.'

'Give us a chance. Now that we know Turkur Tzonov's plans, or believe we do, we're working on it. We're working hard.'

'Doing what?'

'Before we built the Refuge, and while we were building it, we tried to get up the river. Harry had done it in stages, making what he called "Möbius jumps" from point to point. Also, he had help from a dead friend or two, Romanian potholers who had tried it before him and failed. So, we brought in some experts of our own and equipped them with the best possible gear.'

'Potholers?'

Trask explained, and finished: 'Oh, yes. There are people in this world who explore caves for pleasure! As for the people we used ... it was strictly business.'

Nathan gave a grunt. 'Huh! In Sunside they do it to hide — and to live!'

'Our people tried to reach the Gate much as your father had done,' Trask continued, 'by moving up the underground river in stages. Except they were handicapped; they didn't have Harry's special talents, deadspeak and the Möbius Continuum; they only had aqualungs, powerful lights, prop-driven towing torps . . .'

Again he must pause to explain. For while Nathan had read the pictures in his mind, still the technology was way beyond him.

'Since then,' Trask went on, 'there have been a good many developments. The design of exploratory equipment has improved. But up until now we felt we no longer needed it. After the Refuge had been built we felt safer – the whole world was safer! Nothing was going to come out of that subterranean river without us knowing about it and how to deal with it. Anything that got itself caught up in the sumps under the Refuge was either harmless or . . . or it was dead. Or soon would be. Our systems are at least as good as those in Perchorsk, if not better . . .

'So the Russians had their Gate closed off and we were in control in Romania. We no longer had any requirement to reach the Gate itself; everything would be fine as long as we, and the Opposition, were able to guarantee that nothing was going to – escape? – into our world and society . . .'

'Except now something has escaped,' Nathan nodded. 'Me!'

'You are not what I meant.'

'I know. So what's next?'

'I promised you we'd help you, and we will. But . . . what's it been? Four days?' Trask shrugged, however ruefully. 'Well, I'm afraid you're going to have to put up with your frustrations a little longer than that, Nathan. Maybe for as long as four months!'

'Four months?' Nathan made a conversion. 'Sixteen sunups? But if your equipment is that much better now, why delay it?'

Again Trask's shrug. 'It's a combination of knowhow and opportunity. That river is subject to flash floods. Even without them it's a tricky enough proposition, else we'd have been in there long ago. But any sudden increase in the pressure or the depth of the water ... would spell disaster! Four months from now it will be spring going on summer –'

And again he had to pause to explain the seasons.

'– And our weather forecasting will be that much more reliable. As soon as we know it isn't going to rain, we'll send a team up. Then, depending on their report ...'

'... You'll send me?'

'That's a promise. Meanwhile, we learn a little from you, and you learn a lot from us.'

'Four months,' Nathan said again, his voice very small. 'And all that time I won't know what's going on back home. I won't know what's happening. To Lardis, the Travellers, Misha – won't even know if she survived.'

Trask felt helpless. He shrugged again, sighed and said, 'Son, I don't like saying this, but you'd better get used to the idea: it will take as long as it takes. And I repeat, in between times you give us a little help, and we'll give you a lot. It has to be the easiest route. The other way means sullen silence, solitude and sheer boredom – for you. Oh, we'll still get you back to your own place eventually, if that's at all possible, but you'll miss out on a lot of good friends you could have made along the way.'

Nathan had finished with his food. Looking thoughtful, he sat back and toyed with a small jade green clasp, turning it in his fingers. It caught Trask's eye. 'I've seen you playing with that before. A keepsake out of Sunside?'

Nathan shook his head. 'No, out of Perchorsk.' For a moment he looked wistful. 'It belonged to Siggi.'

His words hit Trask like a slap in the face, but he kept it hidden. This was something new, the first time Nathan had mentioned Siggi's name to anyone. 'Siggi Dam, did you say?' Trask was alert now. He reached out and was handed the clasp. And as he examined it he asked, 'Er, *why* did she give it to you?'

Nathan glanced away, shrugged. 'A keepsake, as you said.'

'And does David Chung know about this ... keepsake?'

Nathan looked puzzled. 'Why should he?'

Trask nodded and smiled, however tightly. 'Well, he should, that's all ...' He gave the trinket back, and finished the rest of his meal in silence. It could all be perfectly innocent, of course, but on the other hand Chung wasn't the only locator in the world. And as long as Nathan persisted in carrying that clasp around with him ...

... Did Turkur Tzonov know where Nathan was — his *exact* location — even now? But if that was the case, why hadn't he picked him up west of the Urals? Trask let it go for now and finished his meal ...

They had talked pretty much in circles and Trask couldn't be sure if anything had been resolved. But he hoped so. Finally he pushed his plate away and watched Nathan drain the dregs of his beer. Then he said: 'You were telling me about the new Wamphyri, out of Turgosheim?'

Nathan looked at him. 'Turgosheim lies in the east, beyond the Great Red Waste. They live there now, but very soon they'll move west; and there are a great many of them. The Lady Wratha and the others who have already fled west, they're only a handful ...' Then, pausing to reflect upon his own words, he gave a rueful snort. 'Only a handful, yes, but they've devastated Sunside! Only Lardis Lidesci has the measure of them, but for how long? I suppose he knows they'll get him in the end, and he'll pay for his defiance and the damage he's caused them in hell!'

Trask was eager for all of this. He knew that the men who were debriefing Nathan probably had it on tape, but he hadn't had time to listen to it in detail. And anyway it came better from Nathan himself. 'Wratha and these others: they've established themselves in the territories of the Old Wamphyri? But I thought that Harry Keogh and The Dweller had destroyed all of the old aeries?'

Nathan nodded. 'Destroyed them, yes. All except one. And that's where they live: in the last aerie of the Old Wamphyri, called Karenstack upon a time.'

Trask snapped his fingers. 'Ah, yes! I remember! Harry let that one stand, because in the last battle Karen sided with him and The Dweller and his people.'

Nathan shrugged tiredly. 'The last battle? Not quite; there have been others since, and there will be more. But I know what you mean. Anyway, you'd know more about that than I do, for it was before I was born.'

Trask knew even more than Nathan thought he did. Looking back on it, he remembered Harry's debriefing:

The Dweller had let Karenstack alone for his own reasons, but his father the Necroscope had a different reason entirely. The Lady Karen was Wamphyri, as was The Dweller. If Harry could find a cure for her, he might eventually free his son from the curse of vampirism. He'd tried it; it didn't work; Karen died. And The Dweller had known what Harry had done. Then, because he feared that his father might try a similar 'cure' on him, he took away his metaphysical powers and

577

returned him to his own world. And that had been the beginning of the end for Harry Keogh.

Nathan read all of this in his mind. 'The Dweller was that powerful?'

Standing up to take out his wallet, Trask answered, 'Yes, he was. He knew stuff his father couldn't even begin to understand. How to get from here to Sunside/ Starside, for example, without using a Gate.' He paid for their meal.

'A powerful . . . weapon?' They headed for the exit.

'I won't lie to you,' Trask answered. 'You, too, are a son of Harry Keogh. It's possible you have the same kind of potential. We had hoped to give you the clues to open it up. We still have hopes that you'll join us, see this thing through with us against Tzonov, maybe even stay with us and help us to build a better world here. I mean, when all of this is over.'

'Misha is in Sunside. And that's where I belong, too.'

Passing out into the noisy street, Trask's look was intent, urgent as he turned to Nathan and said: 'Then make Sunside *safe* for her, for yourself, for all of the Szgany! And at the same time make this world safe, too.' Then, seeing the other's reticence, his uncertainty, he turned away and hailed a taxi. Now he must leave it to Nathan to make up his own mind.

But in the taxi on the way back to E-Branch HQ, Nathan told him: 'Very well, Ben, I'll give it a try. Turn me into a weapon if you can. But I'll warn you now: there will have to be a very good reason before I'll let you use me against ordinary people. Against the Wamphyri, that is something else. But not against ordinary people.'

Trask sighed his relief, nodded and answered: 'Judge us as you find us, Nathan. And if we don't measure up, you can always wave us farewell as you enter the Gate.

But I think you'll discover that ours is a worthy cause. In the long ago, Sir Keenan Gormley had just as much trouble recruiting your father. But it was worth it in the end.'

Nathan looked at him. 'To you, maybe. But what about Harry? Was it worth it to him?'

Trask remembered the Necroscope as he had last seen him and couldn't repress a shudder, however slight. But the fact of it was, he knew that Harry wouldn't have had it any other way. And so he answered: 'I think it was, yes. Anyway, that's the way it was and no one can change it now.'

'Fate?' Nathan was quiet, thoughtful. 'Destiny?'

'Something like that. Your father had a saying: "What will be, has been". And we have another: "Like father, like son".'

Nathan thought about that last, thought about himself and about Nestor, and said nothing. There was nothing to say, for Trask's maxim held true on both counts . . .

Back at HQ Trask had a word with David Chung, and Chung broke into Nathan's session with a maths instructor to ask him about Siggi Dam's clasp. The session came to a halt as Chung examined the clasp and felt for its aura. Strange, because there wasn't one. He asked Nathan if he could borrow the trinket; he would return it undamaged, of course; it could be that the clasp was a sort of locating device and dangerous as such.

Mystified, Nathan let him take it and returned to his basic maths lesson. Ten minutes later Chung burst into Trask's office without knocking, to tell him: 'Ben, this is weird!' He tossed the clasp onto Trask's desk. 'You were right to put me onto it. First, this piece is entirely free of psychic probes; it's not being used to locate

Nathan. Next: I tried using it to locate Siggi Dam. Now, I know she's good and has this psychic mind-smog. But with a locator mind-smog works two ways. If I wasn't able to find her, still I'd find the smog! Except I can't. She isn't there.'

'What?' Trask had been busy with paperwork and his mind was only just beginning to focus on what Chung was saying. 'She isn't where?'

'But that's what I'm trying to tell you.' Chung threw his arms wide. 'She isn't anywhere! It's as if . . . it's like Jazz Simmons all over again. I mean, Siggi Dam is one of two things: either dead or disappeared. And . . . you know what I'm thinking? Ben, this thing feels just like Jazz, and like Harry. That kind of disappeared!'

'What!?' Now Trask was all of a hundred per cent with him. 'Disappeared into the Perchorsk Gate? Is that what you're saying?' He got to his feet, came round the desk.

Chung picked up the clasp. 'That's how it feels, yes. Not that she's dead — though she could be; I haven't enough experience of her to be sure — but rather that she's . . . gone!'

Trask found himself wondering about Nathan and Siggi, about what else had passed between them other than her clasp.

And remembering what he knew about Turkur Tzonov's psychological profile, he couldn't help but wonder how the telepath would repay that sort of treachery.

Taking Chung's arm, he said: 'David, not a word of this to Nathan — not yet — but it could be our ace card. We have to be careful how we play it, that's all.'

They were still like that, facing each other — wondering what had happened, what was happening even now, in Perchorsk — when suddenly a babble of excited voices reached them from the corridor. The door stood ajar just as Chung had left it. Trask threw it open and both men looked out.

Half-way down the corridor, Ian Goodly and a group of espers had gathered in a huddle. They were crowded round a door to one of the rooms, looking in. Others were running to join them. Trask glanced at Chung, and queried: 'Harry's room? I had the name-plate taken down. When Nathan starts reading ... it might have proved a distraction.'

But as Trask and Chung started down the corridor, the espers at the door of Harry's room backed off, then seemed almost thrown back by some force from within. And in the next moment the corridor was filled with a white light that flooded out of the room.

The precog Goodly came reeling, rubbing at his eyes as the light faded to a hazy white glow. Trask grabbed him by the arm, said: 'Ian, what the hell ...?' But Goodly was still too staggered to answer.

Next down the corridor was Nathan's maths teacher. Not an esper or member of E-Branch, he'd been vetted and sworn to the Official Secrets Act before they had let him in. A small man of about thirty, thirty-five, with receding mousy hair and wearing heavy, thick-lensed spectacles, he was white-faced and panting. Trask grabbed him and said, 'What is it?'

'After the Chinese gentleman interrupted the lesson,' the man began to answer, 'we couldn't settle down again. I ... I went to get coffee, and Nathan took the opportunity to stretch his legs. He said there was something he wanted to see in one of the rooms.'

Trask went to brush past him but Ian Goodly, back in control of himself, got in his way. 'Ben, there was no warning,' he gasped. 'Suddenly, I knew something was going to happen, and where it would happen. I was in

581

my office but headed straight for Harry's room. That's Nathan in there at the computer console.'

The soft white light had vanished now. Trask and Chung ran down the corridor, avoiding espers where they stumbled about or leaned against the walls rubbing at their eyes. But as the two men reached Harry's room, they skidded to a halt and cautiously looked in. Beyond the open door, Nathan was seated at the computer. Whey-faced, open-mouthed, he looked up, saw them, indicated that they should enter. But Trask and Chung were looking beyond him, at the computer screen itself. And they both knew that they'd seen this before.

The screen was unnaturally brilliant; it was the source of the soft white glow, which still surrounded the entire console. But the pastel-coloured moving pictures on the screen were brilliant, too: sharp-imaged computer graphics, which told a story out of the past.

Trask and Chung said nothing; stunned, they merely watched . . . and remembered.

Remembered a squally February night some sixteen years ago, when every available esper had felt the 'call' to E-Branch HQ, and had gathered here to witness the death of the Necroscope Harry Keogh, taking place in another world, another time, even another dimension. It had happened in the Ops room, and now it was duplicated on the screen in these jerky, angular but accurate computer graphics:

A figure, human, male, in the shape of a cross, tumbling slowly, end over end, down a tunnel of thin neon bars or ribbons of blue, green, and red light; motion simulated by breaks in the ribbons – as if each streamer were a series of dashes expanding towards the viewer, like multi-coloured ack-ack fire closing on an airplane – and each dash blinking out of existence as it 'touched' the surface of the screen from within, giving the impression of falling.

The figure *was* falling, tumbling in space and time towards some indeterminate destiny ... or origin? That last was Trask's thought, though where it had come from he couldn't say. Perhaps it was his talent, defining the 'truth' of what he witnessed.

The cadaverous Goodly had joined them in Harry's room; he stood between and behind Trask and Chung, touching their arms. And: '*Now!*' he husked.

The falling, rotating figure grew smaller, 'receding' as the coloured threads hit the screen that much faster. It became a mote, a speck, finally disappeared. But where it had been:

... A bright yellow bomb-burst! A sunburst of golden light, expanding silently, hugely, awesomely! And not only inwards but outwards, too, as if to break free of the very computer screen! An amazing three-dimensional effect, so that the four observers – Nathan, Trask, Chung and Goodly – gasped and felt the urge to duck, turn their faces away. But they didn't, because they were fascinated and must know.

And it was exactly the same as before, and yet more than before:

Those myriad golden splinters speeding outwards from the sunburst, angling this way and that, sentient, seeking, disappearing into as many unknown places. Those – pieces – of the Necroscope Harry Keogh? All that remained of him ... or of his metaphysical mind? And what of the dart which had escaped into this world? Into our world?

The screen held the answer.

Suddenly it wiped itself clean, and in the next moment a new scene leapt vividly into view: of a building – or the top floor of one – shown in plan, with rooms and laboratories all clearly delineated. A very familiar layout, and so it should be. Trask and his two most senior agents recognized it at once:

The plan shown on the screen was E-Branch HQ!

And there was the golden dart: materializing in the Ops room, lancing out into the corridor, speeding in a series of rapidly mobile stops and starts, as if searching, until finally it paused in front of a certain room.

And that certain room was this one. Harry's room!

The golden dart passed inside, became motionless, shrank to a point of light and blinked out. And even as Trask and the others watched, the screen cleared itself off and immediately filled up again — with numbers!

In the astonished silence Nathan's gasp was clearly audible as he leaned forward in his swivel chair, until his face was only fifteen inches away from the screen. Where the other observers were concerned, this largely obscured the view. But they saw enough to know that this wasn't their scene. And so did Nathan's maths instructor who had joined them from the corridor.

'Now what on *earth* . . . ?' The others heard his gasped query but didn't look up. And for ten, twenty seconds the mathematical symbols and figures flowed and swirled in a hypnotic, sentient-seeming manner, forming rapidly mutating calculi apparently at random on the screen. Then, abruptly, they dispersed and left the screen blank. And the computer switched itself off . . .

Trask picked up a loose electrical lead in numb fingers and looked at it. The set hadn't been plugged in. The others saw the lead in his hand and understood the expression on his face. It must be pretty much like the expression on their own faces.

Chung spoke first. 'And that . . . that splinter, dart, whatever it was, has been waiting here ever since?'

'But for what?' Trask's voice was hoarse.

'For this,' Goodly answered. 'Waiting for Nathan. To pass on its message. Harry's message.'

Trask knew that he was right.

584

Nathan looked up and his face was paler than ever. 'A message? From my father? But . . . what was it?'

No one could answer him. But in Trask's mind it seemed he heard Mrs Wills again, her voice telling him something which her dead husband had told her:

"'Arry's room? Well yer'd best look after it, Meg, me love. I mean, yer never knows when he'll be needin' ter use it again, now does yer . . .?"

II

Nathan's Conversion

The occurrences in Harry's room had been almost sufficient in themselves to finally hook Nathan and tie him in with his new friends. As to his previous reticence: it hadn't been so much that he'd doubted their friendship or even their motives, but mainly that he'd seen himself as being used. Now, however, he was beginning to see how he could use them: their superior knowledge of maths and science in general. For what he'd seen on the computer screen — that final sequence of rapidly mutating formulae — was nothing less than what he'd been seeing in his own mind for as long as he could remember: the seemingly unfathomable numbers vortex as recreated by a machine or some incredibly tenacious revenant of his father.

And if the vortex (the maths controlling this so-called Möbius Continuum?) had been real and worked for Harry Keogh, Necroscope, then given the resources of this computer-geared world in which Nathan was stranded, he might also be able to make it work for him. And not only in this world, but in Sunside, too.

So that now, and as opposed to the selfless motivations of Trask and E-Branch, Nathan's own motives were mainly selfish: since the only way home was to assist his new friends, he would assist them all he could, and in the process attempt to discover his father's greatest secret: the control of the metaphysical Möbius

Continuum. For to know quite definitely that Harry Keogh had been here, worked here, been one of them, was all the spur Nathan had needed. If Trask and his parapsychological organization had been good enough for Harry, then they were good enough for him.

From now on – for the time being, at least – he would play it Trask's way: a game of give and take. Right now it was Nathan's turn to give, and no holding back. But on certain matters ... Nathan had taken vows and there would always be things he could never tell. Or if he did, it wouldn't hurt to obscure the facts a little ...

Since bringing Nathan to London, Trask had cleared most of his more mundane workload; that is, if anything of the Head of E-Branch's work could ever be thought of as 'mundane'. Now he could afford to apply himself more diligently to Nathan's case, and the rest of the day would be spent hearing out the story of his life and adventures on Sunside.

Because Nathan had decided to make Harry's room his own, that was where the session took place. Chung, and Trask, too, had heard something of the story from Nathan himself, or read of it in the first debrief reports, but now they wanted a far more detailed account. Now, too, Nathan was much less reluctant as first he outlined, then filled in a history of the life he'd lived on Sunside, and in Turgosheim's dark and hag-ridden Starside. For in fact it was something he was getting used to: this constant retelling of his story. First to the brown and spindly Thyre, supposed 'nomads' of Sunside's furnace deserts; then to Maglore of the Wamphyri in Rune-manse; and again to Lardis Lidesci during Nathan's brief return and sojourn with his own people.

But this time was different: Nathan had been given sketch pads, pens and coloured felt-tips. And as he talked so he would pause every now and then to draw maps of the regions he named. So that now for the first time, Sunside/Starside was delineated and took on shape and substance here in an alien world.

Zek Föener had been brought in on the session: Zek, Trask, Chung and Goodly, and Nathan of course. Touching oh so gently upon their minds, he knew their excitement and was filled with his own mixed emotions by the knowledge that these people had actually known and worked with his father. Indeed, Zek Föener had been the last person to talk to Harry before he'd left — or been chased — into Starside. Nathan still had to uncover the full story of that, and was spurred by anticipation.

But in fact there were other maps of the vampire world: Zek herself had long ago drawn several crude sketches, mainly as an *aide-memoire*, which she had brought with her out of her Greek island home to give to Trask. But Zek couldn't possibly have known the place as well as Nathan: its rivers, forests and deserts, its lowland swamps and high mountain passes, the Great Red Waste beyond the eastern extremes of the barrier range; and beyond that, sombre and sinister Turgosheim itself. Nathan even mapped a star-chart, showing Sunside/Starside's principal blue glittering ice-chip stars as viewed overhead from Settlement in the middle hours of the long Sunside night. As for Szgany townships: in Zek's time there had been no towns. Just the Travellers themselves, ever on the run from the Old Wamphyri under Shaithis and the rest of the vampire Lords.

So in the course of telling his story, Nathan drew his maps — which matched up, however loosely, with Zek's — until under the fascinated gaze of Trask and his colleagues, Sunside/Starside became real as never before. And its people began to live and breathe as Nestor's life was recorded and his world revealed its secrets . . . Or some of them.

The story was much as he'd told it to Maglore that time in Turgosheim, when the mage and mentalist had taken him into his manse unchanged, unvampirized, a man among monsters. Except this time it included his stay in Runemanse, and his escape on the back of Karz Biteri, a man changed by Maglore's metamorphism to a leathery-skinned flyer, but still a man for all that. He told it all: of his flight back into Sunside, how Karz had left him there in the foothills and flown off into the sun on his own, to end his misery; how Lardis Lidesci's watchmen had seen Nathan land, recognized him and took him to their leader, and how Lardis had reunited him with his mother, Nana Kiklu, and the sweetheart of his childhood dreams, Misha Zanesti.

Finally, he told of a Lord of the Wamphyri and his lieutenant, who came in the first hours of darkness to snatch him from his rediscovered love and dispose of him in the white-glaring maw of the hell-lands Gate on Starside. Of the rest: well, they already knew that. His imprisonment in Perchorsk, his escape, their own part in the story.

As for the things he didn't tell or at best obscured:

He told of his travels with the Thyre from west to east across the furnace deserts, but left out their intelligence, their telepathy, their subterranean society and civilization. For these were things which he'd sworn never to reveal to any man. He told of Maglore and Runemanse but made no mention of the seer-Lord's beautiful human thrall, Orlea. His time with Orlea was for him alone. He spoke of Settlement, but left out details of Sanctuary Rock; for the rock was the last refuge of the Szgany Lidesci. And with regard to his escape from Perchorsk: during an 'interrogation' by Siggi Dam, he had 'stolen' her key to his cell. It was as simple as that. But of the four who heard his story to the end, two at least knew that this last was a lie, albeit a white one.

Just looking at Ben Trask, it was easy to forget — as Nathan had forgotten — his talent: the fact that you couldn't lie to him, for Trask would know it at once. And as for Zek Föener: the fact that Nathan had conjured his own esoteric form of mind-smog, the numbers vortex, to obscure those several vague areas in his story, had been evidence enough of his deception. But as for the *degree* of that deception . . . Zek was as wise as she was beautiful; she knew that there are things we would all conceal, not necessarily out of shame but also trust. And so she, too, trusted.

Then there were the maps. Nathan had been as accurate as knowledge and memory allowed with regard to the barrier mountains, the great pass, fertile margins, swamps, burning deserts, Starside, the hell-lands Gate, the fallen Wamphyri stacks and Karenstack itself, which was the name of the last aerie as he had always known it; but again he'd omitted the places of the Thyre, the location of Sanctuary Rock, and several major Traveller trails through the deep woods. If the time should ever come when men of E-Branch or in the Branch's employ passed through into his world, and if they should ever fall into the hands of the Wamphyri . . . Nathan would not want *Them* to know these things.

Finally he was done, by his reckoning, but in Trask's eyes he hadn't told enough. And despite that it was late in the day, Trask pressed him: 'Nathan, about your escape from Perchorsk. And about . . . Siggi Dam.'

'Yes?' And he couldn't keep the colour from creeping into his pale face.

But Trask found that he couldn't ask his question, and so covered by saying: 'We ... think she's in trouble?'

Nathan had been looking tired, but came awake in a moment. 'Siggi? In trouble?'

Chung quickly explained, and Nathan answered:

'This Michael Simmons, Jazz? He must be the hell-lander – I'm sorry, I mean the agent – that Lardis always talked about. Michael "Jazz" Simmons.' He paused to look at Zek Föener, whose sad eyes were full of memories, until she glanced away. 'Lardis was fond of Jazz. Why, he even named his son after him: Jason Lidesci! I would have liked to have met him. And now you tell me you think that Siggi ... ?'

'It's the same thing exactly,' Chung told him, quietly. 'We have Siggi's clasp, but ... she isn't on the other end of it.'

'One of two things,' Trask spoke up. 'Siggi could be dead, or she's gone through the Perchorsk Gate.'

Nathan shook his head. 'The Gate? Not after what I told her about the other side! What woman would willingly ... go ...' He let his question taper off unspoken.

'We, er –' Trask stumbled over his words, then let them go in a rush. '– We don't think she went willingly, Nathan.'

Their guest looked from face to face, frowning, his flush gradually receding as Trask's meaning got through to him. 'You mean, Turkur Tzonov might have sent her through? As some kind of punishment?'

Trask looked right into his eyes. 'Possibly. It all depends on what he was punishing her for.'

'Ben's right,' Zek cut in. 'Nathan, the Wamphyri aren't the only ones who punish people. It was a different man who sent me through that time, but he was just as

591

bad as Tzonov. I suppose I was lucky: the Lady Karen found me, and she seemed to like me in much the same way as this Maglore liked you.'

At the mention of Maglore's name, Nathan touched the golden sigil in his left ear. Just a touch as he brushed his hair back into place. David Chung noticed the instinctive reaction but it made no impression on him; Nathan hadn't told them that Maglore had given him the earring. Not that he'd been hiding the fact, but to him it had seemed unimportant.

But the earring was one thing and Siggi Dam's clasp – and her inexplicable absence, which it had revealed – was another. Perhaps it was time Nathan told the whole truth about his brief relationship with Siggi. He made to do so, opened his mouth to speak ... but Zek was here. Nathan looked at her and it was her turn to blush. Except she blushed for him, for she had her own suspicions. Being Zek, however, she offered Nathan an out:

'Tzonov and others like him will use any method to obtain information, make people tell them what they want to know. Torture isn't the only way. Don't feel that you can't talk on my account, Nathan. But if you'd like me to leave ...' She made to stand up.

Nathan reached out quickly and took her hand, drawing her down again. 'It wasn't like that.' He shook his head. 'Or maybe it was, but it didn't work out that way.'

Ian Goodly saw it coming and said, 'Nathan, you don't have to tell us anything about that. Well, just one thing. Did you actually steal the key to your cell, or did she give it to you? If she gave it to you, then we can probably reckon that Tzonov has sent her through the Gate.'

Nathan nodded, lowered his head. 'She gave it to me.

Tzonov found us together; he struck me and dragged her out of there; I found the key after she had gone. Also her clasp. But the key wasn't a mistake. She hadn't lost it. I'm sure that she left it for me ...' He looked up and his eyes were harder now, likewise the edge to his voice. 'You people − E-Branch on the one hand, Tzonov and his people on the other − are like two rival Szgany tribes. But you are all people, human. Or I thought you were. What he has done, if he has done it ...'

Trask said, 'It changes things, doesn't it?'

Nathan nodded. 'If it's true, yes. Finally I will know − I mean, I'll be *sure* − that I'm in the right camp, on the right side.'

Trask nodded. 'Well, you are. But we still might have some difficulty proving it. On the other hand, there just *might* be a way to discover what's happened to Siggi. If that's the proof you need − and if you're the man I think you are − then it's all up to you.'

Nathan looked at him, 'Up to me? To find out what happened to Siggi?'

Trask nodded. 'The last time we had this problem, with Jazz Simmons, we asked your father to help us out. He had the necessary ... skills? He was the Necroscope. But in everything that you've told us so far, there's an all-important thing which you haven't mentioned. Nathan, when you spoke to me telepathically in my sleep, in Perchorsk, I got the impression that you knew what Harry Keogh could do, where all of his powers sprang from. But there's only one way you could know, and that's if you can do it too. Do you know what I'm talking about?'

Again their eyes met, and after a long pause Nathan nodded. 'Yes. And I can do it. I can talk to the Great Majority, to the teeming dead in their graves. Rather, I *could* do it ... if only they would talk back to me. But they won't. Not in my world, anyway.'

Seated around him, the others sighed in unison. And Zek said: 'I knew it! Your mind's the same as Harry's. Or it comes so close I could scarcely tell the difference. Not as cold as his, no, but the patterns are all the same.'

Trask nodded. 'That's what I felt the first time I saw you, Nathan: there was no doubt in my mind but that you were Harry's son, and that you'd been modelled on him. And when you spoke to me telepathically ... well, while you're very much alive, still I felt that this was what it must be like, talking to someone who was dead.'

Goodly said nothing but merely gave a small shudder, which Trask sensed as a trembling in his elbow where the precog sat beside him. Glancing at Goodly, he said: 'Well?'

'And so it starts,' Goodly answered, looking more cadaverous than ever. 'My God, but it's gathering now, Ben!'

'What is?'

'All of this. Why, the future is shifting even now. We're not changing it, for what will be will be. But it knows ...'

And Chung said: 'The future is ... sentient?'

'When it comes to protecting itself, yes,' Goodly answered. 'You'd think so, anyway.'

'You should never try to read it.' Nathan shook his head.

And Zek agreed with him: 'For it's a devious thing.'

For a moment they were all silent, until Trask cleared his throat and said, 'I know someone – a dead someone – who will speak to you, Nathan. At least I think he will. And after that ... maybe the rest of them will follow suit.'

*

Trask wasted no time but ordered up two Branch cars, and his party was driven at once to a crematorium, a Garden of Repose in Kensington. It was a chilly evening and already dark when they got there, but the gates were open. This was a place which was never closed to mourners. Trask led the group to Sir Keenan Gormley's tiny plot: a granite slab two feet square and some nine inches high, with a stainless steel plaque which carried his dates and an epitaph reading:

Much loved and missed,
but gone now into a better place.
Requiescat in Pace.

'His family,' Trask explained. 'If it had been the Branch ... well, it could be we'd have done something different. Something esoteric, in keeping with his life. Maybe this is for the best. At least it doesn't attract attention. At least he *can* rest in peace. His ashes were scattered here, but this is his place. *He* is here. This is where Harry Keogh spoke to him.'

When the inscription was read out to him and the last line translated, Nathan shook his head. 'They don't, you know. For they're restless, most of them. They think, remember, talk a lot. To each other. But it's a lonely place there in the dark, and it's certainly not a better one. And they miss much more than they're missed.'

But as the last sentence fell from his lips, so he reeled and Trask caught his arm to steady him. 'Nathan?'

For a moment he didn't answer, because a gonging shout was still ringing in his mind:

HARRY!!!

And it had been so forceful, so brimming with life, that for a moment he looked to see whose mouth had

595

issued it. Around him the espers stood silent, astonished. They had seen his jaw fall open, the shocked expression on his face. But in the next moment he knew, and shook off Trask's hand as he went to one knee in the gravel beside the granite slab. And with his trembling hand resting upon the plaque, using his deadspeak, he said:

No, not Harry but Nathan. My name is Nath —

It's Harry! The other cut him off. *Why, I'd know you anywhere! Your warmth, your 'voice', your ... presence! Don't try to fool an old friend, Harry, but tell me where you've been for so long?*

'Tell us what he's saying!' Zek's real voice, so urgent in Nathan's ear, and her hand falling on his shoulder, caused him to start. She *knew* he was speaking to someone, but it was deadspeak, which was beyond her capabilities.

'He thinks I'm ... he thinks that I'm my father!'

Not Harry? Gormley's 'voice' was filled with astonishment, disappointment. *His son? My God! Has it been that long?*

'Didn't you know?' Nathan spoke out loud, which made little or no difference; the presence of the Necroscope was sufficient in itself; the dead man — his ashes — 'heard' Nathan's spoken words as clearly as his thoughts. 'I mean, about the passage of time? Have none of the others mentioned it?'

Possibly (Nathan felt Gormley's deadspeak shrug). *Time is of little importance ... here. Without you — or rather, without Harry — it's been of no importance whatsoever!*

'You've simply lain there?' Nathan knew that the Thyre were not idle in their graves, so that this seemed to him a terrible waste. 'But what about the things you did in life, your interests in the corporeal world?'

Ahhh! Gormley's sigh. *But little use for such skills here. You see, I was a spotter: I knew when I stood close to exceptionally talented people. Indeed, I was the one who recruited your father, Harry Keogh, into E-Branch. There had been certain great injustices, and only he could put things right.*

'I know,' Nathan told him, 'for they – your people in the Branch – have told me. And now there are more injustices, and I have been recruited in my turn . . .'

So their conversation went, with Trask and the others hearing only Nathan's side of it and making what they could of it. But finally the introductions and brief histories were out of the way, and at last Gormley asked: *Now tell me, what can I do for you? Tell you your father's story? But I know so little of it. I'm sure the new people could tell you much more than me.*

'Oh, I want to have Harry's whole story, from beginning to end, eventually,' Nathan nodded. 'But right now there are more important things. On my way here, Ben Trask told me one or two things about you. And he was right: your talent alerted you to my presence, and my likeness to my father fooled you into contacting me. But would you have spoken to me if you'd believed I was someone else, not Harry?'

. . . *Ah!* Gormley answered, after a moment. And: *Perhaps not. And I'll tell you why.*

'No, let me tell you. There are things which even the dead fear. Am I right? And someone who talks to the Great Majority, well, he just might be one of those things. Do you understand me?'

The one thing Trask hadn't told Nathan was how Sir Keenan Gormley had died at the hands of just such a 'thing': a necromancer called Dragosani, in the employ of the then USSR's own E-Branch. And one other thing Nathan didn't know: that Harry Keogh had used his

Necroscope powers to kill Dragosani, going on to pare the Soviet organization down to the bone.

But now Nathan felt Gormley's unbodied shudder, and knew that he understood only too well. And: *I am the victim of just such a monster,* the dead man told him. *A necromancer, who tore my corpse to pieces in order to get at my secrets. And yes, you are right. These days . . . the teeming dead are careful who they talk to.*

'Which is my problem exactly,' Nathan told him, and sensed Gormley's deadspeak gasp.

The dead won't speak to you?

Nathan's silence was his answer.

But . . . have you tried?

'In my own world? Time and time again, ever since I was a child. There, it was the legacy and the fault of my Necroscope father. For in the end he was Wamphyri and not to be trusted. And so the Szgany dead – Travellers, Gypsies, my own kind – would have nothing to do with me. Only the dead of the Thyre, nomads of the deserts, would let me into their minds. I benefited from it, and so did they. Here, in this world . . . oh, I've heard the dead whispering in their graves, but you're the first who heard me, and certainly you're the first who was willing to talk to me.'

Gormley was silent a moment, then said: *There's nothing to fear in you. You shine in the darkness – the same as Harry in his innocence – and your presence is like a warm blanket over my grave. You do have your father's warmth, or whatever it was he had. For sometimes Harry could be cold, too. Very cold . . .*

He snapped out of it. *So that's why you're here* (Nathan felt his decisive deadspeak nod). *You require introductions. There are others among the Great Majority who you would like to contact, except you think they'll be wary of you. And your purpose?*

'My father was the Necroscope,' Nathan answered. 'Which is to say, he could talk to dead people, and it appears they loved him. But he had powers other than that. I've been told that you were the key to the greatest of those powers.'

Gormley understood, but now Nathan sensed the shake of an incorporeal head. *No, the key was already in place. The part I played was to show it to him. And it was a key, Nathan! A key to many doors. It was this:*

Nathan knew the symbol at once; why, he even wore it in his ear! His exclamation — his gasp of recognition — was automatic. 'My father's sigil?'

Yes, in a way. Harry Keogh's emblem of power.

'But what does it mean?'

I'm no mathematician, Nathan. Gormley shrugged in his deadspeak fashion. *But I can try to tell you something about it. It would appear to defy logic by reducing three dimensions to two, and two to one.*

'Dimensions?'

The planes of existence in which we live. It reduces all places to one place, or makes nothing of the gap between. And when Harry used it, it even reduced time down to NOW. He could go wherever he wanted to go, without covering the distance in between. And as a bodiless wraith, he even travelled in time.

'The ultimate Traveller!' Nathan sighed, and he smiled sadly. 'He was Szgany after all.'

Gormley chuckled. *If you want to put it that way.*

'You called it a key to many doors.' Nathan was serious in a moment, for now he recalled what Thikkoul, a dead Thyre star-gazer, had said of his future as glimpsed in the stars through Nathan's living eyes:

I see ... doors! (Thikkoul's voice had been the rustle of dried leaves.) *Like the doors on a hundred Szgany caravans but liquid, drawn on water, formed of ripples. And behind each one of them, a piece of your future ...*

'Doors,' Nathan said again, as Thikkoul faded into memory. 'What did you mean?'

Again Gormley's deadspeak shrug. *Space and time. Of course there are doors, but we can't see them. Harry could, and pass through them.*

'You said I have what he had.' Nathan was eager now. 'Well it's true, I do. But not all that he had. I want access to the Möbius Continuum. I want to be able to use these doors. Who do I speak to?'

Why, who better than Möbius himself? Gormley answered. *For it was his — what, metaphysics? His lateral thinking? — that brought the Möbius Strip into being in the first place. And I do know this: that your father was with Möbius, this brilliant, long-dead mathematician, the first time he conjured one of his doors!*

'Then I'll go and try to speak to Möbius. Except ... I may need an introduction?' It was Nathan's turn to shrug. 'It's the way of things ...'

Pausing, at last he remembered his other reason for being here. 'Oh, and there's something else you can do for me. That is, if I'm not asking too much.'

Too much? My one contact with the living, breathing world, and you're worried you might be asking too much? Ask away! And Nathan, believe me when I tell you I'll help you if I can. For you're not the only one with problems. If we can solve yours, then — and only then — you may be able to help me solve mine. And not

*only mine but a problem facing all of the Great Majority.
But . . . that would be to put the cart before the horse; first
the teeming dead must learn to trust you, and speak to
you. So for now you'd better tell me what's troubling you?*

'A woman has . . . well, it seems she's disappeared,'
Nathan told him. 'She's very important, not only to E-
Branch but also to me. Her name is Siggi Dam; she was
a member of the Opposition; last known location, Perchorsk in the Ural Mountains. We can't be sure if she's
dead, or if something else has happened to her. Only
the Great Majority would know for certain. Do you
think you could ask after her, find out if Siggi's joined
the ranks of the teeming dead? She was a telepath in
life, and if she is dead should be easy to contact.'

*A telepath? But in that case, wouldn't she have
contacted you? After all, you are the Necroscope.*

'Still I need to be sure.'

*Let me work on it, said Gormley, and I'll get back to
you. Think of me now and again, aim your thoughts in
this direction, and as soon as I have something . . . His*
deadspeak began to fade into a background hiss of
mental static. *And meanwhile* (he was very faint now),
*you must work on your maths. Instinctive mathematician
that your father was, still he had a hard time of it. So I
can't see that it will be any easier for you . . .*

The static took over completely. But coming right
through it – not speaking to Nathan directly, but simply
thinking her own most passionate thoughts, most fer-
vent desires 'out loud' – Zek Föener's telepathic voice:

*Nathan could talk to Jazz, tell him all the things
which, at the end, I was too late to say. He could
actually talk to him!*

Standing up and turning to her, he said: 'One day, I
would be glad to, if it's what you want. You can count
on it, before I go home to Sunside.'

She smiled her wan smile, sighed and took his arm.

And arm in arm, as they walked back down the wind-blown aisles of the Garden of Repose to the gates, and through them to the parked cars, Trask, Goodly and Chung followed on behind. The men of E-Branch wondered but said nothing. This was a good place to be quiet and keep the peace . . .

. . . But as Trask got into the first of the cars with Zek and Nathan, he was eager to ask the Necroscope: 'Well? And was I right? I know you spoke to Sir Keenan, but was it worth it?'

'Yes,' Nathan answered him, and went on to reveal what had passed between them. 'Sir Keenan said he'd make inquiries for me, and get back to me as soon as he has something.'

'Get back to you?'

'If I open my mind to him and seek him out, he'll converse with me at a distance. Apparently that's not too hard, not now that we've been introduced.'

'And meanwhile?'

'I'm to continue studying, improving my maths, which isn't the exciting thing I thought it would be.' Nathan shrugged and pulled a wry face. 'It seems that in Harry, numbers were instinctive. But not in me. On the — contrary? Perhaps because I carry them with me always, without knowing their meaning, they weigh on me and tire me out.'

'We're all tired,' Trask nodded. 'A good night's sleep is what we all need. Tomorrow you'll go back to basic numbers. In Harry's case it *was* an instinctive art, yes, but even he required a final push before he made his quantum leap. In his case it was do or die, and so he did. With you it's not so urgent. In three or four months we'll be ready to send you back through the Romanian

Gate – *if* we can do it. And meanwhile you'll be well protected. My advice: give all of your attention to your instructors. And if Keenan Gormley comes up with a shortcut, well that will be all the better.'

The cars sped back to E-Branch HQ.

Harry's room was now Nathan's room. After eating with Trask and Zek at the hotel restaurant 'downstairs', he retired there with his thoughts. He had been aware through dinner of two men seated at a nearby table, whose flinty eyes in blank, expressionless faces would occasionally turn and stare in his direction. Trask, seeing him looking at them, had warned: 'Don't pay them too much attention. They're not E-Branch, not those two, but Special Branch. And they're your minders.'

His minders. They were like chameleons: ever-changing. He had met several, but they came and went. Sometimes an E-Branch agent would be with them, other times they'd be on their own. They guarded him – against the vengeance of Turkur Tzonov.

But if Tzonov really has sent Siggi through the Gate, Nathan thought, where he sat in an easy chair beside his bed, *then he's the one who will need guarding. From me!* It was his vow.

Ah, but where vows were concerned ... well, he'd made them before. And so far they'd come to nothing.

Outside in the corridor he heard soft, padding footsteps. His minders again? The Duty Officer? Almost unwittingly he put out a telepathic probe, and met with the mind of David Chung. Chung stood right outside his door with his fist poised to knock.

'Come in,' Nathan anticipated him.

Chung entered, shrugged. 'I'm on duty. I was just passing by.'

603

'Really? But you paused outside my door. I thought it was one of my minders.'

'Well in a way I am. We all are.'

Nathan pulled a face. 'I'm not sure I like being minded so well.' Then he looked at Chung more squarely where the other leaned back against the computer console. 'And I think you were more than just passing by. What's on your mind?'

'My talent is on my mind, and this room, and . . . that earring of yours. Every now and then you touch it sort of thoughtfully, like a moment ago, as soon as I mentioned it. We asked you about Siggi Dam's clasp, but not about that earring. Can you free it? I mean, would you mind if I held it for a moment? And would you also mind telling me where you got it?'

Nathan freed the golden sigil from his ear and handed it over. 'I'm surprised no one else has asked me about it,' he said.

'But there's been so little time,' Chung answered. 'I think you'll find they've all assumed it came from your mother, something Harry might have given her.'

Nathan grunted and his look turned sour in a moment. 'To my knowledge, the only thing she got from my father was me . . . and my brother, Nestor.' As soon as it was out he could have bitten his tongue. He'd wanted to leave Nestor out of this, though why he couldn't say.

'Nestor?'

Nathan waved a hand dismissively. 'You can forget him. Nestor . . . he died some years ago.'

'The Wamphyri?'

'Yes.' *Oh, yes – yes indeed – Wamphyri!*

Chung had been examining the golden earring, holding it in his hands, crushing it between his palms almost in an attitude of prayer. Now he gave it back. 'Nothing,' he said.

'What did you expect?' Nathan asked him. 'It's not of this world. It was given me by Maglore of Runemanse, in Turgosheim.'

Chung shrugged. 'It was an experiment. You were wearing it when you came through the Perchorsk Gate. I wondered if I could make a mind-bridge to your vampire world, that's all. I should have known that I couldn't. It was the same with Jazz Simmons. When he went through the Gate all contact was lost.' Then he frowned. 'So Maglore gave it to you, eh? Another sign of his "affection"?'

'Actually, it's a strange story,' Nathan answered. 'For you see, the loop with the half-twist is Maglore's sigil, too. He's something of a mage — a mentalist, as I told you — and on the night the Opposition sent their awesome weapon through the Perchorsk Gate, he dreamed of the Necroscope's Möbius *blazon*. From which time forward he took it for his own.' He paused a moment, giving Chung the chance to say:

'Blazon? It surprises me you know that word.'

'Why?' Nathan raised an eyebrow. 'It's a Szgany word. Many of our words are more or less the same.' And when Chung made no answer he continued:

'Anyway, my father died that night. Perhaps something went out from him in addition to the images which you saw here, and the fragment that entered the computer. Maybe his sign had the power to impress itself into the minds of all manner of sensitive dreamers and mentalists, such as Maglore of Runemanse. But as for me, I'd known it even as a babe in arms, though that was probably coincidental. When we were babies, my mother had given my brother and me leather straps to wear on our wrists, so that she could tell us apart in the night. My strap had the Möbius half-twist.'

'Oh?' said Chung, smiling. 'Coincidence? And your

father was the Necroscope, Harry Keogh? Well, perhaps . . .' His smile gradually faded as he watched Nathan fixing the earring back in place. Then: 'I'd better get back to my station,' he said.

But as he reached the door and opened it: 'Nathan.' Chung glanced back at the other. 'Do me a favour, will you?'

'If I can.'

'When you get back to Sunside — or even before you get back — get rid of that earring. Maglore, this Wamphyri mentalist of yours, he might have intended it as more than just a gift. I mean, you know what my talent is, how it works? I locate things, people as often as not. And it helps if I can lock onto something, such as Siggi Dam's clasp, or an earring like the one in your ear.'

Nathan nodded. He understood Chung's warning. 'You think Maglore has the same sort of talent? That he might have been using me to spy on Sunside?'

'It's just a hunch, but yes.'

Again Nathan's nod, as his thoughts flew back once more to his own world — this time to a man called Iozel Kotys, once in Maglore's employ — and: 'Thanks,' he said. 'I'll keep it in mind.'

Before the dawn, while Nathan dreamed, Sir Keenan Gormley got back to him. Siggi Dam wasn't among the Great Majority. And if she was no longer in this world, there was only one other place she could be.

In his sleep Nathan sweated, tossed and turned, ground his teeth. His conversion to E-Branch and his new-found friends was now complete.

But Gormley had other news for him, too, and as Nathan's resolve hardened, so his plans must be altered. Möbius was no longer in his grave in Leipzig; only his bones were there now; the still-brilliant mind had moved on, gone elsewhere. There *were* other worlds beyond.

It wasn't quite a 'dead end', however. Hope hadn't blinked out in its entirety along with Möbius; there were other incorporeal minds to contact, other mathematicians whose work in life had been just as enigmatic, just as metaphysical. Gormley had a whole list of them. Maybe Nathan should look some of them up instead.

Except ... the old problem might still be there. The dead continued to shun living persons who could speak to them. It was the legacy of Nathan's father; for he had opened the way for them, taught them to seek each other out in their loneliness, only to betray them in the end. The betrayal had worked both ways, it was true, but in that respect the dead could be forgiven. They didn't share the freedom of the living. They were immobile; they couldn't flee before the advance of a necromancer but must lie still and suffer his tortures; they were terrified by the thought that such as Dragosani − and, in the end, Harry Keogh − might return. By the thought that indeed one such might *already* have returned, in the shape of this man from another world. For they knew that Nathan was here, and as yet they feared him.

And so, as Nathan's resolve hardened more yet, his sleeping form grew still and calm again.

Calm, resentful, and cold.

Perhaps even as cold as his Necroscope father ...

III

The Nightmare Zone

In his early days with E-Branch, the daily twenty-four hour round of life itself was probably Nathan's greatest physical and mental distraction. In his own world, where around fifty Sunside/Starside cycles were equal to an entire 'year' Earthtime, a day was the equivalent of four to five of this world's entire day/night cycles! And yet the Traveller physiology had clung to its pre-holocaust rhythms as developed through Szgany evolution on the vampire world prior to the advent of the so-called 'white sun', and the typical Traveller would sleep as often as three times – five or six hours a time – during the course of one long Sunside night.

Here when it grew dark, one slept – and only one sleep, which would normally only be broken to answer calls of nature or duty – then woke up with the dawn. As for the impossibly short days: it seemed astonishing that these people had ever found time to achieve anything. Yet what they had achieved was itself amazing. Nathan could scarcely begin to consider the extent of their science without his mind reeling from the sheer scope of it!

In fact he was suffering a form of trans-dimensional jet-lag, where his body was desperately trying to adjust to time-scales and -differentials far beyond the experience of any Sunside Traveller since time immemorial. But that wasn't the worst of it; something else he must get used to was the foul weather. The seasons on Sunside had varied only marginally over four-year periods, when the climatic changes were so slow and slight as to be almost unnoticeable. Here in the so-called 'hell-lands', however – especially London in the winter – the weather *was* hell! Not as bad as Perchorsk and the lands around, but bad enough by any standards. At least in Perchorsk the temperature had been more or less constant, and the mountain ravines natural as opposed to the man-made canyons of the city.

Nathan had never had a cold in his life – until now! His nostrils had never before clogged up – until he breathed the fumes rising out of the underground stations. The efficiency of his digestive system, his bowels and the solid consistency of their contents had never been in question – until he ate with Ben Trask at various Chinese and Indian restaurants.

All in all, life was uncomfortable here. It wasn't at all the world he'd envisioned as a stuttering loner in Settlement, when all he'd wanted was to escape into his own worlds of fantasy. But at the same time it wasn't quite hell, and when the drizzly, dreary nights came down he didn't have to hide from monsters. Unless they were monsters out of his own past, his own memory.

Nathan's most recent monster was Turkur Tzonov, but at least he wasn't Wamphyri (though well he might have been, if what E-Branch suspected of him were the truth). Separated from Tzonov by many thousands of miles, Nathan couldn't hit at the man personally, but he could do his best to damage his organization, ruin his planned conquest of Sunside/Starside. If not in this world, then certainly in his own. But to do that, and also to avenge if not save Siggi Dam, he must first get back to his own world, and take with him all the weapons he could muster.

Nathan's best weapon, Trask had assured him, would be Nathan himself. But a Nathan trusted by the teeming dead, and one who commanded the metaphysical Möbius Continuum as his father before him. With this in mind he applied himself yet more diligently to his studies, specifically the elusive and seemingly meaningless science of mathematics. And as the first ten days flew by his progress was such that he could be proud of it.

As his instructor explained to Ben Trask on the morning of the eleventh day:

'He seems to have a natural talent for it, an intuitive grasp of maths. At first I couldn't be sure; he was reluctant, easily sidetracked. But now ... well, it could be you'll soon have to replace me. My knowledge goes only so far.'

Trask looked at the other across his desk. James Bryant was perhaps the perfect stereotype. Small and slender, studious in grey slacks and dark polo-necked pullover, blinking owlishly behind thick-lensed spectacles, he just *had* to teach something or other, preferably maths. The Minister Responsible had pulled him in from one of the universities where his term of office had just run out. But Bryant's mind wasn't one-track; it wasn't bound by his subject. He had known from the start, even without the Official Secrets Act, that E-Branch was no ordinary government department, and Nathan no ordinary student. And this morning, for some reason or other, he appeared to have reached the end of his tether.

'Just how far does your knowledge go?' Trask asked him. 'I mean, we've scarcely had time to talk to each other, let alone get to know one another. I know you were at ... where, Oxford? Our Minister wouldn't have recommended you for the job if you weren't worth your salt.'

Bryant nodded. 'Do you know what maths is, Mr Trask? Its definition? Roughly, it's the logical study of quantity or magnitude. It uses rigorously defined concepts and self-consistent symbols in such a way as to disclose the properties and relations of quantities and magnitudes within its own parameters. It can be applied or abstract, can make connections or remain purely theoretical. Do you follow?'

Trask nodded, then shook his head. 'I'm no mathematician, Mr Bryant. I follow you, but I don't follow you – if you follow me. Yes, I know Einstein's famous equation, but that's not to say I understand it. Why don't you just tell me what's on your mind, what's troubling you?'

'Teaching Nathan is what's troubling me, because I can't teach him what he wants to know. Because maths won't cover it. May I explain?'

'Go ahead.'

'Let's look at that definition of maths again. The first word we come across is logical. Nathan's application is hardly logical. He wants to be able to "conjure doors"! He believes that if he can frame or control a certain equation or series of equations, then these "doors"' (Bryant offered a baffled shrug) 'will appear. The physical out of the abstract.'

Taking a deep breath, Trask shook his head. 'Not the physical, but the metaphysical, certainly. And surely metaphysical and abstract aren't incompatible.'

'Exactly,' said Bryant. 'Except I'm not dealing with metaphysics . . . though it strikes me that you are!' And remembering some of the things he'd seen in this place during the past fortnight, he glanced around the office. 'But men can't *think* doors into existence, Mr Trask. Or for that matter anything else.'

Trask wanted to say: *Nathan's father could*, but somehow managed to keep his peace. 'Men can think thoughts into existence,' he said, without meaning to be clever. 'But I take your point, so do go on.'

Zek Föener came to Trask's office door, looked inside and made to turn away. Trask called out to her. 'Zek? It's OK. Come in.' And to Bryant: 'Please carry on. This is interesting.'

Bryant looked at Zek, shrugged and said, 'Good morning. I was just explaining to Mr Trask why I can't go on working with Nathan.'

She smiled and said, 'I'd like to hear that. Any insight has to be better than none. Most have been favourable, but all opinions count.'

'My "opinion" is that he's a nice lad,' Bryant told her. 'It isn't that I don't like him, only that I can't work with him.' He turned back to Trask. 'Back to the definition: rigorously defined concepts and self-consistent symbols. Mathematics doesn't mutate. It grows, certainly, gets more complex the deeper we delve, but even to a computer a plus is a plus and a minus is a minus. Nathan wants to bend maths; if rules don't say what he wants them to say, he bends them.'

'Isn't that what rules are for?' Zek frowned. 'I mean, didn't we once believe that the shortest distance between two points was a straight line? And wasn't it maths that showed us we were wrong? Wasn't it maths that "bent" the line and threw us a curve?'

And Trask thought: *But here in E-Branch we know that the shortest distance between two points is in fact a Möbius door! And I personally have seen Harry Keogh disappear through just such a door!* While out loud he said:

'Is it such a bad thing that Nathan is trying to create his own system with its own rules? Why shouldn't he look at numbers from all directions? As Zek said: isn't that what rules are for anyway, so that people who are clever enough can bend them?'

'Not the rules of mathematics, no,' Bryant disagreed. And quickly went on: 'Look, let's get to the point. The deeper I go with Nathan the less certain I am of my ground. Soon I won't know if he's playing fair with me or if he's ... well, bending the rules. If he is, he won't learn anything. Not from me, anyway. So there's little point in my trying to teach him.'

'Then maybe you should try learning *from* him. Is that what you're trying to say: that he's outstripping you?'

Bryant shook his head, his frustration beginning to show. 'I'm not jealous of him ... Not yet, anyway.'

'Maybe we should get another instructor, then? Someone who knows it all?'

'No one "knows it all", Mr Trask. It just gets more complex, that's all. My suggestion: from now on let him do his own thing, without outside help or hindrance. That way, as soon as he discovers that numbers simply *are* – that they don't govern anything except themselves – he'll stop fooling with them. Then, with his ... well, I can only call it "intuition", he'll probably go on to make a very capable mathematician.'

Trask took a chance. 'You know of course that we *want* him to find his doors?'

'I guessed as much, yes,' Bryant answered. 'Also that you are dealing with some pretty weird stuff around here. Metaphysics? You as good as admitted it just a moment ago.' There was a mildly scornful something in his tone that Trask, despite that he was sympathetic, didn't much care for. And:

'Pick a number,' Trask said. 'Any number between one and a million.'

'A trick?'

'A demonstration.'

Bryant sighed and said, 'I have it.' And Trask glanced

613

at Zek. The merest glance, but she knew what he wanted. And smiling, she said:

'All the nines. 999,999.'

Bryant frowned, said: 'How . . .?'

'I bent the rules,' she told him. 'The ones that guarantee the privacy of your own mind. I'm a telepath. Which is only one of the rules that get bent around here.'

Bryant looked at her, and at Trask. 'E-Branch? ESP-Branch?'

'In one,' Trask told him. And: 'Another demonstration. Tell me something about yourself. Anything at all. Out of your past. But among all the true things you tell me, make sure you stick at least one lie in there.'

'What?' Bryant looked mystified.

'Do it.'

Bryant shrugged and said: 'I was born at about two in the morning on the 2nd December 1975, in –'

'A lie,' Trask cut in. 'You weren't born in 1975.'

The other blinked his eyes rapidly, and Zek told him: 'Ben is a human lie detector. You can't lie to him. Anything false, he sees, hears, smells, tastes and *feels* it right away. We all have our talents, Mr Bryant. Nathan, too. Except his is buried deep inside. We had hoped you could help us dig it out, that's all.'

Ian Goodly's gaunt frame loomed in the open door. He must have heard something of the conversation, for now he entered and said, 'Mr Bryant is right: he can't help. Nathan's maths has achieved such a level that he can now be left to develop on his own. Mr Bryant will be out of here by this afternoon. And anyway, Nathan has work to do. It's coming, Ben. It's NZ time. A week at most, and we'll be dealing with *that* again.'

Only Trask knew what he meant. Zek hadn't been here long enough, and as yet Bryant wasn't entirely convinced that this place was part of the real world.

But 'NZ' was their code for the Nightmare Zone, which was a place right here in London.

The small hairs on the back of Trask's neck were suddenly erect. Despite the comfortable temperature of the air-conditioned room, he visibly shuddered as his gaze transferred from Bryant to Goodly, and he asked, 'You've seen it coming?'

'Yes.' Goodly was like a ghost standing there, features painted on his skull and his eyes sunk deep in their sockets, his voice a high-pitched, nervous warble.

'When?'

'Within a week. I didn't try to narrow it down. But it's going to be bad. It almost scared the shit out of me!'

It wasn't usual for Ian Goodly to use that sort of term, so that Trask knew that he had more on his hands than any problem presented by Bryant's quitting. In any case the precog had foreseen that, so it was going to happen. And so:

'Mr Bryant, you're out of it,' Trask told him. *And you may believe me, you're better off for it.* 'You can do whatever is necessary to finish up your work here. You will be paid for the full term of your contract, of course. But I would remind you, you're sworn to secrecy – always.'

Bryant nodded, said, 'Er . . . goodbye, then.'

And when he was out of the office: 'A meeting.' Trask was back in action, the way he liked it. 'Ten minutes,' he rasped, 'the Ops room. Whoever you can muster from those in the building – oh, and Nathan, of course.'

For this time there was no question about it. This time they were going to need the Necroscope . . .

Those gathered in the Ops room were Frank Robinson, a spotter, Paul Garvey, a full-blown telepath, Ben Trask,

Zek Föener, Ian Goodly, Nathan, and the empath Geoff Smart who was just back from a stint in Glasgow's Barlinnie Prison and a study of its psychopaths. This had been a Ministry of Health job — a feasibility study in treatment and rehabilitation — but something less than healthy for Smart. After three months of close contact with the worst inmates of Barlinnie, Smart looked as if he could use some help himself.

'If I draw NZ,' he'd whispered to Goodly where they gathered in the Ops room, 'it will be peaceful by comparison.' But in actual fact the mere thought of the Nightmare Zone made the flesh of each and every one of them crawl.

With the exception of the Duty Officer, all of the above — the entire on-duty staff of E-Branch HQ, excluding Nathan's minders, who weren't espers — were present as Trask took the podium. And leaning on the lectern he told them: 'Ian Goodly has forecast trouble in the Nightmare Zone. Within the week. He says it's going to be bad. Now some of you have done this duty before, and others have been lucky. The same goes for a couple of agents who aren't here right now, out on field duty, or resting at home. But when it's NZ time, all the names go into the hat.'

In fact, it wasn't a hat but a deck of cards. Trask took the deck out from under the lectern's lid and shuffled it in full view of the assembled agents, telling them: 'Anyone who already did the job more than once can cry off. No one will blame him or her. Anyone else who doesn't fancy it can speak up now and we'll try not to blame him.' He looked from face to face but no one so much as twitched.

'Zek,' Trask went on, 'you're sort of honorary here and so you don't have a card. Nathan, you're in on this job like it or not. I'll explain in a little while, and then you'll understand why everyone is so quiet. So that leaves three to choose. Who has the tally sheet?'

Ian Goodly said: 'I have it.' The sheet matched up names to cards; the first three names out of the deck were it; Trask stopped shuffling and turned up the top card.

'Three of hearts,' he said.

Goodly shook his head.

'Seven of diamonds.'

The same reaction from Goodly.

'Jack of clubs ... *ah!*' It was Trask's card. He had only done the job once before, and anyway he wouldn't have wanted to shirk his duty. 'That's me. OK, two to go.'

He went back to turning cards and the next one up was the queen of hearts. It drew a blank. And:

'Ace of clubs.'

'That's me.' Paul Garvey wore an emotionless expression – always. With his remodelled face, the nerves not quite matching, smiles and frowns alike came out as grotesque grimaces.

Trask drew two more blanks and then the four of spades.

'That's Anna Marie English,' Goodly said, 'but I know for a fact that she's already done it twice.'

Trask looked again at the faces of his espers. 'I'm sending Anna Marie out to Romania, and soon, to take charge of the Refuge. So ... I vote we draw again.'

No one objected, and seven cards later the ace of hearts brought a small groan from Geoff Smart.

Trask looked at Goodly, who nodded. 'It's Smart,' he said. And to Smart himself: 'How many times have you done it, Geoff?'

'Just the once,' Smart answered. 'Which is three times as often as I wanted to!'

Smart was five-ten, blockily built, red-haired and crew-cut. He looked like a pugilist, but in fact was mild-mannered. What he lacked in looks was made up for by what Trask called his 'withness', his empathy, an intense ability to relate. He didn't just feel for a person but became him, experienced his emotions, pains, passions. It was something he could switch on and off like a light, which was as well. There were minds in Barlinnie no one would *want* to relate to for too long.

'Well, that's the four of us,' he now said, 'and the off-duties don't even know how lucky they've been! I suppose we're confined to this place until a hunchman says it's time, right?'

From the podium, Trask nodded. 'You, me, Paul and Nathan, we're it. And when we get the signal from either Ian Goodly or Guy Teale – hopefully with just a little time to play with – then we enter the Nightmare Zone. Teale will have to be called in, if he's not already on his way, and Ian . . . you'll need to be on hand as the time narrows down. I want as much warning as possible.' And as Goodly opened his mouth to make his usual comment: 'Yes, I know: the future isn't reliable. But it *is* your precinct, so work on it.'

And now for the first time Nathan spoke up. 'Just what is this Nightmare Zone, and why do you all fear it?'

Trask took a deep breath, said, 'This is for you and Zek. For you because you'll be in it, and for Zek because she has no experience of it. But occasionally something happens that stops even people like us; something so weird, so extraordinary as to defy all explanations. So . . . really I don't have any explanation for it, except that it happens.

'That's what E-Branch has been about right from the start: the inexplicable, the *outré*, the macabre. In the beginning we were mindspies; we still are, to an extent, and possibly more so in the immediate future, but in between we've sidetracked into all sorts of fields. All sorts of minefields, too! Gadgets and ghosts, that's us and always has been. But sometimes our ghosts do more than just rattle chains ...

'Nathan, you're the Necroscope, so maybe it won't be so hard for you to understand or believe. Zek, you know some of the things we've had to deal with in the past; it's possible you'd accept this too, without letting it get to you. Mercifully, you're not involved. As for the people who *have* had to deal with it – afterwards, when it's all over – they really do nightmare! Maybe that's why we call it the Nightmare Zone, and now I'll tell you how it started ...

'John Scofield was one of our agents. He was the son of a psychic medium, just like Harry Keogh. And John radiated his ESP like a lighthouse beacon on a dark night. Our spotters could feel him coming a mile away, he had that much power. Well, we thought maybe we had a Necroscope here, but we were wrong.

'The power we felt in him wasn't ... what, supernatural? I suppose that's what most people would call messages from beyond the grave. No, his real talent was more properly parapsychological. In fact he was telekinetic: a mover. Not a "nice" mover, but someone who could shift things with his mind. Think about that. Maybe eventually he'd be able to shift *himself*, do teleportation with his mind, like Harry with his Möbius Doors.

'As for John's deadspeak: I still believe it was in him but I don't think it would ever have amounted to very much ... not while he was alive, anyway ...

'We had him for a year and put a lot into him, hoping

that eventually we'd get a lot out. We didn't take our work lightly: on the contrary, we knew what an awesome weapon we would have if it all worked out. What's more, we knew that old adage about absolute power.

'But more about his deadspeak:

'John *believed* that the dead talked to him, usually in his sleep. Now, we know from the Keogh files that this is possible in the case of a Necroscope. And Nathan has affirmed that it's so. But when we put our best espers on John's case they came up with nothing, or at best the very faintest echoes. His talents were less than obvious when he was asleep. And we had to ask ourselves: is his deadspeak real or is he simply dreaming, fantasizing? Remember, his mother had been a psychic medium – a fake, it would appear – but *she* had thought she was real. Was her son's delusion, if that's what it was, something which had come down to him from her? Or did he have deadspeak but in an as yet undeveloped form, which would grow with time?

'Now the other side of him, his telekinesis:

'John was one of the luckiest men alive – within certain parameters. And here I'm talking about London's casinos. When it came down to dice or roulette wheels ... let it suffice to say that he got himself banned from most of the casinos by the time he was twenty-one years old. And he was "lucky" with the one-armed bandits, too. Enough that he made a living from his gambling. But an honest day's work? John Scofield never did one in his life! I'm not moralizing, just stating a fact.

'John didn't get it right every time, but when he was on form it was devastating. I've seen him roll ten pairs of sixes in a row, just for practice. And I've watched the little white ball drop into fifteen consecutive red slots before his concentration failed him. Perhaps the best "trick" he ever performed for me was to move a sheet of paper across a desk, or to close a door, slowly, quietly, just by looking at it. But all these examples were mainly harmless things ... while he was alive. I know I keep saying that, but you'll see why in a little while.

'So he came to us – we spotted and recruited him – three years ago this coming April, and we had him for a year. Until it happened. John had a wife and child. He'd married his sweetheart at nineteen and had a little boy eight years old. I met his family on several occasions and Lynn was stunning. The kid, too, was a jewel of a boy. And I never knew a man more in love with his wife than John Scofield.

'They lived in north London, the Highbury area. One morning after a stint as Duty Officer, John went home and found the house broken into, his wife and child dead. It looked like the kid had tried to protect his mother, and someone had kicked his head in. As for Lynn: she'd been stripped, tortured, raped, and after a lot of suffering her killer had choked her with her own underclothes, which he'd stuffed with a madman's strength down her throat ...

'And of course John came to us for help. Not immediately, for there was help other than ours which he needed first. The psychiatric sort. No question about it, he was out of his mind for ... oh, a long time. Six months at least. But eventually he got it together again, or so we thought, and then he came to us.

'Along with some cash, Lynn's jewellery had been taken. A few good pieces had been stolen, and some lesser stuff. But the thief's mistake was that he left any of it behind. It had all belonged to Lynn, and even the lesser or worthless pieces carried her aura. We gave some of it to David Chung, which was akin to putting a piece of soiled clothing under the nose of a bloodhound!

'When Chung came up with a location, we checked it out and ended up with the name of a fence with a track record as long as your arm. After that, our part of the job was complete and we handed the case over to the police, gave it to them on a plate. But what we didn't know was that we'd also given it to John on a plate. We had thought he'd straightened out, but he hadn't. He wanted the murderer of his wife and child. John wanted him personally.

'It was a close run thing. The police grilled the fence we'd given them. He still had items of Lynn's jewellery, and finally coughed. When they went to pick up the perp from his place in Finsbury Park, John was right behind them. He followed them to a police station in the same area, and was immediately behind them when they took their man in for questioning.

'The perp was as nasty a piece of work as you could wish to find on the streets of London, or any other place for that matter. His name was Tod Prentiss and he had lots of previous convictions. Armed robbery, GBH, burglary, a rape on a young kid that he'd so far got away with. Also, the police had found a couple of pieces of Lynn's junk jewellery in his flat.

'Inside the police station John saw the evidence, knew that this was his man – and cracked. He'd taken a cutthroat razor with him, and went for Prentiss to kill him! The desk officer had a gun. He made to produce it but Prentiss beat him to it, started shooting. He wounded two officers who got between him and Scofield, before a plain-clothes man with a handgun of his own came on the scene. In the shoot-out that followed Prentiss was hit in the heart and died on the spot. And if John Scofield had been a little bit crazy before, now he really went over the top. God only knows what was in his mind at that moment! But we all know what's been in it ever since – *and what's in it right now!*

'Because that was when he took his cutthroat razor and put it to his own throat, and sliced as deep as he could go without actually sawing his own head off!

'Why did he do it? Well, we've thought about that . . .

'You see, whether we believed in John or not – in his deadspeak, I mean – *he* believed in it, just like his mother had believed before him. Also, he'd read the Keogh files and knew there *are* worlds beyond. Now that's a concept which it's still very hard for us to accept. Despite that we knew Harry and now have his son right here in our midst, it still feels very strange to us that death isn't the end, that whatever a man was and did in life, he continues to be and do in his afterlife. The reason it's hard for us is that we're still very much alive. Who knows? Maybe the closer we get to it, the more we'll be willing to believe. But as I said, John Scofield did believe. In fact, John *knew* that Tod Prentiss had got off too lightly, too quickly and easily, and that his evil incorporeal mind was still thinking its evil incorporeal thoughts among all the generally clean thoughts of the Great Majority!

'He *knew* that Prentiss would be thinking of the girls he'd raped and one in particular who he'd murdered, getting his mental rocks off on thoughts of Lynn's sweet body before he soiled it and stilled the air in its lungs and the blood in its veins. But worse than all that, John knew that Lynn was there! She was *there* in Prentiss's dead world, where even now the evil bastard might be whispering to her in the endless night of the tomb, telling her how good it had been for him and reminding her of the hell he'd put her through! And that's why John had cracked.

'For while Tod Prentiss had been put beyond John's reach in this world, he was still very much "alive" and perhaps even available in the next. And what was there left for John here? Not even revenge, not now. But down among the teeming dead . . .? His cutthroat razor had been John's visa into a world where he would continue to pursue what he'd pursued here. In this world he had practised his deadspeak; perhaps with some small measure of success, we've no way of knowing now. But he'd also used telekinesis. Maybe that, too, would have its incorporeal uses. The ability to move things with the power of the mind alone . . . And since mind would be all John had left, there would be nothing to distract him from his main pursuit: that of a man called Tod Prentiss!

'At the rear of the police station where the final act in this drama – or what *ought* to have been the final act – had taken place, stood a morgue. In fact the morgue joined the police station to an old, brick-built Victorian hospital, and served both institutions or facilities equally well. As the mess got sorted out, both Scofield's and Prentiss's bodies were put in cold storage there. And by that simple act – the placing in close proximity of these two dead bodies – the police brought into being the Nightmare Zone.

'That night the duties consisted of a Desk Sergeant and his radio op assistant, a two-man standby patrol, and a car on prowler duty. It wasn't one of the big stations. Some old down-and-out – a drunk with nowhere better to go – was snoring in one corner of the inquiries room; all in all it was quiet, and not a lot was happening. Nothing odd about that, for after all it was a wintry Wednesday night, and the streets were empty.

'All admin attended to, the Sergeant joined his standby crew in a three-handed game of cards behind the desk, and the time crept round to midnight. Which was when things began to happen.

'First of all, it grew cold. That was hard to understand. Despite that it was bitter outside, the station was centrally heated and the heating turned up full. But the cold came seeping from the rear of the station, out of the wide, tiled, cell-lined corridor that led like a tunnel to the morgue. Back there was a door to that silent, grisly place, and on the other side of the morgue another door to the basement of the hospital. Of course at this time of night both doors were locked, and they would stay locked until the morning ... unless there should be business to attend to in the interim.

'Well, it was possible that something had gone wrong with the refrigeration units, which might have started to leak their frozen air into the corridor. But before the Desk Sergeant and standby crew could investigate, they saw their first real signs that something was very, very wrong — and not only with the morgue's refrigeration — and they began to hear the sounds!

'The signs came first: The walls of the place seemed to vibrate like a fleet of articulated trucks had gone by, causing "wanted" posters and other notices to come loose and flutter to the floor. Documents on the desk danced in their trays, and the cards on the small folding table shuffled themselves this way and that across the green baize. Venetian blinds at the windows went jerkily up and down, up and down, like some idiot was playing with the cords and couldn't get it right. So maybe it was an earthquake ...

'... Yes, and maybe the faint, dull *grunting*, the *moaning*, *howling*, and *crashing* that was coming from behind the locked doors of that morgue was only the wind in the old brick chimneys, or the agonized, echoing cries of incurable patients in the old hospital, finding their way down here from above. But it all added up to too many maybes, and finally the Sergeant took the keys and went to investigate – on his own!

'Now, I've read the reports over and over again, so that I'm pretty sure I *know* what broke the Sergeant's nerve, put him in mental care, finally got him discharged from the force. The reports speak of hooliganism, vandalism, and ghoulish activity. But the standby crew only saw what was left *after* the sounds from the morgue had reached a crescendo and stopped – and after the Sergeant's weak, shrill, girlish little titters had started!

'Then they'd walked slowly and carefully down the tiled tunnel between the empty cells and through the open door, to find him stumbling about among all the debris, drooling like an infant, pointing to the mess in the morgue and muttering over and over again what amounted to a confession of madness. And all around him ...

'... Chaos! Most of the refrigerated drawers were open, their – contents? – lying spilled on the cold tiled floor in grotesque attitudes of disarray. It was as if some lunatic had been looking for someone, a dead someone, and in his frenzied searching had ripped open the rows of temporary coffins, tumbling the bodies out onto the floor. But those bodies ... their positions!

'There were eight of them all told, and six of the eight were where you'd expect to find them in those circumstances: close to the drawers which they'd occupied. But the other two ... *weren't* where you'd expect to find them, and their coffins weren't in any condition you'd expect to find them in! For it was John Scofield who had kicked open the bottom of his drawer, slithered out and gone on the rampage in the morgue, and it had been Tod Prentiss he was looking for – *still* looking for, even in death! What's more, Prentiss had known he was coming, for his drawer had been forced from the inside, and the lid almost torn from its hinges as the dead rapist and murderer had tried to get away from his pursuer!

'And *their* bodies?

'They were discovered well away from the other six, in a corner lined with toppled filing cabinets where finally John had trapped his prey. There they lay, frozen again in the paralysis of death, one with his throat sliced open and the other with a hole through his heart, and Scofield's cold hands wrapped around Prentiss's throat as if to choke the "life" out of him!

'And the Desk Sergeant? Well obviously he'd walked right into it; he'd actually seen these two corpses . . . what, fighting each other? Well, whatever name you'd give to their zombie struggle. He'd seen it, and known what he was looking at, and couldn't accept it. Even here in E-Branch – knowing what we know, having seen what we've seen – it would be hard enough.

'And as if all of this wasn't bad enough in itself, then there were the looks on their faces: John with his lips drawn back in a snarl, cording the ligaments of his neck, and Prentiss with his tongue lolling, eyes bulging, "scared to death" of the madman who was killing him a second time! The same man who couldn't lie still but would return to kill him again and again, presumably forever, or at least until we can discover a way to bring peace again to that dreadful place –

'– That place we call the Nightmare Zone . . .'

IV

To Soothe the Dead

Looking down at the drawn, fascinated faces of his espers, Ben Trask stood up straighter, straightened his shoulders. Towards the end of his story his eyes had seemed glazed, almost vacant. Now they focused again and he coughed, clearing his throat before continuing.

'Almost done,' he said. 'These things I've been talking about happened some two years ago, just the way I've told them to you, when E-Branch agent John Scofield took his revenge from beyond the grave. But as I also told you, or hinted, he hasn't let it go at that but keeps right on taking his revenge. Which gets worse all the time.

'Six times now he's been back, and each manifestation has been worse than the one before. The police station has gone — or rather, it's just an old, dilapidated shell of a place now — its area of responsibility absorbed into the larger Police HQ at New Finsbury Park. The morgue's no longer a morgue, just a damp and disused basement. Even the hospital has closed down, eaten up in the Green Health Plan and moved out into the countryside. But these places didn't just close down, they *had* to close down. Because as John Scofield practises his telekinesis in the next world, so he gets better at it . . .

'. . . And the Nightmare Zone gets bigger!

'That's how it all works out, you see? Deadspeak or whatever power it is that John's got on the other side —

628

plus his telekinesis and a dash of sheer incorporeal malice, or revenge if you want to call it that – equals bad dreams, poltergeist activity, fear and loathing and a hell of a lot of dirty work for us on *this* side! And the thing is, John probably doesn't even know he's doing it. Oh, he knows he's doing it to Prentiss, but he can't possibly know what effect it's having here in the world of the living.

'You see, he wasn't like that. John wouldn't be giving us all this trouble if he knew. Except he can't know, because living people can't talk to the dead ...' Trask paused and looked straight at Nathan. 'Or maybe we can – now. We damn well have to try, anyway ...'

After another long pause, Zek spoke up. 'You haven't told us what's been happening,' she said. 'I mean, *how* is the Nightmare Zone getting bigger?'

Trask nodded tiredly and seemed to slump down into himself once more. 'At first it was local,' he said. 'That first time, it only affected the police station and the morgue. But since then it's been spreading. Four months later it was half-way up the Seven Sisters Road, moving down towards Highbury, and into Stroud Green. Another four months and it reached Crouch Hill, moved over into Newington, encroached upon Stamford Hill. Last time it was as far out as Islington, Upper Clapton and Hornsey. At the rate it's growing, it's only a matter of time before the whole of inner London falls inside its perimeter. Can you imagine that? All London the heart of the Nightmare Zone!

'As for what happens, what John Scofield's "talents" cause to happen ... that has to be seen to be believed. Inanimate objects move of their own volition, grave-yards send out foul-smelling fogs in the middle of summer, pet dogs set up a frenzy of howling for no apparent reason. Fires start by what appears to be spontaneous combustion, and go out again just as mysteriously; street lights dim and only come up again when it's over; rats pour out of the sewers, and roaches desert infested houses in their droves! Dead things — I mean people or the left-overs of people, zombies, corpses, cadavers — are seen moving, walking, *crumbling* in the weirdest places: private gardens, behind the plate-glass windows of locked stores, along disused railway lines and in underground stations. Even time is affected. There are inexplicable distortions: events which should take hours are contracted down into minutes, while others of short duration extend themselves apparently indefinitely. And these are just a few of the so-called "poltergeist activities".

'But the morning after . . . never a sign that anything is out of place, and everything back in working order. Except that for the people who saw, felt, dreamed or experienced something, *anything* of it . . . nothing will ever again be quite the same for them, and they're all mortally afraid . . .

'The dreamers are the ones who suffer most.'

'Dreamers?' This was Nathan again.

'Dreamers, yes,' Trask nodded. 'It happens at midnight, when most of the city is asleep. But there are dreamers and there are dreamers, Nathan. Sensitive people know when it's coming, and not just inside the Nightmare Zone. Psychics the world over are wont to nightmare when John Scofield goes on the rampage, tracking down and killing Tod Prentiss — again and again and again.

'A thousand men, women and children have dreamed it: John Scofield after his prey with a razor, an axe, or a blowlamp. Or Tod Prentiss with his face burned off, or with his belly slit open and his entrails uncoiling, or with his eyes dislodged and flopping on his cheeks.

630

John snarling his loathing, while Prentiss screams and runs and tries to protect himself, uselessly. It all takes place in the very heart of the Nightmare Zone, of course, but its psychic echoes are spreading, and its physical manifestations are getting stronger all the time.'

Zek was bewildered. 'And no one has wondered about it? I mean, among the ordinary population?'

'Oh, yes,' Trask told her. 'Psychiatrists, the governors of mental institutions, the police – who get called out to so many "bogus" sightings – all sorts of people. They all wonder about it, but they've no answer to it. For they don't know the cause. Only we know that, for we're the people who have to contain it. We're the ones who have to fight it. Except . . . we're losing the fight.'

'How do you fight it?' Nathan was curious. 'Where?'

'Where else?' Trask looked at him. 'Down there in that old basement behind what used to be a cop shop in Old Finsbury Park – "dead centre" of the Nightmare Zone. They died there, those two, and that's where John Scofield continues to chase his prey back into this world once in a four-month, so that he can kill him all over again.'

'And you want me to help?'

'You're the only one who can.'

'But so far Keenan Gormley is the only one who will speak to me.'

'So use him, tell him what you're doing, ask for his help. Keep up the pressure. You know, Nathan, your father used to say that the dead know just about everything there is to know. Make friends with the Great Majority, and you can consider any other problem at least half-way solved.'

'And if John Scofield simply *won't* talk to me?'

Trask got down from the podium, approached Nathan and put a hand on his shoulder. 'Well, if you can't make him listen to your deadspeak beforehand, then it will just have to be on the night.' (His face was suddenly gaunt and grey.) 'The night when you meet John face to face, and put yourself in his way when he goes after Tod Prentiss to re-kill him, and risk your very sanity trying to keep the two of them apart ... down there in the Nightmare Zone.'

And Nathan's voice was unaccustomedly hoarse as he asked: 'When will that be?'

But Trask's was hoarser as he answered, 'As of now, we're not sure. But it'll be soon, son. Too damn soon by far ...'

For the next two days Geoff Smart was Nathan's constant companion. Trask would have preferred to put aside his administrative work entirely and devote all his time to Nathan; but there were important matters which must be dealt with, arising out of what Nathan had told E-Branch about Turkur Tzonov, and what the Head of Branch had seen with his own eyes in Perchorsk. That was why Smart was temporarily standing in for Trask as Nathan's mentor: to give his boss time to attend to such items as had come up.

For fifteen years now, Britain, France, Germany, the USA and half a dozen other interested countries had had influential men, call them 'advisers', in the variously titled 'United Soviet States', the 'Free Soviet Alignment', or simply the USSR, as some world authorities still insisted on designating their tired old 'enemy'. These men were not engaged in espionage as such but did 'keep their eyes' on things. In a country as vast and sprawling and still as volatile as the no longer entirely 'united' USS, the West's vastly superior communication systems, famine relief organizations, nuclear proliferation and pollution control elements, and a witch's dozen

632

of other aid programmes, ensured that the presence of such men was appreciated – certainly by those people 'in charge'.

Premier Gustav Turchin was one such authority. Despite the devolution of almost all of the countries and ethnic territories within the old borders, Turchin was a central pivot – even a father figure – whose principal purpose was to keep his many squabbling children in order and so prevent the collapse of his great ungovernable estate into further chaos. And since many of these awkward children were nuclear powers in their own right, his was a very important position.

But 'Premier'? Hardly that, not in the sense of Khrushchev, Brezhnev, Andropov, Gorbachev and others before and since them. They had been Premiers, and up to Gorbachev's time at least had been all-powerful from their seats in Moscow's Kremlin. Turchin wasn't in the same league; his power was that vested in him by the people of many neighbouring but separate states covering a vast tract of land which was formerly the Soviet Union, and it could be removed from him just as easily.

Turchin was literally the 'popular choice'; wherefore he must try to make popular decisions on behalf of all of these frequently opposed states or find himself out of a job. In a way, he might even be seen as the East's answer to the Secretary General of the United Nations, except the nations Turchin spoke for were weak and mainly divided by poverty, petty jealousies, and old feuds; while the West was stronger than ever before. In short, the Premier could and must advise, if only to avoid chaos and anarchy – but he could never command.

On the other hand he did have power of a sort. For while his people could be rid of him if and whenever they so desired, they still had need of a representative on the world stage, and Gustav Turchin made an imposing figurehead. He had the charisma of a world leader, if not the financial or physical energy. And while his own people might occasionally threaten his so-called 'position of power', no threat of theirs could ever carry the weight of his – to simply quit.

And because he was mainly responsible for his nation's cohesion and security, he did have a measure of control over certain elements left over from former times. For instance, a much impoverished KGB, and 'the Opposition', of course: Moscow's own ESP-Agency, the Soviet equivalent of E-Branch. This made him Turkur Tzonov's direct superior; and who better for the West to talk to about Tzonov's indiscretions?

The Minister Responsible for E-Branch had been given a full briefing by Trask, and had passed on the salient points of that briefing to a British 'representative' in Moscow, an 'economic adviser' who had the ear of Premier Gustav Turchin. Thereafter there had been much toing and froing by Trask and the Minister Responsible, between E-Branch HQ and Whitehall, and the Minister's scrambler telephone had been hot with messages sent down it to Moscow.

The 'salient points' had been these:

That Turkur Tzonov had built up a small arsenal of weapons in the subterranean complex known as Perchorsk under the Urals. That we, the West (in particular an intelligence agency of the British Government) had reason to believe that Tzonov might be planning a limited invasion of the parallel world of vampires known to lie beyond the Perchorsk 'Gate'. That it was possible he would use the spoils of such an invasion to further his own causes ... whatever they might be. That Tzonov had illegal control of a sophisticated machine whose like had been banned for sixty years, since World War II, when the Nazis had been known to be interested in just such a device: a brain-washing machine which could empty its victims of all knowledge and intelligence, and in fact reduce them to vegetables – and then to corpses.

That Tzonov had planned to use this forbidden machine on a man (a human being, not a monster) who had come through the Gate from the other side, in order to obtain advance knowledge of his intended conquests. And that he had only been thwarted by the escape of the alleged 'alien'. That this refugee, not only from a cruel world but also from Turkur Tzonov's cruelties, had flown to the West and provided British E-Branch with much of the above information.

And last but not least, that one Siggi Dam – a telepath in Tzonov's employ, who might have been partly responsible for the escape of the alien from Perchorsk – seemed now to have disappeared off the face of the Earth. It was quite possible that Tzonov had taken his own 'punitive measures' against her, and disposed of her in such a way that she could never trouble him again. Not in this world, anyway.

These items in brief – plus a reminder that it was Gustav Turchin himself who had requested the Branch's assistance at Perchorsk – comprised the contents of the coded, scrambled messages which had gone out to 'our man in Moscow', and from him to the Premier during several private meetings. Since the preparation of these messages (not to mention their painfully neutral, carefully diplomatic wording) had been left to Trask, he'd had more than enough to keep him busy and on his toes . . .

But in the early afternoon of the third day following Goodly's NZ warning, as the secure channels to Moscow cooled a little and Trask waited on the results of his reporting, Geoff Smart came knocking on his office door to talk about Nathan.

'How's it going with him?' Trask wanted to know.

The empath shrugged, then said: 'Nathan's a difficult one to read. No, that's an understatement: at first he was impossible! I got a sort of whirlpool, or maybe a tornado. And yet it wasn't emotional. In fact it covered his emotions and obscured them, and probably his thoughts, too.'

'The numbers vortex,' Trask nodded. 'We know about that. It's the stuff that's in him, which we want to draw out. You're right: it covers his thoughts like a blanket, blocks out telepathic probes. We're fairly certain it's something come down to him from his father, and we've been looking for ways to improve upon it.'

'Then you're probably wasting your time,' Smart told him.

'Come again?' Trask couldn't tell if it was good news or bad.

'Once he got used to me, accepted me, saw that I wasn't a telepath or voyeur in the common sense of the word, his shield went down. Then . . . I really did get to him. And I have to tell you, that boy has emotions! Passions, fears, angers, hatreds: the full spectrum – but intense! If he's typical of his world, it must be one hell of a place.'

'You haven't read up on Sunside/Starside?' Trask's voice was sharp-edged. His orders had been very clear.

'I have, yes, but it still reads like fiction. That's what I'm trying to tell you: that Nathan has brought it all home to me. It's real now. Only a real place could do that to someone. He's . . . a mess!'

'So would you be, if you'd been through all that he's been through,' Trask answered. 'What else? And what makes you think we're wasting our time?'

'Because you're looking to enlarge him, give him

something, expose something. You're trying to widen his potential. But his nature, aura, everything about him, is already mature. He's at his peak. Oh, you can teach him, he can still learn things, but from now on that's cosmetic. I mean ... he's already equipped. He has everything he needs. That's the feeling I get: that he's like a baby who's about to become a toddler. One day he stands up, takes a first wobbly, tentative step, and walks! And before you know it he's climbing trees. Nathan's a newly hatched moorhen at the edge of its nest over the water. The hen only needs to give her chick a push ... and he swims! Do you follow me? I mean, I know what I'm talking about because I'm an empath, but I can't be sure I'm getting through to you.'

'I do know what you mean, yes,' Trask answered. 'There was a time when all his father needed was a push, too. What you're saying is: he's got the machinery, but he hasn't plugged it in yet?'

'When I stand beside him,' Smart said, 'it's like standing between a couple of giant electrodes. I mean, it's frightening. I think: Jesus, thank God the power's off! Why, he's like some kind of small Nightmare Zone in his own right!' And Trask saw him give a small, involuntary shiver . . .

But his words were like an invocation; for a moment later, Ian Goodly and Guy Teale were shoulder to shoulder at the door. Just glancing at their faces, Trask knew what it was. He indicated that they should enter, and said, 'Tonight?'

The cadaverous Goodly nodded and said, 'Has to be, Ben. We can feel it building even now. John Scofield has refuelled his batteries and is about to give it hell – or give you hell, as it works out. And I hate to say it, but better you than me!'

*

The sooner they got to it the better. Then, as the thing began to build through the afternoon and evening, they would feel it and know its strength.

Driving out to Old Finsbury Park, Trask suggested to Paul Garvey, their driver: 'It mightn't be a bad idea to stop somewhere and eat.'

'Do you really feel like eating?' Garvey glanced at him in the front passenger seat.

'No, but what with getting our act together and all that, we seem to have missed lunch. A couple more hours, we'll miss dinner, too. I for one don't fancy doing this on an empty stomach. By tonight we'll really be hungry. Now that would be the wrong time to eat!'

From the back of the car, perhaps naïvely, Nathan spoke up. 'I'm hungry now,' he said, which settled matters.

They stopped for half an hour at a greasy spoon where their 'alien' enjoyed sausage, bacon, eggs, and a mug of tea, just as he'd had for breakfast. Indeed, the standard English breakfast seemed to suit Nathan so well it might have been devised specifically with him in mind. The rest of them had sandwiches and coffee.

As they got back into the car, Nathan told them his immediate intention, and as he settled in a corner of the rear seat and closed his eyes, they kept their conversation to a minimum. He was talking to the ashes of Sir Keenan Gormley in his Garden of Repose a good many miles away, to find out if the Great Majority knew about John Scofield and the Nightmare Zone, and to discover whether Gormley could suggest some possible solution.

And as the esper team drew up in their vehicle outside the rundown police station in a wide, windblown street where yesterday's newspapers flapped like ghosts and the bleary windows of half-empty shop fronts gazed out on a chilly afternoon, Nathan already had his answer.

Yes, the teeming dead knew about John Scofield; indeed, he was the 'problem' Sir Keenan had mentioned when first Nathan went to see him. And no, there was no solution, not that Gormley could suggest anyway. Perhaps not surprisingly, the place beyond death – which was in fact no place, just a void, or at best an echo chamber for the voices of the incorporeal – was usually quiet and melancholy. People who expired and joined the Great Majority, they took time to settle in, but in the end their frustrations and anxieties dwindled and disappeared, by which time they were ready to take their places in the beyond. And *usually*, that place was quiet.

But it could be unquiet, too. Like now.

Murder victims – people who lost their lives needlessly, hideously, and often at the whim of psychopathic monsters who would go on unpunished in the world of the living, or at best imprisoned but still *alive*, while their victims had been robbed of that happy estate – they took longer to accept their fate. And sometimes they never would accept it.

Lynn Scofield and her son, Andrew, fell within the latter category. Lynn had been used monstrously: her home and body broken into, both violated and the latter destroyed. She had died with her throat stuffed with her own underwear, but not before she'd seen her son's head collapse under the assault of a maniac's booted feet.

As for Andrew: he had seen his mother's rape and had been knocked aside, almost unconscious, as Prentiss took her first as a man, then as a beast, and finally into her choking, convulsing throat. And when the battered boy had crawled to Lynn yet again in a vain attempt to fight this mad beast off, then Prentiss had finished the job and kicked him to death.

Well, and Nathan had said that the dead were often restless. So they were. But in Lynn and Andrew Scofield's case it went far beyond that. These two could scarcely be said to be 'resting in peace', far from it. In those long, terrible last minutes before they died, they'd been filled with a frenzy of fear, furious but impotent, and driven into a state of abject terror. And they still were. Inconsolable, mad with shock and completely unable to accept what had happened to them – this descent into a vast, unfeeling darkness – the Great Majority could not comfort them nor even get close enough to try. They had shut themselves out ... no, they had locked themselves in! Into the security of their own minds, mother and son together. Which had seemed to them the only safe place to be until John came home and put everything right again.

But as for John Scofield himself:

He *couldn't* come home, couldn't join them in their limbo, not until Tod Prentiss was brought to justice. Except John was unable to find a punishment to fit the crime; there was nothing cruel enough, no measure he could take to even the score. Which was why he pursued Prentiss beyond death itself, and would continue to do so for as long as his incorporeal, telekinetic powers would let him. Powers which in his case were not diminished but continued to grow.

And oh, yes, the teeming dead knew all about John Scofield, and about Tod Prentiss. The former who they couldn't reach, for his passion made him deaf to all their deadspeak pleas for sanity, and the latter who begged their mercy, their forgiveness, their protection. For if the Nightmare Zone was a menace in the world of the living, it was no less problematic in that place beyond life, where the minds of the dead lived on.

They, too, felt the build-up of metaphysical pressures as each four-month cycle approached its climax, and they knew the disruption which the release of John Scofield's mental energy would bring to them on their own level: the 'static' blocking their deadspeak; the agony of John's psychosis, which each and every one of them felt as Scofield drove his incorporeal mind to the limits of its potential; even the possibility that in his madness he might disrupt the 'aether' of death itself, and in so doing destroy the very element of their communication. Which was everything that they possessed.

If you could only get through to him, Sir Keenan Gormley had told Nathan across many deadspeak miles, where the Necroscope had huddled in the back of a car speeding him into the heart of the Nightmare Zone, *if you could only speak to him, then perhaps you could make him understand the danger in what he's doing. There have always been 'ghosts', Nathan, pitiful creatures who retain too much of the living world and forever try to return to it, and never settle into this place at all. But they are nothing compared to John Scofield. He is trying to return to your side* permanently, *and take Tod Prentiss with him for his own maniacal purposes! Now much as we dislike it, there is a balance between life and death. And it's a balance that John could disturb forever.*

To which Nathan had answered: *One man? One dead man, with so much power?*

And he had sensed Gormley's patient deadspeak nod as he argued: *But wasn't your father just such a man? A determined man with metaphysical talents? And Harry's talents were also exponential, Nathan: he went from strength to strength right up to the moment when –*

– When he died? For the first time there was a

certain sadness in Nathan's deadspeak voice as he mentioned his Necroscope father's death.

Yes, Gormley sighed. *Even from another dimension, something of his unthinkable pain reached out to us and found us here. His pain, and that of his son who died with him in your parallel world of vampires.*

And: *His son,* Nathan had thought to himself. *Harry Keogh's son, but by another woman. The Dweller: my changeling brother!*

But Gormley had continued:

And so you see, in some men if their will is strong enough, the possibilities are endless ... likewise the damage they can inflict! Just think of it: before your father and The Dweller died, they woke the dead in Perchorsk to do their bidding and put an end to any further agonies! Even here we heard The Dweller crying out for help, and knew how we had betrayed his father. (At which point Nathan had sensed Gormley's frustrated deadspeak shrug.) *And yet, apparently, it is a lesson that the Great Majority still haven't learned. For even now they deny you ...*

Here he had paused, only to continue in the next moment: *I mention this only to illustrate what may be achieved by strong men, even in death. And who is as strong as a madman, eh? Well, this John Scofield is very strong, you may believe me!*

Then Nathan had asked: *What is the worst he can do?*

Again Gormley's shrug, frustrated as ever. *There are those among the dead with ... theories. Except you must understand, they are only theories. Heaven forbid they should ever become fact! But if John Scofield's telekinesis was able to stretch the fabric which separates life from death far enough —*

— It might break?

Possibly. A theory, that's all.

And if it did, what then?

Then? (Now there was a hint of terror in Gormley's deadspeak voice.) *It would be the last trump, when not only John Scofield and Tod Prentiss, but all of the Great Majority would walk of their own volition! Burial grounds would give up their dead, and the world would be full of the unbearable odours of the tomb! Grief-stricken families would be reunited – but in the most monstrous way – when their dearly beloved dead ones came knocking on the door at the dark of the moon! Why, it's unimaginable! There would be plagues, wars between the living and the dead as the world became a madhouse. And everyone who died in those wars ... would join the ever-swelling ranks of the Great Majority in their strange new undeath!*

At that, Nathan had thought of what Ben Trask had told him of the NZ's manifestations. '... People, or their left-overs – zombies, corpses, cadavers – are seen moving, walking, crumbling in the weirdest places ...' Phantoms, of course, revenants forcibly moved by John Scofield's telekinetic powers into an incorporeal or at best ethereal existence on the living plane ...

But an entire world where the living and the dead could only be told apart by degrees of decay ... ? Sir Keenan Gormley was correct: it *was* unimaginable, and as a 'theory' must never be put to the test!

For the dead of this world were not like the Thyre of Sunside's endless furnace deserts. The nomadic Thyre were gentle, civilized beyond their environment and mode of existence. When Rogei the Elder, Nathan's first friend among the Thyre's teeming dead, had dragged himself – or rather, his mummified lich – from his niche in the Cavern of the Ancients to succour Nathan, no fear had attached to his ... activity; no stenches had accompanied it, no malice was implied or intended. And it would have been the same with all the dead of the Thyre.

But in this world and among these people?

In this world there were psychopaths, terrorists, rapists, murderers, arsonists. Among these 'ordinary' people there were those whose thoughts and deeds might even equal the evil of the Wamphyri themselves! In death such men were of no consequence; they were shunned by the Great Majority – quite literally 'excommunicated' by them – but what would they be in the world of Keenan Gormley's as yet theoretical 'strange new undeath'? Monsters as before? Warlords? Psychopaths, murderers, rapists and arsonists as of old? And what of the rest of Trask's 'poltergeist manifestations'? The inexplicable frenzy of household pets; ghost-fires that started and stopped themselves, as by some otherworldly spontaneous combustion; foul-smelling graveyard fogs, and the like?

Merely a prelude for things to come?

Trask's hand fell on Nathan's shoulder and caused him to start. He looked up into the other's face, then at the gaunt, wintry-grey street with its whirling newsprint and sweet-wrapper dust-devils, and its bleary-eyed houses and store fronts. And:

'This is it,' Trask told him, holding the car door open. 'The epicentre. The heart of the Nightmare Zone. And in there ... that's where you'll find the very heart ...' He pointed to the dilapidated police station, where an old-fashioned lamp – with many of its trapezoids of blue glass standing like broken teeth, shattered in their cast-iron frame – was bracketed over scarred oak doors with small-paned, reinforced glass windows in their upper panels. 'We've got something over six hours to get ourselves settled in. Well, to prepare ourselves, at least.'

'Deserted,' Nathan said, getting out of the car. 'But the whole street?'

Trask nodded. 'At both ends of the street you'll find the odd shop or two still open, and a couple of houses still occupied, but mainly the entire area is falling into dereliction. Let's face it, would you want to live here?'

The expressionless Paul Garvey had keys to the place; he opened the doors and Trask and his team went in; the interior smelled stale, damp, strange. More like some cavern lair than a building. 'It lingers,' Trask explained, his voice echoing. 'The smell, the feel, the aura as a whole. But back there —' grimacing, he nodded his head towards the unseen reports room and the rear of the building '— is where it's at its worst.'

Silent except for their oddly muffled footsteps, the four passed through the inquiries and waiting room into the reports centre with its slightly elevated counter and operations area, where Trask lifted a flap gate in the desk to climb a pair of shallow steps up into the Desk Sergeant's domain. 'They were playing cards right here,' he said, 'the night all of this got started. And down there,' he nodded towards an open door at the rear, where a damp-shining corridor led the way into an aching, echoing darkness, 'that's where the morgue is . . .'

Paul Garvey had never been here before. He asked, 'OK if I take a look?' He had the rest of the keys on a large key ring, including the one for the morgue.

Trask nodded. 'There should be a gradual build-up of psychic energies until just before midnight. After that . . . it'll be a riot! Until then, you'll be safe down there. But it will probably feel weird.'

The left side of Garvey's face twitched where, after all these years, severed nerve-endings were still trying to match themselves up. Johnny Found had cut him to the bone that time, so that in fact Garvey was lucky to have a face at all. 'Hey,' he said, 'it feels weird enough to me right here, right now!' And as he started down the corridor between the rows of empty cells, Nathan walked behind him.

Just inside the corridor there was a light switch. Garvey snapped it up and down once or twice but the lights stayed out. The small hairs at the back of Nathan's neck began to creep; he could feel something stirring; it was almost as if a waft of foul air had brushed his cheek, so that he held his breath for a moment to avoid inhaling it. Garvey had felt nothing; he went on, but Nathan held back a little to see if the thing recurred. Then Garvey was at the door to the morgue, and the keys jingled in his hand.

A moment more and the doors stood open. Garvey went in, and Nathan moved to close the distance between them. But in the twenty paces it took to pass along the corridor . . .

'. . . What the hell?' Garvey's shaken voice came echoing back to him; and to Trask and Smart, still in the Duty Room. 'But I thought this place was supposed to be – empty?!' The last word sounded as a gasp. And as Nathan reached the doors Garvey came stumbling out, his face white as chalk.

Trask and Smart came running, their feet clattering on the tiles. 'What is it, Paul?' Trask's rasping query grated on nerves that were suddenly raw.

Garvey flapped a hand at the yawning doors to the morgue. 'In there,' he gasped. 'Containers littering the floor. I saw bodies tipped out, grotesquely sprawled. There were filing cabinets all tumbled in a corner. But the corpses. They were . . . they were . . .'

Nathan looked inside Garvey's head, read his mind. It was easy, for Garvey was a telepath, too. He saw what the other had seen: metal coffins, and the dead bodies inside them trying to sit up – *their faces twisted in horror at the knowledge that they were dead yet still mobile!*

'They were what?' Trask brushed past the others and into the morgue. 'Alive?'

Nathan followed him into the large, cold square room and looked all about. But there was nothing to see. No steel caskets, no filing cabinets or corpses, nothing. Nothing to see or feel at all, except the cold. Garvey, shivering uncontrollably and looking into the room over Geoff Smart's shoulder, said: 'I saw what I saw, and then . . . I didn't!'

Trask grunted and said, 'It's started. And earlier than ever before.' Then, glancing out into the corridor at Smart: 'Do you feel anything?'

The empath's eyes were wide, his red brush of a crewcut seeming more than ever erect. 'The same as I felt last time,' he said. 'Only stronger, much stronger. I feel mounting fear, horror –'

'The Great Majority,' Nathan broke in. 'I can feel them, too. Their terror.'

– And I feel . . . a monstrous anger!' Smart finished.

Trask said, 'That'll be John.' And turning to Nathan, with some urgency: 'Son, I think maybe you'd better start doing your stuff right now. The sooner you can make contact – *if* you can make contact – the better.'

The air was colder still, and the temperature still falling. Nathan's breath plumed as he answered, 'I'll bring a chair from the other room. Then I'll ask you to leave me alone. If I need you, I'll call. But right now I would prefer to be alone. You're all espers. If you can feel something of the dead, then maybe they can feel something of you. Since it bothers them to talk to me, your presence can only make it that much more difficult. Also, I need to concentrate.'

He headed for the corridor but Trask stopped him. 'I'll go and get your chair. You stay here, and try to contact . . . them. Here, take my overcoat. The rest of us, we'll take turns out in the corridor.'

After he had left, Nathan asked Geoff Smart: 'What did you do last time?'

'What we always do: we tried to contain it. I can't say how much good we did, but we used whatever psychic powers were available in us to suppress the thing. I'm an empath: I used my talent to calm the atmosphere of the place, the unquiet spirits which were at work in it . . . to calm John Scofield, I suppose. Telepaths do the same: try to talk the thing down, with their minds. The others do whatever they can. As for Ben, he's good for moral support. In matters like this Ben's the rock that we all lean on.'

'Wouldn't it be better if the whole team, E-Branch in its entirety, were here to contain it?'

Smart's face was white in the frame of the doorway. 'The truth of the matter is,' he said, 'that we simply can't afford it. If matters got out of hand – if it got lethal – this way we know that only four of us pay the price. The survival of the Branch is paramount.'

Nathan frowned. 'Yet you let the head of the Branch risk his neck?'

Smart grinned, however humourlessly. 'Have you ever tried arguing with him? I'm not going to be the one who tells him to go home. Nathan, this man stood side by side with your father against vampires – even against Wamphyri! Now that might not be such a big deal in your world, but in this one . . .'

Trask was back with a metal-framed chair. Nathan took it to the centre of the room, sat down and drew Trask's overcoat more tightly round his shoulders. The cold seemed to have receded a little, but he drew the

648

overcoat to him anyway. Out in the corridor, Smart took first watch while Trask and Garvey went back to the Duty Room.

And there in the heart of the Nightmare Zone, Nathan collapsed his shield of alien numbers and opened his mind, hoping that the Great Majority would sense him there not as a thing to be feared but as their friend. And then that he would be heard and heeded by all the teeming dead . . .

V

Dead Voices

It was a tumult of distant, only half-discernible whispers, a babble — a Babel? — but of crumbling autumn leaves skittering over the stone flags of Nathan's mind. The psychic aether seethed with them: like the static *hiss* issuing from a coastguard's radio as he listens for Mayday messages on a stormy night. Except these whispers *were* that message: the terrified SOS of the teeming dead. Not sent out to the Necroscope but to each other — like the hoarse, questioning whispers of frightened children trapped in a dark place — which Nathan overheard because he had a walkie-talkie, his deadspeak, but couldn't answer because they were too afraid to switch their set to receive.

He fine-tuned his talent to listen to these tumultuous spirit voices, which would scare any other man half to death, if any other were able to hear them at all. But Nathan Kiklu, or Keogh as it now transpired, had listened to voices such as these all of his life, from childhood. And he knew that their owners were harmless . . . mainly. He also knew, however, that to interrupt would be to silence them, causing them to withdraw as from a leper.

It was the legacy of his father, come down to him in two worlds. For in the end Harry had been a monster, and the dead of both worlds had feared him. Or rather, they had feared his necromantic talents. Likewise they feared Nathan, and at any other time must surely have detected him by now, but their circumstances were such that his presence had passed by unnoticed.

So the Great Majority continued to voice their fears in the unending night of death, and Nathan listened in, trying to decipher their deadspeak whispers and uncertain as to his best course of action. And yet if he was to help them, help himself and his new-found E-Branch friends, he *must* break in, must attempt to establish some kind of contact at least. Perhaps by now Sir Keenan Gormley had found the time to talk to them. There was only one way to find out, and the sooner the better.

Nathan cast about with his metaphysical mind, discovering nearby presences in the aether of the beyond. These could only be people who had died close by, perhaps in the hospital overhead, whose spirits yet attached to this place. He would make his first overtures to them; of all the dead, they were surely the closest to the Nightmare Zone.

In this, despite that he'd been born with his talent, Nathan showed his inexperience, his immaturity as a Necroscope. For he was already aware of others who had died even closer to this place, which he nevertheless failed to take into account as he concentrated his deadspeak thoughts directly into the aether. And whispering so quietly that only he himself could hear it, he said:

'Whoever you are, I need your help. I need you to help me now, so that I can help you later. My name is Nathan, and I'm . . . alive.'

WHAT? WHO? NATHAN? . . . *LIAR!*

It was like the shout of a giant or some furious madman in Nathan's mind, causing him to start to his feet. But of course he was the only one who heard it, and out in the corridor Geoff Smart wasn't even looking.

The empath's talent wasn't automatic but must be induced, like a kind of self-hypnotism. Living with his own thoughts and emotions for the moment, he wasn't much concerned with anyone else's. And anyway, midnight was still a long way off. Smart leaned against a wall and lit a cigarette.

But in the morgue:

The temperature had dropped again, plummeted, and Nathan's breath plumed as before. And again the short hairs on the back of his neck stood erect as he took slow, careful steps towards the open doors. For he could actually *feel* the presence there in the room with him, and knew that its powers were as awesome as his own. But where his were harmless, its could only be — devastating!

STOP! The command brought him up short, panting. It was as if he were back in Turgosheim beyond the Great Red Waste, in Runemanse, and the Seer Lord Maglore of the Wamphyri had spoken to him; such had been the force of that single word. But still it had not dawned on him who issued it. And:

'Who are you?' he whispered.

YOU KNOW ME. AND I KNOW YOU — *TOD PRENTISSSS!* The last word sounded in Nathan's mind as a protracted hiss, filled with menace, loathing. And now indeed he knew who the presence was.

'John Scofield!'

And another voice, half-wondering, asked: 'What?'

It was Geoff Smart, silhouetted like a wraith in his own cigarette smoke and a swirling, luminous mist just beyond the heavy steel doors, drawing deeply on his smoke and rubbing his hands together briskly, then more slowly, as he stared at Nathan where once more he inched towards the corridor. But now the empath knew that something was wrong, and reached out a tentative mental probe towards Nathan's aura . . . A mistake!

WHAT? DO YOU HAVE FRIENDS HERE? AND YOU THINK THEY CAN HELP YOU? THINK *AGAIN*, TOD PRENTISSSS!

Smart couldn't hear Scofield's words but instead *felt* them — like hammer blows to his psyche, rocking him on his heels — as the steel doors to the morgue slammed shut in his face. And: 'Nathan!' he found breath to yell. *'Nathan!'* But Nathan was on the other side of the doors.

Trask and Garvey came running. The telepath was more composed now, but the left side of his face was alive with jerks and twitches as his nerves continued to play him up a little. 'What now?' Trask's voice was hoarse with dread.

'Nathan's in there,' Smart gasped. 'But he isn't alone. There's something — someone — in there with him. It has to be John Scofield.'

Trask tried the doors. 'Locked.'

'Impossible.' Garvey shook his head. 'I opened them, and I still have the keys.' Then he realized what he'd said. Nothing was impossible here, for this was the Nightmare Zone.

'Give me the keys,' Trask told him, and a moment later he had a key in the lock. But as he tried to turn it . . .

. . . It was as if a cold, invisible, iron-hard hand yanked his own hand aside — and snapped off the key in the lock! And the key-ring fell jangling to the floor. Down there, streaming out from a crack under the door, a faintly luminous mist began to lap about their feet, causing them to move uneasily, as if they stood in ice-cold water.

Then Garvey said: 'He's talking to someone. I can

sense it, feel it, but I can't hear it. It isn't telepathy but deadspeak.'

'Well, that's what he's in there for,' Trask rasped. 'But we're not supposed to be locked out here. Telekinesis locked this door. And yes, it *has* to be John Scofield. He's early this time. Nathan must have brought him on.' And turning to Smart: 'Take the keys. Go round to the side of the hospital. Maybe you'll find a key that will open a door. If not, then break something, a window, door, anything. But get into the hospital and down to the morgue.'

And as Smart raced off back along the corridor and out of sight: 'Come on.' Trask took Garvey's elbow. 'Don't I recall seeing a bench back there in the inquiries room? One of those old-fashioned oak benches that weigh half a ton? It will make one hell of a battering-ram!'

They ran down the mist-wreathed corridor, leaving Nathan alone in the morgue with the unquiet spirit of John Scofield. For the moment, it was as much as they could do . . .

In the morgue, Nathan began to see things. He knew that they weren't there, but just like Garvey before him he saw them. The triple-stacked container unit with its rows of sliding, refrigerated cabinets; the filing system in a corner recess; a pair of medical trolleys with white rubber sheets thrown over them. A scene from the past, brought into being by the flux of John Scofield's dead thoughts. For a ghost doesn't have to be revenant of sentience; it can also be of a place, an object, a thing other than human, other than once-alive. In this sense the phantasmal items which Nathan saw *were* ghosts, but ghosts of the morgue itself, not its inhabitants.

That was only what he *saw*, however, while what he *heard* and *felt* . . .

... Those things were quite different.

For as the steel doors had slammed shut, closing Nathan in and condemning him to darkness, then the presence of John Scofield had loomed that much larger, until it could be felt everywhere about. And even as Nathan realized his predicament, so the dead madman's voice came back again, so powerful as to be painful in the echoing caverns of the Necroscope's mind:

TOD PRENTISS ... PRENTISS ... *PRENTISSSS!*

'Wrong!' Nathan whispered. 'I'm not Tod Prentiss. My name is Nathan. It's Nathan ... Keogh.' Keogh, yes! Let Scofield know who he was, *how* he could speak to the dead. Let them all know that he was the son of the first true Necroscope. Surely there were friends other than Sir Keenan Gormley out there?

KEOGH? KEOGH! KEOOOOGH –

– *NECROSCOPE!* And for the first time Scofield's demented deadspeak voice contained something other than malice and madness. So that Nathan pressed his momentary advantage:

'Nathan Keogh, yes. I'm the son of Harry Keogh, and your friends in E-Branch have asked me to help you. They couldn't reach you but I can. And I'm the only one who can. That's why you have to listen to me.'

Thickening, the poltergeist mist had taken on a lot more of weird luminosity; sufficient now to light the entire morgue with an eerie blue foxfire. And the morgue really *was* a morgue. Its contents appeared real now; not wavering, insubstantial and half opaque, but solid as life. John Scofield's hatred made it real, as his enhanced telekinetic powers prepared the killing ground for a new assault upon his dead enemy.

NATHAN KEOOOOGH ... His deadspeak voice breathed again – breathed the mist, which swirled about the room and filled its corners, bringing them to glowing life. And: NO, YOU WOULD TRY TO TRICK ME, the voice continued. IF YOU ARE KEOGH, YOU WOULD DEPRIVE ME OF MY PREY. AND IF YOU ARE *NOT* KEOGH, THEN YOU ARE PREN-TISSSS! TOD PRENTISS, YESSSS, AND YOU ARE AFRAID OF DYING ... AGAIN! NOW LET ME THINK. HOW HAVE I KILLED YOU? IN HOW MANY WAYS?

'I'm Keogh,' Nathan insisted. 'Nathan Keogh. How else am I talking to you, if not in deadspeak? *Who* else but a Necroscope could do it?'

THE DEAD CAN DO IT. ANY ONE OF THEM CAN. BUT YOU KNOW THAT, DON'T YOU, PREN-TISS? FOR YOU *ARE* DEAD, AND WOULD REMAIN DEAD – EXCEPT I DRIVE YOU BACK INTO A SEMBLANCE OF LIFE SO THAT I MAY KILL YOU YET AGAIN. AS INDEED I *INTEND* TO KILL YOU YET AGAIN!

Feeling the dreadful intensity of Scofield's obsession – his paranoia, which would not be denied by anything as simple as the truth – Nathan opened his deadspeak channels wider yet. Now he must enlist the aid of the Great Majority, for his was only one voice and theirs were many. If he could only persuade them to talk to him, perhaps he could convince Scofield of his truth. His thoughts were deadspeak, of course, and the madman had heard them.

OH, CLEVER, SO CLEVER! BUT YOU WERE CLEVER IN LIFE, TOO, ELSE YOU WOULD NEVER HAVE LASTED SO LONG. BUT TELL ME THIS: IF YOU ARE IN 'TRUTH' THE NECRO-SCOPE, THEN WHY DON'T THE DEAD TALK BACK TO YOU? OR ARE THEY SAVING THAT FOR LATER – THEIR 'TRUMP CARD' – WHEN EVERYTHING ELSE FAILS? THE ONLY THING

THAT PUZZLES ME IS WHY THEY SHOULD CON-
CERN THEMSELVES WITH YOU AT ALL!

'And what about you?' Nathan found courage to
answer. 'Don't you care about the Great Majority?' (His
words went out to all the dead now.) 'Are you so
unfeeling of them? Don't you know how you're harming
them, how much damage you can do? And not only to
the dead but to the living? You mentioned a trump
card. But would you play the "last trump", John?'
(Nathan had watched an E-Branch Duty Officer playing
patience one night; he knew what cards were, and he'd
learned the meaning of 'the last trump' the first time he
spoke to Keenan Gormley, for deadspeak often conveys
more than is actually said.)

WHAT ARE YOU SAYING? And again there was
other than madness in the great voice. MY ARGUMENT
IS WITH YOU, TOD PRENTISS. IT HAS NOTHING
TO DO WITH THE TEEMING DEAD – UNLESS
THEY WOULD DENY ME MY REVENGE. AND
CERTAINLY IT HAS NOTHING TO DO WITH THE
LIVING. THE LAST TRUMP? TO CALL UP THE
DEAD? BUT SURELY THAT'S YOUR PROVINCE,
'NECROSCOPE'! The voice was caustic, full of sarcasm.

'And yours.' Nathan was growing desperate, and still
the dead ignored him. Or if not that – if they were
beginning to listen to him now – listening was *all* they
were doing. 'It's your province, too. For you're the one
who calls up Tod Prentiss out of death, to make him
pay for what he did to you and yours. Well, and
perhaps you have the right, but why must all of the
dead suffer? And what of the living?'

TRICKERY! Scofield bellowed. WORD GAMES!
MIND GAMES! BUT I WON'T PLAY THEM WITH
YOU. YOU ARE GOING TO DIE – AGAIN AND
AGAIN AND *AGAIN*, TOD PRENTISSSS!

Word games . . .

Well, in a sense Scofield was right: it was a word game of sorts, and Nathan was good at them. The Mage of Runemanse himself had admitted as much. But this time . . . so much depended on the game that Nathan must use every word to maximum effect. And so he fell silent, to consider his next move.

The air in the morgue was freezing now, and it throbbed almost audibly with a barely contained power that galvanized Nathan's hair into electrical life and raised goose-flesh on his arms and back. It was at least five and a half hours to midnight, and for all of that time the power would be building. Surely it couldn't be contained. Not in one room. Not by one man.

Meanwhile, he had inched his way slowly to the doors and now tried them. Useless; there was no give in them; they might as well be welded shut. And tendrils of blue-glowing mist were seeking him out, creeping across the floor and weaving through the bitterly cold air to where his breath plumed frosty white. While starting up again in his head:

HOW MANY TIMES HAVE I KILLED YOU, TOD PRENTISS? NOT ENOUGH, NOT NEARLY ENOUGH. AND IN HOW MANY WAYS? I HAVE CUT YOUR THROAT WITH A RAZOR. BUT . . . HAVE I BURNED YOU? NO. I'VE DRIVEN NAILS INTO YOUR EYES, YOUR BRAIN. BUT HAVE I CRUSHED YOUR SKULL WITH MY TELE-KINESIS, OH SO SLOWLY, UNTIL BRAIN FLUIDS TRICKLE FROM YOUR EARS LIKE THE YOLKS OF EGGS? NO. I'VE GELDED YOU WITH A WHITE HOT POKER, DRIVING IT INTO THE STEAMING RAW HOLE OF WHAT WAS YOUR SEX. BUT HAVE I DROWNED YOU IN BLOOD . . . ?

... NOT YET!

Putting his shoulder to the doors and leaning his weight on them — like shoving at the face of a granite cliff, without moving it the smallest fraction of an inch — Nathan felt the mist damp around his ankles; damp and mobile ... and yet glutinous, too.

Gluey ...

He looked down —

— And saw that the floor was red! Six inches deep in red! And Scofield's words came back to him: 'But have I drowned you in blood? Not yet!'

Nathan sucked in air in a huge gasp, held it, thought for a moment that his heart had stopped, that at the very least he was going to topple over, faint — and knew that that was the last thing he could do. He daren't faint! For he was standing in blood up to his ankles, and felt it oozing, soaking through his trousers, socks, shoes. For a moment he didn't believe it, but he could see it, feel it, smell it. Blood!

On Starside, in Turgosheim, the Wamphyri had a saying: the blood is the life. But here it was or could be the death. Dead blood, like the terrible *juice* of a thousand slaughterhouses, conjured by the telekinetic mind of a dead man to slap in sluggish, scarlet wavelets at Nathan's ankles ... No, at his calves! For the lake of blood was getting deeper by the second.

Galvanized, gasping for air, and barely managing to rein back on his horror, Nathan sloshed through this crimson stuff of nightmares — this stuff of the Nightmare Zone — to make for one of the surgical trolleys standing draped in its white rubber sheet. If it was real he would climb onto it, lift himself out of the blood. And if it wasn't real ... then neither was the blood.

But as he got there, so the rubber sheet bulked out, took on shape: the outline of a human body! And

659

suddenly sitting up – jerking erect like a puppet on a string, so that the sheet slipped to one side – the corpse turned its pale, white, silently screaming face to look at Nathan! Its throat was slashed ear to ear, and its wrists sliced through, and the dead blood was pouring from the wounds in a flood!

'No!' Nathan shouted, shoving spastically at the trolley and sending it rolling sluggishly through the deep red flood, its gruesome burden lolling, then toppling into a lake of its own making. And all a fantasy, a nightmare conceived by John Scofield where his dead mind thought its telekinetic thoughts in the heart of the Nightmare Zone. But a fantasy that could kill, stop a man's heart, freeze the very blood in his veins – or cause him to drown in it!

A fantasy that was rapidly expanding.

The other trolley was similarly occupied with a silently screaming, blood-gushing corpse, and the aluminium caskets had floated free of their refrigerated bank, to drift like metal boats on a crimson lake. And from within them a frenzied hammering of corpse hands on vibrating panels, the lids thrown violently open, corpses trying to stand up, capsizing their grotesque vessels and tipping themselves into the ghastly flood.

The blood was up to Nathan's thighs. He waded to the filing cabinets and climbed them, and sat in the corner with his back to the walls, watching the staggering corpses with their slit throats and wrists where they gradually submerged in the ever-deepening tide. And without even realizing it, suddenly the Necroscope found himself rocking to and fro and moaning to himself. The human mind can only take so much . . .

Nathan! It was Sir Keenan Gormley's horrified deadspeak voice. *Nathan, this isn't the way to go!*

Another dead man, Nathan thought, which was deadspeak, of course. *A plague of dead men. Even Starside, Turgosheim, was better than this.*

And suddenly Gormley was frantic in his mind. *Nathan ... are you giving in? But you mustn't! Your father never gave in. He was a fighter to the end.*

Nathan wanted to laugh, cry, shout his frustration: symptoms of hysteria, which finally he recognized. Somehow he controlled himself, said: *Harry Keogh could afford to fight. His army fought for him. The dead were his friends, his troops. I have nothing, only Harry's blood. As for his 'talent': what good is that if the Great Majority won't let me use it?*

But they've been watching, listening, Gormley told him. *You opened yourself up to them, and they entered. They heard your argument with John Scofield, your plea on their behalf, and on behalf of the living. They've felt the warmth of your deadspeak thoughts and know that you're on their side, Nathan. And now they're ready to help you. Indeed, they've been helping you, or trying their hardest.*

Nathan felt a new strength, new hope. Gormley had a persuasive personality. *The dead are helping me? How? In what way?*

Scofield's wife and son are locked in their own terror, as they've been since Tod Prentiss murdered them. But now, as the Great Majority make every effort to comfort them, they are coming out of it. They were in trauma, Nathan, beyond our reach – and perhaps more importantly, beyond John Scofield's reach! They should be able to provide the element of control which is all he's lacking. Together with his family, Scofield will be whole again.

NOOOOO!!! Scofield was back again, more furious than ever. TRICKERY! YOU TORTURED THEM IN LIFE, AND NOW YOU WOULD TORTURE THEM

IN DEATH. AH, YOU CAN FOOL THE TEEMING DEAD, TOD PRENTISS, BUT YOU CAN NEVER FOOL ME! NOW DROWN, BASTARD, IN THE BLOOD OF THE DEAD!

And suddenly it was raining red!

Nathan cast a disbelieving, horrified glance at the low ceiling just overhead, watched crimson cracks leaking first a splash, a trickle, then streams of blood. The cracks joined up to form a spiderweb whose scarlet threads zig-zagged rapidly, wildly across the broad plaster expanse; threatening blotches and blisters formed as the ceiling bulged under the weight of blood; the plaster tore open with a soggy, ripping sound like wet, rotten meat, letting down its load into the morgue. And washed from his perch, Nathan went under.

Then . . .

. . . The doors burst open! The twin-door leading to the police station, and a moment later the door to the basement of the hospital. But it was as if they were forced open, from within. And in fact they had been, by the sheer weight of blood! Or by the weight of the Mind that had created the illusion.

In the corridor, Trask and Garvey were knocked off their feet, hurled back along the cell-lined corridor clinging to a bench. Likewise in the hospital: Geoff Smart's legs seemed cut out from under him as he was sent flying, slapped down, drenched in blood.

It happened . . . and it was over! As quickly as that.

And nothing had changed, except the time.

Out in the corridor, Ben Trask and Paul Garvey issued simultaneous cries of astonishment. They dropped their bench battering-ram, which narrowly missed Trask's feet, causing him to exclaim and jump back a little. Then, off balance, he sat down abruptly on the softly gleaming tiles – but not in a pool of blood.

Garvey leaned back weakly against the wall; he mopped his brow with a trembling hand, felt the impaired flesh of his face jerking uncontrollably. In the doorway to the hospital basement, Geoff Smart tottered like an infant; sick and completely disorientated, he bumped left and right against the uprights of the wide door frame. But there was no blood anywhere. Not a drop to be seen.

Finally the three espers pulled themselves together, and Trask and Smart entered the morgue. Nathan was seated in a corner ashen-faced, gasping for air and hugging his knees. And the way he turned his head to stare all about, it was obvious that his disorientation was the worst of all . . .

In his time, Ben Trask had seen and been through a lot. Also, he was the human lie-detector and knew that what he was looking at now was the plain truth. First to recover himself fully, he went straight to Nathan. 'Son? Are you OK?'

Nathan could breathe easy again, and as Trask helped him to his feet he asked, 'What . . . what *happened*?' He was shivering and damp; not with blood, but his own cold sweat.

'Out there?' Trask looked over his shoulder at the silhouetted door space. The glowing blue mist had disappeared along with the blood. 'We've been trying like hell to get in. That's about all that's happened. And in here?'

Nathan felt dehydrated. He knew Trask had brought coffee, sugar and milk with him in the car; all the makings. And still shivering, he said: 'I'll tell you all about it . . . but first I need a drink.'

Smart came to help Trask with Nathan. 'I was with you right at the end,' he said. 'God, I don't know what it was about, but it must have been the worst nightmare anyone ever suffered!'

Paul Garvey waited out in the corridor; not cowardice, just good sense. It wouldn't be clever for all four of them to be in the morgue together. But as the others came out, he said: 'I was with you, too. Or I would have been – if they had let me.'

'They?' Trask looked at him.

'I tried to reach Nathan just as we were about to start using the bench on the door,' Garvey explained. 'But there was a telepathic shield round his mind: "static", as we would call it in the Branch. Except . . . it was cold, cold stuff. Nothing living created it.'

'Must have been Scofield,' Trask nodded.

But Nathan said, 'Not necessarily. For there are tele-paths among the dead, too. And Keenan Gormley told me they're trying to help us now.'

'By blocking your mind?' Trask raised an eyebrow.

Nathan shrugged. 'Perhaps by protecting it from the worst of what Scofield could do. And if so I'm glad, for what he *did* was bad enough!'

They were back in the Duty Room. Smart made coffee while Nathan told what had happened to him. As he finished his story there came a burst of static from a pocket radio Trask had left sitting on the reports desk.

'Hasn't worked since we got here,' Trask commented. 'Else I might have tried ordering up some cutting gear for that door back there . . .' Then he frowned. 'I told them not to bother us until 11:00 p.m., and then to stay in close contact. So why are they trying to get through now?'

White as a sheet, Garvey answered: 'Because it's 11:00 p.m., that's why!' He was staring disbelievingly at his watch, his eyes round as saucers.

And finally they knew about the time. All of their watches told the same story: a story of warped time, the extension of a brief episode into something that had lasted for well over four hours. 'What?' Smart wasn't able to accept it. 'We were moving in slow motion or something?'

'Don't concern yourself with it,' Trask told him. 'It can drive you crazy trying to figure it out. It's just another one of those weird things that can happen in the Nightmare Zone.'

But Paul Garvey said: 'It does pose a problem, though. In that we only have sixty minutes left to Zero Hour . . .'

Finally the static broke up, E-Branch got through to them, and David Chung's slightly tinny, worried voice said: 'Sunray, this is Echo Hotel Quebec. Signals, over?'

'Echo Hotel Quebec, this is Sunray,' Trask answered. 'Signals OK . . . but let's junk the radio procedure. We haven't the time.'

Chung's sigh of relief was clearly audible, and then his question: 'Is everything OK? I've been trying to get you for the last hour. I was about ready to send a car over. Most of E-Branch has reported for duty tonight. We're there with you right now . . . in mind if not in body.' Chung was one of only a handful of men in the entire world who could say that sort of thing and actually mean it.

'We've had a few problems,' Trask said. 'But it's cool now for the moment. You can give us a buzz every ten minutes or so, but don't send the cavalry! And that's an order. There are more than enough of us in the firing line already.'

'It's just that Zek wasn't able to get through to Paul or Nathan,' Chung said. 'And I couldn't locate you, despite that I knew where you were. None of us was getting anything! You were swamped with static. And . . . naturally, we were worried.'

'Every ten minutes,' Trask repeated. 'Meanwhile . . . well, you can wish us luck.' He broke contact.

Smart wanted to know: 'So why has everything suddenly gone quiet now?'

Trask glanced at him, noticed how drawn he was looking. All of them were. And Nathan's clothes didn't fit too well. Trask would be willing to bet that Nathan had lost seven or eight pounds in weight. Returning his gaze to Smart he said: 'It must have taken a hell of a lot out of John Scofield to put on a show like that. Now he'll be recuperating, regenerating himself. But that was only the start of it. The finale comes at 12:00 p.m.'

Paul Garvey's face was as expressionless as the unfeeling flesh it was made of, as he put in: 'And if time narrows down again? What then?'

Trask shrugged, but in no way negligently. 'You tell me.'

Nathan finished his coffee, got to his feet, looked at his friends. 'I almost got through to them,' he said. 'To the teeming dead. I need to speak to Keenan Gormley again, and through him to the Great Majority. Even to John Scofield. Especially to him. But I need privacy, and quiet. And I only have an hour . . .'

Trask was on his feet at once. 'You'll go back in there?'

Nathan's turn to shrug. 'That's where it is, Ben. Didn't you name it yourself? The . . . what, epicentre? Whatever's coming, it's coming out of there. John Scofield is in there. And his wife and son, finally willing to accept what's happened to them. Even Tod Prentiss, hiding somewhere in there. And all the Great Majority, prepared to talk to me at last. They need me now. And if I'm ever going to get back to Sunside, I need them. So there's no other way. I have to go back in.'

Trask opened his mouth to make an answer but nothing came out. His eyes went instead to the electric jug in which Smart had boiled water for the coffee. It was no longer plugged in, but the water had started to boil. And Garvey was staring at his watch again. Gapemouthed, he showed the others: the second hand was sweeping round the dial!

Nathan flew down the steps to the corridor of softly shining tiles, and raced along it to the morgue. He didn't want to go in but he must. Too much depended on it: the peace and sanity of the living and the dead of two worlds. And behind him as he entered the morgue, the doors slammed shut again.

PRENTISS! John Scofield's mad, awesome deadspeak voice was back in his mind. TOD *PRENTISSSS!* And Nathan's hackles rose as he skidded to a halt in the blue-misted room and felt again the telekinetic aura of the dead man, a tangible force in the midnight morgue.

'Not Prentiss,' he answered in a gasp. 'My name's Nathan. Nathan Keogh. Why don't you listen to the dead, John? They'll tell you who I am. Why don't you listen to Sir Keenan Gormley? Before you were a member of E-Branch, he was the head of that organization. He was my father's friend, and now he's mine. I know because I can talk to him, even as I'm talking to you. I know because I'm the Necroscope. Would you harm me, John? The only friend you have left in the living world? The son of the man who taught the teeming dead how to speak to one another?'

WHEN I SEEK YOU OUT (Scofield ignored Nathan's pleading), I FIND YOU – ALWAYS. YOU HIDE FROM ME, KEEP QUIET AND STILL, CLOSE YOUR MIND, BUT I ALWAYS FIND YOU. THIS TIME I'VE FOUND YOU AGAIN, BUT YOU WOULD TRICK ME INTO BELIEVING THAT YOU ARE SOME OTHER, THIS KEOGH. EXCEPT I

KNOW YOUR DECEPTION. HOW *CAN* YOU BE ANY OTHER BUT TOD PRENTISS? I'VE SHUT THE TEEMING DEAD OUT, FOR THEY WOULD ONLY MEDDLE. AND THE ONE VOICE – THE ONE LOATHSOME *BEING* – I SEEK, IS YOU. OF ALL THE GREAT MAJORITY, YOURS IS THE SINGLE VOICE I ALLOW MYSELF TO HEAR. WHEREFORE ... I ... KNOW ... *YOU* ... TOD PRENTISSSS!

Cracks zig-zagged across the floor; the room shook with a rumbling rage of its own; the floor fell away beneath Nathan's feet, leaving him standing on a crumbling jut of tiled masonry as the walls extended themselves downwards, changing from brick and plaster to rough-hewn rock. He teetered this way and that as more tiles and masonry fell away, spinning into the blue-glowing deeps. And down there, far below – redroaring fire! Its vengeful heat warmed the shaft like a breath of hell.

You have the wrong man, John! It was Sir Keenan Gormley's frantic deadspeak voice, homing in on the awesome Centre of Power that was Scofield's incorporeal mind. *You don't know me but I know you. I know of you. All of the teeming dead know you, and if you persist in what you're doing the living will know of you, too. Indeed, you may even destroy their world!*

If Scofield heard him at all, he ignored him. But to Nathan: HOW MANY TIMES HAVE I KILLED YOU? IN HOW MANY WAYS? A GOOD MANY, I KNOW. BUT HAVE I CRUSHED YOU IN A FALL, AND BURNED YOU IN HELL'S OWN FIRES?

More of the tiles fell from the rim of Nathan's rapidly diminishing refuge, until he knew that the projecting tongue of masonry couldn't hold him up for very much longer. But was it really possible for Scofield to crush him in an imaginary fall, or turn him to a cinder in imaginary fires?

It was, yes: possible to crush Nathan with the power of his telekinetic mind, and to *move* the fires of inner earth to surround him with their heat, which is such that it will melt steel. Nathan was losing his balance. He slipped, fell, clung to the disintegrating masonry as more debris went tumbling into the mental pit which Scofield had created.

But:

John! (A woman's deadspeak voice, sighing, soft, tender. But tired, too. So very tired.) *John, come home now. Wherever you are and whatever you're doing, stop it now and come home. We're . . . here, John. And we're not afraid any more. The . . . the dead have helped us to overcome. They can help you, too. So please come home now. Oh, it's a strange sort of home, I know. But where we are — the three of us together, you, me, Andrew — that's home . . .*

LYNN . . .?

Now Scofield heard. But did he believe? LYNN? His voice gonged as before, but its tone was different: wondering as opposed to furious. And then . . . a groan! BUT WOULD THEY USE YOU, TOO, TO CON-FUSE ME AND DELAY MY JUSTICE? The pain, sorrow and anguish in that voice would be enough for twenty grieving men. ARE YOU . . . ARE YOU A PART OF IT?

Part of what, John? There is no plot, my love. But just as Tod Prentiss is in hiding from you, so we've been hiding, too — from the truth! And so have you. We've been hiding from each other. But now it's time to come together, John, and it's also time for you to come home.

Lynn Scofield had been doing all right until she mentioned Prentiss's name. But that had been a huge

669

mistake. HOME? (The rage was back in her husband's dead voice.) I SHOULD COME HOME NOW, WHEN I HAVE HIM WHERE I WANT HIM? HE *DESTROYED* MY HOME AS I NOW DESTROY HIM!

The lone fang of rock broke away from the wall with Nathan still clinging to it. Turning end over end, he felt the rush of heated air from the core of volcanic lava below him, and saw the sheer unscalable walls go rushing past. Then . . .

. . . The *pace* slowed down! He continued to plunge – but – oh – so – slooooowly! He floated, a feather with the weight of a man. And he knew how, why.

It was the teeming dead. If John Scofield could do it, so could they . . . Their massed minds . . . The joint effort of a million dead souls, who suddenly knew Nathan for his real value, just as they had known his father in the early days of Harry Keogh's earthly innocence.

And now they turned their single deadspeak voice on John Scofield, telling him:

John, we've found Tod Prentiss for you, driven him out of hiding. And we'll give him to you willingly this one last time, in order to prove how wrong you are. But if you let Nathan die, you'll be damned by the dead for ever! You of all men know what a crime it is: to take the life of someone much loved. Kill Tod Prentiss again if you must, but not this man. For Nathan Keogh is the Necroscope, John! He's the light in what's left of the 'lives' of each and every one of us. Without his father, what would we ever have been? And without him . . . who can say?

YOU HAVE . . . FOUND TOD PRENTISS? Scofield's voice was uncertain. THEN SHOW HIM TO ME. GIVE HIM TO ME . . .

And another voice – terrified, utterly mindless with

670

fear – cried: *No, NO, NOOOOO!!!* The scream of a maniac, yes. Of a trapped, rabid animal. Tod Prentiss's scream.

Nathan, falling slow as a leaf, yet hurtling to his doom for all that, 'saw' the face of Tod Prentiss. As it had been, then in various stages of languid, loathsome corruption, and finally as it was now. He saw it first bloated with evil: red and round, its eyes too small, too close together over a blob of a nose, loose, fleshy lips, and a receding chin. The face of a beast, which leered even without trying. Then he saw the mouth fall open and the leer turn to a look of terror, horror as the flesh began to slough. The lips and cheeks puffing up, bursting and turning to rot; the eyes glazing over, sinking back into sulphur yellow orbits, dribbling sick grey fluids from red rims; the nose collapsing in upon itself, livid flesh peeling back and a crater of jagged bone showing through. Finally the jaws gaping wide in a dead scream, as maggots erupted from the purple rot and quickly fretted the whole to a skull!

Nathan saw it, and so did John Scofield.

THAT ... IS TOD PRENTISS! He knew it for a fact. WHICH CAN ONLY MEAN THAT THIS ONE – (suddenly Scofield's deadspeak voice was shocked, full of the knowledge of its own error) – THAT HE – *IS NATHAN KEOGH!*

The floor was back under Nathan's feet, but he felt that he was still falling. Crumpling to the cold tiles, then hugging to them, he sobbed his exhaustion into the cool air of the morgue –

– And saw that he lay in a pool of blue-glowing mist, and knew that it wasn't over yet ...

VI

Confrontation – Conclusion – Connections

Trask and the others were battering at the doors again, calling out to Nathan, asking if he was all right. He was aware of them – of their voices, strangely distant, as if they reached him from a very long way away – and also aware that he wasn't alone in the eerie blue glow of the place. There were ... *combatants* here, too. For this was to be the final confrontation.

Combatants, and an audience. But never such a silent audience in the history of competition. For they were all of them dead. As were the phantoms they had come to watch.

The previous inhabitants of this place sat on their metal caskets in a ring that encircled the figures of two men: John Scofield and Tod Prentiss. Nathan could tell them apart from the start, for he knew what Prentiss had looked like; his bestial face was unmistakable, and his squat, froglike figure – hunched now in a defensive crouch, or shrunken into itself in fear – seemed likewise to cry his identity. Grave-dirt clung in clods to his hairy body.

As for John Scofield: he was of medium height, sparsely-fleshed, clean-limbed. Both men were naked, and the contrast *was* stark: darkness against light, good against evil. Whether it was an accurate physical representation or simply Scofield and his mortal (or immortal?) enemy as seen from Scofield's point of view,

Nathan couldn't say. But he knew which side he was on. And he was even more sure when suddenly Tod Prentiss rounded on him and grunted:

Cunt! Rabble-rouser! This dumb bastard thought he had me – until you and your dead friends convinced him otherwise!

Then Nathan saw that while Prentiss's basic emotion was definitely fear, indeed terror – of John Scofield presumably – he'd managed to suppress it to allow for a bout of vicious, homicidal rage. Survival, Nathan supposed. For during his life of theft, rape, and finally murder, Prentiss had been a survivor. As in life, so in death; his instincts were unchanged. Prentiss was *still* the survivor. He had survived . . . how many of Scofield's attempts to be rid of him? In his incorporeal state he always would survive them, for men only die the true death once.

Nathan's thoughts were deadspeak, and Tod Prentiss heard them, 'naturally'.

Dead right, shithead! Living men only die the true death once. And you're alive, right? For the moment you're alive, anyway . . . you dumb fuck! Prentiss's sudden lunge in Nathan's direction might have taken the Necroscope by surprise, but not John Scofield. And not the ring of sad, silent observers.

As Prentiss came loping – leaning menacingly forward, with his long arms reaching and his wet lips drawn back from straining, grimacing yellow teeth – so the corpses moved to intercept. They weren't creaking, groaning cadavers but bodies of the freshly dead, and in these metaphysical moments of Scofield's and the Great Majority's creation they were 'alive' and mobile as life itself. Blocking the way, they turned Prentiss back, brought him face to face with Scofield again.

And seeing Scofield's cold, stony expression, Prentiss

shrank down, whimpered like a whipped dog, and backed off. He knew why he'd been called up, why he was here: to die again. And he knew who would be his executioner.

Then Scofield said:

I wanted to show you, Nathan, what I've been up against and why I can't stop. Myself, wife and child, we're here in an afterworld devoid of body, but not of mind. And I for one refuse to share it with such as this! One way or the other I will be rid of him, but until then I can't stop. For the moment — perhaps a brief moment — I suppose, I hope, you would call me sanc. But I know that sooner or later the very thought of this creature still existing, in however limited a capacity, is bound to drive me mad again.

Scofield paused as Tod Prentiss suddenly stopped whining, drew himself upright, shouted a curse and sprang at his enemy head on, jaws gaping as if to bite him, savage him like a mad dog. Scofield paused and held up a hand; simply that ... but it was as if he'd erected a wall.

A telekinetic wall that Prentiss slammed into, flattened against, and slid down groaning to the floor. At which Nathan remembered something, indeed several things:

In life Scofield's true talent had been telekinesis, and it still was. The power to move things at will, with the mind alone. The power to build an invisible wall, or visible spirits from the memories and thoughts and dreams (or nightmares) of what had been. The power to crush, enclose ... contain? Such power that the ebb and flow of its field produced those 'poltergeist' effects which threatened the sanity of a world. Well, and the dead were sometimes a threat in Nathan's world, too, and the undead even more so. But the Travellers of

Sunside had their own ways of dealing with such threats.

Remembering those ways, he now asked Scofield:

Where is Prentiss now? His body, I mean?

What does that matter? Scofield turned his head to look at the Necroscope, at which Prentiss climbed to his feet again and once more adopted his defensive or threatening crouch.

Scofield shrugged. *He was buried close by, else I might have difficulty calling him up. His remains are still there, in the ground, but he is here. This is him.*

Using deadspeak thoughts and pictures, Nathan showed what he intended – at which Prentiss went wild! For he was able to see, hear and understand Nathan's deadspeak scenario as well as Scofield and the rest of the teeming dead. And even knowing what his fate was to be – or more properly because he knew – his instinct for survival rose up in him one last time.

He hurled himself headlong at Scofield again, and again was met by the wall of the other's mind. Except that this time it wrapped around him and folded him in, enveloping him like a fly in a spider's cocoon: the invisible cocoon of a dead man's telekinesis enhanced by his undying hatred. But unlike a spider's cocoon, this one was designed to contain a malignancy.

Then, slowly but surely, John Scofield crushed Prentiss and shrank him down. The ectoplasm which was Prentiss's 'body' assumed a compressed, spherical shape, in which the grotesquely *liquid* contents had his features, but features which gradually melted into the globular blob of the whole. And such was the efficacy of Scofield's telekinetic bubble of pure thought that as it shrank, so Tod Prentiss's frantic screams shrank with it.

The process wasn't necromancy; it involved no 'pain'

as such, only the terror of absolute finality. Prentiss's terror. And search as he might, Nathan could find no pity within himself for the subject of this, John Scofield's final exorcism. For that is what it was: the casting out of a devil, the removal of a morbid tumour which had infected the flesh of the living but would no more suppurate in the minds of the dead. Let it be a warning to all such: death is not the end, and it isn't the end of justice.

Within the thought-bubble Prentiss continued to shrink. His outline was completely spherical now, domed head sliding into bloodhound jowls, into hunched shoulders, into fat arms and vast flat hands which enclosed a bulb stomach, hips and groin that crushed down on concertinaed legs and monstrously curving, crumpled feet. And as the bubble shrank so any semblance of life was likewise diminished; what flesh-tones had been present disappeared and were replaced by a green rottenness, the evil light of Tod Prentiss's soul, concentrated within a small place and shining that much brighter, or so much more lividly.

The telekinetic sphere of containment was less than eighteen inches in diameter now; shrinking more yet it gave a last, frantic wriggle, like a soap bubble disturbed by a current of air, so that for a moment Nathan thought Prentiss was about to break out. But no; he had tried, certainly, but it was his last desperate attempt. Scofield's talent was too strong, too terrible to resist.

And down went the bubble, smaller and smaller, and Prentiss's screams, still furious, less than whispers on the psychic aether. Until at last they were inaudible. Then:

I don't know ... how long ... I can hold it together, Scofield said, his own voice small now in Nathan's deadspeak mind. *What you promised, do it now. For once I'm spent it will be a long time before I can build up to anything like this again.*

Nathan saw how close to exhaustion he was. And now, speaking out loud to the teeming dead: 'Help him! Give him all the help you can. Hold Prentiss until I can see to it, or all this is for nothing.'

They understood, added the 'weight' of their incorporeal minds to Scofield's and helped him cram the pulsing green glow which was Prentiss into an even smaller space; in the end into no space at all, merely a nucleus of sick green radiation ... which Nathan plucked from the air and put in his pocket!

It was as easy as that. He could do it – he was the only one who *could* do it – because he was the Necroscope, because to him death and everything connected with it is different. And now that the Great Majority had played their part, it was up to him to see it through.

The dead and their casket seats faded into blue mist which itself faded into nothingness; the room darkened, but momentarily, before the doors crashed open; Trask and the others stood framed in the dim light from the corridor, their breathing making grey funnels in the cold air. And from some near-distant place in the quiet city, the chimes of midnight rang out, penetrating even here.

But at last, no less than the city, the Nightmare Zone was quiet too ...

In the Duty Room, Nathan wasted no time. 'Prentiss was buried quite close to here.'

'That's right,' Trask nodded. 'Is it important?'

'Yes,' Nathan answered curtly. 'We have to dig him up and burn him – and tonight!'

'But –'

677

'No buts, not if you want to be rid of the Nightmare Zone forever. Listen, time to explain later. But right now . . . can it be arranged?'

There were few things that the Head of E-Branch couldn't arrange. 'Yes, if I can get to a telephone.'

'Then let's get to one . . .'

The exhumation of Tod Prentiss was a speedy and less than dignified affair, and his cremation in an industrial furnace at an engineering plant on the outskirts of the city took place without ceremony – except for one small incident. Just before the bodybag went into the fire, Nathan stepped forward and unzipped it six inches along one side. And taking some unseen thing from his pocket, which *couldn't* be seen by anyone but him, he thrust it deep into the bag where it belonged.

Thus Tod Prentiss became one with his remains, and was one with his ashes when they had cooled.

In the grey morning, the first three airplanes out of Gatwick, and three more out of Heathrow, carried, along with their more orthodox passengers, E-Branch agents on a special mission: to disperse Prentiss's ashes across the world, scattering them far and wide, so that nothing of him could ever come together again.

Also by first light, the remains of John and Lynn Scofield, and those of their son Andrew, were exhumed and cremated, under circumstances and in a manner which were very different. And in the Kensington Garden of Repose, Ben Trask, Zek Föener and Nathan stood with heads bowed as a short but solemn ceremony took place . . .

Later, when the three walked in the grounds of the place under a grey sky, Nathan told the others: 'This may be strange. It may even frighten you a little, but it shouldn't worry you. And it is what they want.'

He carried an earthenware urn, which suddenly he held out at arm's length.

'What . . .?' Trask said.

But Nathan was talking to someone else now. *John, are you sure? This is what you want, right?*

Oh, yes. The answer came back at once. *And it has to be now. Whatever power I have left, it will only just suffice. I know it. I drained myself keeping Prentiss in his place until you could scatter him far and wide. And now it's for me to find a better place for my family. But even if we don't make it, if we're scattered on the winds, we'll be together at the end and at peace with ourselves. We are at peace with ourselves, Nathan, thanks to you. And now . . . do it.*

Nathan did it: dropped the urn, which crashed down onto a red brick herringbone pathway and shattered. And for a moment there was a confusion of bouncing, clattering pottery shards, and grey dust springing up in a cloud. Then –

– The cloud drew itself together into some sort of tenuous whole, which despite the graveyard's blustery crosswinds maintained a kind of cohesion as it rose up and made off in a single body across the perimeter wall, up over the rooftops, and quickly vanished into the distance. And:

'Gone,' said Nathan sadly, in a little while.

Trask nodded, and croaked: 'Gone, yes. I'm not sure what you've done, but –'

'– But we're sure it's for the best,' Zek finished for him.

'For the best, yes,' Nathan agreed.

The best for the living and the dead alike, Keenan Gormley sighed in Nathan's deadspeak mind. *And the dead know it. Nathan, you have what you wanted. You've made yourself a lot of new friends. Now be sure you use them wisely . . .*

*

Trask arranged for Garvey and Smart to have a week off duty, simply to rest up. Then he handed over his own duties as Head of Branch to David Chung for a week, so that he could drive up to Scotland with Zek and Nathan. It would give Nathan a break; Trask too, and Zek ... would be with them. But in his heart of hearts, Trask knew why he wanted her along.

They stayed in Edinburgh for three days, where Nathan took great pleasure in standing in Princes Street and looking up at the Castle on the Rock. 'Men built it!' he would whisper, awed by the thought. 'In Turgosheim it wouldn't be much; it doesn't seem a lot bigger than Trollmanse, Lom Halfstruck's stump of a stack in the bottom of the gorge. But men built this!'

'You should see the pyramids,' Zek had told him, smiling.

'Or the Great Wall of China,' Trask had put in.

'Or the Empire State Building!' Zek had finished it, as was her wont. 'Men have built a good many things.'

Nathan had frowned and given his head a shake. 'Not on Sunside, they haven't.'

'Because you've been held back,' Zek had reasoned with him. 'I've been there and I know. And I'm sure that you know, too, Nathan. Your people are clever and even sophisticated in their way. But for the constant oppression of the Wamphyri ...'

'... But for them — oh, a lot of things,' he had answered. 'I wouldn't be here, for one.'

And Trask had brought the conversation to a logical conclusion with: 'And so it can be seen that they might well have brought about their own doom. You are Szgany; when you go home you can give the Szgany weapons beyond their wildest dreams, and far beyond the comprehension of the Wamphyri. But that's then and this is now, and we've a way to go yet.'

Then Zek had given Nathan's arm a squeeze and told him, 'But we'll get there. I know we will . . .'

They went to see the gutted ruins of Harry Keogh's old house on the outskirts of Bonnyrig, not far from Edinburgh. It was snowing when they got there, huge soft flakes, and an inch of snow lay on the garden or what had been a garden. Trask told Nathan how it had been:

'There was no way we could let Harry alone, let him live here; I mean *here*, in this world. But at the same time I knew that your father was different in more ways than one. Oh, the Necroscope was Wamphyri, all right – was he ever! I saw him, spoke to him that night right here in this garden, and I *know* what he was! But he wasn't the kind who would simply give in and submit to his fate, and never to a fate as cruel as that. So I . . . gave him a chance. E-Branch was out to get him; the Opposition were waiting for him at the Perchorsk Gate; even the Great Majority had forsaken him, but I trusted him. Looking back on it, you would be justified in believing I was out of my mind. But on the other hand, well, who would have known the truth of it better than I? At least I knew the truth *of the moment*: that Harry intended no harm.

'And the proof of that was to hand. He had deadly enemies right here, men who would kill him if they could. One of them was a telepath, but warped and full of hate. I'll make a long story short: the Necroscope disarmed him and dragged him into the Möbius Continuum. Right then I thought I'd made a dreadful mistake, that I would never see that man again. But no, Harry did no harm but a lot of good. Somehow, he took away Geoffrey Paxton's talent – which Paxton had used in the worst possible way – made him "ordinary", returned him snivelling but physically unharmed to me here in the garden.

'All this while his house – this old, burned-out place, his last refuge on Earth – was blazing up in fire and smoke, and while there wasn't a man or creature in the entire world who Harry could call friend. *Still* he didn't betray us ...'

'Not quite true, Ben,' Zek put in, quietly. 'That he had no friends, I mean. He had you, and he had me. I knew what he was and was frightened of him when he came to see me in Zante. Wolf and I – especially Wolf, a real wolf, a Szgany watchdog – we both knew. But the Necroscope and I went back ... oh, a long time, and I was still his friend. Harry was Harry. So I took a chance, too, and gave them shelter, him and his girl, while he arranged their departure from this world. The headlight beam of his motorcycle was the last I saw of him; when that beam blinked out and the roar of his engine was cut off, and the darkness crept in on me as never before, I knew we'd seen the last of him. And I wouldn't be here now if something of him hadn't come back at last.'

Nathan hugged his coat to him, shook off a thin layer of snow from his shoulders. 'You ... loved him?'

Zek and Trask glanced at one another. 'Yes,' Trask answered, 'I suppose we did, in a way.'

But Zek shook her head. 'I'm not so sure,' she said. 'You have to remember, I'd seen inside his head. And while he could be warm as a sunny day, he could also be cold. But a different kind of cold. One that cuts to the soul itself.' And looking at Nathan, *to* Nathan, she said:

You have it, too. I suppose it's what makes you what you are. But be careful, Nathan, and make sure that the cold never outweighs the warmth ...

Trask wasn't party to this but knew that something had passed between them. And so his next statement was entirely coincidental when he shivered and said: 'The cold is getting through to me. What do you say we get back to Edinburgh, the hotel, coffee and liqueurs?'

As they passed through the ruins and got into Trask's car it started to snow more heavily. Grey figures came out of the opaque backdrop and climbed into a second car. Special Branch minders, they were never too far away . . .

Driving through Bonnyrig towards Edinburgh, Nathan received a mental impression of a dog. A big black and white mongrel, all lolloping and friendly, floppy-eared, and tongue lolling hot and wet. The sensation wasn't telepathy or deadspeak but the next best thing, as if he were back on Sunside and his wolves were close by. He had used to 'know' they were there, without knowing how. But here, in an alien world? It was strange.

That night he dreamed of the dog. And in the morning, over breakfast, he asked: 'Can we drive back to that village close to where Harry lived?'

'Bonnyrig?' Trask raised a questioning eyebrow. 'If you'd like to, of course we can. Any special reason?'

'I don't know,' Nathan answered with a shrug. 'It's just a feeling – that someone knows me there.'

'But how could you know anyone there?'

'I don't. But I think someone knows me . . .'

They went back to Bonnyrig, Trask driving slowly and carefully on the treacherous, black-iced roads. And as they passed street after street of neat, terraced houses, suddenly Nathan said: 'Stop! This is it . . . I think.'

The dog-feeling was back, the dog-mind, impinging on his own.

As Nathan got out of the car, he teetered a little. Trask said, 'Careful! That's black ice. I know it looks like tarmac, but in fact you could skate on it!'

Zek, closer to Nathan's telepathic mind, knew that he was suffering from a kind of disorientation, not from the slippery surface of the road. And catching Trask's eye, she said, '*Déjà vu?*'

Nathan was back in control of himself. Smiling, he said, 'It's down here.' And he made his way down a side street to the garden of a house with a shiny brass number seven on the gate, then up a short path to the door. And as Trask and Zek caught up, so he knocked.

'Nathan!' Trask was mildly alarmed. 'Now what in the name of –?'

But Zek took Trask's arm and quietly told him, 'Just let it be, Ben. Nathan himself doesn't know "what in the name of". So let's wait and find out.'

They didn't have long to wait. Nathan's knock was answered almost immediately by a tall, frowning, good-looking young man who was half-turned towards his visitors and half towards the interior of the house. Glancing at the three on the doorstep, he said, 'Just a moment, please,' and called back into the house: 'Paddy – will you stop that?' And again to his visitors, smiling now and by way of explanation: 'My old dog. I don't know what's got into him!'

They heard a tumult of excited snuffling and barking from somewhere inside the house. And:

'Paddy,' Nathan said, nodding. 'Yes.' As if the young man had just supplied the answer to something. And in his mind a sudden vision: *dark skid marks burned into the tarmac . . . and Paddy, a mongrel puppy, dead in the gutter. One of the pup's forelegs flopping like a rubber band . . . its spine kinked and its shoulders askew . . . its partly-crushed head oozing brain fluid from a torn right ear.*

The vision came – and was gone.

'Who is it, dear?' A slender, middle-aged woman

came to the door, crowding the space beside the young man. Her eyes peered out from a dim corridor into the light of day, adjusting to the brightness. Then she saw Nathan and the others – but her eyes quickly returned to Nathan, and her gasp of recognition was perfectly audible. But in a moment, when she'd taken the time to think about it – whatever it was – she laughed and said, 'No, it couldn't be.'

Trask was fascinated. 'What couldn't be?'

'Oh, nothing,' she said. 'But there was a young man we saw but once. A vet, he said. Fixed up Paddy after an accident. He looked *so* like you.' She turned again to Nathan. 'But of course it couldn't be, not possibly. For you'd be younger now than you were then, and that was all of . . . oh, sixteen, seventeen years ago!'

'Did you know this vet's name?' This from Zek.

'Ah! That's something I did know,' the woman answered. 'I have a cousin of the same name, and so I remembered. It was a Mr Keogh fixed Paddy up that time. And he did a good job, too, for the old dog's as frisky as ever. He's near-blind now, but never a day's sickness for all his years!'

Trask and Zek felt the goose-flesh rise and looked at each other.

Maybe Paddy had heard his name mentioned. Whatever, he was curious. And now the two on the doorstep must make way for him, too. It was the large mongrel dog of Nathan's dream and vision, of course. Squeezing out between his master and the young man's mother, Paddy reared up –

– But in no way threateningly. Whining, Paddy kneaded Nathan's stomach with his big front paws; his black and white mop of a head was tilted back; he tried desperately hard to lick the Necroscope's face but couldn't reach it.

And certain now, the woman gasped, 'He . . . *knows* you!'

'No,' Nathan told her. 'But I think he knew my father.'

She sighed and her hand flew to her mouth. 'Of course! Of course! The resemblance is remarkable! But please come in. *Do* come on in!' And to her son: 'Peter, do you remember?'

'Remember?' the young man cried, making way for the visitors and ushering them down a short passage beside the stairwell into a large living-room. 'I'll say I remember. What a day that was. One to remember the rest of your life.'

And when the three were seated, to Nathan: 'Your father was . . . he was like a miracle-worker!'

. And Nathan and Zek together thought: *To say the least!* But out loud Nathan said, 'What makes you say so?'

A middle-aged, grey-haired man had joined them from another room. He must have heard something of the conversation, and the excitement on his wife and son's faces was unmistakable. 'Your father was Mr Keogh, eh? The vet? Well, and don't we owe *him* a favour!' It was a statement of fact, not a question. 'Aye, and doesn't the auld dog there know it! He's no like that wi' just anyone, son.'

Paddy was at Nathan's feet where the Necroscope sat on a couch, his forepaws in his lap, tongue lolling. Trask laughed. 'Well, Paddy mightn't see too well, but he certainly seems to know you!'

'I . . . have a way with dogs.' Nathan shrugged.

But now the grey-haired man was more serious. 'So did your father,' he said. 'A healing way. Ah'm John McCulloch, by the way. This is mah wife, Mary, and mah son, Peter. Peter was just a wee lad then, which has to make this the best aftercare a dog ever had! Can ah take it your father told you to look us up?'

'My father is ... he's dead,' Nathan answered. 'But yes, he did say that if I was ever up this way ...'

'Well, you're very welcome,' Peter McCulloch told him, told all three. 'Paddy has been a sheer joy all his life, yet at the time I would have sworn there was no life left in him. It was a car, on the corner out there. Paddy was ... oh, a mess. So that I was sure he was dead. But Mr Keogh took him away, and brought him back that same night. Like a new dog! Not a mark on him! To this day I still can't believe it ...'

'You'll stay and take a meal with us?' Peter's mother took Zek's hand.

'I'm afraid we have other appointments,' Trask was quick to cut in. 'In fact we have to be on our way right now. It's just that –'

'– It's that my father said I would always find a welcome here,' Nathan finished it, standing up. 'And I did ...'

Back in the car, Trask said: 'That – was amazing! How did you know? How *could* you have known?'

Nathan shook his head a moment, then looked at Trask curiously. 'Ben, are you sure you've told me everything you know, about Harry? He was the Necroscope, yes: he talked to the dead and, when he was threatened, could even call them up to a semblance of life, for his protection. I know all that. You've told me all that. And actually it's no great surprise. For after all I'm a Necroscope, too. But I feel there's something else here, something different. I mean, the dead are dead, and Paddy was very much alive. I tried to read his mind through deadspeak and it didn't work. Paddy *is* alive. Yet after all this time he remembered my father – the *feel* of his mind – and felt something of it in mine. Peter McCulloch told us he was sure at the time that his pup was dead. So ... I suppose what I'm really asking is this: what other powers did Harry have? For it's one thing to make the dead walk, but it's quite another to make them live and breathe again.'

Trask stared studiously out through the windscreen at the road ahead and got his thoughts in order. For Nathan was right: that side of his father was rarely touched upon by E-Branch and had never been mentioned to Nathan himself. It was the difference between a Necroscope and a necromancer, between Good and Evil. And yet even as time ran out for him, Harry Keogh had not been evil. Only the *Thing* inside him had been that, which he'd somehow managed to keep under control until the bitter end.

He had not been evil ... but he had been a necromancer. Necromancy: a dark, esoteric art which Harry had learned from Janos Ferenczy, last of an infamous line, at his castle in the Zarundului Mountains of Carpathia. This much Trask knew of it, and no more – except that Harry had used it to bring back not only a dog but *men* from the great beyond! Even now the Head of E-Branch didn't much care to dwell on it, for he knew terrible mistakes had been made and that espers had died – one of them twice – unnecessarily.

As Trask thought these things so he glanced at Nathan out of the corner of his eye, and saw him staring back at him. Such was the other's curiosity, he hadn't been able to resist it. He had even framed his question in such a way that Trask couldn't answer spontaneously but must think about it.

And of course, Nathan had read those thoughts. Now he saw the truth, the knowledge of what he'd done reflected in Trask's eyes, and said, 'I'm sorry, but I had to know. And it explains a thing or two. Why the dead, who had loved Harry for so long, forsook him in the end. It wasn't simply that they feared his necromancy but the *form* which it took. To be able to call them back to life ... it must have given him a very terrible power over them.'

'Yes,' Trask agreed. 'Just such a power as Janos Ferenczy possessed. For even the dead can only be tortured for so long, until they become dust. But apparently, Janos could call them up from their very ashes into life, to torture them again and again. Harry never used it that way, no, but he did have the power if he'd wished it ...'

Nathan was thoughtful. 'I've talked to several of the dead since John Scofield,' he finally said. 'Even a handful who knew my father personally. But none of them has ever so much as mentioned this other – facet?'

Again Trask looked at him, perhaps with a trace of uncertainty, even fear showing in his face. 'And if you were one of the Great Majority, would you mention it?'

Zek had been silent for a while. Now she said, 'Nathan, I don't want you to have any doubts about Harry. When he was finished – a vampire and necromancer, forsaken by the living and the dead alike, so that he must flee this world into the doubtful sanctuary of Starside – *still* he was Harry. He harmed no one, indeed he cared for ... oh, everyone, all of us! He cared for me, for a girl called Penny who he'd brought back from the dead, even for Ben here and E-Branch. And he never betrayed us, not once. The truth of it is that we betrayed him. So when you think of your father think of that, and act accordingly.'

The slightest nod of his head was Nathan's acknowledgement of her words. That was the way he would think of it – But his natural curiosity remained ...

*

Driving back down to London at the end of their tour, Trask took the opportunity to break their journey with an overnight stay in Hartlepool. This was hardly for the natural 'beauty' of the place, though in fact the once-industrial town's gradual decay over a period of fifty years had now been arrested, but because Harry Keogh had lived here before his recruitment into E-Branch. He'd lived here, and earlier in Harden Village a few miles away, which at that time had been a colliery.

That evening they drove through to Harden and Trask took Nathan and Zek to see Harry's old school. The place was empty, grimy, silent. It stood within sight of a dilapidated railway viaduct which was due for demolition, with the swelling North Sea greyly visible between its rotting brick arches.

By this time Nathan had noticed Trask's attraction to Zek (a blind man would have noticed it), and the fact that she was showing a measured response. He suspected that his mentor would probably appreciate some time alone with her. Which was why, after they had walked round the perimeter of the school, Nathan suggested that the pair might like to go off and 'do something together', while he took in the atmosphere of the place.

It was partly that he wanted them to be free of him for a little while, but mainly that he wanted to be free of them. For as the three of them had walked together down a narrow, cobbled avenue of trees between the old school and the local graveyard, Nathan had felt the lure of the leaning, lichen-clad tombstones and had known that he would find friends there. Or rather, that his father had found friends there. It was a chance to find out more about Harry.

It was a blustery afternoon, but bright and uplifting, as Trask and Zek walked off arm in arm towards the viaduct and the green valley which it spanned, where a stream sparkled in wintry sunlight. But as soon as Nathan entered the graveyard – as soon as the branches of the trees sprawling over the wall from the cobbled avenue shut out the sun – he felt the solitude of the place, its solemnity, and knew that his father had walked here as a boy. It was as if the Necroscope's footprints were still there in the glittering marble chips of the winding pathways, in the leaf-mould and grave dirt, and the cropped grass between the plots.

Then, hearing or sensing something – a muttered word or furtive movement – Nathan looked up, to see a pair of muffled figures leaning on a gate some twenty, twenty-five paces away: his minders, their breath pluming in the frozen air. Keeping a respectful distance and trying not to look conspicuous, still they looked out for him. And reassured, he went on.

It was as if his feet had a mind of their own; they led him on; before he knew it, he walked more surely in the shade of benign trees before coming to a halt where an old headstone stood over a weed-grown plot. And as his eyes focused on the stone's legend, so he opened his deadspeak mind more fully to the whispers of the dead.

Who is it? they queried. Who can it be? It feels like ... like ... but no, for he's been gone a long time now. He won't be back, which is as well. And yet ... this one lives, too, and his thoughts are deadspeak! How can that be, unless the rumours are true? They say a new one has come into the world. But is it him, or is it ... some Other? Dare we speak to him? Dare we ... inquire?

And a firmer, stronger voice said: *Long before he became a threat, the Necroscope was our friend. He was the only friend we had! And now there's this one.*

Well, and are you satisfied to just lie here in your limbo and let the living world pass by unseen, unknown? Will you pass up this opportunity to make contact with a living mind? Harry's gone, we all know that, and we know what he was. But before that he was our friend. And I for one miss him!

You're not alone, said a wiser but fainter voice, as yet another incorporeal one entered his own plea. And despite that the voice was faint, still it was close, so that Nathan guessed it issued from the earth at his very feet, from this very tomb. *I miss him, too. I used to teach Maths at the school just across the road. It was — oh, I don't know how long ago. Fifty, sixty years? But I'd been dead a long time when Harry came to me with the first of his classroom problems — problems in Maths. And do you know, I actually helped him to solve them! Can you believe it? I was the one who taught the Necroscope his mathematics!*

Nathan's jaw fell open; the shorter hairs stood erect on the back of his neck; he couldn't believe what he'd just heard, the incredible gift which now seemed within reach. But finally, as the legend showing through the lichens on the headstone took on new meaning, he had to believe it. For even with his limited understanding of the written word, he could now make it out to read:

JAMES GORDON HANNANT
13 June 1875 – 11 Sept. 1944
Master at Harden Boys' School
for Thirty Years, Headmaster
for Ten, now he Numbers
among the Hosts
of Heaven.

VII

Incentive

'Sir,' said Nathan, unable to contain the slight catch in his voice, the excitement in his heart, 'whoever you are, I think I may have been looking for you since the day I was born!'

For a moment there was a stunned silence, then a deadspeak 'gasp' of astonishment, finally the mass exclamation of a hundred or more incorporeal minds:

Harry!

But there was more than just astonishment in their voices. There was fear, too. So that Nathan at once informed them: 'No, not Harry but Nathan. Nathan Keogh. Harry was my father. That's why I ... why I *sound* like him.'

Sound and feel like him. The voice was J.G. Hannant's. *No wonder the dead have been so reluctant! Your father was – he became – other than completely reliable. I mean, towards the end of, er ...*

'I know what you mean,' Nathan told him. 'I know what Harry was. I come from a world where *They* breed. So there's really no need to explain your fears.' And then, more eagerly: 'But if I may impose upon you, especially upon your time, there is something you can perhaps help me with.'

Oh? The other was cautious.

'Yes. It's what you were saying earlier, about teaching the Necroscope his maths. Whatever it is you showed him – whatever method you used to instruct him – I'd be grateful if you could show, teach, the same things to me.'

Ah! said Hannant. *Well, first things first. And perhaps I should warn you: I did show Harry a few things, yes, but it was quite wrong of me to give the impression that I actually taught him anything. What he had was instinctive; I showed him several shortcuts, that's all; the rest came naturally. But as I said, first things first. Obviously you have a story to tell, and we want to hear it. How is it you're here, Nathan? And why are you so anxious to follow in Harry's footsteps? Perhaps you are too anxious, eh? Perhaps you would follow him too closely. I'm sure you'll understand our reticence.*

Nathan told them his story, the story of his life. He kept it short, picturing most of it as opposed to vocalizing it, but despite that deadspeak frequently conveys more than is actually said, still it took him the best part of an hour. Until at last he finished it with:

'So you see, I need all the help I can get. I have some of my father's talents – his deadspeak, obviously, and even the telepathy which he displayed towards the end of his time here – but they aren't enough. Not nearly enough to prepare me for any sort of real confrontation with the Wamphyri.'

Hannant had listened to all of this very attentively, but in the background Nathan had been able to make out the furtive whispers of the Great Majority voicing their fears, doubts and indecision. Now, as he fell silent, one of these quieter, more fearful voices came forward: a spokesman for the dead.

How do you see your future, Nathan? The voice was quavery, uncertain as its owner. *Let's just suppose that by some miracle of chance, we – or rather some of us, like Hannant here – can actually help you? What will you do?*

Nathan's response was almost automatic, instinctive as his father's maths had been. 'Men should never try to read the future,' he said, 'for it's a devious thing. But since you ask me, this is how I see it. I've been promised knowledge and weapons, modern weapons, to take back with me into Sunside/Starside, to give to the Szgany. Weapons my people can use to fight and destroy the Wamphyri. Except ... even now I can't be certain that I ever will get back. But if I were able to understand and use the Möbius Continuum, then I *would* be certain.'

This – Möbius Continuum? – would give you the power to transfer at will between your vampire world and ours? If there was a point to the question, Nathan missed it.

'Not necessarily,' he answered. 'But it would be a step in the right direction. And it would give me instant access to any number of escape routes, if ever I do get back to Sunside/Starside.'

I see, said the spokesman, but so quietly and thought-fully that Nathan could almost see him rubbing his chin. *You've come here from a world of monsters in human guise – which you have admitted is a plague-ridden place. And yet you persist in trying to create a gateway between worlds. Instantaneous right of passage. For yourself ... and for what else?*

Now Nathan knew what was troubling the other and causing this new wave of uncertainty. 'But can't you understand?' he answered. 'Such gateways already exist! Two of them. They are the source of vampirism in your world, or what was your world when you had life. I'm not trying to open them but close them down – permanently! Or better still, destroy the Wamphyri on their own ground and make both of our worlds safe from them.'

We don't for a moment suggest that you would

695

deliberately use such knowledge to let vampires loose in our world (Nathan sensed the shake of an incorporeal head). No, for it's already apparent that you're neither evil nor criminally insane. But as you yourself have pointed out, no man may read the future with impunity. And if you were to fall into Their hands –?

'– I've been in their hands, and escaped them!' Nathan's frustration was mounting. To be as close as this, and to come up against a stumbling block; this stumbling block: the legacy of his vampire father. 'And after all,' he went on uncontrollably, 'what do you know about it? Have you stood face to face with a Lord of the Wamphyri? Was your father one of them? And has your brother been changed into – into . . .' But now he saw that he'd gone too far, that he'd said and thought too much.

And after a moment of total silence:

Not only your father (the voice of the spokesman was very quiet now, and much more thoughtful), but your brother, too?

But now Hannant was back, and belligerent! Nathan, take no notice. I'll help you if I can, and they can take their spite out on me. For I believe every word you said and I'm sure that you'll be as big a bonus to the dead as Harry was. So what can they do to me, eh? Ostracism? But I've been ostracized before – from life itself!

And another voice joined him in his defiance of the Great Majority; that first, strong voice which had spoken up for the Necroscope, Harry Keogh, and which now spoke for Nathan in his turn. Hannant is right! What's wrong with the lot of you? Have you lain here so long in the earth that nothing can move you any more? We owed Harry Keogh, and we betrayed him! I was one of his teachers, too, just like Hannant, and even after I died I taught him unarmed combat. Why, it *probably saved his life a dozen times over! I did that, yes – I, Graham 'Sergeant' Lane – and I was proud of it! Yet at the end even I betrayed him. And I know why. It's this: that we the dead will only admit to two states of being: life and death. Having experienced both, we understand them. But there's a third state called undeath, a state which we never accepted. And Harry was undead. He'd become a vampire, and so we turned our backs on him. Well we were wrong to do so! Now we've been given the opportunity to square it with his son here. And will you turn him down?*

The background babble of deadspeak whispers came flooding in again. There were those who believed that the living and the dead should remain apart, always, and that the mysteries of the grave should remain mysteries to the living, until they in turn died and joined the Great Majority. These were the bitter ones who had never succeeded in life, and so lost nothing in death. But they were shouted down by others whose time had been good, so that death had cheated them of a great deal. And their argument was that there was much to be gained: to be able to talk again – through the Necroscope Nathan – with loved ones left behind; perhaps to explain that death is not the end, but the renewal of old loves and friendships waiting in the last long darkness. Not a physical renewal, no, but nevertheless a joining of sorts.

Nathan was party to all of this, which showed a certain understanding on the part of the dead at least: that they no longer excluded him from their discussions, even when he and his problem were the business under discussion. And finally:

Very well, the voice of the spokesman for the teeming dead was back again. *We accept you and everything you stand for. And as Hannant said, we hope you'll*

697

understand our reticence. These have been strange times for the dead, Nathan. A great shouting, a terrible tumult from the south, reached us even here. Periodically we would feel it: an urge to be up and about! Something beyond our control! It's not right that dead men should want to walk again, or that others should have the power to make it so!

Nathan recognized the other's subject at once. 'I believe I know what you're talking about: John Scofield and the Nightmare Zone. But that's over and done with now. Maybe if I'd mentioned it earlier things would have been that much easier. Perhaps you would have accepted me sooner.'

You ... had something to do with that?

'I was the one called upon to put John and his family to rest, yes. Though I have to admit I couldn't have done it without the help of the Great Majority. But ... am I to understand that you're not all of you in contact all of the time?'

And now it was Hannant who answered him. It takes quite a lot out of us to converse at a distance, Nathan. Indeed, it's exhausting! Not so hard for Harry, in his time. Once he'd been introduced to someone, he could usually speak to him from anywhere in the world! And it should be the same for you. But you and your father, you're Necroscopes, with all the drive of the living. And we are only dead people. If it wasn't for you, no one would know we were here at all – except as memories. And even memories are sometimes soon forgotten ...

As Hannant finished, so the spokesman came back:

You have our word that we'll work with you as far as that is possible. But Nathan, you should know this: there's a great power in you. And it's not one you might easily recognize. I'm talking about the power of love. In

*the past, the teeming dead loved your father. So much
so that they would do . . . anything for him. And now a
new light shines in their darkness. All we ask is this:
use that power sparingly. We feared John Scofield because in his madness he could have made us walk
again in the world of the living. Don't make us fear you.
Please, stay out of danger, in this world at least.*

'I'll try to,' Nathan answered, as humbly as he was
able. 'But as for your love: I haven't asked for it. Be my
friends, and I'll be satisfied. And as for calling you up: I
would never do that. Any who would come up out of
the earth for me must do so of their own free will.'

Easily said, the other's deadspeak voice sighed. *But
your warmth has touched us now. Harry Keogh is in
you – the original Harry, before he succumbed – and he
was someone the dead just couldn't resist. A bringer of
joy, but a bringer of pain, too. It's no easy thing, to get
up from the grave. But when he needed us, we couldn't
refuse him. And so I ask it again: stay out of danger . . .*

And before Nathan could prepare an answer:

Now then, how may we help?

Nathan turned eagerly to Hannant, tuned in on that
one's deadspeak mind. 'Sir? About Harry's maths . . .'

And Hannant interrupting, with: *Wait! Before you
ask me to show you anything, perhaps you'd better
show me a thing or two. You must have learned something since you've been here.*

Nathan showed him: orthodox maths of a high standard, with one or two 'original' concepts thrown in. It
was as simple as that: a pageant of equations marching
like an army of numbers and symbols down the screen
of his mind.

Standard stuff – mainly, Hannant commented, his
thoughts clipped, precise and perhaps 'typical' of a
maths master. *But if I may say so, you show exactly the*

699

same lateral tendencies as Harry. Which of course you must, if you're to achieve what he achieved. But is this everything? If so, there's not much to work with.

'There is other ... stuff,' Nathan told him. 'Stuff that's inside me. I've been training myself to keep it suppressed. But I'm going to need a lot more of this lesser maths before I'll be able to understand it. It's not the same as what I just showed you. It's in flux, changing – mutating? – all the time. It's ... alive! It lives and works within itself. It's like a whirlpool, a numbers vortex.'

Show me.

'You're sure?'

What? The ex-headmaster and maths teacher seemed momentarily taken aback, surprised. But only for a moment, until he laughed and said: *But of course I'm sure! I mean, do you think it can harm me?*

So Nathan showed him. And while the numbers vortex could not in truth harm Hannant, it could and did shock him rigid!

Swift as thought, Nathan's deadspeak – the issue of his weird metaphysical mind – underwent an almost metamorphic transformation. Like a mental meltdown, it sent near-nucleic energies radiating outwards into the incorporeal aether. And at the heart of the inferno:

The numbers vortex! Hungry, seething, and 'sentient' in its own right, it sought to fuel its own fires. Mutating formulae where they surfaced and swarmed on the whirling rim were sucked back into the core and devoured; caught in devastating collision, incredible calculi exploded in the cauldron of pure maths; evolving equations were fired in bursts from the wildly rotating wall like bullets from a machine-gun.

Hannant took a full burst before his astonished deadspeak 'gasp' registered, causing Nathan to rein back on the vortex and reduce it first to a spiral of valueless ciphers, and finally to nothing.

And in a little while Hannant said: *My God!*

To which Nathan replied, 'In Sunside we have no real God. He died along with our civilization, at the time of the White Sun.'

And when Hannant was himself again: *As I recall*, he said, *the Necroscope Harry Keogh wasn't too sure about a God either. But if there isn't one, how may I explain what I just saw? And how is it that you don't understand it? I mean, to have something like that in your mind and not know what it is? And yet . . . this isn't the first time I've seen it. Something like it, anyway.*

'It isn't?' Nathan's fascination was obvious.

No, I don't think so. But last time, it was . . . what, controlled?

'By Harry?'

Of course. He was in Leipzig visiting the grave of Möbius. Indeed, I was the one who sent him there! Like you, he had come to me searching for answers. But unlike you, all Harry had was an idea, a symbol. Hannant showed it to him: the Möbius strip.

And Nathan thought: *Möbius's blazon. And Maglore's. And now mine, too.* His hand automatically lifted to his ear, to touch the golden earring there – until he remembered that he'd left it in London with David Chung, like a lifeline to E-Branch HQ.

Maglore? Hannant broke into his thoughts. Nathan's telling of his story had been brief, and much of his stay in Turgosheim had been left out. *A friend of yours?*

Nathan shuddered and answered, 'Friend? No, not him!' And putting Maglore out of his mind, he immediately reverted to their original conversation: 'But did you say that my father's numbers were different from those in the vortex?'

Not different but controlled. Where your numbers are wild, untamed, Nathan, the numbers in Harry's mind were like a vast, ever-changing equation on the screen of a computer, which he could stop at the touch of a mental button. Except the power of his numbers was such that it couldn't be contained, which is the reason I compared them to God! Only attempt to still their activity, they spilled over into something else; their mutation became physical as opposed to hypothetical.

'And then? Did they do something? What did they do?' Nathan's eagerness was very nearly painful. Yet at the same time, paradoxically, he was cautious; for several people had already told him that numbers can't do anything, that they simply are. But:

They warped! Hannant told him. Through Harry's eyes, I saw them warp! And they formed doors. Then . . . I saw Harry use one of those doors, saw him pass through it and disappear . . .

Doors!

And once again, as so often before, Nathan's mind went back to Sunside's furnace deserts – to the caverns under the earth and the dwelling-places of the Thyre – and to what the dead Thyre Stargazer Thikkoul had forecast for him in the undying, everlasting stars. The doors of his future:

'Like the doors on a hundred Szgany caravans but liquid, drawn on water, formed of ripples . . .' Thikkoul had whispered. 'Doors, constantly opening and closing. And behind each one of them, a piece of your future . . .'

. . . Nathan snapped out of it. 'Möbius,' he groaned. 'It always comes back to him. An unending loop, like the Möbius Strip itself. A dead end. I've been told that he's moved on, perhaps used his own Continuum to travel to worlds beyond. I would go and speak to him, except he's no longer there.' And remembering what Gormley had said: 'Only Möbius's bones are in Leipzig now.'

I know, Hannant told him, sensing the depth of his frustration. *But you know, Möbius wasn't the only mathematician in the world. Towards the end of Harry's time here, he even asked the help of the giants. And they gave it to him! For of course, they owed him. The Necroscope was the one who showed us how to communicate among ourselves. Since when ... well, there's quite a community of us now: a fraternity, you could say. All the various experts in their various fields, they talk to each other from time to time, and keep up to date as best they can.*

'The "giants"?'

Hannant offered a deadspeak shrug, which was hardly negligent but merely expressed his acceptance of his place in the order of things. *Giants, yes. Compared with such as Pythagoras, small minds like mine are as nothing. Perhaps when I've lain in the earth as long as he has ...*

'Pythagoras?'

As briefly as possible, Hannant explained. And in so doing he humbled Nathan, too. For it brought a sense of human history to him, and a feeling of awe: that the people of this world had records going back all of two thousand six hundred years!

Oh, longer than that! Hannant told him. *We also have the record of the Earth itself, which goes back billions of years! But as for feelings of awe: I don't think you realize your own potential. For while your colleagues among the living have the history, you have the power to actually converse with that history! Your text books are the minds of the ancient dead ... or those of them still extant, at least.* For a moment he paused, and then went on more cautiously: *Except ...*

'Yes?'

(Again Hannant's shrug, this time of defeat, or partial defeat.) *Except Pythagoras has withdrawn back into his shell. For a while Harry brought him out of himself. He had even dissolved the brotherhood and made himself available. But when he discovered the advances we had made, and saw how the numbers he had known were only the germ of current knowledge ... that was too much for him. It was easier to retreat into the safety of obsolete doctrines, surround himself in secrecy once more and await his grand metempsychosis. No one has spoken to Pythagoras for, oh, a long time.*

'But you know where he is?'

Oh, yes.

And buoyed up again, Nathan answered: 'Then it's high time someone did speak to him!' And such was his tone of voice, the weight of his commitment, he might easily have meant now, this very instant.

'Speak to whom?' Trask said, his hand falling on Nathan's shoulder where he sat on the dais of Hannant's tomb. It was so unexpected that Nathan jumped six inches. And startled out of his deadspeak mode, he lost contact with Hannant at once.

Gasping, he looked up at Trask and blurted, 'Pythagoras!'

'The Pythagoras?' This from Zek, whose glance was accusing where she aimed it at Trask.

'Was there more than one?'

'No.' Trask shook his head. 'I think not.' Then, feeling Zek's annoyance, he followed up with an apology. 'Nathan, I'm sorry. Like a fool I thought you were talking to yourself! But now, from the look on your face, I know that you weren't. It's just that ... even knowing your talent, it's still hard for me to believe, that's all. I tend to forget what you can do.'

'Did we interrupt something important?' Zek took Nathan's arm as he stood up.

'Truthfully?' he glanced at Trask. 'Yes. But it's OK. I can get back to him.'

'Him?' This from Trask.

Nathan indicated the headstone. 'A one-time teacher at the school across the road. In life he must have been a very fine man. Later, he was a friend of my father's. My friend, now.'

'Should we go off again?' Trask wanted to put things right. 'Is there something you need to finish?'

Nathan shook his head. 'Later.'

They let it go at that, walked to the car and drove back to their hotel in Hartlepool . . .

'When we drove back through the town,' Nathan said over their evening meal, 'I noticed that my father had chosen to live in a house directly opposite a large graveyard, a very old place.'

Trask nodded and said, 'Very appropriate, don't you think?' And before Nathan could answer, 'I'll tell you something about that garret flatlet of Harry's: it was where Harry Junior — your brother — first used the Möbius Continuum. And he was no more than an infant at the time. So there's hope for you yet.'

Nathan thought to himself: *An infant. The Dweller. My brother by a woman not my mother was a mere infant, yet even as a helpless, defenceless bairn, he knew more than I've learned in a lifetime! But if it was instinct in him, then why not in me? What's missing in me? And where is it? I feel incomplete. Did Nestor get something intended for me? And if so, why hasn't it developed in him?* And a moment later: *But I thank Trask's and Hannant's 'God' that it hasn't!*

And out loud, if abstractedly: 'How was it that time?' he asked Trask.

'I wasn't there,' the other shrugged, perhaps regretfully. 'I was out of it, injured, hospitalized. The Branch was tracking down a monster, Yulian Bodescu, who was Wamphyri, and I'd been hurt at the creature's house down in Devon. Since then, I've often *wished* I had been there, but on the other hand ... maybe I was lucky. A very good friend of mine was there, however – an extraordinary man, an esper called Darcy Clarke – and he told me about it. Also, I've read the reports ...' He paused for a moment, then continued:

'It was night. Harry's wife and infant son were in the flat. Bodescu forced his way in and killed a policeman and two Special Branch men who got in his way. But the baby was a Necroscope. Harry Keogh's child, the teeming dead loved him. And he called them up, to defend himself and his mother.

'The dead of night, no one saw them leave their tombs and come out of the graveyard but Darcy. He was in a locked, barred room on the second floor, and had just seen Bodescu kill a colleague. Then, while Darcy was trying to make his escape through a window, he looked down on the graveyard. And I'll always remember how he described what he saw:

'At first he couldn't believe it: the road outside the house was filling with people, but in no way ordinary people. Silent streams of them were converging, massing together. They were coming out of the cemetery gates, over its front wall – men, women and children – and crossing the road to gather in front of the house. And they were quiet as the graves they'd so recently vacated!

'Their stench drifted up to Darcy on the damp night air, the overpowering reek of advanced decay and rot-

706

ting flesh. Some of them, recently dead, were in their graveclothes, but others ... had been dead for a long time. They flopped over the cemetery wall, squelched out of its gate, shuffled or crawled across the road. And then they were knocking at the door of the house, seeking entry.

'Darcy thought he was going mad. But knowing Harry's talent – and knowing now that his child was also a Necroscope – he had to accept the truth of it. At which he made to go downstairs and let them in. Can you imagine it? Darcy was going to let a horde of walking corpses into this house of horror! But in the end it didn't come to that. Something happened that he just couldn't take and he passed out. And we learned the rest of it later, from Harry himself.

'Harry Junior had already taken his mother to E-Branch HQ via the Möbius Continuum. The dead people attacked Bodescu in the garret flat, and despite that he was Wamphyri, he didn't stand a chance against them. For after all, they had nothing to lose. Changing his body-shape to an airfoil, he crashed through the window. But one of the dead was a marksman and put a crossbow bolt in his spine. Crippled, he fell to earth. They found him in the cemetery, staked him down, cut off his head and burned him. That's the story ...'

Nathan looked at him and nodded. 'And well told,' he said. 'But maybe the dead in that graveyard could have told it even better. I think I should speak to them. There's a lot to learn about my father, and they're the only ones who know. The only ones who *really* know.'

'Do you want us to go with you?' Zek knew he didn't.

'I think I might prefer to be alone,' Nathan answered. 'I can concentrate better. Also, I get the feeling that the dead don't like it ... when other people are "listening in", so to speak.'

'Your minders will be there,' Trask reminded him.

'As long as they keep well back,' Nathan answered. 'But you know, the night time is their time.'

'The dead?'

'Yes. When the world is quiet, that's when they come into their own. What's left of it.' Then, feeling Zek's eyes on him, her telepathic probe, he looked at her.

The night time was Harry's time, too, she told him. *And in profile, when you smile in that oh-so-sad way of yours, you look just like him. Except ... at the end, his eyes glowed red in the dark.* And in a little while: *I know how dangerous your world is, Nathan, for I've been there. But you know, this one can be dangerous, too, in so many ways. So when you're on your own, promise me you'll be careful.*

That was twice someone had asked him to be careful in as many hours. It made him feel wanted, made him feel good. *It's a promise,* he answered. *As long as you'll promise to take me to see Pythagoras.*

In the Greek islands? Her eyes opened wider. *And Jazz?*

Oh, yes. Jazz too.

Deal! she said.

Trask had been watching them, the way their eyes locked. Now he grinned, if a little uncertainly, and told Zek, 'He's way too young for you.'

Zek patted his hand across the table. 'And he's married,' she reminded him. 'What's more, he's a telepath, and we generally don't get on too well together. So consider yourself lucky, Ben Trask. Consider yourself lucky.'

'Can I?' Suddenly he was more than half-serious.

Zek's smile was warm on him. 'Can we talk about it later?' she said. But the look in her eyes was different from when she was looking at Nathan.

And suddenly Trask's heart felt light as a youth's in the arms of his first love. Of all men, he knew the truth when he saw it . . .

That night, Nathan talked to the dead in the Hartlepool cemetery on the Blackhall Road. And of course they remembered Harry Keogh, his father. But there was no reticence in them now; the Great Majority wanted to make up for lost time; they felt Nathan's natural warmth, took him to their hearts and poured their loneliness on him until he felt weighed under by it. Until he felt, indeed, very much as Harry had used to feel before him.

For if being a Necroscope had a drawback, this was it: the fact that friends are not just for helping, but also for *being* helped. And while there were millions of them, there was only one Nathan.

In the ancient Hartlepool graveyard, however, with all of its leaning, moss-grown slabs, their numbers were not so great that he couldn't cope. For a little while, at least. And while he didn't learn a lot about Harry Keogh (for after all, what was there now to be known, beyond the fact that the dead had loved him?) Nathan's honesty and humility did cement a friendship which would last as long as memory. And the memories of the teeming dead are long indeed.

Towards the end, when the cold and a swirling ground mist had seeped so deep into his bones that he began to feel a part of the inscribed marble slab where he sat, a small, shy, deadspeak voice said to him: *Nathan, do you think you could help me, please?*

It was a girl-child's voice, but a voice filled with such sadness, Nathan's heart ached for her. 'If I can,' he told her. 'But . . . who are you?'

My name is Cynthia, she told him. *I am − I was −*

seven. *That wasn't very long ago. But my bones were sick and wouldn't make blood for me, and so I died. But even before that, my Mummy and Daddy were so worried about me! At school, I didn't make friends very well, and they couldn't bear that I was lonely. So I know they'll be worried even more now, because they'll think I have no friends at all. But you can tell them that I do. You can tell them I have lots of friends!*

Nathan thought about it and was stalled for ideas. His new friends saw his indecision – his helplessness – and tried to help him out:

Cynthia, he heard them saying to her. *The Necroscope is a busy man. He just can't be at everyone's beck and call. He has his duties in the living world, too, you know? And anyway, how can he possibly tell your Mummy and Daddy that you've spoken to him? They don't know that we're down here in the ground, still thinking our thoughts . . .* Their argument made sense, but still it seemed a cold one to Nathan.

'Let it be,' he told them. And to Cynthia herself: 'Little darling, if there's some way I can tell them, I will. And I'll be sure to let you *know* that I've told them. Except you'll have to tell me where they live, and their second name. And then . . . well, then there's something I'll want from you, in payment.'

Payment?

'A small favour, that's all.'

Just ask it! (He could see her shining eyes, could almost hear her small hands clapping her excitement).

'A kiss,' he said. 'Just one, right here.'

And a moment later –

– It was as if an angel had touched Nathan's cheek. And in the air, he seemed to smell the soft sad scent of soap and tears and innocence . . .

*

When Nathan left the graveyard he was a man with a new mission; just one more task among all the others he'd set himself, which to most men might seem very insignificant in the greater scheme of things. To him, however, it seemed the most important thing in the world, so that by the time he reached the hotel he knew what he must do about it.

He found Trask and Zek in the bar enjoying late-night cocktails, and told them what he wanted to do.

'Now? Tonight?' Trask checked his watch. It was just after eleven.

'Right now,' Nathan nodded. 'Why should they hurt any more than they have to?'

'But . . . do you think they'll be up and about? I mean, will they still be awake, at this hour?' Trask didn't know what else to say. His mind had been elsewhere.

Nathan knew it and forgave him. 'Oh, yes. They'll be awake. They'll be sitting there in their lonely home, thinking, remembering, grieving. For you see, they haven't been getting a lot of sleep; nor are they likely to, unless we help them.'

Zek said, 'Let me get my coat.' And Trask and Nathan sat in silence waiting for her . . .

They drove through light, late-night traffic to an address on the outskirts of town: a fine-looking house with a gravel drive, well-stocked gardens, and a play corner with swings, a slide and a tree house. The place seemed in good order, yet had a hard-to-define air of desolation . . . or perhaps not so hard to define. Downstairs, the lights were on in the living room, whose glass patio doors looked out on the road. And in that room, a man and woman sat facing each other, apparently in silence, across a table. Their shoulders were hunched and they rested their heads in their hands.

Parking a little way down the road and turning off his lights, Trask asked: 'Should I come with you?' But Zek shook her head.

'Thanks, Ben,' she said, softly. 'But you might distract us.'

Nathan indicated a second car which passed them and came to a halt some fifty yards farther down the road. 'Perhaps you could speak to those two instead?'

'Sure,' Trask nodded, as the two telepaths headed quietly back towards the house.

And when they got there:

'Will they see us?' Zek whispered.

'No.' Nathan shook his head. 'We see them because of the light in there. But out here it's dark. And anyway, they don't see much of anything any more. And they don't *think* very much of anything, either, except Cynthia. Which should make it that much easier.'

'What do you want me to do?'

'Just give me your strength, boost my telepathy, help me get through to them.'

'I'm ready when you are.'

Nathan had given it a lot of thought. He knew what to do, what to say. 'Now,' he said, and reached out with his mind to the couple inside the house . . .

. . . Their grief was enormous. And Nathan knew it for what it was. When he had thought that his mother, brother, and especially Misha were dead, he had felt the same grief – almost. But with him there had always been a hope, however slim, that somehow they had lived through that terrible time. And indeed they had. But Cynthia was undeniably dead, and her parents knew it. They had seen her through her illness, fighting it all the way; they'd stood beside her bed, to be with her when she drew her last breath.

And it was just as Nathan had explained it to Trask: all of the remembering, the grieving and thinking of sad thoughts was still in them, and all of the wondering about Cynthia *now*, where and how she was *now*. It was, in fact, the way it is for everyone who grieves. To see someone in the street who looks like the one who has gone, and to wonder why this one is here and the other . . . missing. For despite that Cynthia was dead, it was too recent; she just *couldn't* be dead! Missing, yes, but not dead. Not possibly. Not while other kids, while everyone else, lived.

Nathan listened a while, until he couldn't take any more of it. And then:

Only to this world, he told them, in both of their minds at one time. *She's only dead to this world.*

'Who . . .?' The husband looked at his young wife.

'What . . .?' Her eyes were big and round.

And with all the force and feeling Nathan could muster — yet with compassion, too, that same compassion which had made his father the champion of the dead — and with Zek coupling her own telepathic drive to his, he told them: *You are right, she lives, but in worlds beyond, where she has friends galore. Don't ask about it but believe. She can be happy there, if she knows that you are happy here.*

Cynthia's father shot to his feet, moved quickly yet stumblingly about the room, knocked a small coffee table over in his haste. He searched . . . in vain. For of course there was no one there. And: 'In my head!' he said.

'Mine too!' his wife cried.

In both your heads, Nathan said. *Now, do you believe? It's a very simple thing —*

'— Called faith!' cried the woman, fainting.

Her husband caught her before she could fall, and

looked up, looked all about the empty room. 'I ... I never believed.'

But now you do?

'Yes! Oh, yes!'

Then she'll be happy.

'But ... where?'

In worlds beyond. Except, you must never think of following her, Nathan cautioned. *For you're forbidden, until your natural time. And then she'll be waiting. But not alone, for all of her friends are waiting with her.*

The man let himself down onto a couch with his wife in his arms. 'Who ... are you?' he sobbed then.

A friend of Cynthia's, Nathan answered, simply. *Just one of ... of a Great Many ...*

And as the man began sobbing, and crying: 'God forgive me that I haven't believed! Thank you, thank you!' so Nathan withdrew his telepathic probe.

On their way back to the car, Zek said, 'Will they be all right?'

'We'll return at first light and see,' Nathan answered.

They did, and they saw. Wood smoke rose from the chimney and the husband was in the garden in his shirt sleeves, dismantling the swing. Cynthia wouldn't be needing it any more, not now that she was with her friends in the worlds beyond. In a little while, as they watched, the man's wife came out of the house and threw her arms round his neck. Talking, and holding tight, they moved inside ...

Returning to the hotel, Nathan requested that Trask park for a moment or two outside the cemetery in Blackhall Road. Then, as they drove off again:

'Her mother and father will be fine now,' the Necroscope sighed, relaxing and closing his eyes in the back of the car. 'And so will Cynthia ...'

*

714

Back at the hotel, a Special Branch man came running from his anonymous-looking car. 'Sir?'

Trask could tell by the look on his face that it was important. 'What is it?'

'Message. Urgent. Came in over our radio.' He handed over a note and went back to his car. Trask watched him go, thinking: *His is not to question why.* Then he read the note:

For Bravo-Tango:
Golf-Tango requests to speak to you about Tango-Tango at your earliest. Suggest you use a blender, preferably ours . . .

Delta-Charlie.

It was David Chung telling him that Gustav Turchin wanted to chinwag about Turkur Tzonov, a.s.a.p. 'Blender' was Branch jargon for a communications scrambler . . .

VIII

Doors!

The drive down to London was uneventful. Back at E-Branch HQ, at three o'clock in the afternoon, Trask got Turchin on-screen; also, in the background and slightly out of focus, the Ministry Responsible's 'Man in Moscow'.

The Russian Premier was short, blocky, apparently unshakable. In his position he had to be. Currently he 'presided' over food riots in Kazakhstan, massive radiation pollution in the Black Sea, terrorism in the Ukraine, Mafia-style gang wars in Moscow itself, and minor territorial and border disputes just about everywhere.

'And now this,' Turchin said, his words clipped, pared to a minimum, allowing for no misunderstanding, no misrepresentation. 'In response to your timely – warning? – I found a way to access certain restricted information. So far as I am able to ascertain, your fears with regard to a high-ranking official of the USS's security services . . . no, let us simply say Turkur Tzonov, are borne out – apparently. There is some evidence of modest weapon shipments to the Perchorsk Project, and –'

'Modest?' Trask put in. 'I'm sorry, Mr President, but we saw more than a "modest" arms cache in Perchorsk! In fact –'

'Please!' Turchin held up a hand. 'I have a good idea of what you saw. But modest, yes, in terms of the ordnance of a full-scale war.'

'But sufficient,' Trask wouldn't be put off, 'to mount an invasion on a technologically defunct country – or world! And let's face it, there is no other requirement. Not in Perchorsk. The precautions against any kind of incursion from the Gate are more than adequate as they stand. So why –'

'– Why ... is the big question, Mr Trask. Yes, I have to agree.' Turchin had gone very quiet, which warned Trask that even his diplomatic patience had its limits. His dark eyes were glinting under bushy black eyebrows, and his thin lips had tightened. 'Please let me finish.' And in a moment:

'I did say that your fears were well-founded, did I not? Indeed, I have had my eye – several eyes – on Mr Tzonov for quite some time. Alas, it is not my position to prosecute but merely to advise, in certain circumstances, prosecution. When the evidence is to hand, then there will be time enough to –'

'– But not yet?' Again Trask interrupted. 'I'm sorry, Mr President, but surely time is of the essence. Tzonov is known to have megalomaniac tendencies, and in at least one instance we know him to be guilty of murder! Or at the very least attempted murder.'

'Siggi Dam –' the Premier paused and his lips tightened more yet, '– is missing, yes.' He half-turned from the screen, then faced it head-on. 'Fled to the West, according to Turkur Tzonov, rather than face an inquiry into her part in the –'

'– Escape of an alien from Perchorsk? But didn't we tell you that would be his excuse?'

'Yes,' Turchin nodded. 'And as excuses go, it would appear to be a good one. For after all, you do have the alien.'

'The ... alien?' Trask countered. 'He's here, of course. But if he hadn't been treated like an animal, not to

717

mention threatened with Tzonov's machine, he could just as easily be there, in Moscow. Ergo: Nathan "the alien" is where *he* wants to be. But isn't that his right, in a Europe with no borders or passports or persecution? And isn't it obvious how Tzonov would build all of those old barriers again, and draw an iron curtain across the world, if he were given the chance to further his cause? Don't give him that chance, Sir!'

'I don't intend to. He *is* under scrutiny. Both Tzonov and . . . his cause.' The glint in Turchin's eyes was now dangerous. 'But slowly-slowly catchee monkey, Mr Trask. Slowly-slowly.'

'That's an old one.' Trask wound down a little, allowed himself the luxury of a strained smile. 'But if I may advise, not *too* slowly.'

'Tzonov's cause, yes.' Turchin didn't acknowledge Trask's smile. 'Treason, if we're correct. But he has many tentacles, reaching out into almost every province of the USS. I can see how eventually he might even use insurrection to further his ambitions – if he could find a way to fund it.'

'Indeed,' Trask nodded. 'And I think he believes that he has found just such a way. Sunside/Starside is rich in gold. There, it's a common metal . . .'

'But just as I have my – what, informers? – so he has his spies, too.' (Turchin still didn't appear to be listening too well; but just looking at him, Trask's lie-detector told him that he was.) 'In fact he controls some of our best intelligence agents. Mindspies, Mr Trask, in your parlance. Or perhaps, "the Opposition"?'

'In the old days, yes. And Tzonov would bring those old days back again. Except we can't allow that, which anyone but a raving lunatic – or a megalomaniac – must surely see. But the damage he could do in the attempt . . .'

'... Is unthinkable, I know. He could destroy what we've all been trying to rebuild for fifteen years, and in so doing destroy my country.'

'My apologies, Sir.' Trask shook his head. 'But you seem to have missed the point. Much as I appreciate your concern for your country, my concern is for the whole world. To be frank, I wouldn't mind a bit if Turkur Tzonov went through the Gate into Starside tonight. I would quite like it – if I could guarantee that he wasn't going to come back. Or that if he did come back, it would be *as a man!* It's not what he plans to steal from the vampire world that worries me, but the fact that he'll advertise *this* world to whatever is waiting in there for him. That's what really worries me: that he'll bring something back inside him!'

For a moment Turchin was silent, thoughtful. Then he said: 'Is the threat really *that* terrible?'

And Trask told him, 'I know as much about it as any man of this world, and you may believe me that there *is* no greater threat! The Gates are doorways to pestholes; they could release a plague that would sweep across the entire planet, and destroy or enslave each and every one of us. Eventually, we must find a way to seal those Gates forever. Even the Perchorsk solution isn't good enough; no way, not with men like Tzonov around. And especially not with him in charge of it! Why not simply recall him, get him out of there, give him a job in Moscow where you can keep an eye on him?'

Now it was Turchin's turn to smile, however grimly. 'Ah, if only it were that easy. But do you know how limited my real resources are? If I told you, you wouldn't believe me. And you advise me to recall him? Tzonov comes and goes as he pleases, Mr Trask. He's a power in his own right. And the last thing I want to do is frighten him, perhaps precipitating ... whatever he

719

intends.' He shrugged, but not negligently. 'Please don't forget: Perchorsk is a fortress.'

Trask was mystified. 'So if we've already reached the same conclusions, why are we having this conversation?'

Turchin sighed, perhaps wearily, and his shoulders slumped a little. 'I love my country too,' he finally said. 'I mean, I love it as well as Tzonov – no, better than Tzonov. Because I love it for itself, not for myself. And so I am torn two ways. You are worried about the Wamphyri ... quite right, so should we all. But there is also this question of the exploitation of another world. What I'm asking is, which is the greater worry? As you and everyone else knows, my country has been desperately depleted. Could it be you're afraid we'll get there first, and that Russia will be strong again?'

Trask shook his head, maybe in disgust, perhaps in disbelief. 'Let me repeat myself,' he said. 'Getting there isn't the problem. Containing what's there already is. If we – I mean, if E-Branch – ever has cause to send men into that vampire world, it will be as a last resort, or an attempt to destroy the Wamphyri at their source. It will not be for exploitation.'

'And you'll let me know if that time should come?'

'You'll be the first to know.'

'Very well. And in future we must speak – like this, face to face – on a more regular basis.'

'We might very well have to,' Trask told him.

'As for now ... well, as you can see, I have a great many things to do.'

'I'm sure you do,' Trask replied.

Throughout, the Ministry Responsible's man had remained a blurred, silent figure in the background ...

Days became weeks became months. Nathan was so

immersed in his studies, he scarcely noticed the days flying by. But that was a cliché, for of course he noticed them. And indeed they flew! Seven complete cycles to one of Sunside's ... the sheer *velocity* of the sun across the sky was a never-ending wonder to him. He could actually see it move!

He studied engines, but only those which would have application on Sunside. Steam-engines fascinated him especially, and he acquired a tiny model to take home with him. The benefits to the Thyre would be enormous! Couple a thing such as this to the long-dead artisan Shaeken's Wheel of Irrigation; why, the furnace deserts could be made to bloom!

Nathan could see it clearly in the eye of his mind: with a bank of wonderful Thyre mirrors focused on the boiler of an engine through all the long hours of daylight – not to mention the heat of the desert itself – the requirement for solid fuel would be minimal. And as for water: no lack of that with Shaeken's Water Ram and Hydraulic Hoist, and the Great Dark River to draw upon where it coursed its way through black bowels of rock deep beneath the surface.

He looked at agriculture, the incredible variety of cultivated vegetables, and remembered the tales Lardis Lidesci had told of The Dweller's garden: its wonderful produce. And every chance that came his way, he procured seeds to take back with him. Oh, the Szgany grew their own crops, be sure, but never in such abundance, with the consistency, yield and high quality of these. The potato was quite amazing, and completely unheard of on Sunside!

He went from maths to science: dynamics, which was simply another branch; or rather, the *application* of numbers. And he enjoyed it, for here at last Nathan could see that they could *be* applied. But of course! No more guesswork required to work out how many cogs were required on a wheel: the baffling mathematics of circles was a mystery no more. Not with the principle of π fixed firmly in his head.

He undertook all of these studies with gusto; for this was the knowledge — these were the benefits — he would take home with him. But not *all* the benefits, and not all of them harmless. For he also studied weapons and practised with a variety of handguns, semi-automatics, shotguns, sub-machineguns, and grenades, on an all-but obsolete Army firing range in the old garrison town of Aldershot . . .

Last but not least (foremost in many ways), Nathan practised his deadspeak. Except now it was easy, for the teeming dead talked back to him without reservation. However unintentionally, he had done himself the greatest possible favour in going to the aid of poor little Cynthia in the Hartlepool cemetery. It stood him in great stead, for the dead knew now beyond a shadow of a doubt that they had found a new champion in Nathan. Whatever his fight or quest was or would be, from this time forward it would also be theirs.

Frequent trips to Hartlepool, Harden, Edinburgh, and all of the many graveyards which Harry Keogh had frequented, furnished him with an almost complete picture of the man who had been his father, the man whom the dead had known as the Necroscope. And despite what Harry had been at the end, Nathan was not ashamed of him. For not one of Harry's many dead friends had a bad word for him, and as a man they regretted the fact that they'd ever turned their backs on him.

In every possible way the dead put themselves at Nathan's command; he received introductions to members of the Great Majority in many lands, and only had to reach out his mind to find them, however far distant. Along with all of his new scientific knowledge, his esoteric talent grew apace almost as if to accommodate the unaccustomed demands he placed upon it. And whenever he met with difficulties, the dead were there to help out . . .

. . . Except in the one area where their help would be most appreciated. For not one of them knew Harry's greatest secret, or was able to offer a clue as to where Nathan might find the answer. The metaphysical Möbius Continuum seemed as far from his grasp as ever.

And suddenly, it was the middle of May.

The changing seasons astonished Nathan, but all in all his senses were becoming used to abrupt changes: the ever-changing concrete 'scenery' of the cities, eye-blurring transport systems such as cars, trains, subways and airplanes, the dramatic variety of the country-side — especially the coastal regions of the North-east, with their crumbling shale cliffs, brooding grey ocean and plaintive seagulls, a species unknown on Sunside — and a hundred other concepts away and beyond all previous experience. Now he was much more given to taking things in his stride.

The one thing he was not ready for, because he had put it out of his mind (his yearning was too great; it was too much of a distraction), was that which Trask sprang on him one Tuesday morning in the middle of the month.

'The resurgent tributary at Radujevac is down to its lowest level in five years,' Trask told him, waking him up in his father's old room. 'I've arranged our flight to Belgrade for a week Friday. Anna Marie English has been out there for months now, and she's really got things moving. She tells me that our potholers have been up the sump to the Gate. They can get you there with all the stuff you've been gathering together, weapons, ammunition, anything you can carry. Plus all that you've learned, of course, locked away in your head.'

'But not the thing I most wanted to learn.' What Trask had said was still dawning on Nathan; he was still waking up, blinking sleep out of his eyes. 'And will some of your men be coming with me?'

'No.' Trask shook his head. 'We've made a deal with Gustav Turchin. We sit still until Turkur Tzonov makes his move, *if* he makes it. Meanwhile, men loyal to Turchin are infiltrating Perchorsk. Turchin thinks he can stop Tzonov right there, on his own ground.'

Nathan paused in getting dressed to blurt out: 'I hope he *fails* to stop him! I'd like to meet up with that man in my own world. Better by far, I'd like some of its *inhabitants* to meet up with him! For by comparison, Turkur Tzonov is only a very small monster.'

'Still thinking about Siggi?'

'If Siggi Dam went through into Starside deprived of her senses, her mind, by that machine —' Nathan shook his tousled head, '— then thinking about her really won't do us much good. But I would like the chance to avenge her, yes.'

'Take care of your own first, Nathan,' was Trask's advice. 'For if there's any justice in the world — and it's my experience that there is — Tzonov has enough of hard times coming without your help.' And as he headed for the door: 'Zek wants you to have breakfast with her, down in the hotel. Something that's important to her.'

And Nathan knew what it was . . .

Three days later they flew out to the Greek islands. Nathan's main interest was Samos: the teeming dead had told him Pythagoras was there, buried on the self-

724

same island where he'd been born. It would be Nathan's last shot at speaking to an expert, one of the greatest ever experts, who might yet help him. Oh, he had spoken to a good many mathematicians, orthodox and 'lateral' thinkers alike, but the numbers vortex had baffled them all no less than it had baffled J. G. Hannant. It was the way the thing mutated, the way it wouldn't sit still — not for a moment — to let itself be studied. And anyway, how could you ever be sure you were studying the right part of it?

Zek's interest, of course, was Jazz Simmons; her husband's grave was in Zakynthos close to her villa. And mid-May in the Greek Islands is a wonderful time; it would be Nathan's chance to rest and recuperate, while she ... would have the opportunity to say those few extra things which at the end she'd never had the time to say to Jazz. He knew them anyway — of course he did — but a last fond farewell couldn't hurt.

Ben Trask had wanted to accompany the pair, but when Zek declined he had understood. He hadn't been thinking, that was all. For despite all that had happened, all of the accumulated evidence, and the evidence of his own lie-detector talent, it was just — no, it was still — a very hard thing for Trask to believe in Nathan's 'art', what he was and did; as it would be for any man who was not himself a Necroscope. But this was Zek's last chance to be 'together' with Jazz, and Ben had to accept that at least.

Samos, between the Aegean and the Dodecanese, proved to be an exercise in frustration; finally Nathan tracked down a disciple of Pythagoras, who had come to his own conclusions about the Master's mysticism and dropped out of the Brotherhood. And so the location of Pythagoras's grave was discovered.

When they got close Nathan went on alone, and as

he reached the spot – a small olive grove on a terraced hillside, above a headland with a tiny white church – so he felt a far dim deadspeak presence; far in the sense of mentally remote, and dim in that of a deep, deep sleep. In a living man, this would be catatonia. In Pythagoras . . .

Shortly, returning to Zek, Nathan told her: 'It isn't any good. He's way beyond my reach. J. G. Hannant was right: Pythagoras couldn't face the greater knowledge of the modern world, the fact that science had outdistanced him. He discovered that while his calculations were right, his theology was all wrong. Unable to come to terms with it, he retreated into his own doctrines. Yet, in fact he *has* achieved a metempsychosis of sorts. But instead of migrating soul to soul, Pythagoras has fled into the core of his own mind. To him, numbers were The All. And so at last he's satisfied with his lot. Finally, he *is* the first and last number: a big cipher, the Great Zero . . .'

They took a hydrofoil to Zakynthos, Zek's island home in the Ionian, and a taxi from Zante town through Porto Zoro and along a winding, rising road that followed the mountain's contours to the south-east. There, where tree-clad spurs descended into the incredibly blue ocean, Zek kept her villa: Harry Keogh's final refuge at the end of his time here.

Then, briefly, they were free of Nathan's minders; the Special Branch men had been left behind in the port of Zante, where it had taken them longer than they'd anticipated to collect their hire-car. But in the afternoon, when the cool shadows of the mountains sprawled down across the pine-clad slopes to paint the sea dark green, and Nathan and Zek sat out on her balcony with coffee and liqueurs, they were aware of the glint of chrome on the road up above, where a last beam of sunlight struck between the peaks. And they knew that their guardian angels were back . . .

Nathan had the guest bedroom. The following morning before he was awake, Zek got out her car and drove into town to replenish her refrigerator. Hearing her return, Nathan rose, showered and got dressed. By then the villa was full of great smells, and he found Zek in the breakfast room where she greeted him with: 'A few of your favourite things.' Namely coffee, eggs and bacon.

And when they had eaten: 'Jazz?' he said, carefully.

'Could we? Now?' She seemed uncertain.

'Whenever you're ready.'

'I've . . . been thinking what to say to him.'

'I know,' he told her, gently. 'I lay awake for the best part of an hour last night, listening to you tossing and turning in your room. It won't be the same for me, either. Not this time. Because it's personal. Because I know how much you miss him. But do you know what you want to say to him? Did you work it out?'

'I think so, yes. There's not a lot, really. All I have to do is . . . not hint at what's come between us. I mean, *nothing* came between us in life – not ever, not even the Wamphyri – until the end of life itself. I have to remember that and try not to cry. Crying's not like me. Not that he'll hear me anyway. I have to just talk to him, through you, as if . . . as if he were Jazz. I mean, he *is* Jazz. And yet it can't be like a simple telephone call . . .'

It was the first time he'd seen her distraught. And very unlikely that he'd ever see it again. Zek was a strong woman.

She saw the look on his face – the sadness, for her, in his eyes – and turned away. And Nathan told her:

'It won't be as hard as you think. Deadspeak can be made to convey more than is actually said. It's a matter of feelings as well as words. We'll use telepathy, you and I, so that we're closer. Jazz won't hear telepathy, but that way I'll be able to straighten out your thoughts if they get tangled, and relay his to you without any . . . pain. If there is pain. But from what I know of him, from what I've heard, Jazz was built of much the same stuff as you. It will be all right.'

She turned back to him. 'Will it?' There was hope in her eyes.

He nodded and smiled. 'Yes, I'm sure it will be.' And he was sure, for he would make it so . . .

Some hours later, on the way to her car:

Zek paused by a leaning Mediterranean pine to gaze out over the sea. 'We loved this view,' she said.

Nathan could well understand that. There was nothing he wouldn't give to have Misha here right now, looking out over that marvellous ocean with him. No sight she'd ever seen in all Sunside could ever compare with it.

Zek had fallen silent. Glancing at her, Nathan saw that she was frowning. He followed her gaze to a boat at the edge of the water directly below. 'A caique,' she said. 'The first of the holidaymakers. They hire boats and find secluded bays, like the one down there. Occasionally they climb up through the trees, picnic, leave stuff behind and generally spoil things. There are more of them every year. I don't think I'll be able to live here much longer, not on my own. I thought I could, but . . .' She stumbled to a halt.

Nathan believed he understood. This had been their place, and magical. But the boat was reality; stealing away the last of the magic, it spoiled Zek's solitude.

'Let's go and see Jazz,' he said . . .

Between Porto Zoro and Argasi, they turned off the road onto a pebble track through the trees. There on a rocky promontory, a small white church shone like alabaster in the midday sunlight and was reflected in the sparkling waters of the bight. Between the trees and the pebble beach, a graveyard was laid out in neat, regularly tended plots. All of this well off the tourist beat, in as tranquil a spot as may be imagined.

'Jazz liked to fish for grouper just off the point there,' Zek explained. 'And when he knew it was all over . . . he chose this place himself.'

And so they went to Jazz's grave.

And Nathan made it easy for them. For both of them . . .

At the end, when she'd said it all and couldn't hide the tears any longer, Zek walked out of the cemetery and onto the beach, and stood at the edge of the sea. And Nathan told Jazz: *We're going now.*

It was nice of you to come, Jazz answered. *And it's great what you've done for Zek. I know that Harry would be proud of you. But listen, I don't like her hurting and lonely. So do me a big favour: if the time comes when someone really cares, see to it that she doesn't feel guilty. I mean, tell her not to feel guilty. Let her know that I only want her to be happy.*

Nathan nodded. *If I'm still here when, if, that happens, then . . . you have my promise.*

But not until then.

Of course.

That's good enough for me, said Jazz . . .

Nathan left Zek on the beach to get done with it in her

own way, and walked back to the car. Before leaving, he noticed that the caique from Zek's place was drawn up on the pebbles, but there was no one in it; and before reaching Zek's car he saw a glint of chrome in a grove of olive trees and knew that his minders were there.

Then, looking closer, he saw one of them – or the arms of one of them – sticking out from both sides of the bole of a gnarled old tree. The hands were on the ground, resting on their knuckles. The man must be sunbathing, but ... his hands were so still. And in the car, the second Special Branch man seemed asleep behind the steering wheel.

Suddenly, Nathan's blood was running cold. Sensing that something was wrong, he reached out a telepathic probe. There were other minds in the vicinity, but strange minds and furtive! Recently, Nathan had used telepathy in partial conjunction with deadspeak. Instinctively, he switched to the latter mode –

– And the confused, astonished, utterly terrified minds of his minders were there! They were dead!

He stepped to the tree and round it. There, sitting in the sun with his shirt open, the chest of the man on the ground was drenched in blood; he sat in a pool of his own blood! His eyes and mouth were open in a frozen gasp, but a second mouth gaped scarlet under his chin and Adam's apple. Nathan didn't need to look at the one in the car ...

Zek! He aimed a probe towards the beach.

Nathan! She was there at once, saw what was in his mind – the monstrous picture he painted – and added her own knowledge to it. *A man – no, two men – in the water. They must have got here in the caique. They have spearguns, and their thoughts are murderous! They're under orders ... from Turkur Tzonov!*

There are others here, he told her. *In the trees. I'm coming.* And he raced for the beach . . .

In the Greek Islands it was 1:45 p.m, but at E-Branch HQ, London, it was two hours earlier and the cadaverous Ian Goodly had just stepped out of the elevator. As he did so, he reeled, gasped, and clutched at his temples.

David Chung was in the corridor. He grabbed Goodly's arm, supported him, said: 'Ian, what is it?'

'H-Harry's room!' the other rasped.

'Yeah,' Chung nodded, licking suddenly dry lips. 'Me too!'

They went there, and met the empath Geoff Smart coming the other way. Smart's face was drawn, eyes startled, hands shaking as he hurried up to them. 'I . . .' he began. But:

'We know,' they told him, almost in one voice.

In Harry's room, Goodly told Chung, 'I saw you plugging in the computer. You, me, Geoff, we were all here. And it's now. I mean, you have to do it now!'

Chung said, 'It's Nathan's earring.' He showed it to them. 'You can't see it, but it's *vibrating* in the palm of my hand. I . . . I've never had signs so clear before. But I'm damned if I know what it means!'

'Plug in the machine,' Smart said, 'and maybe we'll find out.'

And as Chung made to do so, Goodly said: 'I don't think Nathan ever used the computer after that last time – the time it used itself! I don't think he dared. He said something to me once about "saving what was left of it". But I'm still not sure what he meant.'

The screen blazed into life and Chung fell away from the socket, sprawling on the floor. And on the screen, the numbers vortex blazed into life! Golden equations

731

rotated, calculi careened, common numbers collided in a frenzy of motion! And all in brilliant yellow or glowing gold, against a jet-black background. But in the next moment the picture slowed, and froze! One massive, incredible calculation remained, but such a calculation that no one in the room could even conceive of the question, let alone the answer.

Then . . .

. . . That answer revealed itself as the symbols flowed together and fused, forming a three-dimensional shape – a golden dart – which sped from the screen like a fish jumping from water. It was some kind of hologram, or a computer graphic brought to life: a mass of electrical motes hanging in mid-air, forming that translucent and patently insubstantial spike shape. But however faint and transient-seeming the thing might seem, still it was real!

For a brief moment the dart paused, hovered, then sped in a blur of motion out through the wall and was gone. And before a man of the three could move, the computer exploded! Blowing apart in a flash of fire and a shower of hot plastic and electrical sparks, it left the three espers staggered, mouths gaping, cringing back from the reeking, black-smoking mess of the console . . .

Something plucked at Nathan's shirt-sleeve as he raced across the pebble beach, and a moment later he heard the phut! phut! exclamations of a silenced automatic. Zek was running towards him along the beach; behind her, one man was in the water and the other climbing up onto dry land. They were in silver wet-suits and carried spearguns.

There was only one avenue of escape: towards the northern end of the beach. Nathan angled his low-crouching lope to meet up with Zek where she headed that way. But as more bullets zipped overhead, he knew they weren't going to make it. Both ends of the beach were closed off by rocky spurs that sloped gradually into the sea. The rocks were sharp and dangerous; climbing, the pair would be slowed down; they would make excellent targets against the black volcanic rock.

'Into the water!' Nathan shouted. He knew Zek could swim like a fish, and it seemed their only possible route. Hearing him and tearing off her dress, she launched herself across the tide-line and hit the water in a long low dive. And in another moment Nathan joined her. Back along the beach, the wetsuited man on the rocks slid back into the water.

'Hard as you can go,' Nathan gasped.

Get rid of your trousers, she told him, cool as a breeze in his mind. Zek was no stranger to dangerous situations. Now that the emotional times were behind her, she could think like the old Zek again. *You can't swim well in trousers.*

But Nathan was no stranger to danger either. 'I already got rid of them.'

Then use telepathy. You can't swim and talk, but you can swim and think!

Bullets plucked small spouts of water up from the millpond surface close by. And: *Dive!* he told her.

It was no good and they both knew it. The men in wetsuits were already narrowing down the distance; they wore fins, which powered them through the water. And on the beach, two more men in grey suits were sighting along the barrels of squat, ugly, silenced automatics. They could hear the thoughts of all four, which were cold, emotionless, deadly. These were professionals of a high order, and so far the fugitives had been lucky.

Coming up for air, Nathan saw large silver shapes

733

cutting white wakes on the glittering surface. And the men on the beach were shouting directions to their colleagues in the water. This wasn't going to last much longer. There were more muffled gunshots, and something sliced a groove in the rounded muscle of Nathan's shoulder. Blood splashed among the blue.

He felt no pain but gritted his teeth anyway, and asked: *Are you OK?*

Yes. But he knew she wasn't, knew that she was very nearly exhausted.

Then dive again.

Surprise and shock had conspired to rob them of their natural energies. This would be the last time they went down, and they probably wouldn't be coming up again. As Zek upended and headed for the bottom, she saw black flippers sliding under the surface only a short distance away . . .

On the beach, the two ex-KGB men saw their prey dive for the second time, glanced at each other and nodded a mutual affirmation. It was very nearly over. Then, as one of them put away his gun, the other sniffed sharply, wrinkled up his nose and said:

'Shit! I smell shit . . . or something. We must be close to a sewage outfall.'

The other shrugged. 'So it won't matter a hell of a lot if we add to it, right? Those two are done for.' He inclined his head towards the sea. 'Weighted down, it won't take very long for them to turn to slop out there.'

A hand fell on the speaker's shoulder and he jumped six inches, then fell into a half-crouch as he turned and brought up his gun. But even as he had moved, he'd seen that hand – those shrivelled, dirt-ingrained, black-nailed fingers – and he'd *smelled* them!

Behind the killers, a handful of figures came stumbling down the beach from the graveyard. Their leader was Jazz Simmons, but a Jazz long gone into corruption, and one who had known what it meant when Nathan's minders had come suddenly among the Great Majority.

And now through the trees, those minders, too, were on their feet and running for the beach. Running, yes, and full of purpose. For their muscles weren't wasted like the others and they still had a job to do; and what they'd done in life they would continue to do in death. One of them with a pair of bloody holes through his jacket and heart, the other grinning ear to ear – but grinning hideously – with the mouth in his face *and* one other, larger mouth in his throat!

But on the beach:

Phut! – phut! – phut! Three bullets went through the rotten substance of Jazz at close range. And the man who fired them going: '*Urk! Yaaaghh! Akkk!*' as the grimy bones of one of Jazz's skeletal hands tightened on his windpipe, forcing him to his knees. Then . . . Jazz took the gun from him and thrust its silenced barrel into his gaping mouth as far as it would go – and pulled the trigger.

And the other thug, splashed with his Comrade's blood and brains, gibbering and flailing where he re-treated into the sea, finally tripping and going under as a host of shroud-clad avengers fell on him, sat on him, held him down where his air came belching to the surface in a gush of frothing bubbles. They'd sit there, mute but determined, until the bubbles stopped and the figure on the bottom lay motionless.

And they did . . .

. . . While out in the bay where the water was deep:

Nathan and Zek had got separated. He found himself diving into a weed-festooned crevice, while she hid between boulders on a pebbly bottom and looked back the way they'd come. Their pursuers were there, searching, unrelenting, cold. Nathan had disturbed a small school of golden bream, which scattered magically to avoid him. And he'd also disturbed a large grouper, whose sudden, startled motion filled the crevice with a mushrooming cloud of silt.

One of the men in wetsuits saw the eruption of muck from the crevice and came nosing, speargun held to the fore. Nathan needed air; he couldn't stay in here any longer; he had to make a run for it. But run? He couldn't even swim! He was done for. He drifted up out of the crevice and into full view of whoever might be waiting for him. He felt naked.

There had been times in the past when Nathan had used the numbers vortex to hide himself. Now, instinctively – despite that it wouldn't work, because it wasn't a physical device but of the mind – he brought it into being in his head; and as he did so saw a strange thing.

Hovering just above the gash in the rocks, the regrouped school of golden bream swung nervously this way and that. And one of them wasn't a fish but . . . a dart? The thing tilted in the water, seemed to aim its point at Nathan, sprang towards him. It struck him in the forehead even as he jerked back his head, but he felt nothing! Until a moment later, when he felt . . . *something.*

He saw the numbers vortex in the eye of his mind; saw it freeze, form a wall of numbers; saw the numbers dissolve into a shape, an oblong, a door! He could see it, but he knew that no one else could. For even as it formed, water rushed into and through it, and several of the golden bream passed through and were gone. One of Harry's doors, yes: a Möbius door!

The man with the speargun came speeding, trailing his gun to slipstream his body, then beginning to draw his gun arm up and forward. Caught in the rush of water, he shot forward into the door. At which precise moment, amazed by what was happening, Nathan relaxed his grip on the thing.

The door closed, disappeared ... but the thug had passed only half-way through. And the water turned red as the lower half of his body gave a massive shudder and stopped dead in the water, then slowly began settling for the bottom. As the lower torso sank, trailing weird strings of guts and organs, so a ring of silver wetsuit vest detached itself and floated away. A severed hand was visible, too, drifting in the pink cloud, releasing the speargun and posing like a strange five-fingered fish in the water ...

Nathan! It's ... over! It was Zek, her thoughts filled with despair, terror, a sense of tragedy, the knowledge that soon she, too, would be able to speak to Jazz. And it pulled Nathan out of his shock.

The speargun was sinking. He grabbed it, turned in the water, saw a trail of bubbles descending into dark deeps. She was down there, drowning, dying, but she was also in his mind, her agony. And it didn't have to be. He didn't have to let it be.

With every last ounce of strength, Nathan kicked for the bottom. Two strokes of his free arm, three, and they came into view. The thug could have shot her, but he'd dropped his gun and was satisfied to hold her down and drown her. No, he was more than satisfied – he took pleasure in it.

Nathan was behind him, but there was no cowardice in it when he shot the man in his back. It was simply a matter of expedience, for Zek was drowning. Jerking spastically, forming a backwards-bending bow of agony, the thug released Zek's limp body and spiralled feebly into the deeps, kicking up mud and weeds as he went.

Nathan was all in; he reached Zek, grabbed her, and conjured the numbers vortex ... and froze it in a pattern which would soon become all too familiar. A door formed, sucked at the pressured water, and sucked Zek and Nathan in, too.

And at last he was there, in the Möbius Continuum!

Darkness!

Nothing!

Drowning!

Where to go? How to go?

Space without stars, without time ... without space! And a gush of salt water emptying out of Nathan's mouth ... blobs of water, great spheres of it, colliding with him, wobbling like jelly in the absence of gravity. But in the distance − oh, far, far away − a point of golden light. Whether it was there physically or merely in his tortured mind, Nathan didn't know, couldn't say. But clutching Zek's limp body to him, he struck out for it, fell towards it. It grew bigger, brighter. It was a shape. It was this shape:

But as he rushed upon it, so the thing dissolved into golden atoms, and reformed into a door! And together, Nathan and Zek fell through it ...

A moment earlier, Ian Goodly the precog had shouted: 'Out! Get out of here!' And the three espers had scrambled for the door, leaving it swinging behind them. Now, on the inward swing, as the door went to close itself on Harry's room, it was punched as by a massive fist and thrown open again. And three hundred gallons of salt sea water came pouring through into the corridor!

David Chung got the worst of it and was knocked from his feet. He wasn't hurt but simply sprawled there, with his fist clenched tightly on Nathan's earring. Except . . . it no longer vibrated. And Chung knew why. To confirm it:

From Harry's room as the salty flood dispersed along the corridor, Nathan's voice gasping his relief. And a strangled coughing and gurgling as Zek Föener strove to throw up all of the water she'd taken in and start to breathe again . . .

Epilogue

In Wrathstack, olden Starside's last great aerie of the Wamphyri, the Lady Wratha sat with her so-called 'colleagues' and closest neighbours, the dog-Lord Canker Canison of Mangemanse on her left, and the necromancer Nestor Lichloathe of Suckscar on her right. The three were seated in chairs spread wide apart along one side of the banquet table in Wrathstack's great hall, while seated opposite, the Lords Gorvi the Guile of Guilesump, and Wran the Rage and his brother Spiro Killglance of Madmanse, glared their suspicion and Wamphyri animosity across the broad black iron-wood expanse. Wratha the Risen had called this meeting, and out of curiosity if for no other reason, the vampire Lords attended it.

There had been the usual 'banter' – a string of taunts, ripostes and scarcely concealed challenges – but now that her guests had settled down Wratha made no bones of it but launched straight into her proposal:

'I suspect I'm speaking the minds of all present,' she said, 'when I tell you I've had enough of the Szgany Lidesci. Don't you agree? Isn't it high time we put aside lesser squabbles, got together and wiped Lardis and his band off the face of Sunside? Only deal with the Lidescis, finish them for good ... the other tribes will succumb in a six-month, and Sunside will be ours to use as we will! Then we'll have all the good Szgany flesh we need to fill the stack with fighting men and beasts and build an army invincible . . .' She sat back in her chair. 'Well, I've said all that before and now I've said it for the last time. That's me done and it's your turn. So tell me, how shall it be?'

And in a little while: 'Still empire-building, are you, Wratha?' said Wran, scowling and stroking his wen. 'What, and will you bring us together again under your leadership? Aye, and rob us of our get, as once before you robbed us?'

And Gorvi the Guile put in: 'Or is it that you've started to fear us now that our lieutenants are up to strength and our many warriors waxed for war? What brings you to this, Wratha, that you now counsel unity and cooperation among those you've so long abandoned?'

At which, in a voice so low it was almost a whisper, Nestor growled, 'What's that you say about fear, Gorvi the Gutless? Best remember: when you speak to Wratha like that, you're also speaking to Canker and me, who fear no man, for we are united! Frankly, I'm sick of hearing how "clever" and "artful" you are, when your only real forte is cowardice! If it were my say, I'd gladly cut you off down in the stinking roots of this place and let you rot there — except to desert you would leave the stack undefended when . . . if . . .' Here, apparently lost for words, the necromancer paused, gave a snort of disgust, and sat back scowling in his chair.

Gorvi smiled a typically sarcastic, oily smile but made no answer. But Wran, immediately suspicious, snapped: 'What's that you said? About the stack being undefended, if and when?' And then, staring at Wratha: 'Out with it, Lady — what's all this about?'

Canker leaned forward in his chair and coughed, 'Me, Wran! Ask me what it's about.'

Spiro Killglance, usually silent, spoke up from directly opposite the dog-Lord. 'You then. What goes on?'

'I read the future in dreams,' Canker barked. 'That's what goes on. And I have dreamed of an aerial army circling the last aerie ... so many of them, why, they were like stink-gnats over goat droppings! Their flyers were a horde, and their leader – was Vormulac!'

There was a long silence, then Gorvi's laugh – but shaky for all that. 'What, and should we quiver and quake because you have deigned to dream? *Hah!* And why, pray, should we place any faith in your dreams, dog-Lord? All men nightmare ... and you more than most, I should think.'

And again Wratha spoke. 'Laugh all you like, but Canker has the power. To deny it is purest folly. Didn't we *all* laugh at his plan to call down a silver mistress from the moon? Aye, we did. And do we still laugh? She's there even now, in Mangemanse! Maybe she came from the moon and maybe not, but silver she is and real, and Canker's got her. Also, Nestor Lichloathe here swears by Canker's dreams, for he is witness to the truth of them. Now listen: I warned you long ago that Vormulac would follow us out of Turgosheim. Well, he will, and soon. Perhaps too soon! Will you be ready, united, to meet him face to face? Or would you prefer to hang from the battlements in chains, and die in reek and smoulder with the rising sun?'

She looked from face to face, at each Lord in his turn, even Nestor and Canker. And not a man of them said a word but sat there stonily in his chair, with that last monstrous picture she'd painted burning vividly in his mind.

So that at last Wratha was satisfied and knew she would have her way ...

*

742

In Turgosheim:

In the first hour of sundown, Maglore the Mage watched a menacing flypast of monsters, a grand aerial parade through the gorge's blustery upper regions, level with its rim and the topmost promontory turret of Runemanse.

Vormulac Unsleep had ordered the display so that he might review his army's fitness for war prior to its departure westward over the Great Red Waste, hopefully to Olden Starside and legendary lands of plenty. For when next the sun sank down and darkness fell on the barrier mountains, then the Lord Vormulac and his many lesser Generals – and all of their men, mounts, and warrior creatures – would vacate Turgosheim *en masse*, hell bent for adventure, discovery, almost certainly war, and definitely conquest. And to the warrior-Lord Vormulac of melancholy Vormspire, this had seemed as good a time as any to mass his forces and test out their battle-worthiness in the air.

Mainly it was a test of their flying skills in an ordered body. For patently, there could be no doubt but that they were fighting men and beasts: they were vampires all, or of vampire stuff, at least. Even the moderately docile flyers were built of metamorphic flesh vampirized specifically to that end. And as for the carnivore warriors . . .

So that in fact the pomp and ceremony of this grand aerial display was as much for the glory of Vormulac as for any other reason; it was his chance to drill and parade the lesser Lords in his command, and show them his might. And it was their opportunity to rattle their battle-gauntlets, flex their muscles, and feel the 'pride' of their vampire heritage. *Wamphyri!*

And so Maglore gazed out across the great gorge of Turgosheim at gloomy Vormspire with its pale orange chimney flares and glimmery ghost-fires flickering in its windows, and knew that Vormulac stood on a balcony there, watching the parade. And the seer-Lord rejoiced for Vormulac Unsleep, that soon he would fly off with his army into the unknown, possibly to conquest and even greater glory. Indeed, Maglore *revelled* in the thought even more than Vormulac himself ... but for different reasons entirely.

And round the rim in a mighty circle swept the myriad aerial creatures of Vormulac's command: men, flyers, and warriors all, and Maglore smiling and nodding his head as he recognized the various sigils, standards and pennants held aloft to flutter in the hot exhaust of propulsive orifices and the tainted breeze of passage:

Vormulac's own 'hanging man' emblem, Lord Grigor Hakson's 'rampant rod', the virgin grandam Devetaki's 'grin-scowl mask', Eran Painscar's 'spiny gauntlet', Zindevar Cronesap's 'spitted pig' (in fact a spitted man ... right down to the apple in his mouth!), and many another; each contingent led by its master or mistress General, in orderly ranks, proud under its own banner and respectfully distanced from the next flight in line or group a-flank. The gleam of polished leather, golden ornamentation, iron-studded trappings; the cacophony of gongs from all the manses and spires around; the rattle of drums and blaring of golden horns, and the bellowing cough and sputter of warrior exhausts ...

... All very grand, and the seer-Lord hoped that Vormulac took pleasure in the spectacle. But as for Maglore himself: he would be glad when it was over and done with, and even more so to see them gone from the gorge of Turgosheim forever. For once they were gone, they'd never get back in again, be sure!

Ah, but these were thoughts which he must keep to

himself! For a little while longer, anyway. Indeed, for while Vormulac was powerful and dangerous, he wasn't the only one with dreams of empire. And in Maglore's book at least, he certainly wasn't worthy of such dreams . . .

In Suckscar:

The young Lord Nestor Lichloathe of the Wamphyri came yelping awake in his bed, laved in the cold sweat of his nightmare and full of its terror. Even a Lord of the Wamphyri, and a necromancer to boot, terrified of a dream! But this was in no way a rare complaint: *all* men nightmare, and vampires are no exception. For however monstrous a man may become in his prime, the dormant fears of his past will take root again and grow up huge in his dreams, and always have the power to frighten him anew. Except, what was Nestor anyway but a young man even now? There had scarcely been time for the fears of his childhood to mature into this. Also, the terrors of his youth were long forgotten; his youth *entire*, forgotten! . . . In the main.

No, this was a far more recent thing: a recurrent dream which Nestor had dreamed frequently – *too* frequently – ever since a certain disastrous night on Sunside; a dream which invariably unmanned him, bringing him awake to this condition of mental agitation and uneasy premonitions of physical . . . what, decline?

It could be, of course, that he'd supped too well; there were fresh bloodstains on his pillow, marking the spot where a love-thrall had lain until he'd sent her away. Or perhaps his posture had been wrong; had he slept on his arm, he wondered, until it, too, had gone to sleep? Whichever, the dream – or its prophetic nature? – was the reason he no longer slept in Wratha's bed; no, not for all her heat. And not from fear of her, either. Rather for fear of himself.

Getting up, he paced the floor this way and that. His arm still tingled. His left arm and hand. But for the moment he did not look at them ...

And the nightmare still fresh in Nestor's mind. Or if not a nightmare as such, a scene or memory out of the recent past. A monstrous detail of that night he'd spent on Sunside, in the camp ... in the camp of the lepers:

That grey shape standing beside his bed, telling him where he was. And Nestor bolting upright, grabbing the dangling arms of the other's cowled robe – empty sleeves which couldn't take his weight! The way they'd torn at the shoulders to come away in Nestor's hands as he fell back onto the bed. And the sight of the other's twig arms with swollen fungus nubs for elbows!

Now Nestor looked at his left arm and hand, the first grey blotches there on flesh which as yet had not quite taken on the leaden aspect of a Lord of the Wamphyri. The numbness that came and went, making his wrist and hand seem lifeless, or at least insensitive.

Impulsively, he bit the ball of his thumb until the scarlet blood ran. But even so, it seemed to him it ran sluggishly. And as for pain: he'd felt none of it.

But now, before he could stop it, the rest of his nightmare loomed up large as life in his mind's eye; not a fragment out of the past this time, but ... a glimpse into the future? Possibly:

A lone shuffling figure, slumped shoulders, dangling arms, and swaying head with chin on chest. And a trail of footprints in the gathering dust of dereliction, the forlorn track of the lone and lonely figure, wandering like a lost soul through the empty, echoing halls of deserted Suckscar. Everyone fled, save he, and only the chittering bats for company now, in the gloom of this hideous pesthole.

Then, in a chink of wan starlight where a mouldering

curtain had been left open a crack, the figure paused. And almost as if sensing it were observed, looked back.

And Nestor seeing and recognizing that ravaged face: those watery, half-blind eyes; blotched, papery skin peeling from the ravaged bone; fretted lips crumbling over black teeth in shrivelled gums. He recognized the face, of course –

– For it was his . . .

EXPLORING NEW REALMS IN
SCIENCE FICTION/FANTASY ADVENTURE

Published or forthcoming

RETURN OF THE DEEP ONES
AND OTHER MYTHOS TALES

Brian Lumley

Brian Lumley, author of the bestselling *Necroscope* and *Vampire World* series of novels, has for many years been a devotee of H. P. Lovecraft's Cthulhu Mythos.

Defined by such nightmare fables as *Dagon*, *The Call of Cthulhu* and *The Shadow over Innsmouth*, Lovecraft's legendary Deep Ones have taken their place in terror fiction alongside the vampire and the werewolf. Now they are give the Lumley treatment in . . .

Return of the Deep Ones!

EXPLORING NEW REALMS IN
SCIENCE FICTION/FANTASY ADVENTURE

Published or forthcoming

MUTANT CHRONICLES

IN LUNACY
William F. Wu

From the darkness of the void emerged nightmares beyond our wildest fears. As man penetrated into space in the far future, a hurricane of evil destroyed and corrupted all that lay in its way. It was a time to conquer all fears and stand up against the tidal wave of the Dark Symmetry.

It was a time for heroes . . .

FRENZY
John-Allen Price

The Megacorps had long fought amongst themselves for supremacy on Luna, Venus and Mars. Now the Dark Legion have targeted humanity for conquest – and even death offers no escape!

DEMENTIA
Michael A. Stackpole

In a universe of MegaCorporate wars and Dark Legions, even a dead man's mind is fair game!

**EXPLORING NEW REALMS IN
SCIENCE FICTION/FANTASY ADVENTURE**

Published or forthcoming

I SHUDDER AT YOUR TOUCH

Edited by Michele Slung

The secret place in our minds where our fantasies and fears lurk can usually remain dark and hidden. Until, that is, it is illuminated by such supremely talented manipulators of the macabre as Stephen King, Ruth Rendell, Angela Carter, Clive Barker or Patrick McGrath. Then our erotic fantasies become art and the flesh tingles with pleasure or fear.

These twenty-two tales of sex and horror introduce a host of kinky, perverse, bizarre and creepy characters. Terrifying, humorous and wildly seductive, *I Shudder at Your Touch* will have you fighting back a scream – of horror or delight.

**EXPLORING NEW REALMS IN
SCIENCE FICTION/FANTASY ADVENTURE**

Published or forthcoming

VAMPIRES

John Steakley

A razor-sharp fantasy thriller of modern-day vampires and the men who hunt them.

Suppose there really were vampires. Dark. Stalking. Destroying. They'd have to be killed, wouldn't they? Of course they would. But what kind of fools would try to make a living at it?

The Vampire Hunters . . .

'This is exciting and surprising stuff . . . a real genre bender that keeps the best elements of both' – *Locus*

**EXPLORING NEW REALMS IN
SCIENCE FICTION/FANTASY ADVENTURE**

Published or forthcoming

TIME OUT OF JOINT

Philip K. Dick

Every day Ragle Gumm sends in his entry to the competition in the *Gazette*. Every day he's a surefire winner. He's a local celebrity, a hero with a position in town to maintain. Despite having no job, Ragle is under pressure. Pressure to win.

How would you feel if solid objects began to dematerialize in front of your eyes?

Weird things are happening to him, and Ragle's anxiety turns to paranoia. He thinks he's the centre of the universe, then that 'They' – whoever 'They' might be – are out to get him. As his desperation grows, he realizes that it's all very well being the centre of the Universe, but only if you know *which* Universe.

**EXPLORING NEW REALMS IN
SCIENCE FICTION/FANTASY ADVENTURE**

Published or forthcoming

THE
DIAMOND AGE

Neal Stephenson

'The Quentin Tarantino of postcyberpunk science fiction'
– *Village Voice*

Far above the diamondoid bedrock of New Chusan, a power-ful class of neo-Victorians is ruling twenty-first-century Atlantis/Shanghai. John Percival Hackworth, a brilliant nanotechnologist, has created an illicit, magical book for the education of a young lady: an interactive device crammed with folklore, science and the martial arts that teaches young women how to think for themselves.

What will happen to society if it should fall into the hands of someone like little Nell, a poor orphan girl with so much to learn?

'A brilliant, tricky, twenty-first-century version of *Pygmalion*'
– *Guardian*

EXPLORING NEW REALMS IN
SCIENCE FICTION/FANTASY ADVENTURE

Published or forthcoming

TIGANA

Guy Gavriel Kay

Tigana is the deeply moving story of a people struggling to be free. A people so cursed by the dark sorceries of the tyrant King Brandin that even the very name of their once beautiful land cannot be spoken or remembered.

But not everyone has forgotten. A handful of men and women, driven by love, hope and pride, set in motion the dangerous quest for freedom: to overthrow their conquerors and bring back to the world the lost brightness of an obliterated name: Tigana.

EXPLORING NEW REALMS IN
SCIENCE FICTION/FANTASY ADVENTURE

Published or forthcoming

BEGGARS IN SPAIN

Nancy Kress

The time: a not-so-distant future. The breakthrough: gene scientists who have discovered how to produce children who have no need of sleep. At first, nothing about their lives seems extraordinary. But as the Sleepless grow to adulthood, a disturbing pattern begins to emerge.

Severed from their last evolutionary link, the Sleepless are free to realize a potential no ordinary human can match: a potential that will see them banished from the confines of Earth ...

EXPLORING NEW REALMS IN SCIENCE FICTION/FANTASY ADVENTURE

Published or forthcoming

THE ARTIFICIAL KID

Bruce Sterling

Shallow seas, coral-atoll continents, flying islands – this is the world of Reverie, the Artificial Kid its most notorious video star, a professional combat artist who tapes his acts of violence for sale to an avid public.

But the kid's affluent lifestyle is less predictable than he imagines – especially when he has to flee from the Cabal with Moses Moses, newly emerged from seven hundred years of suspended animation. Then the mysterious forces that come into play have drastic effects – both on him and on the lovely Saint Anne Twiceborn.

RoC

EXPLORING NEW REALMS IN
SCIENCE FICTION/FANTASY ADVENTURE

Published or forthcoming

TEMPS

Devised by Neil Gaiman and Alex Stewart

To the tabloid press the Department of Paranormal Resources is a scroungers' paradise, issuing regular girocheques to a motley collection of 'talents' with questionable results.

But for the 'temps' who place their bizarre abilities at the service of the State in exchange for a miserly stipend and a demob suit, life with a very British League of Superheroes leaves everything to be desired ...

Hilarious and terrifying – *Temps* takes you to the cutting edge of Superhero fantasy!

EXPLORING NEW REALMS IN SCIENCE FICTION/FANTASY ADVENTURE

Published or forthcoming

VAMPIRE WORLD

Brian Lumley

BLOOD BROTHERS

In the beginning, on Starside, Harry Keogh was the Source. Ultimately, he would also be the Doombringer – to the Old Wamphyri. But death is not the end: not for Harry, nor for the vampires whose tenacity is legendary . . .

THE LAST AERIE

Nathan's lot is to venture into the world of his father, Earth, there to seek the source of Harry Keogh's awesome talents with which to return to Sunside/Starside, defeat the Wamphyri, and destroy the Last Aerie!

BLOODWARS

Concluding the epic Vampire World saga by the author of the internationally bestselling *Necroscope* series. In the field of no-holds-barred terror fiction, there's Brian Lumley – and then there's the rest . . .